G DAY
Please God, get me off the Hook

By

Neil Baker

authorHOUSE™

1663 LIBERTY DRIVE, SUITE 200
BLOOMINGTON, INDIANA 47403
(800) 839-8640
WWW.AUTHORHOUSE.COM

AuthorHouse™
1663 Liberty Drive
Bloomington, IN 47403
www.authorhouse.com
Phone: 1-800-839-8640

First published by AuthorHouse: 06/03/2010
ISBN: 1-4208-0822-2 (e)
ISBN: 1-4208-0821-4 (sc)

Printed in the United States of America
Bloomington, Indiana

This book is printed on acid-free paper.

Cover Design by: Neil Baker.

I would like thank Denise Baker for her assistance in typing and editing G Day.
I would also like to acknowledge Marilyn Harrington for her assistance in typing the final
manuscript.

Divinity

The final murder took place while god was running down like a watch; exactly how a watch serves man, by running down. Everything is held within the same ephemeral construct: we are dead, already. We simply are! As he had neglected to tell you before (or perhaps his words were just cleverly disguised), he was *meant* to be born. For what was ever meant to be born that did not fail in time to grow? Beginning and ending in a day. What for? What for? To swell, slug, and later hang me at 9 a.m. midday. Know: father will fall. So say goodnight, Gracie, and I will murmur, "Good mourning to you all."

As I get ready to battle god in the last gigantomachy, I speed read through science, history, religion, myths, heroes, beasts, journeys, falls and downfalls, and I marvel: what purpose did it serve? god's guilt supplied the curve to physical reality. Nothing physical is served. Not even complex atoms, molecules, nor dust. Not anything that he had ever brought forth: grass, cattle, beast, man, nor dust. In leaving the earth behind (days of lore becoming days of *is*), skip the wars, skip the space age, skip the final atomic damnum fatale . . . O . . . god is grinding to a halt! Though it has taken billions upon billions of years, his yolk is finally being consumed; he is forever undone. I now define for you my name . . . by number: None; but not as it has been taught to you. Divinity consists of nothing the world has ever read, heard, nor thought of before (ugh).

So climb the ladder past god's knowingness, into the dark. What you are will light for you, all-knowingness. I know. Because I now become *'thy will be undone, O universe.'*

Beware all ye who enter
IN THE BODY OF THE EARTH
On the Couch in Cloaca

In two days he will be dead. And I will kill him.

Last night I was watching him sleep while sitting on his right side, clothed in a long, white hierodulic garment. I could feel his breath on my cheek coming from across the secret chamber. His breath tapping ever so deliberately on my left cheek. It isn't that I haven't visualized his demise before. It's just something I care not to talk about. Such an idle *moyenâge* tale . . .

Have you ever watched a moth butting itself against a light? Just a moth, a simple *arzt* moth, butting itself against a big, bright light? The way it keeps coming back, as though it were trying to find a door. A way inside the light. I know of another creature who constantly butts itself against the light. A wingless soul, without a scratch to its name, desperately, anxiously attempting to find a door. Or at the very least to create one.

Actually, he was different before. Younger, yes. Lighter. Full of less worry and fatigue, but nonetheless troubled. Killed a quarter of the population then, he did! Oh, yes, always troubled. He would come home from work, smelling like olives on a corpse, with enormously plodding steps, tear through the threshold and cast a black ominous shadow across my nigrescent vision. "Sweetheart," he would say, "are you ready to go the distance? You're not going to keep your cadet waiting, are you?" Seconds into minutes. Minutes into hours. Hours into stretches of time that tested the polished episodes, the extended nobblers, the very breath of nocturn existence. Ask her and she would say, on stage, wailing like a sorrowful farceuse, "Vitus, I'm ready . . . I'm always ready to play the discobolus, my dear old Jephthah."

He's near me . . . he's washing me farley maidenhair again, and my pistic head is beneath my feet. If I could only grasp the two-edged sword on the counter that I dusted yesterday, I might find myself folded over like a letter, fleshly unread.

The duality of existence eclipses my very memory. Swaying ever so slightly. A town lasts three years, a dog outlasts three towns, a horse outlasts three dogs, man outlives three horses, an ass outlives three men . . . I lose, lose, lose an anovulatory legacy, and then find myself again a phoenix at 83,052 years old. Light to dark, day to night, order to chaos. *Rinnnng!* The wonderful ring . . . red for day, white for disease, green for nothingness. I try in vain to hold onto a tangible thought if only for a moment. Ogam letters in stone (my father was into lithochromy). *And no more.* Just long enough to whisper a prayer of accumulated survival. He beckoned at my heels. Like the fox. On hands and knees he bleated *Gall*, his soul pleading for a breath, a sigh, a belief on vapour. The years before fell over me like a sticky bark, morning mist of sabbath. I cried, "Moth...er!" Silence drummed my ears like the blood that pounded me into existence from two tossed dice. Disseminated among wo/ men. Why am I left slaying my very own soul, when my setup is lost in his rosy, bedded eye, his hidden, preying eye gladly digesting my 8:16 innocence? This time the patzer must be of the lowest rank, and his foot must be in his toss. His best cast were three sixes; his worst, Canis. And now his Venus has turned out a whelp; he has spent his ambo.

THE SOUNDING OF THURSDAY

In the residue of last night's tumbled weed of intoxication and regret and pleasure at the clit of an amnesia-clogged artery blown wide open by the sudden spasm of one thousand and one forbidden, airy fantasies, I creamed the bedding glory beneath me. I wept. The shortest come and see. A drop of blood . . . drops of blood . . . he didn't care. I wasn't to let go of this tumbler until every last drop was downed. In the long run, it was a less dangerous route, one pass not plagued with worry or pedage, less thunder. Oh, regret, where is your sting, your blade's penetrating point? Where is your passe partout? Hidden, vanquished, under a veil of crinkly skin on a little hill; unnecessary; loft, cardboard, glass, and strips of fabric holding the whole being together. The crest of my heart mothers a moth cracked from an egg so small it refuses to fry. Nucleus of my eye, as I stare into your mirrored afterglow of deflection, I ask, *What black, mighty pool of non-syllabic thought did you spring from? What fleshly pigmentation cursed you forth? What pedagese brought you senseless? What widow's weeds left you falling this good mourning?* god envisioned, I dive backwards into a murky, fathomless appeal of displeasure. Asked the passing stranger: *What crime did bring him lifeless?* I just might lose myself, solar-eclipsed, luci-tailored plight of my soul pulled free, and not be found again until three Thursdays come together, and I am discovered, a lepidopterous spirit.

I could cut the juggler, watch his balls tumble to the earth and roll pathetically to some long-forgotten corner of the room, and utter, *O'Sis' dear me, I cut your b. juggler all right.* Oh, crust, oh, scab, I picked to bleeding last night. It was on a Thunderday, was it not, that I chewed you to a pulp and spit out the pit and sent it shooting, gentlemen-and-ladies? I regurgitate the aftertaste. I slice your essence to crumbs of cheese crusted with mold and offer you cheese and bread as a light, unfolded meal. So long you have played king to my deuce and called it fair from the pulpit. When the tables are finally overturned and the belly of your foundation is cut asunder, I will cry three tears from my left eye only, like a joe miller crisscrossed on a crimson-soaked cut of wood. I will play the weeping philosopher clit because I will see into the folly of it all. I will be the pedagogist teaching you toward *dies irae.* I will dive not sounding swans but queen's nails into your cuticles, and get at the scales in your bread; gog, I will do a dive in the dark and make all swans geese, and then we will see what there is to your glory and your righteousness and your comforted, eloquent sense of balance.

G SAYS

A child visited me last night through the threshold like a thief in the night. He formulated a plan, like an epure, on the wall. His edges were sharp. One only needed to tip the scales ever so lightly and come back a Sisy, a glistening bead of blood waiting to be born, a pedagogue created with love, displayed as a sacrifice, worshipped as only the banquet of an unerroneous heart can be in order to see the traces in one vast connection of blundering spirit. If it be pleasing to a god to cut the quick, to cease the flow, to crumble the chocolate momentum of life's holy matrix, then let him at least do so without a lip curled. Better yet, allow him passage. For is he not here fresh from the café? Does he not gather stores in Athens and sell them as Tiffany's? Does he not mingle with the massive tons of ruinous history, and promise not to tell a soul? Is he not like Adrastus, surviving by his wits? His secrets are sacred missions locked away under tongue's reservations, where truth is kept quieted by seven convictions. For I have uttered my oneness with a horn, blasting asunder the very heart of the matter. I have sold myself *con amore,* and his acceptance of my flawed decree nearly leaves me sightless; but with eyes closed, I can still read joe doakes in a cacodemon. And I can research seven: sleepers, warriors, churches. I glimpsed his laughing, unctuous face and his devil-driving drumstick drowning my thoughts of dowry. An odd space for a rescuer to occupy. It wasn't until I saw the two-edged lifetime he held bonded in his right hand (both past and future rolled into one nondescript ball of opprobrious imminence) that I realized that I was witnessing nothing more than creation's first simple act of pure epuration getting downed. I don't give a good flying A for the forbidden zone, the foreboding, forewarned, don't-you-dare-dwarf mentality that was suppose to have worked as a sports' appetizer. If only god had put a bit more oomph in the recipe. Call us both man and woman, nothing more than a bad case of unleavened bread. Pretzels, at best. god spoke too late . . . man acted too soon . . . And too many blessed, infamous angels with folded wings clogged the route . . .

ONESELF, alone

My mother slept like a cyclops, one eye burning in crimen. I reached out for her left hand, a ringed hand calloused with nicks and curses. A hand that talks: "You there, and I here." One bite of the certificate, and the secret of the riddle turns into excrement basking in the sun. I'm certain no one heard but she. Could this be the legacy she handed me with a crippling finger? A doubting heal? A temporary amplexus? Somewhere in a dark recess between classes, I will teach the teacher another kind of lesson. Somewhere between the light and the dark, the order and the chaos . . . the master's cutting brain globe of glass . . . the mirror of man's salivation . . . the ampelideous therapy . . . I will politely scorch the sour tongue. Like smooth and shiny paper it will rip irreparable, and I will be as foxed as wooley ol' blaize pretending to see it all through a helmet.

It is not the contrary sighs between tides that caress and smooth my pores into a gleaming landscape of unblemished serenity – it is the rootless cry heard silently, the primal liquid exclamation erupted from the depths of a chasm long bellowed out before spoken tongues broke words on the ears.

LORD G. DARKNESS

His voice first resounded in my ill-formed, womb-watery eardrums like a tinkling cymbal. *Be fruitful over fish.* I was all but six months before the mast, sailing, floating, like a sightless buoy, a chained cow grazing in the flow of my mother's sublime satisfaction. If she offered a comment, it was wrapped in French salty silk. My mother's message-laden sealed cocoon on the qt. My father's voice growled with a duelistic formula. His countless fingers probed like the heads of quean serpents from the East, like amphisbaena barely scraping the bottoms of my soles: *but the message is not here!*

"Take it to heart, darling. If it turns out to be a girl, we will call her Mme de Tiffany, after the jewel that I planted on your index finger. The dollar jewel you'll watch grow into a wet Medusa with seven heads." My father.

The new creature.

As noisy and as stately and as illicit as a Lafayette.

And I, all but seven crescent moons in a twelfth night cry, fell to beating my blood against the walls of my mother's stronghold. "Feel her kicking," my mother said. "She should resist the ravages of time that are capable of dissolving whole empires into dreams of sand. If we should decide to raise her like the first and last forgetful flower of our garden, I suspect she will grow to blossom virtuality like Cornelia, be full of spizzerinctum, and Ana Biosis, and grace and joke the drawing rooms and the catered halls and chamber rooms of the protected and fancy elect." My father could only cough his disapproval, speechless animal of the species that he is; as much as he tried, his foxy manners could not be hid. And so cunning in court before the Lion. Naked, slippery and full of dust. Bending the truth, resurrecting himself after death. I adored him nonetheless, adorned in the precious furs of his primitive protection, where his concern was imbued with all the melodious rapture of a fingernail consuming chalk, which in the end would be thrown down, ashes to nought. I really had no choice in my prelude to *Amen,* in *my* pre-face to the *Vision of Judgment,* whereby I assigned the Lord G. Darkness his selfish prayer for light, to and fro, upon the dust. Gorging she was, the universe; and Bysshe's Ozy at Thebes, cold command, lifeless things in the Satanic Schoolana. The diamond of my mother's pride was really the dessert of my starving Cock, even before the world began to rise, when pancakes were the craze, and eggs, flour, salt and milk the malaise.

The clock is ticking. Its sticky minutes broken down into cakey seconds; flaking into tired hours, years, dust, in layers of minuscule bones. I review my life through the chipped rim of my drinking cup. The anachronic pieces begging to be put back together again. O, Father, in his bell-shaped cloak, said it so well; his tongue lapping at the bloody bowl of my womb. Yes, father said it so awfully well. Abashed he stood in the goodness of my shapely shadow. My father, my one and only beloved, devoted, connected slab of love. O my amphivorous father, he had the sticking ticket. My father said, "No man is an island, but" (and always but, over and over, again and again, resounding in my ears like a stubborn tide, forever reaching, on its belly, either reluctant, resistant, or just plain obsessed with its own pull of the seas; whether onto sere rock, or back out to sea again, coming and going the awful way) "he had better explore the territory he owns before he seeks rescue from outside survivors. Yes, he had better know the basking territory, so no man can say that he was the pot calling the kettle black."

O, my father, how you own and possess my lot in life. Your sign, your name, your mark, your hands planted smugly, firmly depressed in the soil of my smoky breath. Cash my life, my love in, my father, my landowner, my translucent gardener. You stake my residual earth like the splachnaceae claims its entire fold, unchallenged, unmatched, on a dirty fork.

Mother! I cry. My land is occupied by one flesh. For better or for worse. Confusion worse confounded, like the splathering vow you took preceding my creation. How you tore the leafy pages of my prologue and my denouement, and chewed and ate; the ink still wet; the glue, pseudepigraphic. I gave up the host. So, sore, O father, the dogs. You could take any sacred word and smear its identity and make it look like a stranger code wandering through the phosphene frontier as on a dramatic pellucid checkerboard, marking a trail of black rhetoric across the watery page of my own innocence.

*   *   *

Last night my fingers left the bed. They crawled like crafty spiders down the bleached sheets trailing to the floor. My fingers crept into the bowel, beneath the numberless feathers of my quenched slumber. I gripped the barrel marked 'desuetude.' My stealthful, playful fingers tapped the trigger, each played their part, and I cried! a somniloquist, "The maid is not dead. Sleep on now and take your rest. The hour is at *cheiro* . . . Elemental; short, thick, crude, slow, instinctive. A prominent mount of Jupiter, Apollo, Mercury, Mars, Venus and the moon." The aim was unfocussed, off-balanced, and the target misplaced, though firmly routed between the division of humankind dilemma. I visualized the black seed exploding in the epilogue, ripping through the stonewall and embedding itself in the heart of the matter.

Around the bed there was a harsh conclamatio. *"Corpus nondum clamatum!"* howled the heads.

The room uttered its noxious annoyance at my consistent inconsistencies. I had but a one-track mind to chaos, lending a baptismal howl of perfusion, granting me three golden wishes of tarnished content: *Conclamatum est, he has been called and gives no sign!* I, bathed in a liquid intoxication of bemused sedation, scratched the shoreline of my pixilated desires, scorched the barriers, scoured the blocks, cleaned up the debris and restructured the skeletal design of my behemoth wantonness. During a bout of contorted-restitution, in which my father had me pinned to the mat of sublimation, I cried out in vain for the child within me to come to its senses, let go and rise and thereby bestow upon my ego a sense of equilibrium, of delicate balance, as once the playwright suggested after a three day struggle with some still undiscovered, interworld code, after which he received a measure of wheat and three measures of barley in a psychedelic zodiac of the internertamid. Actually, during one of my innumerable conversations with old, bloody St. Nick (a conversation, bare in mind, that barely scratched the surface of my mirrored image, cracked though it was with paternal credibility, or so I thought at the time, for how in god's name can the paternal be anything but credible when you're actually talking to the blood of a dead man?), there was a knock upon my front door. A knock so imbued with the desperate suggestiveness of a jetson seeking shelter from the storm that I was not at all surprised to find standing in the threshold of my cloudy domain a boyish, one-eyed titular, his mist-brimmed palm outstretched like a waxen doll's, or like some sad-eyed amoretto put out of house and home; his initial voice at first slipped past me but returned again to my ears with a message so endowed with piercing appropriateness that I could barely pick out my breath.

"You're not mort."

*   *   *

If, but for a moment, time stopped, traffic lumbered to a halt, eyes tired at the crossing, the inner noise in the hollow of the earth stopped bleating, brittle voices against the walls of ears' lost chambers ceased to share a room, I would at once dare to question my very existence, bone-bleached, weary clod that I am. Morbid is not the quintessential word that I would use to describe my formidable condition, although vicariously I have otherwise done so. I stand like Brutus concealed, lochetic, dagger-happy ready for change, eager for

7

restitution, hungry for the pit in Caeser's stomach (hallowed be thy name forever and ever. Amen.). With steady hands I operate on gas, on those like Archestratus, who when placed in a dish weighs no more than an obolus. But I am not a numismatist, though I am well aware of the image and superscription. So I write on the epistle side with outstretched hand: whomsoever I shall kiss, the same flesh shall be cut off. Neither am I a gastriloquist, though I take from the stomach food for thought, and reify the mass. Note my rehfuss tube and its slotted endpiece for juicy analysis, and my team of draegermen to the rescue.

"You're not mort."

The child who is the man, the man who is the child, bleeds epistaxis like a sought upon rock star high on vinegar. I will not listen to the oxygenated cry of a child – the soft, muted, tender, finished heartbeat of a thousand year reign. Nor will I stoop so low as to be tickled by the milk-curdled voices of a dozen babes in arm swimming in the lochia. As it stands, I am thoroughly unimpressed with what occurs on the ground. But as it stalls to order, I will be a physician . . .

"You're not mort . . ."

But let us go to Gastronia to wipe out the G on the walls of the estates, and then pay a visit to Gastonia to see a man clothed in soft raiment go mad.

For in that day – that dry, dense, tropical, run-on afternoon – I will lay my brow down upon the blood-stained grass beneath the graffiti, and seek revelation: one, the soul; two, the body; three, the very fact that four you're old . . . marked: unmarked; oh for four I take one Alborak; *reihengräbers* all in a row . . . ("But he didn't clarify . . . classify the categories . . . nor the territory . . .")

Mort.

BOUND FOR A THOUSAND

After the bells, the salutations, the courtesies, thankless enough to creep out from between clenched teeth; after the hound bays in the night, blows out the candle and throws it to the ground; after the book is nail-closed on men and the blank back is facing the eye; after the *how do you dos,* the *oh, reallys,* the *you don't says,* the *naturallys,* the *but of courses* have graced a knight's passing; after the extended hands, the subtly raised knuckles, the elongated fingers sliding like operatic, new, other unknown tongues have given into the quick; after the smile's half-retarded reach of antiquated eloquence has found its third seat at the table; after the ventriloquist has possessed half the pop. of New Haven, Connecticut *Qui transtulit sustinet* and proclaimed the lot dead; after cows' bells suckling teats bleed from the endless wavering sucking of toothless totterer gums; after the whales' wail, the forlong empathic fog-shroudded, manimalistic cry screeched from the sands of earth's first and last flowing grass frontier, alpha and omega; after the eye atop the apex of pyramids' transcendence blinks, bleeds, and bewails eternity's death-defying mystery in one single fall down leap; after the riddle spoken solemnly – Solomon's secret super ejaculated like one-half of civilization's half-crazed tails – has swum into Opinicus' gaping mouth; after Astaire's Daddy-Long-Legs-sidesteps straight off the set into dancer's oblivion and resets its bones in Archaic letters; after Abel raises the dirt and slains Cain craniumlessly, cutting his second head into little dainty hors d'oeuvres, enough to nosh the multitudes (excluding all barbers and surgeons), I will simply, and most deliciously, blow his pebble-strewn brain to kingdom cum. It isn't that I don't utterly adore the manliness of man. I would be but a speck of unwanted dust in Belial's right eye if it weren't for the first burst of ejaculatory cumuppance. Oh I am forever indebted to that involuntary spasm of white honey musculatory pleasure that I have in my later years personally experienced under the weight of a foul mourning breath, heavy as the brick of old ironsides some mornings. And if I may be bold enough to add to this document of devil dribble, I am also most indebted to the god-bestowed creed of fleshy fatherhood that entered our good man in heaven, who also found it heart-wise to add to the overall plan the grand design master scheme as only Old Constitution could devise it. But in this blood-splattered cry of embryonic anger, I do spy from the canal my old saviour dressed like a three-year old prostitute in Sunday school. I will back down and draw my Medussa-serpents'-forked-tongues inward, silent seconds enough to hear the innocent explanation. The voice that does lightly tap upon my eardrums is devoid of such mishap. The child's voice is so soothing, so refreshing, so reassuring. I could cry for thirty-three years without so much as taking a breath. "I love you," he says. "I simply and devotedly love you."

It pains me, the manner in which you receive him. If I were but flesh and bone, I would fling nonce and his load clear across Atlantis, like Hercules disc-skip-riding the childish waves to death. Flesh and bone do amount to something, given how much havoc it can create and ingrain in so short a breath of time. Your eye . . . your wonderfully stunning eye atop the salty mountain is regrettably half-crazed with shock; under a hazy gaze of ingratitude, the anger reduced to frustration, anxiety's clogged exclamation, the promise half-whispered at Pisgah mount. I would stand and adorn my walls with idols, photographs of daddy's little child among the dear antelope, developed, signed, sealed and delivered; except that I have a bone lodged in my seat.

"QUICKENING"

In the beginning of things, chaos was created. So said Epic. with *cacoethes scribendi;* but holding his own to the point of death. Suffering from epistasis. The suppression carries at its root the sup and the scum of cheap wine in retentive piss. One thing over the other. But as Archetimus tells it in the age of seven wise men, most men are bad; consider the end; except I know nothing of the wisest.

Messenger of Troy, winged Hermes of fancy flight fatality – thief in the night – take the steps you have gathered around you like so many dropped blossoms, and bundle them up into clusters that you might wear as soft clothing. Like undyed maco. Tell Helen in her ear (the ear marked right) that she is nothing but a fraud, a harlot on ice clinking her glass diamonds against the bridge of her wrist. Damn spurious fool that she is with child in winter. A diamond and a prison on each hand; knees clutching the earth like two fists curled up with leprosy; immovable mound of trapped breath; unleavened soles. Rahab stalks her corn-rimmed garden like chanticleer in the morning searching for god knows what. *Prison? Death? Spies? Armies of aliens in the night? An hypostomatous fish with an active lower mouth?* There is nothing edible in the midst of the bowels of earth that one can obtain nourishment from. Except just the other day the sun uncrossed its legs and lent me a view of Pompeii.

Colon of hens: Know thyself. The beast lingers in the hypostasis of the sediment.

The curator barked, "Don't touch!" I spoke to him about it, his office dripping lines on agonized intent, the color of his eye still wet from the master's touch, and his *via lascivia* leading up a path of intensity. In broad strokes he obliviated common sense and flung his threats at me in such a way so as not to disturb the quiet restitution of a vagrant mind. If I could only gather enough roughage in the essence of his hypostasis (leaves, sticks and stones) and build a wall (a fatal necklace, however frail) and stand on the other side of the sea, blending into stone, matching my wits with a twig.

The epistatic G in the dark, undoing.

That boy, oak-framed, stood directly akin to the man whose palms tested a fire on a pede cloth. He stepped into my father's shoes in a dreamy, hypostatic union and suddenly I could sense the coming of the just one. His pederastic steps, top-heaviside with rage, as vented as Velnias, would not move for me though I pleaded innocently. Dancing belly-down, gnashing on me edge with his teeth, my father was finally done, and pulled himself free as though he had been trapped by me. On the brink of thin ice, I dislodged the sieved Margarita bait that was embedded in my cheek.

Meanwhile, Mother kept placing a feather in the drain, disquieting the disposal. "Mother!" I screamed. "It's me! I'm your inn's keeper, your gate to the seven wonders of abuse! Sister to Mercury! Holy Cow! But he drives me all along the long sea strand. He will not let me sleep."

Cut!

*　　　*　　　*

The dust roamed, and in its midst, the code. Originally from a turmoil, the dust rose and randomly floated through the galaxies, the seas, dimensions unseen from the nooscopic eyes that later gave a new structure and meaning to the dust: Motion saved man. From whence his origin began? Far, far away in the midst of a world of disarray.

G DAY
THE LIVING NOVEL
A Stage In Three Acts

ACT 1

god sits in an old, dilapidated, broken down, green cushion chair in the middle of a spacious living room surrounded by penates. In the left wall is a tele surrounded by built-in shelves that display rows upon rows of various books. The tele is on, and the channels are constantly changing via a remote control that god is holding in his right hand. From the sounds emanating from the tube, it is clearly evident that the programs consist of topics ranging from drama to comedy, laughtracks to newsreels, and variety shows to talk shows, all of which are attempting to roof the void with words and images. Directly beside god is a round table upon which rests a lit majolica lamp adorned with sparkling pendeloques. Actually, the lamp is something god retrieved from earth before its final destruction, the lamp being a victim of a somewhat virtuian obsession. It is a well-proportioned table lamp that was made by a small company in the Abruzzi region of Italy where, once upon a time, less than a dozen pear-shaped employees created beautiful reproductions of historic, ceramic museum works. This handsome hand-painted urn features majolica patterns from the 1500s. Retail price value: $265.00.

It is probably of some importance to make mention of the table upon which the lamp is mounted. This is actually a tôle tray table that god was able to swoop up instances before destructions' hungry flames could lick its fancy. It is a little table created by furious Florentine artisans faithful to eighteenth century vesuvian methods. It features a fixed tray top with a ring handle and gallery rim. Anthemion designs accent the sturdy table's octagonal base. With an added feature of tôle paintings, combining both detail and rich color. Retail value: $295.00.

Behind god stands a magnificent folding frescoe screen in the style of a Renaissance diptych, hand-painted with faded frescoes. The back is finished in an antique terra cotta shade. Actually, the frescoe serves as an excellent backdrop for a dynamic duo, William and Mary (both looking absolutely splendid on trumpet legs). Retail value: $7,600.00.

As god stretched forth his hand over the earth, his eye simultaneously fell fancy to several material sights that he (being a wee bit disposed to oniomania) was able to sweep up, and thus save seconds before the final destruction – the bulk of such sights currently surround him in the living space of his domain. Clearly on display are various other items ranging from large to small, flat to round, shiny to dull, hard to soft . . .

Those are Billy bookcases holding those magnificent volumes of books! They boast proudly of a cherry-stained, red-oak/ash veneer finish, with convenient glass doors built-in for *dust*-free storage. This combination retails at: $816.00. (Apparently, unbeknownst to god, there is still a red sign taped to one of the glass doors advertising: **Wilder Hot SALE 20% Off!** A clear clue as to just how much of a haste god was in during those final moments.)

At god's feet sits a dainty crewelwork bench, stitched in wool, with a colorful crewel-embroidered top from the tree-of-life design. The turned legs are breached with a mahogany finish. god's feet are quietly resting upon a crewel-embroidered top but . . . take a look at those slippers that god is resting his feet in! Those are the hard-to-come-by, quilted cashmere, faust slippers from one of France's leading manufacturers! Yes, that's a silky soft cashmere god's curling his toes in for well-deserved warmth and comfort after a hard day of work. Suede-over-felt souls provide good footing, and the quilted cashmere uppers are detailed with suede piping, with a *vici* hammered into a strip of leather. All in white. Value price: $666.00.

Yes! Go ahead. Blink your eyes! That's a for real silk and terry cloth robe god is lounging in. Elegance and practicality meet congenially in an all-white robe of washable silk charmeuse. Lined with soft absorbent cotton terry for that 'grab-me and give me a hug' look. Detailing this is a shawl collar (currently turned up) and French seams. The only thing missing from the spectacular elegance of this robe are wings! Retail: $900.00.

Oh-oh! Has god gone trans!?! Take a look at what's happening in that Oden wardrobe of sturdy, antique-stained, solid pine against the wall behind god. That's a Victoria Royal rayon and silk dress with rayon-velvet underskirt in mink color. And that's not all! Hanging beside that is (if you know your fashions) a Carmen Marc Valvo, black triacetate and polyester charmeuse bias cut dress! Actually (as rumor has it), this was the same dress that god was adorned in during *earth's final moments.*

But wait! There's always room for more! Yes, that's an Evening Wrapture. This was the piece god was suppose to have worn in his role as Redeemer, Destroyer and Saviour, but just never got around to it. Still, it's worth noting for its ruffle Duchess satin evening cape. In striking cross red. With black satin gloves. Perhaps another time, god.

Dinner at eight? god did. That's a new silk tuxedo with jacket, pants, and tank for that special armored look. The quintessence of destruction!

Two antique bergère chair prints done in a vivid impressionistic style are mounted and framed in gold upon the wall. (By the way, that's a Gold Louis XV chair and a Blue Louis XVI. And squeezed in between the chairs is a monumental bed of gilt splendor with bedposts carved with bees, and a carved canopy topped by an eagle.)

Incidentally, that old, broken-down, green chair that god is plumped down in is just a little something he spied at a meager mizpah garage sale while going about his rounds, and took an instant liking to.

Total value of the room-at-large (including items of virtu not aforementioned): *A Grand whopping* $20,018.00!!

ACT II

god stands.
god sits down.

ACT III

The setting is in the same living room as before. Sunlight (or at least some kind of celestial light) is streaming in through the window to the left of god, washing the room in brightness. If birds were chirping (which they're not), if tree branches were visible through the windowpane (which they aren't), if theomachic voices shouting from the not too distant were heard (etc., etc., etc. . . .), the atmosphere and the lighting of the stage alone would have suggested that its setting was somewhere in Rome on a summer day in 1881. But Italy is gone. There is no England. Africa is definitely a lost continent. China? Iceland? the North Pole? the South Pole? Chile! indeed!

Mrs. Alving (whom god chose to save as a part-time strumpet, partly due to her cup-shaped mouthpiece, partly due to her fine twice-curved tubes) enters stage.

Mrs. Alving is most upset for she has lost her country estate in the west of Norway, as Norway is now *Noway.* But she is not about to taunt god, nor raise him just yet, because he has already proven to be totally phonomanic by turning the world into an empty lot. Actually, she is a succuba cursed. What she has gone through (the loss of her individuality and freedom, not to mention her house of assignation) one would not wish upon a dog. She is but a victim of examination and judgment – a chambermaid to god, with the responsibility of attending to his passions as well.

god's tele is playing old reruns, some of which are in black and white, some of which are in color. There is the Stoned Age, and two burly men comparing tools made of icy rock rock offence. One man plunges his tool into the mund of another man and a title flashes across the screen: *Weapons one.* Two troglodytes on holiday share a mind-shattering experience while filming on verglas. There are the Hyksos, shepherds pouring into Egypt from western Asia, torturing, murdering, looting and keeping Egypt enslaved for two hundred years. Three fierce Hyksos swing their metal weapons against charging chariots. With a sweeping hand the tide turns and the Egyptians drive their foreign rulers out of the park. A title flashes across the screen: *the Age of the Umpire* or: *Strike the triumvirate and they're out!*

Mrs. Alving putts about the room, grasping the pope's head, *dusting* the dust here and there. There is Grease and Sparta. There is the Peloponnesian War at Hens Falls. (god laughs.) There is a soldier in a meager garment; barefoot in winter; eating what looks like Cream-of-Wheat with asparagus tips; walking in silence for miles with eyes to the ground; and receiving daily whippings in public to prove his worth. The soldier is seven years old. (god laughs harder.) Servitude to war until sixty years old! . . .

god chomps on a Pelops shoulder . . .

Mrs. Alving steps in front of the tele as she goes about her cleaning. god shouts, "The play is to be like a veridical picture of life and all I see before me is one great fat ass! Sit down! Get out of the way! Move over!"

Mrs. Alving turns about and apparently has something she's dying to say, but all that comes out is "Well, you may be right about that."

god perks up and gives Mrs. Alving a smile. "I don't deny that."

Mrs. Alving moves off to the side and starts to dust around the books, while god commences to watch more of the tube. There is John Wycliffe, who pokes his head out of the tube and says with a snarl, "I was dead some thirty years when a Church council ordered my body dug up and burned, and my ashes tossed into a river. Condemned as a heretic! All because I had insisted Logos was to be the highest authority of all, and not the Pope! And all my disciples thereafter, the Lollards, got to be . . . headed."

Instantly, Wycliffe gets sucked back into the tele, and flashing across the screen are human scavengers robbing churches, while cannibalism, famine, and disease wipe out half the German population; and the war goes on for thirty years with shouts of "Reincarnation!"

And it's "Do as you please" as Thelemites from the abbey rise and ad-lib off the cuff with ease.

Mrs. Alving stops dusting and picks a book off the shelf that has caught her attention, *Mortality is a Matter of Taste* by T.E. Cyclops. She opens the book to the first page and reads, "We stew in our own juice and get seasoned in a bail of self-hate. Our taste is rather repulsive and can sometimes come back up sour before it is finally digested. We seem to be derived from a recipe that once put into motion becomes a definite no-return concoction."

god catches Mrs. Alving in his eyes. "I don't deny that such books have a reasonable fascination, and I really can't blame you for exposing yourself to such intellectual matters as mortality. But, after all, Mrs. Alving, you are my servant and you're not to dilly-dally between the covers of a book."

Mrs. Alving stomps her foot down. She glares at her adversary. Her nostrils flare with scorn. "Your servant?! By god, I'm not your servant! I'm a free and independent employee hired on because you're lacking a John Panegyrist to sing your praise and glory! I am a woman! You think, like every woman, I have to be a servant? You conceited, self-indulgent, phallicistic *twerp*! You think I should fear you even as I oppugn you? Go ahead. Decap me and end this hurt, because while we're on the subject, there are certain goings-on around this sphere that I don't quite admire! I do not like slaughter nor burning worlds up like potato totters! I realize that in your eyes there is clearly fire, and in your pursuit of pleasure you have cindered all I treasure. And I would beg to leave this place and your godly, ghastly face. For shall I tell you what I think of you? You're spoiled! As only a god could be. That is, a god of mediocrity!"

god laughs haughtingly. "You know your lines. How delightful. How you can jump from stage to stage. It's utterly quantumfantastical! What a leading lady. I kid you not. Here. Allow me to grasp your encolure as we ride the night. For there is no time any longer, and the once configurations of physical fields in space are but in a knot. That is, my dear, without a trace. Ah, but how I love to see the duality . . . Anna in Helene's face."

Mrs. Alving lays the back of her hands securely upon the built-in ledges on either one of her hips. "You think you're quite the director, don't you? Well . . . don't you?! Back there in time when I really knew my place, when I really knew my lines, my place on the stage was so well-defined. Compared to your acts! Oh, don't think I don't know those lines. Showing himself alive after his passion . . . taken up by a cloud and disappearing. All those special effects . . . the mighty wind and the cloven tongues of fire sitting on tops of their encomic heads. And in the last days pouring out your spirit so everybody can prophesy and see visions and dream dreams and jactitate all about. And then in the middle of it all blood and fire and smoke, and the sun going black and the moon turning into blood! And they don't just stop there! Your acts go on much further!"

god jumps up. "Mrs. Alving! If that's the way you see it, then consider your duty to me for having spared your soul! At least, show me a little gratitude!" god turns away with a melodramatic sweep of his shoulders.

Mrs. Alving swings god around in order to face her. "My duty? Indeed! Whatever you profess to be, right or wrong, I rebel against as false and ugly. When I started to think was when I started to analyze your teachings! You are one to speak of eyes and ears, conscience and duty, when you yourself make ears dull of hearing and eyes shut with blindness. The living, the living . . . Is Ai! Ah! I cry a palilogy of parchment! All you stand for, all you preach is artificial and dead! And as far as your kingdom everlasting being lined with streets of gold goes, why that very chair you've been sitting in was lifted from a garage sale!" Mrs. Alving glares sarcastically at god. "Dear god, nothing in the universe lies so soundly as the tongue in your mouth! Honestly! Anyone who would think it fair to say *the first shall be last and the last first* can't help but get his own name backwards each and everytime his tongue awakens. And lest you should forget from having gulped babel too rapidly from an elephant's trunk, *the first shall be first . . . and the belluine bell St. Ill tolls like a dog!"*

god clasps his hands together in delight. "Delicious. Absolutely delicious. It's no wonder why I chose you to end this long, dreadful act. Dead ideas, dead beliefs, dead hosts. Countless, no doubt. Dreadfully afraid of the light. But you, Mrs. Alving, how I admire your courage. Where would my colossal drama have gone if it weren't for martyrs such as yourself? It brings to light the line 'Suffering is said to be salvation's corn'."

Mrs. Alving mumbles (beneath her breath), "And death a lubber's liberation."

god blinks. "Ah, she does know her lines well. Let me increase the illusions so that my lines are not so easy to tell, for the parting hour has come, and as the posterior appears and the end draws near and the puer makes for god's softening end, so does the dreaming child of god who sweepeth downward the dust of my lot. For salvation was never a must as long as the king felt discord among his kind, before the throne did flush the mixen. So, if you'll allow me to quote your train of thought: thief, liar, forger, adulterer, perjurer, glutton, gasconader, drunkard. Now, your refrain, *my* blame? Hardly. For not one of those names fit me. Can you guess my true title? Oh, come now, Mrs. Alving, 'tis easy. Very well then, I'll allow a clue. For where does glue derive from? Guess this, my dear Mrs. Alving. And as a prize: eternal rest. Otherwise, dust up to your very breast. Now, think wise. Glue is derived from hides. Hides, Mrs. Alving, *hides!* And who in kind needs those hides to keep their very name alive? Oh! Come now, Mrs. Alving! Think well of the prize!"

Mrs. Alving wiggles her finger in front of god's face. "It isn't fair! I'm not a sleuth in your tree of knowledge. To be every leaf, every branch!"

"Oh, yes, if you fear the circumstance."

Mrs. Alving cocks her eye. "Don't you mean consequence?"

"Yes. But it didn't make for rhyme. Now, Mrs. Alving, keep on track. The clue is but the name of eternal celebrity. Think of one man and a cyclone of voices. Open it up, Mrs. Alving. Think of a Harpy Hadleyburg in one breath, that is if you can stand the stench of a poor, published devil with a harp and a chicken's breast shouting: *'Order! Order! Lead us not into kistvaen!'* The name leads to the title, and the title has within it something akin to refrain. Destroy. Break up: But also to resound tornados, whirlwinds and storms. Now let me tempt you. One who relies on hides to carry on a name is a . . ."

Mrs. Alving suddenly displays a smile as broad and long as the once magnificent city of Chicago. And with an eye as wide and pink as the one that privately suggests *we never sleep,* she exclaimed, "Why, a tanner!"

god applauds. "Bravoes! Checkmate! You see, it doesn't take a genius to turn up the nose and make god's dream. To convert: Beat and Whip. That even his hired creation could rise to the occasion and stomp me good."

Mrs. Alving stomps her foot down and bears her teeth. "Oooooh!"

"Like a cow you screech, less a cat. Closer you come. Just a little further reach. Be positive. Perhaps, Mrs. Alving, you just might break my back with the stroke of your hoof, and thus compel me to will my very own trial."

"Fullfillment in my eyes!" Mrs. Alving cries. "Don't think I wouldn't spring now if I could. What scruples I would be abandoning I could stuff in my hip pocket. I will refrain the very lines of the role you so playfully obtain. 'But a lifetime of happiness, no man alive could bear it: it would be hell on earth time, times, half a time.' And as for heaven? No! Heaven is the home of the spoiled masters of reality? Isn't it a shame, dear god, that behind my tongue I hold another name?"

god gives Mrs. Alving a scornful look. "Out! Out! Out! Come on, out with it! Don't keep me waiting long. You with your infinite variety could surely spare one rod."

Mrs. Alving snickers. "Since you be the king of infinite space, cry all you want. And since we are jumping from stage to stage, you sing your song, I'll sing mine. Let's not fool ourselves. You ain't got the stuff. I discovered your line, so now it's my turn considering I'm still in the game, stopping short of the name. Let's put you to the test, and should you lose your rest, eternal be thy muse. This is so delicious. So nutritious be this theme. My clues come clean having been spoken by a herald, an archbishop, a chorus and, in darker terms, four who stretch much as you bid me to do stages ago. Time be of the essence even though the clues be hard to find. For should you prove right, it would be by way of doing wrong, whether by promise of pleasure, or gain, or by way of ancient song – to make trial of, to risk the dangers of, or to lure with seducing arms. Come on! Good god! Stretch as you bid me to do. Why all the fuss? Your kind of stretching hints more at tenesmus. Shall I give you a second to evacuate the strain? For, indeed, my clues are boldly plain. Four there be with attendants in tow; in a hall; on the second, of twelve; and most important of all, eleven comes seven with zero to fall. Still in a fix? Let me see whom I've nixed." Mrs. Alving starts going through her list counting each one on her fingers. "A chorus of woe, men in tow, three priests in a psalm, one herald, Singalong! his last name – a crier or messenger go – a T.B., A.A.C. who, in particular, brought out a highly variable, communicable disease of men at sea. Dearest god, does thou know the play?"

god scratches his chin, ponders a moment, then jumps in with, "'Tis not fair! 'Tis not fair! I gave you a line. All you give me are a cast of characters in a play I imagine divine."

Mrs. Alving chuckles. "Oh, if you only knew how divine the line marking the title atop its messenger. P.S.: a *t* before *s*. Then, most important of all, the first three as in divinity, as in Hebrews, as in a judge and priest of ancient Israel, as in the first three, with two, to, follow: *Eli.*"

god still appears flustered. "Nuts! Whim! I'm the one who set up this game! It is you who's in tow, and therefore *you* who must know the riddles I sow."

Mrs. Alving appears to speak matter-of-factly. "I grant you that title such as you are, for I can think of no finer a sow than you. And as long as you're sowing to set in motion your game of one kind or the other, what's a misplaced '*h*' for '*d*' when they stand so close to one another?"

god steps up to Mrs. Alving and attempts to overpower her with his size, which is double that of Mrs. Alving's, both width and lengthwise. "My fair chambermaid, is it? The peasant becomes the bishop and tries to take the king by check; however, diagonally, she moves across stages in an effort to diminish the force of my authority. And as long as you speak of dogs, beware, lest you stop in your chase for having lost the scent. For so I be, forever I change."

Mrs. Alving scrutinizes god. "No doubt. But underneath it all, it remains the same. As for losing the scent, please, a much harder game! But let's not tarry; the game is still undone. And in order to fully realize 'thy work is done,' you must advance yourself from between the formal stages of time, events, and lingering, transfixed, ethereal states of the mind."

Mrs. Alving catches a glimpse of Christ on the tube. He is crying his best upon the cross. Mrs. Alving says, "Destiny waits in the eye of god, and god is at rest. Tell me, *did you sleep through this as well?* Were you awake when the king gave in, four winks to a nod and a split in the shin? You best pray, my lord. As long as I'm awake, beware, lest I wake a dead world and be the first and the last to hold the keys to heaven and hell."

god laughs. "Worthless keys are those. Hang them around your neck as forgotten monuments. For without the doors to venture through there is no mystery and therefore no history."

Mrs. Alving steps backward until she is up against one of the bookshelves. She grabs for a massive enchiridion, and shakes it in god's direction. "Crime, oppression, indifference, eploitation is what I know of the history that has brought about your demise."

"My demise?!" god barks. "What makes you think your eyes to fall on such a prize so unattainable that an entire globe did explode upon attempting to challenge me at my omnigenous table? You speak of demise and you allude to a play on Christmas morning, 1170, when all on earth were ensorcelled and did Glory to my name in the highest. For the salvation of all! For his tormentous body in blood bursting sacrifice! For the sins of beasts breathing finite intellect! You, dribbling, that you cast as divine. You, rib, that you cast as fine. Your pale white natus. Your mind, a strange and insubstantial thing, carelessly plopped between your ears. And you think that you can challenge me with my demise?"

"What's the matter, god? Did the overall design of man slip through your plan and leave you with a close-ended plot in which you piled all of your mistakes? What I fear, god, is that when you die there will be no man to bury you, for no one will care except the tombic creatures that crawl across your grave."

god takes a deep breath. "You challenged me to a game, Mrs. Alving, so let me find an extemporaneous line. 'Death will come only when I am.' How, dear prey, can those doors be unbarred? Whether heaven bliss or hell charred, they do not exist. Neither one. Toodle-oo, good-bye, all done. To the loo."

Mrs. Alving looks shocked. "What is this you are conducting? You take so lightly, destruction, no less than suicide rendered from an unsound mind."

"Precisely, my dear most charming and sincere Mrs. Alving. That is why you must take pride in your calling, for it is I who summoned you here on knees to wash the blood of earth that I tracked in, even into my own hearth. Remember the broom, the back bent in laying the fire and in cleaning the hearth. Under sin, under grief, winter, birds and beasts, and most of all the blood of mactation. Your very own allusion, my dear, have now become a prophesy fulfilled. In cleaning this, the evidence of the universe, like me, a god, you'll be. Come on. What do you say? Let's turn and mix."

Mrs. Alving folds her hands before her. "Now you tempt me twice, and unless it be a third, I'll be falling without a safe journey."

god puts his arm around Mrs. Alving. "But consider this. Things are different now. You can be made full, and since you are so hungry for gain, howbeit salvation be its name, I should think it wise for you to grab at the chance."

Mrs. Alving steps away from god. "What am I to you? A second Eve? What apple is this? Offered by a haje? Perhaps you should have picked a deeper passage and given me less the advantage, for the water is shallow at the ford at Hajlah and not half deep enough to hold your sins."

"You think to entrap me? Or at least confuse me with your morbid attempts to say a simple thing? Please, Mrs. Alving, spare me your feeble attempts to confuse the mystery any further and simply cleanse the scene."

"Now I look back upon my life in stages," Mrs. Alving muses, "and I consider the first time around when, from the ground, god formed man, and from man, woman, and from woman, the tree, and from the tree, the serpent, and from the serpent, the downfall, and from the downfall, promises, promises broken all. The long, hard struggle based upon a play, nay, more a drama with a price to pay. But what good to fall? To what avail? Therein are martyrs numberless – saints, heroes, villains, all. If there is any room left, it would hardly matter. Conscious or not of rest, perhaps the alternative is best."

god smiles fondly. "That is why I call upon you to be my child, to begin a world anew, and to put into it what was lacking in the former residence. Come now, Mrs. Alving, surely you must have a clue. Does this not ring a memory? Does this not feel like the beginning at the end all over again? You're to be reborn, godsend!"

THE WHORE

On this level, in this room with a throne, she was five feet two inches tall. She was lean and loose; and although she modeled, her legs were somewhat crooked, and she looked a bit pisgah. She had a bizarre upper canine-shaped head. But like a strong, majestic, volatile bird with outstretched wings, her upper lip presented itself like a climax to a flight of fancy or a dropdead look. Like a cat – the glass-like eye of a parricidal cat named Dinahvindicatus, her lower lip displayed itself in an equivocal pout. In the beginning, she was skinny to the point of famine-shocking anyone whose eye rested upon her, if only for a fleeting moment, if only to skin the cat. Like a needle, a vertical line with an eye for thread at one end, she bore herself; a needle-shaped leaf from a tree, such as a well-oiled tree with various grape-bearing branches. She was a total; a natural one hundred per cent inner-lit beauty – mark of sobriquet; his answer to sobriety. But she was, in essence, perfection itself, worthy to loosen and seal and open any book, and thereby burn it.

Turn the fascicle.

The camera that is the representation of the eternal eye loved to image her in its paludous chamber, its dark room of the low lands. Her cheekbones were slanted ledges that held the salt of her origin. The sensuousness of her mouth balanced the gentle slope of her great shoulder blade. Her eye seized the observer with a subintelligential language all its own that dared to suggest *'come be a part of my bailiwick,'* that even seemed to change as her gaze became a stare, hard and soft as rock, penetrating and intense, loving and wanting, forgiving and compassionate, holding the salt that was locked within the watery depths that was also an idiom as primitive and as old and as significant as the birth of a child, or the sweeping walk of a nun with a special purpose toward mariolatry. She was waiting in camera, now in *sobornost.* She was waiting for him. In a stand-by line she stood, waiting for a certain season when she would finally be spotted by an important agent. Her mother (a true devotee of the Norman Theory), who had lived in her house and had worked as a housewife, and her father, who had worked as a professional Boxer, had been her dramatic teachers. Throughout her existence, under their roof, even in their bathtub, she had been a troubled, salient child, eyeful as a scan daisy, as probing as a scutiger, but ever so rationally troubling to the *dokladchiki* under a load of birchbark documents, business notes and amadelphous messages.

This was the dream, the modern tale that hit humanity. Cocks and Box. She grumbled and moaned and cried, and spoke bowls of plastic poetry (. . . *box the Jesu it and get cock roaches hot shit* . . .) and illusions, thoughts and symbols, desires and revenge, redemption and despair. So impressionable, and yet so creative. She was the girl of the movement, a lady of ton however imprisoned as a *skomorokhi*, alone, to face herself, face-to-face, two bears in a golden bowl, in a challenge that she alone must rise from like the air breathing baby bears rising out of the sea on big rubber bowls, balancing music and elementary theater in immoral and paganistic terms. She wasn't about to get stuck in a pigeon hole. Oh no! Or at a table knocking over a saltcellar. But she meant to escape into an image; to change herself.

But it is not easy to move from grime to glamour, and remain steadfast, true and noble throughout, without suffering dromomania, wandering beyond the three seas. And for this reason, she stayed inside of her own thoughts. She could have been taller, she could have been shorter; it mattered not what others said about her as long as she had her *kormleniia*. She was certain of one thing. In the world that Peter Bogatyr Imperial had made on his own, with not one entity higher than himself to look upon, one must finally be directed by oneself, alone.

THE TWINITY

The pillow that I rest my head upon, the cranium coffin of goose-feathered compactibility, can barely hold the massive barrage of activated gray-mattered weapontry being manufactured for purposes that only top personnel have access to. The blue print is half-revealed, half-completed. And, at the tail-end, cautiously peering from around the sun-saturated corner that leads via canal to the celestial den, where god sits in his favorite easy chair, back to the wall, blocked, but nonetheless puffing vanilla-scented swirls of saintly thought, I stand ready to intrude upon the almighty – ready to venture forth with full disclosure, my most honorable and irretractible plan of assault.

The burning bush that smokes before my eye – the fiery ball that melts the burning bush that smokes before my eye – stands the test of time to an upright position. And I kneel like philomel in allegiance to sweet retribution. Were my tongue retrieved and my voice composed of the same oak that felled Babylonian steel, I would clear my throat like a forest ripe for harvest, scoop up the um suff, pad my pseudoglottis, bare my branches three false ways, one apart from the other, and entwine god in a grip that might just render him crying 'Uncle!' and put the dog right under the Pawnbroker's sign, trading in three golden balls for three green frogs with a note from Momma: *Don't come the umquhile uncle over me.* For if there is to be an elimination of fear, then it must and most crucially be an elimination of all fear. For consider this: if I am to succeed then I must be bold enough to come down in the likeness, as on a mare, and tap god on the shoulder, and say with a voice as melodiously sweet as a nightingale, "Might I please have your seat for a spell?"

SPACESHIP EARTH

The final perfect twist to the tale that is the earth, to the reality that is the universe, to the spin that is the curse, to the burrow that is to all that there is beyond earth, is that overthrow, overcome, recall and dissolve would put such needless limits on spotless existence.

They looked half-crazed, half-awake, these creatures of temporary space and time. They had moved in their deliberate and well-spaced paces through endless streets foul of spirit, odious to the energy that had composed them. They were walking figures once – always being somewhere at sometime; whether dashing to a cab in a driving rain or shopping on a clean and well-lit floor; whether composing before a sea of instruments, all eager and nervous notes; whether dining above a cityscape, a skyline faintly streaked with remnants of dusk and filmy mare's-tail; whether embraced in limbs, soft and sticky twilight sweat, lint and dust; whether fighting storming torrents of words wished were never said; whether crying, laughing all in one wet breath – they had taken the journey backwards, as far backwards as the involutional cry of god merging in his own space, grasping his own guts, entangled in his own design, coiling inwards, with or without the returning face of time.

Now, each in a silent way was occupied in imagining how it might have been had god been *without a doubt towards humanity.* How it might have been had god not pointed the accusing and punishing finger at anything. In their own silent journey backwards, as each was occupied in imagining the gaseous cry of resignation, a quiet but most frightening wave of nausea came over each one. That they walked and moved and went about in the flesh as prints of incarnation suggested that they were but by-products, like shipwrecked seamen in plight beckoning to beautiful Nausicaa playing with balls. Even as some of them spent their existences out in a condition of sleepwalking, neither aware of their fellow human being, nor of themselves, nor of their surroundings, nor of their wants, nor of their desires, they were essentially alone – drones – entombed within their own isolated states; and behind their drugged and filmy eyes, a plea for assistance, a chaffy cry of despair, a feeble attempt to find a last trick in the tale of empty existence.

In the journey backward, before the bear cry of risibility, into the journey backward, into the chamber of sanctimoniousness, Spaceship Earth crept. Inside of it could be felt a net of wants and needs, impossible to escape with perfection – could be felt hooks, snags and traps galore. What abundance of crops! What arcane plants! What bushes! What trees! What samsonian logs! What pomaceous decrees! This was not a clean and empty space. This was a space cluttered with debris, refuse, bits and pieces of cutting glass, bleeding creations of thoughts bursting forth like big proletarian bangs. This was a violent space – spontaneous explosions, constant as driven waves upon distant, forgotten shores; pulled by gravity, by the moon, by the system that is solar, by pieces of massive rock hurdling and colliding with spheres as gaseous as worlds . . . but worlds, dead and cold, with a quietistic purpose.

Each was occupied in imagining how cold and distant a hesychast could be to the substance that rests inside of his/her very own head. Each of them, alone, yet side by side, longed to ask one another the question, *What god be this?* The good bad book creates in one's mind a sort of false map of the world into which one can retreat at odd moments throughout the rest, and which can survive a visit to the reel countries that they represent. It's a double trip, as is the book laid before, where myth comes true and is believed in by one-eyed saints, who should always be judged guilty until proven otherwise. But in the quiet mission of their trek, the question could find no proper place to emerge. Each one of them remained alone to ask, "What is it?"

As Spaceship Earth ventured forward, there was much weeping and gnashing of teeth within, and some imagined this to be the hell of an original plan: *to Timothy (and Tender?),* whose A.M. call 419-1995 to fedbldg was made clear by the obstreperous suffering in all ears as a wind swept down the plain. For these were not only the cries of the guilty on the Frankfurt horizontal but of the innocent as well, alternating with each other, and on display, each exchanging their vows of good and evil as is typical of the numerous shitty journeys of the skull. What loving spirit bid them to make haste dwelt within each and everyone of their souls. A brute race perhaps. Without a trace to the sea, a fleeing animal might escape the gallows, even in the form of a 3.2, or, after having eaten lousewort, eructate, and be cleansed at the porch at Bethesda. But sheep, in themselves, cannot only be saved or slaughtered, they can also *disguise the measurements.* Yes, they can hide a man curled up underneath its belly;

"G, o see Gagarin rushin' by"; moreso, they can shield an entire troupe (tied beneath) from a one-eyed germ, or outtower an immoral universe stressing rules of desperate passion, or blend the leftovers into lientery.

And so this was the case of the troupe within the belly of the ship gliding past the blackness of this ill-hearted universe, as the blackness ran its hands along the back of the ship, as it sailed through the threshold in pursuit of the *right* angle, or, at least, the mark on the left shoulder of O! To be one of the 25 brightest stars on wood! To have a balance > power and a sackcloth of hair. To have a mag. of 1.63, being made of kings and priests over the blood of a dead man! Yes, the past can come back to haunt you and hook you by surprise and expiscation, like a female warrior in erubescence (or a Geronimo inquiry), if you do not buckle to and row with the will. For the past is nothing more than the backwater of an isolated backward pool in one's heart that would long to drown a less than fearful soul. Now there were far too many victims to count. Far too many nizyes. Forget about hares (or sheeps or swines) – chasing them and losing them (especially around 8:30), you tend to forget why you are here. 3.2 knew this, as elusive as he is. It takes much more than a bellatrix hunt after the fox to find the most vital clue.

Spaceship Earth sailed everso motionlessly through the magical darkness that marked its transition. Its occupants could hear a distinct cry; and even though the cry uttered no words, the sound of it stayed fresh in the minds of the travelers within, so that it would seem like each and everyone of them was bewitched, simply by the motionless state that the cry put them in.

There is no approaching home for one who is locked in a trance, wherein the consciousness is unaware of the state that the unconsciousness is in. The unconsciousness is only the soul reminding the body *alter idem*, howbeit in an abbreviated whisper, or, perhaps, in a curt cry, what its ultimate purpose is. It does not matter if a man surrounds himself with wife, children, parents, or possessions. For there is no 'welcome home' available to a man who has not first found himself; no home in which to brighten his return, nor Paraclete to overshadow him. *Mystery, give us your oil, for our lamps have gone out and it is the last hour.* If a man comes to the end of his journey without having fulfilled his superior quest, he will find, in place of a home, a ruin, if nothing at all. For the total cries come out *6626*, where *in*=666 with 2 left over.

. . . Spaceship Earth appeared to relax in what now seemed to be the music of cries that the enveloping blackness contained, however hidden, like an embryo. If 3.2 were present it was not evident. Numbers, like rabbits (or little snakes), can escape the grasp of any probing approach. As Spaceship Earth hung suspended in 30min space, like a drop of moisture that gave up in the ghostly night, each occupant was piled high to the walls of Spaceship Earth, straining to hear the skeleton cries of Souls in Agrypnia, disembodied from what was an encasement of weathered skin clinging tight around the sioux bones. If these were the cries of lost human endeavors, the living occupants of Spaceship Earth would search them out and, upon finding them, open their hull, which is only the concealment, more at hell, and bid the tortured souls to come in and rest and listen to themselves think eternal, and to thereby solve their individual dilemma . . .

THE CRIES ARE RESTLESS AND HEADLESS BUT OCCUPY AN ANCIENT LINE

One always takes a risk when one picks up a straggler or two, a desperate soul longing for a ride to the nearest paradigm. Like a moth encountering $C_6H_4Cl_2$, the straggler nearly always wears the cloth in secret. Every human being on earth – that is, every eye – followed his/her own course depending upon what life had handed him/her in the way of *givens*, as opposed to what he/she had *earned* through his/her own efforts, be it through good measure of all power in the body of a wise masterbuilder or a thorn in the flesh. For this is the record: For anyone who owned his/her own vehicle, there was always one who lived solely by foot. But then there was the middle ground – those who lived by foot and bummed their rides. This seemed to be the case with (eleven) *thecries*, as they will henceforth be referred to. They were not just *thecries* sounding unto themselves in the dark; moreso, they were *thecries* that beckoned. One could even say that *thecries* provoked; though upon hearing their forlorn wails, one need ask oneself, *Should I heed thecries and choke this vehicle and beg them to enter leaderless; or should I forever shake my head less; or wagmore, accelerate, and leave thecries standing in my dust?* When your actions finally support your thoughts, you will know for certain your current course. Anything less is uncertainty – a jockey on a dark horse.

The travelers within Spaceship Earth were serious about their quest. Yes, they did want to find home; a rest to the struggle. O for the love of history and the loss of what once roamed. Finding god – *there* was neither the answer nor the question; either course suggests that one's destiny is contingent upon his whereabouts, believing here is there. Lo, come and be hol.

And, yet, there are more ways than *two* in reaching home. More ways than merely acceptance or rejection, present or absent. A third course neither considers nor dismisses god. Its 101 path is strewn with: *god can be who and what he says he is, just as I can be who and what I say I am.* Each to his/her own, devoid of consequence. Whereas some believe that god leads to paradise, the alternative in such a scenario is a place where sheer cliffs lead to fiery rocks below, where nothing lives in safety, and where there is no escape. The middle ground, however, suggests an irous sea where the foam is but a blanket for flotsam. In some respects we are very much a vagrant, impoverished, obsolete, breathing race heading for still a greater wreckage than the worse mishap at sea, where the rose waves lend their own steps to the ghost dance, unless one considers the trance that comes and goes during coitus at the tanged roots.

Know this: god's cry is the cry of everyone, since he professes to be all things. Those in Spaceship Earth therefore wondered: could *thecries* we hear out there really be the single cry of god? And if this is true, could these cries be meant to tempt us, to deceive us into still yet a more confusing room where we, not unlike tawny timbers and assorted debris, will be tossed in doubt and fear, into a kind of death anxiety to the nth degree by the waves that kick us and herd us like cattle to the waiting flames licking the mists of eternity? Of all we are, of all we breathe, we are still the noble ship "T", the Enyo of light – Ida, nadi & pingala – that goes down to the sea to rest forever in the liquid contents of a deep and unseen passage, that is otherwise known as seasonal destiny.

BLOODLESSBABEUCHAINNOWAYREDEMPT

It was difficult to say exactly what these cries were. Heaven could keep her sheep, hell her hounds; but it did not seem that the ship was likely to keep each and everyone of her own souls. For *thecries* not only reached into the depths of unconsciousness, they threatened to snatch away the brittle spirits within, leaving behind only an empty shell standing rigid and transfixed, like the dead in their horrible way. The husks left behind would never tell any stories on their own, unless the living put words on their deadened tongues and bid the dead, dry figures to speak only in the seat of their evocable imaginations.

god walked here today, in the garden progeria of whose bloom came early, god brought incipient dotage upon residuum as soon as he uttered 'forbidden.' In the cool of that afternoon, when questrist and resignee could both talk as friends, one moved and felt an urge to condition the other's placement in earth. For how does a creation of love stop evolving and growing as long as it is a creation? Does not a seed take root to grow upward? Does not a seed become the bush, the flower, the tree? In the late shoot of that afternoon, paradise shoots took to bloom, uplifted and transplanted none too soon.

One certain woman, in particular, who had been a part of the whole of the world, and a seller of purple, was occupied with her own special encounters as she proceeded to go backwards. Soon enough, the journey would lead her to a far place where, in the laughter of rebirth, ugh, goddesses never die, fig trees never wither away, mountains are never cast into the sea, and the population-at-large is never answerable to god. Glancing at all humanity around her, catching the first stone, this woman who was imagining slipped in and out of the realms that each one occupied; the cities of everyone's dreams, the dreamdump as it were, millennium after millennium – names, ads, dresses, disguises forever changing, forever riding from stage to stage, forever shaking off the dust – the slime – shoeless, staveless, spentless – the tables of stone.

Earth seemed distant. She recalled once looking down at it from a passing plane, thinking how small everything seemed to be. Shining city lights, the darkened theater in; complete eutaxy. She recalled flying from place to place, attempting in between to connect the standing dots. So much happened in each space, in each place. Did it take more than a god to solve the geometric puzzle of any one clouterly Mystery? In the faint streets of her youth, she had dressed in shapely evening costumes (marveilleuse fashions with picturesque hats, flaring brim, décolleté gowns and skirts that hung down in a tube as though bound for a ball), stepping over the puddles left by passing johns. Sometimes, in a trance, she had stood like an eumoirous statue herself, her gloutos a visible assemblage – a light, filmy mass, undone, gazing down-raised up – until like a poor pilgrim on a holey journey to venerealation she had turned around to face a hospital wall, billed as a billiken.

A tenebrous hospital where she had been fed stolen sweet waters and secret bread by quest nurses from the myrmecophilous depths, who also grasped 1080 tubes for the chisel-shaped edge of gnawing terata, beginning a fetal attempt at teratgenesis in some of the deeper wards of the institution, among the HIV (deposed and excommunicated) and the consecration of O.

To the one who imagined in her own way while traveling back before the birth of god – she thought to have read in a faded, yellowing headline page that an ad angel had drowned in a flood. They say that angels can only drown seamen. Perhaps it is true. Difficult cobblers often do. Some battled, some died in the tabloids. Other drowned in wine. *Little men at sea often do.* But seamen break up, retreat and fall back into a dry and flaky reside . . .

She, among the multitudes, wished to dissolve god, because with him there was a silent partner who did not protect her from the poison gas that leaked from her own chiromantic hand. She recalled, in various flavors, the very tralatitious words that served as her last earthly visitors. *I did not have a mother who born me; but a father ruled my heart. And I spoke as an adult with a baby's tongue.* The one thing that delighted her now as she gazed from face-to-face, as she thought about the various plane trips over god-forsaken earth, as she thought about the many attempts to take up her own little pantophagous life, was that she would never have to return again. (And yet again, behind autumn shades, she went down on Hades and kept her mouth glued to him for months.)

She fancied herself a discoqueen in a G-rated film, wearing the best of *haute couture* – reinforced leather gauntlets, a fur moiré napkin to catch the drops of her cycle – surrounded by masked warriors and plavusa cigarette girls fusing with the net, telling fortunes by reading coffee grinds to the rest.

Why am I mad? she asked. *What birth, this disorder in mind? It hurts, it's foolish, crazy, silly, mad and senseless. Did I give birth to such a state? Scum with blight on the dress. Do your part. Spread out the rumors and throw down the darts. But this only leads me to ask, what is it?*

That was why she allowed herself to be seduced. She was hurt, foolish, crazy, silly, mad and senseless at god for having reduced her fractions to bread.

A WHALE OF A TIME AT THE LAST SUP.

Another who was occupied in imagining how it is to be while traveling in Spaceship Earth through the 'deli' of god was in the midst of truly knowing deordination when he happened to glance down upon his menu matricula and saw the words *order rare Christ deo volente* fade in-and-out . . . fin . . . time on his hand . . . Should he wash his hand clean of time like Pilate within the courtyard before the pavement? Or should he deorder a *pasch straw me* on rye? 'Tis a bit of whiskey desipience for a gypsy gentleman waltzing through the rye ballroom in duple/triple time. But *G wiz, fin!* . . . for this was the late judgment . . . The last order . . . *(rye and mayo?)*, and he was to be part of the pi with respect to the deontic menus plaisirs of his inanition.

Now it occurred to this one who was occupied in imagining how each holey one upon the earth had his/her own role to play, that each and everyone had an order to make. Even those who typically take orders, in turn, have an order to make. *Ladhere . . . a bowl of red lentil soup to rouse us . . . Say, let's all have a lamb da'cism and sing a Martial's line: Sol et luna luce lucent alba, leni, lactea, labor lady laid life and lettuce lich fowls while we lich-wake.*

And then he thought of himself as a Titian, being served. One of a family of scient giants whose name, in short, could have been Tit. Now he could see himself as the son of a Tit who came to dine. Seventh in order at the table: O. *A bon chat, bon rat.* And, too, as he drifted through god's deli in pursuit of god, he began to feel like Spartacus in the gladiator's hold, waiting to fight the good tat fight to death; dog to the bloodhound; waiting to unionize the broken mass with a soldering nipple; the radical germ; the radical anus.

And in the center of his trek, he called forth the distant face of

Christ

in order to give himself strength of allusion. *(Were not movies magic?* he asked himself. *"A gift for a champion dwelling in a dark church with water leaks?")*

The watchfulwaiter, a ladhere, kind enough to follow through the menu.

O the earth was the first to emerge from primeval chaos and bring forth the starry sky.

Delicious barley bagels, garlic, onion, egg, water and rye. Two white fish among so many locks. *Number two!*

"... ladhere, there's a seed of tares, just how watchful are you? What new ale you have?"

O Gaia, you brought forth the sea. Pontus, deep and barren, without any sweet act of love. You brought forth Oceanus which flowed around the whole table: flat cakes, popcorn, figs fresh from the boil, "Dr. Is, such a plaster! such a heze fix! such a big eye!" O. The better to see you with. Light-stepping Oceanides. You put fifteen years on a man if not a day. Holy S. sq., eleventh at the table. Six thousand feet deep. Take the bitter with the sweet, E saiasth at the last sup. *Must acknowledge the corn beef, take another slice of mea culpa, me dear. Now don't protest. I insist mesaint . . .* And exactly where to place the salt shaker, the contents of which gets spilled on to the table, like one's guts, one's bowels, one's meretricious destiny – destinies in which histories are consistent with the beauty and the love of the ones who came to sow while Spartacus slept with his mesail up, *try the lamb, RIP, it's been boiled in its mother's milk,* just as there are also other histories leading to other pleasantly observed states of the sprung up blade in which real historical characters ceased to exist under the guiding wings of elected senators. "Sir, the bitter with the sweet? Wolf it down with meat. It's better to wake it through into the barn than bundleburn before its due. Pass the Jud," as G got up here in order to look down upon the old world as it was.

And then he who was occupied in imagining all that is saw how god had rearranged himself over time, over the histrionic paths, to create false memories at the abracadabra table – be they human, written or transfixed in massive monuments of stone; be they dreams of a Final Theory or of a Universe, six stages long; be they images of Revelations or visions lightly digested through the senses of neology. *Sis boom bah* and *sodelong.*

"Psst . . . Pass me the mustard and tell Ladhere he's got to be more watchful if he expects a good tip. Burp. Tell him the plaster won't do for the gas, nor the seltzer. Tell him to come and see. Burp. This won't do. What's this?" (Dip. Dip.) "I smell mint jelly!" G proposed to disposals of man. *"Burp. Do quickly."*

And while he who was occupied in imagining all that is drifted forwards/backwards through god's deli on a wave, he knew that his destiny would bring him to the given location at the given time in a given land, where he would find god poring over and ripping out every page of every book wherein god was forever and ever Bible-backed, and having a neonomian-neophrenian fit. god's face was ashen, puffy and deeply lined, and the eye seemed to be glazed over with a massive film. The left leg trembled violently, and the left hand clutching desperately could not stop the trembling. The shoulders were caved-in and the look was smaller and took on that negative suggestion that one might equate with recrudescence, where there would be a return of an undesirable condition, manifested in the increased severity of a disease, as is evidenced by a totally shrunken look, a hunched head and a deeply buried, lifeless eye, crazed and hungry, like that of an old, old vulture dining on the dead; and a lurching walk, almost irrecoverable, like a last drunkard's trek toward some ill-defined destination, where there might be a cluster of half-concerned doctors awaiting in tired attendance with a simple two-word prognosis: *crux medicorum*, among whom would undoubtedly include Dr. T. Morelle, Ch.B., a total creeping baca-type with a rank smell due to an overexcessive nicotine habit, and a cloak that was manufactured by *Belladonna* that was never washed, even in spite of constant deaths in attendance, and sleeves that were undoubtedly poisonous due to blood-soaked diseases that would splatter and leave star-spangled splots of purple decay on the cloth, who was also infamous for his special contribution of brightly arrayed pep pills, not to mention sex hormones and thousands of Köster's Anti-Gas Tablets for chronic flatulence. An other-worldly shuffling man, well-versed in pulverized bull testicles and shambles, as that term applies to meat markets and slaughterhouses of mass destruction and free-flowing bloodshed, as well as being at ease in scenes of monumental disorder and irreversible confusion; a man of overwhelming, formidable ugliness devoutly disliked by butchers-at-birth who found the doctor's long-winded discourses on pharmaceutical tonics (i.e., bright anodynes with strychnine base) to both benefit and *verhaftung* the actions of the nervous system.

He who was occupied in imagining how it is pondered this stage deeply. The thought suddenly gripped him as he stammered like battos – this was all part of the whole design. That god should intervene and attempt to stop the spirit of humankind from being all there is was indeed a crime, the very essence of aid itself. How god could have been so hypnotized, so jealous, so envious, so fearful that he would obstruct his own childrens' minds from clearly knowing their own distinct placement in the universe only proved to show that god had become the milk of his own galactophagous comeuppance, and had thusly turned an offensive belch into that which demanded to be reverend, respected and honored as the only worthy eructation. Yes, indeed, he had created his very own empire out of one historical burst of wind, with the order shouted, *"Bis peccare in bello non licet. Receive thy Siseraras!"* It was no wonder that he could not accomplish this feat without first experiencing a sickened world in the process, with all therein taken to their sickbeds under a dire decumbiture in the *horo-heavens*, thanks to psychopompousness. For it was known in every human being's heart that there was indeed something even Higher to attain to, something to Become ("nor the way in meal or in malt"); but that only by belching was one likely to find it. Indeed, when god cut humankind off from this Absolute state of wind and threatened humankind to never seek It unless he first receive Death in the face or, at the very least, one of Adam's excommunicated Mazikeens condemned to a purely Mudspiritual State by having received only a portion of the Meal-of-the-Universe, god was neglecting to share with humankind one of the most important aspects of Unconditional Existence; and that is the Energy, the Pomaceous Power that comes from the Eternal Belch; the Power of Release. *Requiem aeternam.*

And that was why, in his own consciousness, in his own unqiue way, he who was occupied in imagining was going to go in as a warrior, a giant, a Ulysses, a David, a Judas with a questionable sway, so unlike the singsong Lambach solemn splendor of his abbot-adoring youth. *Auf nach Cannes.* The others around him were going in too – to dissolve god in their own unique way as well. And in so far that he was part of the whole, he who was occupied in imagining could feel, could smell, could even taste the distinctive spiritual essence of each and every pocket of gas around him. What a beautiful sensation. *Annus mirabilis.* To know at any given instance the *actual* sensation and distinctive impression of all of existence all at once as it moves inward to dissolve god, to plague and to fire, and to thereby become a beloved all-powerful movement unto itself. Once in this state, all humanity would evolve and simply become the essence, the creation, the absolute, the eternal state of the universe, all-in-one.

Leaving behind the drama, leaving behind the absurdity, the humor, the burlesque, the satire, the tragedy, the classical, the reform, the abstract, the impressionistic, the renaissance, the restoration, the monarchy, the democracy, the dictatorship, the astrology, the astronomy, the *glazialkosmologie*, the cosmic fire and ice, the ancient nors, the modern nords, the wet nors, the baroque nors, the rococo nors, the Hoer myths, the wet bigers, the saturnic fables, the deaths, the dreams . . . the dreams . . . the dreams . . .

ENTER OBIUS VERMICULARIS

O to bore deep into the universe of the eye, the Oceanus of consciousness was what he, doup among the magnitudes, was now destined to do. The power and the glory of his own mawkish genius was (even by manner of his past) predetermined from the hour of his birth. As he stood naked in his own essence, he could feel the divine element that had originally been placed in each heart. And in another tongue he uttered, *"en cueros."* The molecules, the vapors of his genius (indeed, he was about to undergo an OHG fart) would never again be separated from the Unique Entity, nor from the fact that *he is more than dung – he is well-dung – for he now comes into being with one particular code: All-and-Nothing-in-One-Fece.* To beget the Hole. The sentimental journey of the Maggot to the brain and downward ho! to Os, where Mag will meatus in a fanciful dance of 'Balthazar's maggots.' And in tapping into the total consciousness of his essence, he could also feel the rock-breaking power. Luno Dun Cow. Birth of the saxifrage. *Pare au continuum . . . Gottago! Gottago! . . .* Wherein each soul is the *pater familias.* The Bull on the Dunghill and the *fyrdung* prepared for war in armoured birds. Even now he could recall the offerings of cakes, honey and milk; the first strike of the knight; death and the devil hanging on the wall; and the copies of *Ostara* on his nightstand; and in recalling this he could feel the Genius of the Emperor Prior revered with sacrifices throughout the Empire. What a guy! Pinned to the wall, chewing myrrh in a preagonal twist of fate. O to be god and not have to beg nor break for bread at your own castle gate like a pri-mate. How each and every human had longed for this.

Now a corporate Genius was floating through the interior blackness of god, and in this odyssey, this parenthetical journey (actually a perergon of sorts, an ejaculatory, episodic, incidental digression, a *dictum* of the judge *[genetrix]*, a *scholium* of the producer, given to sudden fits of parerethesis), he who was occupied in imagining could sense a specific kind of divinity guarding god's effervescent existence – a divine power ruling over a particular spot over the stall. G . . . all. And just as a flaming sword had guarded over the tree of life, a riddling shield had been kept over the Capitol of Rome, the Throne, bearing the inscription, *To the Genius of the city of Rome, be he male bone or female fustilug.* Is genius not an abstract, divine thing . . . the same tractable formula encoded into prayers, into visions, and into dreams, both male and female, coded in the mind's map to the *arcan caelestia . . .* where one is likely to encounter the ancestor Abbot Hagen presiding over his haken with punious pride?

And as he who was occupied in imagining connected to the energy of parodistic events having come before him, he experienced a reckoning. But these were not such ancient times.

This was the twenty-first century. Dregs of scared saints were in style. Loosed seasons were in vogue. It is the next stage – which made darkness feel very dark indeed – loosening, declining, and finally falling like a dry leaf with a dead message. All he needed to do was to imagine (in his search for the Ultimate Dissolution) and behold! he found himself looking at . . . a Cyclops! And his thoughts circled around his head like so many pieces of brown, toasty bread smoking in a christloss dream.

He who was occupied in imagining stepped cautiously toward the Cyclops, for he knew that this Cyclops was more than a mere vision in the path toward god, and must be dealt with delicately.

"Cyclops," he who was occupied in imagining said, "god had us believe that he ruled over the earth as a trinity. Beside you I can see the severed heads of three gods in all: father, son and holy ghost. Might I gain entrance into your kingdom, I, too, might slay god with a knowing hand. In secret I tell you this. I am the one who sacked the New Look during the last sup. I drew a line in death and impaled a lamb on a stick. How I would love to finally slay god to dust without receiving punishment and tedesco furor, without being driven insane and having to cut off my yellow-fleshed member, as well as the tenth part of my brain. If I seek your assistance, Cyclops, and gain all that I quest, perhaps I'll be able to avoid the pine in my breast and be forever honored-reborn into life from death. To be able to come down from the heavenly spheres and be freed from the ties of matter where existence's hounds lie in the street beyond the recurrence of both life and death."

The Cyclops blinked and his wet eye went in and out of sight; but when it was out its exposed pupil was black and penetrating, and its surrounding white orbit was crisscrossed in red.

"So you desire to kill a god?" the Cyclops said. "Simply said, that's simple enough. However, I give you much credit for finding me, for I truly am a killer of gods and hold no fear nor reverence for any of them. Howbeit, I am hard to find. Expensive disguise, this murshid, and my sanbenito painted black dev and tongues fit to size. See my limb? Fruitful, *par pari refero.* And my sign: the Charnel House. Consuming them is my pastime. Indeed, with my very own hand I squeezed Zeus into a kind of juice that was so much sweeter than what you normally get from the can. Those heads you see that number three were my latest kills, biten off their triglot. Having cut off their members, their bloods within did spill, with which I used to wax my floors and coat my door; take notice, *religio loci;* and now the heads that bore their passing I will use as aurelian pieces to string. And sing such phrases as:

I remember you.

You're the ones I plopped into a stew

Such a brew

Oh, let me tell you, I remember you . . .

I'm still working on the chorus and plan to turn the entire work into a living epic, a medley staged and filmed to both highlight and rectify the current acculturational and parsimonious problems of the ecumenical movement. Which reminds me, *esquamate*, did you happen to see Doris of the lovely hair? Not in the style of a *day*, but more the daughter of Oceanus and Tethys, kissing cousin of Ceres, cornball queen and all? I hear her meat is particularly lean from having lived in a palace in the depths of the sea for some thirty-three years, roughly 3.14159265 miles from where Dallas Trinity use to be, not a stone's throw away from Palatine Hill, where in August the weeds spill over the ledge into the Palatinate on the Rhine, where a bunch of swasies play the Crystal Palace, an orthodox cellar for fish in general. Which brings me to a vital point: I simply love country music and honky-tonk joints."

C. REFRESHMENT

He who was occupied in imagining (who from this place forward will be referred to as Dr. Sseus) – his heart sank within him. The commanding voice and the *pas seul* dancing rhythms of the Cyclops's mind were quite alarming. Aside from the fact that a crest of golden hair adorned his shoulders and his lower extremities took on the likeness of a sprightly goat in pink pajamas, there was something quite altogether ominously reminiscent about the manner in which the Cyclops spoke. It was more his accent, first starting off somewhere in Brooklyn but ending deliberately in an Irish brogue.

All the same, his vast and specific vocals grounded his scrannel-forked tongue with a root befitting a hyaina lapping whiskey.

"I'm sure your pat tastes and interests are each your own," Dr. Sseus said. And for this I've hardly a quarrel. *Quid proquo.* Having come in legs, both wild and wooly, I understand perfectly your seedy condition. This being the great resurrection of dead and buried words, my covered words of contempt be for another god – the god of circumcision and oil."

The Cyclops yawned and stretched, though not particularly in that exact order, and responded, *"Mutatis mutandis.* As for gods I chew them like children's vitamin tablets. Indeed, my belly's been stuffed with so many arms, legs and heads, my dung's come out like fairy dust, I'm afraid due to an imbalanced diet. Too many combustible gods down the gullet. Too many fall guys. Too many stuffed effigies handled roughly, dropped 'n fire. Too many hard-shelled wagfs with a chewy mutawalli center. I haven't an ounce of resistance when it comes to those light temptations." And then with an eye that did more than just spy, the Cyclops askewed Dr. Sseus over for perhaps pinguis dessert. "Hmm . . . you say you're a hero and not a god? Good heavens, mother night! Might you be a priestess of Aphrodite who was loved by Leander who lived on the island of *Sex Toes* in a tower on the seashore, alone with winds and waves?"

"Feizit forbid! For one, Hero is a woman and I a man. Two, in her grief and despair, she tore her tunic and fell from the tower to her lardy death. A fatal gift."

"Good lard! Ida see a nixie, fixed, and a Fata, hiss! In printer's slang, *hell,* the program's setting. Then your breast would be smaller and not as tasty as a dears, I fear," the Cyclops yawned. "I shouldn't want to eat you if you truly be a man. For men taste much like Spam, and I hate that spread!"

At this point the Cyclops rolled over and made to go back to bed. He yawned and belched and farted, too, in that particular order, starting first at the head. And the wind from his farts bowled Dr. Sseus over into another kind of Gastro journey and, in consequence, made him look a lot like Hero, who after all rolled over into the sea pinned to her own untimely death.

"Excuse me," Dr. Sseus said, picking himself up and approaching the bed, "but I will be frank and lay my cards over on the table and step off from this fable that I find myself stuck in. The god I seek to dissolve is the father of ham – a titman neither you nor I understand."

"Man," the Cyclops said with his back to Dr. Sseus, "if it's desolation you seek, simply plop this ham of yours into a glass of cold water and wait for him to fizzle out into a fuzzy-wuzzy sudan, as I've heard those crunchies slave between my molars many a times, and have used their fat to heal many a wound."

"No, no. No, I don't think you understand. He isn't a tablet. It isn't that kind of fizzle. I meant to say that he is the supposed creator of the obtuse earth, both night and day . . ."

"Then you are speaking of Zeus. I told you, he's been seduced . . . or rather consumed! You should have dropped by sooner. I might have given you a loin, and a bit of bile for drink, none too sooner."

"No. No. No. Still I compel you to think. This is not a late god that you know of. For this be first a god of the Jews."

"Then *chew* him if you must! *Sero venientibus ossa."* The Cyclops sat up and emoted dust, along with rage, scorn and impatience that, in turn, made Dr. Sseus hush with trembling yearn. "A god can be drunk, dunked, chewed, swallowed, sucked, dissolved or burned. Whatever you choose, just do it! or at least put on a manducus and play it, and let me doze and lose myself in musings of meals of womanly flesh washed down with butter-n-milk-n-suet."

"Allow me to put it bluntly for I fear you're about to crunch me. And howbeit I'm a hollow shell, this meal would never do you well. My respect for you is the highest for I sense that you will gracefully fit the bill, unless, of course, . . . *Benedictus benedicat . . . gratias agere . . . male parta, male dilabuntur . . ."* (Dr. Sseus was attempting to employ a bit of prandial psychology on the Cyclops in an attempt to entice him to challenge god before supper) " . . . you are in fear of him who claims to be leagues above Zeus on the till."

"Fear!" Dimensions here and beyond shook from the utter force of the Cyclops's roar. "We Cyclops have neither fear nor reverence for the gods! We care not a jism for Zeus, nor ham, nor any other long-necked goose of a god you have at hand. For we are much stronger than they, this day, and let me warn you that you're starting to look tasty after all, *Benedicto benedicatur!,* and my entrails are beginning to roar, less than stall, for a little company, roughly five-foot-three, like the Greek you be."

Dr. Sseus took a gulp of diplomacy. Mixing Greek with Latin could get quite explosive. Delicacy, he thought to himself. I must employ delicacy, lest I quickly become one and all is dung. For he recalled that this very same Cyclops, ages past, was prone to seize a couple of men at once and dash their heads against the floor until their brains ran out onto the ground and soaked the earth at last. And more! He tore their limbs apart as well, and made this all his meal. And less he end up a fart in the monster's bowels, he must think before he starts to swell.

"Oh, Cyclops. If it's your entrails that roar, a measly morsel such as I would hardly score your appetite. But on the other hand, I know of a course that is like a thousand-in-one; and if you truly be the base Cyclops you are, I should like to say, and thus carry the tale to countries far, far away, that you found this massive meal and in one gulp alone did steal!"

The Cyclops rolled his one round eye up and down and up again. "I abhor! How dare you tempt me, little tyke! Little pseudoblepsia! Irish maneen taking on an ancient tale! I had a brother once, Ohhum, next to bore. When he was my size, once upon a time, a specie called Nobody, who came but up to his knees, stole my brother's soul while he too did sleep. And when my brother awoke and opened his eye, it appeared as though he were still in the dark. Yes, dust to dust became as dark to dark. And throughout the remainder of his life he did wail and seize a fylfot in the rain beyond the pale, as far as the pale in Russia of seventeen ninety-two, or the pail of ette-one. The Imperial Jews couldn't settle for less. O.

I'm missing.

I'm missing.

The best part of me.

My I

My I

My I.

I can smell another man's brother, insofar that I am a brother myself. A willie-boy. Well-versed in brontology. What happened to he, my Cyclops sibling? In his old age he turned into a terrible monster, shapeless and vast, and suffering from intense entropion. Each day that he remained to live he walked down to the seaside with cautious steps, feeling his way with a generous staff until he finally came to rest at the ocean's edge, at which time he washed his eye-socket in the salty waves. So sad to think him sightless when he had so much to give, was so much on the ball. A great goat-keeper he was, and as kind as anyone can be. Many copious friends round about he had. But the best numbered only three. I can still recall the last time I saw him; he was tapping his way toward his destiny as a mahdi, and was as common to the island that he inhabited last as a fly on a stall. A strong rain did fall which prompted him to sing Placebo for a better state of mind: *Domino in regione vivoram;* for the dead, sycophants take a liking to. And for a moment he did stall the hands of death between the margins, singing bread in agony, a canticle for bread and circuses under wine. They say a Cyclops never dies and oh, yes, 'tis true. They lust. Just step right up beside me and press your ear to my own palm, and you will hear my brother's voice captured therein. That's life, for Sunday's eternity."

Dr. Sseus could show no fear if he was to expect the Cyclops to assist him in the death of god. And so, with hesitant steps, he got within ear's reach of the giant's pimply palm and listened as the rolling notes of his little brother's immortal songs drifted out as of a two leav'd book, melodious and strong as an opened shell.

"I'm sinning in the rain

Just sinning in the rain

It's the glorious blame.

No man escapes sane.

I'm dapper again

Like Darby and Joan

All my eye, and Betty Martin alone

Let the bosh winds chase, the rubbish from the place

Come on, O mihi, beate Martine in the face,

It's all for gain

One-eyed refrain

Just sinning, oh! sinning in the rain."

The notes were so melodious, so Kellyish, so civil yet so without Christian faith, so Arimaspian, that Dr. Sseus begged to play it again. The Cyclops nodded, sighed, humphed *such is life, Sambo Galilee,* only this time the song that emerged went something like this:

"You must remember this

An eye is for an eye
A tooth is for a tooth
This will be the only truth
While I watch you die."

Suddenly the Cyclops gripped Dr. Sseus up in his great pimpled palm and made ready to dash his brains across the galaxies, and to thereafter stellify him in the anals of history. The muscles in his arms flexed with decretorial, decrowning cruelty, and there was a clearly visible flame flickering from within his solitary eye. Only a green flame it was like the color of a cocktail olive with a baalistic bloodshot center.

"Your gift to life shall be that when your skull cracks and breaks apart, your traduced brain will splatter its deleterious energy across the fifth dimension and brilliantly glow back like chaton foil ever after before it cakes, the yolk of your youth. Naturally, you will have no consciousness regarding your own passing, but rest assured that I will wax new the words of Telemachus, who is but only dust in my own begotten memory. 'With arms around my father's burning neck, I licked him good, as good a dog his milky, drooling, industrious head.' Ah, then, very well, the bishop will have put his foot in it."

Not a moment too soon Dr. Sseus regained his senses, having previously lost them in the reverie produced by the desolate conditions of the songs, all, for the most part, charivaris. Because he was gripped in the Cyclops's upraised hand, he was now within inches of the monster's ear, and this gave him a grand idea. Unbeknownst to the vast majority, a Cyclops can be hypnotized by words alone; just as long as they appear like new wine to the nature of their sounds in order to confuse their mock reverie. But if Dr. Sseus were to succeed in such an endeavor, and take the bishoprick, so to speak, then he would need to act fast and use his tongue in a yentzer fashion.

'Tis a Warming!

Eat her in the warm shop. Did not Mabyer eat the cornhole that promised knowledge as well as life but which in the end granted only death? Pullorum disease. It's so traducian. Cornwall . . . Pull it! Remove the icing and all you have is cake caking. And a jarful of honey-apple marmalade. Not bad for a rock and roll band you say, who all love to catch a buzz now and then. Perhaps. But now it was time to eat, so to speak, yet another fruit and thereafter live in the dreamy indolence it induces: Zizyphus lotus . . . *ether* . . . Sing in the air an aria of insipience. And use the tongue as a token.

Dr. Sseus said:
"Come, my faygeleh.
It's not too late to seek a newer world.
Let go and sit me well in order that
I might make my purpose stick, brace and bits.
A pretty doll, a plaything just for kicks.
To sit beyond the fifth dimension and the visions of Bristol City
Of all the english dreams he promised before he died.
It may be that your anger will keep you down
And you could suffer an Irish toothache
It may be that you'd destroy he who came to send you up.
Broaden your outlook, me eye, me tutor,
To see the great Triskelion, whom you'll know as Sup.

And . . .

How much is that god in the window?

The one with a wandering eye?

Empty-headed, impertinent black pupil

To be sold, I hope he gets by."

Upon hearing Dr. Sseus's words, the Cyclops recalled three spirits who each fell under a spell after the partaking of a particular other fruit. Jack Horner, Miss Muffet, and Tommy Tucker who sings for his supper. O to never have to return to the past. No . . . never again to butter me ass like fallen bread. But to linger, always, in reverie, watching St. John eating his tuna sandwich on black and white TV.

And to learn the secret of the C. refreshment.

And to recite the octonary. 1) I will meditate in thy precepts. 2) Open my eye that I may behold wondrous things. 3) I am a stranger in the earth. 4) My soul cleaves onto the dust. 5) I will walk at liberty. 6) At midnight I will rise. 7) My eye prevents the night watches. 8) Plead my cause.

Dr. Sseus could sense the Cyclops leaning toward compliance. A perfect time to strike and eat after the shivaree. Now he would don a maieutic analyst and midwife an obsession.

"How knish sweet it is, hearing the downward scream of god! Mata Hari.

Take me to the sea

Or *out!* to the ballgame with the apple of the earth.

With only one eye to dream ophthalmos in nature's veil

Lift the velum sail

Falling asleep is mean while Maud goes unwatched on TV

Open the oculus, spot the prow, let the gubernator be

Land! To scream, and scream, like Joe Eat Brown

Who did not leave a single bone on the ground

To hear oneself's whispered burp

Chippie, *chirp chirp*

Soon after the jaws did work

Red light, green light, *squirt*

On the crispy brittle fleshy middle catch-of-the-day

And the rigid members' delicious creamy spray.

To suck and lick, and lick and suck all day

On the kosher dill that nearly spilled off the tray

To the tune of consuming, mild-mannered Homo sapiens.

The kind that muse and brood and live to only sin . . .

And take pride in the bull's eye that they sling

And the *Juif* that French-kissed a king

O where have you been, C.C. Cyclops C.C. Cyclops?

O where have you been, charming Cyclops?

Heeped over a mound of grass

With two handfuls of white dust up each Mass

And dreams, tuned-in, to cheeks of rippling ass."

Dr. Sseus was delighted to see a smile on the Cyclops's face that stretched from here to kingdom come. Now one part of his sanctimonious work was done. Review: Counsel, fear, fortitude, piety, understanding, wisdom and knowledge. Ghost words as valid as the Sampford Ghost. The Cyclops was almost, nearly, completely hypnotized. Another few steps to go and the monster would be under his full command!

"Let me now give you the full and honest recipe of man. You might as well know of what parts you eat. For it is much more than just meat, organs, bones, heads, hands, toes and teats. There is a secret to this entity called man, and that is what he was originally made out of. Which is to say basically . . . sod. Now mark my words and mind my jussive. Replace the *s* with a simple *g* and you have the extra hidden secret of the recipe. The ingredients are diverse, as such. But pay attention. For I am certain if you do, you'll learn much."

The Cyclops with a love-long glance uttered these words, although still in the midst of a trance. And these three words danced across the stage like grease itself.

"tell me more"

And so Dr. Sseus carried on. "Dear Cyclops. The recipe for man is much like the recipe for god, for both whine incessantly. Whine. Yes. In the en-sof agush. We'll need to evolve the word by first dissolving it somewhat into cakes that

Whine . . . wnine . . . wiine . . . w,ine . . . w.ine . . . WINE

Down

a long way to

Winnie's poo and Tipperary too.

Now, Mr. Cyclops, we must discover and thereafter review wine's origins."
Pheu.

The Cyclops released his own hold on his tongue, and in so doing allowed it to hang sacrificially out of his mouth . . . much like a dog's on the run. Clearly one could see bits of human flesh hanging off the tip, obviously remnants of his last supper.

Dr. Sseus cautiously cleared his throat. "First think upon a paper-white glass of liquid. Next visualize it being shot BANG! with greeny-gold. Good. Now imagine smelling wildflower scents and tasting fruit raised on spring water freshness. Excellent! Now think of a burnt-umber fluid as smooth as the juice of apricots, as rich as butter to melt, and ocean-dark as an ocean forest primeval spray. It is the fluid of the main ingredient of the first stage, with each drop drawn out of the ground by the roots of a vine."

The Cyclops's eye seemed locked in some dreamy, monumental zone. It made him seem even more strange and mysterious than he actually was. His eye envisioned crushed grapes, the juice of which grew aged, mellow, and was thereby transformed into a *sent* and *favour* beyond mundane comprehension – that is, as far as wines are concerned. All its own, a flavor relaxed, contented, but full of kaput ideas; free-flow in form the texture was, identical to a friendly contact, a warm embrace that comes to form a swell and thereafter burst, its natural sugar shaking the tongue. Thank god for the trapicheian.

The Cyclops's mind lingered on all the wines he had ever known – table, sparkling and fortified. And as Dr. Sseus spoke, the Cyclops recalled a tramontane cousin of his who would sit under the shade of his own vine and all day long sip the ripe clusters of a dark blend hanging just within his reach. And in the intoxicating visions of his own dreams, of his own foreign sights from beyond the alpestrine, the Cyclops fell into a spell of omniscience, both crimson and green. And in this vision he saw sights that meant hardly anything to him at all; and words with pictures, rehoboam, six bottles strong, like Mr. Hellstone in his shovel hat,

burying the dead of the enlarged nation after refusing one request; but, nonetheless, he felt he could identify them as much as he could the severed head and the tappit-hen hanging by hook on the wall of this hook shop, among the other offals and measures of men.

"Gancio." The Cyclops uttered in a bent whisper.

One of the visions just so happened to be the decline and fall of the Roman Empire, which thereafter left the church in power. And as his vision traced its way through the storm, he witnessed new races from the East coming to take over the Empire. And then he saw how the knowledge of wine-making and vine-growing became a monopoly of the church, and how all the biggest and the best vineyards were both owned and operated by religious houses benshing, *"Shabbos goi, Shmuel Bukh Shma Koleinu mama loschen."*

"What visions be this?" the Cyclops yelled, while his red eye was about to jell within the rapture of a barmecidal dream. Even the wall of his mouth did swell, ballooning over his white milk teeth like some mighty arachnid. And all the while he could hear the arachnophagous voice of Dr. Sseus hypnotizing him with obtuse lessons in the art of wakefulness in the hub. As the words filtered down, his vision dug even deeper still, spilling forever down into *vitis vinifera;* and the vine snaked its way like a worm, an iulus, gallying to the gall of bitterness – from the East of Persia, down the Phoenicians and into Spain, through the Greeks and into Italy and Provence (with a tourists' trip through the Villa Vignamaggio, a posh Tuscan retreat, where was mounted a smiling La Gioconda, amidst 600 year old cypress trees, crisscrossed with vines and rooms, eighty-five in all) on the quest for perfection, through the Romans, through Gaul; and then down into the French Revolution, which deprived Miss Nancy of his lands, the vine crawled; and then into Germany where many of the monasteries were secularized by Anonpole; yes, the snake snaked onward, into Bergen D., where it waxed rich, savory and ruby-red; then down into the Mountain of Reims where it became full of glittering foam; then onward into South America where it went through the conquistadors; and then through the Cape and around through California and Australia, the vine snaked. And all the while it was being pursued by the phylloxera, the worm, in due time the beetle, which later found its way into France, where it virtually consumed every vine.

The Cyclops started to repeat a-line of don dior; for in falling into a state of omniscience, he knew don to be a libertarian, a once forgotten Roman slave now manumitted and unrestrained by unbridled morality. Much to be learned from a cynical devil. "Do you know the way to Dis?" the Cyclops said. Oh, such a rakehell – such a slope – such a scale – nearly perishing, greying tree, falling, falling into a slant; that was how the Cyclops was to go, to travel down a long and oblique course, all the while both searching through and censuring all he could in an English autumn that had no vines, except for the few that stood at the feet of the red grape in the sunny lands of stygian song. The claret light. The Madeira strong. *Life cru.* The very best of old vineyards in the Cyclops's new cave. But by way of song – the cellar, the room of the unlearned, where all is lost and preserved.

And it was, as Dr. Sseus continued to seduce the Cyclops with intoxicating rhyme, that the Cyclops stretched his sights to England and instantly witnessed the ental/ectal marriage of King Pulletry II to Queen Light of taint, which befell the best red wine of all. Yes, the swad infant was overlaid at birth by its immensely vigorous Gallic mother. And they all came to see the swaddling babe in bloody arms with nothing to eat. "What gall!" the Cyclops said.

Which prompted Dr. Sseus to refrain, "What gall you say? I hardly think there is any bitterness of spirit in wine today. Unless, of course, it has turned rancor with age. But we're in the business of transformation. For this is the New Rage! Take care you do not hurt the wine, 6.6 proof in '39. The anil of aromatic schiff base with a good hyde affection toward the reddish violet color of salvation. Old was his mutton and his claret good. Firm and erect the highland chieftan stood singing, 'Thou shalt drink port when I come.' Being a passageway for safety, at least this was what was understood. However, he cried. And thereafter he drank the poison, and his body died."

"If this be the god you speak of," the Cyclops said, "then why bother to get me out of bed? After all, what would I want with a meal that's already quite dead?"

"Ah, but Cyclops," Dr. Sseus said, "I speak of one who is living, however dead, and is as red as that Sherry that you took to bed and licked the very drops out of."

"O, yes, I remember her well," the Cyclops said, dwelling upon the very bud of her essence. "And insofar that it takes a grape to die in order to give birth to new wine, could this be how you speak of god in whom you seek of so sercial a mind?"

"Quite so," Dr. Sseus answered. "And the taste, though somewhat bitter, should be sweet as down it goes into that great tavern of an apocryphal belly on tap. That is, assuming you can hold its load, its belly-timber and all its members without croaking silly."

"Now you surely have me horny for this toad you call a god!" the Cyclops said. "He somewhat reminds me of a manzanilla I had. A very tart pale finos it was from Sanlucar de Barrameda on the sea, the broad estuary of the Guadalquivir. Delivered to me by a seaman from a dramalogue disembarked from a weaker vessel from afar, who just so happened to lend himself as part of my thirst-quenching meal, so that I might have me meat, with drink to steal. A bit salty they both were, being as though the sea air had somehow impregnated them both so earnestly. However, the salty taste vanished as soon as I stepped foot into my sepulchral cave. From salt to just plain fancy, the thing was a mystery to me. Something about the Spanish character – a rare and superb thing can suddenly turn as salty and unsavory as a shark's fin. And dim the ears to empty depths *O ventre affamé n'a point d'oreilles.*"

"I don't think I understand you," Dr. Sseus said. And then it suddenly occurred to him that his spell was wearing thin, and the Cyclops was once again attempting to do the devil in. Quickly he acted, imagining only words that bore an intoxicating, nearly permanent effect. Once again he spoke of wines, careful this time so as not to let his a-lines slip their foundation and meet with bad weather, as his own stalwart logic was infused with sips from illogic's glass, the bull's eye express expelled to the letter. Now he took the Cyclops through the golden age of wurine and had him stay in a cheap estaminet in Bordeaux, in the year 1894, and tempted him with intoxicating visions of a haven in order for him to drink up a storm; and in the midst he saw a King, Tom, and Mahu directing flibbertigibbet to sing-a-long with chambermaids and waiting women, light-minded, gossiping on puck, mo, motar and motte – mowing and mophy, too; and thusly, the fall of man continued; and as each grape died in the downpour of its sea amongst the tentacles of *hero-in-distress*, so did each man who took his own life into his own hand. For Dr. Sseus knew of one fatal drop to the persistent mystery: The best way to a god's liver was by Intoxicated Suicide. IS at hand. 10:10 p.m.

Hours it took. Even days, blending into years that lay around like lazy summer dogs. It's difficult to space time when there is not one solitary clock to find. Indeed, his scaturient talk with the Cyclops could have lasted a millennium, for a great deal of wurine was drunk with much a transfer from bottle to glass allium. So much so that it left the consumed wurine in a shocked state and caused the Cyclops up-bottom sickness, prompting the beast to regurgitate a lakeful of garlic aftertaste. Only words relating to retsina, with its spirited taste of turpentine oil, could quell the titubant Cyclops, as that word *quell* has a double-spell meaning – to kill as well as pacify, be it either heaven or hell. M . . . a shudder . . .

> *Be sure not to hurt the oil nor the wine,*
> *Cest action Gist.*

And the rest should turn out fine.

And then onward to the region of Cyprus and a race of holey Superwurines that set the Cyclops's head spinning in order to increase the monster's winnings over god. A little bit of Ouzo which, when neat, is clear and slightly yellow, as is known by any good Greek fellow. A really fine muscat, whose scent does attract dear to dear in a girdle. O the perfume that lives, lives as well within the fruit; the same that did indeed cast another kind of spell over other kinds of beasts; namely woman over man, burning flesh, cloven feet. Dear to dear in a lodge. A spell that held two in just one bite. The apple rose, which long, long ago had the same haunting, sweet quality that can also be called musky,

testes testes

O the Crimea is a strange place to find a Cyclops drunk in the face. But the first vineyards were established here (as was the War!) from cuttings of the same vine from Byblia in Thrace – (the moscato in rhyme! What a burden!). What is better to kill god with than the smoothest, most delicate and best tabloid? The very sweetest Cyclops on the block.

And it seemed to Dr. Sseus that he was talking to none other than himself in the form of a beast with one-eye on a Rock. A god to put a god to rest. A chaye to rise in the afterdust.

At least it was a very long reign. For nearly five billion years an insanely hubristic host with lyssophobia had hosted the *herald* universe. (A locum tenens; *lo! cum ten ens!*) And even though this cocksure host had created the world with a shock and had started the ballyhoo ball rolling, it was only befitting that this host would be disposed of now, enlocked in such a likely manner. For the transfer of power goes hand-to-hand, and the published changes therein can stretch far beyond the dollar. For the germ can bud from any womb; change can come in many forms. Consider Io and her own change into a cow, even though she happened to be the bride of Zeus who took out a lot of time to pee; loosen cock. You see, instead of one eye, a hundred eyes followed her, each named Argus. Like Odysseus, loose, she was made to wander, pursued by a gadfly on a gander. Over the whole world she fled, swimming through the Ionian Sea, roaming over the plains of Illyria (thriving on bread), ascending Mt. Haemus, crossing the Thracian Strait and arriving at last on the banks of the Nile with her head in a strait. The wandering itself is sane. For whether it be man or beast, it takes a wise soul to know that one does not grow without wandering through waste; even as the vine had wandered the earth, east; even as its path had coursed the dirt, east; even as the bread had risen the yeast, east. It was so. Just as it was so with the Cyclops and Dr. Sseus, who did know.

IN

But replacing god was not going to be easy. First of all, there was this matter of taste. The trial. How to handle the death test? The end of dinner (e.g., *la dernier souper; la ultimo cena*) is also a good moment for *Asti Spumante.* To the Italians it is the equivalent of champagne. It possesses a musky quality and is excellent as a sweetner for any type of drinking-party. Actually it would be a superb drink to serve upon a hasty death. For is not god akin to sparkling? Bursting forth, thrown out by a body in combustion for a little season? Exploding in light, falling in order to incite the young, beautiful and witty women and the brisk, showy, gay men? The hot-tempered, hurried, rash and fickled masses of the dead? Has it not been written so that he glows and scatters his tacks so as to stick in the tongue? And would it not suit the Cyclops so to have such a sweet drink with such a strong smell? Even its skin is perfumed, the most honeyed mouthful imaginable. The mere suggestion of it prompted the Cyclops to dream of lazily blinking in long scented grass, perhaps by a stream, with the sun winking in the ripples of his bare ass. There is so much to say about the *Asti Spumante*, particularly in how best to serve it. Unlike god, it is best to serve Spumante very cold – much colder than champagne. When it is warm the taste seems to get out of hand and brings grief if nothing but; but when icy, it is nicely balanced and slips down easily. Imagine serving god with such a coldness and still feeling balanced all the same. Nay! Serve god cold and expect the blame with his finger pointing in your hangdog face, and at best shouting, "Luke Warm!" Ah, but the *Spumante*. Such grace! Such style! It's characteristic taste is like a musical tomcat singing in the night graveyard to peccant rats. Shortened, as such, to muscat. Should we dare disturb god by boring a hole in the universe? Set upon our journey on a white horse?

Dr. Sseus thought the Muscat would be a grand grape indeed to break considering its reputation, for it was getting near time to make his move outside of history. Certainly time had stopped from existing within history, just as age had stopped a certain wine from being as syrupy as it was in youth. It was not altogether a different god that greeted the world on that fateful day after he destroyed all that he had made.

OUT

Nothing could be more difficult to deal with than a god who exists outside of himself (even though gods often do come *out* in the wash), who, in turn, reduces his creatures into schizophrenic states which are nothing more than tumble-down journeys into inside-out oblivion.

Now . . . what to serve it all in? How about a dark and strong Setúbal, just meters away from Lisbon? Yes, why not! Simply go across the Tagus by way of the suspension bridge and then twenty miles up and over the Arrabida Mountains, just west of Sesimbra; to be more specific, we'll make good our *outre* visit, and we'll grab up an ancient bottle that barely exists. Namely, Tornaviagem, Setúbal. What is it? *Chateau Lawoff 1666. Saint Devlion Grand Cru.* The yellow wurine that rubs its muzzle on the label Appellation SAINT-MIS EN BOUTEILLE AU CHATEAU-RED 14% DEVILXIS Oenophile, licked its tongue into the corners of the bottle, O for ullage space, a little emptiness, but recall the bunghole and the hogshead, the mouth, the neck, the shoulder. And seeing that it was the Muscat Family after all, mulled over the bottle and fell asleep.

– *But what time is it, without time?*

It is almost the time to make a toast to a fine host gone blind mad; crisp, hot and surely brown.

The Cyclops took his vision with a vergence both intoxicating and dizzy into the next provence going East, from a mere crack, a sort of meuse in the mounting Alps where the river Hiddekel flows; and beyond that the Euphrates, where the sixth angel trumpeted four in a sublime vision to slay the third part of man which is made of wood and stone; and hunting further still into Babylon and some widely scattered vermiculate mounds supporting some bloody drunks stoned under a limb bearing a couple of Lloyd's bushtits praising the tracks of J.C. superstar.

The Cyclops was going to speak but something stopped him. Something foreign down around his toes. (A Cyclops has immensely hard, strong feet in which to support his bones, his very vola, and toes roughly 8 1/8 inches long.) It seemed he was much too lazy to speak or even to think. Perhaps if god was served directly to him like a piece of pie, then the Cyclops would wine and dine to his heart's content, taking it all in without ever having to leave his bed. His eye in the last few moments had grown to look rather hard and vinaceous, much like a strong and well-aged wine – a Sfursat left sitting on its shelf. A wine meant for drink on Saturday, with Sunday time to sleep off Quinquagesima.

O Cyclops so supine. You look more like a flat, unpromising country – sleeping as you are from head to toe – much more suited to the production of the Maseratis and Ferraris.

No, it is certainly not easy to make acquaintance with a Cyclops in bed. They tend to get cranky and sour in the head. *Phre no sin.* What Dr. Sseus was attempting to induce was to channel the Cyclops's crankiness unto god.

god: last seen in a scruffy little café in Sorbara, where he was plotting the world's demise with a little bottle labeled *Lambrusco* at his side – his disguise bearing the crushing circumstances was somewhat wise: all dressed in white, exactly the size and shape of . . . Sidon Greenstreet! in just one of several pleasant pictures he made – in this case, one where his co-star was heard to utter, *"Führer befiehl, wir folgen!;* and a host of ravens fluttered overhead and fed Sidon flesh continuously, along with a black widow with a drumstick who fed him wine enough to make his bed; and Sidon cast it to yellow dogs who died with their boots on, custard and all. In sackcloth, he plotted the lites.

As Mr. Greenstreet sat sipping, a dwarfy waiter approached with a second bottle in hand bidding him to test his palette on its uncorked essence. The waiter was wired, of course, as was his offering, accounting for his finger being on the *coiffe*. In tiny writing underneath the label the bottle read: *This wine was squeezed, fermented, and aged with the upmost care, and is exclusive to Sidon Greenstreet's table.* Amazingly so, the bottle was dated exactly six hundred thousand years ago; that is, 66 millenniums prior to the piacular moment, as it here now occurs; and the ravens scattered at the falcon's approach; and the mystery read: *Barnone.*

Upon reading the label, Mr. Greenstreet said, "A prophetic wine! How stable! An ancient Beaujolais with a dash of black current put through a sodasyphon. I can recall from before the false Fall, a certain sauce from a quaint little village with the lovely name of Romanèche-Thorins. There I had me an infamous chicken dinner, domestic drumsticks sinfully bathed in *Moulin-à-Vent,* to accommodate my *wire hood.* Beside it on a separate plate reigned a family of deliciously sweet potato pancakes. *Crepes Parmentier* in a mas of elymus. Queens pimped up like fagots fit for fodder. Still, beside these rested a cold *Cavaillon* melon. And just brushing the sleeve, crayfish *à la nage.* Simply piaceful. And like ancient, delicate, complex shells of early spring, milky disks of *Parmigiano-Reggiano* come to top the list.

Almost. Dare I say, each bite from that glorious dish of *Volaille de Bresse aux morilles* made me wish that I would not crumble the world like so many bread crumbs over my *tartelettes aux framboises,* falling from the table to the jars below, so like a piaculum I did know. The raspberries sitting on that magic custard that makes 11-12 tartlets after meat 'n mustard were easy meat to eat. And, but of course, the *Chante Perdrix Compris Derriére.* The Partridge Song, which left me at the bar a total mess, turning this way and that, however subtle, with the right- side in a misty darkness I could not explain – bar a hand to lead me to a proper refrain. Or, perhaps, I'm wrong. For I'm certain that a falcon belongs in there somewhere, insisting with some seasonal mockery, *'Noli me tangere!'"*

And to the waiter's utter amazement, god disguised as Sidon suddenly turned into yet another figure of immortality. Namely, *the man who played god* (touched me not . . . They're both condommed). With piano solos by Salvatore Santaella. O, the connections to god were simply uncanny for *the man who played god* involved a king, an anarchist, a battle, an attempted assassination, a deafening, a woman named Grace, a farmer, a suicide, a faithful servant, some eventful eavesdropping, an actual attempt to *play* god in the guise of *Arledge,* a dweller at rabbit lake (the same where rabbis played and danced to mystic music made by frogs eating French chews who certainly had the nose for a long French-inhale), and a whole lot of shaking going on under the table over the rights of an armagnac that the jars each felt entitled to. Purely a matter of *droit d'aubaine* being the poor alien *'died'* by his barren hand over a brown, dry affair stamped close to *droit du seigneur* with a proper jark. In spite of the fact that Grace spoke way too rapidly for the microbes, she was, nonetheless, a sure Bet vision of wide-eyed, blonde, baldrib beauty, mumsieing her salad with all the speed of an escaped prisoner. Actually it would have been better for Grace had she played the silent voice fricatrix and kept it on the stage where the good man rabbi resided, on Greenstreet, along with Benny and Brown (in the underworld: King and Lorre), Ida, Kitty and Faye, the complimentary trinity fricatrices in chorus – with all the gang (the whole damn mishpachah) finally meeting at one particular Hollywood canteen during years darker than the world had ever seen in any one quoit. Otherwise known as *Sickleave-Red Frog-Sticker-god.* And while millions cooked across the seas, Morgan, Patton and Woods, ménage à tree, tried squeezing in a jesus or two, singing, *'You Can Always Tell A Yank By His Tumblin' Tumbleweeds,'* a tumblin' fu under a Voodoo Moon, with a Bee Ketengban tribesman stinging the General who jumped at Dawn from a sweet dream about having a baby . . . say . . . *creamcheese* fella . . . frog up! *'Mr. Jones! what are you doin' the rest of your life?'* Running time: 124 millenniums. With John in the Field getting in a lick or two as one of the *moving spirits* who later left the scene doing the French walk with a phallocarp. Which brings us to yet another exitisin, an Exitious of Alpha & UA . . . 220 m . . . *Otto let go!* (The Cyclops rolled over here, lost in a spin of *moving-past-dreams;* and a trio of *sturmabteilung* suddenly storms in to divide the notes amongst themselves: *Wein, Weib, und Gesang,* and yank the *present* from under the tree.)

Speaking of the falcon aforementioned; *he returned* from a nasty stint in Maltese having served a serious misdemeanant, and thereafter reappeared on a train en route to San Fran with Engineer Tiphys, only this time donned as Shayne Warren William in search of the mysterious Barabbits (himself a madame in search of a ram's horn encrusted with priceless gems and rare photos of the Upper Ten, including the creamy Spencer in a close-fitting bodice and the irritated Liz with her sharpened ten commandments). *H'm. H'm.*

Upon a heap of cowdung she was bound
The greatest Gdayallday she had known
The greatest alldayGday that had sound
Of the nails in the palms that, too, had grown.

And here everyone joined in the party, for it was not everyday that Satan met a lady and got stoned on gin and water *and* did the world in.

"How convenient!" the critics roared in the aisles. "How simplistic!" "The scene packed quite a wallop!" "Disconnected and lunatic!" "Irrelevant and monstrous!" "Full of sin! And yet, there is really no story. Merely a farrago of nonsense representing a series of impractical, heavenly compromises with a whorish script . . ," commented two tossed critics. "O, such is the isle world on stage when viewed from Robinson Crusoe and Friday."

"Release Barabbits! Release Barabbits!" a mysterious woman in scarlet suddenly shouted. She was insisting over the *vorspiel* that she must find Barabbits for reasons she kept "obscure," only she belched gas on "obscure" and pronounced it "tcure," which could have been a verbarium. *"Weiche, Wotan, Weiche!"* Perhaps a misquote due to a choke.

O Madame! The ram's horn is holding a valuable secret!

. . . Come see the vorticist do his best J impression! rest

Which all brought the Cyclops to dream on and on, and thus to enter a banquet hall, the cenacle, belonging to an intimate little restaurant, *The Last Stall* (the missing S-water-logged fecs) renowned for its long, rectangular dinner tables on legs like viticetums, with accompanying dogs underneath to lick the soles of all them foolish, loose, longfanged, chauliodontidae. (And an active *wurstmax1* in the far right-hand corner kept yanking his pork.) Each seat was a toilet complete so as not to get up off your feet while you eat. In the center sat Bogart himself, portraying G. Sus with a clenched jaw and a grocer's itch. Too much vanilla brings on vanillism. Hardly in Anna, and you get the vaginsatans. He was busy talking amongst his guests; and among the clamor of dishes, and coins in the till, and common waiters on running feet, Bogart did squeak, "Lobsneak. Take, eat, is this not our hobby?" At which time, upon his seat he farted, and was quickly departed, ushered out bum's rush by horse to the Lob's Pound. Nag! Shit! as it were, by way of the lobby.

. . . So much for whining in the Garden.

Now this was a large, upper room, both furnished and well-prepared as any delirium. And upon each toilet seat (each therein serving as a machnical chair) sat twenty-four feet, that is twelve bodies in all, in a meat (excluding Bogart, who occupied the most elaborate stall having returned to his census from A fall, that was all adorned with colorful stones each having come from the kidney region). And he was saying to his guests with an upright cup in his hand, "Take. Drink. Squeezed fresh this morning from this zit on my chin and mingled with me mudda's very own breasts in fresh from a babcock test, which had me all buttered up to the neck, whirling acid silly. Read me vally-tilly." And his guests all round-about stood up right on their feet, turned away, and sang in *unisin* a villancico with accompanying translation. Or a rare facsimile thereof.

"Le veré cuando venga.
Ojalá que lo halle.
No vino anoche, lo cual nos sorprendió.

An fué invitada por su amiga.
Se ven muchas cosas en las calles.
Se debe obedecer la ley.
Tarda en venir.
J . . . E . . . S . . . U . . . S . . . *Apostrophe* . . . S TU QUOQUE
Mother's MILK is the ABSOLUTE best.
Sueño con mi madre
HARLOT"

At which time the dinner party was entertained by the gene *Harlow* herself, who suddenly appeared clad in briefs and a tight brassiere on loan from a demimonde; and she commenced to dance around each stall, singing, "Give me, give me, give me, give me it all." And Bogart cut in, "All of you shall be offended because of me this night. – For it is written, *I will smite the cidevant shepherd, and the emeritus herd shall be scattered* and thereafter lodge with incorrigible strangers.

¿Qué piensa Vd. de este libro?
Another Fart and . . . open the Dyke!
Don't cook tonight
But . . . *tengo ganas de comer*

Bogart's extended, otiose guests were a varied lot (an obstinate Aragonese or two. Throw in, for a paradise full of lice, an Andalusian, with music and wine on the arm. . . . *Aprenden el francés*). That's nice . . . including Holiday as in Doc, Randolph as in Scott, Hudson as in Rock, Basil as in Rathbone, Franchot as in Tone, Lewis as in Stone. And to the left of him Madonna (as in Ida sin), O.J.! as in Son, and Georgie Raft as in 'has-been'; and to the left of them, so far away from Bogart the translation was terribly thin, were cloistral Ed as in Wynn, Buster as in Keaton, Charlie as in Chaplin; (and all alone, Columbus as in Sevilleian, buried up to his colón) and the three of these fought amongst themselves, *lucha por su vida* tugging at one another's lapels while they squeezed out the best of their meal and bickered as to the precise translation (insofar as they knew eisegetical Gothic) of all that they heard.

No lo creas

"I heard him plain and simple," said Mary Diana Lee (as in Crosby). "He said, 'One of you shall bring a silver tray for me straight from the philosopher's tree.'"

"That makes no sense, I tell you!" Buster said. "I'm certain that he said 'Virgil and Lee, I sing to thee, of thee I see! for wandering in meadows of fish and apples, and street preaching while shaking needlessly.'"

"No, no! You both have it wrong!" Chaplin stormed. "He said nothing about singing a song. What he said was 'Vile are we who eat muffin and tea, and thereafter to be or not to be.'"

"It couldn't have been muffin!" Ed said. "Maybe mutton, but you can see that he isn't serving muffins tonight!"

"I think he said *matzo*," Buster butted in. "And let me tell you, the matzo tonight is stale and awfully thin."

"If he said *matzo* he couldn't have said *tea*," Chaplin said. "Jews don't drink tea!"

Suddenly O!J! stood up, though his pants be down around his knees. First, releasing gas from *"Alas,"* he boldly said to Bogart, "Is it I?"

"It is the one that dipped his own into my stall, for these two feces don't match at all."

At which time the Cyclops rolled in and out of sleep, totally confused over the meaning of his dream.

And Bogart said, "The son of man indeed goeth!" And to make good his words, his bowl runneth over after flushing. And all his guests did dip their cups and drink of it. And once again Bogart said, "All of you shall be offended because of me this night."

To which Doc proudly boasted, "This has got to be the damndest supper you ever hosted!"

"We'll all die from the stench alone, if not the drink!" Randolph moaned. "But here's to you, Bogart. And to independence! I bottomup my *cuba libra* with trans end us."

"If that be the case, then I'll go straight for the bone and its one eye, and make the cock crow thrice by my tongue alone!" Madonna shone.

And the evening lasted well into the night. But ask Buster and he would have said, "And the night lasted well into the evening nightie." Whereas Wynn would have answered, "And his bite bit me, where once my circumcision." To which Chaplin would have argued in turn, "And Eve Arden lusted well into Aphrodite."

"What does it mean!?" the Cyclops screamed, while in more than just a doze. And then his vision rose into a most horrifying scene. All thirteen stalls overflowed, and the room was filled like a red sea with chunks of loads of digested meal. And as the room was filled to the ceiling with watery debris, all partakers swam frantically looking for a space of latitudinarian breath. And the sight was so confusing the cast managed to swim directly into yet another pietistic scene. Now swimming in this religious mess were Roddy, Carol, Gene, Red, Ernest, Shelley (with two exposed breasts) and last of all, Irwin, who just so happened to be filming a remake: *Allen, The Cripple of Lepanto in Stall.*

Rest.

At this point Irwin swam up through the *Mess* (i.e., Mass) to where Jesus was thoroughly engaged in a serious breast-stroke. At first, considering they were underwater, Irwin attempted to communicate by way of sign language, but Jesus couldn't seem to get the bowels straight, and when Irwin communicated with a marred left hand, "Follow me . . . Hurry, or it will be too late," Jesus thought he was stating, "Follow me, Harry. Let's go get a steak." Jesus picking up that cue remarked, "Sorry, I'm a vegetarian of late and this is pure navi, dad, with lots of Gallo," and slapped his hand, despite his face.

If it weren't for Franchot, who understood sign language impeccably, Jesus, via Humphrey, might have been trapped in miscommunication for eternity. But after all was said and done, and the sign language was clearly understood by all, Irwin gladly took control and proceeded to lead the entire cast to safety, which meant finally emerging head-first out of a vacant stall. (And this in spite of the fact that he was portraying a country gentleman, however unbalanced by a maimed left hand.)

First appeared Irwin, followed by Joseph, John and Paul – then Matthew and Mary, and a crew of minute neustons in the surface film. But that's not all. Larry as in Moe, Curly as in Joe (don't let go!), Nancy Carroll, Phillips Holmes, Ted and Alice and Cyrano, Cierva and his autogiro, James Kirkwood, the fiery feet of Escudero (just the feet), Bori singing Goy, which brought down the House, *el mendigo, pordiosero,* begging for *limosna* in the name of *por dios*, and still more to *la tertulia;* Ezra Stone; Zasu Pitts; and then the exit was stuck due to Shelley's left tit; and then Gene came on the scene. "Not this woman, no!" he said. "Oh dear god, a toilet shouldn't be her eternal bed!" And swimming back down around, he swam up underneath her gown and shoved a fist up the brown dung hole. And Shelley with an astonished start burst up and out of the toilet, aided, no less, by a massive fart. And her finish: "First Dylan at my breast, now Gene in my beam!" Then it was Gene. After him Mr. Clean, minus his faja and his enemizer scheme. And then Crauford Kent, defense attorney. Ivan Linow, Harry Earles and Lon Chaney, *the unholy three;* Paul Luke back fresh from *the devil's holiday;* Fay Vila Wry, her beautiful self all twisted out of shape, dripping wet from a night with *the sea god pelando la pava;* Leslie and Clark, each fortunate enough from their star trek in the dark to be *a free soul;* and Dorothy Mackaill, still apparently *safe in hell,* complete with mantilla and a dash of hairgel. And then the bell rose and the toilet bowl closed, and those fools caught below drifted down to a most tragic death, down to the Buena Ventura in shit, in a pure defecation of Disney swell, a Mass of noyade and tasty bits.

O silent debris, what a mess you be.

The survivors, dripping wet, with their features splashed with bits of excrement, stood over the toilet . . . tsk . . . tsk . . . tsking goodbye sweet pets.

Poor Ernest, poor Red, poor Buster, poor Fred. Finer souls couldn't have found a more disgusting end or stone to be their enfin bed. At which time Bogart spoke up and said, "Don't bend and mourn the dead." And with that he flushed the bowl one final time, and concluded with "Royal."

"This is perfect." Irwin said. "Rather than death you'll all do my sequel instead! What I'm planning to do is a *parody* on death. Swallowed up in teratology. Why, it's perfect! Such breath! I'll cover in one sequel alone the entire spectrum of decay. Caducity in one gulp. Eat your heart out, O. Stone! If you can swallow it. This time I'm going to do the big one, all on my own! with or without an olive leaf! Here's what we'll do – in perfect tune. We'll combine the plots of *the devil's holiday* and *Independence day,* wherein a young woman will be forced by circumstance to reform from a hard-boiled, man-hating fortune-hunter and party girl to a serialized nun in order to face the responsibilities she owes the now seriously ailing husband, alias *Alien IV,* whom she had once deserted. In the course of time she'll meet up with the unholy three. Insert: father, son and Topper's Three, who will be played by Earles AZ Tweedledee the midget, Linow et Hercules," (upon hearing this the Cyclops thought for an instant that he was beginning to understand the dream) "and Chaney as Echo, with Constance ringing the Cosmos . . . 'O dear god, get me off the Kirby. . .'

"The young woman finds herself falling in love with Echo, alias the icy holy Cary (get the drift), who has the uncanny ability to employ five different voices while on the glacial stage, including a sweet little old lady, a parrot with a peculiar furfuraceous itch (closer to a cacoethes), a little girl otherwise frozen in time, and a bitch dogma (get the hook!). It just so happens that Professor Echo works in league with a pair of side show ice-freaks: the strong man Hercules and the depraved dwarf Tweedledee . . . father and son, respectively. Black and white. In actuality, the three of them operate a pickpocketing sideline. In time, Echo opens up a pet shop that he runs while disguised as Mrs. O'Grady, and operates as a front for his pickpocketing ventures, along with the aid of his two side-kicks. Needless to say, the victims of their clever burglaries are the shop's unsuspecting clients, alias the world-at-large-left-hanging-at-the-crossroads-with-the-President-of-the-United States; I . . . eeee . . .

Jefferson IV. All of this, naturally, includes a subplot that revolves around an utterly fantastic tale of South Sea adventures, ventriloquism, pearl diving amongst submerged UFO's and three cannibals in a dock Trine. A handsome bogatyr adventurer will fall in love with a local moonlighting Russian barmaid originally from Kuibyshev, who is additionally trapped in a dead-end day job on Catalina Island as both coordinator and operator of a modest vertep. When she hears about the adventurer's exciting life in the South Sea Island, she will call him her yelpsin seadog come to save her, and quit both jobs right there and then. But not before handing over her Vertep to Nebu, Chad and Nezzar – three stooges who put on a puppet show called *"Baby, The Zed Must Fall,"* which, needless to say, went the same way as *"Oedipus My Visionary Optometrist Queen."* Oblivion! On the island, amidst an army of blind cannibals, both she and Sin will meet Abbott and Costola and delve into seventy-five minutes of innocent, hem . . . hem . . . fun. Meanwhile, Echo, via Lon Chaney, dressed up as Mrs. O'Grady, will fall under the comesee eye of an alcoholic lawyer-father, a defense attorney (who, in turn, falls under the alias of "Blythe"), who will relentlessly pursue her through the underbelly of New York City. In order to get him, the defense attorney, off his tail, she, referring to Echo, will succeed in killing him, that is, Blythe, via strangulation and carbolic acid/tar injection into the veins, and thereafter encounter hell after she/he is struck by a car and wakes up on the *Original* South Sea island in a pot of boiling water with a *hundred* hungry cannibals zamacuecaing around her, all obviously 'mad' from consisting solely on a diet of grass since their last human meal roughtly 3 ½ years ago, a Catholic named Charlie."

"Say, wait a minute! Where do I fit in?" Bogart said.

"Why, at the end. You'll sample your Chow Mein on the Plate after pounding the pavement clear to Catalonia."

"But then shouldn't I be in . . . Jerusalem?"

"That's just it!" Irwin exclaimed. "This is all taken from the $ venene test a mint $, wherein you and Judas, played here by Jon Hall, will be much like two Indiana Jones'-in-one going after twelve, if not a multitude! And your meiny will have an entirely different animus catch. You will say things like 'Blessed are the cannibals for they eat the dead along with their mein, to a cluster of semen.'"

"Will there by any tunes?" Curly Joe asked.

"Can you sin?" Irwin inquired of the stooge.

"No. But there always a *beginning*."

"That's good enough for me! I've got it! In keeping with an Hebraic theme, how about you playing Nickodemus, and your signature song will be:

Three Jews on a mountain

Three Jews

One-two-three.

One is named Alvin–

The others, Gould

And Borenstein.

Curly nodded in earnest and went off practicing his lines.

"I'm not going to take this! No way, Jose! I'm not going to dance! Not for the sun nor the moon, nor eleven stars! If I don't get top billing I'm going to pick up my coat and sabotage this entire production! Bogey, my ass! *Sinnlos!* Since when have you ever worked with bogie? Doesn't devotion mean anything these days? Devoutness, devolution, devitalization, devirgination, deviation or, for that matter, devon wrestling, as long as one's loose linen jacket and trunk on hold is permitted! You've got to be one son-of-a-bitch to stand me up like this and not even give me so much as a second glance, short of a fall other than on my back!"

"Gene, Gene. Calm down. I haven't forgotten you. I'm planning on you playing the part of Gilda Carlson, the lost lady safe in hell covered in gold and rigoletto. Not to mention Nabucco."

"Gilda Carlson!" Gene screamed. "I'm not going to play some goddamned woman shoestring to a bowstrong peaceful Hun! Success is impossible to me if I cannot rule as *my* eirenic heart dictates. Even my head *va pensiero sull ali dorate Wach!* gets off on golden wings by the Baby waters. No! For as TV will have it, I am king for a day if not a lifetime! To the Huns I must be the universe, short of Italy. For coming without spontaneity is premature thinking. *Fame! Fame! Morir di fame!* One must perceive new worlds beyond the dry chaos. For I am a man! A pool player! And I'm mighty proud of it!"

"A-ca-de-my A-ward. Think of it, Gene, gene dancing machine. Your opening line as Gilda on the South Sea island is, 'Holy Joe. This place is one son-of-a-bitch, hell of a drink, dirty rotten, cock-sucking stink! So, let's devant in a forward link at the masked ball.'"

Gene's eyes suddenly sparkled. Gina, daughter of rig, an ancient Irish king himself as well as a mere wanton, immoral woman. Already he could envision himself playing Gilda with a Popeye Doyle wry twist to the accent, and simply hacking up the scenery.

The Cyclops, though still asleep, suddenly sat up in a hot sweat. The dream was too much for him. The only part he understood was the reference to Hercules and the bit about the parrot possibly being a fallen angel with knemidokoptes on its wings. But aside from that the dream was a horrifying vision which probably had something to do with the total breakdown of existence itself, wherein miscegenation becomes the *in* thing and everyone's tossed in a salad as a force of destiny.

Dr. Sseus quickly jumped into action and subdued the Cyclops, invoking him into a much deeper and more hypnotic state by speaking monotonously into his ear, however, patetico. "Learn the meaning of history, my *soldat Clio.* In industry, power means the force or energy that can be applied to do work. During ancient, medieval and early modern times, work was accomplished through power furnished by man, animal, water, and wind. Even the first machines of the Industrial Revolution were operated by hand or water power. The Industrial Revolution spurred man's dream for a new and practical source of power that would grant all would-be ergomaniacs freedom from hard physical labor, as well as freedom from the limitations of wind and water power. The steamboat was invented by Robert. The locomotive was invented by George. The rocket was first propelled on wheels turned by power from a steam engine. Towards the close of the eighteenth century, John first stated the atomic theory. All matter is composed of small particles called atoms. Niels, Lise, and Enrico helped to prove that the atom itself could be split and that in the process tremendous quantities of energy could be released. During World War II, the United States inaugurated the Manhattan Project in order to produce their own atomic bomb . . ."

O Geheimnis . . .

The Cyclops did indeed fall into more than just a mere deep sleep; he fell into an omniscient sleep wherein time and all knowledge of events were contained behind his solitary eye.   "Khufu, also known as Cheops, built the Great Pyramid of Gizeh," he continued as though in a deep, *tief* trance. "Osiris is the judge of the dead. Amenhotep IV tried to introduce the worship of a single god, Aton. The Egyptians are credited with being the first people to employ a system of writing. In the sixteenth century, the Turks advanced deep into central Europe. Under Suleiman the Magnificent, they laid the siege to but were unable to capture Vienna. Consequently, Pope Urban II in 1095 issued a call for a religious war against the Moslems to restore Christian control over the Holy land. Due to this the Bolsheviks, led by Nikolai, broke with the Social Democrats and founded the Communist Party. Proceeding this, Pope Pius XI urged that working men share in the management and profits of industry. Remember, in the meantime, G.W.C., an American negro, discovered over one hundred commercial uses for the common peanut. And Thomas did much to spread Darwin's theory of evolution: IHC. Gautama the Enlightened taught that control over one's emotions and desires results in right living. Confucius despised soldiers and war, and Andrew provided funds for free public libraries, while Susan B. Anthony led the struggle for women's right to vote. Elizabeth led the movement for better treatment of the insane, while in Germany minnesingers gracing the earth as wandering poets on all fours, with two longer and two shorter legs for walking on hillsides gray with gyascutuses, preferred the Nibelungenlied, relating the adventures of gods and warriors and wolves and shepherds and hungry centaurs from Thrace and Thessaly. O, where are the poets wandering now that the world is gone, and Gargantua and Pantagruel are in the arms of the city of Agrigento, as Siller Sea as the Isle of Man, and a comic world of common giants whose antics satirized that the evils-are-all missing has vanished, and the most divine one of all has taken a detour on an imaginary trip with a famous hard so-and-so with excessive GMP, and is somewhere in a far country out-of-control? Ask Donatello where the four erect horsemen are and he is likely to answer, 'Somewhere behind St. George in the right Centre party'; but then he might add after searching through his dossier, *'Stabia quocunque ieceris.'* O, I could cry, although I can't say exactly why. Somehow I missed the *Laughing Cavalier*, perhaps because he was a real horseman and I but a substanceless myth. Why do I cry? What did I miss? *Füssen* with an erect arm and three bent legs? A Clintonia de interruptedly pinnate witt? A Dr. G. Eros who would use a planet to wit love of the masses? A wittol who is also a Pen Pres? Or yet . . . a 3-faced pebble faceted by wind-blown dust? I could ask Zwingli to define me; but despite his good intentions I fear that I would cease to exist altogether. What is really supreme? What be this? I dream symbolic *dreikanter?* Rotation in the extreme. *Sich dre hen.* The autumn breeze blows leaves upon the sea, my soft and moving tomb."

Dr. Sseus began to think: *What have I done?* As director of religious education (A.K.A. D.R.E.), in allowing the Cyclops to eat of the tree, he had opened up to him an awareness of his own transparency. For indeed was he not a myth and therefore not a living form? Much like Thomas Rowley chattering up a storm? Only now the Cyclops, within his own dream, had come to see himself beneath the left hand of god, based purely in myth and storytelling, traveling with a yram and a baby tsir to the Linear Gasthof, and asking the Besitzer Tod for a room, and getting *non c'è spazio.* Such is the fate of having eaten of the forbidden tree; making sleaze blossom into art along the way, with sit-comsncelebs the electronic clamor of the Age. The Cyclops knew he was naked of John Doe facts, eaten as it were to the core. And yet it filled him with dreddour.

"How can I consume a god that does not hold me in his beliefs?" the Cyclops cried out. "I do not exist to him, and therefore I'm less than paper-thin. How many heads have I dashed against the rocks, drank the blood and crunched the bones thereof? How many sailors? How many warriors? How many kings? How many objects have I consumed around the *gancio*? How many Its of its own accord, all undressed vines in rest? More than my stomach can hold at any one feasting. But this is certain – everyone, be it god or man of whom I did consume, did believe me to be a Cyclops, a doctorate of Freude. What room be this where a zoilist god does sit upon his throne and swears a Cyclops has no home? Worse than Zoilus. Absurdity may be his lot, but certainly it cannot stand to reason!" Drop. Drop. Drop.

"My dear Cyclops," Dr. Sseus said, "forgive this crude state of affairs. To be certain, I did not wish to grant you such misery with such spontaneous knowledge. Do not stare. Or may I say, do not linger too long upon god or you might find yourself stuck to him in sacrifice of yourself, with not meat but dreich, sir, men dribbling off your chin. In this beware: the devil is thin; and therefore god encompasses him in much the same way; his words are only weighty should you grant them concentration."

"But this hardly matters," the Cyclops said, his solitary eye transfixed in a dead stare that looked as though it were gazing from out of a black pool of oblivion. "I never thought a Cyclops would die simply because he was never born. This sole thought could bring the first tear to my eye alone. I have only known the salt of skin as I gnashed it from the bone; but never the salt that comes from sorrow as it glides out one home and into another. So, I could die, marrow?"

"No, this is not true," Dr. Sseus interrupted. "Do not allow this thought to rule, for you are indeed a mighty monster and the ground floor upon which you roam is certainly your own. What dares to stand before you and dictate your creed? Think rightly! Whom can a Cyclops fully trust in if not himself? I only make you aware of god so that you might add him to your shelf of bones on the storey level with the ground. That is all. Take heart. Smile and be forever as long as the night is dark. Go unto this god and consume him. Roar! Chew him up like tar sops, Cyclops! Euphemorize your senses! His blood congeals same as any man, no matter his stand on whether you breathe or not. For indeed behold! The tree to eat! The dream, Cyclops, is one's long home, and the living shall not make an end of it. Venture deep inside, quickly, and thereafter become your own *D, IOU Die!* Make the bottom exemplar of your *X* sample. Frit!"

And in his dream the Cyclops began to descend a staircase. From the manner of his walk he appeared confident enough. His torso rippled as his muscles worked even onto his calves. His strength was revealed in the sculptured contours of his body which defined him as being fierce and commanding; but within his mind he was lacking a certain confidence he had once possessed, and he was wary of encountering a god who bore him no credence, neither good nor sin.

The air grew colder as he descended the stairs. *What crepuscular purgatory is this?* he asked himself. And even though his awareness had granted him knowledge of the word, *purgatory,* he was still somewhat lost as to its significant meaning. Divine justice (incomprehensible to reason alone) moved god in his threefold attributes of power, wisdom and love in order to create hell in any one of three primitive languages. The suasive Arabic, the poetic Persian and the Gabrielish Turkish. Could this be the city of *Dis* – the city of grief wherein every hope is abandoned? The Cyclops could not allow cowardiceness to endure.

What cries he heard round about were of a language far beyond him, more menacing than Turkish. And yet the voices belonging to the cries seemed mediocre, like voices refusing to take sides in a major dispute. Like voices heard half way up a mount *im*, the heterophemistic words were not totally discernable; one rose in fall. Sorrow. The bleeding one laid at the gate found no one pleading for him; instead they cried for their own poor spirit, for their own silver chord broken and retwisted into a triangular shape, like three penned rabbits whose ears when pinched together form a *dreieck*.

These are the voices of indifference, the Cyclops mused while emitting tiny farts. Voices who care for nothing beyond themselves. Even I care for my sumptuous meals as to whether they are all eating well. For what good does it do me to consume celery-sticks? Even as I deeply come and see the dogs lick and dip the tip in this great gulf fixed, I throw a tit to Abrahamman feigning Lou to gather alms. Certainly I care for the health of my meals. Even as I venture into the valley of the abyss I hear the word of the first son speaking to me, *"Se dió por vencido"* or "Be ye able to do the work that must be done and not claim unemployment?" And it seems to me a great force of crowded trees did sprout, which left its shade returning upon my shadow so as to make my image last long into the night. When my voice is silent but my ears are filled with wax I will learn how to strip the gobbledygook essence from the word, and thereafter become the stripper dunger. O my heart is much too fresh for a Cyclops's breath. Instead of its odor reeking of old meat and bones, I pass onto the air a meadow of fresh verdure. I can't, nor I won't say I do not exist, for therein lives my mephitic company – Electra, Hector, Aeneas, Camilla, Penthesilea, and one Zasu Pitts crepitating like a certain raven with a mordant tongue.

Upon reaching the bottom of the sechste stairs, the Cyclops found himself before a great shade wherein he felt a great familiarity. And be began to *read* the shade like one skilled in dermatoglyphics. It was strange indeed. For within this place he felt an immediate onrush of rapture, a sense of *déjà vu,* where just beyond the shade he would find his own grave under a Pale Stein, bearing the crackling spirits of Jove the Sicarian, a kerygmatic proselyte posing as *gai saber,* and all the *crémant* thunderbolts that the giants ever threw covering his lifeless form like foam in a hardcore cell. Could this be where those who knew not god found themselves confused and supine, feeling hour after *vide* hour the overbearing power of his eternal absence? Should he check his keraunograph for clues?

Cut!

Mt. Etna is no match for Phlegra, the Cyclops thought. But if my contempt, if my defiance, if my arrogance, even more, if my *mauvais ton,* my *mauvaise plaisanterie* should lead me to god, I should hope to find him a proper host on whom to vent my rage with a properly raised *Mont de Saturne.* How dare he exclude me from his own page? Was I not mentioned in a *Comedy* wherein the trinity did spin thirty-four for the inferno whine and thirty-three each for the remaining two? All-in-all, bearing three lines of triple rhyme. Certainly this is a vast architectural structure that I be in, with all parts fitted symmetrically together. So, simply, I do exist; howbeit, in an exedra I sit and talk and kiss the sediments of my weaknesses. For this is where I am in regards to a reduction of god that nonetheless bears within it both his name and tree rooted to the eminence in the palm of my hand, a place relating to the wine aforementioned, wherein there are nine circles plus the vestibule. This be my most pleasant surprise scrambled in the bones of Jack Riparare. At one moment to feel cold, silent and repulsed, frozen to the waist in ice as if in the midst of a *zastrugi;* and the next moment to feel the tears of man's sufferings flowing down my breast just moments proceeding the evening of a very good Friday. For there I be as in an eye's reflection looking back at me; a movie *zvezda;* and beyond the glass I sense to see a bespectacled revelation repairing a knight in the form of a woman; and her name sounds like be-thrice; and she has beautiful eyes I feel I can see; and her tongue, her sinuous words, behold an army of all the untapped fruit gathered from the circling of the spheres; and she holds the lightning like the thunderbolts I carved; and her smile comes down in a morbidezza of mona lisa, monkey and fish to greet my tears. I am so moved as to suggest that buried secretly beneath her imperious breast is the name *from the beginning.* Danse . . . Danse . . . Danse . . . O, ten-pounder.

The Cyclops was continuing to grow fuller in the knowledge that his vinous dream bequeathed him; perhaps he would even evolve as a Cyclops top full of gnosis. As it was before, that is, in the myth of his former placement, his lines were forever being repeated clear back to daubenton's plane – marking the landmark with three outward digits, all identical, much like a record with a broken groove or like a visible message traced on the skin in a condition of dermographia. "Help, help, good Vulcan, in your cosmopolitan warm sea. *Da en el blanco.*" But what quadrum leap this beast was taking, compliments of the irrisory dream bestowed upon him by Dr. Sseus, could prove to become his own redemption. Now at least he was part of the evolutionary mystery – wet, clamoring, crawling, bowed, nearly in air, like opisthotonus, head back and, in time, walking soundly through the dust kicked up by those whom god had thought to put to bed – the faces . . . the spirits . . . even the raised bodies of familiar names, like a troupe of transients raised, as well as unfamiliar strangers bearing reddish marks that the Cyclops passed by as he lumbered thickly through the tenebrous corridors of this buried design that he felt absolutely no thirsting for. No, never once did he think to consume any form filling his *sub rosa* view; rather his incrassate appetite lingered only upon that which he thought to have conceived: The future was his con-souling destiny, for it was too difficult to say the same for his past. Oddly, somewhere within that future he felt there to be a woman, although with how many eyes he couldn't be certain. And then while moving through a grid of dark, decaying streets and red lights, smoke-choked bars, and limbs of wild theatrical gestures, a dizzy confusion of gaping societal wounds, *and* rooms let by the hour to one particular wet chamber of his mind, reminiscent of a muebles not short of *una habitación sin muebles,* he caught a sideward glance of himself in reflecting glass; and just as if the reflection had a life all its own, he thought to see it suddenly break away from his own reflective movements, and whisper, "As I was dead, so am I alive." And thereafter the Cyclops cried, but A-bomb.

Why should this possible dream within a dream of the Cyclops's mind bring forth yet another dernier tear?

And rage, more at dust.

Perhaps it was only for the protoplasmal food for which he had gained a new appetite.

The Cyclops seriously considered this new appetite and began to think of how the old protoplast might drain out of him. Certainly in order to make ward-room for the new, quite a bit of furibund draining was due. Relating matters to his own mad realm, he began to envision the overflow from Phlegethon as a river of blood similar to the blood of his own bedlamite body coursing through his veins and overspilling. Old blood for new. And as he crossed each threshold of each succeeding certifiable room in his dream, he compared it to where the bloody overflow from Phlegethon crosses the apodictic plain and enters the dereistic plain; and then the woman whom he had previously envisioned in his distant, noetic view suddenly appeared in his mind's eye, sighing the word, "Bulicame . . . Bulicame . . . Bulicame . . ." – appearing like William with the little flame, like an *ignis fatuus*, a foolish fire, phosphorescent, like a whore, a pale misty light in the shape of a logomachic warrior; the kind of light seen mostly hovering around graveyards and marshes; the kind of light only fools would follow in a hazardous debate, misleading wandering night travelers into a refuge of neither heaven nor hell; erratic; unbaptized; a light wanting to be heard for its earthy desires, too innumerable to count; for this was where a hot spring thrived, where spontaneous gas arose from decomposed matter, where iniquitous women shared among themselves a clientele of hypocritical men, some of whom were even hotly sterile so as to offer an adequate passageway, since blood without sperm cannot quench a fire that would otherwise cause much fury and suffering.

Desire. In what room? The Cyclops came upon a sign that read

MOUNT IDA. IN CRETE. THIS WAY. . . ☞   ☞   ☞   ♪

The Cyclops considered the meaning of the sign as the possible display of a compendium of all the fashionable substances likely to be found in a myth, and especially noted the aberrant position of the arrows. And soon his imagination (after visualizing having mounted Ida in the position called for) was playing a most lively tune on the head of his in-n-out. Hurriedly he moved ahead, and shortly thereafter he found himself in a large drawing room with such infinite riches as Corinthian columns and Palladian windows. In one section was an Oxford library in miniature with antiqued oak paneling. At least part of the floor featured Italian marble and there was fine French and Continental furniture throughout, including rococo decorations and Oriental carpets. A tapestry hanging on the northern wall depicted a scene from seventeenth century Belgium – a bearded 36-inch ruler with a grand procession of rock pens and coral pencils – while other lustrous paintings adorned the foliage ceiling, including the Adoration of the Lamb (of which the Cyclops helped himself to a gigot, as in a eucharist), the big "T" Descending, and Anthony's Temptation by Fish and Rats. And glittering chandeliers, like wicked eulachons, overlooked an extravagant fountain in the center of the room that sparkled with gilded lions and statues of ancient gods emerging with numbing intensity from some innocuous realm in a time prior to the drowning sea. (One being the late Venus Callipyge with the beautiful 'tocks from the Musco Nazionale.) And all of it receiving the kindly spray of a Lamb's jet of water shot to a height of six feet in the air.

The south wall was encased in agate and jasper, decorated with malachite, lapis lazuli, porphyry and alabaster. Still another painting on the eastern wall depicted the *Church on Spilled Blood*, which was built at the turn of the century on the spot of Tzar Alexander II's assassination. But the item that most struck the Cyclops's fancy was the Marbles' Arundelian statue behind a fountain chiseled into the shape of a zoic woman with bare breasts and an aura of *the extinction of existence-kind* trailing around the crest of her head, below which was an engravement of the Proverbs of Standing Statues.

IDA

A standing statue makes a seer stay: but a moving one makes a seer flee.
A standing statue makes a seer blush: but a moving one makes a seer birth.

A standing statue makes a seer think: but a moving one makes a seer blink.
A standing statue gives time for a seer to ponder: but a moving one steals
the thoughts and makes a seer to wander.

It all seemed interesting; however, in the Cyclops's omniscient mind, Ida was meant to represent the entire history of mankind, the chassis of his consciousness, and not a mere abridgment of it. Her back was bare and turned toward the East. Her face, barren, yet fair, was also made of gold, and meant to represent the Golden Age of the Ancients in the Garden of Eden and the silent stones in Olympia's temple. Her paired eyes depicted the Roman Empire and the Papacy; the same eyes being pale and blank with reverend exhaustion, the cold wet heat of the Piazza della Republica, the surviving power of the Ponte Vecchio, the G of Santa Maria del Fiore, Donatello's Crucifix, and, in Salon's terms, the resurrected musical-dramatic art of ancient G., via Peri's lost Dafne, lost under the tourist's choke of the bus's dust of the guide's cackle, and the sweaty tide of food's fast channel. The same dust, once cleared, that revealed emaciated men in moving cars, women under piles of steely parts, one-armed operators soliciting trash, men on crutches making toys work, men laying bricks, digging graves, mixing cement, their individual movements describing a pattern within arm's reach of time's exposure. And from this the eruption of wasted motion and fatigue and compassion and sweat. There was a sudden distinct crack in the statue and from this fissure tears dripped at Wannsee. Immediately the Cyclops yelled, "Ida!" to which the statue looked up with sudden lifelike, cryptic movements. And after spreading her arms out invitingly, the Cyclops plunged forward into an 1170 eight-armed knight, and sank his erect cock into the bloody primate T.B. fissure that was Ida. Wide enough (but just wide enough) to hold him snug. And remembering the irregular course of the arrows, the spaghetti entanglement of lights, the cross-reference of his liturgical plight, the Cyclops made mad passionate love to Ida until a stream of bulicame overflowed like the drowning mud of Flanders, and thereby creamed Ida from head to toe.

"Oh Ida! Ida!" the Cyclops said, collapsing in ecstasy. "You are the dream I dreamed since CAD30! How I love thee! How you have made my heart joyous with water and leaves when once it was a heart deserted. Other Cyclopes of my kind would no doubt find my speech here sickening, but Ida . . . Oh Ida! what do I care what the others think? Their diet is still meat and bones. Their solitary eye serves only to grade the hides of any man or beast they come upon. But my eye, Ida, though there be only one, lives to feast on the very beauty that I currently penetrate, and to wander on in a childish crusade over your soft curves to the hole I desire. O, you are a safe cradle to me, and this be my new diet of meat. To sing! To dance! The wedding dance! And to sue to divorce me from mary for my new appetite. Until the circle is complete and I kiss your feet of baked clay and enhance this trance!"

Ida, the statue, said in return, "All of your words rest as comfortably as the ten eighty-six compilation of my census for the day of judgment. Therefore I offer no contest with your lay. But had you come yesterday I would have been expressing a much different tune. Yesterday I was not quite the same lay considering that I do represent history. No . . . had you rested on me yesterday your cock would not have found such a welcoming crow's nest. For yesterday I was a great Old Poker and one not prone to homosexuality . . . But today call me Baucis."

"Then my timing is impeccable and only goes to show me that I'm on track." And upon saying this the Cyclops planted three gentle kisses on Ida's back which be made of brass as far as to the ass. "And you may call me Phil, my heroine." Whereupon they intertwined like hydraulic trees on a grassy hill.

So far, upon quick review, the Cyclops had finally come within his newly realized dream to experience tears, love and the willowy veil of a woman's form as it silently rains upon the old, indign life around it. Yes, even now, the Cyclops was drenched by the endless needle tears shed from the fissure in Ida's immortal bust.

And the Cyclops never imagined such a passion could ever exist. To kiss the lips, the breast, the feet of one who could accelerate or decrease the beat of his own ineffable heart was but a mere alien thought legions ago. Cyclopes don't exist to love. They feel and sense the heat of skin only in how soft or tough it will be once their very teeth sink in. Nor do Cyclopes mate out of love, but simply to perpetuate the race. One to another, Cyclopes do not gaze with love nor brush the hair back lovingly from one another's solitary eye. They do not express words of warmth. Neither do they reassure one another of their perdurable worth in staged whispers of ill-content. Cyclopes are a cold lot indeed, living simply to mold and carve their thunderbolts, to tend their flock and to guard their keep – as well to eat anything that might otherwise breathe. Simply this was how they were made. And if ever any woman or man should happen to encounter a band of Cyclopes, either high upon their cliffs or down along the banks of their circular island, he/she could be certain that their last site would be lost among the decomposing pieces of meat in the monster's belly.

"O my Ida," the Cyclops moaned, for he was tired and had spent all that he could for the moment. "As much as I can, I beg you to rest awhile with me. In the last hundred years, whenever I had consumed a meal, I would lay back down and allow it to rest while I digested it somewhere deep beneath my reposeful bones. That is all I ever knew of satisfaction. The only thing I waited for was a final belch to let me know that my stomach had done its intussusceptive work, just as it had done one twelfth night ago on a reckless, roistering knight named Sir Toby. The only thing left beneath my breast thereafter was nothing more than a most sublime kind of rest, which compels me to recall still another Toby, only this one was a dog that wore a frill garnished with bells to frighten the devil away, sort of like a Heath Robinson of sin. Ennui he was meant to represent, with leishmania about his head. And just as Punch was meant to represent Pilate, and Judy was meant to represent J . . . Judas, the beginning was meant to represent the end as it is dead and alive again. O, for rigid abstract humanoids wielding sponge, bone and string. Beating the matter to death is no small thing. Such is the sweet re-play of events when it comes to matters that are flagellant. But now what seventh hour fever has gripped my mind and has informed me that indeed, most willingly, I must follow your own skirts wherever they might go, even if it should be unto eternal punishment, I am certain I do not know. But of this fact I am most confident – I would surely grouse and die if I could not follow in your wake and attend your resort, seeing how the heavens have been most gracious for allowing me to have this very vision, and to open up to me such savored lemanry."

"Cyclops, you make no sense at all," Ida said, her mouthpiece obviously working in spite of it being composed of pure stone. "Of this I know. Insofar that a Cyclops can fall in love, its mind thereafter can seem to grow as on a dung heep. Far better that you stick to meat and bones. At least both your control and your dignity you might be able to keep. I cannot relay your love back to you just as I cannot teach you how to evolve. Allow me, for a bit of sound education is due. Statues do not love nor are they made to receive love in turn. They are only prepared to sit or stand, and thereafter stare. Such words of love as yours are not new to my ears as I keep one foot in the world of men. But let me say they will find no way into my heart. Therein you'll find no lekach nor will any lenis of yours so smooth find an entrance. For you see, there is no heart here, honey, but merely stone that I keep like cold and hardened clay. Might I say that love is filth. Yes, you heard me say correctly. It exists only for ill-strained muscles that connect to bodies that must piss and defecate. Do you see any statue doing the same? The only way *you* can mix with stone is to become like stone itself, even as you pray to love. For as for love, keep love where it belongs. On the penny. In the exergue. On the reverse side. Below the design. Marked off by the line containing the date *in.*"

"But I saw you move as I called out your name!" the Cyclops's eye welled up with tears and he experienced closure in his breath channel. "With your arms outstretched you opened your nest and gave unto me not a perverse city but a waterfall of tears and passion that fell like the wine that pursued me while I was but a belsen beast. Nay, I, belswagger, who am even guilty of committing sodomy with my fellow beast, experienced in this sudden turn of a leaf a hum as onto a beehive, where three bees running together left a bit of honey upon the tip of my member, and fiery torment spurred on by love did cause me to deflower you. If not your love at least your pollen might I reap? Yet may it cling to my limbs and weigh me down like soiled stones. I care not as long as I am buried in your dust like the prints of buzz; whether it be living, naked, oiled or dark, breathless or scorched with lunacy's misery, I stand pictured in your soft powder for eternity, wired to the erect: windless wind."

Now all this time Ida had been holding a secret unbeknownst to the Cyclops, for indeed she was meant to lead him into the next circle(s) 000000. For you see the story, the mysterium, forever continues; from the birth of creation to the destruction of the earth and beyond; from god in dirt to god in air and beyond; and thereafter – in exactly how existence progresses from beyond the destruction of myths and fables to the creation of new stories, new truth, new flesh and new stables.

Id Est, Abinu Kadescha Papa: your tiara is but a beehive on the back of a *camel, au cum,* on the back of a *camel au cum,* etceteras, etceteras, etceteras.

Let it be noted hereafter: WORDS ON THE PAGE WILL NO LONGER TAKE ROOT JUST AS WORDS ON THE TONGUE WILL NO LONGER HOLD TRUTH. If anyone expects to survive by evolving beyond god then one thought must be contained: One must keep moving by circling around one spot – the eternal eye – G – the consonant *pgnslrw.* Without discord but consistent, congruous and sympathetic – an open and shut case as far as David in Philadelphia is concerned; for therein the Mystery's key answer lies, and the translation of it will be revealed once falsehood is finally put to rest.

But how does one put all falsehood to rest? First one must be cunning enough to decipher truth from lie. But more than just cunning, one must be wise and captious if not outright omniscient. For wisdom alone does not *see* all there is. Wisdom can only rely on what it knows. And what it *knows* may be lacking truth. What actually holds truth from being fully revealed? The limitations of one's own mind could not possibly be its root. More due to the *stealth* of knowledge and truth by a superior jealous mind, man is left in doubt no matter the job. And if this be true then would not lesser mortals do the same to one another to foilow suit? What game of cards god directs with man in mind, wherein the one hides *all* in his hand from the *others,* no man will know until that god be put asunder, and/or confused to a blurb on dust.

Darkness. How soon before it will let go? Must man wait forever, a victim of fate entrapped and entangled in the web of insidious argument? As subtle a bite as on all eight if not four. Was it really a case of sodoku? Ask the jap who took a nip. He'll tell you so. What will it take for man to grow beyond darkness and to be as much in the light as omniscience itself? How soon before the sun is more than the image of melting, nay, bleeding yolk? Eight? Four? The smoke of the incest? Which came?

a rat's bite, nay a kiss . . . ho lleh
Somewhere man still dwells beyond the concept of this.
26 twice . . .
a man in culpa levis
in too tight a fix . . .

Quite an iniquity.
continued on back flap
And the secret is close to this: To destroy truth as it stands to control, to overpower, to stifle, to hold, to impose fear, to impose obedience, to impose allegiance, to impose servitude, to impose threat, to impose death – before ever administering love onto the rest of the flock – a Gobbler who crows for Cripes must be fixed beside a gulf. For one dead rose will not raise the ears of the deaf.

The Cyclops arose with these thoughts in his head. And as he arose he caught a glimpse of himself in a mirror framed in gold against Ida's northern wall. And for an instant he saw not a Cyclops at all but a man in a dusty jacket, and the dead impersonating the living in self-praise, making a noise like a pub.

This was more than confusing to the Cyclops. Cyclopes cannot be men. And yet what he saw in that brief instant was the *exact* image of one man in his own reflection. Like a G coining itself. And then it occurred to him that perhaps his image as a Cyclops was changing. Even his very head felt thinner – rather bare and hairless like a J.C. emperor he once ate who had come to land on his island by mistake. An ex-act. Upon a second glance, however, his former image was restored. And yet the monster in the glass was looking backwards into time with an eye burned, choked and overcome with fear. But what does a Cyclops have to fear aside from his own mortality? A month's mind? Hastily the Cyclops groped through his mind for some basis for the change that he thought to perceive in his image. But the best he could muster was that love had done its honoured deed and had cut him to the quick.

Requiem aeternam . . .
He was now compelled to consider this: if Cyclopes are not capable of love and love was the thing that he was experiencing, then he mustn't be a Cyclops at all; and if by chance he was not a man then perhaps he was some *new* kind of beast. And then he got to thinking that, perchance, for all these years he had been wrong and had *never* been a Cyclops. True he played the part well, insofar that he looked like a Cyclops, performed all the duties thereof and had certainly eaten more than his fill of human flesh. But still something did not feel right. Such an illness of confusion was gripping him and refusing to leave his virile world. And then like a sudden gush of wind, he began to cry with his face upraised. And the words that spewed out of his mouth seemed to come from a place in his heart that was totally foreign to him. "Amen! Culmination!" New people and sudden gains bring fortune upon this humble creature. "Amen! Amen! Amen!" And then he looked down upon Ida, frozen as

polar stone, and said, "What I am waiting for will soon come up, and what you are dreaming about will soon be revealed to my nourished eye, all in red, ready to take peace from the earth. For the lie which appears to be the truth will be struck down. Carry on. That is what I must do . . . Carrion."

And then Ida spoke up and said to the Cyclops, "Everything you say has truth, except your pronunciation is atrocious. For your very words have taken root inside my stone and I must inform you that the one you seek is Geryon. So far as truth is concerned, Geryon has an honest look even though his body is winged, three-bodied, reptilian, leafed and debossed with devious designs. Nevertheless he is an honest beast with a pointed tail who can break through walls by the thrust of two hairy paws, and who also wears a culotte with the words

GERM, ANY?

printed on the back. And in that panspermic word you can have three bodies in one
germ, man, many."

Ida's words had a strange effect upon the Cyclops's mind. He could feel his brain buzzing. As well, he could visualize men burning, and one man holding a torch who also had a tail that darted from left to right, which had a tip on it like a scorpion's; and the men burning were like sad souls with long cascading beards; and each man had the legs and paws of a dog; and each man was shouting, "Reveal nation! Reveal nation!"; and each man swore that his name was Valentino after a well-known pederast of old; and each man kept insisting, *"You've got to catch my zoro, Norman Norell! It's full of pleromas!"* At which time the Cyclops twisted his mouth and stuck out his red tongue with a dark-brown matter on its tip like a dog with sordes about to lick its nose (as well as the crumbs), and grumbled, *"god's son ties."* And meanwhile, all the sad, costumed, sordid souls were burning to the ground. And within 1,300 separate shots, scratchy Odessa casualities filed into an empty studio on Fransuski Boulevard.

For sanctitude. Scared but purty. Report to the Lot.

And then Ida said to the Cyclops, "Go on, big boy. Have a dream within a dream. Only be strong and bold. Like Element 43! Like Ma! According to the rules of Art!"

And the Cyclops did as he was told. And soon enough he found himself mounting Valentino and fumbling for his zipper. And the demotic thoughts that poured forth from the monster's brain were like butter, only a raging shade of blue, like a wet little boy foaming at the mouth with exhaustion or, perhaps, with pursy, driven to bay by a shadow, swelling up with emotion, with a vague, strange, menacing sense – blind, but not yellow, more like an obstacle in the presence of a large mass being dismissed, rising in relief like an embossed head on a coin.

"Take out that big hairy zounds of yours and I will lick its shade," Ida said. "A purple head it made. A purpurogenous purveyor with a purpuriparous purulence. See how I hold it in both my hands and stroke it and rub it and beat it and aim it so that the sheep spurt out and form a circle on the ground. And if I am quite right, yes, I can form a decagon like a communional wafer stamped with a simulacrum. Aye. And after all of the sheep, the countless sheep, have been pumped out, I will descend slowly, thinking of all the obstetric changes I have made – the decalogue of my binding authority as I stand ready to receive your seed and carry it dnally about like an obstetrical toad until it's ready to transform. Such as . . . what I have learned about love I could say in ten words. And in doing so I will change your name from Valentino . . . a likeness – dashing silent movie star . . . to: *Jes the cow in the corn is who you are.* But it is still unfortunate that I should blow my horn and come an executant. For in the end, we are all stripped of our loins and melted, excoriated to the living end. But, nevertheless, let me read your load, expelled, splattered on the ground."

And then the Cyclops got down on his hands and knees and among the dust and the ashes of the bones of those who had been burned, he licked up the circle of sheep and consumed them all. And the millions, totaling six, went on swimming, swimming down his throat – circled and descended until at last their journey ended somewhere deep south beneath the Cyclops's bones.

"So this is my new diet?" the Cyclops said. "From dead men to love. And now to life! Sheep in the meadow. Cows in the corn. Vac! Vac! Gadwall! Grosbeak! Galliwasp! *O-O!* You all must die to be reborn."

And it seemed that the Cyclops was *beginning* to understand that this was still part of an edacious plan. What was his original mission? To seek god and then consume him, howbeit his flesh was already collapsing as in an endoxerosis. The Final Act. Alas, are you coming down too, god? Descending wearily through so many hollow circles to where it all started out. Sound, the earth. So you can set your foot down on the jagged rock and hold your head up in your right hand. "O, by the way, god," the Cyclops said to the image of god in his head, "there's a place you threatened the world with and you called it *right in the middle of a baleful, pathological space: dnaia.* Wide and deep. The new womb. And you said this place is reserved for those who disrobed you. And you promised, once entered, there would be no escape. And you said the prophets dwelt there who have in their power, hereby granted by you, new torments and new howling miniseries to administer unto those who disagree with you, even though they may have already suffered their full due while upon the earth. In addition, you promised there would be cursing and noshing on locks amongst assorted props for eternity. And that this be compliments of a loving god on channel seven. My good master, I think I see one coming my way now just as he was prophesied to do in a faraway, ancient land. Like a god, but a man noshing on news, fangled strange and contemptuous for a gewgaw effect. And his name starts with '*J*' and is followed by four other letters, the third of which is '*s*'; his encounters upon earth have been written about; he was made unto a sacrifice and is likened unto a ram; upon his return from a land of death and decay, a golden halo graced his crown and went down upon his shoulders; he battled evil and righted wrongs. When I met him he was followed by twelve other men each bearing bees in their ring-like bonnets; he took out my brother's eye; and his name was *Jason* from Itháki. Now I come in his place. For slowly I, too, am learning how to be a god who is a *bon vivant* man among men, dreaming intellectuals treating one another with allusions to island aromas and erotic spices. I will cross Al Sirat and pass through the island of Lemnos where bold and stoney women give men their first death at seraglio. Here, with gifts and loving words, I will deceive Ida for having deceived me first; I will abandon her, pregnant, forlorn and worse for wear."

And upon saying this the Cyclops began to ascend the hole that housed his unclean dream. For the dream was the earth and his ascension was a resurrection. And when he had come out of his dream he thought to see heaven, for the place was exceedingly white and clean; howbeit looked like the drawing room of *before* with a bit of dust (or more) upon the floor. And the first face he saw upon ascension was Ida, only with dry hair less the Breck and the *allée*. And she was squatting naked and pissing buckets *fall*; and all the Cyclops could think was what a lovely bladder she had and how good it would be to eat, especially when cooked in butter and leeks.

And while she peed he crawled beneath her and turned over on his back and drank full her urine as it flowed, even going so far as to web his mouth to the draught so as not to lose a single drop. A regular nipcheese he was. And because she was a honey, Cyclops picked up a bit of melituria in the rum. O Supreme Wisdom. This hole could lead to a tomb, in fact, an *allée couverte*. This woman of livid stone covered with holes (one for the soup and one for the rolls) then took hold of the Cyclops's head, planted it on her second hole and gave him her body – a brown george hot bread to eat, a germ paradise of sauerkraut pizza. The mother load gushed down his throat. And afterward the Cyclops licked clean what bits of aftermath clung to the grooves surrounding her hole. And in between Ida took hold, jerked and layered cream over his face, and said, "O come, let us golden worship and bow down. Let us kneel before the board, our maker. Yes, come. Let us take our fill of love until the morning has undone the um bra. Come. Let us red sup and fulfill the emption of stuffs."

O Ida! O Cylcops! O commissioners of peace!

Lend us your demimondaine that we might see her bathe the baby.

You would become like god if time permits. Time is somewhat wedded to occurrence, which in turn is somewhat wedded to evolution. Emit and eliminate time and, thusly, you eliminate permission. For as long as there is time and all of its *up-to-date* limitations, there is a conditional god; *annos vixit;* and as long as there is a conditional god there is a major contingency upon ultimate freedom as it stands in a permissive broadcast. For as long as man is beneath god he is subject to his authority. Being subject to his authority induces a natural state of fear; for therein is the fear of pain, the fear of loss, the fear of death; and god holds authority over each of these coded conditions. So the answer to the dilemma is more than merely becoming like god; indeed, it is even much more than going through with a commodious mission. The way to transcend time, the way to transcend permission, the way to transcend EAR is to transcend god.

The Cyclops couldn't stand it any longer. He couldn't bear to think that he was so close to something he loved so much; and yet he wasn't allowing himself to do all that he wished. The Cyclops could feel himself breaking bonds, barriers, walls, even expensive dinner dishes. He saw the livid stone wall covered with holes. On the sides and on the bottom and riddled all around. Holes through which he could bore through and thereby make his way onto the other side – whether to save a drowning child or to deceive all men, mostly all stars, who knew their work, who each had a name and who art dead. Whatever. Such is the right of a god. Just think. Into the mouth of each watery hole, each inciting hole, he could place his tongue and speak words beyond any gatecrasher language known to man – whether it be a new language or an old and dead one, long since forgotten. For the gate is but a hole – as the greeks would say, *chezein,* which could be construed to mean a state of separation, where one might give one the 'gate' for being late or, if on time, 'the path itself.' The journey could lead to defecation and thereby a watery brown gate – a previously consumed revelation. And into any one of these holes, the Cyclops could baptize even Rexist in the Gate of Tears, made redder by Menagogue, and piss and hold him there for as long as "Christus Rex" occupied Belgium. Whatever. The Cyclops was getting ready to play the part. He was going to smooth the transparent serous membrane that lined the cavity of his heart and mind. He was going to bite the sloes. He was going to suck the squids. He was going to connect the numbers with the periods and do his part. From beast to man to spirit to god, with atomic numbers displayed above the symbols for the elements and atomic weights. He must act hurriedly for this was the periodic table before the break! In short, he was going to squirt an unknown origin.

Xnty . . . Xnty . . . Xnty . . .

The Cyclops was becoming sharp, but more at the edge. O yes. The Cyclops was becoming an element that is found as free as a colorless, tasteless, odorless gas in the mass enveloping a heavenly body as a dominant appeal, as an overall aesthetic effect of a work of art.

The souls on his feet were suddenly on fire, and his legs up to the calf remained within him as a power that could break withes or ropes if given the chance. His mind, however, was vesuviusized with Christi bliss up to his gray matter in feverish mud. O how the Cyclops twitched betwixt and between a rock and a hard place; if only to move over the outer surface and glide, ever so gently, his tongue into the bunghole of his love without losing his hold on his own res erection; to take the chance and to venture into the fourth ditch where Anacreon was choked by a grape stone, Fabius was choked by a goat-hair, and Otway was choked by a loaf of Wonder Bread.

And, so, the Cyclops wormed his tongue deep, deep down into Ida's dainty bunghole, and wormed it up into the colon, through, and Roto-Rooter-arized it into the maze of twisting corridors that composed the large and small intestines, and continued it on, tight squeeze, through the duodenum, around the bend, the stomach, too, and a half chewed mortadella, and then barely squiggled through the esophagus until it sprang like mort come alive into full view from out the mother of all holes, the mouth, wherein Ida now had two tongues to rule; and both worked simultaneously, each dancing upon the other's surface as words were exchanged in due course. Hymn: Dithyramb: O! heil

I got plenty of nothin'	Organs one two three
I got me a stomach	I got me a heart
I even got me a spleen	'Cause I'm mean . . .
'Cause bein' human is somewhere	
betwixt and between	a statue, a god and a tinseltown queen.

A disembodied laughter erupted in the midst of this dense, wild, entangled scene. It was a pitiless laugh and the sound of it renewed a sense of fear in the Cyclops. With his face still glued to Ida's crotch, where his tongue took root and had worked its way to the threshold of Ida's mouth, he cried, "What will it mean? *Requiem, dona pet eat lux!*" So heavy was his cry that Ida could feel it tingling in her very teeth and could only think *what divine love this must be.* For it was setting beautiful things into motion such as: the hecate beast with the gaily gaily spotted eye, like the coluber on the front page, one meter shy of one international candle whose tongue had found a sweet golden street to clean.

Suddenly she let go her bowels and gave him a solid squirt in the face. And lo and behold! the Cyclops jumped up and immediately sprang back down to his knees. For indeed with this new mask, sort of speak, he was suddenly transformed (though still a Cyclops) into Asa Voelson.

It was true. Another Momma's boy. But to have to return to such misery was more than any race could take. The Cyclops (scratch, scratch) had certainly brown-faced himself into a miserable state of indignity and overindulgence. Slavery. O Mass. O Brown. You played with a deck of secret sixes and clubbed the bearer like Periphetes. O what man has done to man. Bondage. *Cut!*

Think upon the ew. Think upon the ergo. Think upon all the gee-gaws that have ever had to serfer needlessly to the point of surfeit, and you will be shocked to learn that slavery and bondage still continue well after the bogus destruction of the world. The laughter resounded for a little season and then made an acid drop, as in a surfer's term, ass in dropping into a wave and having the bottom suddenly fall out, followed by a sense of weightlessness and helplessness, only here the wave was the season, loosened as it were, and the Cyclops was a grumpy, old longboarder who burns everyone and never looks back, and says, "She's death," a lot, "fer sure" and "go down on Kathy Kohner," while getting tubed, going to church while hanging ten, and while on the hook in the Pope's living room, as it were, mingling with all the surf dogs and surf nazis as they come and go with papaphobia, speaking of El Niño, according to Big Wednesday. *Cut!* And with a scream that could have shattered glass, the Cyclops started talking to the seals, and bolted forth a song that even brought forth a golden tear from Ida's eye, and a *take off* and *die sindrome* attitude.

"Swanee
Behold her, single in the field
Brown body
Reeping and singing Œnone
O listen! For the Vale
Guess who first put amn in jail?
Save the munitions, but not the man!
O Swanee
Breaking the silence of the seas among the farthest Hebrides
Borborygmus on the go. Propulsion, not slow.
Will no one tell me
For battles long ago
From Timbuktu to Jericho?
My Swanee
Natural sorrow, loss and pain
That ever has been, has come again
I'll strike a match in sin
For the gaseous song that has no ending.
And o'er the sickle bending
The Luz is still ascending
My Swanee."

Ida leaped upon the Cyclops, yelling, "What does it mean?"

But to this the Cyclops was speechless and dark. For not even he was certain what force, what inspiration, what calamity had given birth to his gerontic song. One thing was certain however. His hoary head was spinning round the colulus. And the intensity created from it brought forth to his mind a bizarre assortment of whilom words and images. For instance, he mused: *I know everything, even though I cannot define anything. SHI. SUSEJ. If Mary is not available, may we call upon Igraine?* To which Ida recited her refrain:

"What does it mean?"

"If you really want to know then know that once I was clothed with the great mantle. For I was the son of the Earth-shaker, who just so happened to be *one of three*, all quite contrary. The other two being the Father and the Invisible Ray. By way of the cap that I gave him and the staff which he holds to lead, just a couple of old folks at home as directed by *Whale* and *Hillyer.*

Again there was a disembodied, pitiless laugh in the midst of them.

The Cyclops ignored it for he felt it to be nothing more than the cosmic, pre-recorded laugh track out of court. Another Hatbox Mystery solved in 44m. "The one that held the symbol of three, the trident, was very adept at changing himself into a recurvous ram or, in the case of Caeneus, from a woman into a man," the Cyclops said. "Just as I could be mistaken for Pope III or, better yet, considering this mask of excrement, Boniface, I can state exactly the same thing as before, only upside down like Latrodectus. Consequently, one could also say that I be one of three: first of all, me – secondly, vulcan – and thirdly, jove – god of the Ancients. Mysteriously just. Dark, marked with red, of medium size, and a tad venomous. Like the koumiss I sucked in bed before night mares rode on high. Fetch me my cuneiform cup, the one touched with krasis, so that I might strike down a rioter, a recusant who has lost control of his watery son. And get in a few extra licks without a tongue. But let me see what I can do with a long and wirey leg and a globular glossy abdomen or two. Moo."

"But what does it mean?" Ida asked, bending down in order to face the Cyclops's head upon which the beast was standing.

"Is ca riot? I think it must be," the Cyclops said. "For hasn't it always been our calling since the beginning? When we as candles, as oolachans, were but bright candidates in white togas, roaring like anguiped hounds for a curious prey. Check out my rennet."

"You speak nonsense," Ida stormed. "From standing upside down like some insidious desmodus, your head is spinning round and round."

The Cyclops laughed. "Revolt like Judas. Follow my strokes and kick against the pricks. Stand upside down and you'll see red and get the joke."

Kick

The cock-boat sails on the stroke of gallicinium, cockcrow, he, the time is three.

Ida again picked up the sound of disembodied laughter. "What the kcuf is going on? I feel so confused. Perhaps the only course to take is the one you advised." Upon saying this Ida stood on her head and at once a kind of vision was restored. "This is Bolgia! But of course!" she said. "Now I understand. But allow me to translate and to channel the spirit of Jud from the mud as to the giving of a bit of information. Your call to riot is nothing more than Iscariot, restored. Yes! Now I see! Another aging son of which you spoke. Phaethon. Of course! There be the joke! He scored a victory. A sign. Standing upside down, it is plain to see. And the joke's on poor old anaclitic me! For you have taught me something I didn't see before, rather than the other way around, which I abhor!"

"That's some Vamp I be!" the Cyclops said, taking delight in his abilities. "You see, I was not just jesse with a rod rising from my loins. I was Remus raised by a shewolf. I was

Romero raised by a shark. I was Sebastodes Mystinus raised by a *prete.* I was Rena raised by a queen of cards, shouting *renegation,* failing to follow the rules. Now I think of another revolt, namely molasba who, too, hung nearly upside down even as he did revolt, and was finally put down by three darts to the throat. *'O my son, my son, my son.'* That carries us to our final revolt of which we must all take a part."

Oyegevalt.

Ida, who was turning red in the face due to the blood rushing down, looked almost Scarlet. "Baby Lo! I will help you," she said. "For I see there is yet some hemoid piddle on the ground upon which my head sits. If you could get back up on your feet and between my outstretched legs give to me your meat, I will then grant you six more as long as there is life to bore. Pray tell me. Where's the missing *n*?"

"The same as where the free course is. In Athens. Where the wicked men are all plain men and there's a patient waiting for man's bread. Note that man!" The Cyclops kicked hard with both his feet. And finding that his leader was pleased, he positioned himself rightly between Ida's legs while she stood upon her head. And with both arms he took hold of Ida and planted his eager barrel and shot, rested, and shot, rested, and shot, rested, and shot, rested, and shot, rested, and shot, rested, and shot, and thereafter got back on his head and sighed, "dog si doog sa daed."

(Pause)
Meant to be noticed

Oh Baby! Three stunning originals. Meticulously created by a little master, an old master, a past master, a master raised to the third degree, all-in-all nine, a trinity of trinities. Thoroughly unique to you. Your life. Your style. god & sons, Ltd. Heaven's premier joaillers where we feature an exquisite fine jewelry watch that changes with your mood and occasions. This exclusive design lets you easily change from a gold to a red, from a green to a baby blue, from a lizard strap to a swan white, from a man to a wolf . . . Oh! lou, baby! Priced at only $20,018.00. And together with a fine cleaning oil (retail value $45), it makes for a fine gift. Start your engines. *Rev. Rev. Rev.*

(Pause)

No ifs, ands or buts: An issue of blood? A jugal entanglement? You can change your bottom line in smoky hours for that small personal touch. We can put a dent in either cheek or widen the cleft in between. Reduce your saddlebags. Contact g.O.d. That's *get Off dough.* That's paradise, lady. Rolllicking heads. That's jugate-coined. And if you act now you can wipe away those suffering lines with a complimentary gift of Veronica's™ handkerchief.

(Pause)

Spellbinding! A wildly hypnotic thriller! Thrilling! Frighteningly romantic! A dazzler! It's impossible to take your eyes off the page or the ball. Innocent, yet erotic! A masterpiece! An elegant, fascinating puzzle! Even better than parousia! An indisputable masterwork! An event that happens only once in eternity! A review of earth, after the facts. Lucifer's final lament as Satan according to the devil under god's authority. While Lu waits for the new season. Beyond genius! Wow! Indescribable! "What does it mean?" asked the beadle Jack, the schizophrenic sax/trumpeter with the fat lips and the battered brain. Don't ask. Just read and buy everyone you know a second copy. And let us go and make our visit. "The spirit is ready." Not Athens, not Greece, but Olympus. On Peachtree Street. Near the park. Where Coca Cola has done its part alongside the viper militia.

This is it!

Rip!

The Final Book!

Everything written before it is just plain schism. Nothing will be written after it! It's impossible!! A review of the universe! A review of heaven and hell! Daring in its analysis. *. . Please, what is it all about? I fell asleep on page thirty-three! Disgusting! Amoral! Banned in Iceland, Pasadena, and Bryce Canyon! Sickening! Sacreligious! Should be burned and its ashes used as lawn manure to spread over White Chapel.*

ALL THE CRITICS DON'T AGREE!
Better to see *Jack's Delight In His Lovely Nan*
YOU READ –
RACA
AND DECIDE FOR YOURSELF . . .
SATORI
Peek a bòo!
I see a beard

Page 1

gOD!
PLEASE GET ME OFF THE HOOK!
or
what's it all about, az?
or
how to stop worrying and love bm
or
G DAY
or
The Ultimate Scoop
or
The Missing M
or
Credo Ut Intelligam
or
That-than-witch-no-greater-can-be-thought

There will be a little 'tan year intermission.
'Tis the season to be loosened . . .

god scooted his chair back within a room that posted a soaring ceiling, Italian marble floors, high archways, Roman Doric columns like the type that commemorated the Great Fire in one 666 . . . treachery and malice, bronze kouroi, tempting, muscular and sly statues, a hollow boast, a six-pack of Coke, a Cincinnati refrigerator that also makes toast, strings of floating freestyle rhyme and massive moldings. The click on kind. A hand-carved fireplace of wooden marble was currently fireless, but an automatic air freshener kept the room dancing with the scent of fresh winter pine and ashes. A biometric palm device was situated at every door frame for either hard or easy access. On the walls were autographed portraits personally signed and addressed to god, celestine pro in sneakers; he walked you through basic allusions and references, his anthology was narrated via a Master game. Art Rupestre. Among the faces were Will Rogers, Gloria Swanson, Tom Mix, Pinky Lee, the Emperor *Marcus Aurelius Antoninus*, Napoleon, and Martin V.S. of Palmdale, famous for the shuttle private table dance, a pie in the sky experience this side of a senator's pants, wingless except for a sheath with a pointed angle, and an aerospike named Shedu. There was also a group photo of the Valdez family with the inscription, *Dear god, thanks for the mecca. Though the land is sand, we can really use it. "Hostile takeover, CG romed over the land, and the Hill imagined hearing Eleanor conversing on the air (S.O.L.)."* Another photo showed George Burns and Gracie Allen posing with god, with all three waving at the camera alongside the pool in their Beverly Hills backyard. *"Area 51. You in? We got a house to think of. A sacred text. 1947 account. What is it? A lion, a calf, a man?"* Yet another photo displayed Charlie McCarthy sitting on the lap of Edgar Bergen sitting on the lap of god atop the inscription, *'One for all and all for one'* in the right hand, a *within* book, and on the flip side – seven seals. Beside this was a gold framed photo of god, lockjaw, chatty, otherworldly Agnes Morehead, and Joan Crawford in a Scotch drag having a swedge on the rim, and Shiteing the Al down stonecohol – all posing in a king-sized bed atop the heading, *Bob, Carol, Ted, Alice, Andy and Aunt Bee: the pollination crisis.* To be declining . . . Other photos included god on the putting green with Bob Hope, with Hope remarking via cartoon balloon, "Watch the birdie, Shirlie"; god on the back of a motorcycle with Brigitte Bardot with the inscription, 'Easy Rider,' to a planned retreat up shitsleak, wingding, San Die, go Tibetan, but watch the rays and Mumy in hot pursuit; god in top hat and cane with Judy Garland, "No, *You're* The Tops! Pops," as in Poe after glow in Baltimore; god giving Cesar Romero's head a big, wet kiss on the lips in steed on the set of *Lust In The Dust*; god with his palm over the lectionary in a rare bit of dicacity; and god on horseback with a group of Mexican settlers (among them, Pancho Villa and Mumy), all entering California at once, shouting, "Where's Wallace?" Say *leman*. (Noting that this was *not* the same Wallace who was hanged, disemboweled, beheaded and quartered at West Smithfield.)

god stood up, curled his toes in his faust slippers, and stretched his last legs, although not beyond his V measure. His TV was still lost in a sea of commercials, regions beyond the dolose inscription: *in search of religion,* mikey! Psychogram-digression: Energizer, Pangloss, Ajax Pixies, Tony, Speedy and Chevron. From his window he had a grand view, for it seemed as if this whole world of Mondialisation was his stage. There, over the hill, was *Saks Fifth Avenue* flanked by a couple of fifth columns. Not far away, *Gucci*, staffed by a host of wild and savage gubbins. In the far distance was *Roxbury Park* where some rare and ancient manuscripts were buried. The streets and the avenues were deserted. There were empty parking places everywhere. god sighed. For just a moment, a split second, he thought to see Mary Pickford (or was that his favorite, Shirley Temple?) on her front lawn posing fashionably beside a spruce tree, a coquette holding an Oscar; but, alas, it was only his imagination trying to make something Moore out of Mary. Commercials, he thought. Local party apparatchiks! Bah! Talking heads, Diesel cum superstores, global flashdressers. O I hate them skeins, except when they lead to Spitalfields. A man named Ralph (not Farmer

George as in fyerm or kolkhozy, but the comic Roister Doister – on the one hand a badchan of sorts, on the other a former 'protector' and a member of the MVD Ministry) was trying to sell god a car. god remembered the day he created Ralph. Granted he had intended to make Ralph a star, but at the last moment he changed his mind and made him a car salesman instead, selling comedy on classical lines. MOyez! TOyez! MOyez! *Such is life! Cram den, though Dis' always room for more.*

god walked quietly through his Lord Mayor's mansion, his *pied-à-terre*, past the walls faced in brilliant white marble or, depending upon the room, covered in pastel silks that tempered the otherwise cold conception of the place, with his steps supplying a hollow echo on the wooden parqueted floor. Here and there a foralite marking broke up the geometric patterns at his feet; and upon glancing down at the worm's burrow, god was reminded of several things, among which included the variegated, ophic themes of parquetry itself. For this was, in fact, the state of his mayor's mansion. The dining room featured a suite of Russian chairs and a settee circling around a rosewood dining table set with imperial Russian porcelain plates commemorating the coronation of Czar Nicholas II; not to mention the intricate patterns in the mahogany, birch and oak braunsteinan designs; and the ceremonial hall with the Pillemental greek gods looking down below as four elements; and the Ostankinoan gilded theater palace/ballroom, state of the art, surf status, overshadowed by a TV tower. "O hum," he said. "O hum an I dig aquarium." And viewing a copy of *Burda*, West Germany's fashion magazine given a Russian edition in 87, god added, "I loved to dance in *Burda's* dressmaking patterns, to Kruise with Eva, the feminine face to bizinesmen, alias Bortchik and Zaitsev – myself, and my house of models, *Dom Modeli* style, never fopling, but Ruthenian, whom I later took for an old McDonald's on Pushkin Square with a wait of two hours. Most pitiful." But his thought became split up. Looking around

there were so many things he had stolen while a guest at the homes of the famous and rich. There was a fur stole, the ecclesiastical vestment with the ends neatly crossed. There was Nat's very own stole, now *his* privy. There was that Turkey at thanksgiving. *Stolen waters are always sweeter and bread eaten in secret is pleasant as long as one cleans around the edges. Entjudung while chewing on Levant.* There, in the corner, were Jack Warner's George III mahogany armchairs. O. god recalled spending the night in a white raiment at Jack's home back in '35 with a vigil of hi-fi dweebs, a pair of normals (slightly mixed), 2½ conspiracy theorists still somewhat at the breast, an undead bloody mary, Christ of Lee, Warwick, a min black ort, and a mint in out-of-body experiments (Chars to be accepted if domestic and have the notes to prove it). Jack had had the gall to say to god, after just eight glasses of wine, "I am what I am, captain, and I will probably never change so you may as well paroles me!"

The George III armchairs were not the only thing he took that night. He also bagged a three-seat, Louis XV style confidante, a kingly encoignure done fit for a corner, and the entire grand two-story entrance hall that featured still another parquetry floor. Jack hated him for it, especially when all that was left in its place was a *note*

"I'm not a butcher,

I'm not a yid.

I'm just your light-hearted cid

Cast upon the earth in birth and sinister amphi-gory

And to rig-ma-role to Bend the story."

Perhaps he did miss it, just a little – the world and all its playthings. All the little Jack Sprats licking the platter clean. He loved to amphimixis. He remembered lean, wrinkleless Lana Turner saying to him one Halloween's Eve at her home in Brentwood, "It isn't sex you're afraid of – it's love." A year later she was nominated for best actress for *Peyton Place*, but lost out on a lie to a bright raven type. Poor, poor Constance. Double-crossed. Madam X got hel and was rammed. Just go and ask hyde. Why, he'd say her vision was but an end to the Great Schism of Holywood, as all's hell that ends well and sprightly. Backstage *she* was overheard to say, "god blocked that award, 'cause he od'd on onomastic paronomasia!"

Minced on o mastic. Could it be the risen from the tree? Or is it the Bar Reich's Theory on hypnotism? No reply.

god's eyes fell upon a T. Sheraton bureau. It once belonged to Joan Fontaine. She went insane the morning it was missing. Lifted up and out of her bedroom while she was fast asleep. She had always suspected it was god who took it, for she had refused to scratch his old runed back that very evening while they lay in bed. Three years later he gave her *Suspicion*. Beyond a reasonable doubt, she was born to be bad. Forever consistent . . . to the ear . . . Exodus! and bear left.

god patted down his aggerawator and settled back down inside of himself. So many ailuropodous memories. Funny he should still be holding the house keys to Sammy Cahn's Beverly Hills home. Together they had composed "Three Coins In The Fountain." Other working titles at the time were "Three Spirits in One," "Three Jews on the Run," "Three Bar Mizvahs on Sunday," "Three Sincere Ovey's," "Three Daisy Mays in October." In the end, Sammy rested and said, "Let's just keep religion out of it! We'll make more money that way." After Sammy won the Oscar for "Coins," he locked god out of his home along with all the pussycats, and said, "Who needs 'ya?! Go back to the fountains and lick the pidgeons! Ya strigine tongue!" and threw twenty-seven cents at his back. Three years later, Cahn was still searching for his lou-sy keys with a runcible spoon. During this time he managed to compose the main theme to *Hole In The Head*.

god tapped his knuckles on top of an African drum that was serving as an end table in his sun room. Instantly he recalled '37, Sammy's missing key, which he had hid in Philadelphia on see st.; and thereafter *A Star Is Born*, just as it was written in a book, in an open and shut case regarding Orion's vanity and a particular scorpion's rise to heaven, *another* revelation. Janet Gaynor had told god that being with him that night was like being in *Seventh Heaven*, listening to gay science. Actually it was '27 when she had first encountered god eating Van Gogh's *left* ear. It was all part of an amatory trilogy, along with *Sunrise* and *Street Angel*. All in the silent era in which she did her finest work in the space of half-an-hour. She had carried on a glorious affair with god in a "particular corridor" of a train during the janney coupling, which she later referred to as "another side of life." No, god did not take the drum (although he did manage to bag seven trumpets). Actually, the drum had been a gift. Secrets between lovers. An eternal kiss. The kiss that emanates time with parts of space, with shape, density and mobility. It was all there. Yes. The love between god and his creations was quite apparent. You give and take. Tribulation and poetry (but you are rich-ard's indicator, with a hammer in your hand and steam on your forehead). The experience of knowing god can only be temporary, for god gets stifly sickly bored after just seven days bearing that sickle . . . *If only they could have understood this,* he lamented, *they might not have loved me so much.*

god turned away; his orectic memories were filled with voices in the millions, all sounding at once. The vibrations were vibrant. The past came to life: god was sitting in the blinding, sun-washed garden of his creation, lounging in the cozy shade under the pitch of spit, seeing men, as trees, walking, while, in the near distance, at a fork, Adam and Eve, the little rascals, frolicked with bare red tushies near Oxford. The birds above him soared and glided in and out of his aura. Sitting there, god resembled a hilltop Greek temple, a fabled place, surrounded by flowering shrubs in full bloom.

god moved gradually into a room with shoji doors. It was an entire Japanese bath complete with silk screens carved and painted with doves and flowers. The sound of trickling water continued to evolve into the sound of trickling water. god removed his slippers, put his feet into the Mystical Essence™ of the bath, and sat down at the edge. He was traveling light and unrevealingly. Rest was rather vulgar to him now, for it made him realize what flaws were inherent in the second chapter of his original book, when the children fall at the edge and grasp the words on the night stand.

I can't see how they didn't see it, god mused. *I guess I was just lucky. Ol' lord Lucky by a curious fluke, a most important duke living in a grand hotel, rose in less than half an hour to show off all his filthy power. For as it was stated, I rested on the seventh day from all my work. If god is god, then why should he need to rest? god shouldn't get tired. It shows a weakness. But, in fact, I was exhausted. I wanted to be alone. People come, people go, but nothing ever happens. I wanted to be alone. Not only that, what wasn't written was that I had a migraine. My joints hurt. Made mention of it in the book of beasts. The one inhabited by a chelifer. Such a sick volume. Orbis terrarum. I think that was the time I thought to create . . . a Hit King.*

"So vye did you make me vait so long to come onto ze zene?" Hit scooted closer to god. Jabbing him in the rib, he said, "Vell, anzer me zat!"

"I don't know . . . So, how's the water? Is it warm enough?"

Hit curled his toes in the soothing liquid of the Japanese bath. "The vaters fine but my toga iz zight. I zink I'ze got toga viriliz. Iz yourz zight?"

"No, mine's fine. But I think the water is too hot."

"The vater izn't too hot! Vhy can't you do zhings to blend?"

"I don't know what you mean. I have always tried to do what I feel is right."

"Moral codez are made for ze ztupid and ze inferior!" Hit said. "In vone zense I vas ze greatezt Zerm of all time. I did not folloz a moral code. You made me zoo-*zat!*"

"I wanted you to have the freedom to choose."

"I spitz at frezdom! And don't give me zat choozing buzinezz! You maze my every move. I zed ve vill have no ozher god but Zerm alone! Your ozther nazure, the von you called Chriszian, the von you programmed to zeach ze brozherhood of man and merzy and kindnezz vas juzt your otzer zide. Opprezzed peoplez are never unified in a common empire by meanz of flaming prozeztz but zhrough a zharp, unzheated zword! But in ze zame manner I find myzelf zhaking ze duzt of your zip of my feez like all ze zift-necked peeplezes wiz caz-iron dezermunazation to lay ze foundazation of ze new exizestzence to ze new vorld."

god looked hard at Hit.

"Vhat are you looking az?" Hit leaned over and looked at his reflection in the still waters of god's bath. The reflection looking back at him was unmistakenly *Jesus.* "Vhy do you make me to look like him all ze dime now? I much prefer ze muztache and zhort hair alone!"

"I want to test something out," god said. "It always baffled me how I could put two different kinds of souls in the same body. I planted seeds for debate, but I cannot accept any of my own explanations, except that I should return as an angel of light with a driven stake. I am depressed Hit. For I am a god with conflict." god started to cry. he buried his face in Hit's lap and sobbed like a baby carpenter hitting www.nail.comm. without a response.

"Zoo muztn't cry. I forgive you for zer own veaknezzez."

god lifted his face up and looked into the face of Jesus. "This is me!" god said, his face a veil of tears.

The moon rose next to the rising sun. The ocean was in the desert. The first day of the week was big Wednesday. god took Jesus's head in his hands and screwed it off and tucked it under his arm.

PEEK-A-BOO

This is the hidden chapter conceived.

god's contents in the same hour.

Chapter 0 in a bodily shape.

This is the chapter regarding the story of god's inability to control, though there is a fan in his hand.

What god cannot control he decided to call sin.

This is the mystery of god: as long as one believes god to be perfect with all body, mind and heart, existence will never make sense. One could spit and then attend a buffet, engulfed by fans. To allow oneself to believe in god's imperfection, one must first know with all body, mind and heart that it is not a sin to think so.

In god's own ultimate realm, thank heaven there is a flaw: there is not total belief in god because of his imperfection, his missing chapter, which puts belief in toto tortuosity.

What does it mean?

It is the question. Just as god questions himself, what thinks you?

There is no answer as it pertains to god.

How about a devotee to blow on, excite, separate and cast away?

There is only the fact that what god creates breaks down. Just as what man creates breaks up in a common hall. How to solve the puzzle?

To become the missing piece. god is a natural child. The G according to nature. Which is one. Total O.

Finished.

It is impossible.

As long as god exists in one's mind it is impossible.

But how does one eliminate god from the mind *in?*

This is the challenge, the missing chapter.

It's frightening out on the porch, gazing through this fanzine of waking dreams.

*   *   *

god stood up and started to walk back to his television. god was thin, a bit awkward.
Nowhere in his eyes was there any sign of joy. There was an odor of sour wine on his breath,
explaining the origin of ozostomia. Actually it was the fermented juice from the grape he had
chewed but a week ago and was still holding in the pouches of his cheek. "I'm nothing but a
war correspondent," he mumbled. "Wandering beggar . . . in black and white . . ." Still, he
was determined to survive. Crawling along the floor, an umbrage, he slowly made his way
over to the TV, perverting the nation.

WEN NEVAEH

Scene 5. *Jüngstes Gericht.*

Cut the light!

Armageddon in New Jersey. It is 8:50. There are voices, and thunderings, and lightning,
and an earthquake. Do you know where your children are? Six million are missing. The
farm is the camp. O and St. John the Divine are at odds – not to mention the Meridian of
spirits is at odds in New Jerusalem with G, where Raquello I. John plays music for the bride
of Ha' Eve, in the key of
St. John awoke from the dream with a horrendous fear more intense than real life itself.
His head was blocked with an uproaroutcry, and it drove him to curse before the bench.
"Do you swear to tell the whole truth and nothing . . ." with a twist of scotyid in the final
benediction 'ido,' all in the spirit of Esperanto. With nothing to hold but his baculum, the
ercles rectitudinous vein would not leave him, even in his waking state. And in his current
form he was prone to bombast the proceedings with excursus.
St. John thereby entered the synderesis, as a sort of espiègle espier, an origenian, a
schauspielerin, but also as a chapman disguised as a chaplain, and found therein his platonic
father lying upon a bed with hornets flying around him. Big, black, saber-tooth hornets
– buzzing mad, their heads full of eyes, their stingers fire-conflagrant enough to burn down a
throne. And they spoke as of the voices of men in Sanktus and said, "Holey holey holey be
the soul once we're through with them." And beside where his father lay was a book, the title
of which was half-obscured by the resting of his arm. But some letters did lay exposed like
a baculus, which, when put together, added up to BOSEVSEALS. And there was red on his
father's body where the hornets feasted and chomped on his staff, paper-thin. And through
the holes in his chest the hornets crawled. From within to without, a path they carved,
leaving frasses in their wake, straight to the crosier.
St. John fell back against a wallingog, for the sight did sicken him, and the hornets did
five-month him, half paving a way from Texas to a syntexis. And then one creature landed
securely on his father's hand and from its mouth it shouted, "Wasp, you fool!" and took a
bite and drank his fuel. (Really one blood-red dumb locust with scorpionitis and delusional-
grandeur-megalomaniatothemax.) Drinketh did the wasp, with saber-sharps. More than
this, through muscle did it chew, straight down to the bone *grindgrind*, the syn stone like

grain grown from a sin genesis, where the Germ contained the germs of all subsequent grains, being exposed to a sin for disorderly intake. And having once emerged from the depths within, the wasp said, dribbling flesh, "Remember agent *roman à clef* – the inventer standing in for a matter-of-fact. Just a long and complex sequence of events with a key. And remember this . . . ," it said with bone, flesh and sinew, liquid dripping off its head. "When you emerged from the sea holding the key of hell and death like Isabella offering the grape to Brooklyn, you had your servant write the last book. In itself, for seven to behold on their bastard TVs. You *see* yourself so *far* on the screen, and yet there are billions listening to the same joke at the same time, and yet remaining so lonesome that each one could scream out to god, and still be unheard."

And upon saying this, it plunged its head back in, and tore sinew, and *chewed chewed*, and rising once again, it did shout with grinding sabers, "I do!" And revealing both rows like a two-edged sword, it roared its effectual calling, "Repent! Or I will feast with the wares of my mouth! Dream a dream and see yourself, even as you cry your tales."

St. John stumbled back and shouted, "I am your chapman and this be my chapbook. Come see, have a good look. It's free!" And stumbling yet further against the wall, he landed flat. But never losing view of his father. And this he saw – a figure added beneath the covers where his father lay – a figure working, as it were, with rapid movements in what was gauged to be his father's lap. And above it all the wasps flew. And nay did another moment lapse before a woman likened on to a *mal de mer* fish emerged above the blanket waves. Too, her mouth was dripping fluid – a bloody seed mixed with special leaves chewed to a praiss. Shirley Schrift from the Poseidon! Disease is sickness that does impair the performance of the vital functions – much like a malady or, closer yet, a bad melody as it relates to limbs and songs with trumpet voice, *la matriz*, a diablerie ableeding.

Harps, vials, chorus.

And the wasp said to him, "Look on. The first estate is but your own nightmare. And in this *you* see your destiny which you alone do own."

And the head St. John saw which did emerge from the blanket wave with semen clutching at her chin was Izebel cast in a labored role all her own.

And once more she arose from the blanket wave looking like a long cylindrical tube, curved and ending in an upright roar that vibrated and gave forth a ringing sound when one did strike her crown.

And still the wasps rose, and dove at her who did arise as though on a merry throne, with such broad beams, eyes to and fro, swish, swish, devious. And before his eyes, four more heads were grown upon that throne. All stinking beasts, like skeletal horses, each and everyone. And each did pleasure to his father, beyond which couldn't be measured.

What is the book upon which the right arm rests with signs thereof?

TRISKELION

For eternity. It is this book. Of which you now read and look upon. No weeping here for here everyone is worthy to open and to read and to look thereon. Especially Ray, Reginald Truscott-Jones, with the X-Ray eyes.

triskelion

And as St. John looked upon his father, he saw his father rise with three opened sores festering on his knees. And then before him arose a sea, like a white horse, the focus of public hopes and expectations. And the four beasts and she did leap into this sea, and with a busy hand they did drink the wild waves.

And from out of the microwave, St. John pulled an eggplant bathed in cheese, with a side of buttered buckyballs, 60 carbon toms, turkeys not easily swallowed unless accompanied by milk. While the ads finished on TV.

BE MY GEIST
OASIS HOME MODEL
(III in I)

And in this scene, St. John looked upon his father and saw the four beasts eating his scepter to the bone. But this did not stop St. John from venturing forth, clothed in a sheet like an Old Slavic cloud. And with one foot upon the sea and one upon his bed, he cried out loud, "Do not write this dream, but guard it with your life. For my mystery should never be found." And with that he did stuff into his mouth the book. And in the midst of this, he sprouted yet another cock, only without skin and bone, merely an oleomargarine vein that dripped blood, and stood erect as a refrain. And when that cock did crow, blood was its seed that turned the ocean red. And all that was in the sea that had no business *but business* did catch his great diety disease. And opened oily sores released remote poisons that the wasps devoured most greedily.

And St. John cried, "I see myself, all-in-one, a three-letter man. Three in one." And now he saw Izebel rise, a mother malkin with a rod sun behind her belt and a querimonious son inside her. And from her belly appeared a xiphoid tail that whipped about like a cig fish. But upon closer view it was clear this was neither tail nor fin, but a long, living thorn, a B52 stratofortress, that was connected within to a man-child. And the man-child's name was of three letters. And his name was Cin. And his brain fell into rotundity at the temporal lobe.

Ripping through her stomach to Shay, *touché*, with intestines wrapped around his feet, and trailing behind, Cin took his mighty sword in hand, his scramasax, and beheaded the taxing mother scram who gave him birth. And a fatal castration be the norm. More an execution – like a fatal nuclear kiss. And with her head detached, he lifted it above his breast, and the bloody mane that showered down did mingle with the refrain, and the refrain was thereby given a name by St. John, and that name was Accuser. And without a trial or a jury to speak of, the Accuser wormed its way down inside the torso of the body that lay at the foot of the sea neath the headstone. And as the Accuser chewed through the entrails, it claimed as its own the morsels of war. And once it chewed its way through and emerged out the liquidy pit, and wiped the foul matter, the black mud, from its raffish vein, having fully emerged from that chamber within, it shouted in a hoarse voice, "Everything, both small and large, should have a formula to live by. MGM. The shrewdness of angels."

And it was here, again, that St. John fell once more. And he said from within his soul: "O. This is my mystery. To bore everything I see, air interdiction, incrassate head or headless be."

And with that St. John shot forth a fart so loud, so strong, it actually tore through his loins (as well as the loin cloth that adorned his loins), and sent a rumble and a quake throughout the universe so potent that it rattled the cage of god's chambers, and lasted for well over an hour (as time had returned for a brief CNN space). And in secret (in a mirror as deep as any girandole reflecting skyrockets fired together), he called the cause of the quake *'eurt dna lufhtiaf,* and afterward said, "Make pajonism a djinni affair." And in the book he added: *'eht drow si ton, resal-dediug sbmob, htlaets'; BOMFOG, BF.* And then he bid the hornets and wasps to fly and feast upon his nates (in order to cleanse the nates of rude red aftermath), which he helped to expose by ripping and tearing apart his own *corpora quadrigemina* by way of the finger bone and a rough unpolished stone. And of the flatulent men and horses that lived therein, both large and small, free and bond, smart and dumb, all did become part of the feast, and fell in a fatiloquent corner. And much learning makes one mad, makes one kick against the prick. And the shouts and screams and gales lingered on until the dining was done.

THE FRESHMAN

The Cyclops was attending Yale, having made a fortune in India selling keys, locks, and bagels. Currently, he had a lot on his mind. (C. Real Estate. Sec. 6.66. 6BC-30AD.) His suit was tailored in the best Savile Row tradition – a regimental tie, leather shoes – quite the courtly Cyclops. So neat and trim he was, so balanced in dress from head to toe he was; he even acquired the nickname of Trimmer. With a wry sense of humor, he spoke in coherent paragraphs, choosing his words for their quality as well as their quantity. He listened interestedly to others, just one sign of his unshakeable good manners. He performed impeccably at large functions and enlighted all with his wit and charm. Currently, he was studying law and was even in the midst of writing his own autobiography, *Reflections in a Cyclops's Eye.* His wife was a woman of consummate good taste. (More on her later.)

Thus far in his climb, the Cyclops had delighted the boards at Alcoa, Gulf Oil, Bank of America, and Proctor and Gamble. He had grown to love rare books and horse racing. In addition to this, he had become a collector of valuable art, and owned original canvases by Klee, Seurat, Degas, Renoir and Rembrandt. He was well-versed in literature and lectured friends on the virtues of writers from Chaucer to Samuel Johnson. In actuality, he had become something of a financial genius and could consistently pick the budding entrepreneurs who would blossom into great industrialists. Indeed, due partially to his scholarship and the fact that he was so well versed concerning *The Seven Pillars of Wisdom*, he became known within certain circles as T.E. Cyclops (T.E. standing for *The Eternal*).

Small details helped to define the exquisite Cyclops. For example, he was prone to wearing little pendent trinkets that clinked like delicate, little regal bells as he moved most assuredly through the layers of high society, the *grand monde:* the Palaces, the Courts, the Chambers and the Tribunals. Oftentimes he would delight a party by arriving in a powdered wig in addition to a gold lace coat, pumps and white silk stockings. His entry into any hall might further be accented by a spontaneous quote, "To the devil!," upon which he would get a burst of applause, even though half didn't get the joke. Traveling through a sea of guests, one was certain to find the Cyclops bestowing a word of promise here and a smile there, a snatch of whispered advice or a roll of mumbled caution. His solitary eye could catch an entire room in a single glance. And given a list of fifty names, he could recite them back hours later without a single misplacement. He was prone to carrying snuff which he would inhale through a nose beautifully formed since he had had its irregular lines redone by the renowned Dr. Doitlittle, so it was now slightly pinched at the top of each nostril, and hardly, if ever, did run. The orbit of his eye (depending upon the *light* socket) was typically horizontal and thin; still, should he ever make a face, a grimace or a sign of displeasure, his eye would become inflamed with that old Cyclops brawn, and either turned everyone on with excitement or caused them to cower in fear, drained of any ounce of courage.

As a matter of fact, he even had the ability to peer, and to find behind the face of any honest man the buried person within, the shadows of which others less able could never understand. He could confront a man of five-and-forty years, well respected and established, a literal triumph among his peers, and secretly suggest to him his most hidden fears; whether they be in the passion of the soul, such as pride, contempt or stubborness, or in matters more bearing upon the body, such as a corn on the bottom left heel, a boil on the tailbone or a mole above the left tit; and thereafter prescribe how best to get rid of it. His face was one face, just as his brain was one brain and his eye was one eye. But the passengers aboard his presence would more certainly than not view him in different lights: doctor, broker, lawyer, historian – depending upon the view, he could simply satisfy everyone; even father and son would share the same conclusions, and in this manner he brought families together. For it always feels good when two on opposite rungs share a common view.

And even though matrimony was his stable lot to the women round about, he was quite a rogue. External luxuries throughout, cruel anxieties within, so many women were thin, poor creatures hungry for love from husbands they had had to steal from to make possible that satin dress that graced the halls of the most current balls. These were poor women, emotionally starved, who were better briefed on the backs of their husbands than on their fronts. Women who cooed and fell at the feet of a beast, who, in turn, admired each and everyone her beauty. For with every hand the Cyclops took and graced with the plant of his lips, he would extend the respect with a wink or two and a promise to later get a better view upon which to plant his compliments.

Generous on all accounts, the Cyclops grew richer in public view by donating valuable art to institutions in debt. No one had given more great art in donation than the Cyclops. He had a knack for saving managers of sound judgment but little luck, who found their respective businesses in the red; all to help heal their shattered world. He restored life, and replaced even the lord in the common view.

His wife was Ida, and the changes in her frame were too numerous to count. But, for strangers, we'll define just a few. First of all, consider her small, sparrow-like form, an hourglass in flesh, a subtly sexy red wear on her skin, a soft silhouette as thin as peeled silk. The stone – black, cold and hard – had been replaced with a triangular face, framed by a luminescent mane of flame-red hair. Her speech was soft, though intense, light almost transparent, but dense with poetry and *power*. She had an arresting presence, and upon entering a room could capture all eyes with a curve. She didn't hold conversations as much as she held court, expounding upon any subject with such style and seduction it would seem that gravity had left the room. She could disquiet the dead simply by her breath alone; as fanciful as a Box flower, which is to suggest that *hearts are meant for beating and not for rest;* but dare don't relax too soon, for she held within a rebellious combination of daring determination and sin that was no less naughty than running naked through moonlit gardens heavy with yews before the shades are raised and eyes can gaze on the forbidden. Her headquarters could be either a master bath or a smoky hall. But everywhere she created a feeling of powerful awe that otherwise strengthened her lily persona. But it was more than etiquette she was attracted to; rather, sunglasses with Day-Glow purple frames, a scented pomander, and a warm, powerful gun at the end of her mane.

Ida loved weapons. It stood as part of her evolution, her pingala consciousness. The AR-15 was her sport, a link to the association between metal and flesh. Akin to an army rifle, the AR-15 had blonde hair, rosy pink lipstick and evergreen nail polish as a reminder that femininity is entirely compatible with the world of destruction and guns. Ida was a part-time attorney general in a state of Mass between Fairfax and La Brea. She had achieved this position after having quickly learned the ropes of the military and working her way through the Pentagon, and eventually joining the private sector where she commanded a salary far greater than her modest contemporaries. Perhaps her relationship with Rocket Impact Fuse was due to her origin in stone. Light years away, preceding the events that eventually led up to her transcendence of god, she fell upon one of the most beautiful sights she had ever seen – the M-433, which blows up things and the Gator Raid Antipersonal Mind Bending Pup-Ray, which blows people up. She was interested in using it in her future work with the House Armed Services Communion, a religious organization based in the seventh house of god, whose division was subtitled OCTR (for Oil, Chemical, and Tobacco Rings).

On Capitol Hill everything was linked. (This was in the year of the AP Market which started the Anti-Presidential Act of 2010.) There were ironies and contradictions regarding the future of the Dairy Association at the time because its major spokesman, P.E. Milkmane, was refusing to acknowledge the clear evidence that milk and cancer were interlinked. Ida's book, entitled *Thank You For Not Breast-Feeding*, which had the backing of thirteen thousand lobbyists under the age of two and twenty, clearly was the instigating factor in the creation of BADD (Babies Against Defensive Defecation). Because of the negative repurcussions supplied by the press, Ida was forced to slip undercover, and for awhile became an actress, and did a remake of *Candy*, entitled *Candy with a Sword*. Only in this remake, Candy worked her sexuality in the arena of public relations campaigns, wherein she was implanted with a CS-69 vibrating dildo that was pushed in a couple of inches beyond the vaginal track in order to give her a more political point of view as she pursued legislation at Honeycutt, which was nothing more than an institute for clitoris stimulation, via masturbation, regarding anything higher than .10 percent Standard Sufficient Fund Radiation Due. Rev www612. bs.

During this time, Ida fell into the hands of Mizrahi Kamali Variazioni, an industrialist who owned a large planning commission steel-based enterprise at Votre Nom, where decades before a major war was fought, being one of many thereafter wherein America lost face. His partner in kind, Rizik Calcinai Mirabella-Weitzmancoft, took Ida through the underground network of their organization in the hopes that they would be able to make use of both her talents and knowledge in Seikosha LT-20 Envoy RAM network Intel and Ericsson radiomodems-graphical interface-technical programming. The Woman's Information Resource and Brain-Exchange was going through a major restructuring at the time on account of the abrupt assassination of its twelve-year-old entrepreneur founder, a padishah by claim of birth who ran up a string of debts totaling in the billions before he was eight, due in part to his unquenchable taste in Iranian waste. In order to separate Ida from what would have been a certain death sentence, she was taken to the Nibelungian German restaurant in Muzak, where she dined on flaming shrimp and eggplant souffle in a setting amidst carob trees, jasmine and lemon blossoms, far from the range of Hi-Lo TechnoRadarBeamFeminine Detectors, after which she was taken by HiPowderRadarFilledSecurityVessel to a destination extended from and beyond the Minoan temples of Knossos and the Byzantine and Phaestos palaces with the ruins at Archanes, where she was briefed on the double lingo *copa de oro* haven at the Dictean Cave, the purported birthplace of El Zeus, the king.

Because time was of the essence, she was flown to Las Alamandes where she was given the title to a secluded piece of property that currently accommodated a vast array of condos, a dramatic golf course, and an ornate lit-fountain centered within miles of leafy vegetation that stretched forever along the Pacific coast. Here she shed her dusty clothes and waded bull naked into the shimmering white in an effort to nurse her essence, for by her very nature she was given to fits of aficionadaism. It is impossible that the entire concept of espionage can be fitted into such a small frame; but in the world, everything is within easy reach as long as one circumferences the sphere of plasma-god.

GET ME a J-J BEAN

Ida – drying off, walking out onto the lawn flanked with chaise lounges and lace-edged umbrellas; Ida – knowing that the minute she steps off the plane, she will be whisked into a two-hour odyssey that could easily become forty days; Ida – in her room in the Hotel Gazzo Brad Flamm, supplied with a map printed in Cyrillic that is going to lead her straight into the lap of Oni, who describes herself as "a cherub in cyberspace"; Ida – well-familiar with electronic salons, feeling that the four faces of power need a lot of technie decoration with "attitude," similar to the karibu carved on the palace gates in Babylon; for if Ida is going to transcend, it is best she doesn't think of god as a bloody wheel. Oyez. *Ida . . . Ida . . . Ida .
. .*

Ida's name was greeted with shock and dismay, as was her brain which was put on public display, via x-ray, during a lecture that I. Rapalot, a noted activist and hardcore pantagruelist, gave during a bloody upheaval, wherein the entire U.S. government was impeached for selling carnage to Hong Kong. Rapalot was attempting to enlighten mainstream America along the lines of bestiality as it pertains to random acts of in-house violence, the origins of which can be easily traced back to god's early acts, specifically those denoted in 'sis I, wherein god attempted to establish a franchise in Eden with the hopes that Adam would be his general manager and part-time keeper.

It is not news that today blood is sexy. This was the case with Ida who was currently dominating the tabloids with her reality-based exploits. American reporters in tattered-tailored, six-to-nine-o'clock-evening-business-suits sat around in the food courts of Jigoku shopping malls downing Big Emma-hoo burgers while attempting to work out fashionable laws best *suited* to gut-reaction intestine white noise, which included plotting merchandising strategies in the Far East to best sell the papers they were basing their quantitative headlights upon. Gallows humor and perverse glamour were hot-selling taradiddles in intestinalinteroceptive interviews, which naturally put a grand old tradition on the luminous cross sections of high-concept interstice as it relates to common doo and steepy statistics.

Consequently, Ida was given an assignment: to intervene between god and all of his creations, disguised as *Space Itself;* and all this while being accused of a double-murder while being pursued through not only the seedier sections of Argentina but through the third floor of an abandoned Random House, where she realized it would be next to impossible to be apprehended due to an entirely indefinite plan on the part of her pursuers! Fortunately, Ida was a member of a sect of elements who went under the code name *Ramadan*, named as such for its daily references (from dawn to sunset) to the axiom – *everything has a definite probability of occurring within a specific frequency, as long as one refrains from feasting.*

Americans by the millions were being monitored by their very own computers, and informed upon via the internet by buttons, numbers, codes and discs. The franchise Ramadan was spherically disguised in the chain *Dunkirk Donuts.* Tactless scientists had created a surveillance system using hidden microphones buried within the very donuts themselves that listened in on flagitious customers as they discussed rapacious plans to do one another 'in' by blood-based measures. Ida had had the misfortune of finding her hidden microphone buried within custard hanging off her chin; only it was too late. She had already articulated objectionable messages to a rival government fellow employee, Missedya Dublanchit, regarding the new Black & Blue Ball SM Vexillary device that was installed on TACHYMETER in order to establish intimacy between distant objects, using the web of a feather to house the computerized Clipper Chip, thus allowing it to eavesdrop on digital transmissions. The impact on Statue-Evolution was devastating because so many clay figures were coming to life after having learned of god's secret plan to put breath into dust and vice-versa. There were still a few mars in the system, and its workings-out were being supervised under the code name *Mars Bar*, which was also linked financially to the International Development Association (IDA) in order to promote capital projects such as PMS (power mobile stations) and CHILD-ELEMENT 43, techily speaking the first synthetic MAPA Enterprise to hit the globular chart. Currently, Ida was conducting several AERobic classes to zombie-like, subreptitious denizens that set their stony features into expressions of quiet vicissitude in order to avoid easy detection. Before a surveillance team was able to land upon the premises via Viking Air Rovers, Ida and three clay Phrygians (all named Midas) were able to round up from behind counters freshly baked donuts – enough squeezed jelly and chocolate to lubricate and wax-slippery the floor behind them; broken bones and a strained neck in a heap of human collision resulted as five thoughtless, *misprision* policemen ended their pursuit drenched waist-deep in rasberry-late jelly. In order to keep in contact with her "public" (for it was in her nature to *lay* low during altercations, hid-in-night-and-obscurity), Ida appeared (in Light) during a Product Promotion Campaign on a David Letterman VIII adult quiz show, *Fiat Lux!*, before a live audience, in the guise of Jesus Sounds, winking knowingly at Daily Variety's hallowed reporter, Isaac Newton John, knowing damn well that he would be unable to prove anything close to *mens rea* in the tabloids without first exposing the fact, via J8:7, that David and Johnathan were so much more than just good friends.

PRESENT TENSE

The media coverage of violence, toing and froing, implicates viewers and guests alike, even if some of those guests happen to be one of the mini-echelon lifted out of context from a series of steps (as of rungs of a ladder), who will be whisked away by a dark rapture via violins, leaving only the original subjects alive to the end.

Within an eye's twinkle the blast of a trumpet shades a violent posture. Ida puts on a show that is pure Grand Guignol; meets heavy metal established a quarter-century ago by channeling free-floating angels frustrated over the loonydove dance that god had involved his host to learn, a sort of fabulous facsimile of the tarantella that requires thrusting the head and torso forward a hundred times a second while spreading the wings apart as wide as the Mississippi, all while the hips hum in 6/8 time and the legs are set in stone. The one exception is a throw-away rhyme from Danse. *I will tell you the mystery of the woman, rick: The slug spits in levis to sea men(t), the stones together to repent, the lion cop u late, so the unicorn got it straight, and the acid pulp was Irish sent, right up to the gate, where peter acquaints with mirabelle, shots mirabile dictu of late.* Ida bores a hole in a place where *death crowds hope* is in short supply, and the biggest possible shadow to ward off enemies is a hook well-hidden within the fiery bush. It is here, all before the bloody rapture, that so much is revealed so the chosen can get a hint as to when the Big-Lift-Off-Of-G is to take place, and not get caught unfueled. It takes Ida's work in espionage grace to see the true *esprit de corps* and to find the hidden graveolent spirit who (once dissected) contains mostly stuff rankly misogynistic in content and not dissimilar from stool. Those unfortunate enough to be drafted into the plot of *G Day* will be split; half will be raised in a gentler and more refined ward (suckled), while their parents watch Beaver in his baseball cap leaving it up in June; while in another ward, the other half will be biting nipples red, while sixty parents watch Beaver going down at the tail end of June, with Ward behind subservient Beaver making him live up to his livery. It is all Ida can do being cosmic-minded with a heavy shadow over the eyes, knowing what god has put her through, being set on a classical-style stool with all the myths and images dropping, beautifully spaced.

3^(RD) DRAFT

'Knowing' women eventually eat out men, nibbling testicles until working them back to the molars, eagerly waiting to crunch the bastard pods and feel the burst of squirting hormones, testosterone, and interstitial cells trickle down the throat even as the molars crunch and chew the gummy deflated sack that once hosted its very own civilization of wannabesomethingorothers Jills and Jacks. Insufferable neighbors all day long smoke penis pipes, suck on cock cigarettes, muttering to one another how bad the world is getting – so many misocapnists, so many misopolemical misologists, so many misotheists misfeasancing the system – why, just the other day, two kids named Beavistic and Buttheadin burned the house down on the corner with three pinheads inside, staying there while the Circus played in town. *O say can you see by the dawn's early light, the flames caused by Buttheadin's gas . . .* rit-plight to save three screaming pinheads on the second story of 424, *'sorry he's busy bagging twenty-four groceries at Barnum's sardine,'* so Ida, though busy, drops everything brown, crosses the English Channel, jogs the Mojave Desert (huff huff huff), forget the taxi, kiss-off St. Fiacre, dashes through Las Vegas down Highway 5, sweat stings, fucking eyes, gets slowly to the corner, hears a thousand inspired voices pleading, *"god, oh my god, what so proudly we heil"* on the second story, the pinheads are jailed in flames, sobbing big fat retarded tears on Times Square below. Ida goes down on Forty-second Street instead of Forty-fourth, jumps on the back of Pontiac's Rebellion, kicks hard in third, leaps off and slides into home, and firearm umpires yell *"Safe!"* as Ida scoops the pinhead trio in her arms, a slapstick trinity with one to spare. The flame is obviously real, but the blood on little Nemesis's pointed head is Hollywood blood-bag-technicolor-fire-engine-special-effect-red. No matter – 'Sus-n-Go still out of town, fifty billion miles removed from the jukebox that played "What Makes Sammy Run?" Guess what?: the strong-waxed Holly shade that promises to take us all after breaking us all like sleazy recalled toys will do so after two witnesses cloud-rise in a mirifical score.

Darwin hands Ida a water-soaked cloth to wipe the grease, blood and smoke off, and says something about *'monkey see, monkey do,'* and stuffs a primate tract in the breast pocket of Ida's coat, and suggests she read about monkey eroticism, especially as it applies to sucking the monk, as soon as she has the time, but, fuck, what the hell, Ida no sooner has time to find her breath when beep! beep! message instructs her to repel two flanking teenage boys from dashing a four-year-old's brain on the railroad tracks. Shit! all the way over to Liverpool, Ida blasts off in a horizontal tunnel of smoke, reaches the East Coast before the two buggers have their hands gripped around the toddler's limbs, no time for the boat, Ida dives headfirst into the wake and strokes her way to England, shit! the fog's as thick as honey-syrup cake, turns left, not right, the two buggers swinging t . . . t . . . t . . . toddler in the air, cracking jokes, joints and all that jism jazz, the blood's rushing to the lids of the toddler's eyes, and the tips of the fingers; watch out! it's not Hollywood after all! There's the correct passage! A nice little season. Northwest! Toddler coming down to meet the tracks on a fatal crack, Ida measures forty feet and dives, no water, stalls but hits the bare bones of Beavistic and Buttheadin, and together all four land in a sea of dust, the bones Je' makes of all of us, only this time toddler gets softly released and finds a new lease on life, while Beavistic and Buttheadin get it on with a mighty fling thrown clear across Timbuktu, and land head-first on the second story of the burning house. Adieu.

DAYBREAK

Ida stumbles out of bed in a riant suite in the St. Francis Hotel in the City of Hills, use to be a landmark Gardens Hotel, its sign sometimes read *maison close.* Bladder currently holds 50 millilitres of urine. *Get off! The dog's nose.* Urethra cries, "The sphincters closed! The anterior walls got mold!" The facts are dizzy, simple statements: Al Jolson is being accused of kidding his ex-wife, Catherine Eddo, with the bottle in room 105. Wes and the gang sort of sent a kid in spirit from Hell Catch Can, *liquor to the vigilance committee!* white chapel, the edible root; and a young man whose link to her is nearly equal to mass times speed, wrote, *Fried, licked and/or ate it. No, you ain't heard nothing yet! So lend me an ear!* And then the phone rings. Headquarters. Ida's got to save Aunt Sally from the pipe in her mouth or, minus that, aunt Jemima from a job well done; we don't want another orgy; so she tries to learn a thing or two; so she cuts across town *per saltum,* San Fran to London Town and back to the rialto, makes a leap and bound, in the grand canal, lobe to lobe, over to the City of Hills brothel café, such duality, but remember we're breaking the rules, so here we are, the marketplace; exchange den for bed, blessed St. Francis for blessed Buck Jones; and he's the fattest star by Occident in that vast silent screen above us, the Loyola, the Paradise, on St. I, the theater district, the one whose lights only come out in oriental darkness; it almost makes you want to cry out *rapture!* but instead it comes out *rape!* only its spelling is *rappe;* and St. Francis has a bloody virgin on his hands with a bad case of stigmata and Flower Drum; but the blame is on the buckler due to some fat idea of a midday game in the hay; and Ida's learning acquittal, and realizing what setting free the guilty really means; so rapture becomes the ultimate acquittal; down on his knees. *(O Jesus)* you got yourself a spectator sport long before TV. *god help me, I'm dying of laughter; brother, have you got some broth?* or how about 40, that is, a first monthly check, say, for 22:54, so that May maybe fuller than she was before S.S. came through the door. And everything gets greatly magnified like the spectres of the Brocken. First with – the woman shall not wear the men, nor the men put on a woman's garment; to: abide with the ass; to: hang the chief baker; to: they made light of it; to: they took him and led him; to: there shall be no night there. This is a tough one for Ida. For the crime is theater and popular sympathy for the star. And then Don makes the comment (that's John): *the world has narrowed to a neighborhood.* The bosses even block Ida from singing of brotherhood, so she goes yonder to an earlier ballad: "James and Floyd and Dillinger," and souvenirs and beer and a sixteen stanza ballad to "My bonnie lies over the ocean, my bonnie lies over the Clyde"; and then Ida recalls what myths surfaced after her unemployed carpenter-husband was but one of the falling stars in the mirror of human salvation, the Speculum Humanae Salvationis, where the troubled waters carry the blocks, the t's with the concealed Spanish worms, to the thunder below after the testi is opened, and jars the teeth on what they saw; and everything gets boiled down to the broth of a careless Sunday boy.

And then, going back to 58, Ida looks at Sinbad and his *Seventh Voyage* envisioned by a crew (all *loving* 24 men – a very *special* crew). The effects are amazing! Four hydro-aqualic beasts, roc to cure the blues, harps and golden vials. Kerwin's got his cyclops blinded, a little jet-black *Ray-mann*, one spinning off the rock to his death below, to satisfy a Sat. afternoon; and then there's Lang insisting *you only live once;* and Ray specifying that *they only live by night;* so during the night, call, Ida gets caught in Blockwood; and she could swear that god lives around here somewhere, some kid on the corner says he'll sell Ida a citizen's map to god's home and his entire cast for $20.10; and on the way to the lake she can view dynaclay Taylor, Lamarr, Mature and Rosebud tormed to the max, which is roughly nine and a quarter million dollars under the gun. Too bad, when originally 10 thousand talents had gotten off the hook, and Max had guided them as all souls to the garden. Ida's got only four so the kid sells her a map without Rosebud, and Ida says it's okay because life is a series of doors we don't always get through; so she tucks the map under her apron, and in a spell that lasts for but a twinkling she sees the map turn into the head of Adolf, and asks, "What the hell is that bud all about?" Questions can be thoughts even if god won't answer every one; so Ida starts to think of statements like *A-OK; it's old Kinderhook!, there is but one reliance,* and things like: the boy, the girl, the trunk and the eats; so she thinks of Bonnie's death in the Clyde, and she thinks of resurrections – the Bradbury in Blade, the Alph in Bel, Churchill in mgm 9/28/29 *there arose,* Claud in Cleo, tee hee on the hill – and she thinks of Badlands, and she thinks of natural born killers having a true romance, and she thinks of Tim, and she thinks of the newest little digital magicians, Ida and Cyclops, and their whirlwind heat, fire, brimstone and meat dance. And for those who have never sinned cast the first igneous stone, an essexite, at a direct Hit. This one will be so popular people will be begging to get through the special effect doors. But how can a saviour superduper diner, patron cenacle, lover of children, birds and beasts turn over such a leaf? Ask the red fox, celluloid. And sure enough, Ida grabs a hold of Cyclops; she finds him this time upsetting a cheerful full house marking everything with a *666 a must!* and presents to him a situation for a new kind of sit-com wherein she and he come from dysfunctional homes, and then take to the road in their hunk of junk that they seed in and swing, in trinity, while they rob America to pay Peter, palming their way through Chicago, Baltimore, Mayberry, Don Diego and Vega, where they rob a banquet, make a fortune and kidnap the sheriff, and take him on a wild spree through the back roads on a J. trip to the moon. Cyclops is driving a Henry Ford down Hershey commenting on the excellence of its getaway form, because the Ford has got every other car skinned, especially the V-8 on the fair banks, while Ida puts Black Lightening against (he confesses) Sheriff Andy's cheek in the back seat; she's humiliating Andy, and reaches in and cops his bullets, and is giving Andy a toss, while her other hand jack tunnels down into his back pocket and pulls out a wad that Ida flips open, Wow! even a worm will turn; for inside is a three-dollar Bill and a lot of pictures she flips through; and if Andy knows what's best for him he'll tell her the names of just a few *minties,* even while his seized trigger is in full view. "T . . . T . . . T . . . that's Aunt Bea and t . . . t . . . t . . . that's Opie and t . . . t . . . t . . . that there is my partner Barney and me p . . . p . . . posing with Billy the K . . . K . . . Kid." Ida says, "Aint't that cake?" fingering his twins and "O! Andy nasty nasty you got it all over me"; and the Cyclops steps hard on the brake, by three inches barely misses a tree. They pull Andy out of the car, plant him in the dirt and take pictures. O! What a trinity! Ida, the Cyclops and the Holy Ghost Andy G. of Mayberry!

But T . . . T . . T . . . never knew J.

This is now! Hear ye! Hear ye! Listen to the story of Ida and Cyclops and their semenistic careers on TV. Poor mythic mumpsimuses barely kept their family fed. Later Andy, having risen again, head-shoots them both to smithereens between commercials for Mr. Clean, as overseen by St. Bernadine of Siena, and Quaker Oats, as overseen by a son of the right hand Freeholder. Three seasons later they turn up again, only this time Cyclops is a Boston Jack cop and Ida is his crusty ol' Australian New South Wales Ma St. Zita, who heads the entire precinct with a laugh-track cutting up the gut and a pure Zen-like monologue slicing down the middle. The show's called *Om and the Boys.* And NBC (where N is Any number and is always Before Christ) is hoping for a big Hit under the guidance of SS. Boniface. The Cyclops is older and fatter, and Ida (How-now, Aunt Bea?) has got lines that are nauseating, but just plain loveable nonetheless. "You're entitled to my heart, you're entitled to my spleen, but for god's sake keep my paps out of it!" They don't get much to solving crimes but their precinct is always kept spotlessly clean, that is, aside from a few drops of residual cleanser.

During the third season, the Programmer bursts into the episode wherein Ida catches Cyclops in the Park by George, cleaning the bottom of a 9th grade queen, in uniform.

His name is Pangloss the Programmer, in charge of ratings; his left hand is literally an axe (the original fixture had been amputated in the close of a car trunk); too weak to cancel anything out; but now it springs into action (minutes earlier it was holding the Niflheim ratings); *Om and the Boys* falls seemingly overnight to number 6, having been steady at 3 for *time, times, and a half* of twelve. "None too soon!" he shouts.

"Cut the Act! Crazy Kat, cut me another *Felix culpa cabana* and set the stage for another wash. *Metaphysicotheologocosmolonigoantipasto!*" Fortunately, Pangloss speaks with other tongues. For the Programmer is the utterance in the wilderness who is known to prophesy with his tongue (like St. Gabriel and St. Clare) the general outcome of any given show that would otherwise (if ratings fall low) cut asunder the prophet, whether by revelation or by doctrine. For even shows without life giveth sound, whether hard sitcom cachinnation or dramatically slow ululation, disposable dialogue or hollow words that do not know the saint from the barbarian, the destructor from the healer, the magician from the charlatan, the irrefragable Doctor from the mellifluous Doctor; no! there's no use praying in an unknown tongue to matter and form or to a kaleidoscope eclipsing a beautiful beholding reflecting a groupie's hind of lamb if the audience does not understand Dan's, James's nor W.B.'s marked card or, at least, is not willing to do so; perhaps they could reproduce their presence in a new unanswerable tongue, Baby Lon a new incontestable frame – Neb dreaming dreams braking wet dreams forever – cut in pieces – heads, hands and toes – all thrown together onto a dunghill half-made of shit, half-made of clay; yes, why not – after all it's not the personalities but the ancient plot that counts. So the Programmer gives *Om* the axe and throws the 9th grader to the amative crew in the back, who drag her off to the back office, Chaney Pandemonium, and douses her with paphian wolf saliva; and by way of pan-genesis, the Programmer creates them a new show: *I'm Solomon, She's Sheba*, with a sidekick, Pelias, and a next-door neighbor, Pandora, snug-tight in a shirt of Nessus. Biblical hysteria laughs-in-tow. Act I, the episode: Cyclops playing Solomon Pingala (with only one sandal on) is tied down to the bed in an act of bondage, while Sheba exerts her secular dominance and expertise equestrienne and, remembering Bonnie, rides him like a centaurian Clydesdale-draft, net and hook. "O god, get her off! She's bending my implement!" Solomon screeches to ward off this female impetus, riding him to the hilt like Elizabeth Mutton. "O Lord Apollo!" Solomon cries. "Hear me as she turns. That from her swollen belly you should spew the blood that you have sucked!" Turns up . . . 666 on the N scale. Heads drop beneath the axe.

And the board – Rhadamanthus, Minos, Æacus – stamp it a *Guarantee.*

And then Ida playing Sheba, the peregrinator, travels an arduous fifteen hundred miles across deserts and mountains with gifts (shit! the ice cream melted!). For in between the scene, she has to dash and block a bullet aimed at the prime minister of Jerusalem (herself a marked queen), the motion regarding mass and space so swift a commercial couldn't get the best of it; and by the time the second act is in motion, she's armed with a cunning riddle: "What starts with sir but is *confined*, and can best be found in a burning bush?" Cumrotating while she speaks (and as a further hint), she extends the answer to a metaphor by rolling out her tongue, and serving Dick.

"Serpent!" Solomon roars as he shoots his venom into the plum whore. The Programmer is delighted. The ratings soar to sesterce! because you have two and a half asses, which, rounded off, makes three! The lucky number for a Hit series!

Backstage, Ida curls up to Cyclops like an insecure schoolgirl, like a soubrette in the third act, like a grisette in woolen cloth, like a water of ice, even though, so far, she's played, via TV, a *potpourri* of prostitutes and other assorted lemans – a bottomless dancer; a phone sex operator; a New Age, love-hungry, virgin queen Scot. high on leasing; a coke-addicted, usquebaugh-afflicted, gusset-conscious fashion designer; a biped arctophile into quadruped beasts; a headless housewife torn apart by four pitbulls in her own weedy backyard; and an ebony-lacquered Gloria Swanson Fifty-seventh Street streetwalker with a Marilyn Monroe birth mole on her fresh vinyl-slicker chin. Cyclops is all in a dizzy working with her so low, he's gotten on with a teufel afterglow. There's never been so much pandemonium before, not since Uriel had sharp-sighted Urania into an act of wisdom; but, after all, this is a paronomastic paradise lost in a wild uproar of smatterers, where a pair of dice can lead a *Hind You* on a roll to Kali Yuga, or where an Ace can die getting a hole in one. Cyclops plants his lips to Ida's ear and whispers, "When the trumpets blasted and god scooped up his crew, why did he leave so many down below?" To which Ida responds, "Because to god we are the pap smear of civilization, so we might as well go deep within the dark well and take a quaff. In the water of existence that is given unto us, the water that we birth in, the water that we drink from, the water that we make, there is sadly the hook by which we are quartered and skinned. Can this be where our travels end? How I wish *fin de siècle* could be so easy," Ida says in full, with darker French lips than the slick, scarlet lipstick like a beacon of rescue she is use to.

It's all about balance, no, not only of the soul, but whether one's ultralucent, X-rated lipgloss balances one's vivid hot pink, collegiate hippie-chick eye shadow. Life and death in the postlapidarian wilderness. This is where we find ourselves, *röntgenstrahlen*, now disguised in a corporate vision that blends into the soft brain spirituality ragout. A merry, yet underscored, musical number. And a new lesson in the secret of successful programming. *To be continued . . .*

2:08 tick . . . tick . . .

That was when the Apple came in, a little over an essence ago. Ol' Jack Brandy, Andrew – manhandled and served on a *crux decussata;* where 'X' is any number as long as it's one, 1130, and crosses like a warship or a man of war. *She's a rock, a corn off the Scilly Isles, a frigging frigate if ever there was one.* Streetwalker speculated that the dandiacal Apple was an attractive take-over target. Apple was wallowing at *66 and one-sixth*, and it would appear that all hell was breaking loose and storming the door of eternity via the ionosphere and the F layer. So . . . what's the matter? Apple had seen turmoil before. Fallen objects (could we safely say sea shells, bones and kitchen refuse?) had been raining down upon Apple for eons, bruising its very core. Objects which even went by names like AT&T. (Go . . . jump to conclusions. A Triskelion Trademark.)

And the pomme served as vert for the forest of information.

You see . . . take a breath . . . *SEE* . . . Apple had fallen short of divine ever since: *Sa . . . Sa . . . Sa . . . Suntan. My beautiful suntan. You're the only angelic outline the eye abhors. And when the son shines over the bounty, they'll be kicking Sa . . . Sa . . . Sa . . . Suntan out to the kitchen-middens* had become the most popular and adored tune, which meant that Apple was holding a hot new single despite a lack of rhyme. As a result, every last Laodicean predicted that all would be grand once the door had slammed shut on the matter altogether.

And poor old Rabbi Schneerson-son, old boy, got his fingers caught in Apple's gate. Johnny Darbies put the darbies on him. Sch. was busy reporting to the great central mind (Sam, Scratch a verse or two) his prediction as the late, great, grand Rabbi of the Lubavitcher sect of Hasidim that *"yes! there will be a major discovery in diamonds and gold, with a buying frenzy resulting in a common share rising from 18 to 21!"* Grand Central knew (damn fucking well) that the streets of Apple are lined with gold and a wide assortment of precious stones and, depending upon theft and other likely acts of old, such as separation and purification, the stones would occasionally need to be replaced. So Rabbi's prediction turned out to be *gold in itself?*

Maybe it was due to the Rabbi's fingers getting smashed, but the diamond find that was predicted proved to be hardly enough to cover the cost for a common engagement ring. Perhaps, like old ned, Schneerson-son had bitten off more terephah than he could chew and had gotten a trichinotic worm/pork in his head. A teredo from the first crew. Rabbi blamed it all on Apple's bad rep and no! . . . ah . . . drift toward more regret. Being mitnagged to death, was it? But how can such a nice vert get a worm in it? Rab had a point because the worm, after all, was the link to a mirror-universe on the other side of spacetime, where anything unfortunate enough to fall into a wormhole would indeed encounter infinite curvature, wherein any material object (and that goes for both rabbis' and pieces of gold) would be crushed like gooseberries (the black coats literally ripped off the shoulders, the tallithim and the yamachas torn apart, the beards and braids up-rooted); shuddering force beyond . . . no . . . *before* the beautiful universe could find its exact replica in numbers as they are mirrored through to the other side, having first encountered the engagement ring of death that the good Rabbi had not predicted.

"It is a wo . . . wo . . . wo . . . wormhole!" The last thing poor Rabbi Schneerson-son remembered at the point of total disintegration was strolling (swimming) down New York's Fifth Avenue one Black Sabbath Mass day during the month of Veadar, musing upon the gentler themes of primordial man, such as one Adam Kadmon, but otherwise minding his own business, when a strange floating television screen appeared in front of him at 1300. He stepped up to the screen to grab a closer look and was horrified to find himself staring at the head of a nasty-looking Cyclops, at 1:00, which, for a brief moment, Rab mistook for a giant penis in need of a giant mohel and a good sucking. Curiosity drove him to circle around the floating object; but when he peered at it from the backside, he found that it possessed the uncanny ability to transform. Now a woman's head was staring back at him. And almost instantly the rabbi knew (being a rabbi, he was more than a wee bit linked to god and was therefore more than a wee bit linked to omniscience) that in some faraway universe the Cyclops and the woman were squared off in a life-and-death confrontation. "It seems that everyone gets thrown about," the Rabbi mused while chanting a few bars of the Kolnidre. "But if a person is lucky, before he or she is crushed in a wormhole, he or she might just be able to utter something, have something important to say as a final departing statement. For the Rabbi it was: "Arbitrarily advanced civilizations construct and maintain wormholes in the core of the Apple, the heaven brain of the mind, the bread from heaven, the Starry mills of the beating fist, which in total cost exceeds the gross national product of the earth." This makes it possible for a duo, such as a Cyclops *and* a woman in the form of a statue, to act as badchans, and solve the riddle of the transversible serpent/wormhole, so that the statue in her own separate universe can bridge the pure vacuum of empty yoni-space by the cosmolo gicalconstantantipasto, and thereby form a perfect *O* with a spin of zero like a singlet. The infinite web of interlocking serpentholes in the sea of the universe prefers to ride quaker on a wave like a graceless grasshopper that has zerocosmologicalconstantantipasto, that will thereby connect an infinite number of live universes to an infinite number of dead universes, which, in turn, is essential in order to cause god *and* gravity to eat up and swallow, and wrap itself up into a tight, tiny ball and Sinatrasize, and explode outward at fantastic rates, and thereafter fucking hydrocoffin die (for . . . *That's L'Chaim! That's what all the people say. Schlepping high in April, kaputtin' down in, . . . Oye vey!),* which was exactly what Rabbi Schneerson-son did at that very instant, which helped to prove his come-to-the-burning-bush-of-no return-Euclidian-as-according-to-Legend point, in the twinkling of an eye, and thus terminate a line and all its parts.

Ida and Cyclops stood sadly before Rabbi Schneerson-son's memorial reading his epitaph ("So . . . where is the body of Nobodaddy?") etched in stone.

"Do you think we could work it into one of our shows?" Cyclops asked. "Call it *a ganef in the night* and leave it for the Histrios to tongue out?"

Ida remembered another epitaph by a fellow known as Dr. Pangloss the Programmer. He was a hard man who was only *just*-so, and a sad man who was only *wise*-so (*so* sounds so promising); but those whom the gods would destroy nearly always are so-*promising* at first, so . . . Ida turned to Cyclops and said, "It is up to us, the consolers of the human race, the preservers of the universe, the souls of all tender monoceros creatures, gentle love, exquisite grace, to follow the map to the stars' abodes in leather shoes and ring the doorbell of the horned one and not run away, but finally greek god cheek-to-cheek, and shoot him clear down to the core with Final Judgments. It is *meum-teum devoir.*"

Ding-Dong . . .

A STRANGE GENEALOGY

Ida will pose in this Episode as the fair, cruel maid servant of our August Barreness, who, in turn, will be played by Cyclops, in whose arms she will enjoy the delights of paradise that have produced the tortures of hell by which *All* will be infected and devoured in this Greek tragedy if *Action!* isn't pronounced soon and angels laid to rest.

Ida and Cyclops received this information from a most learned monk, who had gotten it from the mysterious Source, after the Source had received it from the Accusor, who had gotten it from a Director, who had owed it to an actor, who had derived it from an actress, who had received it from a writer, who had obtained it from a lover, who had borrowed it from an ex-lover, who had sold it to Grace, who had inherited it from Homer, who had stolen it from Mary, who had slipped it to Mrs. Alving, who had granted it to 19; for 19 had received it from an old smoking whore, who had gotten it from a sea captain, who had derived it from a dictator, who had snatched it from a saint, who (when a novice) had received it from a direct line of one of the colleagues of Dr. Pangloss (who is also Dr. Sseus – one-in-the-same).

Currently, god was holding part of the secret inside his Hollywood Hills home, disguised as a page marker in a *livre de chevet*, but he was not going to give it away to just anyone because three sets of three words each were now added to his trilabiate lips, which made for a whole lot of difference. *"I am dying! O Dr. Sseus. Such holey French letters, I'll never forgive!"*

And the Cyclops cried out. *"A strange genealogy!"* And he started to bellow out a tirade, but short-windedness got the best of him during a rapid run between G and g, which left him panting in a smorzando interval.

Wasn't god at the root of it? For if god wasn't at the root of it, there would be no devil, no demogorgon, no demiurge – there would be no awareness – there would be no chocolate nor cochineal – no mundane shell to dwell upon. When thirty gold pieces from the Rabbi's eye can buy a god in entirety, there has got to be a führer sale made in order to attract a noteworthy prophet. You cannot be a god without paying the price. The Cyclops paid the price. Being worshipped became his single vision for the future, played out with all the elaborateness of a soap opera with themes of stupidity, cruelty, greed, honor, venality and deceit. *Parvenu!* And for having only one eye, Cyclops was taught by Dr. Sseus to write and to speak fluent Turkish, and to grace the upper echelons of fashionable society with his tails; for the god in the dog makes the public good everytime.

Ida was seeking only one goal, caring for only one result while she stood at the grave of Rabbi Schneerson-son, facing the west wind and the racing shadows, and looking deep into the Cyclops's eye, past the film on his grate. She mused: was it not always the task of the hero to enlighten the otherwise confused and depressed, pestilence-stricken multitudes, the atomies, so that they might be mindful both of their origin and destiny? She, grown from a statue, enveloped in her own evolution . . . *so many minds* . . . she was able to question, challenge, dig, and seek beliefs, concepts, and theories; too, she explored, measured and probed the movement of the stars, particularly from hill to hill: Beverly to Holly; and sea to sea; Indian to Red; and chemicals, elements, and physics in bed; and even gossip, cast into the wind; from clay to flesh, she pondered: why do we need air to breathe when as stone it is not necessary? Can words be exactly defined? Not so long as empty words can fill the air. Impassioned, eloquent, deadly serious – in the single eye of the Cyclops she saw it all – friend and foe – mark the eye, alone – fried, ugly, vain, ruthless, kind, considerate, selfish; the eye that in its younger day consumed the arrogant indigestibility of kings and captains alike; the eye that crunched the bones, that munched the myths and mysteries of the Church (see BS); for not only flesh did the Cyclops eat but bigotry and barbarism as well, wadded up in a ball of barbed wire at the Cheslea Hotel.

Cyclops was not alone. For he could read her script and see that not only were her pages his own but her words as well; as though stemming from them, he could also divine another place and time, perhaps somewhere deep in the Mediterranean – uncultivated but not infertile – where wheat, corn and vines grew naturally from the soil from which also grew sight, around which numerous treks of goats and black pupils in the guise of boy servants and motel managers roamed the interior in the mirror of the eye of unpleasant chasms and crags – just a hop, skip and a jump from the Hacienda Motel, where St. John was livin' it up with a stroll when he ran into a last judgment out of fear that there should be time no longer.

Somewhere in the Ocean (a blank verse representing the sea with two Insurance Policies against fire and hail, both equiprobable), the Cyclops saw the sayings of Rev. Elation and the Karaite with seven heads and ten horns – a hairy Esauian island rising up out of the sea; a hexagonal sign proclaiming to make war with the saints and equiprobability, and to overcome them in order to deceive; *odium theologicum*; cum to give life unto the image of the blatant beast, that it should speak in one hundred tongues – *'jubjub in the tub!'*; it's all personal, apolitical religion – an avocation in the likeness of sinful flesh; for even as they stood at the grave of a prophet, the Cyclops stood grave at a pun:

The third is a slowness in taking a jest.

Should you happen to find one he'll be wearing a vest.

In ecclesiastical power his words nonetheless:
be a mess,
For, in spite of the rite, he's entirely sleeveless.

Ida could feel the Cyclops slipping into a place unreal, myths bounding like pursued deers tearing through the ruins of a palace-principality of the Nowhere Dead Sea. A magnet school, drawing in all the fish in order to pursue their lessons. Shaking the Cyclops out of a state of Skip Ophirnia, hearing Dr. Sseus instead (" . . . We were looking for new ways to breathe life back into sequestration, because in the spit court the issue is death . . ."), guiding him through the golden journey, together, Ida and Sseus, rooted Cyclops to the reality-myth. Cyclops fell willingly, sprained Tarsus, and took root in the bushy V of one in particular – Her Imperial Highness, the Grand Duchess, O – now thinly disguised as Olga, the eldest daughter of the last C-pizza delivery by Paul the Pizza Man of ten t makers, who was not really murdered with all the other members of her family in the red zone, but, instead, traveled erratically amid the chaos of a civil war on angel's wings *above* the spiral twining counterclockwise – that is, sinistrorsely. Yes, traveling, as Ulysses traveled, as we all *must* travel – through the chaos towards our personal, glassy destinies.

It took Olga three years to scratch safety in the form of a queen, wherein she found love with an officer, some jewels, a pavillion, and a gambling den where the pips fell silently and defeated the mass of innocence. The Cyclops recalled swarming to the casino with the crème of Alexandrian society; and it was he, the Cyclops, who advised the king to grant Olga a palace on a small, horse-populated peninsula on the Red Sea which she called: *Eye. See a clear marked view of nothingness.* After three monks labor, water trekked through the groves in the courtyard and across the many uppermost rooms, and into the marble basins (both water and its accompanying equilin); and all the most corrupt from Heliopolis to Petra frequented its halls, and dipped endlessly, to their disinfectant delight, in the provided stalls, all their little ailments. Madame's court became an instant deluxe whorehouse with transvestism its roaring fashion. The ladies of the court (bull, gentlemen), and the gentlemen (ladies), all spoke with rapid-fire tongues: *"Bandersnatch!" "Toves!" "Borogoves!" "Raths!" "Tumtum!" "Scot! Gone Dutch!"* and *"Eatupalltheoxygen."* For as there will come a führer day – wherein man battles the Great J Wood Beast who, fresh from the querencia, hosted its own old party battle between a young man with an eye like Lynceus and black balls short of delight, and a monstrous creature named Lyme – there will also come: *O god, for your eye of flame, your catching claw and your biting jaw. For anyone who does not take your third name: Off with its head!*

And . . . *it's off to see the Lizard, the wonderful Lizard of . . . Ho . . . Ly . . . Wood . . .*
+ Dr. Besetzung: "Do you suppose this is a psychic thing?"
– Dr. Besetzung: "I suppose it is three things. Noun, verb and adjective. Object oriented, like Cathy Exis and in-fidelity. Or trilingual lines to fission."

HEAD

Today it seems as though Hate should have chosen Hollywood's tabloid as its scandalous birthplace, for this little ivy town lied on the green boundary between Ever Hills and Angel, which the younger owls from Ludgrove had made it their destiny to survive in. One blood demands that one people stand before their god through a sea of glass, in their black swallowtail coats. The needle will become their plow, and from the tears of hustling deers the daily bread of future Does will grow. And so Hollywood on the border is the symbol of a great Miss ion, as G takes over the sun on 12,25, and a great wonder woman takes over the show and twelve stars. Statues and Cyclopes are twins in union after all, just like Dionysus and his counterpart, Exi, g, uus, who, high on wine, made an era in error. Under one skin they prosper, in disguise; but, nevertheless, their smooth skin underneath might not be the real thing either. A week earlier Statues and Cyclopes were not facing the battleground at all, cluttered with smokestacks, oil tanks, refineries and such. Instead they were alone within one another, unraveling the secret thoughts, disguises and desires buried within one another's heels.

Yes, Cyclops longed not to have just his soul tapped but his intellect as well; and while we're at it, tap into Poland, Denmark, Norway, Holland, Luxembourg, Belgium, France and o hell, Diana, the goosegirl, and all the gnat ions of the world, rolling their *I's* most conspiculously. Yes, in fell all the sects, under the hand of Hit, who sought Lebensraum. *Today we rule Holl, tomorrow the room for the living!* In Red: *Rub Riche.*

LINES

Extra! Eden moves into Home Guard and has a civil arm guard the plate.
S. We dish: Sue Cism. Mass. Age. Swejism.
Needless to say, the Cyclops's receiver oftentimes went off its axis. The stain from his armpit definitely made him look awkward in degrees of learning. (When the second vertebra of the neck that serves as a pivot for the head to turn on falters into an unlocked position and repositions the atoms, the time scale of events become array.) This was exactly how the Cyclops fell into such a bacchanalian state of existence, and for a space of time it could have been said about him that he *mot sterven wood.* The intoxicated mind tends to lump dissimilar events into one lump of time. It comes about as a result of omniscience. There was a general implosion that stormed: *death paves the way for evolution! This is the marching season!*

The Cyclops knew much of death, for some of his ritual dances were inspired by the movements and life cycles of the vultures, choughs and other such puttocks. Indeed, once he wore a leafy loin cloth made from the bodies of dead robins, and danced upon nothing while doing the Tyburn jig. Vaguely, he could recall the last dive, John at T. Tree Motown, and dancing for the Lord of Hollywood, while the crowds looking on clashed in a Corybantic dance, ogling one another in their gump fatigues, rocky trunks, guille hoopshoes, marvel green mania hiphuggers, rainforest blue suedes, cap n gown, harley shades and hardrock underpants. He could hardly have imagined what bird carnage would occur toward the middle of the century, when the slaughter of races got out of hand. But death takes many guises, and where once robins covered the dead with leaves, the white devil hovered picking out thorns at Calvary, not a stones throw away from Drury Lane. The names of the slaughtered and the tribes they originated from all faced extinction in their various positions, but this could also be blamed upon the skin frenzy of *plumassiers.* For as it stood, Hollywood was infamous for ornamental invention of the barbarous kind. Eatertainments had their own commandments regarding souvenirity, and the Cyclops was receiving a rich history lesson in *IMPOED.* Once he got past Ginger Rogers spinning so violently that the air grew thick with fallen lashes, once he got past Disney and Elvis on Capitol, 241481677, and Marx three days thereafter, once he got past all the beggars on Sunset Lane, the Cyclops was finally able to view the scratchy herds filing through god's eternal promise to *delice* the multitudes (misconstrued from delight); it was all part of the germ's smattering education of man ab initio.

Ida's classes were difficult, vague and abstract; half the time the Cyclops felt as if he were flunking in his attempt to understand a language totally foreign to him, even though he comprehended the words. Time and its various elements were not following a particular order in *houres* and it almost made him feel plebian (his worth), of a common lot – impotent and inept, as though he were suffering from aspermia. Ida stressed that it was necessary to capture and to hold and to thereby expel the entire battleground of civilization in *any* one breath; for such is god – the *Bocca della Verità*, the mouth of truth on the seventh block from Sunset past the seventh hotel (where Harry Bailly, the Ghost, will gladly take your cents *and* your tabard should you get High before your time), past the seven houses in the country divided. The map should lead you to the spire, the pillar, the Schreckhorn, the peak of terror, *O! burn niece!*, and the punishing dome; the mean geometry of the inevitable, and all the tears you have ever shed and owned.

It could be that god's division began so long ago it is now impossible to locate the whole (diaspora scattered about), although this conclusion would make Ida very mad; for with such an attitude god is nowhere to be found, with or without a map. The Cyclops wanted to belong to Ida's school not just in name (as in marriage) but in spirit. He looked at her and closed his eye, and in that single polarity he saw Medusa and her serpents all doing the St. Vitus's Dance with argus eyes; and every man who saw it turned to stone and smiled like the boy Gwynplaine; and the Cyclops saw discursive maenads, women driven mad by Dionysian bacchanals, loosely chattering like an army of locusts at a klatch for stoners; and he saw Hellenic goddesses teaching Jews their Greek; and he saw Mary Magdalene's red waves, free and mad, and nearly insane with immaculacy. O the untapped energy of the imitatrix of god – the houri-femininity that bore god even before he was given a name – long, bound, banded, omnipresent waves of the sea. And the Cyclops saw Marie and her court of cages atop the cranium, complete with lovebirds and glasses of wine, and a pot or two of Heavy-wet; and he saw Irene Castle, walking, bobbed, with a bit of Osmund in her cheek, and a cigarette, over to Ion, but on the cutting room floor; and he saw himself sitting in Leman's lap, living up a storm and stress; and he could hear Ida cry, "Row me over and I'll beat you into shape!"; and he saw the Harmattan-wind carrying Vivien Leigh all the way to St. Martin's Lane, off the pavement; and it occurred to him that he would need to cast Verwünschen, and to thereafter transform himself into the *cut* blonde.

The theater of credibility had changed (. . . *adieu, Aschenputtel, au revoir, Rotkäppchen, Shalom, Dornröschen, my little der Gestiefelte Kater);* and the end of time had evolved into assassination, stunning (if confused) at best; and when he looked again, the polar opposite to the obvious presented itself as a shorn head – a naked head – before the tree was nibbled, and the Cyclops could also imagine Ida on the Supremes' Court, tombesteres and baudes gently hovering over the bench, leaning way over to say, "Stop! In the name of Eros! This is not a gun-flagging, wild-haired daughter of the afterworld but a Cyberspace riddle, a bibitory dream, a one-eyed wet saviour! who requires loads of hydrotherapy!"; which made the Cyclops think that the Book of Revelations was entering a new chapter which indicated that one was about to have a spiritual illumination.

It was a handful of ripe revelations. One of the handfuls of good revelations ever made about the future of civilization. Dr. Sseus (himself a revelation critic) just so happen to have given this handful of infinities a thumbs up! To encounter revelation, one must either be guided or somehow guide oneself into the secret pre-occurrence world without ever letting the on-occurrence or post-occurrence world discover that you have somehow departed from their respective realms. One must learn how to die if one's goal is to grasp dominion over god by a scribbled verse. For death is not a cessation – rather, it is nothing more than a queasy moment when we discover that our horror dies in inaudible laughter and that all of humankind is a likeable, entertaining young thing whose only sin is that collectively it does not seem to understand the riddles behind the universe.

There is one-way: dare to get inside the teenage mind. Between the ages of thirteen and nineteen all human beings take on (in both mind and body) the exact likeness of god. Anyone who has properly studied religion, philosolphy, theodicy, theosophy, theurgy, thremmatology, toiletry, tomfoolery, tortuosity, or totaldepravity would automatically know this to be a fact. Anyone else would naturally fall under the category *a la couplets threnody:* Azrael playing the thrombus in a sweet diapason of transcendence.

Actually death's ultimate deliverance can be traced to a physical plane, wherein one can best define it in comparison to one's fondness for the latest Paris fashions. Consider, in fancy, the millions you might have earned from movies, ads and pin-up calendars; consider "Christie"; consider "Marilyn"; consider (jesus!) sucking at the she-bear's breast and how, in Paris, he offered the codling to the sweet and fair smile for beauty's sake! Somewhere along the line, in terms of death, everyone possesses a bit of *Garboesque,* shunning publicity, and meanwhile suffering from a bit of c.g.m. (christ glamour and mystery), at best.

Art in terms of the mass moment. Never a care. Nothing lasts. Wear, bear, digest and throw away. The medium is the coated special of the day, and That is the mass moment.

The Eye has it all in order – in order to prepare himself for the life and breath of god after the zipper has fallen to a rest for a fast stop and a little pud dance. Several seasons of black hordes of fashion watchers must be internalized and witnessed as a tyranny of high heels and an ostrich-like walk that adds a sense of popular depth to tiny toroidal slips (holes for the head! cracks in the egg! curves to the profile! arch to the back! requiem to the dead!). Perfect mere mortals of penury, starving for the fashionable silhouette.

Achilles's ten *dons,* Marlon, Ulysses, Alphonse, Paris, Brando, Lucky, Muni, Café Colosimo, the golden pomace and *For the Fairest One of All* – all of them traveled back to mount Ida, for what else? power and and riches, but without leaving a cumshaw. Ida and her beautiful V, the sacred bush. O do we not all seek to be mad in order to meet our persecutors of the not ungentle bad race, from which there is no escape from badinage, except within the depths of the sea (or a sidetrek to Novocherkassk to view the Don C. safely under glass)? For the youth, the son, was just sixteen years old (the down just beginning to darken his cheeks) when the fierce giant (Hit, the terror of the woods, from whom no stranger escaped unharmed, and whose fingers and toes were twenty-four, six on each hand and six on each foot) learned to fell what love is under the t-shirted guise of *derzyklop.*

Beyond this, touched with passion (fashion), the Cyclops forgot his flocks and his well-stored caverns, and began to take care of his appearance and make himself amendable, cutting to the quick his beard with a sickle, getting a good tan, via good rays, and restoring himself to a finer grace. His love of slaughter, his thirst of blood prevailed no more. He even took up an instrument of numerous pipes and made the hills and waters swell with ebullient music. The Cyclops gave the river a name (Dis side), a song *(The Pome of Harmony)* and, once given the proper keys, a *klavierstück*, composed as an apology *(Amende honorable)*. Yes, he who had handled a weapon and had thereby betrayed himself to the keenest eye with a wet kiss was now exposed to the flower passion of Ida.

Fashion *(all have fallen)*. For all women, lost and raised again on that most unrealistic of female icons, *the toothpick slim styx*, which makes every hateful part invulnerable by the aid of celestial armor. O Mother, dip your vanilla cone into chocolate and harden it lest we all die on the spot where blood sank into the earth, and lie speechless for a year (no thanks to involuntary anorexia). A flower has sprang: Judgment. *Ai – it is for suffering.* (Lebensraum-Larkspur.) If not by intuition then by pure dianoia.

And enter Achilles's ten noblemen (all restless spheres – the masters to the christian name). To the persons of consequence, the parsons and the clerks, and all Oxford grandees fleeing from the City of Destruction: Dear Sirs, will you please kindly place yourselves into wear, and become fashionable. All heil, and envelop the Kleagle. The end is near. Even ol' Dod, the would-be godfather, who also refused Alice her son, knows this, dear. Nevertheless, adore the heel of life *(Heidelbergo man)*, who knows the salty business which over time can lead to an actual cessation of breath, so that by the time the hour is up O dad's sparkling heels will be underground, his lot of bones mingled with breast and dust. G.

These are the dons: Experts in metatarsal-bursitis (the excessive force of jamming a rectangle into a triangle). Childless father. Fatherless child. Damn that whale! Ram it with a man! Loth Peck! And let them both go down! Hammertoes, compliments of the don Mortonius Neuroma. But Achilles had ten dons in all, the tenth of which was Frank Stilettos, who could drive the end point home. The scene-stealing spike, high-tapering-heel-in-the-sky, who could also draw conclusions into the breast of an opponent on the target of a period with his *Mackerel*, six inches long. *Take a rest.*

Take hands. Therein, the duality of god. Some can spike, some got the soft touch on grunion babes, Veronica Lake, and Lauren Bacall playing a saint who wiped the face of a god in order to leave a good impression. And a valley of weeping tears: Cleo, Baca, Taylor, respectively; even though reel life isn't always so fashion-sleek, cool-cat, waif, laurel leaf, crown, baby-fat, mouth-wash clean, in order to counteract the damage done to skin and bones.

Flash!

Due to overexposure to god, the evolving Cyclops and Ida had to create *Revelation Restructuring Construct* (i.e., Zonal drilling into the zona pellucida involved squirting an acidified solution into the entrance for spirits, sucked tailfirst into an extremely thin glass needle, the sharp, angeled end of the tube-tongue-gullet, which is next to the membrane, Suzi Subzono [. . . by the don's early light which so proudly we heil . . . the lillies bursting in flight], Gianto Paténumana Reggio, and a crew of antioxidants, emollients and paternal-triple-fruit-alpha-omega-gel-cream finality juices), thereby making it possible for the Italic type to grab a piece of the pi and to add to the slope of the Deity. For everyone wants to get into the Act it seems. How else to survive the inevitable consequences of the Negativity? the otherwise comic plan to the Decline and Fall of Legs Diamond, who was in between two thieves with *meow* stitched into his crotch.

What was needed before their odyssey could continue was a place in which they could 'sit-in' for seven days, and thereby generate enough boycott energy to give them the ability to overcome the influence of god (which, in itself, would be a sex cathedra miracle). A temporary structure made of cloth and lumber, and topped with tree branches, where one can overhear the latest gossip.

"*. . . use to be quite a dancer in Philadelphia, that is true, and later, at the Hotsytotsy Club, Cassidy got really red laid by the smash and grab thief in the night. He's got little strength for being a clay pigeon of the underworld. Ah, spittle on the light of day, shot six times and still potter power over clay . . . Don't say? Not the way Kiki tells it. Jack's always got the last to say on kike . . .*"

The precept of sitting demands that one becomes a sort of existential operator. Yes, in order to enter into the household of god for the purpose of making a domiciliary visit, one needs to become quite the detective. Quite the spy. Quite the sharpshooter. Quite the unraveler. Exercise the brain. Flex the organ. Stretch it. *Domify.* Open it so that the ability to interpret and correlate is at its optimum level. Think Virgo – beyond the whore scopophilian substituting for Mary. Think beyond Gilgal, and the first encampment of the lites. Sextant. Sex. Sex. Sex. Measure. *X* is to obliterate, which only a higher power can do, just as so many Roman criminals were banished at Gyaros. *O* is perfection. *Dis* is another name for sat' or sat an . . . what? A chair? A throne? A pile of dung? The cyclopum scopuli, on the eyes of the needs? What correlates when you put it all together? *A mass departure.* How many seers departed Galeotis? >3? Remember: the belief that god created this departed material out of nothing is a long-sitting part of the Bowelstine doctrine. For if god did not create matter, it would imply that he was limited in his work by the nature of the raw materials available to him in times of dire trouble. In regards to this evacuation, one must consider the abrupt organization of matter from a chaotic, structureless, Gasosaurus-Gallimimus primeval form into a complex order and activity. Mass has energy. Mass is the quantification of matter (e.g., a little mass is worth an awful lot of irreligious energy; just as the mass of a particle is a measure of its inertia or resistance to change, such as body and blood into bread and wine; just as the mass moment can overreach the 100 million mark and then sink and, if lacking an 'm,' make a complete ass of itself). In motion, a light particle is more easily moved by a given force than a heavy one. A large body is typically of a Mass that is so heavy and ponderous that at the dismissal of a religious service it would naturally move slow and labored. In other words, the more massive the messenger particle, the shorter the range of the corresponding force. This is because the mass of the messenger – sagamite pies, loaded and sodden heaps – is uproariously related to the range of the force. And because 0 mass particles travel at the speed of light, which is a hell of a lot faster than the speed correlated to a Mass upon dismissal at the end of an earnest service, this naturally brings us back to the theory of *X O Dis*, insofar as it pertains to a mass departure. The *rest* is rather simple for all together it equals: *EXODUS* and a mass departure that took over 200m. to sit through.

GOSSIP

The purpose of sitting was to connect both Ida and Cyclops to Exodus. Man to Saint! "Suck it!" Cyclops exclaimed. "Of course!" he shouted with omniscient energy pounding in his head. "It's a warning related to the Numbers! I see it all now because my head is swarming with tao-tieh images of the Feast. Before I leave, I must understand godsibb. Just as I once kept and sponsored goats on my island, I see what obvious connections there are to me! The fallen star! Risen!"

And yes! He resurfaced in film. *IS.* T.E. Cyclops hr. 9:00. Boxoffice opened. Son meets girl. Girl meets son. Lots of hubba-hubba-ing. Tombesteres. Dancing girls. Lama. The blade. A fight. *r-r-r.* A kiss. A trial. The snarling dog letter. A death. A life. Music. Some tuneatics. Credits. Alcairo, baby! And, ol' my soul in Ausonian land. And despite the critics – appeal to the Masses! The Greekest Stooly Ever Tooled. Kink of Kink. Love me kissin' jail blue John new suede shoes. Turn to gold again so there'll be peace in the valley O little town of Bethlehem. Bottomless key. Fifth Fallen star. Precious Lord. Suffer the children because I want you. For in my father's house are many mansions. But Ito also eats girls! girls! girls! for this is my heave in and out! there is no god but god asleep in his shoes. Lawdy jus' tryin' to get to you, promised land. O Memphis! O loyal legions of followers! O Cadbury, canal me down!

Ida could feel the eye of celebrity upon her temple. And she could see T.E. Chnicolor visions of victory!

Introducing . . . the god of Memphis . . . Electrically charged and all! The Cyclops!

REAL A T.E. CYCLOPS

Cyclops, with a few wet coins in his pistol pocket, ventured down, knuckles scraping the ground, to Century 21, the local realty, and requested a plot of land upon which there was rumored to be a good god tug of war. Sam Sham, the Realtora man, looked up from a copy of *Le Cahier Jaune,* and said, *"Sa raison en fut ébranlée.* You're sure a man I can gladly see, but if I look askew the view of you looks more to be like that of a dew beast gazing up into heaven. What kind of plot are you exactly looking for, my friend?"

"I'm looking for a plot to be *full-field,* some living space, which H.G., by the well of Dave, spoke of concerning another fellow, Jud, who might have looked a bit like me, but not fulfilled, napoo to the gills," the Cyclops said genteelly. "In other words, I'm looking for a real tor, like the one come from the real schule."

"O, you must mean that lot in the midst outside of town on that midsty street . . . what's its name . . . *Sicarius,* or something near insane, not more than a baetylus's throw away from here. O don't tell Jud was a dagger-man-beast on one hand, Ish' on the other? Sure . . . I know the fellow . . . He's sort of an oddball. A stewer. A gusher, by dram. I heard tell he never married. Lonely Jack and as misunderstood as an old relic of a clown, miraculously speaking, as all pure hell bapted in beer. And all on account of drink and meat. Pity. Why, he's sent lots of people to me on his own recommendation, in spite of his delicate condition. People, such as you, devising a permanent plot."

"Devising? Hardly. I mean to succeed where the others have failed."

"Then you found the right man, my friend. I must remember to thank the old Jew and slip him a ten. By my book he's not so dark after all, for the blackness of him makes everyone else's grayness less noticeable. I'm sure. Yeah, he used to be a treasurer or an accountant of a little arbitrary company. But some of its members got arrested in the first world and it's all hush-hush now. On my brief encounters with him at the train station, where I'd often meet him en route, I took to see what a passionate fellow he seemed to be. But that was three years ago, and since then you know how plots go once under way and there are no brakes to apply. Actually, I deadly recall now. He recommended another potential buyer to me, and for all his Herculean efforts I gave him eleven bucks 'cause I was lacking twelve, not to mention a girdle for me Hip. Tell you the truth, fellow. The same eleven bucks could have bought me a young, wet pussy from Allahbam, like you see over there on the corner at 8:30. But what the fuck. It's the least I could do for a little bit less than a friend who was going through such a still life. Stagnant. Vulnerable. After all, I know a thing or two about Achilles' heel too, you know. Just as I know a thing or two about cleaning lig stables. Ugh. *Ar give us this day our daily bread and forgive us our uxoricide and our infanticide as we forgive our Ju.* No!" Sam said with a wink. "Feet problems. No! Arch problems. No! Fashions and all. Mind lifting your heel?"

"Yeah. You seem to have a knowing eye, too, just like my muletta before she took to rocks," Cyclops retorted, standing directly behind Sam the Sham. The Cyclops dug into his pocket and dug out a hardened piece of gum spirits. "You like to chew?"

"Don't mind if I do," Sam mused. He unwrapped the gum, stuck it in his mouth and chewed, and must have had an instant sugar, friar rush. For as he chewed his eyes bulged out like a lobster's and a goofy look appeared on his face like a devilish grin. And the roof of his mouth collapsed. And his hair turned baked brown. And the sun went behind a passing cloud in the shape of a beast with four hoofs. And for a second or two it got real, real dark. And the second hand on the wall leaped on its face like a theopathetic locust.

"Mister," Sham said, both somewhat delighted and overcome by the vigorous effects of the gum in his head. "Didn't get the name."

"Cyclops. T.E.!" the Cyclops exclaimed. "The same."

"Well . . . step into my holy office, T.E.. I've got a lovely plot of land I think you'll be interested in. Over on Highway 119, there's a field the locals 'round about call *I sell ta' Ma.* Got its nickname from another local, years and years and years back, who originally sold it to his very own Ma, hence its nick, *I sell ta' Ma* . . . Get it? Get it? O . . . it proved worthless to Ma so she sold it to a pottery company that died off real Pd quick and had to let it go to us for nearly nothing, for it had originally fallen from heaven, the old wooden T, that is, upon which the safety of us all is supposed to depend. But to tell you the truth, the whole thing is simply Brit, and a bit of a circus. But, still, it's a noteworthy piece of land by god, at least insofar that it has rich soil, almost light red. Now I don't know what you may need it for, but listen, my friend. It's a good place for a truth-teller, a know-sayer, like yourself. So why don't we go and have-take a look?"

"Sure. Why not?" Cyclops gave a patient shrug. "No harm in looking."

"Sorry there, friend. You have to speak up. I don't hear so well in my right ear from a drunken, parotic blow in a fight over some smartass kid in my past who is now in a wing locked up tight in a white garberdine."

"I said . . . sure . . . why . . ." But Cyclops could not utter a further word on account of a sharp, spontaneous pain that occurred in his side, and continued to cut deeper still, like a dog's nails, into his gut, which, in turn, made both his skull and bowels crack and burn in unison. It felt to the Cyclops as if a sharp-toothed jaw was biting down into the four corners of his stomach; as if his very stomach was a quadrilateral, a 150 and one-twelfth inches across. "Via dolor rosa!" he cried out as his bowels seem to split from within and a gushing, gurgling musical whine from deep inside his rectum took him for a spin. "The chaff shall perish with a double heart. The lips and the tongue cut off from my right mind!"

Sham leaped forward. "What is it? What's the matter?"

"I think it's my taenia coli. I'm sure of it . . . It has a lot to do with the trinity, as it is present only as three bands!"

"What are you talking about?" Sham said. "What three bands? What are you? A musician?"

"No! No! No! Not those kind of bands! The islands of Langerhans!" Cyclops grabbed at his stomach moaning with each grunt of pain. Vertigo, nausea, and indigestion shot through him like triplets of bad poetry. But even more than that, the uncomfortable sensations came on so suddenly and with such dramatic intensity that it felt *more,* more like *coup de théâtre, coup de 'état* or, at the very least, *coup de grâce.* "Maybe it's the Big *C.* I can't tell. It keeps traveling in legions. Oh, Thomas! Moore! How you do take the cut, divine tree. Cast a leglen-girth and baby make three. The Big C!"

"You don't mean Christmas, do you? A visit from St. Nick? Harpers, musicians, pipers and trumpeters, craftsman of whatever craft he be, craftsman of domesticity. Is Christmas moving through you in *July?*"

"No! No! No!" Cyclops winced with another spasm of blades in the gut. "The Jew doesn't lie! It's the duodenum!"

"Are you talking about the duo perchance? The Denim? They made a splash in the fashion world awhile back, but it still makes no sense!"

"Of course it doesn't! The duodenum, you fool! The one that produces three enzymes, next to the jejunum . . . god! Must eye be empty after death?! Ba Ba soulroaming the cinerary screen after a harrowing journey. O! Sir! Is this it? No! It's the cecum now! In the right iliac fossa! Oh! For Troy! It's . . . its got my pylorus and it's going for my sphincter of oddi adjacent to my ampulla of vater!" The Cyclops squirmed on the floor. "O, in tharm's way! No, no . . . not my . . . peyer's patches! Peristalsis!"

"What can I do to help?" Sam cried in confusion. "What Sphinx are you talking about? With your one eye I took you for Greek, not Egyptian."

"Fistula-in-ano!"

Sham rolled up his sleeve. "I don't understand! You want me to put my fist in your . . . *ano?"*

The Cyclops could bear the pain no longer. Like an involuntary reflex, it was beyond his conscious control. He attempted to struggle to his knees, but the pain shooting down into the very rocky crevices of his anus dragged him back to the earth as though a ceremonial iron cross was bearing down upon his shoulders, lumping him to the floor in a cromlech heap. His hairy, mythical body became locked in various military positions. One moment – his ass was elevated upright into the air; the next – it was pressed against the very floor boards beneath him. Pain, pure and simple, was taking this moment to live up to its disguised name of Ol' Mummer (B. of B.K.). But what pain! Soldiers, martyrs, legions, prisoners of war, accused heretics and witches never experienced such agony! Not at End-or? Nor in combat, nor on the rack, nor the stake where the butcher makes orts for squeals. In the vortex of his rectum, he could not only feel but also hear the *Symphony Fantastique!* blasting *March to the Scaffold* and *Dream of a Witches' Sabbath* all at once, the secretions playing havoc with the bits of gristle and bone in his descending colon . . . the ministers of the go spel (the key jumped 1619 to 11891) carrying glasses filled to the rim with French wine that actually turns out to be the blood and slime from a mass slaughter of chewed glasses . . . Nazi guards carrying buckets of abdominal muscle juice, perforated stomach secretion, *Borscht*-style, several moist flakes of digested meat, severed limbs, tongues, brains, vaginas and testicles all reduced to a uniform, modest brew, a brown stew that resembles a fat, unwashed Caddo, rather eyeish, soused in Moctezuma's diarrhea, resurrected into a soup, hollandaise-sauce, but a gravy-brown, chunk fruit cocktail . . . unwarranted pis in the anal track (maybe due to the shattered French wine glasses), cutting, slicing, jagged pieces swimming downward like piranha poop with jagged teeth and rivose fins toward the Isle of Anus, and forming mountains, dangerous precipices, sanguinary cities, BMs the size of Berlin – red-drenched, serpentinous veins in the hardening walls that held within the soft, syrupy, polymorphous centers of Puce liquid, of gram-negative bacteria – a Polyphemus – fiery volcanic shit that squirts like serpents' spit after an excessive appetite of beans, broccoli and baby calves' head, running snot mix of green ice cream, asparagus tips, chopped spinach, minced garlic, whole oysters, sturgeon, Sauerbraten, eggs, yolks and ovaries, yid kichlach in the shape of diamonds, holey paper bags of genital vomit, reconsumed, chunks of polypoid membranes grounded with meat Paraclete, papoose-style, with shreds of sauce *a la pap smear*, blue-ghost tuna, mucous, shell-shocked, carnage-scented cream with slivers of cannibal crap, cardinal, car-sick, sperm-filled, chocolate-coated catechumens with cat distemper anal grease, smearing, in his gums and ears, and one gigantic belch from within the Cyclops's depth drags off the bottom of his terminal ileum – (and shoots up through the esophagus!) a warm, urine, shit-serum dribble that leaks out the corners of his mouth and down his shoulders, *drip, drip, drip. Couldn't put the kibosh on?* Another belch *urrrrp!* and the implosion from within sends up a BM W(hale) in disguise, like the birth of Rushmore, rushing to the throne; his intestines, an instant runway for desperate, backed up anal debris that instead of shooting out one orifice finds freedom squirting out another. Chunks of yesterday's casserole, gaseous, pelvis-shocked buttermilk thickened to a brown, crude crumb cake helplessly got wedged between his teeth as he coughed out sticky flakes of it that sailed forth on a short-term voyage that terminated against the wall, the same wall rising above the common level. The wall of lamentations, enclosing the inside, assuring the delay of both the feminine matter and the masculine spirit. And then the Cyclops's widened mouth became an exit for a black trumpeted tidal wave that rained across the room, and Sham got doused . . . nay baptized . . . in a dirty deity that he somehow misconstrued as being the abdominable wash of the body.

Zero in

Cyclops could hardly withstand the pain, and he needed assistance badly. But now poor Sham was reeling about the room, miserably coated in bacteria; round, rod-like spiral filaments by the thousands were clinging to his skin, body, and bones in true rupicolous fashion. His clothes were soaked in a defecation aftermath of backwash – regergitated, basted BM coats. He was screaming and could barely see, his eyes secreting an ex-laxative serum; the stench . . . *a la delirium* . . . like cabbage spittle from a heated cow.

Sham vomited instantly and proceeded to slip in his own makings; and everytime he attempted to stand he slipped yet again under a new reign of the Cyclops's vomit, now intermingled with his own emesis.

The Cyclops's colon screeched crazily and broken debris began to slide down and out. Hastily, Cyclops unbuckled his pants and pushed them down to his knees. Where he lay upon the floor in a sideward fetal position, his exposed dong stretched longer than a pussy galore, brown-skinned and rivulose. The sprout was still glistening from past nocturnal emissions; his penis was nearly the length of a boulevard, flimsy, but growing, forever buoyant, bounding forward, even while his rectum shot forth dangerous hints of deadly gas. An inflammatory sore sat like a just-fed horsefly on the left cheek of his hairy ass. His lively farts smelt like bochilism, threatened to scomfish, and he tried, in spite of himself, to warn Sham that a mass of anal mud was about to christen the room. Sham could sense it coming too, and with desperate cries of anticipation he managed to climb to his knees, but not before a black, monstrous wave exploded and caught him *smack!* against his face, wheeling him head-over-heels in the tide against the wall. Out of the absolute darkness that was now his head two stunned and disbelieving eyes reappeared; and the poor fellow choked as hot, turdy soup scrambled down his throat.

The Cyclops groaned (or was that the resounding cries of his anus as it shot forth a complete round of despair in a backended reversal *macabre musical* of helminthemesis?). The Cyclops was thinking *he's sorry, he can't help it,* but his Zulu penis wouldn't dare let him apologize, and the outbursts of sickness had become the flow, the black jet river, hosing Sham down to oblivion. Alas, no fire was ever put out while sin abounds; and, furthermore, mixed in the mess was not only an elaborate composition of fecal matter, but an *arrangement*, the color and texture of death clothed with an Al Jolson resonance. For now the black, liquidy catastrophe consuming the office began to move in various places; for, indeed, in the muddy river were the living, wiggly forms of expelled tapeworms, sowbugs and medium-sized crustaceans (forms of a *foreign disease? . . .* invisible alien crabs inbred?) that ate the male fernseed that was originally grave meat for the tapeworms. And like an army of Lapithae locked in a wild frenzy of tarantism, hundreds of the creeping forms swarmed over Sam Sham and started to consume his flesh, now made soft and chewable under a warm blanket of discharged rectal lava. Sam didn't scream. He shrieked. He howled paranormal sirens of pain coupled with a hypermimia, more like an actor's truculent curse. The tapeworms with enemy counter-offensive teeth drilled through Sam's cheeks in a *coup de main*, while swarms of pugnacious worms made their way inside Sam's mouth; they used his tongue for a slide in which to course down to his stomach and gorge on the *pièce de résistance* (his twelve very vital organs within, plus the vantage loaf). Barely inaudible, indeed, barely comprehensible, Sam managed to express a primitive, bitten-through rendition of plain English. "Cy . . . clops . . . pl . . . ease . . . hel . . .p me!" His last words as Sam Sham were mingled with blood and pitiful bits of battle-broken organs, now reappearing in spasms that Sam's throat continued to spew. With his tongue he mashed wounded tapeworms against the roof of his mouth and began to chew, thickly, in a last desperate attempt to defend his very inner fortress; but a fresh horde of creatures, soaked in defecation, stormed through the chewed holes in his cheeks and slid straight down to get the last remnants of him; the gurgling sounds they made as they descended made Sam Sham appear as though he was gagging a mournful, expensive tune from a lost, needlepointed Camelot.

The office fell into fatigueable silence. Sam Sham was no longer Sam Sham. He was now a miserable mass of cycloptic waste; one millimicron of a man, a most dubitable fatality. Whatever form there once was within the disgusting quagmire, now not a limb moved nor a muscle twitched. It was safe to say that Sam Sham was gone. Time was the only thing beating, the only thing able to transpierce the massive silence. The office itself looked to be the disaster sight of some catastrophic soil pipe explosion. Bloody Gettysburg, the morning after the note perished, could not have looked much different. Still recognizable, the Cyclops lay upon the floor, double-jointed, contorted in such a manner as to be locked in a position of *soixante-neuf*. It was obvious that he was still alive, as his heavy breathing suggested, and there was certainly no question as to his state of exhaustion. It appeared as though the worst of the deluge were truly over. All the Cyclops could recall, aside from the pain and the utter spontaneousness of the cyclonic attack, was the manner in which he had farded Sam's face to obscurity with his own special brand of torrential cosmetics. Nevertheless, it was a perfidious tragedy. One preinnocent dead man, one bowel-angst Cyclops, one modest office fallen in decay. In some circles this scene would definitely stand as an unquestionable offense; while in other settings, perhaps less official, it could have been misconstrued as a bizarre, nightmarish, bestiarian offertory. Clearly what was needed here was a scullion to wash away the overwhelming spill. And who better to do it than the mother of mayhem herself – ol' Moll – the same who gave birth to what later became known as the Mohock Gang of Twelve.

Cyclops felt his head pounding with purposeful (and not so purposeful) facts and figures, even as his bowels pitifully made a last ditch attempt at a feeble fart (though, in 'deed,' there was not a shred of liquid waste left in him).

How similar the words: *parasite* and *paradise*. What clearer duality of the words is there than that of the very scene before the Cyclops? For was not man born of the mud, the clay and the dust? Did he not rise from such, even as god had formed man and had given him breath, transpiercing the very dirt of his primevous nostrils? Yes, it was more than just a mere paralogism. There was some basis to it. For as stercoricolous monsters come, so must stercoricolous monsters go. Was it not demonstrated here, to be so?

Such a time to get philisophical, Cyclops thought. It were as though the Cyclops had somehow fallen into a sudden parashah, and was dividing the circumstances of his accident into five appropriate categories: one of which was origin, another was law, another was priests, another was fighting men, and still another was departure. But was not law, in *itself*, a synonym for science? For even as Cyclops lay in the dung of his own bodily expression, he was seized by the thought that the brown, dark gray color that formerly had been concealed (as are heaven and hell) was actually a parapet of sorts. For in its massive state it was like a wall, an elevation of earth (howbeit, waste) that served to protect. But protect what? The dead? Possibly. After all, what are coffins for if not for tombstones, cemeteries or fences? And continuing on with the paralogism of this plot – didn't god transpierce those very walls of the dead in order to raise again the spirits paraffined in various seals of sleep?

Why shouldn't the Cyclops give it the old college try, being an old collegiate and all, with a degree from New College MulliGrubs, after having waded through all of the pseudodoxes briskly expounded from that particular institution, and reemerging with a Doctorit in British, American, Scientific, International, Commercial English? To raise the dead and to bring up a new Og form, likened unto his own, up from the depths of the body – the body god, the body earth – just might prove to be a nobel deed in disguise. How much time had elapsed since the deluge? The Cyclops was not certain. But already in the mire he could see parasitosis taking place as countless numbers of procercoids and other indefinable parasites wiggled, swarmed and infested the very mound that priorly was Sam Sham – the very black mound of Mullock from which springs the cities of the giant Paraponera. From the primitive waspish mother with a differentiated brood of young daughters to the highly complex cities of modern Dolichoderine – from a single primitive cell to colonies and tribes recapitulated to glory, the general fashion in which the great majority of cities arise, ward life was warpish. The city is born from the egg – the mound – and from the long lived-by nature of the mother does each succeeding generation grow, whether in its lowest form (a pack of loosely Associated Carnivorous Creatures exacting immediate social service from all its members) or in its highest form (huge and independent communities investing immense reserves of energy in the perfecting of its members). Both shall be noted in one breath: Dinoponera erectus. Bellum internecinum.

The Cyclops rose to his feet. Indeed, there was pain and exhaustion. His bowels creaked, still rickety from the ordeal. In a standing position the Cyclops felt ramulose, as if just so many invisible yet formidable paradise shoots were attempting to pull him down. But they all seemed too young, still too new to do the job right.

And so Cyclops stood before the shittah, the uncertain roots of yet another formidable tree – in this case, the body, the temporary abode of the soul, a shit-ornamental sealed box for reserving the host – and sang

"We'll roll, we'll roll the chariot along
If the Devil's in the way we will roll it over him strong
The collection, on to the morgue, is our marching song
It's a song, where it's been, is full of sin
It's the same the whole world over:
Just roll me over in the clover."

No. Cyclops was not suffering from some fashion of *tabes dorsalis* that typically presented itself in three stages, but was specifically experiencing a synoptic problem regarding transformation, especially as it pertains to a specialized dis-harmony between the marks in Lu's mat. *Welcome.* Stretching forth his hands, the Cyclops proceeded to wave them in six circular motions, three times above the mound that was formerly Sam Sham. *Warmed-over rist can taste just as nice as when first consumed with butter in ice.* Chepe – the warmonger. Richthofen – the warm spot. Stalin – the xenogenesis.

"I'm so sorry for old Adam
For he never had no mammy
Though he had a horse named Sammy Bill
Who kept him mighty still
Two white horses, and the other one was 'nil

O paradise!"

Communicating to a nonvigorous movement that is now commanded to rise on webbed hind feet, and take fuehrer form, and bark back snappishly, and whimper and moan with quick erratic movements, and yawn and yield to further evolutions, the Cyclops hovered over the mound once known as Sam Sham. Even as the Cyclops fancied himself as a massive Yggdrasil, a great magical tree of life, did he bind the molecules and cells of the mound (the parasite, the beast, the waste that fell yestreen, and took another day to grow into an ongoing, forever evolving *Ugh*) together.

And the Cyclops said, "Let me make Ugh into a strange new image, after a likeness that is composed of all there is in one. Let him be of service, as his numbers show. Even locks have their parr marks. *Âme de boue.* And let me spit a wise Kvasir to answer all questions. Niaiserie. Spit! Spit! Spit! And do away with It." And the very walls of the parapet did stiffin the lifeless body, and shield the viscera not only from the rib and the heart but from the deep instinctive appetite buried secretly within.

The Cyclops conjured up assorted opening inspirational statements that leaned heavily on glossolalia. The first words spoken were related to the one who loves butter and honey. The one who loves to french cook and eat. "I say, *Ahhh!* Salute! Sniff. Suffer it to be Julia *Batakusai.* So now the time is fulfilled with a holy kiss. Melissa, how is it that you sought me among all the saints? Buzz Ida and tell her that I am in my secret chambers with eagles overhead. For I am he who follows in a triad from raw food to cooked food to consumed food. I had started with a shoulder of mutton. It was a butcher's dream. A recipe kept secret since time began. 'Tis a mystery. From there I went to codfish heads and salmon fillets. The catalytic mouthpiece of a fairenough speech. For the sea myths that surrounded you in the desert. The poor, the mournful, the meek, the hungry, serve them their belly. I came up with a certain recipe to treat the sickness that I found to exist down below under my bruised feet. The wound stripe of civilization, cut up by ensis.

"First of all, be sure to season your ground steak with salt, tomato juice and onion. Cut thin slices of three-day old bread into various shapes. Toast the bread on one side and spread butter on the other. Spread the buttered side with a fat layer of the ground steak mixture and broil for a short time until the meat browns. The second phase consists of codfish balls. Take the heads of the codfish and mix them with equal parts of human testicles. Add one cup wine and form into balls. Bake in a 666-degree F. oven for 6 minutes; until spring. Serve piping hot with refrigerated cumuppance and pickled relish as a condiment, with locks on hand."

(The Cyclops had actually applied this very same condiment along with an added mixture of lemon juice, egg yolk, and apple extract onto a large condyloma near his anus years ago and had found it to be, when applied generously and over a week's period of time, an excellent treatment in the removal of warty growths.)

It is a well known fact that a good cook is actually a happy mingling of both scientist and artist. One who knows something of the compensation and the acceptable behavior of foods, as well as the bodily functions resulting from the consumption of such, must always remember that within a theory of relativity all measurements are level. It is also important to note (as in the crowing hen) that a skilled cook always plans meals in triplicates. In order to last, one must plan three suppers around, for example, boned, smoked shoulder butt, called by some as daisy ham or bacon (with salt and alcohol under a bed of lettuce . . .). Assuming, of course, that this course has passed the rigors of any related concordat. For, indeed, 'rigors' is an entirely appropriate word here, as it is nearly impossible to get a Bacon and a Fryer to see eye-to-eye, on the same plate, at any given time of consumption, no matter who may be being served at the table.

Specifics here should be considered. For one cannot do anything that includes raising the dead *or* creating an entirely new recipe from scratch without first getting a firm grip on the fine art of specifics, such as the Principal of Hamlet, which states that *all things are possible*, or the Principal of La Place, which states that *the weight of the evidence ought to be proportioned to the strangeness of the facts*, as they might relate to both syntaxic and parataxic experiences according to Harry and Dr. Syntax. Cyclops took his cue from Archbishop Ussher, who was able to pinpoint the exact date for the creation of the earth: (4004 B.C. at 9 o'clock of a

Friday morning). He discovered this by first arriving at the origin of the American Indians by simple *de-deucing* of the composition of the red skin Sequoa of any select number of subjects by dissection, and applying his findings with any given number of variables available to him at the time of his study of Pretheosophy, and thereby divining the American red Indian as being the direct offspring of Egyptian, Phoenician, Greek, Roman, Chinese, Japanese, Welsh and Irish blood, and the Lost Ten Tribes of Israel; *wink:* hanky-panky, channeling, while consuming a herring freefloating from India to Mars before 1997.

During the Ice Age, which was an Italian happening, meaning that it took place in and around the region of what today is commonly referred to as Mt. Etna (Caduta! Quack! Quack! Quack! Heads up!), the Archbishop, contrary to religion, was of a complete scientific mind, and thereby based his aforementioned calculations not upon divine inspiration, as once believed, but upon an ancient technique of carbon 14 dating, whereby he used home basement tests of organic substances to compute the residue of a radioactive isotope of carbon, designated as carbon 14, which is present in fixed proportions in living organisms, and which disintegrates at a constant measureable rate after the death of its host, thus acting as an atomic clock pinpointing the specific essence of the subjects tested, and thereby came uppance with his own overall conclusions while stigmatized in an M.B. waistcoat.

While Cyclops rotated his hands in circular motions over the mound (which he referred to as *Ugh,* for *ubiquitous gorgoneion hitlerite*) and concentrated, most diligently, on raising the worm-infested mound into a living form bearing height, breadth and depth in pure triadic fashion, he extended the metamere to include the triad of the offspring of Uranus: the deep-breasted earth as envisioned by Elijah J. Bond and William Fuld in Baltimore.

"Top of the world Ma!" the Cyclops cried with a faithful Jamesian tear in his eye (like a tear shed from the work of a sclerotome) as he proceeded to carry on the most important work of creation thus far. "My Trinity: *Brontes, Steropes* and *Arges.* And my grandkids' stew: *Cottus, Briareus,* and *Gyges.* Such beautiful kids. From their shoulders' cut sprang a hundred invincible arms, and above these rose fifty heads attached to their backs, and a rumprack. Cute little Centimanes. Nice Scolopendra. Precious Scolytids. In their winter coats. And there you have it. My family tree, à la seeded Revelation*ee.* A scobiform gentility. I bring them up from the depths of Ugh with gleaming steel, a sharp sickle, the Absolute Plan, a kielbasa, and a kickstand. *Dochaku!*"

Cyclops knew one thing to be certain. This was a secret matter, this matter of creation; mystical . . . thaumaturgic . . . with Cyclops, the thaumaturgist, presenting the origination of Ugh by a series of hierarchically descending radiations from the godhead, through intermediate stages, to matter. The method employed was by a cipher. The symbol *0* denoting the absence of a celestial body on a logarithmic scale, reduced to a nonentity – the only method of transforming a holey text into a holy text in order to conceal its ultimate identity, *ex silentio.* Adam and Eve playing AZ and 19 playing Cyclops and Ida.

Cyclops was going to call upon his wife, Ida, so that she would be able to witness this berserk act of creation and therefore be very proud of him. But once he had connected to her, via omni-waves, she responded that she'd love more than anything to be there, but at the moment she was caught bare between the Scylla of her spiritual animus and the Charybdis of a whirling spirit, which was demanding that she reject consciousness altogether and identify solely with the apologetic Christi feminine in the walking streets. For in the realm of anity, love means never having to say *'mi scusi'* while standing framed and bearing a geometric shape into the dark and early hours. She did, however, promise to catch his act much later on Fool's Replay – during the Morris Dance, when the Miller's son bangs the heads of the gaping spectators with a bladder full of peas, with their eyes all hollowed out by the chisels of stonedeaf Kings.

TAXIS!

This is the night journey through god's mind; death-and-rebirth, find. The darkness here represents not so much the *mystery* as the dubitable condition of god, the shallowness of his atrabilious existence, the futility of his ideas, and the trivial routines of life as he had designed them, like a hungover physician compounding a prescription most extemporaneously. Here rests, in darkness, the tragic idea of the earth and its concomitant universe, the father ocean in whose depths all ideas are bred; herein rests the absurd notion that the displaced body parts of the world can be restored simply by sliding back and venturing deep into the contrite darkness where each and everything was born – that to go beyond the first birth, to venture deeper still, until one comes upon the seed of which *all* becomes unborn, past the symbols, the strong, sober souls not ready-made that nonetheless sleep, rocked to unconsciousness by the heartbeat of some long forgotten tragedy, is to begin to solve the riddle of the spirit of Mindererus; herein rests the absurd notion that the mechanical formula encrusted upon the living (roughly speaking, piss and sweat) *saves*. For *nothing* really dies. It merely returns to the mind of god; howbeit, there are countless minds to encounter, some of which interflow into an interdictory goulash.

THE DEATH OF DEATH TALK

Act III, Scene ii

They're shooting a film.

AZ is still suffering from a tremendous hangover from having lost a $5.00 bet (the agent and symbol of *his* death) that he had made six nights ago, insisting that he could drink 19 under the table. 19, meanwhile, has just passed out upon the floor directly underneath the table where the two of them had been courageously drinking, somewhere near the Three Taverns.

AZ proceeds descendingly over to the small round table and sits down upon one of the three chairs positioned around it. There is still a distinct mycodermic scum above his upper lip, although it is distinctly bubbling away even as his cloudy thoughts pop inside of him. He rubs his forehead like one suffering from a massive hangover is prone to do, and groans like a pelican in agony that can find no place to rest on the cliff, due to lack of a proper hyperfocal distance. He mumbles an assortment of complaints pertaining to the burning pain in his head, and stomachs a borborygmus, and follows this with a further loosening of his tie, as well as his *dülfer rappel*, to lessen the pressure of an active mormal on his left sin. AZ's look is completely disheveled. He is in need of a shave and a clipping, but by the look of his corrupt good manner, it seems likely that he will not be attending to either one soon.

AZ looks to be about thirty-three, six feet, broad-shouldered, deep-chested, slightly off-balanced with a boy-scoutish quality of head, with his hair parted down in a jagged middle line and held transfixed in a raise of butch wax; his face is clearly broken down with frozen lava folds of skin, thus confounding his otherwise blazing-reddish hair. He has a mustache with a bare spot in its center like some kind of offensive crack related to a monk's tonsure; and he is sucking on a khella, i.e., bishop's weed. Actually, AZ is sir alpha-omega, a discussant and/or one-eyed cus if ever there was one; and the heap on the floor is in a strange evolutionary way a sugarcained Mrs. Alving/Sam Sham. It's clear that AZ's/19's marriage has gone sour over thyme; howbeit, it's been thousands of years since thyme has seen its flowering time.

AZ is forever watchful and kicking the heap, 19, in the foot.

AZ: "Get up, you old broad! Sleep is all you're good-for-nothin'. Nothin' except you drunk yourself high-strung-donecumpoop for the past few eons. Get up, you cad-a-lack ewe. You old bunker, self-destruct, water-logged sea biscuit. You gimmer you. Get up you fustilug before I sips ya' another drink and makes ya' lay down again for a thousand years. You're a fine armful now, why, with those forty-four tons you gained in your seat. I should gives ya' a scrambled egg breakfast like a hole-in-the-head, god damn it to hell with gas! I would hope you're not as big a glutton as you sound; but from the stench alone, you could hardly be stenophagous. I should gip you good and clean right here on the peer. This here is the longest journey I ever took, with me bone in a pentad and me legs and feet in a jodhpur, off the book, whilst you're breaking wind in a constant gale. You see, I kept my rhyme so's to cock up some new sin to touch . . . No! No! No! Ain't that a shit in the pants with a dog's tapeworm thrown in?" (AZ digs deep into his back pocket and pulls out pages of the script, all worn and wrinkled. And as best he can in his hungover state, he commences to read off their folds, word per clumsy word.) "I'll . . . bet . . . they're . . . cooking . . . up . . . some . . . new . . . scheme . . to . . touch . . . the . . old . . man . . ."

AZ reaches into a hidden pocket of his jacket and pulls out a long green cigar that he lights up.

AZ: "This cigar tastes like scorpion shit. It's no wonder I got it dirt cheap from a stand up on the corner of Serpent and Vine. Eme Tom Cob Uttocks . . . Leigh gone desire . . . the last of the seven worthies. Who took a loan on Tom's grey mare on which to ride to Wid Cum Fair? When the wind whistles cold all down my knee, appears Tom's old mare ghostly white as can be. It's all so rev rev revelationary. Grasshopper gherkin corn eatin' plague. Chew me a husk . . . Say there Sadie, Sadie, Sadie married lady. Come on you ol' sadducee. Get up before I make you a quick turnover and plug me in for a fine profit. You know it's bad luck to sleep in your own stupor. Get up before I bite you a hung-strung that will have you smarting for a little season. Or I just might eat the fat of the land. Soil and all." (AZ pauses while he takes another puff off his cigar.) "Wow! What a fat and beautiful end you've got. What jazzy gams. It's like looking at a sick whale on the floor." (AZ starts to impersonate a foghorn. He cups his hands over his lips, thus turning them into a crude megaphone.) "Beached whale . . . Beached whale . . . Khidmatgar . . . *Omega! Omega!* . . . Come. Take this behemoth off my table." (Makes a noise like a foghorn again.) "Look Ma . . . it's the Old Man of the Sea in the Navel Academy. O for sin. Bad. Drunk as Nereus. Forget the lint. That's-a-some-a-big-ga-fish. With a tail like a cedar. Look at you there. You can draw up Jordan in your mouth, but as soon as your head smacks the floor you're off and out. And ten foghorns couldn't wake you." (Does four or five foghorn impressions.) "I'll bet me eyes you're up-and-out snoring, god damn racket what you make. The Whale . . . I'll know her trumpet. If I can remember John Dunk, a dim fog off the beach. But far back I'll recall a trumpet talking with me on the backside. On the throne. A book. Seven horns I recall. She runs out with *Het Achterhuis*, the house behind the stall, and seven and a half guilders bring about her fall. Seven trumpets to sound. Angels all cast into the sea like dark whales. When they begin to sound, the mystery of god should be finished . . . whatever." (AZ starts to cry. He raises the pages he clasps in his hands above his head.) " . . . And take the little book, Miepgies, that is open in the hand of the browned angel that standeth upon the sugary sea, and take it and eat it up along with a dose of liveingite with a male virility to lead to sleep. Bit herb me to ob live, he in." (He stuffs the pages into his mouth. While he cries he begins to chew and chew and chew, and very soon his belly becomes bitter. And still crying, he begins to fart and fart and fart anew. Again, he kicks 19 in the shoe.) "Get up you sea cow so we can start to plague the stage with resurrected angels. Get up you dung buggy and drop a few. Farting like a trumpet you. In one hole and out the other like two fricatrices doing a bread and butter. And me, in me good jodo fashion, crying *Amida* as pure as you please. If you don't get up, smack on your head I'll jap-blast a tune and it won't be some enchanted evening Les, I promise you that. And your nose will be pierced through with a smoggy afternoon." (AZ farts high and sweet.) "Not some, but maybe . . . I whistle a happy tune. Come on, 19, you old witch with a broom, antihousewifegoon in the catsup sky. Remember when you said in your heart," (AZ starts to mimic her.) "I sit a Queen and am no widow, and shall see no sorrow. Well, it's just the beginning of sorrows. While they're all making cakes to the queen of heaven and pouring drinks to gods, I'll be devouring your black chamber in the backrow. Wake up, toot-toot-tootsie. Don't cry. Yuck! Yuck! Yuck! Don't lie. You're gonna be sorry. Just wait and see. Death and mourning, famine forming, Ba-by-lon that migh-ty ci-ty." (Reprise) "One ho-ur and judg-ment come, burn-ing smoke fumes out the bung. Ba-by Ba-by-loony-here-it-cums. In one hour, judgment come." (AZ's little song ends in a throng of trumpets' blast, accented at the end with a tiny fart. Compliments, the Ass.) "You remember, honeybun? When I bellowed out my numbers one-by-one playing the zyklon in B-flat? Berime. Such formulas. How they poured forth my tongue. Material things exist only in so far as they are perceived to be symbols of authority and regimentation. O George Hollerith, George Holy earth, how mutilated your branches . . ." (Recites the following in Shakespearean tongue.) "And the city lieth four square, and the length is as large as the breadth, and the city with the reed, twelve thousand furlongs, and the walls a hundred and forty and four cubits. To the measure of a man, of an angel." (Starts to cry dramatically. Nay, melodramatically.) "And the building of the wall was of jasper, and the city was gold, sapphire, emerald, topaz, and a pinch of amethyst, with a bunker fit to size without any roaches." (Kicks an unresponsive 19.) "Get the jist Kicksy-wicksy? Formulas too old to worship before the cracking feat." (Kicks her feet again.) "This is some cardan joint we're in. Universal bowel motion, unchanged. Here, let me give it the old cardan shaft and a bun of power. I am Alfalfa and Omelet. Beat me to a froth. Spank me. Serve me so that, half-round, my buns are brown and bounce back with just a lightly pat. You remember? Don't look at me like that, transfixed with risus sardonicus. Vacantize those raised eyebrows. Sanitize that tetanustic grin. Bubbles, Monstro, where you been? Sin with your smile? The trial? Draw out leviathan with a hook. Speak soft words to me. Play servant and play with me bird. Look up." (19's face is still unseen.) "This is the kid's story." (Starts to cry.) "My dear, beloved Clops. Dreadful thing, but he was funny. Did you ever *peep* in and catch his first show like the pasty sparrow did? Alas . . . I was his Landlord and his rating was . . . low." (Sighs.) "Dear Clops, I tried. Oh Lord Peter. You'll really have to do something courageous. One for Jud Suss Riot, the other for the author of the general letter issue who did treat all trials and tribulations as a privilege rather than a blame, and yet a third for the gideon sleeping on the gueridon. In my embellished name, I wish to thank the Academy. In the garden of Play Toes. A crack in the mirror and the tongue aflame." (AZ looks down at 19.) "How dare you sleep beneath my lines. In my afterglow. Take the hook, my dear landgravine, and honor me, a landgrave. *Achtung.* Chirp. Peep."

AZ *transitio:* (He gives her another kick but to no avail.) "Nothing but a pig. A fat Irish pig that eats her own farrow. Could lick any bone and lap up the marrow." (AZ leans forward and shouts in her ear.) "Broke down my fence, did 'ya? Had a free swish in me pond, did 'ya? Too much lick her? Too much water? Got the belly ache? You should have been a real whore is what you should have been. Then you wouldn't be looking so foolish, fool that you are. Damned rot-turd in the gr . . . ass." (AZ looks around aggravatedly.) "Where's me shovel? Where's me thumbs? There they be with the meat under the table. Do you think for a minute your quietness fools me into thinking you're unavailable to me? Don't stir me laugh. The way you've spread yourself way over the universe like a price on a bed . . . a sailor over a map. Plurivorous, are ya? Come on, ya' ol' queen of the south. Jackson's Island, Glasscock's Island, eroded away. So civil of you, Miss. Rise up and condemn the lot. You filthy cotton tongue rotbutt. Talk about Broadway and lead roles . . . that's lead, Hershey dear. As in metal. As in metal in me affairs. Thick as lead. A bung slide to a room with a bath and a great big bar over the frame. It's a damn shame your mother can't see you now. The fust to keer fer ya'. Why I outta call the perlice. Gets the aunts involved and let em all eat out the müllerian body." (AZ mimicks a foghorn two more times.) "I have all the picnic pits in my heart for her especially now seeing you, Broadway Street loafer, flaunting your unconsciousness like this. Didn't it suffice knowing everything there is to know in the universe? Wasn't it good enough, you old egg scrambled aphid? Wasn't it good enough for 'ya? Not enough creature comfort? No. You're only impaler now and your eyes shine like two corn kernels in a roll of dogbless. Whatever manner you possessed was lost in some *pregenocized* scene from a grevious act. That little speckgrain of awareness you kept hidden between the skin of your teeth has slipped down, deep center green into the blubber bowels of your ungainly existence." (AZ makes another sound like a foghorn. It is obvious that he is in some kind of drunken condition by the badger-like squint in his eyes that he displays each and everytime his lips fall on the vowel *E*.) "The final curtain B.W. Then we pass the gate. Get ready, ducky. Get the speckfall. Get in your stool. You pegh like a cow in heat without a sonny to keep her warm. This is where you need to be. 9.99% down the path that leads to the tumbling sea, the fog so thick one could trip over a beached whale. Nay, I didn't meet a sole along the way. Everything lies so dead and unreal. Flat bottom marsh true, it be, purely palustrine. Nothing was what I was. Bottom weaver alone with myself on another stage where the word is untrue and a soul can hide only in what is false. You're nothing but a flipflopped prolepsis embued with proctitis." (AZ kicks her again in the foot.) "How much for ye blubber, B.W.? Out beyond the tide with the sandy bottom, was once the sandy shore. I lost me fiery bride and the feeling that I was part of the high sea and not the fog that is the ghost of the sea. The ghost, that is, a whore." (AZ stares down at 19 with the combination of disgust and pity.) "Don't look away from me. I'm who I was. Looks to me like you're the fish in the Pan. Living like a ghost. Don't you feel just terrible? Refuting the only question you would dare to be burdened with. Time weighing down your breasts so low to the ground even snakes can quench their thirst. Shoulds I succuss ya and see what's left to wet me kisser? On a mattress the bounce is more delightful, like on a wave as opposed to the shore, where I could dip my dainty tongue in the hole of a shell and taste tuna and salt in one gulp, while my finger socratizes the lower senses. Drunk, drunk drunk, drunk, drunkie drunk. What does it take to beat upon your drums? You never heard me bark before? Softly, like an obfusticated flower, I spread my petals to the piacular sun. O Satin, patron of the arts, whereforth art thou? Confused as the queen's tarts?" (AZ farts.) "O, there you are hiding, slipped out. And the stage stinketh even more than before, with heavy vapors full." (AZ looks down at 19.) "The vulgar audience has yet to understand what filth, despair and pessimism I hold in my hand, even to those morigerous handmaids who got down on their knees all night long. The weak-kneed Laodiceans. Even my buds, the Lao, upon their hearts they did search for a warm heartbeat of god as they read the Wicked Bible and the seventh commandment: thou shalt commit . . . And here he was, kissing mother above the knees somewhere between the trees of her forest green, where her red mouth was sweet as sea bread and the shy lock, butt wet with dew. And it was only 4:57 in the afternoon." (AZ kicks her again.) "Poor far burlesque queen. Doesn't get a word of it. Does she? Just lies there kidding herself, denying me my just rewards. Just lies there like an ill-formed mortorio." (AZ falls on top of her and begins to engage in a dry fuck.) "When did Mama go to bed and leave us alone in her stead? You cicada, I, killer. Dig her. From downstairs, had there been anyone there, they would have heard me chuckling, moving around." (AZ increases his rhythmic humping on top of 19.) "All are running, playing freely, getting the serpent to dip its head in the drink and have a shot or two. Drink hardy, moby hunting fields, drink the dog's nose dripping wet and hope to god she doesn't come dragging down and spots us messin' around in the white house 'cause we know, 'cause we can pray, she's nothing but a dry ghost haunting the past, back before I was born." (His humping increases and he starts to moan on top of 19.) "You make me say . . ." (AZ sings) "thanks for the memories. Of dicking in the grain. Of grabbing on the mane. A dash of salt of course. A cock the size a horse. Hiding at three to eight. After the dinner plate . . ." (AZ stops singing.) "Your father is great, generous, and noble. And my dear child, such an innocent dear kind, when she came bobbing into the world among the trees, all moschate from a previous squeeze, she showed such promise, such a mind. When I think upon her, on top of you, now limp, then fine as a string taut on a violin, god bless her beautiful find. Bursting with the kind of sea a ship could go down in, gleefully. What? Did you take me to be a fugie? This, a fighting cock, dipped first in Scot?" (Begins to hump again.) "We're all alone, ducky, and there's no cure for this kind of poverty. O, let us go and cut the shrubbery." (Mocks a cry with tears.) "You lie again? Didn't you have enough before? Didn't you learn enough before? The truth was, you promised more cakes 'n' pancakes. Shrove Tuesday over in the clover. Ashes to ashes, having burned the housewife's loaves on Wednesday." (Starts to laugh.) "Poor thing. What's happened to our game? Whose play is it? *Bicorn and Chichevache in the Same Pen?* Push comes to shove." (AZ hollers as he apparently climaxes and collapses exhaustedly on top of 19. He slides backward, dragging himself off of her, and sits up. He still seems to be suffering from a tremendous hangover, even though there is no clear indication that he has actually been crying or drinking. However, he goes through all of the *mouillé* sounds one would make in repairing themselves after a heavy cry. He speaks now, more in a reflection; and though words can be heard, there is a sense that he is speaking only to himself. His voice is low, somber and heavy in tone, and seems full of regret and remorse.) "My kindgom for a telotaxis. The only escape. All hail god. Father don't lie. I am a liar. But blessed with a good memory. Ever since before I was born to earth, I was but a seed in the sea of a vast universe. Not my own. What growth I found. What form *I thought* to find on my own; yet, in my way, I felt struggle and pain. Who could place the blame for such a state on anyone but myself? Still, I evolved from that original seed in the universe. Floating . . . O . . . such a Floating Academy. The hulk of which were the source of much lively communications. Wiggly worms. And I do recall having been something more even before the seed. *What things?* An image falling. I can quietly define, even in my own mind; but I felt a plan imposed, but not without a maze imprinted in my mind that later became the seed in the sea of my composition. If I could only tap back into that floating place, elusive for even I, a god, a maze to find. I always feared it would change and I would be taken away and put into a place of blame. And no matter whatever I made thereafter, I would still be cursed for having perfected an otherwise imperfect universe. Such is my lot, having the tiniest of spots upon my heart. I do grieve, being a true theopaschite. I know, because I fell. O, A stab to the heart, and they dared to say I gave up the ghost. I failed, and from it I tried to commit suicide; howbeit, I failed, a god, murdered, impaled *nos*, I called my own. Liars all. They wrote the words that would stand-in as signs and wonders. But I know that in holding back the price even my wife got a start of the blade. If only I could have faced-down to the world, even now thawing out in hell. My devils get wrinkled as I draw up my sanbenito. And I, a creature in a foreign land between the sun and the moon, I fell, a part of me hoping I could cut off what I felt was a loose string. Even later, when an image and a likeness fell, and even later still, when a sleeping brother fell, there was no compensation for my own poverty but twelve stars in my head. Alone, I cried, 'Why me?' A jib rat, holed out in a ho' tel, coming and going, to and fro, the tvtobath, giving info to the Mass, purring me game, an optimistic progress to enriched fields. A god who had created an earth in order to dispose of his own hulk, bred of a universe, well-done, where there was no warmth. This goddamned play doesn't have much the same punch as before. In essence it ruined me. A small broken king on a terrene stage with an easy fortune – ten billion graves and a queen who loved enough to rave, this god of dust. Whatever hope I braved I lost, even before I was tipped from the shelf. What I keep to torture me? The word I loved to hear. *Subtile à fond.* The poetry of my gifts, I beared. How they sang for me." (AZ suddenly thinks to hear something in the darkness.) "Who is that? What the devil is it laughing at? What audience? At life there is none, god knows. She's dead asleep upon the floor, desition on the brain. Not even the salpinx roars. My estranged glumdalclitchan bedfellow. For glory-hole's sake, who laughs? Who speaks? Moving above and beyond me on this small stage, amidst the junk, a tailing ghost haunting my past? Straining my ears, listening for the slightest sound with a finger plugged in either one. The fog dripping from the universe like hurried alcohol, full moon, half gone. Water foaming the spray of the sea, gone. Masts glittering white moonlight, gone. Dissolved in the sea, gone. Past future, gone. To life itself, gone. No sound of human, kind or not. But a laugh?

Dreaming. Not eye. Not even from where we slept together, she and I. Lying alone on a beach, a staged garden."

AZ listens intently in the darkness. "I think I hear her moving about . . . moving above me and perhaps just beyond me. Yes, I have been waiting. And how she may strike in the dark, I know not. Massive, inconclusive attacks, clouded in dust, gas. This obscure warfare races with forspent sounds. But me seeking in hide comes to a stop now. I doubt if she will knock; howbeit, the power was never lost. She only held it in while she lived a tired child beneath me. She will not knock for me. This I know. I did become drunk with the glory that I created. And the exploding rhythm of it I did envelope. I remembered being anchored to a rock like a crab. I remember being covered by glaucous angels and saints, cheap renditions of seaweed and kelp. A mass burned for the ashes. Swaying in the oily tide, they did serve to conceal me as I dissolved in the sea. What becomes of the king when he is left exposed upon the ocean and every chamber is bare but his? All of his delights are lights turned down, except in darkness. Pieces, inferior moves, but with an ability to destroy. Prawns with a stroke. Without a kingdom a king is toyless and waxes old as moss. I can feel them closing in, slipping over the rocks through the darkness, into the bog. Truly, at one time they wanted to belong. But I, a king, kept them at Arms distance. A god does not live in his kind, just as a poet does not live in his words; for soon as they are spoken they have left him, and are devoured by all. The old sensations swimming back – surprise, wonder, mystery in irreverent order. First come, last served. Follow the acolyte's candles if you come in a mass. I should have put a lighthouse out there in the darkness to warn the oncoming dyslogia of its tagging awareness. What Black Hole cannot stand a little blindness? But no. When I thought of earth I fashioned the dead waltzing with fellow prancers, dust to dust, whirling, the prickly horses. *The state that man was in, both with the voice, both with the world – a cheapened stage with doors as paper thin as fusumas, man did at one time pursue me, in fact, but more in order to know me than to do me in. Noli me tangere.*" (Laughs.) "How I did run from man, quickly, strapping my traveling bag and dashing backward whenever he was close at hand. Leaping from the stalk, touch me not. What I feared was being known and exposing my character. Wet weary roads, I detoured man north-on to get him nowhere slow so as to give me a spell of a good time to vanish to Glubbdubdrib and grant me my nugatory visit. I had my days of glory, my days of pain, my irenic days of rolled-up creation lighted by my nugae. I dreamed, o, but I never dreamed the end would come so suddenly, being subtle as I am. Omega, the piquant winter of my senior year. So it is with me, a biloquist god in tender." (AZ looks down upon 19.) "How foolish of me. So easily I forget. But, of course. It's all free! There's no cost involved. You can go ahead and do as you like. Do as you please. At the lowest point she slept, entombed within. And smiling yet. Like the matter pertaining to proctology, good-for-nothing stool. Let me change her seat, accordingly, to *happy*, and thereafter take a libidinous seat upon her rump upraised for me, a smiling stool; and wait like earnest for destiny to come with her arsenal Black Lightning-Final Judgment. O do I smell characin?" (AZ puts his head in his hands and waits.)

CHORUS

Chorus: Dichotomy. How god does see with one eye; one closed; whether A to Z or Z to A. It makes no matter in the circumference. There is no way to see one way. We are the Chorus throughout time. It may be hard to find us, but nonetheless we exist on the line. In the circle of the celestials we are fellow citizens, bright shiny flies that do observe the deeds and characters of fishing men, as well as hobo gods who start false lawsuits with fake evidence, and who win in court by perjured testimony over topics one through ten; all-in-all, to be later fined with a heavier penalty than what was sought and won in court; of gifts and sacrifices, we cannot be placated, and to tempt us is to only warrant your suffering slow. For this we know: AZ fit the bill, 19 carried the show. This is meant for you to get your bearings straight, for each of us acts out of pride. 'Tis a mistake. For clues here belong to justice, without a chance of escape.

This is the conflict, necessity; of life's smallness, absurdity and fragility. Pass away. To he who sits upon the stage under his gibus hat, limitation and mortality mark the graves in the tens of billions made. 19 does not speak as yet with her gibson girl waist, for god does sweat a sea, and until he has stopped perspiring the essence of all will keep still. *What is done. It is done.* The decision – to create an imposible situation that each and all can be fulfilled by. Do not let this challenge fall. For each and everyone demands an answer to what is justice. Justice is an answer to existence, all. Now let fall the line. It is the last time.

THE BANQUET
ACT II, SCENE ii

19, who is played by Mrs. Alving, is fifty-five, a little less than medium height. She still has a shapely figure, is nearly callipygian; but she is beginning to show some evidence of a multi-dimensional waist and hips. Her face is distinctly inter-planetary, but in earth terms is still quite striking. Her nose is long and thin and has yet to take on that bulbous shape that will later affect her autumn years. At this time, she is using so much rouge that either side of her cheeks looks like the planet Mars in miniature. Her high-forehead, which in later years will become low and Neanderthal-like, is framed by thick straight hair dyed the color of weathered brick. Her blue eyes appear black; but if one squints hard enough, they look to be yellow depending upon the light. Her breasts are large and commanding, but three sizes too big for her standing. She is a striking presence on stage; howbeit, she occupies three-quarters of its length. From afar, her hands are beautifully finished with long tapering fingers; but closer examination reveals that arthritis has twisted the appendages into angry knots, thus giving her members a strange and crippled sinuous look, in spite of their illuminant reputation originating from the mezzanine. She is dressed in a quick and dead floral design two-piece bathing suit, a piece of which is caught tight in the outer reaches of her podex; and she is currently straddled upon AZ, who is played, in turn, by a fable; a fable concerning works, labour and patience, as well as bearing *them* who have been tried and found to be liars. As the curtain opens, 19 is riding AZ like a horse, listening to all he has to say with radish, itching ears.

19: "I've gotten too fat. This crew I carry in coach must have whacked my spurganum. Can't you feel it in my brain?" (She kicks her heels into AZ's side and gets the claque to applaud as one body in kind.) "In my jabber, my squat refrain? How about a *little* breakfast? How about eight fried yolks swimming in margarine with nine slices of bacon, stripped of their meat, thirteen buttermilk pancakes served on two plump beds of French vanilla ice cream, and a slice of toast crisp with cinnamon?"

AZ: "None of that kosher nightmare jive, milady. We'll have no talk of reducing, silly. Is that why you feel like eating so little? Void of sparganiasis?"

19: (Laughs. The rieurs join in.) "Hardly. But there's barely room left on the stage. And you're so strange about expanding it. And you're wanting children yet?"

AZ: "I didn't say that I wouldn't expand the stage. I simply said that a stage is a stage, and nothing more."

19: "Pus for little brains! Book it!" (She kicks him again in the ribs and rubs her elbows against his sides.) "Meow. Meow. You need to eat in order to keep up your strength. I keep trying to tell you that your appetite is like a bad afterthought."

AZ: "How so?"

19: "How-de-do! So you must perish too! What's an afterthought?"

AZ: "An afterthought is a future."

19: "Dummkoph! A future is an aftertime. I'm talking about an afterthought."

AZ: "Oh, an afterthought? That's at a later time."

19: (Hitting him over the head.) "Dimwit! That's afterward! The slaughter. I'm asking you for afterthought. Afterthought."

AZ: "Oh, that's the persistence of a sensation after the stimulating agent has gone."

19: (Giving him *quite* a hit on the head. Actual stars appear above AZ's crown. The bisseurs cry, *Bis, Bis*.) "That's aftertaste! Don't raise your milky cup quite yet!"

AZ: "Well, isn't that what cums after eating?"

19: "Yes, but not after thinking! So . . . your definition of afterthought?"

AZ: "Afterthought?" (Clears his throat.) "All right, this is my *final* definition. Afterthought: a short comic entertainment performed after a sixty minute play."

19 suddenly goes berserk, and after shouting, "That's afterpiece!" she cries, "Howl! Howl! Howl! Let me crack your crown and give you a little bit of holey afterlife *and* aftermath! One plus one equals zero!" (Upon saying this she starts to strike AZ with closed fists. Her strikes are hard and fast and delivered with such force AZ can feel the blows all the way up into his afterbrain. Three pleureurs manage to shed invisible tears neath their chiefs.) "Kosher gelatin is hardly gentle! What with bones and tendons and skin! What with explosives and that transparent sheet of bloody red over the light! How about a taste of lady's-finger this night?"

AZ: "Stop it! Stop it!"

19: "I don't forgive you, so don't tell me to stop it! Do you remember our wedding day, dearie? I'm sure you couldn't have forgotten. You couldn't even supply me with a wedding gown. I surmised that gods just don't notice such *little* things. They don't think it's important." (Hitting AZ on the head again with her fist.) "Well, it's important to me. How excited I was when you proposed. How I wanted to run and tell mother. But where the hell was she locked? I'll tell you! She was dead, along with everything else! And I was left with my pink rachel trailing in tears down my cheeks!"

AZ: "So just the two of us. Down on the wall, entangled around the 13th pillar. That's quite a tanning. What do you care about a wedding gown?"

19: (Hitting him on the head again. The rieurs' refrain.) "Piss for brains! You don't think it isn't every woman's dream to have a wedding gown done up for her alone? Especially when the bridegroom is god? You couldn't afford a dress? You could have said, 'Never mind the cost. Let's dip into the bursary. Let's go all the way. Let's eat and drink to our heart's content.' You don't think a girl loves to be spoiled? I don't care if the wedding gown would have meant the death of me and the dressmaker! So what if there's no one around? Look at me! All I've got is one hour and a dusty costard to shit on! Not to mention the shards of metal, bits of glass, traces of paint, and the frigorific, grievous facts of physics!"

AZ starts to speak sensibly but 19 interrupts him.

19: "Look at you! Your nose is too long, your mouth is too big, and your ears are starting to stick out. You're coming off looking more like a rache with a gruesome psydracium. You're wooden! Plus you're pissing pins and needles and missing the *t!* You make one damn fine groom! You're lucky our father and his jury of twelve, plus one with a tail, were not alive to see this. I could cry . . . I could just cry rabbi tears!" (She starts to sob. The pleureurs back her up.)

AZ: "Oh baby, take out your frustrations and put them on your tongue and let's have a ball."

19: "A wise mouth, huh? Talking back are you? Arguing with your mouth full, are you?" (Gnashing her teeth.) "Well, that does it!"

19 cocks AZ's mouth open with her hands and whistles; and, seemingly, from out of nowhere, foods of all varieties suddenly materialize in mid-air and begin to stream into AZ's mouth and down his gullet. Everything from roast pork to broasted chicken to rabbit to veal cutlet, from vegetable oil to lard to creamery butter jams down into AZ's gut. This goes on for quite sometime; in earth-time, a thousand years, give or take a little season or two.

THE SUPPER CONTINUES
ACT II, SCENE iv

AZ is pacing to and fro. He has taken on so much dead weight from his last feeding (from which he has taken a temporary break) that 19 has started to call him 'Big Daddy' (and behind his back, *Brutum Fulmen: Ghost Writer*). As much as AZ despises the baneful reference, he is agreeable to putting up with it mainly on account of the fact that he hates getting hit on the head, and in his pacing seeks only peace and an Easterer way. Surely, this is his period of adjustment after the battle, and he is trying his best to move with the punches and evolve into the form that 19 has reconstructed for him. This, in spite of the fact that he was originally intending to appear in the hereafter as a commonplace stone angel standing forever rigid as a locust in the background of an interior scene of *dictum de omni et nullo*, and as a *lucus a non lucendo* icon representing Eternity brooding in quotidian silence over the nothingness state of the universe.

Upon closer inspection, one should notice that the jud books upon the shelves in the background have either been replaced, transformed or cooked down into an entire collection of cookbooks, except for one loaned title of a key play (most obscure), entitled *Conversation Among The Ruins on St. Lucy's day; the Short End of the Stick According to the Wrong End* by Lapsus Calami. The stage itself has taken on the appearance of a room, perhaps a library, in a mansion of Victorian-Gothic-style-earthly-delights, with a lot of room for backstairs gossip (i.e., "Did you hear about Lucy Light? She got Barnaby Bright to perk up at 12:13

after catching him sleeping at 6:11. And that's the long and short of it." "I heard tell he was none other than the casting director, in the earth, yelling 'Cut! Cut!' to the female lead for breast feeding on the set during a crucial scene." "Well, let me tell you. She got the white robe for it anyway, and she and her servants were dumped for *more* than just a little season." "Son of Consolation, glory be! When you have it, don't sell it or bring it to the feet. Just goes to show you, can happen on any day of the week!") in what was once the Hanging Garden District of New Orleans among the gods. It is important to take note of the fact that New Orleans is where a hooked fish might tire itself on a line, which is somewhat synonomous to New Jerusalem, which is synonomous to New Heaven or, pending a small typographical error, New Haven; with a further note pertaining to 'con' as in 'criminal' as in 'AZ' as in a backfriend who carried the *lebhaft* melody to its bombastic tune; continuing with 'Net' as in 'fisherman's net' as in 'hook' as in 'saviour of men' or 'fisher of men' who carries men to their plates; continuing with 'cut' as in 'sever' as in 'god cut larry' as in 'death by sword, death by confusion, or death by noise.' Thus, we have 'Connecticut'; *qui transtulit sustinet;* the true meaning thereof.

Thus saith the Chorus, "Amen."

The room AZ is pacing in looks CUTE ('cut!' with an 'e' which, in turn, stands for eye; an eye of carnification that turns bread into flesh; good enough to eat once the carnifex has made the split into a shift, which is not the end of it; an eye of mastication, obviously of great value – canine, yet kingly – *carpe diem* to the appetite, never mind the digestion as long as one can chew sight to a pulp, swallow, and feel all the better for it; an eye of pleasantries – fearful maybe – but definitely emerald; an eye of anti-neuronism that stresses the discontinuity of a heavily flow – of a positive degeneration when severed from the cell body [at least for a little season], which could turn out to be an eternity onto itself; an eye of celtic-gogo, design-milk, blood and meat people – with an eye on sham-memory; black and white). A Christmas reef is high on the wall. The TV set is turned on with the sound . . . off. There are empty cans of small beer on top of it where H is hardly Holy. (Could this be the Flamingo where she canned the bible with her holy tongue?) 19 is sitting on the bloody stool with the remote control in her hand giving the placental sign. In this scene she looks a bit like a risqué rendition of a hot Deborah Reynolds number. She is singing snatches backward to herself from several dramatic and musical bloody dramas under the shade of a twig and berries, but settles on one in particular. The chorus of "Twat a White Christmas in Bee," accompanied by a Sting Band and Somebody's Aunt on the eunuch flute. Except her bloody lines are as follows: "I'm dreaming of a white crisis. The king we've never seen before. Where god the schlob spits up upon the floor. And quotes the angels, 'nevermore.'" And because she is singing this all bloody backward it sounds thusly: "Crisis white a of dreaming I'm. Before seen never we've king the. Floor the upon up spits schlob the god where. 'Nevermore,' angels the quotes and."

Cut!

AZ, who has been pacing continuously, is trying not to pay attention to 19's *cute* lyrics and is, however unsuccessfully, continuing in his efforts to upstage 19 and cut her off, even though he has the Government upon his shoulder and is remindful of his earlier muzhik days in Motherhood as a minor. He is being extremely cautious, however, for one more knot on his bloody head will make twelve, and he is already key-cold at the nose. Because he is pacing most deliberately across the stage, one could be moved to label AZ the KeelHaul

Thinker. He is deep in thought, like a miner stretching his leg – a hero in place – even as he paces from wing to wing like a popillia Jap with milk disease – stretching his leg – sternly bowing as he goes. The stage itself displays various props quite different from those in previous scenes. There is now a double-bed in the room with a purple wicker headboard both shaped and fashioned into the masks of drama; that is, one mask laughing hysterically and the other transfixed in a weeping lament like a plot in a garden. There is a stack of parted garments, *schmutters*, atop the floor, in a mass, along with a seamless coat. A teak night table, wood on legs in the form of a skull, is at the left of the bed; but its authenticity is somewhat questionable, somewhat insincere. For printed across its frontage in gold glittering letters is the phrase, 'Visit Palm Springs Soon – And Work, Eat and Play in the Open Dark.' There is a sole glass of water on the night table for holy consumption. The bed itself is unmade, that is, unprepared, and indeed looks the victim of a heavy burrow of lodgers from the night before. There is a primitive scent of peziza breaking wind in the air. Suddenly AZ stops right-dead in his tracks before the hole like a risorial-masked crab suddenly nailed and contemplating its carapace.

AZ: "Look, baby. Maybe I don't got a wedding dress but I got a couple pieces on two hooks you're gonna love. Guaranteed to give you an era of good falling. You'll look absolutely flagitious. How about the white flowing dress Monroe wore in *The Seven Year Itch?* That should put a smile back on your face and a sense of formication on your wrist, and perhaps a botch of deut's kiss."

19: (Looking at her fingernails, declining.) "Uh uh."

AZ: "Okay. Try this one on for size. An odd little trick. The blue jumper the immortal Garland wore in *The Wizard of Oz*. And, of course, we'll have it . . . tailored to size."

19: "Uh. Uh."

AZ: "Okay." (Smiling.) "You're gonna love this." (AZ sort of rolls, due to his weight, over to 19's hole.) "It's perfect for a finger man or lady. The gingham dress O'Brien adorned in *Meet Me in St. Louis*. For bringing in a little English vice and flag elation. St . . . *saint*. Get it? You could wear it as an understudy in the gang scene."

19: (Sighing with utter boredom.) "No . . . szmatas won't do."

AZ: (Appearing totally flustered but still maintaining, ever-so-slighty, his composure.) "Dun blasted encephalitis! Keep the Pole out of it! Okay. Listen closely or I'll be tempted to dress your droddum. The greens plaid suit Temple wore in *The Biggest Rebel*."

19: (Smiling.) "Don't you mean littlest? Honestly! Stripes on your leaf! Must I teach you all over by the book? And the answer is, no!"

AZ: (Pleadingly.) "Baby doll, please. Something's gotta do. I can't come up with a wedding dress. More or less a cake with a baker. I didn't think to snatch one up before the Final Yearning."

19: (Daintily.) "Your mistake, Karl. If I told you once I've told you a thousand times. Hook in the body, not the mouth for the fish in the lake." (She puts down the remote control, picks up a nail file from beneath the stool, and proceeds to file her nails.) "What else you got? . . . Come on, Big Daddy. Look at me. Let's get on the ball here."

AZ: "I got it! I got it! I got it! The red-feathered mass gown Deb wore in *The Unsinkable Molly Brown*. What a match! And, if you like, I think I got put away in the back the white nun's outfit she adorned in *The Singing Nun*. Then you wouldn't look like such a common whore when they all take you in the common hall."

19: (Stops filing for a moment just long enough to ponder.) "Hmmm . . . maybe. They could make nice May red apples, screaming black dogs all the way to the 19ᵗʰ hole. Put them aside. And when the time is right I'll put my finger in the takers' ears, spit, and probe their tongues while they're standing in the green way with their swords in their hands, and make 'em all disney. Now how about something sassy? With a nasty bark? A little daring? Adorn me in an early sax if rage. The latest-greatest Mashed Potato Rock. Plus, on the same bill, a little honey to spread over my son's ass when I cry *Ephphatha!*"

AZ: "Daring you want? Daces' devils!" (Hits himself across the forehead with his own skin-palm.) "Have I got daring! Grabbed it from her water closet seconds before she cindered brown in a spontaneous combustion birthday gown. You'd look superior in it. Doris Day's mermaid costume from *The Glass Bottom Boat* with the tight fin tail. The oceanic one washed up on plage. The cosmopolitan *Nudi branchia* with the retractile tuft around the fiery eye."

19: "And with a scarlet mandrake on top?!"

AZ: "No. But we'll strip and improvise. I'll even throw in some pajamas from *The Pajama Game.*"

19: "Meow Meow. Go ahead, John! Put them all aside! You know, Big Daddy . . . I want something elegant. When I walk I want to feel new again." (19 stands up and starts to parade in fashion across the stage.) "I want to look like something more than a monstrous iceberg adder. I want to feel ravishing, devilish, queenly, saintly. I want to feel like a raven straightening her pall with a terminating beak. I want to feel like a mondaine with fine feet. Like an emerald with eyes. Like a ruby with thighs. I want to be tasteful, pa. Can't I, pretty please?"

AZ:"What I got! What I got! Plump! Thigger! Beg in shame for the body in the palla! Bertholde in a furca with accompanying carnifexes! Two-in-one! You can wear them both at the same time if you want! Like bookends! And when it comes to balling you'll be quite a slugger. Quite . . . seminiferous. Taylor's headdress from *Cleopatra*, beneath which falls, most majestically, in time and motion, by a fixed piece-rate for both man and machine in white management, Hepburn's hot, red-velvet, high-speed, pearl gown from water, *Mary, Queen of Scots!*"

19: "You actually have those?"

AZ: (Licking his fingers and crossing his heart.) "Was there a murder in the inserterection?"

19: (Going back to filing her nails.) "Very well. You're getting better at least. Mene, Tekel and Peres. Plus, I trust, a pashmina for good measure. Numbers finished in the balance should want to be divided. Granted it's dated material and we've got a lot of costume pieces, but as long as everything's fashion's ghosts from the past anyhow, it should fit. In or out of bed."

AZ: "I should have kept a tailor . . . however, when it comes to great authority, I find that a eunuch makes a better charge of treasure. So, I'll take a candied yam from the raining sky and open its skin so that it cries a sea of butter without the fat confessor. Fall on 8:32 if you need the time to end the story in a simple slaughter without the mouth to carry the pash blues. The books have been cooked and the accounts well-buttered. Oh, well, I think most of what I got will stretch to kingdom come."

19: (Coyingly.) "Big Daddy . . . come here . . ."

AZ: (Pensively.) "What child? You're not going to hit me again are you and have me singing like a suffering servant? Expecting blows makes me blind as a bessy."

19: "Oh, Big Daddy, why you acting so scared when I'm the daughter in bed? See. I'm entirely dehiscent which should leave you open-ended. Come . . let us blow the kazoo."

AZ: (Burps and releases trapped gas which fouls the air.) "I think it's all that beer and Jack Rose, usquebaugh, milk, liquor and beastings you've been feeding me from the bottom, along with all the other lagan. I feel all bitter soaked with it. After all, I've been carousing liquor alone, straighthead, wet and erect, without drooping for the past forty years. And that's without stopping! For forty years! Why, if I were Cromwell I doubt if I could kick me own rump right now and hope to cumwell."

19: "The desert . . . dear Big Daddy . . . the desert . . . straight, wild, doleful ostriches eating ghost owls and man until dead while satyrs dance all round the head . . ."

AZ: (Wanders over to the far side of the stage.) "During the exordium the hills around here use to be quite a site to see. They made creature wandering easy. For it was easier to sit on the camel's back without falling off than it was to enter and get the best out of her, and that made for an easy mark for an easy rider, and all my grass children running around those sandy hills in their split barefeet howling and scratching in the heat, and manna laxative exuding sweet drops, and dead-in-childbirth hooting for their offspring in sunless nights, and how fat the top ash guns were, and how Peter played an example. You know, I could have fed that whole dusky tribe corned beef hash. All my eye and Betty Boop. All them precious stones. Yup, I had food enough to feed that whole AssArimaspian wandering tribe. Ugh. Ahasuerus, Cartaphilus and the whole damn cavalry with their asses in tarry and their peters in various stages of salt content. But, you know, the whole lot of them onagers were so beastly annoying, blowing their horns, I could have come and sat each and everyone of them on that there bare stool you're sitting on, one stacked upon the other, and appear, and feed them good and proper gold from this here banquet for forty days, and still I expect I would have found the whole mother bunch of them just as annoying as when I first laid eye of them underneath the fig and all that anal's dust." (AZ walks back to the stool where 19 is sitting, filing her nails.) "Forty years can be a sterile long time, old odium theologium."

19: (Smiling, looks up at him *de haut en bas*, sticks out her hand, reaches up and begins to unbutton his trousers.) "Quit talking, Big Daddy. You sure are shooting the breeze, and god knows how you can talk through one's hat, talk one's head off, breathless, and let the ligure roll cross the floor from up high and, most surely, talk to death. But tonight you're going to take a load off. First seat, third row." (She starts to rub him inside his trousers. It's obvious from AZ's wide-eyed expression – his eye in the pie-triangular-spectaculum, his reaction to the mass, the proportion, the color, the motion, the picture, indeed, the very pressure now being applied to him . . . squeezing, forming, straightening the eye to see in the open, fashioning him into a qualified speleologist – that he's finding a great new deal of pleasure in her cave-in message. Relief from depression! A holiday! Emergency Acts of Mercy! Bowels of Mercy! To Save Confidence! To declare Death in Order to Restore Life! But 19 has something else in mind. Exactly what it is is unbeknownst to AZ.)

AZ: "Wow! 19, hell, you found me! Like I never did before! It took the shadow of the day to do it, but you found me like I never did before! And you keep that up, honey, and we're going to have us a Bull's Ball! Like infants in the light with no ears to hear *Amen,*

Amen! You bet! I can still have pleasure for the women and kick against the pricks! And I've never seen death yet!"

19: (Her arm, up to her shoulders, is down inside AZ's pants.) "You like that, Big Daddy? You like the way I drive, El Sweetheart? Go, Big Daddy. O, you got yourself one big lion appetite, Big Daddy. You done got yourself one big servant mouth. It's by time you got a big load off, Big Daddy. Wrestle Big Rock. Big D. Come on, Big Daddy. Shoot for 19. Sweetness and light. Get a Bull's eye! Fall into my red demanding mouth, Big Daddy, and let's complete your run, your grace, Big Daddy. Because we all want to see that big perfect load in you go out."

AZ: (Giggling so violently his whole body shakes.) "Big Daddy just getting all worked up. He's all giddy. You're just full of surprises, 19. You're quite the fox. Did you notice what a real country dinner I had three days past?"

19: "I sure did, Big Daddy. You broke the century's fast and now I'm just waiting for something like a bomb to go off. I don't think I'm going to rest until I see your big bomb go off and have you shoot all over to kingdom come. Why, I better get all my brood under my wing or they're all liable to get desolately soaking wet!" (Even though her arm is buried deep inside AZ's pants, it's easy to tell from the movements within that 19 has greatly increased her fingerspring.) "Should we take him out, Big Daddy? Can't deny he doesn't exist. Should we take him out and let him take three paces?"

AZ: "You do whatever you see fit, 19. You're the anti-pas and I ain't never been one to stop a flood or the *dégringolade* of anything."

19: "You're gonna make a flood, Big Daddy? Why not? You've got the biggest, richest piece of land this side of the River Nile. And being a lone star myself, I just love a six-pointed star man. Should I subsidize a dam, Big Daddy, and call it the Nihilistic Dam, Is Wirklich, and give it a floodmark if you're gonna make a flood?"

AZ: "You do whatever you want, little girl. So long as you keep rockin' the boat."

19: "I'm gonna take him out, Big Daddy. I'm gonna take him out all in one piece, Big Daddy. And make him streak equilateral triangles all over the floor."

AZ: "I've got three other rooms upstairs we can go in, little darling. How about us going upstairs to cool off? I've got a room upstairs that's sweet as milk and honey with a fine cool pool besides. Stocked with fallen britt."

19: "What's wrong with down here, Big Daddy? Seems like you're doing fine down here, Big Daddy. Where the red flood draws across the path a fine fault, and the fox escapes with the hanging mouth. I ain't never felt such fiery sardine basketballs before. Not in a hundred years. And the way those two hoar honeys are rolling in my hands, it's no wonder sardine is just one of seven letters, although five are fallen and one is left standing in a short space. Wow, Big Daddy! That's quite some passenger! Mama here is going to have to put both hands down inside." (19 takes her free hand and plunges it way down inside AZ's trousers and starts to coo.) "Ooh . . . you're just all balled up, Big Daddy."

AZ: "I ain't balled up, honey. No, never!"

19: "Was so."

AZ: "Is not."

19: "You are, Big Daddy. You're all balled up." (19 is shoulder deep into AZ's zipper, working her arms like a piston. The smile on AZ's face stretches beyond the stage.) "How 'bout we make a bow?"

AZ: "You sure do have working palms, Big Mama."

19: "You like that, Big Daddy? You're just growing an inch per second. You ain't going to be able to keep your garments at this rate."

AZ: "Couple of more inches, 19, couple of more inches and you're going to spill my drink. Maybe you better take him out before it pours."

19: "I'm going to take him out, Big Daddy. Been locked up a thousand years in a penial institution. Spent a thousand years in there, he did, caught in a pleonastic gnosis." (19 starts to make certain adjustments in her body movements, vulgar twisting and contorting, and after a minute or so she hauls from out of the darkness within AZ's trousers the head of a penis so large, so monumentally formed, that it actually looks more like the head of a bald-headed man; a sort of penisless piety.) "Oh, my god, Big Daddy! What in the world!" (19 starts to laugh.) "Where are your numbers? Ooh . . . wee, Big Daddy! Ain't this a surprise! Speak of the devil! Ain't you full of surprises . . . I had no idea, Big Daddy! What's his name, Big Daddy? He's so pretty, Big Daddy. Such a pretty eye. Oh, such a pretty eye, Big Daddy. Such a cute nose. And such fine, quiet lips. And such a burl on the limb. Can he bark, Big Daddy? Can he bark if I perch on him like a tree? Like a tree in a mighty close wind? Barking is such an acquired thing. Not like howling, whinning or growling. But, here, let me put my hand around the bark, and block the punk book, *Apocalypse*. Oh, Big Daddy, I've got to give him a kiss, Big Daddy. I've got to give baby a big wet kiss, Big Daddy." (19 holds the head of AZ's penis firm in the thicket of her hand and plants a long, wet, piercing kiss upon it.) "Wow, Big Daddy! Rictus saltpeter! What's its name, Big Daddy?"

AZ: "Troubles! Whew! Grab it! He hurts! Hold it tight!"

19: "I'm going to grab it, Big Daddy, and I'm going to lick it clean with my lambitive tongue. And I'm going to call it Skipper, Big Daddy. I'm going to call it Skipper because it certainly arrests my heart and makes it skip a beat or two. You think me and Skipper make a fine pair, Big Daddy? You think we could play the crowd at a rout?"

AZ: (Murmurs.) "Till death do its part. Now hold it, honey! Hold it tight, honeybee! Feel it labour in the wind!"

19: "You excited, Big Daddy? Is it time for Skipper to shoot the curl, Big Daddy? Is the figure of him about to come? Can this iron whore get an alloy to induction-harden? Fast, then slow?"

AZ: "Hold on . . . hold it on the loose. In a minute!"

19: (Pulling more of AZ's penis out into view.) "Oh, he's got a face like an angel fish, Big Daddy. Take. Eat. This is my head. Don't mind if I do. Hook. Sniff . . . sniff. You may come kiss the rod too."

AZ: (Murmurs.) "Ba. Ba. Ba. In a baaling minute we'll kiss the rod and both make mary in the hall."

While 19 is busy working her hands and her mouth up and down, over and upon AZ's tremendous organ, busy working up a dust, lambasting busier than she really was, AZ falls back into a deep and sensuous fantasy; howbeit, there is a distinct vein of reality intermingled with his indulgences in reverie. Seemingly with each stroke, each beat, each suck and delectable lick, AZ's mind falls upon his past angelic loves. There was Jael, a dear stripe of a woman, whom AZ knew while he hiked with a 'k' on his forehead in the desert under the bright stars, southeast of Akaba. Even though she was married at the time to Herber the (Kidder) Kenite, this did not stop AZ from carrying on a most passionate and perilous love affair, most of which was performed in the head behind any given sand dune at the time of rapture – so unlike his typical fornix, where the hookers traded in-the-wet, near or about the stops along the highway, sometimes referred to as the suck-in-a-truck. She was a broad-chested woman with a gleaming bosom the size of Jericho – where she was prone to go and to tell lusty jokes in three different dialects, giving the key punch line in French whenever alluding to the three bad K's and the five tasty spirits. During negotiations she'd often jest, "Brag is a good old dog but Holdfast is the best." AZ loved her for her goodly air, her dainty table manners (Jael would eat her meals by balancing a fork, a long spoon, and a knife on the bridge of her nose under onlooking sighs, while at the same time eating with like utensils her own tasty fruits), and her thirst for blood (especially Cretan blood), which gave her a bit of a Jack Brag air on the hook. Even though Jael did carry on an illicit, wailing affair with AZ that lasted well into her lickerous nineties, she is perhaps best remembered at the gate for her bomb-bursting actions performed while she was away (in the Alps at the Innocent Children of Israel Musical Summer Camp in 1814) whaling. It was here in the midst of twilight that she took a tent peg and in a fit of burning rage drove it into the temple of a camp counselor named Sisera. No one knew the reason for such infamy on Jael's part. But when Sisera's body was found in fine linen and purple by a group of camp counselors, he was clutching a note in his lifeless palm that read *Drink to disparted Jerseymaids*. Indeed, beside his body was a cupful of kumiss, untouched – and just outside his tent, the camel which possibly lent. Jael was later put on trial but was never convicted due to circumstantial evidence, and remained forever active within her community as a broadcaster for a seedling television sect *(the Pat RIP Ass Ians, Crosslines in Death,* the same that was formerly into telephones and telephone poles, as well as headphones), until her final rest in the classy chest of mobocracy. She was best known in crowds for the phrase, "I am a lamia with a Finnish accent, and you're a lamdan with a Yiddish."

Then there was Gomer, which means ember. She, too, was a loose fast woman, a direct descendant of the Broad Church in the Lowlands, where she was referred to as 'a little pinworm caught in the digging finger of an old maid.' Gomer managed to carry on a hot affair with AZ under the very nose of her husband, the prophet, Hosea, without getting nailed at St. Paul's. One reason this was possible was due to the size of Hosea's nose, which happened to be of such generous proportions that it was difficult, if next to impossible, for Hosea to see anything that was going on beneath it. It is important to note that Hosea was not only a prophet, but quite an influential mocky one at that; for he vigorously denounced both political assassinations and moral and religious laxity as definite and most definitive "no-no's"; more like sores or pests or plagues or wounds, even though he pronounced them: "No-nose" – that is to say, "No nose of mine is dead," which, regarding his own nose, made everyone laugh. In fact, the prophecy he made that had a whole tribe in and out of stitches before going into battle was "Let the seamen come. In the end we will wax them limpet and after a good licking they will bore no further erections, as we will nail everyone who noses into our business." Hosea also referred to his woman, Gomer, as "the wife of The Harlow Tree, from where a lapwing did leap, crying farthest from its nest with yolk dripping on its breast," when, in fact, what he should have said was *harlotry. A real hell's angel on wings. A real nancy bombshell kicking up red dust.* But being a prophet whose 'gift' was rampantly oligodynamic, he, nevertheless, foresaw the births of Harlow, the milky way, and the entire shapely Hollywood shell (as it continuously revolved around her head) as all one in the same.

Before his patibulated death, he even had time to write a questionably humorous book that absolutely no one of his time could make sense of, entitled *Harlow: In the House on the Fortified Hill of Pulsating Selznick – d.o.s.-à-dos style with a broad in between*, but which he insisted was totally prophetic – that is, between the sheets. He also predicted the magical degression of Jannes and Jambres, a.k.a. Janus and Deanus, and went so far as to draw supine, proligerous images of ten boards in the sand on the shore of the Red Sea, and to demonstrate the art of "hanging ten commandments on a stiff board in a strong, soulful wind," as he was also quite the animist. For miles around, he was considered an absolute lunatic – howbeit, an agent, most nauseant. And it was no wonder that his wife was going down on AZ (who, anon with joy, received it), and was mooning daily in a surfeit of positions eight to ten times a day under his very . . . nose (which in some circles was affectionately referred to as 'Jinnee-Duranda,' which in ancient dog Arabic means 'the demon-Katmir sword in the poisoned womb left seven sleepers snoring soundly well past noon').

And then, for some odd reason, *Sanballat* popped into his mind (nearly shot upward) three times. Sanballat, which means 'sin save the life, sunningfags-on-the-pad,' was actually the one and only intimate experience AZ ever shared with an anguiform man; although he cannot be held totally responsible for this historical fact. For, in fact, Sanballat met AZ at a Samhain eve's party, when Sanballat was costumed in a most ravishing rendition of Sarah, in honor of the forking of the male/female psyche. AZ, who had always found Sarah (which in Hebrew means 'princess') to be 'quite open,' thought it a good opportunity to pick up on Sarah's/Sanballat's provocative elicitation toward him, while in the kitchen beside the bloody pots and cups, and in a favorable wind. But when AZ finally discovered Sarah's 'true' identity, he was so aghast with him that it was like two bulls locking horns in a wretched pen, which, in fact, did occur; for AZ and Sanballat actually got interlocked, via erections, under the clay pots and pans. Afterward AZ was so enraged that he rebelled and sought the *real* Sarah out on Sam Hill, and successfully impregnated her on the pavement with what turned out to be an anguineous seed that she later gave birth to when she was all of ninety years old, and in a laughable state; a colubrine seed that budded into a perverse, stiff-necked, cross-grained, bonehead, diehard, dickey-jack-moke-cuddy-dolt schlemiel of a son, fruit on a vine, whom she came to call Assis, which in labiodental Hebrew means 'he brayed to god in vain.'

All of these images, and the women surrounding them, file past AZ's mind as 19 works faster and faster, double-time, the sweat leaping from her brow while she waxes vigorously the godly organ, managing to sing, "It's the sweet second coming, Big Daddy! The burst of everything!" Even as the stonyhead fills to the brim (and thensome) with hot blood. And then in an instant, the organ starts to spew out words like a pencil while it remains engulfed in her mouth; such words rained as – "Behold my number" (although due to the intense sucking going on, including the teeth *and* lips, there's some question as to whether that "number" spoken was actually "member") "in whom my soul seeks terrigenous delights." And again the organ utters, "The living cast of the kingdom of god is at hand"; and again "Live! *Carpe diem! From:* the kingdom of god! is come upon you! a cast of thousands!" And all the while: 19 interjecting, "Yes, Big Daddy! Yes!" as sweet as she could grasp a spectacle. And the organ shouts, "I grow fast like the bustard seed! I am like leaven in the lump of his lap! Look for the *signum* for it will poureth out and all shall quench their thirst by seed! I cast my line, C.B. Semele!"

Reserved seats. Intact. 2719; 1410; 282; 236. This way, please. Moving in a dream, in judgment, in the midst of the sea, to the chief seats, respectively.

It is difficult to say exactly how slowly or how quickly time was going by during this intense activity; for it was indeed a cosmic fact that time had lost its meaning – meaning that time was no longer a thing in itself, whether linear or not, ear or not, *anno regni* or not; however, unbeknownst to the majority of mortal minds that indeed were all but gone, time was still of the essence.

IS IT TIME?

As AZ's *corpus cavernosum* is stroked, and the cries from the cock outside crow a depth theology that is meant to recover the original awe, mystery and wonder of the in petto-universe, of, literally, bottom disease in the garden, faith did spring back into god's temple. Remember to capitalize. The Pen is an immediate *comprehension* that has nothing to do with rationalism, but has everything to do with beat, rhythm and vibration.

This time, 19 fearlessly pulls AZ's 'entire' pal out into view and discovers to her utter amazement that not only does it possess the head of a man but the arms and trunk of one as well! Even as it becomes fully exposed, it becomes an apostle of infinite space. Its arms reach out and seize 19 in a restrictive hold like a heister with his hands full of cowworkdoneintoil. This sudden movement, however, does not appear to alarm 19, but, in fact, has quite the opposite effect upon her. She seems to take delight in the way the snakely arms spontaneously spring into view, and dwarf her, and grab her around the waist, and embrace her. "Be a lover," the head commands, "and I'll be your red prisoner hot-at-large." And while the arms curl around 19's frame, the head transforms into Pope Alex III, and sings a quiet, almost seductive-ridden song. The commencing words are familiar, as is the tune. But somehow the words together with the tune do not quite match the current fruitful proceedings. Nevertheless, 19 takes it all in stride, for she is more concerned with her own state of excitement and rapture in regards to the strong, thick, rigid and throbbing member in her palm. AZ is making her nest crack a no-nonsense beast, slobbering and drooling saturation bombing. Her own excitement and involvement is getting the best of her, and she is feeling totally vulnerable to the wild enticing nods of pleasure.

She drops right flat down to her knees, quickly lifts up her platyopic apron and exposes herself, which is easy to do being that she wears no underglue. "Tirrits, your naked weapon!" she coos.

Her body stays on her like a kid's glove on a peak July afternoon. No matter what position she puts herself in, there appears nay a fold of fat in her thin skin, nor upon her inwards, nor anywhere near or around her calves. And all the while the eye of AZ in the face of the yellow, perorative pastor burns holes in 19's common compartment, particularly in the drawer between her left and right hip, where there is a scent of dust-powder in her pants and a hint of Mrs. Aitchison's rose in the midst. The arms extending from either side of AZ's male factor travel down her torso in jerky but, at the same time, sliding motions – like two summer cats working their way down a walnut tree to sniff out Miss Willmott's ghost.

Squeak! Squeak!

"Who Shot Cock Robin?" the numbered head whispers in a closing discourse. A question intending to receive an answer, or so it seems, hanging on the line. Obviously, 19

cannot satisfy the bird's rail nor the bird's mute with an effectual response. For with respect to conventional moral/bio patterns, she hasn't a clue *who* shot Cock Robin; something amiss; indeed a puzzle – the sudden appearance of seeds sprouting – but for want of appearing witless she responds, "Whoever it was must have flown the coop, so shoot! Big Daddy. Shoot! Open up the hole in your crown and get your nuts to release the monkery puzzle. Be nasty in your pen. So nasty that you shoot words, serums, from here to the ground and back up again."

AZ responds to 19's words in a way that seems odd, given the fact that 19 is working so hard to get the job done. He lightly pushes 19's head back, places his own tight mouth over the head of his pen and blows like a fanfaron, such serious, steady notes. The arms extending from the pen instantly let go of 19 and wrap themselves around AZ's shoulders. From somewhere deep within the embrace there comes the golden sounds of a pig's squeal. AZ mentions something about the hole opening, and his words intermingle with the noise coming forth from the head of his pen. *Squeak! Squeak! Squeak!* The words are clear and distinct: "Hell, I can't breathe. All my life I've been squashed up like a fist on a tramp. And now my business ends are released, and I'm ready to thunder and be let in to whatever room or body I might cross in the clouds. Like a soul going through metempsychosis. Dick, Dick, Dick, Dick. Dick. Dick."

Suddenly, AZ shouts, "Jesus! What's gotten into you?" To which the head of his pen balls, "You don't see the point! I just can't let it go!" "It will come," AZ shouts. "You sure in hell will know, Laszlo. It will come!" But the head of the pen doesn't agree; for it's got to be quick-drying if it's going to come. Although it is difficult to know if the head is being wholly sincere or just plain obstinate. Irregardless, the pen begins to bicker and increases its hold with anger and resentment – as if (considering the odd connection) the pen is intending to somehow kill itself, being attached as it is to AZ via bickerstaff. For, indeed, the hold is now a choke. And a life-threatening one at that.

"Get me my crutch and lick my throat so I can wrap this hanging cock around it! This pile of flesh scratched together!" AZ hollers at 19. "And cradle it like a crossed baby grain! And let it finally sleep in grain!"

But 19 takes sides and suggests to AZ, "I hear orgasms are more intense while being choked. Morning, noon, or night. It makes no difference. As long as the words flow forth in the book. So go with it, Big Daddy. It's getting exciting to see. Hold on, Big Daddy! Stretch it too and with yourself do sodomy!"

AZ shouts, "Dom Pinchon almighty! Give me a hand, old salt. It's caught in my throat and swelling. Grip your palms around it before it becomes my sepulchre. By any artificial means. Fertilize my schemes. Get the box to release the egg and let a brave new soul emerge!"

But this is impossible for 19 to do, for her own hand is busy stirring the dew in her own garden, her own paradise, her own dippitydew, with the baby in the nest and the dog with its head resting upon the master's breast, salt lick dead, flat as the surface of the earth, without a counterearth to accompany it and to shield it from the fire within.

Do you think you finally have a clue? This is the place to find some. Weeper, loser, monk in stealer. For this is the soft birthday. It binds like wage. It leans like wage. Bricks smashing on the straw skull of a soft birthday . . . Thump! Thump! Thump!

Arrest

Layer by layer, the release of old calcified rage, brickbat, piece by piece. Peel them away. Nonpeneseismic finesse, letters and words, anon with joy, buried under millions of leaves of garbage; muticous pages. And shouldn't it be stored in a bloody gardevin? *Fin-de-siècle.* Address 151515 @Ma 1320: to 19, to Mrs. Alving, to Danse, to Eve in the leaping house: Take this body out into the field in order to detonate it. The secret place where the voice spills thunder gushes: *if only god could change the scenery.* Blood is a length of *time*, literally pushing forward, outward, divine . . . me. There is a much needed place for clear water. Water calls attention to pain. Pain covers healing. What pleasure is there in the Acts if one suffers from hyphedonia? The refrain: water is a divine substance. *(Shouldn't it be copyrighted?)* A beautiful liquid space, where a woman captured naked and suffering from a gardez aftermath can dip her heel (vulnerable place) into the pool of treatment and get clit-cured of any residual her-a-clit-eanism, which might otherwise be clinging to her nest in flux, nonfixed on all but the pen supplying the logos, which is at once law and fire. Deeper still, 700,000 leagues, set down and let rest. And then drag your troll across the sea bottom, embedded with a 3-ring hook. What will be fished up in the soul of woman? A condition known as hebetude. The heal? Treatment: One Anchovy meal for twelve. The heal? The hook on Pinchon on Fishing. On the artificial fuck. The business foot, the stinky sole embedded with dog stool. The dom heal in a pinch arrest by a guddling under stones. The whale's fin protruding from the clamp of an oyster; 3 rings. Do they all mean the same? *Rinnng! 'Be careful. Every imbroglio slurred over will be a ghost to disturb your sleep later on.'* The sound is there, layer upon layer. The sole rests ZZZZZZ, just as the soul rests; just as the sole wrests upon the ocean bottom much like the monkfish. It is a *circus neronis, maxentius* and *septimius severus.* The sole (unmarried) is used chiefly by wowowo men coming. Layer upon layer, the word takes form. Woebegone. Knot away, Gordius. Send him back home with a sewer brick and a bone. And let the dome fall so the basement turns upright by the grace of god.

him! christ plays in the midst of this eating of eternity because he insists!

AZ is choking on his own soul. Meanwhile, 19 removes herself from the hook of the fisherman. Dipping her fingers into the nether mouth of her own well, *19 fishes for the shrimp!* But lest one think it irrelevant, this is also the act of beginning a recurrent disease. An itch that won't leave well enough alone. *Ugh.* So it is for the wise to sin along for the full of wonderment – to appreciate and recall the bewildering, rapid, chaotic songs and musical tones of the history within these words: recapture and re-invent the probity of eastward, the signs which are longed for in the marvel solution to the ultimate mystery. *Ugh.* 19 is singing in her bones. And the vault of her watery dreams becomes a leap to yet another cell.

One continues to grow. To evolve. Stepping back, one parts, floats, holding in secret a renascent universe. One has seen the world, been in the earth, and has lived for a spell with Dr. Fell. (O! T.B. tell John what *Non amo te, Zabidi nec possum dicere quare; Hoc tantum possum dicere, non amo te* means to remit the sentence). One has experienced the pain with a stinger in the tale like Telegonus's father; that is part of the realm of the unknown world. One has (among other things) been born and has suffered a broken home, barely able to see out the cracked oriel. One has (among other things) been torn and has been violated by RIP. And through all this, One doesn't give a tinker's damn for blasphemy, and has remained a mysterious longing, like the *old longing* that both man and woman have forgotten. In a term: salvation. For all humans have sought salvation-in-kind; one even to the point of *felo de se*. Even now, if one stops, stops instantly, and listens to the sound that is quite unlike a sound, listens to the sound that is beyond the prevalent sounds, beyond tinnitus, beyond the prevalent silence beneath the sounds, then one can hear the moon call from the sea within the spirit; the sound of many waters; the feme soles' calls that beckon to venture out over the ice and the broken sea to the mark where creation dwells. *Nekumonta. Genetaska.*

From where 19 sits, she sees the cock probing deeper and deeper into AZ. This is AZ's encounter with simony. Head-on. Choking is good. It is all right. Choking. On his own seed spewing from his own cock. Is this cock the chief person? The LEADER? Old cock of the walk. What you did you did overbearingly. Now it is time to think of yourself as a device to divide, to tell, to deceive. Does it not carry the sound of a bad don? A polly on the repent? The learned class, priests, magicians and astronomers fallen into fortunes? All chaldeans grasping a chalcedony? Certainly it falls in between the leaves. And to further the device, we move to the final judgment; we move to the reference previously spoken of before the face *I'm, in time, in word*. O the tribulations!

AZ can barely breathe, being shot with seed.

The arms rise, take hold of AZ's neck like a hook around a cacophonous act of cabotinage, first of all groping, and then finding the nape, and the apple falls, forever tightening its grip. This, the befitting quest of dipping in the dish and making a wish to be unborn.

"Arrest him!" AZ coughs.

But it is more than any simpatico god could suffer. For even in the realm of supremacy, there is pain and abandonment. With a sense of forboding, AZ goes down on himself in true anthropophagous fashion, and chokes.

MURDER IN THE FIRST

. . . I need change for a dollar. Not that a dollar was all I had to my name. For the issue had nothing to do with money at all. After all, I also had me my old man and a basket with two turtledoves. Words rarely find their correct course once they have wandered into the lackadaisical confines of mankind's malignancy. The current flow of thought that careens down the windpipe of man's expansive resonance has absolutely nothing to do with currency. To break down change into compartmentalized slots of bureaucratic tedium would be to miss the point entirely. For change can come by way of a quarter, a dime, a nickel, and a penny. This we all know to be a fact: all dollars are created equal, being made up of one-hundred cents. But to need change for a dollar could, in all likelihood, be a trademark for much less worldly men. To sing, to dance, to perform, to stretch the notes far beyond their limits, and to place them in their respective realms, could actually mean that one could *change* for a dollar, or a nickel, or, what the hellbomb, nothing but *change* itself. For what is *change?* It is quite emphatically transformation. Under duress? Under sleep? Perhaps. I can tell you only this mystery: If given the chance, I will take Hades' head beyond the grave and return highly evolved, highly wrinkled, and none the worse for wear.

. . . If I could stamp my forehead with a plan of escape, I would slip into the mailbox and wait in utter darkness for my delivery man. Where is he? Does he exist? Dung is the slip that first was the sacrifice to the body's fire. Is the world only one man, one center, one nucleus? Or is it one hound who slipped his collar and dug his way down through the open sepulchre to the Adam's apple, and bit and chewed to pieces the bloody flesh? Might there be a counterpoint to this shame? Might there be a contrast to the reflection in the windowpane that I glance from? the pain in the glass where the reflection stands as still as stagnant water?

I will lie here dead to the earth, dead to the spirits in the earth. I will lie here dead to the heart beating frantically against mine. No matter where I'm touched, I will not be moved. I will be as steadfast as an old oaken dresser holding bricks, a tree of license refleshed of meat and blood. I will lie dead to the foul invasion of breath in my primal nostrils. I will clamp my mouth shut, shove my thoughts into drawers deep in my mind. My tears will leave no trace inward; rather outward the salt will trail a path like a true mother decoy. And if I should fall like Troy, knuckle-wrenched dethroned, fall to my knees defaced like a badger at the kill, my lemuroid mask ripped from the flesh, suffering like a jeremiah without a pill for the consequences, I will not render nor leave my baggage at any doorstep traceable to my name.

. . . I stand a thousand miles away from any hand that I might touch with a harmonious surrender of peace. If I debate the issue, tread water in a dish and ask my father, *What depth might this be? A dog's tongue lapping would scrape the bottom,'* he would undoubtedly answer back, cynocephalous in face, *'Depth is a matter of exploration. One might explore 20,000 leagues under the sea and consider the depths thereof or, on the other hand, one might examine a single molecule of the 20,000 leagues and consider this to be both the beginning and the end of depth.'* J . . . V . . . Fr . . . Father could draw lines along any desired path and claim his boundary; his domain. If I am a bit disorderly and possess my farouche being, then I am without a being. For to possess by-being under such borderless circumstances would render any human being crazy-on-burton. Do I shed my soul like so much dead skin? If I am forced to handle my father's rod must I stay inside and risk remaining cyprian? Or a thousand miles away from any hand, etc, etc, etc.? I can feel the growth. My father grows . . . old. Old narbo. He likes it like this. Changing in and out like a loup-garou. So he says: the hand is but an instrument. The hand caresses, strokes, placates, stimulates, explores, restrains, opens, closes, pumps, throbs, crosses, stings, beats, beats . . . beats . . .

My dear father, what a perfect facsimile of pride you make! How you stand like a pioneer, musket in hand, eyes ablaze on the new frontier. Everything in place once you've cleared the way. Not a thing unruly exposed. I am but your lifesome grindel child. Watch me approach you, father. Here comes your little lioness on fire. Your coprolaliac with the dirty tongue. You're so strong, father. Your hands tear the trees, cut the forest, hammer the metal, build the cities, clear the skies, connect the continents, crack the whip, hold the musket. Land where our fathers died, here comes your little pride. Watch, father! My mouth sucks the muzzle of your musket. Blow my brains out and I will sing the sweet melodious exchange; my declaration of resignation on the air.

This rib – this rib that dares to think, to act, to ponder – hustles with the sublime notion that all men are created equal. If this be correctly alluded to, I stand a thousand miles from your crap-infested face rustling my leaves in your forsaken wind. Sue me. What the fuck. It comes out free. For once you find me, there will be nothing to collect. My soul after all is a pitiful wasteland of chiffon-reynolds-wrap-absolute-twine wrapped in care, beginning and end.

If I brought my child back, that is, if I literally yanked him from Beelzebub's bloody bath of muck, and breathed my own life back into his bloody bleeding heart, and made him reappear, we would cut this cock asunder, paint the town bloody red, and move our hands not up the shaft of life but down into the bloody bowels of the earth where god himself stands diligent, preaching to the lost slipped souls of his heavenly kingdom how to let fools rush in.

Faster . . . faster . . . faster he wants it. 19 ways. My mind must have slipped a disc. My fantasy had visualized him tucked away. In the bowels of Malebolge. But no. . . . Scarlet Scent *on dit*.

Faster . . . faster he wants it squirting his seed across my face . . .

On such a pluvious day.

FIND THE HIDDEN SCENE
*A HINT: C

Maim's morning mist marked the middle of my life.

I was all of eighteen; motherless, void; farouche. And so I became my own best friend having been a refugee of the interior war with a lack of polish, but, nonetheless, a fortuitous survivor. You could tell – there was a certain look in my eye; a vacuous, thought-sucking fastidiousness that simply knew where to place the benefit of the doubt. Naturally, I had resisted defeat having been brought up to believe that one does not relinquish one's holy gift to the world, whether it be that of tongues, rings or robes. And so I loved, desiring to make my life useful. I returned unto danger for renewal, having first been a slave, second a thief, and third a fugitive; but forever in the bowels of all three.

Late one afternoon while polishing up the brass, mother crossed my mind as though she were an uninvited saviour, and asked me, "How would you prefer to be saved? Do I dig you up out of the earth? Do I spoonfeed you a fool on a chip of wood? Do I spread you across my lap, rake my fingernails down the length of your lunar-surfaced seat, call you my sweet-faced, dimple-dented, overseer Plautus honeybunch and ignore the split-egg, runny yolk film of gobbled gook ooze issuing from your eye?" Come on, Mother. How could you have not noticed? Judge correctly your own baby in the sink, scrubbed. In the vestibule, Pandora's Box was opened, vests were tossed, and secrets scurried into the deep, royal-blue partition separating neotenous girls from neoteric women.

Note: Daddy longlegs Freddy-Freddo freestepping his way to the forbidden zone; the brooks of honey; motor-running; butter-buzzing heater heating the forbidden, finger-licking, solid red knight, eating and eating and sweeping the commensal clean. Toss me three coins so that I might fountain-fling them into dreamland and bring forth butter in a lordly dish.

Back to mother; I stand facing my own sorrowful reflection; Deborah; Call Girl: Seven-eleven; the mirror cracked and left me a jagged jock underneath an oak tree, nonetheless eager for play. Get the buzz? It can be most deceiving up until the very end. Rumor has it. 3 shots were fired. What was a little girl to do? Solve a mystery all by her little lonesome self? (Oh, by the way. Bought a May dress today. Going to drop-dead it off at the laundry, spearhead it over to Mom, and ask her to wear it for Dad's sake; he'll just love its space for two cocks, and getting milked three times a day.)

Father's head was round. Purple like the crown. What a revolting idea that the body, the beautiful full god-in-his-image body of mankind, can be transformed in true associative fashion into the plugged-in body of man's pleasure.

Dong. Man's dong. The body of man as symbolized in the body of man's dong. Dong! Dong! Dong! Father said: "This is my head. Take. Eat so that you may live in the bitter spirit of that head. This is my seed. Take. Drink so that you may grow in the image of my head."

If you ponder deeply enough and allow your vision to become more profound, you will easily see the answer through this chaos. Here come the passing bells for a nifty passage *in extremis.* If I must arise to this position and thus condemn myself as an irreproachable murderess relapsed into discomfort for mankind's sake, nay, for womankind's, humankind's, animal's, fly's, even for flea's sake; for conduct, contemplation, effort, faith, occupation, resolve, self awareness, speech; for a book, coin, mirror, pearl, artemesia leaf, jade gong, musical lozenge and rhinoceros horn; for anything that might fall victim to such a force spreading life open, widening it beyond repair, then I must reckon with the notion that not just *any* old living shaman will find himself reciting the hidden answer, word for word, with a troop of talking trumpets in niflheim, but only those shamans who are multiscient when it comes to matters relating to mortality. The mannered door is opened. Come on in and sit a spell and I will show you things set in stone. For this I stand alone, headstrong in the position that I could kill if necessary and leave as the final discernable trace one knowledgeable thought: to die is to transcend the laughing pain, to let go of the fear that shapes the distortion of the smiling face, and to embrace the sin against the ghost dove.

LIGHTS

In my private apartment in the hall, the company, along with the cleaning woman, took bread after the performance, and thereafter saw the head rise and vanish, even as they celebrated the closing night of *G-Day.*

Frozen, I stopped in timeless grip to ponder that which I could not comprehend with sunlit mind. The fingers, each subjects of the force that drives my heart to unbeatable rhythms of breath, grabbed at the oars that propelled the vessel to its ultimate designation. Bare-breasted sailor of feminine depths – liquid, lucrid, lanquid, damsel-dorsel mermaid of the sea – G's frozen words came undone. I began my watery voyage, unglued, ocean-fed, nurtured on seaweed, long and flowing seaweed of the flesh. I called the ancient arms of Mother's embrace, the widow-black morning veil, falling in tisty-tosty leaves of dismissal: *To Swim Back To Where The Sea Kisses The Lap Of The Earth Is For Now The Most Heartfelt Journey This Mermaid Could Ever Undertake.* Scales as fresh as salt, sunwashed clean in the sea. I, but a minnow, fell upon the six inch hook of Daddy's pull.

ACTION!

Dad rolled off the cushions of my Mother's protection . . . my Mother's flame . . . and plunged what little he had left to spare into the belly of my totality. Enter Nuntius. A message? From the page I ripped the Fantasy of my life-story, the books of the four kings, and unearthed the truth. The hierophant, the old man, the pillar, the V-sign was the *telum*. Sound advice – *Apellous' Table is the Lord's* – with words as discernable as the numbers on the face of a clock. Dad said to ears too heaven-turned to comprehend, "Be still! Be still, my baby, queen, Daddy's coming, the roytelet terror."

With his *caucho* dangling from him, *muerto* makes him a has-been.

Dig! Work hard! Search! Then eat!

It wasn't an invasion, nor an assault, nor a massacre, nor a slaughter, nor a blood bath, nor an air raid, nor an execution that started and ended the story on Grub Street, where one was prone to hack out a living, despite a lack of goods. No . . . all of these would have been too simple, too convenient to make last. It was a *tabula rasa*, the removal of a living soul – *lucus a non lucendo* – immortal, omniscient, and omnipresent – the heart of the fruit in the heart of the tree in the heart of the wood that served as the clean moment of circularity, even as a russin' wind came in and performed a baptism of fire. *Absolvo.*

Above the pyramid She sat eating Her curds and ways, nursing a nasty mormal, when up from the bush sprang a spider hatched from a cockatrice's egg that pushed Her into hell's cockeyed maze . . . Tapping on my shoulder, a little boy of shreds and patches handed Me a dagger. "If we make the incision . . . cut snugly . . . closely around the heart, and quarter it in Cosmopolitan-style fashion, I think it would serve us well. Please . . . Let us try to offer Daddy on a tray before April breaks her morning cloud-strewn skies." *Absolvo.*

April's branches are still leafless. It is not open, being *too* young, and it is folded. It is a *gowk* searching for a crazy echo reverberating in dead daffodils. Spring slumbers almost to the heart of hotter days when the tuberose of the night rises and makes a pleasing embrace. Daddy, the Magician, spread me like golden margarine across the blue sheets that Mother wrapped me in before her sleep. *Coq-à-l'âne. Vac . . . Bath Kol . . . Acco . . .*

Cut!

HUNTING THE GOWK

Such fearful days lie ahead. Still, these will be days of awe as mockers seek higher ground . . .

In the heart, beatless in the night, through the open window that yawns flower frozen in the indigo, in the star-splashed placid night, the first hint of *fleur du mal*, the gopher snake is wailing, lamenting, burning, hating and forgetting it all with but a sip and a sly sense of line hissed as a fricative vilification. After dad's moans have left their vibrating residue of love in my ears, I blink and break a thousand angry tones into one monotonous hum. Let this be my hymn for the dead, my villancico with which I am well pleased. As for myself, I mumble a poem of sixpence. I ask, please, please wait, Mother. I just want to say goodbye to an old friend who wrapped my heart in crushed velvet one wintry-wet afternoon after having shot down an albatross bearing an olive leaf. Remember how you permitted that Ancient of days to stay beyond dinner dropped its plates, pots and pans into the sink? To stay until a light lunch of meatless spaghetti and salad was had on the following day? I love you for that, Mother. I love you for fingering my desires and picking up my job so that I might linger along the edge of pleasure fearless with amazement. It was my labored childhood in a mazy almondshell. When your back was turned, Mother, I kissed the boys and made them cry. And their rods yielded almonds. Now, while your spirit glides alongside me like a pilot fish, I recall how you taught me to stand tree-sturdy, forever ready to pinch the nostrils and shut the mouths of my enemies. You gave me thought, knocking my trunk as though I were an amelus. Tucked in dignity is what you brought me from. The isle of afterlife. Chewing on Ahmed's apple all the way up to the front door. What is that? Who's there at doors? Where are you going, Mother, with that bony finger? Correction: Where are *we* going? Up and over the clouds on a lion with eagle's wings, on a bear, on a leopard, on iron teeth that chomp! chomp! chomp! the only element of truth left over from the day before. Clouds go on, speak, sit up. Ma, your flesh rises – goose bumps up and down the length of my arms. Other mortal beings might hear me playing long midnight notes in the wind from a g . . . cave. Something beyond the first notes of the Third Eroica. Not quite here. I'll be damned if I allow the victorious roar of the crowd to bowl me down. Here is my life. The little golden book is open. Take. Eat. I give you my aurivorous spirit underneath my breast, my vinaceous veins, blood-soaked with the best intentions. Not because I am speechless – rather, because I am a horn who wonders still – beyond the burial of childhood – still, I wonder, with a thorn in my beak like a finger pushing the pen: Where else can one dash-day their life away on burning wheels of fire and not feel the power of an arthritic condition hung on a sexpenny nail turned into some kind of glorious afterglow of candleflame? In a fippenny bit motel, I, *ma mere L'oye*, gave a six principal Baptist a golden wash in order to make Providence Island heb. Who would have ever thought that I would have knelt beside your name, Chiseled-in-Stone, and utter a prayer of submission in your image . . . flawless, Mother . . . flawless . . .

I only wish it could be so easy. I gaze upon a picture of Daddy's image in my yearbook: the intricate design, the interlaced lines, the flower, the fruit, the animal disease, cancer productus, geometric in character. 'Most likely to be fruitful.' So long. Hold your peace! *'The One Most Likely to Challenge.'* I admire your arabesque. (Dong!) I read your sleaze in low gear. The seconds ticked on. Your firmamental features change over time and the *L* in your line becomes an *S* in your flesh. I listen to your basket antics. N-A-T-U-R-E-A-F-I-C-I-O-N-A-D-O. A clown on the court! A devotee of fices. Charged and bustling. I gasp at your accidental misadventures in the final chapter and pout . . . "Is there a room for me? Is there a place for me at this table in the midst of villeggiatura? Will there be time for me to play in the street? Will I count for anything if I should protrude and land like a stuffed pigeon at the picnic, as pigeon-toed as a caliper? If I come, will you bake me a cake? After all, you are one busy son-of-a-bitch, beyond measure. And where sleeping dogs lie, by god, that is where you will be tapping on my shoulder like an emmet."

My fingers are moist with my own dew. Abalone-scented residue cakes and crusts along the ridges of my mouth: Anti-gone. I dare not wipe away the evidence that spoils my sense of substanence. It would be far better if I flung the sling out of shot and made the organ sling limp in the fist like an Australian virescence. Daredevil Sue Aside leaping into a glass of purified drinking water from a height of fifty feet. The crowd of two thousand gasps as I plunge headfirst and land compacted as a legion of sardines into the dare-not-add-to-nor-take-anything-away-from these my words. Tomorrow, if you're still around, if you've decided to spend the white night because your belly would not allow you passage through my threshold after such a rich cholesterol-colossal meal, I will rub the sixes out of your back and smuggle you into the gates of pearls, flanked by two dinergates, and we'll have us a feast for having done such a wise, noble, self-sacrificing deed.

THE HOUR PASSES

In true Cyranoian fashion I take the liberty of bisecting your buttons before the final fall and the curtain drops. Here we pay homage to his majesty, sigmoid flexure. For without him where would our passing be? We engage him to take full command of his title – partaker of a deep and dark language of old, oftentimes conducted as the rhythmical unit of an utterance, best put under by anagoge – and stand as proud as coprolite in the sun, surviving the ravages of time. Like a saint you are s-shaped. However, your particular kind of curve takes you on a path quite different, quite unlike any such illustrious departed of old. More like a great movement, matter expelled at one eruptible passage, you are the tantara long since written about in lore. Coprolalia reaching deep into the lower extremities, wealthy with fruit receding backward. Should I excuse myself for a moment in order to exorcise your magnificence, your preponderancy, and should you be bold enough to occupy Siege Perilous in my absence, I should first warn you as to the fatalities attached to my seat of destiny. Synonymous 'S'. Shhh it is the silence before the blast that is a carriage of the body. Show me a heavy load, dear father, like the one you carried at Carri On, hauling earth and crushed stones, leaving hen tracks in your wake, and I will dismiss you from service in due time with a good cheer reserved for our genial host from afar. And watch with pure gramercy your own grand expulsion, your inwards externalized for all that there is to see.

He, being G, being himself, being mankind (with emphasis on man, deemphasis on kind); he being the gait in a Long John Silver's prance; he being the barbeque in a seamen's aftermath; he being the flint in a dove-piece of eight; he being the rack meat at the social gathering; he being the struggling fish in the slow belly; he being the great mystery we love to hate – the kingdom all onto itself; he being the *malentendu dans naissance*; he being the stride in a midget's waltz – the sway, the dip, the fall of mankind itself on one leg; he being the sideward glance offered to one as fair-skinned as myself, myself being a lady, a fair maiden of three ages – myself being a blemish in his eye, a blemish in the pupil of his eye; he being the prick that bled a twitching finger to shame – a kingdom to open; he being a cock who awoke an entire kingdom with a mourning cry; he being an Ernest-Robert, a policeman of sorts, but more a highway man, once a devil of Normandy, a wandering ghost until Judgment Day, restless, an exflier having gone for a burton and is still swimming in the melancholy drink of the holy book; he being a beast who tore a beauty asunder without the rose to fill the heart; he being a beast who was never transformed by a kiss nor an intracutaneous test; he being the warning at the beginning of any black oily book one might read in darkness with an argand lamp; he being the good lesson one might learn in an earnest attempt to stretch the soul beyond the dreary confines of the body; he being the G in the street who took a *K* and pushed all the cats and monks into a K-hole; he being the date with Rohy Pnol who *roof-roofed* his calling; he being a Liquid, G, who followed a line into *série noir* complete with fog, dark alleys and secret meetings; he being the expectation of the creature waiting for the manifestation of the purchased possession; he being the weed that choked blue the garden of the throat; he being the weed that strangled the serpent in the garden of the throat that sealed the great agony-sweating-drops in the flocks of *alto cumulus* – he being G cannot despair nor dally too long at the public mailbox slip, holding all the letters above: don't add to, don't take away, don't eat, don't touch until the day . . .

DODGASTED NATIVISTIC AGENDUM
Contemptus Mundi
Glimpses into the Mystery of G Day

"O, tell us more, tell us more. Show us if you will, Danse, god digging in the mud," the universe-in-hiding said. "As much as it hurts us to gnash our teeth in agony watching god be what he is and always was, irregardless of what he proposed to be, we are delighted to view the real drama of our destiny. And even though not every scene is explainable, the end result of where it goes *is* the ticket, the show we paid to see."

"Paid, indeed," Danse agreed. "For surely there is no life beyond time that can take as much credit for its own struggle. And in this you have won merit as a form of life that strived to reach beyond its limitations. So as long as god falls where the branches diverge from the trunk, let us glimpse backward further still, to a quick stop, when, as a baby, god was cradled in the arms of a would-be lady. god is wrapped in a diamond coat and is barely one month old; his mother is a music master. As she cradles him in her arms, she is dancing gracefully about the stage in a real turkey of a play, almost fit for the gallows. Remember that the first two acts are a series of gags with no suggestion of a plot. However, there are clues throughout one should pay attention to, if he or she is wise. For such is the way of creation. 9 A.M., 26 Oct. A song, a dance, some gall, a misnomer or two, and then all is through."

"But what of the third act?" the world-in-question asked.

"O, but of course. And that is where love slips in like a koodoo dancing in moonlight. Catch the lace of her gown and her breath – multitiered fluff, ivory-corseted train, cream cardigan, violet chiffon, cleavage-spilling and two brown beans – and you will catch the fragrance of love as it swirls into the nostrils, unbeknownst to pain. The fashion of discovery!"

"The refrain?" the world-in-earnest asked.

"No, not quite! Although there is a certain delight about the stage as two pursue one. The dance! Like the nameless wanderer – anonymous, untitled, and elegiac – a desolate chill can send one to the fire after dreaming upon a freezing sea, the sound of horns, the loss of fellows, the lord's death . . . sung in C."

"Such is your very name," the world-in-light observed.

"The same," Danse said, taking a bow with no arrow intended. "But, a rainbow, yes! You see her dance, but in this act a plot is more important than the gags. The dance will tell a story. For the baby is a noble thing, simply by presentation. But look deep within, you'll find that nobility is thin. The tongue is stifled. And the parasite, liar, and crook be the story. For starters, take the declaration of life through movement, channeled through parable, as it pertains to myth, but more to belief. Here be the third act enucleated: *sohtym*." Danse starts to giggle and sneeze, almost simultaneously. "In the inner we have Saint-étienne among others, such as *Dickens-n-son on a poem*. Holding her baby, whether it be honor or words in crambo or, even more, a wandering, beating heart. The treatment toward all is that the time-scale is distorted through the use of a curved mirror. Flashbacks and glimpses of the future as interpreted by the dancer."

"How so?" inquired the world-in-tow.

"What is important is that the dance employ the entire stage so that the work can be viewed from almost any angle. Even when viewed by Echegaray's folly or Saintliness – dead bodies after a murder on display look like $E=MC^2$ in the classic theater of heads and tails. For here is thrown off a dazzling, complex sequence of steps. Take one – the *Book of Beasts* – an eccoproticophoric feast if ever there was one, in order to get a loosened lease on life. Take two – *Cruel Garden* – with a head that becomes greatly enlarged. Yes, the movements seems to come from earth. Limbs curl and intertwine. The tree. The dance. Divine. So you thought laxly at the time. But in the second act of the dance the garden is cruel and the limbs are curved. Twisted steel for fools. And so it goes as such: Saint George – not the day nor the mushroom, but the duck. Saint Ignatius's bean – not the seed, but the soldier, mean. Saint dipper – with john's bread run through with a German comb? Limes with rime. Locusts honey . . . *and jam instead?* Well, why not? Break boundaries in bed. And dine. With a bit of wort to ward off Barth, throw in some Crisis, John's fire, Joseph's lillies, Mark's flies and Martin's birds into the hearth. To burn – Saint Nich's clerk cleric-gladiator-hatter – and finally collapse from too much solitude in a Saint Vitus's dance in order to finish the martyr via the pot. A ding-dong matter with a *pitter-batter*. In feasts of charity, keep the spot. But as long as you're in tow and I'm in front, think *nuf.* It was too late. Not late enough. Universal, from dust to dust. Twenties, wiggled, bounced, pugilistic Black Bottom, break away wind. O Marquis of Queensberry rules! Lindy, smoothly, violent, sexy, thin, twist and contort. Are you with me? Keep in toe. And an eccyclema is wheeled in just for show!"

"Why?"

"I saith so! Moonlight, stardust, roses and bleeding hearts. Wig Walk, toes together, knees apart. Eagle, pueblos for rain, Iroquois calumet for mimicry. Wiggle and waddle like a teleost leptocephalus at sea. The jungle snaps! and swings, a pumping action. Mushroomed in the fifties! Sing! As the stage was set the movements went, provoking screams and fainting dreams from the masses. *Wings!* Life and death. Featherweight. Genesis. Fascist éclaircissement. Do you see a dent? Life cannot be *spent* dancing my friends, my children, my love-in-tow, burning off the oblong puff of *whipped cream* stripes best platitude."

Danse closed her eyes and breathed so vividly that it was like a dance all unto itself. Dancing all the while, *folie à deux au naturel*, with an eldritch, improvisational laugh. *Flash! an eschatological conversation in morendo movement on a celestial line is transferred to the spirit without a hook.* "I love you all so much! I do! My nation-divi! t . . . sweet land of misery . . . If I could add to my list, I would add a waking beauty, an angel's lake, a rose of black water. A second take. Notice how your spirit evaporates in a jump so complete that it is in contrast to all the laws of flight, balance and movement as they were once perceived. Think: to jump and to breach the stars, and you will never again leap with a limit in mind. Whose story is this?"

"*Call io! Pe!* And if that's busy try *Is A Gog, ics!?* That's our side of the story. Our very own. For we are beginning to know the power of the dance," said the universe-in-trance.

And so, the third act of the dance opened so . . .

"Programs!"

THE COMEDIC BALLET
or
AN OPERA, TAN WART in DISGUISE

The vorspiel to this opera was formally disapproved of by the Church. Brought on by a lazarstink four-day journey through the wilderness.

Everyone means to be loose it seems, but most of us come out looking quite unclean.

See the *MUSIC MASTER*. His eye, his pupil is working at a table lined with dull hagstones. And therein he sees the reflection of a puppet on the stage bound about with a napkin.

HIS

muc

RISE

The mother, a music master, was busy waiting for her man to get up. Yes, all day long she had been waiting. And over and over again she had told herself that he would come as long as there were lines to recite. She was wanting him near her, mainly due to his sense of precog. In essence, he was able to see into the future and thereby foretell events far ahead of their time. The music master was most interested in knowing the fate of her baby, and was willing to pay her man a healthy sum if only he would peer into the future and tell her all that he saw.

Now much to the delight of the world-in-tow, there entered on stage a most welcomed surprise: Danse, herself. The world-in-tow was so beside itself that it accompanied Danse's entrance with an uproarious applause, which in turn stimulated Danse to say, "I find it an absolute delight to perform for kings and queens, all. And to wear their salutations upon mine own crown like a diamond shawl."

To which the mother bellowed, "Bullshit! That's a grand how-do-you-do coming on this stage like you own the whole lot."

"I do," Danse said with a smile, and a heart-warming approval from the audience. "Such enlightened praise! And all from . . . graves!"

The mother, cradling, uttered, "Listen. I enjoy praise as much as you. But what good is it when only the dead is your due? The dead can't speak, nor rant, nor approve. No, no! I prefer something a bit more alive. Like my baby here with beautiful sleeping eyes that suggest not death at all, but life, rave, and all its noble due."

Danse, with an upturned frown, adjusted the envisioned shawl upon her crown, and stated, "As a rule, your baby's fat, and tends to drool. Its ears are extended much like a mule. And if I'm not mistaken . . . isn't that stench, a stool?"

The world-in-tow let out a grandiose laugh, and from the far reaches one hollered, "Tell it, to the last!"

The mother pointed up her nose and said, "So. Parrot, expect your end. The trailing rope cuts short the joke of prophecies scratching scoffers walking after us. So you can flap your tongue with redundancies. Bursting in here without so much as a please. Talking such nonsense as *sailing on a weatherly breeze*, when you should be addressing me on your hands and knees! Or, better yet, on your head upside down, to help establish that smile down-turned on your crown. Why, who are you after all? What entrance this? Who bid you to come? This scene calls for only me, he, and my beautiful piss of a son! There's nothing written about a country lark who just so happens to plop in from the dark. And as far as your insults, I'll have you know, I don't think much of that hair on the end of your nose."

Danse laughed, "Ha, Ha," and again and again, "Ha, ha Ha ha," like a comical refrain, until she had the whole audience doing the same. "It gives me delight to please my universe. To sing! To laugh! And then repeat the verse. Eternity long, such a splendid song. Ha ha! Ha ha! Care to join along?"

The mother uttered, "As long as I have to wait for him, I'll correct your simplistic melody, and do it one better, for the sake of sin.

"O, grievous is my woe, I am dispirited day and night
Since my domineering eye has lost its future sight
And that is why I am waiting for he, who knows the direction so
Of what must be my fate, whether be friend or foe."

At this, the baby made it first utterance upon the stage, by blowing a fart out his ass. Upon which the stage shook with an outburst of laughter, from the graves.

Danse, fanning herself with an imaginary segment of a circle, much like a series of vanes radiating from a hub, muttered, "What a pleasurable and delightful song. Anyone out there care to join along?"

What followed was but a long, long, long silence upon which Danse picked up her merry tune, "Ha ha! Ha ha! From June to merry June!"

The mother, knowing that words wouldn't do, straddled her baby in one arm, and with her free hand did proceed to glue her fingers into a formidable fist. "One kiss from this and you'll be flipping through the same direction you came into."

Danse, feigning a heave of despair, stated most gravely, "Your rhyme is about as fine as thy utterly most profound, densest of minds. Now . . . how did it go? O, grievous is my woe? How about, blatant is my bah? You see, that's used to express disdain or deceit. Utterly perfect for a wolf dressed up like a sheep."

The mother, forgetting all about her baby, now placed both fists on her hips, whereupon her baby performed a complete flip and landed as it were locked in the grip of her forearm. "Sheep, is it? Well, I'll have you know," she bellowed, edging ever closer, "as for sheep, they are cheap, and that is why a peasant leads them so! What a bungle to be cast as a beast that feasts solely on grass. Behold! Neither wolf nor sheep but a tiger 'neath these clothes."

"Alas," Danse said. "She speaks like a beast. Isn't it so? Did I not pen her right from the start? Which reminds me . . . while we're on the prefix, let me extend the letters so and complete the spell from pen to penal, and then further, attach it to code, and there be your load."

And edging ever closer, said the mother, "A code is it?"

Danse interrupted her, "How she repeats herself so. Isn't it pretty? Isn't it swell? The intelligence of it all makes me absolutely dizzy. Pray tell . . . From what school of merit did ringeth your bell?"

And again the stage was hit with a quake of laughter that utterly jelled.

The mother responded, "My school is life! Disorders and wars! Appalling chaos, stabbings and errors galore. And variations of fuss, all in the name of dust-to-dust."

"Lovely, charming, most grievously. A school born of war, death, decay and misery, evermore." Danse faced the audience. "Care to dance? Why not? We'll use mother's mighty roar for music. Therefore we can step over bodies as they fall to the floor. Titus and Gaius and Xamore." She turned on a wave of laughter from the audience to the mother. "But before we begin huygenings, one more statement, however thin, it be true. Better take notice, for that beautiful baby of yours is now turning blue."

Shocked, yes indeed. Mother screamed and released her grip, and voilà! one more flip, to the floor plops her *'amor.'*

"Is this what dancing's all about? Tsk, tsk, tsk. I think not," Danse said. "Must just be your shout. A false step, no doubt. Come, come! my dear. Start again . . . turn about."

The mother picked up her screaming baby, but didn't so much comfort it as she did brush it off. "Scaring the daylights out of me is what you've done! Ranting about like Miss Number One with your ass in a run! It's no wonder all here is in disarray. And speaking of donkeys, it's you who doth bray! Now look what you've done, you deuteragonist. My baby's a mess. Thank god I am still supple, and it can nurse at my breast!"

"A breast fest is it? So glad we could visit. Go ahead," Danse said. "Go expose, so the audience can doze."

"Don't mind if I do. In fact, I'll expose all that I've got. And just to show that I'm generous, why, I'll grant you a sock."

And upon saying this the mother transformed her hand into that forever formidable fist, and swung at Danse but missed, and twisted, and spun around and around with mighty saltations, from stage door to stage door, until *whoosh* through the air flew her beloved *'amor.'* And the audience roared.

"Quite a dancer. That's the stuff. Now, tah tah . . . Once again, soutenu if you must."

It's anyone's guess where the baby flew. So much for it having turned utterly blue. After all, mother's the music master and is much more into tunes. So we'll forgive her for dancing like a contemptible loon.

(But offstage in the dust, there cameth a shout, "Here, come get your baby, it keeps bouncing about!" But mother kept spinning. Such a swing that she took. And all the audience could do was to stand, laugh, and look.)

Danse stepped center on the stage that was bare, and bid her audience, "Everyone now, have a care. Settle down in your seat, for there's still quite a feat for your eyes all to rest upon. So take a load off your feet and enjoy this Dutch concert, according to a Dutch widow treat. Now," she said, "this lesson is short, for the words are quite pat with honor, grace and love to counteract each and every tort. For, indeed, dance is brilliant and powerfully true. Like a lively lavolta kicking in shoes. The flip side to such? Witness mother still spinning, and a vanished baby, last seen blue."

"But we thought music was part of everything right," shouted a voice that was amplified by the use of a mike.

"'Tis true. 'Tis true. I should never disagree. But the science of muses goes beyond musically, to the reaches of heaven where angels' harps hum like bees in the sycamore trees. Take the nine sister goddesses in dreamy abstraction. They sought to bring lightness of harmony into a kingdom of dark winsome. Know . . . no dreary larks shall obscure the stage where souls in melody arise renewed from their graves. Now isn't it queer as we get ready to sing, that in the court of Louis XIV, better known as the Sun King, the dance of ballet did fling into birth, and completely revolutionize the artificality of earth? And revoke the edict of nantes for all it was worth. And victory, fame and peace, together with persecution and mirth, did lend story to the dance, thus its second birth. Plays, ballets, banquets all as you've witnessed thus far. Gardens, theater halls, tyburn trees and full-fledged bars. Yes! Let us all make a toast to the art of song and dance as they're properly combined to compose the most accurate trance. For wisdom and foresight to jump, hop, and prance – to sway, tread, and tiptoe, with sybarite partners we hold like a lance. But, ladies and gentlemen, centered below in this realm of merriment, you'll see neither gun, spear, nor bow. For unlike as it was in times long ago, both destruction and death will finally let go. Yes, dance, speaking music, singing will be the one and only sect, and will be the source of all nourishment to the eye, ear . . . and intellect. So with steps slowly controlled requiring both lightness and depth, we will make with wondrous music whose lyrics are best! As mother spins, spins, spins like a world twirling in flight, let us all clear our throats and with full knowledge, delight. Grimaldi is a race, as a race against time, for the bones tell a story, and the comedy is divine. Life is a game, we're happy to play. The wise enjoy it much for there's nothing to pay. The lovers uphold it for in love there's so little to say but coo, woo and dine me in the most sensual of ways. The winners can laugh. That's their rightful, good way. The dancers can prance for they're no longer clay. No, it's essence and light and lyrics delight, and while she's still spinning, just toss her your fright. And forever release yourself from the leash that father did strap you with while preparing his feast."

And with that the universe leaped right on stage, and danced up a storm that turned delight from rage. And she, *who is Danse?*, shouted, "All right all, let's hear it! The dance and the song that grants yourselves merit."

And the universe-at-large joined along in a dance and a song whereupon ALL could belong:

"We are a heart, all beating as one
We are a Sun, all getting it done
They say sighs are raptures that lift men from earth
And so we all dance, sing, and sigh,
Our glorious rebirth."

"But a sigh is for sadness as Melpomene would agree," said a little child, dear, with a feeble bowed knee. Upon which all did answer, "Yes, but only when mingled with fear. For a sigh is a passion of warm ecstasy. And with it three hearts and a hind can most easily flee."

And over their graves the dead did a minuet dance while Grave Merlin, Vivien Lake, and Veronica Bull wiped the Holy Face. And death so did melt under its own blackened taste.

And then with a hush and an abruptness of dust – from the left wing of the stage appeared the baby blue brave. He crawled on his knees like sceaf in an ark to the center of all, and stood on his feet most laboriously and unraveled a scroll, and started to talk. And he read as such in a voice born of dust, corn, and VeraIcon, and a bit of bark.

"Dear ladies and gentlemen, without making a fuss, I appear before you for the very last time as a sign on a bussock, as is only befitting, for my sentence is due checking my crime. I need not remind you of my sad regret upon which sickness and infirmity has happened my way, and has held me fast to this token day. And all tied up to a tee as they say. And I can no longer wear this halo above for it got dented in flight after ma gave me a shove. Needless to say, I'm dizzy o'er the brook and nauseous indeed, and in a second or two I should be back down on my knees. The clothes that I wore were whisked out the door, as I prefer to be stripped within the coffin I'll bore. Suffice to say, I did try my best, but a fowl in the pocket is as good as one at the breast. And believe me, dear friends, ma's milk ain't the best!" (Laughter and applause from the audience. *Woof. Woof.*) "I thank you, I do, for releasing me alone. I thank you much. For if it's hell where I'm going, I prefer not to go dutch. Let mother begone, and with her that abominable song, *woe woe woe* all day, all day! and all the night long! I jumped my last jump. I bumped my last bump. And now my poor head will dump its last dump. So feast on clay eaters and Hippophagi by the fours. Have a ball. In your stall. And daresay, try never to remember me at all this Wednesday. For I am gone. All is free. My gift from me to thee!" And with that the baby crawled, and was soon gone entirely.

Danse alerted the crowd by clapping her hands to prayer. "Tah tah. Look this way. There's still so much to do. Baby blue is now gone. The clapier flew to the deep-mouthed sea. Shed your tears . . . tah, tah, tah . . . no more than two. Mourning the belated is now all quite dated and *lay me down to sleep* is yesterday's news. So pick up your feet! Let's carry on with the tune!"

"But mother's still spinning," said a little one tugging Danse's train. "So fast that I fear she's producing a flame."

"Oh, you needn't mind her spinning, as such is her call. And to tell you the truth she'll now fit in at the ball! So dancers, get ready! Let's hippodrome to the beat. Winning is losing a terrible streak. And if you haven't a clue, pivot thrice in a dizzy . . . That's it! Up on your shoes!"

How they spun and they spun and they spun, everyone! Doctors and lawyers, and even their sons! Brokers and accountants dressed in mock-turtle furs. Spinning faster and faster, shouting,

"Obsolete all num*burs!*"

For dancing was Master. No plot had ever turned with such switfness, such fashion as a *La Fille Mal Gardée* yearn. For the mother was nasty therein as we've learned, spinning faster and faster, allowing omniscience to burn. For in *La Fille Mal Gardée* mother kept lovers apart, as mothers often do when they thrive in the dark. And even though that ball was lost in the midst of time, we captured it to help us define the reason for being, and the reason is fine. For love is a power that childish souls do possess, whether naked as death or gravely dressed up to the best. And *nothing* will conquer a love in the nest, a fat mother spinning, or a baby suckling a breast.

It's the *Skeleton of the Graces* that does mother best! Feminine forever, such a marvelous breath! Flying ballets the *Apollo of Dance*. Whose very leaps through space could put all in a trance! A candle, a fire, a flame evermore! Mother spinning and spinning, "Fire! Water! Earth! at once is called for!" But none was available, and the king flame did sustain the manner and fancy of a mother insane.

"Does this mean we're *evolving?*" asked a once-washer woman, sweating and fair. For she was weary and broken, and in need of a chair. And had housemaid's knee without turning a hair.

And the words thusly spoken from Danse, fairest of all, were, "Get up! Quit your bickering! And join us at the ball! For the fire is magic and it will burn mother through, like flying in the air or disppearing, too! It's romantic! It's grand! Passing the cup is so sham. It is finished. It is done. It is a know-not-what-to-do-for-pun. The King's place, a stage jammed in Raspberry flames that neither burn nor scorch the frames of tongue spirits in long-winded games. There's no risk to a dance . . . Bid those flames to soothe and enhance the magic of us delicate sylphs all in a trance!"

And bidding her words the washer woman emerged, and spun and spun until her ravaged clothes were undone. And tears shot forth from her eyes, and in its place a prize! A wispy gown graced lightly with lace to her feet.

"Oh, so wonderful! So grand!" The shouts filled the air. And as far as flaming mother, not one seemed to care. For muscular dancers, both so tall and so lean, were like water to the flames that just feigned being mean. And grilled in her dress, mother spinning at best, shouted, "Stop! Someone help me! My performance . . . a mess!"

But the laughs only heightened to cock a snook widely spread. And those who ran to assist on the mesorhine nose sharpened the gaiety by shouting to mother, "Slow down and gives us a kiss instead!" O, the feet without hurting, the breaths without breathless, such is the manner of dance ever restless!

Yes! Imagine a spin until no one can count just how many turns are being made all about! Whether short-kneed or knock-kneed, cumbersome or stout. Translyrical, light fantastic! was what it was all about!

FIGS! CAST THE CREW!

. . . Pleasantly, at the ball, entombed temporarily while all that was falls. But clearly. A new code to install into the hands of merry, gentle souls, all! Take positions, light beings. All take delight in being equally fastidious about the accurate depths of your reverencies. Mix the elements to make your manniferous energy such, a kind of theater parting on its own. Break the code, spill the beans, onanism and deflower, and spread garments across the stage, even to far Cathay, where the luxurious court thriving on fruits sway like dancers. Roads, bridges, and canals flawless. Rubies, thick as a man's arm. Floors and roofs of gold. Mannheim gold. A stately pleasure-dome where the sacred rivers flow to a sunlit sea, and gardens bright where dancers delight under incense-bearing trees.

Danse lives! Rising from the page that gave birth to verse. Immortal maid. She will thrive as long as god thrives. But once he falls – and the gravestones beaten smooth by centuries of New England weather vanish the letters, and lanes opening onto playing fields fall, and meadows dotted with calves and sheep make lions of their meal, and teachers who favor wool jackets and Homer in leather miss the legends, and dents live without walls in infamous cubicles of decadence, and dashers dash to rehearsals, lectures and readings, leaving the eucalyptus and yucca lined pathways to bend in their wind – the gay, the proud white lovers of music and dance will chance the shades of darkness. No distant age will conquer, for fading beauty makes a tear to fall and dry as it courses downward to the lips.

One form resembling all at the ball will never lie nor die, but will float above the waves and caves of ice. What form divine? *Virtute et numine.* Those wakeful eyes singing on the Mount a symphony and a song, with a dance to play along: all edentate grandchildren drinking the milk of a loving paradise of pellucid elements.

And from this point Danse took center stage, coming forward with measured steps, tripudiating in the act, and then slowly raised her graceful arms covered with triangular scales, and opened and extended her naked breasts, and granted all the ball to feast with precision and lightness upon the nipples of her ghostly wantoness.

And the ball-at-large did charge! with urgency, most diligently. Creaming wet with pirouettes. Until one leaped above the rest shouting,

"Surprises galore! Aint't this the best?!"

And with that he made a dive back to the breasts. The divine harmony of his movements did find no rest.

And in that ridge that did compose *her breasts*, a hoofer went a-riding, and homed in onto the range, and did quite a bit of sliding. And up, up and away you could see it in his sigh. A buck and wing his gallop. A Highland fling his eye. And nay that eye did ever tear, but dripped emotion with haste. Yes, indeed, even down onto his waist.

And from this union with her breasts, a new garden did hereby grow. With not a warning, not one at all except *to reap exactly what you sow*. And sow they did from head to toe, and drenched her quite the same, and all Danse could say dripping wet was "Isn't this a lovely game?" Now listen close if you need a clue. More certain than not, you probably do. And let these words fill not one hemisphere but two, as homily we go.

"Acey-deucy for a start. Blindmen's bluff if it's in the dark. Balloon ball on an expanding course. Shuttle propalinal cock for moving back and forth. And in the realms of balls, we needn't stall at merely two. Consider the following, and if you more, I'm sure they will all certainly do.

"Association football. You play this on your shoe. Together, with football, now that makes two. Baseball, basketball, now there's four. Bowling ball, captain ball. Have we anymore? Handball, Pushball . . . let me see . . . Softball . . . the eighth degree? Tetherball, trap bat and ball, all-in-three. Quite testy. And in the way of disciples, twelve makes volleyball. Twenty-four plus one. And now, you're free!

"And of the twelve, could you find Judas? *Psst . . . Psst . . .* disguised as a hierophant . . . slipping thirty mazumas in his hat? Hint: feathers radiating from a center, under the guise of friendship. And while we're at it, as does this garden grow, a tree with purplish, rosy flowers that is part of what they sow. In the belief that the guise did hang from it, after having hung so low. Seek as many Judasses as you can in this highlight of a show.

"But yet another word squeaks out me lips, although one need . . . one must pastiche! Peer in, for the word is synonymous with three letters. Pronunciation: *sin*. And the very word in question has several meanings pertaining to its spelling, from the way it sounds on the ear *pssts* . . . come and see. The word in question is *hole*.

"First, we have a hole-in-one. And then we've got *one-in-the-bun*. From here we take a walk around, and slip inside the hairy crown. With holes you have a 'w,' but in this case that will never do. So, let's continue on. Let's do! And in the course test icicle.

"Now insofar as a hole's a shape that looks thusly like this O, let's see where it will go. Take a breath. Bolero. Cantico. Fandango. Mambo. Saltarello. Tango. Gambado. Now misplace the O and you have: Heel-in-toe. Pigeon wing and Double shuffle. Two-step and Sir Roger de Coverley. Scotch reel. Schottische. Round dance. Astronomical. Corybantic. Floral. Abbot's Bromley Horn. Rigadoon. Portland fancy . . . must be nearly noon . . . Polonaise and Polka, too. Morris dance, most vigorous. Costumes and bells will do. Long ways dance, that's missionary. *Penché*, that's not, which is proper for the church, even though you break the cherry . . . Burst! Religieuse! Jota, that's a bit obtuse. For beating meat, what is edible is distinguished from the common shell. Horn pipe . . . there's a bit of cock. Hootchy-Kootchy . . . haven't we done this before? By lots? Gallopade. Fox trot . . . but not out the door. Conga and Shimmy dot . . . I dare you. Want the answer? *Fuck you!* Now, take *that* word apart. Let's do! Take *o* and eliminate the *u* . . . Still haven't a clue? Then borrow the *c* and double it: *coc*. Still no clue? Then steal the *k* and let go the rest, and what's left? *'Cock'* as in *cock-a-doodle-doo* . . . which is exactly what he did before *he* denied him thrice. Stay on track. It does get that nice.

"A cockatrice is a serpent with a deadly glance, much like a cock in a rigid dance. The tyburn jig, the Gregorian tree, gory be! It's Bull to me! Or, better yet, considering a serpent, Gadreel in a well-wrapped turban. Now a cockatrice according to holes fits the bill, because they're actually hatched from a cock's egg on a dunghill. And while we're at it consider this: A cockalorum is a self-important little man, much like the one that took the grandstand at Azazel, with 7 heads, 14 faces and 12 wings, who refused to bow before a dam. The first – fire before clay? What the hay!?, rather be Eblis, or a tall cherub well-hung any day. The remaining universe was O . . C . . . Cupid. Need a rest? You're out! Must keep abreast! The game is up, as in orgy. Twenty-one or thirty-one or . . . vingt-et-un. She loves to have them all undone. And then play stud poker just for fun. O . . . please do! spread me wider, stupid, there's still some room. Straight poker, if you prefer, but gobang if you have the nerve! Blind poker if you're a bit shy. All fours if you're into *bi*. Now a dog is smart, but so is a banker in the left pocket when the head pokes out to view the power of the air. Tremble there. In the dark. O, I love to play by the rules of the game . . . that is, as long as the game has a tinge of shame according to the course in the socket. So, lock it."

And it is finished.

VIBRATION IN PARADISE

Now this was where all of the soles in the sea totally parted from their existence briséing in the air with god's shoes, and thereafter did cleve onto Danse and become *one sobornost vibration* in Paradise, alias Pennsylvania, settled by Dunkards and Mennonites, with the name Paradise given by Abraham Witmer, long since lost. And even though it was all in the spirit of song, dance and merriment, and all gay religions full of **Dis** play in dawn, each soul opened its second chakra and bore Danse, and encouraged her to mount Rainier, which is the same as mounting Paradise (or Ida), if you happen to be Grace or Russ and know your history. In view of all the wigs and masks on stage, it was difficult to move in the Tao House since there was a great demand on 1st principals, eternal order and cosmic truth. But near Danville, CA, there was a still, long journey into night to make a canterbury to. Souls danced male and female roles inside of Danse's womb. For it was here that the magnitudes burrowed, with some swimming in the canals, others shooting the tubes, and still tens of thousands more hanging on the bathroom door, flushed, and just outside the boundary condition, esp. on the wall of a rigid conduit where there might be still more, clinging to climbing sumac, and a mass wife or two clothed in pamplegia. One named Mlle. de la Fontaine even went so far as to excuse herself, scratch, and lap up the juice oozing from one of Danse's inner shelves. In minutes (and those are timeless minutes), she was drunk with cumuppance, as it was the first time she had ever fished from a woman's well, and had not as yet developed a tolerance for *anigav suocum*, as in music, viola. Needless to say, there were thousands lined up (including seven Australian cliners) just outside her bmow, parallel to the wall, waiting their turn, each bearing a capital *'G'* on their foreheads. And down the line could be heard Danse's dancers, all in turn, awaiting velocity of escape to M.mmmmmmm. AE:

"I heard it's delicious inside. All slippery wet with a billion and one places to hide."

"Like in a beehive, I'm sure."

"Sure hope they don't take prints. See mine are not usable burned down from red-hot."

"But BGee, outside, inside, meeting or breaking, cracking seven miles a second, one can move outward inward and still vellicate."

And from the uproarious gaiety inside the gibbous mood, buzzing drunk, bawdy words were added to the songs on stage, morals grave, here lies wer, full belly of wormwood.

"I heard inside there's a catchy tune being played about. It smells of South Pacific and, yet, with an altogether different sprout.

"I'm as horny as a lizard on the prowl

I'm as beaten as a bitch getting mauled

Much more than a tart, I'm a girl who won't start

'Till I got me an interrex by the heart."

"Believe me, honey! The lines inside will move much faster as the tail spins on a hook."

"And O! I hear the smells and the tastes within are just heavenly! Formidable reeb and akdov still-hot-mecca, mart iniold No.7 Jack Sazerac, slimmed down, deflated, little water, *nip* pressed against the chest, the rim, hipbone-thigh draped with loose wavering silk. My. My."

"Mon, I's hopes yous cans efi insides."

"Where you been? Deef is it?"

"Why just outside the door. What for?"

"What for!? You need to know more. It's the teeth of a boar."

"There is nothin' like a whore!

Nothin' on this plane

There is nothin' you can name

That is anythin' like a whore!

We've got spirits in the stagelight!

We got a god kicked out none too soon!

We've got numbers runnin' crazy!

We got months stacked up in June!

We got movies, we got musicals! We got dancers *in   interregnum!*

What don't we got?

We don't got Joel!"

"Joel? Who's he?"

"Joel is a minor prophet of the old Testament, but brother! he ain't nothin' in comparison to me muddah! . . .

"There is nothin' like a whore!

Nothin' in this realm!

And once we make it through this door

We'll be banging our Ma once more!"

"Do you think our verse will improve once we are inside?"

"Interesting you should ask. For what is a verse but a line of metrical writing. And what is a meter but a basic unit of length. And what is length but the longest dimension of an object, preferably an object in space. And what is space but a period of time, a boundless *three*-dimensional extent in which objects and events occur and have relative position and direction, i.e., R&H, which brings us into a space that is directed into a verse that is, in effect, one of the short divisions of space into which a chapter of the wisdom of the Minerva Press, like a fascicle, was traditionally divided after having sprung with a tremendous battle-cry, fully armed, from the brain of Leadenhall Street, London, a trashy but most complicated plot of bloody Mary space, where the hangerons glue their shoulders to the walls outside of brightly lit cafe's, *'have ye any change to spare?' asked T. Hunter, to which Janus responded, 'In the beginning was the Gate, opened for late-night snacks, whereupon 2 faces ate . . .'* Which once again brings us back to Joel, who is the Judicium Crucis incarnate, the trial of the cross, the ordeal of stretching before the bar, the ring of Champ Agnes, Mart MadCock Tailset, on the tab, *Shake Shake,* the Silver Goblet, Port, bon voyage, every color – which is all that the Music Master was waiting for at the time she was holding her baby before Danse, the Dancing Master, Moody Chaos, came unto the stage performing a sort of stick dance of India, having just stepped out of the undulous puddles, imbued with gnacs, very ree, with a Shaker's Guarantee in J.J. Wardley-Captn' Morgan and Son, Beefeater-Non and Ann Lee, the Bride of Frankinte-Quila-Glen-livet-as-a-werwolf-on-holiday-in-Manchester. He, known as Joel, wrote a short prophetic *heils geschichte*, a Doomesday Incident Report, that was divided into four chapters. The first two being devoted to the realm that was ravaged by a swarm of nasty insects with beating sticks. The last two describing the judgment executed against all enemies of the aforementioned Booking realm. Was it a symbol or not? First, remember there are *three* stages in regards to the insects: the great cloud darkening the sun black, and also the stars; the noise of the wings whirring and the jaws crunching like old Big Bertha herself of armament fame; the futile Garden turned into a wasteland by seventy-five insects, megatons shaped like stick horses. Yes, it was like a siege akin to labefaction. For the stick insects, Phasmatidae, leaped upon the Garden at 1600 and devoured it whole. And insofar as there was sole punishment in the manner of bastinado upon all oppressors guilty of opprobrium, regardless of their rank, there was also a rebirth and a restoration. However, after Judgment a new era dawned in which a *Geist* was poured forth after having completed pelotherapy. Sons and daughters prophesied, old men dreamed dreams, Waldo's brahma screamed, and younger men saw giant visions starring Anak and Og, the teutonic twins destined for wag along with the whole wagang."

"Achew!"

"Gesundheit!"

. . . Meanwhile, deep inside the womb, life was being born anew under the very eye of G. At first glance it was short and not pretty: a skeleton, knees drawn up, gaping jawbone of hollow scream, slug exiting through the hole; but charm, vivacity, and dance made up for those defects. Some of the early growths caught in the midst of their journey, who went by names, *Moreau, Maupain, Subligny,* and *Huretti*, all ballerinas of the Pear Is Ope Ra, wore large panniers, roughly two inches above the ankles, in order to give a pleasant cross view of their beating entrechats, in order that all might see them leap in a fury from one stage of evolution to the next. Crowd scene: organza skirts, microminis, attenuated Duchess skirts, hostess blouses in autumn-prints with a springtime hint, a thirties boudoir theme with a forties sprint to droopy pinkwhite rising mush. Indeed, speaking of furies or Disir, vengeance was the very action considered to be justified in regards to AZ's undoing (that is, his black skirt). And it was these very furies that did spring forth, like budding fruit, out of god himself. Only this time they came forth without the plague of unwarranted moral, and stood like giants in the earth fashioned after Bergelmir, Gilling, and Thiazi, each holding candlesticks.

Maupain just so happened to have many lovers as was befitting a ballerina. Moreau was rich as was befitting a ballet queen. Subligny was both dainty and beautiful as was befitting a prima donna. And Huretti was well-mannered and gracious as was befitting a Hostess. It was Huretti who caused a stir by wearing a see-through muslin dress and a fascinator on her head instead of a pillbox, which proved to be rather awkward, in (so, *being*) that the Moslem she bore was nude beside/atop her as was befitting a battalion and/or Italian beaten at the plate. (Incidentally, there just so happened to be another Muslim, unrelated to the first, who did wear a solid muslin dress that had nothing at all to do with religion as it pertains to surrendering oneself to god, even though a *god* to a Muslem is not the same as a *god* to a Christian, insofar that each firmly believes his *own* god to be the only *true* god to surrender to, and looks upon each other deuce to deuce, *de haut en bas*, or as holding a fool's bauble.) Which brings us to the very nature of formal dress as it pertains to god and stercoration, *l'oeuf* and *amour, love the 0*, irrespective of which god one is referring to at any given moment in time (i.e., time is timeless, 0, so there is very little formal time in which to view anything, solid or otherwise, that is within infernal time, unless one, such as a prophet, ventures across the board to Rolland Garros and views the 'F' opening in 't', or to Asturias and views a Mantis in a mantilla saying, *"Yo rezo. Olé!"*).

Now, work the mind like a muscle in fasciculation till it hurts and has you shouting, *"Crux criticorum!"* Pump the brain of Gallimaufry. Disregard insane, even though one may find it hard to blame D-O (to Jell-O) with anything but insanity. (However, when one takes into consideration all that *affreux Diva* the Gourmand has done in order to make sure that the world was truly animatedly mad, and beating itself, affrettando-style, into *aischrolatreia* arrest, it makes it so much easier to cope with the insanity therein – *ad unguem,* at least until one gets beyond the 'insanity' and realizes the quantitative drama, the intense conflict of forces at work, and thereby avoids being gorged by implementing a farol swirl, such as a whirling mass[messa] or a spiraling mark[6], or by taking the charge[card]in hand – if one can quickly cut through the bull.)

The surface of existence has a meaning – *de integro.* Naturally, the meaning goes much deeper than the surface itself and takes on a whole new definition the deeper it goes, so that in time the meaning of existence is indistinguishable from one depth to the next. Consequently, one cannot comprehend existence without the aid of paros. It is only proper that one seaman is forced to investigate (i.e., re-search) the causes for *bellum internecinum* if one is to discover the true meaning, the origin that forever changes within this book, which is both significant and vital to all existence *à la aition*. Insofar as we are speaking of the G region, we must take into considertion, in our analysis of stercoranism and its hidden buried secrets in onomasiology, the Heaviside layer that contains free electrically-charged particles of light, by means of which special communication is transmitted throughout great distances consisting of several regions possessing one or more layers with varying dimensions but with associated concepts, including space, time and solar cycles in the > E layer of the ionosphere, approximately 60 miles above the surface, where can still be hard amidst the *astuto* notes of *Oración del torero*, "*E'li E'li . . . Albert Herring, Red tick tick tick across the page OOO* the *corrida. Quisiera una localidad de sombra.*"

Witch vampirish succubus going down Hexameron to Hic . . . Hic Jacets . . . Gytrash comes upon Habe (as Corpus) flaccidly manustuprating on a cross-row with the letter G, dreaming wetless dreams and dispossessed prophecies.

JEST BECAUSE YOU'RE YOU

Four heads down the line of those waiting to get into the New Womb was a man who, by way of abbreviation, was referred to as *ist*. (O henry's law: *Don't act amish.*) *Ist* was famous in his own time for having made an enormous *discovery* – namely, that all he had man-made and owned on the earth 'grieved' him in his heart. In addition to this, his 'fame' was kept intact (posthumorously) due to all the movies that were made about him, particularly by one made in the realm of *March*, while he was doing a stitch of time in Ohio for embezzlement and for fainaiguing a good-hearted Jack under the alias Joseph *(Amen)*, which was synonomous at the time with self-inductance while in a state of inertia, which, being-at-rest in the lounge suit of a faineant, meant that not only would the weight of his gas become dissolved by liquid through the digestive track, but that all of his ten fingers would get classified as a unit, as prints entitled *Sophia: The 400 Million Marks* (Surprise!). Needless to say, *ist* had converted many Jerries in his quest. In the realm of eternity he most certainly favored the *O* and found it to be perfectly logical in the Brit sense. There were, in essence, many sweet bredmen beneath him known as afikomen-famuli, but forever a dancing Queen above him. Some said that while on his journeys in Ahasuerus disguise, *ist* literally walked on water and ate bread while on the runs (+ half a dozen ghawazi in the street), and that he journeyed with a garden on his back. *O* he was a commander – all right – awashed in gouache. And even though that which *ist* commanded were but midges in comparison to the light horsemen – both Australian and Turkish at Beersheeba – *ist* was still a noble admiral, sonorized, and was 'spotted' as far east as Salt Lake City, locked arm-in-arm with a *dame de compagnie*, still breathless, though still much the opaque snail into sod.

Certainly exploration of the soul became the rage after *ist's* major work was done, and many followed suit in his name. Perseverance and encouragement were *ist's* virtues, and his hell of a harrowing presence in the line leading into the New Womb was well-deserved. It was said that *ist* was well hung – no matter the house, no matter the specially designed Babylonian pubic *tuft* – and that his dowry was thoroughly modern and rogynous, youthful and anti-camp, and anti-ball, and somewhat of a drain on the installment plan for wardrobe plerotic replenishments once-eaten by the household dogmoth, which first attacked anything with a Julie green tinge of Georgian paste to it.

Behind *ist* stood another cinematic moment: *Hud aka duh* – who just so happened to still be connected to his never-before-mentioned seven-year old son, Nut Capaneus. Eavesdropping, one is able to hear Hud utter to his son, "GeBurt, ain't this better than the freezing waters of H.B. and going for a burton?" To which his son replies, "Duh, but I sure hope that in this new Womb there aren't going to be so many poverty-stricken mumpers and vile berries under the new broom hanging around as there were in the Old Womb, which can leave one old broom in a clear state of cataplexy, or even duh paulocardia after having eaten just one berry."

"Undbaremezacruzforzemumpsimusofzit," Hud said.

"I'll drink to that. We'll get C.R. & Hopefully to help us," his son replied.

Stop! Momentary pause.

"Do you think it will stir a revolution? Like Robert the devil overturning the pages to Palestine? Or Don the Cos sacking them in the middle and lower part?" his son asked.

"Perhaps. But all in the name of jinete, son," Hud said.

"Just as long as it doesn't cause too much of a fuss and we get some rest before Judgement Day," his son said.

IN THE NEW WOMB

Last night while wallowing in the inner depths in search of god, I was able to slip off the hook, as it's often said, and, by balancing ever so lightly on my ligament of zinn, climb through liquid waste to the surface, and reappear, almost in harengiform guise . . . with a spruce frankincense and a noble llautu wound about my head. A new inner depth I found there – the sky, the sea, and minor divinities.

I finally located god in an oasis of sorts, over seas – midnight seas rolling in soft bodies twenty to thirty feet high; rolling over desert sands yielding to winds, demanding advice; rolling over slippery cities in the moonpath; agitated cities washed in moon soap; docile, sleeping cities easy to handle; cine cities caught up in the light moist night air carried to the tops of crescent hills, cries mafficking, but really only cries protesting the will – I found him draining tears, inspiring horror, repugnant. With wilting eyes I saw him unbalanced, with the face of a man commanding nothing but his very own voice, solemn vows of poverty cracked, hard, external and so small in scope you could fit it in a nutshell. I caught him in my eye and he fell into a state of nympholepsy.

THE ELEMENTS OF MURDER

Suffering, pain, negativity, expulsion, exception, blame, guilt, shame, hunger, thirst, mourn, corruption. Ida sat and wondered. She was about to leave for a spell and allow Cyclops to tell the world his story. It was all right. After all, every healthy gaia woman has a deep holy need to submit to a benevolent phallic power, and to receive and contain it – the sword-like, aggressive phallic power that is able to transform itself into an instrument which opens up a channel for the circulation of burden, of blame without parents. But wait! G Day! which can bring humans more happiness than anything else in existence!

Ida closed her eyes.

She loved Cyclops, and in her absence she was going to send him a vision.

THE VISION

ENTER: One of the soundest casts you'll ever see this side of Thebes! Bry! McQ! Horst! James! Bron! Vaughn! (a.k.a. Ugh) and Dex! And their stand-in: Toshiro!

THE M-SEVEN AGAINST THEBES

Bry. A good old boy. A member of the old establishment composed of vision, decent values, humble manners, and a love of hats; but dashing, courageous, a swashbuckler of the Manichean Age (though not above making fescennine comments on festive occasions at idle, bending girls). A firm believer in a syncretistic religious dualism that preached the release of the spirit from matter through asceticism, which warranted an ample amount of self-discipline, especially since it involved the fusion of three different inflectional forms, all of which naturally conflict in an illogical and inconsistent platform that involved a further union against a common enemy.

Bry was also the founder of *Uniwise News Corporation:* The Healthy Solution, which ranged from Twentieth Century Fox to Asia's Star TV, to more than five thousand lying newspapers in eleven couchant countries, to *Lyra News*, which had within its breadth both the lyre of Orpheus and the glare of Las Vegas, and was best read while on the John from 1 A.M. to 10 P.M. with the head raised.

McQ – who ran a $28 billion dollar a year fiefdom in Memphis that encompassed Warner Bros., Doubleday, Amway, Noway, Mad, TeenBeat, QVC, CBS, and Takearest – a man of three thousand contracts, who has been involved in almost every major deal of the past three decades, including the sale of Columbia to Sunbeam, Matsushita's purchase of the MGM Grand and Madison Square Garden, Trotsky & Co. Inc., a firm he spun off from his father's and uncle's revolutionary holdings in East Prussia during the Backwash of 1929, with the backing of a family embezzlement scam worth well over 3.5 billion, and the transference of Gog to god into the corporate *Goggodgoogoogeegees,* a fathersonolénterprise.

Dex – essentially a hard-driving mongrel-cowboy nicknamed the Bulldog, who, earlier in life, was a giant earl in the home-shopping network industry – an acknowledged programming genius who spent the weekends at his four-level house in the Fire Island Pines, spotting every houseplant and chair, while entertaining various members of society renowned for worldly success.

James – James was a good man to have on anyone's team for he knew how to network, surf and enemate into most any hole of society, and could just as easily rub cheeks with secretaries of state as he could with full-blooded, long-limbed Ashantis in the bush. Nevertheless, upon closer examination, we find that James came to represent different things to different people. Certainly, there were several who laid claim to him. Zebedee the Great insisted that James was his son, but so did Alphaeus, as did Clopas the Younger, who thought most everyone a stranger, while Judas insisted that James was his brother, but so did Jesus, and yet Yermak was positive that James was a loyal Cossack with financial ties to the Stroganovs, however Darryl F. Zanuck could have sworn he was only an extra-long in *The Longest Day*. James's title actually included Chairman of the Council. (Case in fact: he was responsible as well for writing a letter to the Twelve Tribes with Dysentery, wherein he advised the members to eat only tails and entrails, and to refrain from eating baby tongues and mother tongues as they can both set the belly on conflagrant con-foundation.) When James was sixty-two, he resided in Memphis and was given the nickname *King of Thirty-Three*. One day out of sheer boredom he decided to better translate the Vulgate from Vulgar Sow (that's *sermo plebeius*) to Earitant English. For as it stood in Vulgar Sow, Genesis currently began:

"god was vulned in his very fundament due to a fumble among his fruits giggling on the vine; therefore, he created a buff-ball and placed therein a sailor from the sea in search of a Mist. Shore, who both finally met by daily mail, signed and delivered to the coachman in the inner-box. And the lord went thereafter by Cap, and he did sail about the Cape of Good Hope in his G boat, which had a leak due to two missing seals, compliments of a blood-thirsty serpent; and he did set his pen uprightly in order to come a rightly dux, so as to bury the hatchet in the may flower, so to speak *rev*, and get off the musical rock."

GI: I www.Vsnot

Cut!

GAWDBOX WHIZZY

One must first ask oneself *what forces are at work that thereby necessitate a need/feeling/ desire to be not only pessimistic about the present but, beyond this, to foresee nothing but truthful calamitousness regarding the future without having to lie as flat as Ananias?* In other words, why can't we simply live in a dimension and/or society whereby every member, every citizen, bears a calathos upon his crown as a divine symbol of temporary fruitfulness? Simply put, the answer is: because god as we know him is a cadelle, a dust to duster, who thereby spreads amathophobia to one and all, and who apparently feels quite justified in having set up a system whereby man as an innocent, bewildered mass, a pastry vernix of dead cells, gets the blame for nearly everything – whether he is in cahoots with this or that pitcher, with this or that dodger, or with this or that scandal. It is no wonder that mankind roams aimlessly from place to place like so many seeds dispersed in an east-windy wind, landing wherever they may to flower. Certainly despair is a common lot in which to put seed *in;* but for that matter so is nome – first as an ancient province, last as a fish on top of Hat-Mehit. Nevertheless, for those of us who have been able to find a euphony to existence and have in their own hard-wrought battle been able to produce a pleasing, harmonious succession of words and sounds of life in spite of the judgment in arms – the death, the ruin, the dissolution of forms, like Anthony of Padua speaking to the fish, even to the one-eyed variety, on his day, 6/13, when the stars fall into the earth, and the figs cast untimely green in a mighty wind, and the little fishes in the pool of tears blindly swim into the crocodile's grin – there is still a chance to come into league with the strike-breaking operations of *the Magnificent Seven* (Theme music), and to cry stinking fish for the wares in the streets, and bidding birds for the fowls in the air, and to realize that as it pertains to their Japanese stand-in – Toshiro – G means talent/ability, and is specifically a classic Japanese dance-drama that is heroic in both subject and in the use of measured chants and movements (LOUDER theme music).

THE STAND-IN

Toshiro, the stand-in for the M-7, was involved in nothing less than an *agon* with god. Clearly, Toshiro was driven to lay the record straight and to once and for all clarify the meaning behind the fatuous diversification of god's plan of creation.

It is common language that what is evil is strictly relative as long as there is duality and the do's and don'ts remain interchangeable; just as there is a yang of life as opposed to a yin of death, just as some of us eat no fish and just as some of us do, just as some of us fish the anchor and pick up the cat, just as the mother spanks the baby because the baby has crawled into an oncoming path of traf-fiction (i.e., fabrication-in-transit or fabricated intercourse), one must ask the question: *Is the mother instructing or punishing? Or should it really matter as long as the holder's weight in spirit remains the same?* Naturally, god claims justification for his actions by putting forth the same dualistic premise when it comes to war, famine, crime, sex, disease and injustice. To punish or to teach? But in a deeper sense this is more analogous to the divine and universal language, the mystical code that is defined as only pleasure and gain. The quadrum leap that surpasses the experience of war, madness, destruction, separatism, feudalism, communism, democracy, murder, mayhem, turmoil, abandonment, abuse, the aerosol bomb, the long range missiles, the atomic bomb, biological and chemical warfare, Armageddon, floods, famines, pestilences, a belief in pain and martyrdom – is the very quadrum leap that must be made over god himself. In essence – to quadrum leap over the very thornes of the shrinking/expanding Universe, and thereafter to work backwards, to amphibianize, de-transcending both the mechanics of time and the activities of a tyrannically advanced civilization, in order to find the exotic worm of existence by boring into the transversible hole without getting ripped apart in the process, and to thereby avoid any upstanding *verruca acuminata.*

SMOKIN' G.

Toshiro say: "Remember seed. For Pop will put germ between he and she. It will bruise their beam. So goes royal head. So goes brain. So goes meal. Hah! Got fernball caught in throat! Rise! god is on the way. But first . . . key history lesson."

And with that Toshiro reached for his copy of *Die Kunst Ciromantia* by Johan Hartlieb and read:

Catch Torii Love Dance of Sperm Seed, put in pocket, save for rainy day

or

Catch Falling Star Lu in hand! Commode est ta Perry?

. . . In the floppy disc fits bedsheets of Fallopian fields – in the roving, rolling, windswept clothes of a strong gush of trophoblast – in the soft midnight bed near old Cowper's gland, adjacent to Farmer John's prostate gland, where vulva met Corporeal Cavernosa out of uniform and had a whambang-thank-you-ma'am in the incised meander, with the sword erect and pointed at the moon behind cervix, the rampaging sperms met their gushing geisha ovum, militarily lashed her with their tails, and patted her like a group engaged in *poor pussy*, rotating her to 6 RPM; crop rotation clover balls of sperm pirouetting silly – piscatorially – around and around the pisiform – waiting ovum for several suspenseful moments – 3 – until one hoofing tango country dance Fandango, one strathspey-spitting Snakedance closed in for a reel-in Scot kiss short of scugging, and a moody, femme, pea, butterball, poached-egg plunge fling off the old Baby Ziggurat Tower. Ba Ba Black Sheep, a various uproar, a pig jangling on a chain, a hideous gas bubble burst into flame, a whore, have youse any wool? Ba. Ba. Ba. Fuel. Fuel. Fuel. Just like Zeno of Elea and the tortoise and Achilles spiel. O! how two lovers do spin a chemical quickstep ziganka that inhibits any competing sperms from cutting in. O motion and plurality . . . and something plural . . . become something singular. Self-transcending after time and space into an ultra-localized motion of the most radiant, beautiful war theater that there ever will be between molecules, eggs, spores and seeds. Concretely and abstractly. Visibly and invisibly. O! how divinity soars beyond Elysium fields.

Star fall by reason of smoke.

Amour propre. The sphere of mortal life transcends the sphere of spirit life by way of self-love in the palm. (Meddling in the girdle, Sol got his ring stuck in Venus, which actually put him in a fine mettle.) The reedy people of the planet earth pursuing the interests and pleasures of onanistic life essentially means that the entire area in which man thinks of himself as living encompasses a position than can be applied to the whole space present to experience, including all visible celestial bodies, with special emphasis put upon the third in order of distance from the sun, and the ninth, especially as they involve the entire system of created things as a total (metaphorically speaking) unit in its arrangement and carnal operation, all contained within a piscina with a proper drain for the sacred reedy disposal.

Chill

"*Howf! Howf!*" barked *Let's slip in the dogs of war*, for he was accustomed to marking as his haunt the pisciform gates of heaven. Indeed, every morning, *Let's slip the dogs of war* would appear at the Piscidia-garden gates. "*Howf! Howf!*" He was eager, for it was a well-known fact among the strays that god, gazing, would often throw a tempting bone or two to wandering, outcrying dogs living on the pavement among a scryer or two. Wagging his tail, hearing the footsteps approaching as god descended the stairs, *Let's Slip* was salivating worse than Pavlov's dogs, just dreaming what bleeding pieces of meat this butcher might throw, spiked with *caedere*, that is, Piscidiaerythrinajamaicaoverkill. Ever so closer the steps echoed. "*Howf! Howf!*" Just thinking: what meat, hot from the burial, would come? What tree to baptize when done? Ask Anubis. He's usually under the XVIII Moon, howling up a storm. He's a regular psychopomp that one. He's got the odor of sanctity. He sniffs your behind and tells you what's up front. There he is now! Only his mouth looks dumb and from his ruby lips he Cries Havoc. For indiscriminate slaughter bears his mysterious reply.

Such an exposed, cryptic tongue. On its tip, it's well-dung.

*   *   *

Serious business this, thought Toshiro. god thinks of indiscriminate slaughter standing in for revenge at Armageddon?! So much like sixteenth century novel where brownnose

147

villagers hire professional warriors to beat off bandits. god, you fire-breathing lizard, Zilla, threatening civilization with atomic-fueled energy, seeking revenge for son, very acute Ahasuerus movements directed by team of experts overseen by archon director, Honda himself, could easily be confused by letter O for tough, wily, heartless cavalry scout, Hondo in Devil's Saddle, forever warning of Apache *zuknallen* dance uprising. John say first misfortunate word. *Grace.* Hondo made for him, without him could not be made. In him was star and star was light on screen and light shine in darkness. *Gnade ne.* If this business of kamicide come clean, will be necessary to consult Katari-be, At ha! pascan, T. lingit, Ha! Ida, and E. yakyakyak experts in relating ancient devious legends about gods during Shinto festivals. Same who sang dance song at Imperial Court with B-girls led by B.V.M.

Mary had little lamb
Fleece white as snow
Everywhere Mary went
Lamb never go.
Follow her school one day
Observe Golden Rule
There heard him say
Earth filled with dancing fools.
Think not I come send peace on earth
I come not send peace but sword,
I come set man against father lord,
Daughter against dear mother, yet further reward.

Toshiro sipped his tea. "Such business beyond me. No keep bad man down. We cut him in heel. That where he peel." So Toshiro called upon O no Yasumaro to set up a Committee whereby O no would have to work at learning all the secrets of god by heart, under the code name: tv godjak: the Bejesusfile. There must be a way of keeping humankind from wrongly being committed of sin. If successful, some dear tv guide would appear, and the pilot would evolve into a long running series, and go on to win numerous Emmys, capturing the image orthicon, even if the series should involve Nazi spies with a fetish for lollypops, and Russian émigrés in Belarus with a fetish for vodka, and British Tommys in tow, and Hod as in Odin (not Hud as in Paul), all inspiring a lost class of heimin to scale the heights to becoming heinies in their own reich, with a fetish toward anyone named Heinrich Henry-Tojo, residing in Ginza. The 'code' itself would need to be made up of white Russian/Chinese characters used with a radical in order to form a new character as the phonetic equivalence of syllables, wherein two or more are gathered together at a stag party in an effort to establish an Orphismic orthodoxy in order for purification to occur, but only after successive runs to the body head (the Surroyal Crown Jewels). And could go something like this:

"Four April saviours may come your way
They'll bring Big Fires, a flame in May
So as to burn, the earth away . . ."

Toshiro sipped his tea. "What combat such force? Perhaps Shichi-Fukujin. In Hotei Luck, fat dine. *Joie de vivre* as watchmen give long scholar good eat, good fish, good venison, good music on goodship lollipop. Perhaps Kami. High mountain, tall and ancient tree, river, all Kami, all Bambi. Samson Hirsch, old R. So too-great J men more highly placed. Music master Benzaiten! Obviously, god schizoid. Toshiro not need be doctor know god possess two souls – one gentle, one violent . . . nigi-mi-tama and ara-mi-tama. Aries! *Mazal tov!* But positive and negative make negative. No doubt, god has power. Can leave B.O., Body Obsolete, with gentle or violent energy. Manifest into any given object."

Toshiro recalled having stayed at the Hotel Osho, one of the seven hotels immediately surrounding Dis Knellland, where god had manifested in an ashtray and had taunted Toshiro by blowing out his cigarette each time he went to flick his ashes into the ashtray. god could be tricky, even devious. *Eh . . . yeh . . . as her . . . ash . . . er . . . eh . . . yeh . . . that . . . I am.* Yes, this time Toshiro would be certain to bring many matches.

Toshiro sipped his tea and pondered. A 'ma' means 'mother.' But it also means 'Danse.' There is a heavenly river: Ama no Gawa. Yes, he would cross the *Ama*, accompanied by his piqueur *(woof! woof!)*. For on its other side was a sloping and winding robe leading to an abyss, wherein all sins and all impurities are swept down into its depths. The Me sisters, Shiko-me and Hisa-me, ugly and frowning women, sit at its threshold. They would, in turn, serve as perfect lures for god, for they held in their hands 1) god's favorite food: Fried Chicken; for he loved to see himself in a rowdy resort for thieves and beggars, indulged in a hot game of forfeits with a wing in his fist; 2) god's favorite sport: Rock, Hud & Son vs. Fish Pond, Inc., wherein a Rod Angle gets tried for putting the screw into a particular fish market where the catch is always fresh. Yes. Now was the time to coax god! Perhaps even a *flyer* promoting a special 2-for-1 coupon with an expiration date! And a jingle: *Yea! It is I, Col. Shamshiel, arriving on high to offer you lip smacking licks of our breasts and thighs.*

And on your way out, drop a seed or two in the poor box . . . bone dry . . .

Toshiro sipped his tea to a t. Suddenly there was a burst of violin strings. Toshiro stood up and began to sing of the crossing.

"Twenty-six mile across the sea
Take-Mi-Musubi awaiting for me
Pisgah sight promised gleefully
Amaterasu O it gonna be
Menage a trois.
What glee! What glee! What glee! What glee!"

Toshiro immediately sat down and sipped his tea. Leaves. *Must snap out of it,* he thought to himself. *Brake bone and un-hinge. Walk away from a t to a u, turn to view double u, x mark spot, my broken business destroy god. Eight hundred myriad of female goddesses in universe and I get stuck sticking only male stamp. Crazy meshuga deity. Kill self to right wrong, tracing his steps, bad gumshoe. This earth business give me geisha ha ha consciousness . . . I no give Shichi-Fukujin! Nein! If I start thinking about them, I be here forever.*

Toshiro allowed himself to relax, for the *menage a trois* idea had given him an enormous erection, and he was beginning to look like one of those great lords with extended three-foot scepters, so prevalent in Japanese wang-wank drawings. Indeed, in the grounds attached to the Shrine at Ise are a large number of wide-awake cocks sacred to the sun because they salute the dawn like so many naturalists high on jamoke. And then it dawned on him! hook! get me off! of course! Hikohohodemi went to the bottom of the sea to look for his brother's fish-hook! The sea! where is washed off all the impurities of heaven! And, as well, the nasty effects of moor ill, moon-spilled with moo's milk of kindness. Yes! Toshiro would lure god down into the sea where owhadaboutatonighta would be waiting to lock him up! Perhaps he would entice Sae-See-no-Cocki to flank him in order to keep him in checkmateo. After all, in ancient Shinto, cocks high in seed were set up in the middle of fields to protect the rice from both locust and rice christians who were constant in looking for sempiternal handouts while on the road, which, in turn, reminded Toshiro that he owed Uke-Mochi-No-Kamiment (she-who-possesses wine-rice krispies is hardly silent) two condommints from the night before . . . *pop . . . pop . . .*

Toshiro sipped his tea. He recalled that as a small boy he was forced to recite backwards, while standing on his head, as many Buddhas and Bodhisattvas as he could without blinking in a sixty-six-second time-span under the threat of a heavy shillelagh, held by none other than Emma-hoo? himself, flanked by two decapitated heads from whom nothing can be hidden. All in order to demonstrate discipline, devotion and concentration. O Jigoku! Why not give it an old college try . . . for old times' saké. Toshiro stood up and with salacious ease, flipped over, hands first, to the floor, and with his head properly in *extremis in perpetuum immedias res,* in *equilibrio* with the earth, his feet pointing northeastwardly, directly six feet above his head, he preceded to talk backwards – one word per second. "iaroyN ukuhsA. iaroyN ihciniaD. ustasoB neguF. iaroyN ohsoH ustasoB nonnaK nonnak ujnes. nonnak nir-i-oyN ahkumasadakE. aravsetikolavA. nonnaK iednuJ. ooyM. ukuF. ahbahtimA. Ooym-Oduf ooyM-ahsayognoK. ustasoB oziJ . . ."

(Phew . . . phew . . . phew . . .)

According to the theory, Cross-Referenceality (which had its origins in both the crossedchristian *and* [vis. dna] the Illusion Consultational Source Information Denotation Field Theory Book of Equation Gravitation WormHole CosmologicalConstantProblogical Unified Theory Dialectical Materialistic References), life is *Deus avertat!: Damned Nutty Abbau.* And so Toshiro decided to confront some latrine fannia scalaris issues from the fourth dimension, namely, Beel the psychopomp, Acephalus the pealess, David, Goldblum, Stoltz, J.D., ibid., Qued, Goliath the Headless, RIP of GOP, R. of G.S.A., Man of Uncle, and a few other salty bubs as well in regards to *faex populi*, and thereafter to recite from the Assyro-Babylonian *Epic of the Creation* and to come off sounding as purely psychagogic as possible: 'They marched into war, they drew near into give-battle-head. The lord spread out his net and caught Tiamat into it. The evil wind which followed him, he loosened it into her face. She opened her mouth, *ad libitum, lapsus linguae, coup de grâce,* to swallow him. He drove into the evil wind so that she could not close her lips, but compelled her to employ *lingua franca* nonetheless. The terrible winds filled her belly. Her heart was seized until . . . *immundity!* A common tale.'

Toshiro sipped his tea, but cup was empty and in need of an incast. No leaves, no Phyllomancy. No Phyllomancy, no deal. The noise made from his sucking of empty space was most undignified, especially coming from a sailor born in Batavia who had stamped on the crucifix four times in Japanese blood. And dogs and black holes pinching a piece of space-time circulating in a hyper-sphere bending light into a full circle were only a part of the order that accounted for the hidden, undetectable missing mass (X – shame on you.) Dark matter (indeed!) – that that tad *is* the 'T' of Tea and . . .

Two for T
And T for two.
You for Me
And Me for You.
Add One more

And that's a brew,
Adieu! but first . . . *quem deus vult perdere prius dementat . . .*
And pass the hot cross buns, if you please, newly risen in my vision.

Toshiro realized that minus the tea that was formerly in the cup, the temperature of the tea that was not there was at absolute 0. Naturally, this called for the increase of entropy, which measures the total amount of chaos and randomness in the universe. Eventually, the universe would cease in a formless death, the ultimate state reached in the degradation of matter and energy, just as the order of tea and water would turn into the disorder of consumed tea and water and be converted back into the environment as urine. *Dochaku.* Toshiro peed.

Toshiro flushed the bowl. "I smell Jizo," he cried. *Vehimur in altum.* Ah, such a strong gush-release brought on utter relief. Some say the world will end in fire, other say in ice. Toshiro say it end in great elimination, like piss in bowl, a yielding gratification. But a noisome wound to all the little fishes of the sea.

His urine had sparkled within the sphere, before it was finally flushed to still further entropy. Had Toshiro been of an astronomical mind, he would have found a way of measuring the mass (urine) of a galaxy (toilet bowl) and, hence, the mass of the universe (sea). It might have even lent him some added insight into the mind-dimension of god himself, which might have proven to further assist him in his battle against god. For as it stood, MASS (murder) was the property of not only the god of this world and the beasts, wicked Crowley and Kramer of Belsen, but also the Beast of Exmoor. It seemed as though everyone was wanting to get in on the act! No, Toshiro had not forgotten that he was not alone in this endeavor (for indeed he *would* need assistance) and was part of a mass unto itself. A team known as the Magnificent Seven. (Theme music.)

Yes, Toshiro could have counted the number of beads of glistening urine in the bowl and multiplied that number by the average weight of each bead, but it would have made for a most tedious fashion show as it would have only served to demonstrate that the average density is less than the critical amount, and that god would continue to expand forever, rendering us (f)all fashion victims. Far better that he sticks to tea in its original state.

Now it was time to look deep into the problem. Now it was time to act. The issue here was that, aside from a battle, god was giving us a further dilemma: either the universe *would* contract and eventually collapse into a fiery ball or it *would* oops! expand outward and thereby explode! thyine wood, and most precious wood not excluded. Toshiro must become aware. Otherwise his performance could result in another fine mess that could haunt him for forty-two months, with hardly any laureled consequence. He had already received the phone call.

6 A.M.: *Ring ring ring*
"Hello"
"Tomato? That you?"
"Toshiro! No tomato!"
"Is this 212-Ylon? The Great Tomato?"
"Yes! But no tomato! Toshiro! Who this?"
"This is B.S."
"I should say so! No waste time for me!"

"No. You don't seem to understand. This is British Service. We've got an assignment for M.S."

"No Ms. here! I complete male chauvinistic pig! Anyway, I give no money women rights unless she laying right on back!"

"No, no man. This is British Secret Service contacting Magnificent Seven. You know. 007. It's time to ring up epiclesis on the g."

"Yeah! Yeah! I know you guys plenty good. What you did Oddjob I could spit! Good Japanese fellow, getting fried! No go!"

"Listen to me, man . . . Forget about Oddjob! That ket working for Goldfinger Gert was a *German!* It's a whole different era! We've got a whole new Goldfinger to contend with! And the gold of that land is Havilah! And the magician said this is the finger of god! And as a sin offering, Spectre shall dip its finger in the blood and sprinkle of the blood seven times before god . . . before the veil of the sanctuary of kerygma! There's going to be a battle in Gath where a man of great stature, who has on every hand, six fingers, and on every foot, six toes, four and twenty in number to make six in all, and who was also born to the giant, will fall! Now get a grip on man! You and the six others have got to be there! It's the Last Battle!"

There was a crackling of sorts in the receiver. Much static and interference. Suddenly, the lines got crossed and Toshiro was listening to Bobby Vee singing "The Night Has A Thousand Eyes" from a grimoire.

"What this? Some kind joke?"

Above the crackling: "Toma . . . you th . . .? This is no ti . . . to be sin . . ."

"I not sing! I got much better voice!" Rather abruptly, Toshiro broke out humming the keynotes from *The Flower Drum Song.*

"Get a grip on, Tomato! That's Chine . . . mu . . . you're hum . . . now. Listen . . . Tomato . . . Listen closely . . . Be sure to bring Mother of C . . . C . . . arlots with . . ."

Regrettably, the connection was lost.

. . . Toshiro walked laboriously into the kitchen. *So much easier to destroy than build. Yes,* he thought, *it may take year to construct house but only hour to destroy in fire.*

So it is with . . .

TEA

How many man hours does it take to grow, cultivate, harvest and export tea from the time of its conception to the moment that it is brewed and about to encounter human lips? It is almost immeasurable. But on the other hand, consider how long it actually takes to consume a cup of tea. Creation and deliverance versus elimination. Yes, perhaps, tea is a great deliverance. Business in the commercial capital of time. Why, even in America tea has played a vital role in drawing back the veil.

Go C. thea; in fact, go *see* Thea.

Revel, because once again we're at the ball (or, at the very least, a legitimate variation upon its theme, as in Vivian of the lake Emmy, holding up a shining ball), for we are dealing not only with a roundish body or mass, a conical projectile, the rounded eminence at the base of the great toe and a perforated metal ball that holds leaves, but a large formal gathering wherein dancers masquerade (T. Vivian) as well. And just as ballet historically moved into professional theater, still incorporating into its themes mythological subjects, even to the point wherein Louis Dupré was dubbed to be the *'God of Dance,'* and in the opera *Les Fetes Vénitiennes* donned a wig and mask, so did a party of disguised pilar men invade the tea ships of Boston and dump the bowels into the harbor under the full moons. And all within an hour or so of time did the leaves go down to the sea in shits. Art vs. war. Ah, humanity!

O Toshiro. The entire business of disarray really started as soon as St. Francis Xavier had led his Jesuit missionaries into Japan in 1549, and began converting the people to Catholicism. Toshiro was nearly ready to call upon Mutsuhito power and to get into full uniform and do some serious desmonizing within the Big Almighty Dude himself. The speed in which Toshiro would transform himself from a feudal consciousness to a powerful, unified, industrialized force would amaze the universe! Naturally, there was still this business of blackholes and worms to contend with, along with a hushed up, entitative, dipsomaniacal, dipsey, episodic existence that B.A.D. was personally responsible for.

1945: Waking up to the enuretic nightmare of a wet teafull East Asian dream-empire wormhole without an entire sanctification on site. In 1946 twenty-five war leaders were tried before a tribunal. *And hung?!* Not quite. The prisoner of Spandau was the prison's sole inmate and the last to be held in the Tower. Fishes . . . souls . . . both small and great . . . well, Hess could be regarded here as a sort of *ens rationis.* Toshiro was ascribed to the honor of bushido, and was reminded of the illogical revenge taken upon the poisoners of the wells. Jews mercilessly slaughtered, *fall down* in Freiburg, Nürnberg, Königsberg in 1349, until finally at Worms the Jewish community of 400 turned to an ancient tradition and burned themselves to death inside their own houses rather than be killed by their enemies. What trials resulted to further aggravate the condition of Christian against Jew occurred with yet another St. (Augustine), who declared the Jews to be outcasts beyond the spheres (the mass) for failing to accept redemption by Christ due to some rare variety of ens reale bacterioly sin.

"HEP! HEP!" cried the dog, **H**ierosolyma *est* **P**erdita. Actually a monster dog with fangs filled with hatred of the human race, bearing a banner: *Jerusalem is lost. "HEP! HEP!"* The call for murder. *(Step back three paces.)* At the gates . . .

Toshiro turned on the stove. Bacon was sizzling on the grill, sprinkled with a pinch of gregory's powder. Yes, Job himself stated rather inductively – in correlational proximity to the origin of vapid-voluptuosity as it might be scientifically controlled by obsolete-human-progress-through-intermediate-generalizations with regards to negative output – "I have said to the worm, thou art my mother. I am a brother to dragons and, by Spear alone, actually wrote them off the shaken path. But here, make merry. Grip Dipsas and have a drink of tea."

The water started to boil – the swelling of cells, the sprouting of seeds, by the pressure and friction of water in motion. For water is not just a drink but an agent of transport that enables the encasement of seeds to stand erect, in order for the movement of life to take place. Toshiro mused: "Daily water flowing through body. Mysterious combination of thesis and antithesis into higher stage of truth of vital substances from each of Three Kingdoms gives me courage, upon tasting of first fruit and donning of first clothes, to utter physicotheologically, *'She (hehe!) ya nu pu.'"*

Toshiro's musings stretched even beyond this – even to the extent of Toshiro disremembering his urine just moments ago, in and out of breathing consciousness. Being one of the stand-ins for the Magnificent Seven he knew all, but often forgot the Lord knows what. He knew, however, that the key unit of the kidney was the nephron (sounds like napälm), and that under a microscope it (the nephron) resembles a worm (more at dictyocaulus) with a round mon skull of geometric design, like a pillbox, that dribbles (shoots) out of tiny, wormy, concrete tributaries (i.e., urine). Toshiro had no trouble carrying his mind even further . . . to the sea . . . the beginning . . . where he could locate the fecal pellets of mollusks that from this particular beginning are later responsible for turning out a little Oriental temple roof, compliments of the pagoda tree, with bottom edges cutely turned upwards toward heaven like a little shirley poppy to help brighten up the meadow of *his goodship lollipop,* which, if consumed in vast quantities, will result in poppycock – soft dung, and void – and empty talk, foolish nonsense and the suchness instead, as in middenstead.

Toshiro allowed his mind to drift down past shin, and to dig to the absolute bowel of the deep, and to rest gracefully within the convoluted, ancient, Oriental script composed from the excrement of worms in a deep mysterious conveyance of the arcanum of the outcasts of benthos opusverm. O off the hook, O energy cycle, O physic movement, Oceanic Intelligence, off the record, *How long it takes for H2O to go through animal and vegetable cells amounts to two million years.* Toshiro *knew* (he was hep as well). And within his swelldom, zingy, holly, woody, bubble-dancing, pansophical mind, he *knew* that H2O loves to dance. (Check out free, colorless, tasteless, odorless, chubby partners who both embrace by extended arms, and who both depart and twist – rolling, mixing, milling in a whirlpool of clouds of dust, water and space, even as they boil, even as they eliminate, venturing deep deep deeper into the infinitude of a shapeless force, beyond the veil of woven nothingness . . .)

Sniff. Sniff. Is that a trace of piperonal? Mr. Hyde inside the sunflower? Or Jack inside the prosopopoeia? Dead, yet alive? A thing, well-spoken for? Pish!

Toshiro sipped his tea and burned his tongue. Too hot. Too soon. Break down. Get done.

O. In Savoy, in September, 1348, the Jews' properties were confiscated while they remained in prison on charges of poisoning the water in the wells. The water, un born. O christ, give me something to drink other than hematometra. This is my blood Spilled. Poison-filled confessions, extracted by torsion, proved rabbinical instructions for sprinkling the poisons in wells and springs were true. Duly found guilty, eleven Jews were immediately burned alive, and by lottery, another sixty. And every month over the next six years countless more were burned, *ya nu,* numbers unobtainable, names unknown. And even though now obsolete, several were nubbed disgusting! business! And the would-be shock on January 9, 1349 – wherein the whole community of several hundred Jews were burned alive in a wooden house especially constructed for that purpose, in a room, a night-reverse mare, a womb of a house on fire, *tathagatagarbha ha ha* gone amuck on an island in the Rhine in Basle, all burned down in butter and milky residue – lasted well into the night. All several hundred herded like domestic dolphins, all fell like old news on the hardened ears of the populace, on the old abandoned sea floor. Sea cows submerged in the milky dew. Leaves submerged in the tea. All dried up. Pisgah Mount the promise and lie low . . .

What Jap to the rescue of these poor peasants in villages oppressed? What Jap stripping down to his poplin? Toshiro smiled for Kurosawa. The conductor. The tempo. The mood of the appropriate passage of movement in action, space, drama, and music. The pipes! The pibroch playing a martial, dirgeful, and yet proceleusmatic rapture of the deep. *Armageddon.*

Comeandgetsome. It had given Toshiro life, purpose, essence and meaning simultaneously. And somehow made him feel less guilty for having spent a good portion of his past in secret as a quadrigamist.

Not so ridiculous, Toshiro thought, as Kung-Fu met Dracula. Seven brothers to vanquish the bloodsucker in a mixture of warrior-whore-supernatural womb and Dracula themes. Yes. He recalled having seen the movie on *Español* cable TV. That's the key! The scottish key, peck, in war torn *China*, posing as a famorian of the deep with a pilot fish singularity. Yes! Funny how fiction, however ridiculous, can become, gradually over time, fact-in-saltus, and fraction the bread box of *Vida.* So to better help him prepare for the encaustic battle ahead, he would rent *Hercules and the Haunted World, Hercules Against the Sons of the Sun, Airport '79, The Killer is Loose, Wee Willie Winkie, Pirulí, de negocios, mujer encargada de parar el tráfico en un paso de cebra para que crucen los niños,* and *Toshiro Saves the Jews,* yes, rend them all in one night, and pop in a tele meatloaf Banquet and turn the oven on *hi,* and bind and loosen the meal at will with the 16/19 keys, and a rowan stake (steak?) with which to seize the berries of immortality, smack in the center of the testa, the old ferronnière . . . Punch! The commercial catch! And protrude the tongue! *And Mccaughey has seven!*

Toshiro sipped his tea . . .

GRACE FEODOROVNA (a.k.a. VAUGHN) AND THE MASTER RACE

Enter, in process, Grace Bacall Hartley Feodorovna, a succulent fruit if ever there was one. It was a solitary existence for a peri carp child of six, a descendant of fallen angels, excluded from paradise and enclosed within three carp walls of her lonely domain. Raised by her mother, the Robe, a Browning version of that most distinguished body of well-born Ephesian matrons, the Mistresses of the Robes, Grace was forced to abandon her childhood prematurely, and literally become a student-at-home surrounded by the same sauropodous tutors year after year, who, in turn, were obligated to answer to the Robe herself – cold, stern, withheld from head to toe, and positively quite theropodous in both structure and disposition, and somewhat akin to a *rejoneador,* if not a downright minotaur.

Obviously, Grace was an unhappy child – a jack of clubs, a matador at the bottom of the deck – due to the fact that the 'home' she resided in was so dark and was as chilly as an ice age. Confidentially, it did not need to be so but the Robe was much too spendthrifty to pay for either lights or heat. At night it was perfectly dreadful for the household-at-large, as restless up-and-about knees continuously smacked into the ends of things, including *rejons,* thus causing so much pain as to prompt their interconnecting pieces to all at once *saut de basque* in midair. Naturally, it was not uncommon to observe at any one time half a dozen bruise marks on either of Grace's dainty little caps alone, clear evidence of her attempts to move about the house in utter ignorance, somewhat like an auroch in a china shop.

The Robe died when Grace was all of sixteen, an excellent time to break away from her formal lessons in history, English, French, calculus, gardening, cooking, music, toreo, geography, fashion, philosophy and micropaleontology (and take up phonintology). Finally, she could break through the formidable French doors that led out into the terrace of the Farnese Palace where she was living at the time, and be free to . . . falsity. Unfortunately, at the moment of her departure, the palace was being fumigated for SP. housekeepers, for so many of them had been fired over the course of time but had refused to leave the premises and were generally loitering about the more than sixty rooms of the palace in secret. *La lucha por la vida!* Oddly enough, the fumigation procedure (ugh!) revealed that not only housekeepers were hiding in the cracks and crevices, as well as along the borders of that most magnificent of structures, but once the poison had cleared, there was also discovered lying directly beside the housekeepers, a handful of House of Lords, Bishops too, some with trousers, some without, and cupfuls of cats and mites.

A lot of sixteenth century hype! bull! as well. No, it was not uncommon the amount of needle pricking that was going on back then, as well as a lot of gimmicky, old-fashioned advertising by needle women for knightly effect. Still, no wonder that so many temporal and spiritual peers of Parliament would travel to Rome for a *quick*, both by way of arm and bone (one for the pulse of the temple, two for the show in the tail, comes to three in the accommodation home). Upon further investigation it was also revealed that several of the lords were actually pee-eye nellies traveling with their peg boys-in-tow. (Roughly translated: Abrahams traveling with their young Isaacs for the sole purpose of backward acts of kindness and nonlethal shoots in the tail.)

But why not to Rome? After all, the Farnese is of a design of classical balance and symmetry, the most sought after elements of the spirit. So what better place to find it? The long rectangle of the smooth facade is framed by quoins and cornice, and across it march the long lines of windows broken only by the strong central location of the doorway built of rusticated stone and surmounted by a balcony and the Farnese coat of arms, Odoardo-style. To the likes of one from Parliament, the court is strongly classical in design, combining alike the Colosseum, the arch and lintel systems, and using superimposed orders: Doric engaged columns on the ground floor, Ionic on the second, and Corinthian pilasters on the third, each order being finished with a complete entablature. In fact, it was the interior furnishings of the palace, currently sitting out in the open air (deep plunging breaths with the nose! due to the fumigation occurring within the palace), that Grace was forced to literally step around-and-over to *been around* as she faithfully made her hasty retreat over-and-around the cardinal shins, armed with nay but a wee spray bottle containing not more than 12 squirts of pure farnesol.

O by George! now Gracie did run away from the regal, gilded, coffered ceilings, the Michelangelo-designed cornice, the velvets, brocades, damask, taffeta, the pompous and grandiose display, the lessons, the formalities, the cooler air of the hills, the formal gardens laid out geometrically, the masses of trees, the cold stone statues, the reginal fountains, pools, and cascades. O how she did run, hopscotch even as far as to the Arch of Tits, with its solid masses of masonry hanging over the titular lord of erection, and a bronze four-horse chariot surmounting the Arch (O Mass! O Revelations! O, M'ass!).

"This way the king will come; this is the way," Gracie said, echoing the Quean Richard. "For where the king comes, there's surely to be a display of children disputing, and if not chill-I-will then at least a farthing, and if not a fart thing then at least an erection, and if not an erect shin then at least . . . Ah, wiltshire, here comes your sheep-herder in green body pastures of paederasty, railing accusations at the three: G (reek), tinbrew superscription, **A**." (So, therefore, the crim. con. would go as thus: 'This way the king will; this is the way.' 'You mean the way it was and is not and yet is?' 'I mean tongues marvel in a short space for an hour.') No, Grace was no pure-white, one mind fool. For there was no telling what the king would be inclined to do if he did not actually come to stead a reign of terror. Indeed, if what is being spoken of here is actually the King's will, then this would naturally imply that the King *expects* to die and is planning on leaving a legal declaration as to the manner in which he would have his property or estate disposed of upon his Death. Of course, Grace was no fool by knight. Certainly she would not mind taking advantage of the King's inevitable demise in the hopes of acquiring his estate, be it heavenly or earthy (or some such secret sphere he's been holding caulpily behind him). This is exactly why Gracie decided to become, while she was in-waiting for the King, a streep walker. O and what an actress she did become! What a beast! A regular (or shall we say irregular) Thespian, Simon Legree and Chorine, all-in-one. But certainly it was not beyond her to throw in a bit of Harlequinade, and even blacken out her teeth if necessary, and secure a merkin in order to have her own private counterfeit hair on stage, in order to secure the best comic effect of all.

Certain places attract actors and actresses just as they do angels and gods. (Places such as Get-mane, Go-ha, and GolGonooza, which gives form to all uncreated things.) Gracie knew this to be true, whether sitting under the huge old trees, relieving herself into Abel's skull and the massive pools of shadows of Palmyra, where one was inclined to receive *palmy* for such open acts of voluntary incontinence, or stretched along some thirty square miles of *reihengräber* mysteriously bordering the Brandywine River from Levis Lane, Colorado to Rod Rocky High, Road Louse, California, completely stinko wooden habeas. Grace owned a share in Go Do Stocks, and was well aware that god's legions numbered 0000 strong in lobcock, and also knew the place was centered in Los. She even was aware of what it might take to kill god, napoo! stone-dead, and could, in fact, give place to it. Indeed, she knew his tricks, his evils, yes! There he is now, posing as that pothole on Scrounge Around Boulevard! Yes! There he is! Over there! non-camouflaged in the rush-hour Angeles traffic. And there! as old duke of limbs crosspatch, grinning on a cycle between a Greyhound bus and a Union 76 12,000 gallon oil carrier. *Ab initio caco tikkun.* Yes! god was everywhere! (check *every* pigeon!) and yet he still had not appeared. Media elites were anxiously awaiting his arrival but were still clueless as to what angle he would finally arrive on. Some felt he would choose to slip in on a *Becky Sharp* and do a little balling before the big battle with Lu; others were certain he would sort of slide in as *The Gay Desperado* and deal freely with thieves to the left and right of him. One columnist in Washington, who was known for his expertise in reading between the lines of cyberelectronic spiritual representational claptrap vanity press periodicals, seemed to insist that god would abruptly burst onto Broadway in the musical, *Pion!,* which, Off-Broadway, was a short-lived meson with an unstable pi in the face plot concerning a last mass in a spinning cycle, although without a consistent point of view, but which had won enormous popularity among the echelons of venatic society known as hardons (or in physicycles as hadron or "had one, no thanks") – people who were only too eager to flush out god, whatever Bath room he be hiding in bashing the Bishop in solitary.

No wonder, wise move on Gracie's part to become an actress and thereafter wait for him to arrive breathless at parties five, ten, fifteen, or twenty or more arms strong,

Oh, yeah! Now, three basic facts in relation to the Quantum Mini-Nap-Superspace Model with an Omega Point and/or Fact in the Form of a Question – i.e., who's on first? 1) The wave function of the universe is a function of the scale factor of the universe and the conformal time in terms of how long it takes one to scale the universe, given that the one is allotted a full conformal dress ahead of time, and a long ladder. 2) god loves to be invited to parties, point-blank, especially when they are being hosted by an informal super-Hamiltonian construct of a deranged asymmetrical composition made from unequal shapes of common distrust. 3) Jefferson corrected the Deism of the Jews and gave them jester notions of his *jefe* attributes in government in regards to the doctrine of a future *chef* state, and wielded it with efficacy, which he went on to further define in his wee little book on theology, *Wee Willie Winkie, The Philosophy of the French Baby Chef, Julia,* wherein chef Baby states, *"Judenschädel – hollow howling, chinless, void of kranz. There is only one souffle! Blow uppers beware! But please do have a shrimp!"* Fuhrer along, Baby screamed at another blower, "Syphsive Morbus Gallicus! Where did you put your Saint Peter last?! Girolama! Shame on you! Three in one that you are! Go wash your hands at once!" Baby Julia was all of *three months old* at the time of the writing and Saint Peter was syph. but a babe himself. Simply AMAZING! Nor Man-Sant Peal, upon studying Baby's philosophy, went on to further elaborate in *How to Interpret the Seven Bells Without Really Trying* or *The Game of Cards is Vanished:* 'Study to get the scratchy elements out of your body, even if it takes a little digging. Just be sure to dig it out before the third stage in order to avoid grocer's itch, vanillism and other such grossosities.' In time this proved to be excellent advice for those inflicted with pinworms, among those being one face resembling *Rufname* – Stalin, Beria, Hitler and Mussolini. This, in turn, can be traced back to the Gullah "gri-gri," the doll-like, babyish image used in voo-doo rituals to represent the *image* of a person (see spider, man) in which pins (i.e., worm in a Crucifixion) are stuck in to cast an Evil Spell on anything having to do with a *guaranteed retired income*, as well as to the game of prediction *oh hell II* and all the tricks of the trade of the car salesman, B. Cheka, alias Ralph *Narr*, whose motto regarding dissatisfied customer satisfaction was *Wegen Reparatur Geschlossen.*

This takes us immediately to the first role Gracie ever graced upon the screen. G-G. She was coming close to encapsulating god at the time. So much dichotomy was at stake. The production itself concerned a charming, turn-of-the-century, country French girl (G-G), a complete gallomaniac, who was crossed-groomed to be a francophobe-courtesan who could turn tables and heads by the use of her hip. During G-G's engagement, Grace literally graced the Hollywood scene and popularized the slogan, *Grace be on to you, Abuladze.* G-G went on to win nine Academy Awards, including *Best Pic,* which naturally became a lure for god. For not only was god a wolf sucker for Awards, but pictures named G-G as well. For what most interested and lured god was the tabooish connotation behind G-G. For, in fact, the word 'GG' suggests the general orifice genus and is usually applied as thus: "up your G-G." So a great grossing picture for the orifice could put humankind *evermore!* closer into figuring out One important Piece to the intricate puzzle of Life. G eewhiz – god's into showbiz.

Gracie discovered, only a second too late, that god had actually been *in* the production of G-G; hiding, as it were, in the body of the late Hermione Gingold (*Alien*, Hermes ion E plain spirit in the free state). It was his way of snooping, while at the same time getting in on the *Hollywood Acts*, which also had a lot to say regarding 'lical circumcision and the cutting up of babies' bibs (Jee-gee-gees!), which in its own right suggests a lot of bibacious, recrudescent horsing around.

Grace was actually proud (fig. prone) to be one of the Magnificent Seven (theme music). As an actress (actor), she meant business! (And not just business in great waters or wonders in the deep.) For in her mind she was (simply and truly) an empress who ruled an empire with poise and discipline, being hortative, homiletical and pedagogic, all in one. However, her favorite 'role' was as founder and inventor of the cereal trademark, Prozac Puffs! Chocolate, Vanilla and Strawberry-flavored prone-floats (no go-down-to-the-sea-in-chips here), which not only became a huge success in milk bhang (particularly around the Beverly Hills/Palm Beach A.M. elitists), but even filled the bowls of many a con-verted mid-westerner, bestial or otherwise, and furthermore caused quite a stir in the saponification department at Autoicous-Witz. In Idaho her cereal was known as *Prozac Potato Chips*, in Oregon as *Prozac Apple Peels*, and across the seas in Italy as *Prozarizzios!* (dropping the c with all due respect to christ). And then, in a sudden rush! a whole new generation of non-masturbatory children were forming. Worldwide! Little girls were naming their dollies, Anhedonia, and a global shut down of desire was becoming a craze with its own particular flavor of *joie de vivre*. Literally, by the tens of thousands, teenagers were yawning upon viewing anything that even remotely suggested sexuality. Indeed, an uncircumcised presentation of *Deep Throat* put everyone at a Prozrock party to sleep. Social groups were forming with names like TWOP (Teenagers Without Pimples) and ENNUI (Erections Never, Never Unload Inc.), which, needless to say, were also stirring up god's anger in the matter, for his people were assuming a *laissez-faire* attitude towards sex in general, thus allotting god impotence in the area of *Judgment on Vine*, and thereby (literally) undermining father's business. No one was sinning! Even Giovanni De Seingalt was spending Saturday nights as a dux in his castle on the leaden roof glued to the Lottery Discovery Channel in the same time zone that 1) the Golden Spur Bar and Grill (owned by Sam and Paul in mohawks) threw tea to the intolerable masses, 2) John took off with his flying shuttle, *The Come Up Hit Her*, and 3) James founded deep time in the rocks, which meant that *no* vestige of a beginning could have *usshered* in creation, even on Saturday, October 22, 4004 B.C. (unless one was alluding to *J and J* blowing a lot of hot air over the map).

And then Grace landed the lead role in *Prozac II: the Search for the Down Regulation of Norepinephrine Receptors,* wherein she and William Shafther III ventured deep into cyberprozactic space in order to retrieve a 'chip' of depression and a 'quark' of sexuality that was threatening to penetrate earth's sexagesimoquarto zone. It was Grace's and William's responsibility to not only apprehend the chip-quark, but to perform *prozactus interruptus* upon the social erectus sensitization separability of the too little cherubim chip-quarks, and to thereby erect a nonerection in the place of an ongoing erection that, in essence, was both cuming and going. *I'm Age Less God. Speak!* Be East of Wisdom. XIs'. In addition to this, Grace was able to both compose and sing the title song, "Ye Vet! on E-ye TV," accompanied by the 33-piece band in general dis-array, complete with cats, dogs (includ., a GoldeRetriever), a Jewish vet named James Jismwet, and plenty of Japs to comminate the Princess (i.e., Mary, Mary full of grace . . .).

"If I lived on Prozac
Daidle deedle daidle
Digguh duxdux deedle daidle dum
All day long I'd biddy biddy bum
If I only Lived, Prozac!"

And a salutiferous remake of *The Ten Condiments,* retitled *The Ten Prescriptions,* even had Mo (as played by Gracie) shouting on the pavement, "Let my Prozac go! Open says a me or suffer from T-radition and a healthy dosage of pilocarpine-pissasphalt ala plum."

Gee, god was unimpressed, and forever, breaking down . . .

oye

Each (in his/her own way) of the Magnificent Seven was discovering new and better ways to break god down in the hopes that as a pistic group they would ultimately find him in such a cracked state that the final dismantling would be a dumptyhumpty cinch and a holy ointment, to say the least.

To continue toward this goal, Gracie changed her name to Pauline Prozaccovovich and created a one-woman vehicle for herself, entitled *Garbled Ink: The 4-Wheeled Chariot, Replanted,* and took it on the road, with accompanying milkmen's carts, doing many a dinner theater coast-to-coast. In her show she actually took on fifteen different characters, both male and female. Each had their own story to relate regarding federal crackdowns on computer breakins, the hormone DHEA on lupus and diabetes, and demagoguery among the political right. One of her characters was named Penologie Penuche, whose aim was to create a sweet prison system, whereby god would be enticed into confinement by using fudge as a lure. (The clue for this tactic was originally discovered in Gen ate twenty-one after smelling a sweet flavor.)

In downtown Manhattan her one-woman show had already taken on a hound of publicity, combined with rousing reviews. Stepping out of a limo, she was greeted by a butcher of a stray pit bull, Razal Flow, wearing a yarmulke and a prayer shawl, and then by a swarm of reporters, an Ute plagued with no-see-ums cameramen, assorted fans, and the League of Spencerianism that just so happened to be in town promoting the mechanistic evolution of the cosmos from relative simplicity to relative complexity, with violin accompaniment.

PRESS: "Pauline, what's your opinion of the current state of American drama?"

PAULINE: "In my opinion it is no different than European drama. No matter where you go in the world, human beings are nondistinguished from the lower animals in that they both speak, as well as control their waste, by way of an intricate dramaturgic network. Except in American drama, the flush of material is much more abundant."

FAN: "Pauline, what's going to be your next role?"

PAULINE: "I'm in the midst of producing a script entitled *Rauwolfia, the Sinamon Roll* or *man da lay I had last night!* In it I'll play the part of a notator in the guise of a poisonous musical tree plagued with plagal melodies that just so happens to be growing in Mick Jagannath's backyard. In the story Mick is residing in Ireland. He is married to a dusty old Okie whom he detests and is plotting to kill by way of jagging her with a dagger in her kip. It just so happens that the poisonous stem in his back bears luscious Indian fruit, along with cyme clusters for that somewhat pregnant effect, for in deed the whole thing is meant to be a spin-off of Adam's and Eve's kiplingesque attitude toward god and every lowly creature on site, only with the roles reversed. This time *Mick* will give birth to Cain by way of Snatch. I'm hoping to get an unknown to play Snatch. And then go onto resurrect its sequel, *Edelweiss Pirates of Cologne,* which was actually written five years prior to *Rauwolfia,* in forty-four, when man was armed up to the hilt."

PRESS: "Pauline! Pauline! Is it true you're currently having a love-fest with twelve former Klansmen?"

PAULINE: "Bullshit! It's strictly a physical thing with the clan and me. Love has nothing to do with it; howbeit, with twelve you get a pizzle of a heart-on and a white-hot-

slavery cast upon a certain prejudicial island where Paul knew man in a little way. And Melita was a honey of a Lolita who brought on Malta fever to the barbarous klan, a meliphagan cast of vipers if ever there was one."

PRESS: "How do you feel about those rumors that you may be nominated for a Tony in your work last year in *Papuan: Two Gals from New Guinea?*"

PAULINE: "Rumors . . . wa! I loved doing *Papuan*. I thought the music was marvelous. Hats off to Sol Shylockovitz for writing such witty lyrics and for making the whole affair into one endless palindrome, back to front. *Eros saw me ere em was sore.* O! Not only would I be honored with a nomination, I think it would be entirely voguish seeing that it was such an earthly production, so ostentatious in expenditure. But please don't bring a simpleton into it as foolish as Antoinette, for the loss of her head was hardly beholding theater."

MEMBER OF THE LEAGUE: "Pauline. What's your opinion of the relative complexity as it pertains to the cosmos in a bi-urinary mode?"

PAULINE: "I'm glad you asked me that. It is my belief that a duct that has the nerve to carry away the chief excretory product of the universe, so rich in end products of carbon, hydrogen, nitrogen, and oxygen, the essential constituents of all living cells, has no business calling itself a proselyte! I could give two shits whether he's Jewish or not! That's got nothing to do with it! But duck I will accept. Especially on the urinal."

PRESS: "I understand you're taking *Garbled Ink* to Ojos del Salado."

PAULINE: "You heard correct."

PRESS: "But, Pauline, isn't that a mountain 22,539 feet high in the Andes west of Tucumán?"

PAULINE: "Yes, but look. They haven't had decent theater there since St. Anthony met St. Paul and toured the mountain ranges doing readings from their book, *The Hell With Halos!* Getting our equipment up there is going to be one Hannibal-and-a-half. But, by god, we're planning on taking *Garbled Ink* into all the world, to every living creature and thing, even if it should come to dyvourcy. This summer we do two weeks in Novaya Zemyla, two islands in the USSR between the Barents and Kara Seas, and three weeks in Molucca. We're also planning shows in Oubanguy-Chari, Toowamba and Alhambra, California, where we'll be giving away Dry Ice to the first hundred patrons as rumours have it."

O! Pauline was wined and dined by fashionable cigarette-smoking elitists; cyberspace experts in *Information Forget* (IF) with the infamous motto: Me Not, Age, Name and Social Security Number 666 respectively; the vice-president of YOWL Savings and Loan; the chairman of the board at Chiquita, Ban Ana, Graceless; and two Secret Service wire tap experts whose slogan was: You'll give us 66 seconds – we'll destroy 600,000,000 lives.

Pauline had no interest in anything as venomous as the downfall of humankind. Her aim was much more venial. Actually, no less than the downfall of god in total; and to thereafter become purely venery, with or without a cock. Yes, Pauline was proud, proud in a rabbinical sort of way. For it was far easier to be involved with rounded characters than square ones. And this was precisely why the evolution of consciousness itself would fall briefly, but most significantly into the hands of the Magnificent Seven! (Theme music.)

O

fade to

THOMAS BALLOU the Kid

The alarm went off playing a trumpet at 10:42. Thomas rolled over and with eyes still asleep in the back of his head, his chin dribbling Dixie spit from the gaping mouth in the kip of sleep, his nostrils clogged with fifteen cubits of snot, the size and shape of wild crottels, he punched the march out of alarm and took in two and one-half breaths of life, with another half getting gobbled up in a yawn. It was late. But instead of bouncing up on the balls of his feet, he just rolled back into his dry nest and let two boulders of a fart clash inside his bowels. Kate Smith echoing, blowing the alarm, *god Bless America!* that Thomas had punched! to nearrear destruction was still reverberating in his head . . . on this . . . the seventh month of the seventeenth day of the month of living fountains –

O dove shit! Thomas rubbed suspicious bird-adieu out of his eyes. *What ostrich blew a trumpet fart in my mouth last night? What walrus belched sardines? What cow golden showered me? What guerrilla hand-dropped poop down my gullet? Cry, thank god for dry land!* even though his living fountains' place smelled like it was meaning to air a rat out which could have died in some dark corner last night, however formless and voidless in the midst.

A stiff kind of wild morning, broken down with it raining fierce angry mad outside, *patter patter, beat beat, beat beat.* A lone voice sang, *'I 'za cumin' I 'za cumin' though my head is hangin' low. Jes' git me to the church on time before a raven does a full end doo-little on my forehead.'* And *beep beep!* the sheep! Shit Lamb. The head rises! "Ah, no rest for violence sake," Thomas moaned.

Watch out! the water became a horse flood that spilled all over his trembling flesh; his chest sticky-wicky swamp of polywog crud. Somewhere in there was mixed urine, *wine-lime* that Thomas had consumed with ham the previous night, due to there being three hams at the time, which meant one extra to horse around with.

her kos fit right though it was a little tight around the windpipe . . .
loosened by a belch of pneuma.

"Can Margaret Ann be my servant tonight?" Thomas cried, beating himself, flattening his pride. *"Or how about Geli Raubal?"* Gloating over her like some servant with a rare and inflamed bloom.

No wonder his other name meant 'rest.' This was where Thomas was. On the second level of his three-level condo, resting with some of the best wine bottles this side of the Mississippi, drunk to his toes in drink; Southern Comfort; thanks to his trusty butlers-in-tow for shaking up the cockintails and serving Hudi-bras, Luke in tonic with a butt of Hudibrustic flesh thrown in; he returned a bit post-puritan, *nowhere* revisited, except in his mind where Chinese waitresses in bras served tsui-chi drunk chicken in backward Hebrew rhyme and *poisson bleu,* for so many of the waitresses were not only cats but totally blue to boot. But everyone in his dreams was walking backward, quaking. And seven clean dogs that he took to be heroes kept reappearing, beckoning to him to think:

"Tho' What's 300+300?"
"Two hundred?"
"No. Ha! Guess again!"

Poor Thomas went to and fro. He was trying to make a fresh start, and from there see how things would grow. Isn't that what man's been doing all along? Making fresh starts? (Although in Thomas's mind it sounded like he was thinking: *flesh tarts,* which naturally made it seem like he had only commerce on his mind, and was a bit of a pock pudding.)

PLEROMA CINEMA

Thomas Erastus (Zwinglian theologian, forever advocating theodicy while crossing his fingers with an indefinite singular antecedent of theophany) said, "I'm also known as Bron, the same pseudoprepotent bloke who stood up for whacking off the head in the secret shadows of a vomitus bed where the miserable, horrifying darkness was impregnated with plenteous impressions of dread."

What's this?! Thomas kicked Horst out of bed. Thud! to the floor! He mistook him for the 1-900 Fairy whore he had had the night before.

"Time is relative and the earth is expanding into the ice of eternal infinite space," Thomas said. But an inebriated *Eratosthenes* was not a good enough excuse. So Horst took his hand and thaumaturgically transformed it into a PM Book that had the recipes for Long Liz and Drunken Lizzie (and Afternoon tea), and thumped Thomas on the head, and said, "You cheap, drunken outlaw detectives are all alike. All folly!" But this only made Thomas feel as though he belonged to a group of Erasmus's soldiers coming under the altar of Morgan le Fay vituperations, contrary to how sad he felt to be all alone in the world once his work was done.

Perhaps Horst was right. Perhaps. Perhaps. But perhaps not. After all, Thomas always did fancy himself a bachelorly Phillip Marlowe-type (as opposed to a Desi-Lu) with a dark shadow on his prodigious face and another more ominous one following him about. Yes. Bred from a long line of Mongrel-bloodhounds tracking down black-and-white, dead-or-alive Western cowboys, symbols of the CD battle as played in the pages of Ma. Being naked and tempted. 'Tis only human. Thomas imagined it many times before.

*   *   *

The saloon doors swung open and closed on an old honky-tonk squeaky note of watered-down praise for the cowpoke who was out to clean up the town. (Boots were creaking, stinking leather was squeaking.) The Kid took steady ready *High Noon* steps into the center of the dust-choked, *lousey* cowboy-concupiscent street, grasping a *non est inventus.* The sun beat down on his lordly brow. Chow was an hour ago. Watermelon. Steak-'n-beans. Burrrrp! The air, the scene was for a split second in time a cabbage patch. The Kid sniffed the air. Nothing like smelling your own tarts. It's so exclusively des-potic. It's even better than speaking in your own language on the throne. Two innocent bystanders lay flat in the darkness of deadly gas and would have obviously benefited from a stronger dose of restrictionism than to a bitter end. "Sorry, partners." The town, aside from the Kid, looked deserted. *He has not been found.* But behind the curtain there! was Ellie May! walking after her own lusts. And behind that door over there! was Doc Joseph! (in his own house, begging for god knows what). Everyone else was clean out of sight.

The Kid had itchy fingers. He cracked his knuckles inside tight fitting gloves and dared anyone to perform chiromancy. O! Above him a dove flew by holding a live branch in its beak. *Reis,* the Kid thought! *He's still lookin'!* The Kid yelled, "Land already!" But no one in town got the Gist . . . no not even the dove, nor the one or two dud sensa floating somewhere above. No matter . . . this was another town, another story. Suddenly, behind the wind-swept silent dust! the strong, heavy tension of the afternoon! appeared two horses, and behind them two dogs, and behind them two hens, and behind them two roosters. *Wouldn't you know it,* the Kid thought. *So much for fresh starts.* And this was the fashion, for where the flesh ended the fresh started, and the raven nowhere returned fresh with a pantywaist. But two horses came galloping in after 6:00 PM, more like 7:00, and collided most untimely with Gad.

And now the air was like a short catch of the breath, a faint shadowy trace, a deaf conversation, a heated argument between two small fish on a skillet. In still darker words, the air *was* gibbous with solitude. It had to mean only one thing! The gloves fit tight. The Kid cocked an ear past tense. Yes! Faintly, but growing louder . . . the high-strung cling-zing of the stirrups . . . the flat, trampling, edgy step of the boots . . . the apparent displacement of an object as seen from two different points not on a straight line with the object!

The Kid exercised his fingers just inches above the holster – like an Ab-Liberactinstein before a concert. Stringendo! The chorus that came from nowhere suddenly halted in space! The death dance was about to commence. The last picture *Vorstellung.* Better mind your pieds and queues. For there in the dusty, slanted street of a homeless Texas afternoon, dressed to the hilt like Bat Masterson with a borrowed Homburg, a curly black mustache, an eye as burnt as coal, and a teeny-tiny bead of fan-g blood dripping on the chin from too close a shave, stood, in full view, the holoblastic, lickety-split, damn good gunslinger El-Shaddai.

"You ready to draw?" the Kid asked.

"Son, I'm always ready. But I suggest you mind your P's and Q's with me."

The Kid cracked his knuckles. "You mean my . . . pistols and quicksilver?"

"No, I mean your Paradoxes and Quips!"

The Kid and El' were but two little forces, fourth on a scale of five, which is the quintessence, the highest essence in ancient quietistic philosophy; the substance composing the heavenly bodies and the special revelation of the tossed aside masses. There were greater matters in existence to worry about. El' was not the *only* El', the Kid was not the *only* Kid. There were others. Some far nobler, some less so. Indeed, if the Kid only knew that El' was presbyopic (which accounted for his perpetual squinting), the Kid might not have been so nervous with knuckle-cracking quirkiness. Perhaps it was only a ploy in a quixotic effort to stall for time. For, indeed, time had yet to arrive on the scene but was somewhere in the canyons beyond, galloping frantically on Grizzle, hoping to put a stop to this most dreadful of showdowns. For as it stood only time possessed the power to change what would otherwise be regarded as *bha-bha* fate. For time was like a presentation, particularly in regards to the position in which the fetus lies in the uterus in labor with respect to the mouth of the uterus.

Uhmmm----There must be a third element, a *prochein ami* if you will, acting as a *sui juris.* For just as the Kid was at one time positioned sweatily in the uterus in labor, so did man labor in regards to the sweat of his brow. So, therefore, allow the Kid to fan the fire with a tic.

Meanwhile, inside the saloon, the town had come to life, a micro society of quidnuncs, including B-Girls, bhats and bhangs. It seemed as though everyone was talking about the great showdown outside. Whoever was actually directing the show had decided to equip it with a cast of thousands. Details. The saloon scene alone was potable and called for 200 thirsty faces (excluding Perry Como), all of whom were staying at the local motel, registered under bhaktas.

HUMPHREY BOGART: "Do you think they'll be having a gunfight?"

LUCILLE BALL: "Who knows? It's still so incomplete."

JOHN WAYNE: "Bet there will be, stonk and all, bhai pilgrim."

RANDOLPH SCOTT: "You can say that again."

GROUCHO MARX: "That, that, that, that . . ."

TALLULAH BANKHEAD: "That's enough potting already, darling."

FRANK ZAPPA: "I thought I was suppose to be out there in the role of the Kid, mooning El'."

W.C. FIELDS: "Shut up, Frankie. You had plenilune time when *you* were still a kid in your mother's eyes. Anyhow, can't you see? You're bothering me."

RONALD COLMAN: "Tobe or knotberry? The garment or the fruit or the fish? That will be the question when this is all over."

ZASU PITTS: "O dear gar!"

MAE WEST: "Save it, honey. Someone's got to go."

AL JOLSON: "And it might as well be Mammy's kid, or some such meliphagan Slubberdegullion suscept of a tV plugola."

C.B. DeMILLE: "You're wrong, Al. Take a look. There's no Mammy in the scene and El's shaking like a leaf in hash. El . . . Let go!"

JUDY GARLAND: "He's scared."

EDDIE FOY: "He's nervous."

VERONICA LAKE: "He's old."

MOLLY PICON: "He's shy."

GARY COOPER: "He's a needle in the camel's eye."

CARY GRANT: "He's bluffing . . . Jewday."

JUDY GARLAND: "Whad'cha say, Cary?"

Outside, in the canyon beyond, Time© was forever drawing closer. The lid was drawn shut and the sewer was stitching the last stitch. It was a *renewed* subscription. *Come hither, the Brief Trager.* Even now, the sun was filled with bells and whistles and other dazzling special effects praising the scripture and the crimson-colored chalk on the pavement. But this was a hyper-technological production far beyond the special effects of the words in the MAG of Life. Clouds just didn't roll – they *roamed* across the sky. The sun's rays bounced off of literally *everything*. It was a miracle how they did it. Even Time got into the act and took on the appearance of the Campbell's Soup Kid, only the hands on his face were traveling *counterclockwise!* and his *leaves*, so to speak, were lined with *world* events. And the horse he rode on bared its own personalized plate: *Trig her.*

CONCEALMENT

In this room marked revelation – in this room marked trumpets and souls and headless wingless things with teeth as mean as battle-tanks; in this room marked doubt and fear and hope, everlasting faith skewered for the masses; in this room marked angels and devils tangolizing their way agitanado to golden crescent moons; in this room marked surprise! Behold! the bride shines in shimmering, shivering colors of redemption; in this room marked: I am Percheron. I am balanced with a branch and a fish in a *livre à clef.* I have spoken so therefore I suppose we all ought to listen; in this room marked retribution, hellish be thy name; in this room marked bewitched, bothered, and bewildered – I grind my teeth to molarmadness and dyspareunia, and feel the circumference of the universe coil itself around my crown like a Jappent tightening forever and ever in a heroic dance of no, tightening itself around in measured chants and movements until Pop! Pi! out springs Pattycake, Bakers Three, Shite, Kyogen ha! and Old Waki. (With an emphasis on the former shite shitepoking when flushed, or whatever Lola wants.)

I have sat at the teacher's feet along golden shores and I have listened whole-heartedly to his musings and revelations of hope and despair. I have lent a full ear to his sermons and orations on existence, his definitive solution and its twelve easy guidelines (instructions intact, warranty clause noted, some pieces not included). I have studied his bombastic gestures and given great thought in consideration to his japygid symbols stretched mysteriously across his postbellum-visualized sermons. I have held my breath in haste as I've witnessed the teacher bleed and recite purity simultaneously; the first part disguised, the second part partial, the third, truly in the soil. Yes, I have washed the teacher's feet with my tears and have opened up my box of deep secrets and have said, "Here is my heart – take it, eat it, it is all mine to offer." I have been the lowly student. I have taken the tests, both past, and failed miserably to my utter regret. I have pondered the imagination of man's act and rendered it godly. I have walked the streets of the glorious city for blindmind not on sale. I have spread myself across land masses in patches like a geographic tongue. I have crushed the eggs' warm dust upon blisters on the souls of my feet with a jagged stone. I have knocked on 'entrance' and have not been quick enough, and have found my fingers seized and smashed in many a closed door. I have memorized the dirty lines that the teacher fed me from the conductor's manhole, and threw them back into the faces of my evaluators with all the force of a desperate child caught in the clutches of the drink. Master, oh my mast . . . take this wandering rash. Oh, my mother, my father, my life. Where is the map I need to blanket my motley heart with? And the mat I need for genuine genuflection?

The sun is setting. The sun is set. The impressionistic colors of the third act have vanished behind the closing curtain call. The doorknob rattles and I shiver in a lukewarm bathtub, all thirty-three trembling purple inches of me. I cross my sudden nakedness with two defenseless limbs and stare in breath-silent hesitation as the door parts like a nomore sea before me, and opens inch-by-inch oly urbs!

My face under dirt-tainted waters, I feel his hands investigating like eels the length of all that is attached to me. What I do now with the help of tail-swift mermaids is to detach my head from the body and let it roll like Sis's boulder to a deep cavern of a sea upon where there is no return, while my body left behind is the dead hulk of a drowned ship consumed by wantoness, authority, and utter dominion. Sarcophagid feasted on organic material. I can see my body crushed in a climax . . . the boat, the bones of a once beautiful vessel of destination. Sarcophagus burkes.

Daddy fished. How many sardines he collected in a month was anyone's guess. I know. Once neglected in the backseat of a black sedan, I watched Daddy scour the seas for a little fin. Bonded with fear, ignorance crashing over me like a violent wave, I could only respond to a trembling connection with habit. What I thought I knew I did not know at all. What I thought was right was wrong. How much knowledge should be stored in a child's mind? I didn't know her name, nor did I know what the real connection was between her and Daddy. Nor can I recall exactly why I was in the sedan in the first place. But the memory remains vivid and correct and unchallenged. Daddy stopped the car. And using me as his accomplice, he lured the fish in.

We drove, tire-beating the pavement, up and down quiet neighborhood streets specially lined on either side with quiet, white ash planted by the polis. Daddy commented about those trees, making a wrong turn, getting the little fish to gasp out of its element. I wanted to ask how in the world do fishes cry? but I hadn't the slightest notion how to stretch words. How Daddy could lock the doors and keep them locked throughout the entire time simply amazed me. Daddy was a 2-pole magician from Olisipo. An ex-citizen of no mean city. Don't ask him how or why he does it. He'd never tell you. And then he made the little fish disappear under his massive bulk.

Where were we? It was a road, dead-ended in a field no one cared about. Over there was a tree, over there was a tire, over there was a part of an old car. Daddy rocked the boat. The little fish was consumed by the same fire that burned my thighs inside. Effe Min ate. She should have been Hep. She should have been a crab. Perhaps she could have crawled away on land with one claw trailing, snapping behind her in defense. Or if Daddy failed to strike deep enough, he might have fallen backwards and been thrown. However . . . fish get eaten. It's a fact. Daddy's eaten lots of fish. 100,000 in fact. Tossing what looked like bones out the open sedan window.

Trailing behind in the aftermath of foam, swirling along with the multitude of microscopic organisms, tails whipping, heads throbbing, rolling with the force of an army of Spartans after Mochadick, penetrating spearheads reflecting the sun's output, the desert's scent of ancient, sea-scorched seashells, crushed history, little fishes enlarged by the bait on the hook chasing frantically the stoic on the stern pulpit, I blessed myself with bowsprit bed ignorance. Embryonic amnesia only a fool could partake in. Stepping sideways off a crime-crested curb, the same curb where Louis had his jaw locked onto and was kicked vigorously in the back of the head, his teeth smashing like a wine glass in the fireplace, lending his blood to the gutter, the life-happy crimson cutless draining the life out of lifeless *siècle d'or,* I whipped my sidley thoughts together, spied myself husking in an inner eye of glass that one of the gynecoid sailors must have dropped while blinking apologetically at the captor, and formulated a measured plan that none of which my three seized souls had the slightest inkling of. A plan pertaining to the control of forces responsible for movements in and deformation of Daddy's lot.

Daddy hummed alongside a Broadway medley, crackling coarse accompaniment on a piano. Mother was vacant. A vacant lot, Mother was. Clothed, according to the season, while she took her ceremonial right bowssening bathyal cornwell for purification of bathyesthesia. It was the least one could do. The hour smashed my vehicle like a bad driver on the losing end of teetotalism, and I put my life in the hands of a compass. Bi-polarized. I, and a couple of cons, that is, wet our gizzards at Fair Havens, entering like a bee a tee-hole, seed feeding with our backs against the thick wet walls, conversing, cocktailing, dancing away the honey hours until it was time I called over Euroclydon to let her drive us to Night Club Viper Heat in Lisbon to hand-ski on the hand. Obviously, it was the least I could do in order to fool this master, get him to think *I am*, naive, hopelessly ignorant while singing my te deums, and make shark-fin soup out of him and his daily summation of altruistic blabber. Waiting for yet another victim to shed its skin, to peel away a flimsy coat of the soul, is the only thing I need to carry along with myself, at least until death.

What I need is a hammer. Nails to keep the body sticking to the wood. All day long, willingly, without a break or a sit for a spot of tea, as busy as a puli on the farm, I would pound, pound the head so that the point would do the business needed in order to complete the ordeal. Pound, pound, pound until I had me a *katzenjammer*. Paul-apart rib seeking resurrected interruptus, the unattached rod that stiffens – stiffens the walls of the body – can, in turn, move and break the walls in two, and bring the body down into its own fluids pouring profusely life's sauce into the earth. Get wise in tectonophysics. Count three and play: Count Bassie. Count to the Monte Cristo. Count to the false Baby making a profit. Count three and pray van harem. Count four. Count in. Count on. Count up and out. Count the syllables in the coffin text. Py-ra-mid. Count the hairs around the head wound that counts for nothing. Count the Dead. The pus. The god. The midnight vamp impaled nape. With this blade, I count the seven knotches made in the belt of the whale, beached bleached behemoth moby-white ash dick of ages that swallowed a skhul man, ape mounted in caramel.

(Skip four lines)

D. Erectus,

How are you? I am fine. I thought of you today and just wanted to drop a line. Fish. Hook-line and sink her with dear dick, that he-man puissance of dead weight. How are you? Your leather apron bib etc., etc.? Hammer – I meant to say *ham her*. Daddy's such a pig on the mount of corruption. I entered him in the trampling out the vintage state fair. Oh, yes, really. It was my bid in pignoration. He came in second. Quite wasn't on his pettitoes. Seems he couldn't pork the can quick enough, intimidated by the crowd throwing figs and pips. Apparently, there must have been a hundred onlooking cow-whales in the bleachers (dung as pat as pawns in trade), and in front of them a hundred more doodling vans, creeps, banshees, and pipits – drooling three times and leaving slimy trails, this being a state fair and all.

L. Mashhit.
aka Erect us

(Skip four lines, if not three)

It wasn't always this bold, you know. As a child I was don't-touch-defenseless. The very idea that one could counteract the count did not even exist, just as the seed did not exist till the third-day-soaked-to-life-bursting-forth. Here we take-out time and have it delivered directly to the house. Ten minutes later the doorbell rings: *Don't Cook Tonight. Call Chicken Delight*

stands in the threshold, her *Juive Kartenlegerin* shadow dancing jagged lines inhuman across my face. My god. I blink not once but twice in a lifetime at thirty Asiatic dolls. *Why . . .*
    dog with mus . . . mustard seed!
    Eye can see the *Judenhetze.*

It is in the corner of certain designated spaces that I find my consolation. Whether these spaces exist within four walls – a bedroom, a kitchen, a library, a den; or outside in the vast, boundless musings of the sky; or in the tiniest chapters of the brain (quadrants of the soul); or in one of the four parts of a plane beyond the horizon; or in one of a quadriga; or one of four yolks, eggs scrambled yellowwhite blendings of a quarreling duality wrangled with illogicality; or whether they abide by the rules in the book of elation, a sea of cockfoot's grass mingled with fire, clothed in pure and white linen; or in one of the four beasts consuming liver and salt, their riders drunk on the blood of the wilderness; or in one of four precious stones rattling in the cavity of a JB jaycee head, like dice turning numbers in the palm of a ring-racked hand full of abominations and glory climbing to/out the womb-wet stage haven of lower face, two weeks shy in the midst of a puerperium wilderness; or in one of four camels, each a sackcloth of black-matted hair, sweating passion fruit before the lamb tongues knitted in knotted stitches, before salvation does not matter to god eating hoppers and flesh honey – there will be the burial mud lair or anyone of seven thousand shouting, returning men quartered in the clamp of a diver's quake. Men with heaven's paintings scribbled on their foreheads, still wet, voices mumbling plenty of troubles in thundering, darkened rooms consumed by midnight malice and Magdalene water pleasure and pure dreams of pulchritude-panting penance.

Children do not simply tumble out of bed into the world with bits of blood on their chins, cradle in mother's washbasin limbs, and lap pearl-nipple drops all winter long. Jump rope, jacks, rubber balls, dice, doll accessories, Monopoly, Pachisi, Zephyr Worst do not count as legitimate criteria nor as water sports. Sunday nursery noose, doll panties, jack's balls, aitchbones, red paint, aleatoric rolls, head toss were the scrambled emblems of my patibulary infancy. "It is not for you to figure out," Daddy would often howl in my face. "Don't you dare even try to figure. I will grab your pri-vatic and give it a good vaticide trick of the wrist, I will. Good private twist!"

One cannot go back to collect what was never collectable in the first place. Childhood occurred I am sure, for I have come thus far and I am old. I am as old as a great, great, great, great great great grandmother still clutching her *vade mecum.* I can recall the Civil War, and the Centaur and the Monitor, and eight souls saved by water, and doing hand battle with any Indian, bare-chested, beating prison heart bleeding beads scarlet red with ponceau R. It is all one in the same. Before that the red was in woolen coats covering body parts too young to die unnoticed. British longjohnpriapia Acid red 66, jacking Jack often, benimble, all french blue thumbs. The thought then was to break away. Slavery, bondage, or escape could not be taken lightly in the hands of a jacklight. Instead, reality, passing by, poked its wagging head out, bit me in the nape of the neck and scooted me, a head, forward eight spaces. It was cheating to be sure. Who doesn't cheat? Jack Horner Pie apple-crust dynamite of my heart imploded into untraceable circumstances. In order to do the job right, one must call upon a power, a linking of the yolks – good shaking down jack ketch leaking labels – so that I just might bend the rules ever so slightly . . . reevaluate the goods, the cloth, the strips, the marks, and inventorialize five . . . of the most important criteria I could muster, including the planes, the senses, the elements, the virgins, the cinquefoil. Fingered licking good. Ack-ack the loaves, the talents, the kings and, of course, the smooth stones that adumbrated *Rev. Ver* in a nutshell.

The wind winnowed the leaves.

I found an accomplice – Daddy's gone a marsh hunting, stalked by an *ignis fatuus*.

And in the midst J. Baptiste sounds the word.

RESURRECTION AT A COST

Let's put it simply like this: ALL minds are marbled with normalacy. Oh, yes. Open up the cranium with a nasty tooth surgical saw, release the obnoxious gas, pry apart the bone, elevate the organ (taking care not to sever it from its cable), and marvel, at eye level, at its marbled pattern. Like clouds, visualize and revel at its various shapes taking the form of animals, peoples, places, and objects familiar to the pages of historical fact and chaotic fiction. Even the most sadistic, orgasmic-grieving human entities confined in the darkest, dampest holes of the penal system possess such contrasting textures of the brain, otherwise known as legions of normality (see, 6,000; making 12,000 feet in all). Radioactive, radiant energy as intense as eve's constant.

Take my father, for instance. He wakes up after seven, makes a cup of coffee, puts on his slippers, ventures out to retrieve the paper (minding to bid good morning to whomever may cross his path, even manages to nod at jack in the pulpit addressing a mass of bright scarlet berries), returns to the house, puts on the television, catches the morning news like a million and one other law-abiding, fingent citizens, makes ready for work, ventures forth to a well-paying job within the right angle establishment, is well-liked and respected by all who share his working hours, and I'm sure bears a yielding smile, and holds nay an ill-word toward anyone in his immediate environment.

That is the thing – how we manage to create our personnas, and thereafter present them in a state of eversion to the world-at-large. What seed of degenerate growth permeated man's souls from being consistently and inherently evil? It would be so much easier to digest if man did not have this seemingly irresistible urge to look good and/or dead as a telamon turned inside out. It only adds confusion to an otherwise linear and simple thread of existence. Mother said it in her best patois verse when she cradled me id in her arms, when as an infant, like a ben, I was so hopeless and helpless and so egg-yolk vulnerable to the prongs of existence. She said: "Rock-a-bye baby fly in the treetop. Don't you cry. Go to sleep my little baby. Jus get a whiff of me adulticide."

Sleep, dear weary god. Sleep (if given a chance), I could sleep all life long as a column. Born to bed by breath in deep, uninterrupted, toss-free slumber. Put the dog rose to my nose. Look, I'm snarling the dog's letter. Hold me, Mother. In blissful softness, hold me as you once did, when as a fast child on the fifth Sunday, as a *bim*, I gazed at your loving, adoring features and wide-eyed security. Your particular kind of goodness not only permeated your blood, it flooded your entirety with an essence that made your exterior glow like second heaven. Take up the any-deadly drink. Be invincible when pierced somewhere-anywhere in the cold, unchartered whereabouts of the universe. Perhaps it would take billions upon billions of journeyed years to fall clear into the castfire house, *la casa calda*. But in those confusing sections of existence, sections in which I expand my logic and wonder illogically about this condition-labefactionledlife, there is a craftsman waiting who both devised and designed life with tools unfathomable to the mind of man.

I failed . . . I failed . . . you, Mother. I failed . . . you, humanity. Upon leaving the house I nailed (the house of biltmore), I attempted to follow Daddy as he prowled the city on wheels. Oh, what a pathetic duo we made. He encased in a vehicle of heterodromous movement, me following so far behind on feet much too small for the world-at-large. I read three days later in a tossed *billet-doux* smeared with red (dye or blood, I know not) that a child was missing. Daddy exploded on my stomach like a spurred mysticete in the dead of night, while Mother slept under the influence and caress of a golden brew. Meanwhile, Daddy drew his heavy breath, *nematode bursa copulatrix* surrounding me.

Note.

While wandering in the wilderness, I came upon a kiosk. The headline shouted: FIFTY ATE. I see BM (the Blame of Man). Whereupon, I descended into the subway station.

I gathered myself up like a bundle of sheets, tossled, and turned into the heterodox hour. And minutes beyond – steadily ticking away, drops of glue sticking to black fear, a moment of febrile anxiety, courage mustered in my breath consumed by elongated fragments of history interspersed with flashes of insanity – I surmised, I know naught. Plunging a blade like a carlisle into the heart of a clio, a myxoid welsh rabbit, whose seed split the code that established the atoms of my consciousness, *and* still amuse, is by itself the most difficult act of sublimation. My feet do not take me anywhere where I am forbidden to go. So on my muscular foot I creep. Death is but a coelom that exists within the powers to be and follows upon my heels like a doppelgänger visible only to me. For it is not an act of completion, but one of ghostly continuity to the living walls of my toasted soul, my interior, however long the belly bough might linger in the cave, *that that that that that that that*

Daddy sleeps on his back. His stomach is exposed to the tory world like a big ripe melon, a watermelon with lots of seed. With each mouthful the seed slides across the tactile tongue and becomes caught in a holding pattern above the bilophodont molars rising from his gums. Like the fish in the sea bottom that holds its young in its mouth whenever danger lurks as a process of the floor of the very mouth of existence, I harbor a million unborn, plus one on my knee, like a sandek. Oh, humanity! Must I be chosen a bloody, lucan, Yehokhanan martyr in order to shelter your children from the cold? See the Cook. Prepare the blithe meat. A rolled big cheese blintze with lots of light cream. Mary Mallon would call it a carrier of disease. She would say: Seed freezes when exposed to the air. Six inches long, erect in my hand, ready to incite and beat him to the punch is Daddy's most effective rival. Consider this: with one childish thrust I could make a bee-line down to his bowels and cut him a porterhouse deal for the sake of surmising the known from the unknown. Outside, the living moon shines, squats like a billiken about to rise, and I could swear smiles toothless: 3 wisdom, 4 incisors. I believe I read somewhere of a case that consisted of two cop killers, reapers of the dogberrys, who had had just about enough of changing shapes. The wronged rarely believe in limits. My own platitudes reek of foreplay. There is always that *calm* before the storm – that place just outside the realm of human endeavor where greatness resounds in the tree with a thousand *dure* acts of will, only to be disheartened by the disharmony of mankind's inhumanity upon itself – that serves as the bearer of bad tidings. I destroys me every chance it gets. It is not a battle but a downright insidious act of kindness. With steps as silent as a stage of evolutionary change without apparent measurement, I transform my tangibility into an energy quite intangible. Is it not better to transcend cognation and dwell in a realm that bespeaks of unknowingness? After all, what is murder but a gentle act of ascendance? My blade depresses itself into the skin. The tip is sweet, the back bitter like a well-looked tick. I cry, but naught a soul picks up my endecha pitch.

Instead, Mother descends the stairs. Down *Middlesex.* In her arms she holds a drained child, a has-been sigil, I know not.

Consider me other half. JSICASICK R.I.P. In May the brick is erected, just as James would say at 12:00: *fall into divers temptations. Like a wave of the sea driven with the wind, a double-minded man is unstable in all his ways.* But everyman is tempted when he's drawn, shadow of turning. Mother knows this, as does the child. Fair of skin, this child she holds with such a gentle persuasion so as to render her Absolute Time – liquid, onto liquid, liquid blood transfered from body to body, body to soul, by a family of tabanidae, oh, the eye, the eye liquid – has as its reproach a built-in gauge for measuring the art of a man's empty walk. A man of no reputation. Holy! Holey! Holy! Is, the Wonder Loaf of Kenosis! Landser. I fall in the chorus. The hole world full of dough, throwing at me their golden do-re-mis in green notes.

It has been said that a newborn is nothing but a soul plucked out of the mouth of god's reluctance. He does not flip and land flat on his feet like a familiar Liberty cat; nor does he coil in order to stand; nor does he crawl in a diagonal manner. It is next to impossible. Rather, he takes that which has been given to him and compounds it with an energy that, for want of a better term, could be termed *crime passionel,* whether by armies of frogs seizing meat via a prehensile organ, a head and a cake of bread or, better yet, a boiled son at a banquet *or* a feast. It is sound. Just eat and drink. For tomorrow we die as experience goes and

take your pick: 1) *crimen in nominatum* 2) *carnaliter cognovit*

How many times does one go over the lines? Until one has memorized the code backward and can recite the language by way of tongues, ten in number. An agent once said: "Restore your hindsight, onocentaur." So pick up the pieces and ask yourself this: *Can a thought be changed? Can it have a great deformity by time?* If there was *only* time attached, like a clause, to the proper length of our wasteland meetings, then I *would* have time to collect the world's wild limbs into a common heap and burn them in such a way that only smoke *would* leave a trace, with coffin nails trailing like a bone-destiny to the coffin joint. My killing crew speaks not a word. Nor do my emotions offer a reply to questions only fools would ask.

INTROMISSION

It wasn't warm enough today. If dismissal is to be discernible to all of the senses but one, then it simply must be warm. For life is a reflective circle in constant need of an incident, perhaps an incident of light itself as captured in the albedo, the rind of the fruit that thrives as much in light as in darkness, as long as there is a body that understands its specific cultivation as well as its specific limitation. And beyond the darkness, upon the face of the deep departed, there is light. Not 'light' per se as in the incandescence of day or the coruscation of a flame but 'light' as in awareness, apperception, electricity, power. And before there was anything ascertainable, there was solar light. Solar Plasma. The essence of Pleasure. So, de-part in de-light, and *lights!*

Come and see Archimedes, the soldiers of fire! Come and see Lavoisier, the sun! Come and see the solar at Paris and Ashkhabad in the midst of manure piles that play a highly respectable role in the landscape!

Seat twenty-one . . . pips and all . . . 'cuse me.

Warmth – it is not to be felt nor seen. For this would greatly dilute the power of that which by its very nature is indiscernable. One does not go through the world without warmth. Dead works, being alone – that is the very heartbeat of our existence. Were it not so I would not cry for the warmth of humanity's soul on a rood. Nor would I bemoan the howl of the dog, nor the suggestion of the moon as it is reflected in the pools of pupil fire that captures so much waste. Last night I was imbued with force. *Vis inertiae.* I created my universe as on a shoestring. There wasn't much in the way of leafage time. Three stiffs. Time had lost its leafy meaning. It was dashing destiny and salvation that beckoned me from my warm throne in order to swat another knat too dumb to realize that life has its consequences. *And if one is to do something wise, then one must be devoid or rather free of consequences.* It is a great dilemma – a sorrowful contradiction solvable only by way of wisdom's seal; a six-pointed star.

Flash! TWO hanging on a rod are able to regain Joy of Life and Hope through deflation. Relief is only one hour away!

Where is warmth? The heart speaketh not. And yet it is the only organ of humanity that repeats its single sound, twenty-four hours a day.

While Daddy slept she shredded his garments, starting with his crinet. Never mind the six o'clock steel in the sky nor the codes duello. She posed as the soldier in the body of an incognita.

A thousand years to come. The fire is hiding. Plumb the depths leading the mass of lead. The sea is nowhere to be seen. Where the ocean pats the shore, caresses the beginnings of man's solid foundation as though to make amends with this foreign element, the sea excuses itself for its transparency, its refusal to transform. From where I stand the sea is far too distant for the plight of the feet. The dead earth, man's endless code of asphalt, stretches beyond sight to somewhere beyond thought. If I close my eyes I need not imagine. Instead, my sense of smell is heightened, and I can breathe in from the salty depths of that bodily form the seaman bursting forth from the sea. He smells of salt and sand, of library words liquified like mercury across a marbled table, like Hermes figure skating with the fish that fly above the glass and dazzling eyes of the sea, before jc on animal bones in and around Philadelphia, where the first club was born under the watchful eyes of nine judges witnessing the starlight and the camels. And, too, I can sense the fragrance of creatures unseen, behemoth monstrosities sleeping at the bottom of volume. Above all, weight plays a heavy role in this, my scenario. For weight is but the seaman's plight of fancy. The heavy toll. The fold. The gumran flock – to bet. The smaller creatures must pay for the presence of the giants. Mews cry. Concealed in the midst of things, they sound like newborn babes.

THE VULGAR NINE OVER SIX

This transgression is caked on my belly. From here it looks to be the outline of an island (or perhaps of two islands, considering the cancer productus). Its curves and irregular contours denote where the body of my bloody soul connects to the release of his bloody darkness, kept in the beginning as a bloody word. Angiogenesis.

The thought came first?

I am pervaded in all directions by his wantoness. And yet I am concentrated in fylfot form by his assaults and his tails, and by my associations with defense because of them. For a breath of time I connect to my dilemma, a symbolic contest so stultifying to the soul as to render me utterly exasperated with logic. *Cut to:*

In trails I see what's hep and extra spicy. Jacking it up to Ant Hropo Mancy. I say, as a cutup, beware the ides. Cut to:

Insofar that we were a family, that there were three of us coexisting side-by-side, at arms length to whatever trauma was being enacted at the time, there was still a sense of inordinate movement revolving around our unit. It is not an easy task: to fill vital time up with wayward insignificance – nor is it easy to snap the back of motherhood, of playthings long since forgotten about, neglected, or pushed aside like so many soiled linens. It is rather frightening to be doffed and exposed by one as powerful as a god. Exposed to public contempt. Exposed to public disdain. Susceptible to scorn (as in a pillory). Susceptible to community corruption. A teasing quodlibet, as a man of the cross advocating docetism. If reel. 3,2,1

Madame Blavatsky,
The five basic questions will only serve as a deterrent to unity. Consider the who, what, where, when and how as enemies of the people. And again I ask, "Who will take suit and serve to protect? And with a little bit of espionage, guide one as beautiful as I to wound?" In bed it is the survigrous breath of Procrustes that gears me in the proper direction. And I fall short holding in my hands the very seven tools that I was meant to work with. Supposititious tools which have no definite explanation. In regards to physicality there's even less to speak of. For as father encroaches, there is no room for communalism. Adjectives will keep you alive and stagnate your blood, depending on their usage. But they are in the end, dependents. And so I am left subjected to a voyage amongst (loved?) ones, only because I care, only because I keep my journey as promised.

G

Not shaken by the letter. But falling away. Showing himself off as the mystery of equality. Showing himself off as the sign. The *wonder* lying in a strong allusion.

IN THE BEGINNING
YOU AIN'T HEARD NOTHING

– He is de-parted. He is not the disciple in each and everyone of you. Never shall there be another moment when creation and death, love and murder, turn dreams to dust in one breath.

One day, long ago, in a world that was cyclopean, the Gestapo hanged a child. The child had the face of a sad-eyed seal; and although he was silent and shallow-eyed and never uttered a word of protest, he was led to the place where he was to be hung, stripped bare, and needlessly tortured. Three days it took him to finally die; but in those three days the pain was immeasurable and neither the world nor the universe had ever witnessed such suffering. Omnipotence would have prevented it; for love, akin to omnipotence, is neither impotent nor useless; nor does it rationalize why misery must be, but spears the rod for clemency. For if one is to pay for one's past sins, the finger must still be pointed at the creator for all spoiled things.

LOOKING BACK AT THE TRIAL OF god

god: "The generation of my forgotten. Sire, let me speak. I am all I'm claimed to be. Originator, author, lord. Singular slaughterer. I am neither formed nor developed. I am beyond. Father was never a name I gave. Upon a call I have heard it gravely spoken."

Take note: the jury scratches their chins bearing witness to his words.

god: "Because in that day and age the earth was corrupt and full of violence, and flesh was everywhere, and it had to be destroyed."

PROSECUTOR: "So you did destroy the earth!"

god: "Naturally. It was bad and full of stale jokes."

PROSECUTOR: "What are you talking about?"

god: "I'm talking about the earth!"

PROSECUTOR: "Yes. The earth that you made."

god: "No. The earth that I created."

JUDGE: "Answer the questions specifically!"

god: "That is what I'm attempting to do. But to be more precise, allow me to get round and get up before the hour is due and we all weep three short tears and faint blind. Now, if I may go on, if it so pleases the court and that lovely jury as I do waste time."

PROSECUTOR: "So your method of ending violence was to do violence upon every holy living soul. And you have the nerve to brag of good deeds! More like good debts! You were responsible for every living thing that walked the earth! And what did you do but go and destroy everything and everybody simply because you were annoyed and didn't like what you saw! How convenient. We should all have such a field day watching that which we detest conveniently vanish under a blanket of gas. And what of the children and the babies? What of the animals and their babies? Cockerels, nymphs, nits. Did it not occur to you that they were totally innocent." The Prosecutor redirects his line of questioning and attempts to focus on god with a line of facts. "I want to get back to this business of destruction. I think it is more than difficult to justify the phrase which you implanted in the mind of men: an eye for an eye, a tooth for a tooth. I have it on record that you stated that every moving thing that lives would be meat for man and his kind! And even then you weren't satisfied to leave well enough alone. You even . . ."

god: "Stop! I don't mind being put on trial. I can take the humiliation *and* the degradation that is being imposed upon me on this day of all days when I'm 'spose to be quietly resting, and put it in the palm of my hand like so much . . . so much dirt, and blow it into the four corners of the universe so as not to make a mess in any one particular corner per se. But at least get your sacrosanct finger straight!"

PROSECUTOR: "Don't you mean facts and figures?"

god: "As a matter fact, yes, I mean those too!"

PROSECUTOR: "Speaking of hands, since you're so compelled to speak out of turn and to interrupt time when there should be no interruptions at all, I would like to ask you a question regarding another statement you made in relation to the life under your jurisdiction. Did you not require that the blood of all life, at the hand of every beast, woof down the better part of man, excluding the hand of his brother? And before you could pause for breath or make a Left on East, also state that who should ever shed man's blood, by man should his blood be shed in turn? For in your image did you knot-make man to confuse the language?"

god: "Well, isn't that a dunghill ton of words for such a bantam mouth? A mouth, I might add, formerly perceived with hematophobia. I'm surprised your jaw didn't shatter upon the floor from the load whilst you spoke."

JUDGE: "Order! I'll not tolerate you running sentences into life term statements."

god: "Sir, please." (Clearing his throat.) "I can't say precisely that which was said I saith, for what I had apparently saith was but a quote thereof, as perceived and imperfected by the ears of man, living in confusion or not!"

PROSECUTOR: "So you *were* insinuating that you didn't say that?"

god: "I'm insinuating, my dear Coattails de la Plume, *chien de garde,* that I was misquoted."

PROSECUTOR: "Misquoted?"

god: "Ah, had man but ears to mirror like thee, we would not be here today but rather yesterday, which would have left today in the wind with all work done as finished. It woes me, the utter diversity of man. My heart is heavy with missed conception, and all on account of an atheous reflection."

PROSECUTOR: "Look, my patience with you is waxing thin."

JUDGE: "god, you will kindly refrain from being petty and witless or you'll be facing a charge of contempt! Counsel, you may proceed at your own risk of pace."

PROSECUTOR: "Thank you, your Honor. Now, god, you state that you detest being misquoted."

god: "I long to interrupt but there you go falling away into the same old ditch as all the other nincums have before you."

PROSECUTOR: "Clearly this is nothing but a cheap ploy in order to evade the question in an attempt to disrupt my train of thought."

god: "Loco, to be sure."

JUDGE: "Order! We are not going to waste time while you two argue. Counsel, proceed with your line of questioning and mind your contempts!"

PROSECUTOR: "Thank you, your Honor. As I was saying, it appears that our witness loves to confuse language and would change the very confessional into confusion if permitted to take the pledge or plunge. Why, he could be counted on to dismantle the common words of a people with but a bending of his knees."

god: "Well done. But on the contrary, my dauntless little Din-n-Dabbler, I would go no further than a ledge to dismantle the wares of one's body, for I happen to love language and have given it gleefully as a gift to both grownups and grunions alike, grounded in the goodness of gracious earth. I swear. Such is the way of gay trivia. Does poetry not ring in alliterative terms? Does a tiger not have teeth? Does a lion not lay around a lot? Does a human not hum when he's happy? Does a streetwalker not screech when she's squeezed? Now I ask you, how could I ever confound the language when I bestow such beautiful blessings of blank verse upon the tongue? Am I not mental after all is said and done? O man, go fast and catch a falling Star and lie in one place."

PROSECUTOR: "Your Honor, this is an utter hypocrisy! Such nonsense I refuse to tolerate! We might as well end this trial here and now on grounds of total insanity alone!"

JUDGE: "Counsel, it is the duty of this tribunal to uncover and reveal truth as it stands in the face of adversity. And not a second before nor after will this trial come to a close as I see it."

god: (Drumming on the armrest with his fingers a wearisome number of times.) "Well put, sir. Well put."

PROSECUTOR: "Then let me warn you. If you so much as even think about confusing the issues-at-hand and transforming such a serious and somber topic as the state-of-your-universe and all the inhabitants and living things contained within it as sheer mockery and nothing more than your helotic playthings, bearing no more weight nor sustenance than a mouse to a cat nor a helminth to an intestin-time, and if you continue to ridicule and insult your creations and make light of the fact that there are contemptible, sacrilegious and downright brutally abusive conditions to contend with, and that it is your very acts alone that are on trial here, and that your role as supreme ruler of your universe is at best shaky in its conditional security, and if you insist on responding to my questions with nothing more than satirical sentences of such sheer irresponsibility that you might be blamed for reasoning within the maintenance of your own sanity, and if you continue to treat this tribunal as though it were established solely for your entertainment and amusement, and if you cannot resist distorting the facts and twisting events, then I with all the checkered power invested in me to persecute to the full extent of the law will, in turn, show no mercy whatsoever as I pursue the persecution of this most serious of multi-universal-dimensional-fish cases. Now, I hope I've made myself perfectly clear?"

JUDGE: "Order! Counsel, we are not going to sit here while you blow hot wind across the courtroom atop the hot wind that you have already perflated! That's enough! (Pointing to god.) "And as for you, if you don't buckle down and listen better, I'm going to impose a mark on your hide that will really have you smarting, and then we'll see where that puts you Mr. High-In-The-Pi-Eye-Sky-Do-or-Die-Utter-Lack-of-Attention-to-the-Sixth-Degree. Counsel does make his point perfectly clear and I for one happen to be in total agreement with him."

COX: (Standing up.) "Oh, excuse me, your Honor. *Excusez-moi.*"

JUDGE: "What is that ruckus coming from back there? Who is that speaking out of turn? Come to order!"

COX: "It's only me, your Honor. A mere speck amongst spectators."

JUDGE: "Well, what is it? You're speaking out of turn."

COX: "Oh, excuse me, your Honor. I don't mean to be improper, but I have been holding up my arm for twenty minutes and no one's bothered to call on me."

JUDGE: "You've been holding up your arm?"

COX: "Yes, your Honor. Holding up my arm."

JUDGE: "Well, what for? What's the problem?"

COX: "Oh, no problem, your Honor. I just had a question."

JUDGE: "A question?!"

COX: "Ah, yes. Questions . . . aren't they allowed?"

JUDGE: "Aren't allowed? What do you think this is? This isn't a classroom!"

PROSECUTOR: "Your Honor. As counsel for the persecution I must protest this outlandish interruption. Now I don't know if god's responsible for this present chaos because god only knows he created enough of it down on his own planet. And I'm not even sure if this gentleman back in the seats isn't in cahoots with god himself to further spread chaos and confusion throughout the courtroom. But this outburst from the bleachers from Mr., Mr. . . . "

COX: "Cox, sir."

PROSECUTOR: "What? What was that?"

COX: "I said my name is Mr. Cox."

PROSECUTOR: "Mr. Cox, is it? And just how in heaven's name did you gain access into the courtroom?"

JUDGE: "Excuse me, Counsel, but as presiding judge over these proceedings, you'll beg me to ask the questions." (Clears his throat.) "Now, Mr. . . . Cox, is it?"

COX: "That's correct, your Honor."

JUDGE: "Well, Mr. Cox, seeing that you have succeeded in breaking up the already questionable momentum of these proceedings, may I ask just what this current interruption is all about?"

COX: "Well, your Honor, I really just had a question to ask. Forgive me if I was amiss."

god: "You are forgiven."

COX: "Your Honor, I hate to be causing all this trouble but my question was only a brief one. And I'm enjoying this so immensely that I didn't want to miss a moment. But nature is a-beckoning the piping times of peace and I don't know how much longer I can ignore the pole's call. I simply want to ask is there going to be some kind of intermission?"

JUDGE: "What?"

PROSECUTOR: "Your Honor, please, I employ you. This has got to go beyond certain inalienable rights. god did the same deliberate thing to everyone down on earth. That is, he had them all speaking into thingy air. And now you're allowing him to exercise his insanity upon us, even here."

JUDGE: "I understand that, Counsel. Now, Mr. Cox. Just what is your purpose here?"

COX: (Taking his place beside god.) "Well, actually I don't have any real purpose. I didn't mean to interrupt the court. As I was saying, I was only inquiring whether there might be an intermission in order to give us relief. Funny thing, I always thought that once the body forum passed away it would simply take with it this business of elimination. I don't know about you, but as for me I always found it to be such a bother actually having to stop whatever you might be doing. Sometimes, mind you, very important things, vital things, things even relating to life and death, just so you could get a load off and *rupt* so to speak. Oh, I never thought there was much need in it myself. I was shocked to discover that it's still something we souls need to do in order to expel all that excess synergy."

PROSECUTOR: (Crying.) "Your Honor, how long do we have to put up with this? I can't take it anymore. Look at that. Just as seven *thats* may follow each other, and make sense, so does my hand shake seven times per second! It's nerves, your Honor. Just look through the records and count how many ulcers and nervous conditions were prevalent upon the earth throughout its ulcerated history. Billion upon billions! And he showed no mercy.

No, not even to the apple of his eyelid. He showed absolutely no mercy! He created the atonic conditions and watched his creations grow literally mad, depressed, confused, angry and spoiled from overexposure to zooerastia!"

god: "How could any spirit who is supposedly as wicked as I create someone as innocent as Mr. Cox?"

PROSECUTOR: "By simply being thoughtless. Your Honor, is it really necessary for Mr. Cox to be sitting alongside the witness in the witness box?"

COX: "If you'll please excuse me, I just want to know when there is going to be an intermission, that's all."

JUDGE: "When god levels with us, which I insist he do promptly."

god: "Very well then. Sit still and listen good, all wise members of the court. For what I am about to tell you are but the words of my heart. I am a humble lump of soul with all the humility of a liliom who but loveth his planet from the heart. And if I be a loving father, where is my hour? I have created and I have been cursed. And if I be a master to my flock, where is my key fear? I do not shed a tear from my own well according to my own whims but from my heart. Do not my tears rise like dew and moisten all humanity with my compassion and still they despise my name? They who have polluted the air I breathed to give them life. They who have polluted the wheat I milled to give them food. They who have polluted the oceans I spilled to give them sustenance. And at my table they call my food contemptible. If I give you eyes to cover blindness for light, is it not good to also have sunglasses? And if I give you limbs to cover distance with a healthy stride, is it not wise to also have a compass? I pray you who call my name in vain that I am still gracious unto darkness and racious in the race to death. Even the bird sings at night, its love song. *L'amour et las fumée ne peuvent se cacher. Vitulus, vetus, ve by ve, sus, bos, revenons à nos moutons.* Who is there among you who would wisely put out the fire with water? Far from the rising of the sun, I dwell behind not to hide but to protect the risen fruit of the earth. But they, my children, have profaned it. The fruit is mixed with meat, and neither will be kind to the other. I am weary. I am torn supporting the lame and the sick, and I starve on the offerings, a mere dot on a plate. I am and always will be a marked king of great pride, and those who think otherwise will lay at their hearts broken pieces. Lumps, heed my words as *flatus vocis.* For even in my hour of empathy, remorse withstanding, I will curse the blessings rising nonmellisonantly on foul air to my ears. I will corrupt the seed buried deep in the heated nest I built and spread dung over the mouths of those begging for food and even spread dung over their feast prepared without my name. The truth, nay the law, is in my mouth, and on my mellifluous lips slipping spirits walk keeping guard of my single tongue. For I bestow knowledge, and that which is sought is hidden within me. Yes, many have departed before the heart's breath has ceased. Many have stumbled and fallen, vanished forever, although I will find them in a moment's twinkle. I stand near all souls, not in judgment, not in fear, but in love with standing pieces. I do not change, even from the days when my giant sons ran unclothed. I have kept silent regarding fear and words stuck in the ear. Often I said I would return, and I have left my house unlocked in my absence. Will a being rob god? Who dares to fall in order to find treasure without a note? My trust is robbed of its security. Not only with one, but even the whole earth in parts spoken of old."

JUDGE: "god! Will you kindly refrain from such long-windness."

COX: "Gee whiz! That hardly seems fair. I was touched by his speech. I don't think that's fair at all."

JUDGE: "Shut up, Cox, or I'll have you in contempt of court as well."

COX: "Dear me, it's awfully strict in here."

PROSECUTOR: "Do you have any idea what he is being tried for? What tricks? What deception? What *prestige?* To dazzle, to charm, to manipulate the very essence of the word. Do you know what incest is? Torture, humiliation, lies, violence . . . mendacious retort, fashionable despair? He garmented the world with these and so much more."

COX: "Yes, but, your Honor, did you not hear him speak yourself? He is so filled with love, I could break a leg in spite of him. Why must he be punished so?"

god: "Hush, hush, sweet Cox. Thank you, but hush. It is a strange land we're in. 'Tis a fair and all the rides cry bumpy to the *fin-de-siècleth* degree. And as for punishment, why, ipunmeish every chance I get."

JUDGE: "Order! Counsel, do you have any further questions to ask the witness?"

PROSECUTOR: "I don't know exactly where to begin. This is most irregular. Two bodies in the witness chair at once. I beg your pardon, your Honor, but this is all very quite confusing. Whatever business Cox has with these proceedings, could we kindly get it out of the way."

JUDGE: "Well, Cox, do you have anything else you want to add?"

COX: "Who me? Well . . . no. Well . . . yes. *Ad captandum.* As a matter of fact, I do. I simply must protest. I think it's abominable the way god is being treated. I can't say for certain if he's guilty of the crimes he's been accused of, but I can tell you that on earth he was revered as the one and only god. I do not condone any of those terrible acts that god is being accused of, but I cannot see how he can be judged before he acts. Now I may not be of this realm. True, I am but an outsider from another world below, and true my feet have departed that world as well, and I am but a wanderer in ashes, the lowliest of kind with no true place to rest my head or unburden my feet. And true, I did not come here with great stories behind me. My physical walk was meek and insignificant. A few laughs, a few tears, I put into the souls of my fellow human beings. But still, as I sit in this chair and am asked questions, I find in my heart that I have many things to say, and I know that when I prayed upon the earth I was comforted by a knowingness that bore no distinct words, no distinct voice, no distinct preséance. Even my own father was silent when as a child I searched for his love. Still, I could hardly judge him for being distant. He was my father, after all, and he lent me passage into the earth. He was big and strong in my childish eyes, and I never thought I would taste death as long as I stood behind him. I suppose that I was wrong. It's funny, but sitting beside god now I could almost feel the same."

god: "Such a wooden beggar, truly you be, Cox. You know there are dragons in the wilderness who would consume an entire forest in one sitting, just as there are vessels that would attack from behind the ball. They always think they've got all the answers, and then afterwards hurl themselves into a sacrifice. If you want to uphold me, Cox, you may try, but don't think for a moment that your dagger goes undetected."

JUDGE: "Just what is going on between the two of you?"

COX: "god works in strange and mystagogus ways – his words are but the strangest part of him."

god: "My words, you call them! My words are your bed to swim in, but beware lest you drown in dreams."

JUDGE: "Honestly! What are those cryptic undertones between the two of you?"

COX: "Your Honor, I can assure you that I wouldn't know where to begin. It's true. Winter nights I slept in cold rooms. They finally found me in a motel, stretched on a bed, a wooden frame defaced with initials carved in crude letters by dull knives that tolled a secret. The life of one between ultimate success and the crack of doom is but a lonely one, neither here nor there. But more like in pieces, in a maze."

JUDGE: "Here now. What is this all about, Cox?"

PROSECUTOR: "Your Honor. Don't you see what's going on here? Cox stood behind god and fell under his spell; just as god has seduced and abused his universe, so does he to a single soul."

JUDGE: "Is this true, god? Have you cast a spell over poor Cox here?"

god: "If it so pleases the court, lift up your eyes and look upon me. Both the width and the breadth of me. In my length is every grain of dirt, every speck of dust that has ever touched the earth. Arise! Resurrect the words! Pitch your tents in my mud and keep watch all the night through and see if there is but one fallen star that burns into nothingness."

PROSECUTOR: "Your Honor, how can we ever conduct a trial as long as god speaks in a language all his own? I beg pardon of the court, but you are dearly responsible for the words of god bursting forth excessively."

JUDGE: "Silence, Counsel! You are treading on the most dangerous of grounds. This is not a bloody hand-out nor is it a lighted menorrhagia! I am the highest of high here, alone, and I will judge who is responsible or not. You dare to tear my cloak and stain it by your deed? If words topple worlds then you best conceal yourself from the page and make your words scarce or you'll be found in contempt. Do you read me loud and clear, Counsel?"

PROSECUTOR: "Loud, undeniably. And clear as grit, your Honor."

JUDGE: "And as for you, god, save only that which is comprehensible to these proceedings. I demand logic!"

god: "Your Honor, my words are full. There is no room for anything else, redundantly speaking. I speak what I am, nothing more, nothing less."

PROSECUTOR: "Look it, your Honor! god, he smirks. I swear, he smirks. Now I know the dirt! *Tel père, tel fils,* howbeit Greek!"

JUDGE: "Yes, Counsel, god smirks. But there, a tear."

god: "I volunteer this now. You are both wrong!"

JUDGE: "Wrong? How so?"

god: "Your smirk. My smile. Your discovery. My pun. For my work, son. Should that not bring both a tear and smile to the eye? Does not a tear carry both bitter and sweet, severity and levity? Between me and thee there is but space, but space to fill with thoughts invisible to the eye. Had I not loved I would have not destroyed, for blood is but joined with blood by the brush."

PROSECUTOR: "Spare me. I have done my research well, and I know you can thrive in darkness and die and live again with just the lightness of a word. Fortune spins your wheel. And if not fortune, grandeur. Beg you a smile? Ha! Not even upon this special meeting pursued by a policy of confrontation short of reassurance! Your poetry is the dirt beneath the soil and it renders every man a wild man against himself. What I have seen of the earth is what I have seen of the sun going down, into a deep slumber, into the ground. And a horror of a great awakening in a great darkness upon the same earth as that one awash in endless light!"

god: "I beg your pardon but if I may interject, being as wise as I could possibly be, I see that there is only despise in your eyes, and that envy seems your ploy. Your Honor, your royal holy magistrate of miraculous highness, is it not apparent to you that there is more than myself on trial? This is between all that is here and departed, born in the same puerile house, one and all."

PROSECUTOR: "Heresy! You alone were born in this house of judgment for crimes committed against your kind!"

god: (Interrupting.) "Kind? You yourself admit to that which I am. Let it be noted in the records that even prosecution recognizes me as kind, and that my actions are born *and* bred of unharnessed love, and that good precious energy is exhausted under such scrutiny as this."

PROSECUTOR: "What nonsense is this? With such suffering why would you defend? If there is really such comfort in your heart, why would you present pain for consideration? Does not meek and smileless Cox stand as a witness to this fact?"

COX: "Please, I beg your pardon. My suffering was not meant to be an expression of resentment. I am not a mad murmuring in the wind. Actually, I suffered lovingly, gaily unto god, in spite of his vastness."

PROSECUTOR: "Barbaric and brutal for god to do as such. I would allow the court to bear witness to the fact that even his subjects breathed pain as justification of love."

god: "Please. What pain I granted the body is visible only in the soil. Pain ends at death."

PROSECUTOR: "And so, what of hell?"

god: "Hell? You ask of hell? It works when nothing else remains. *Non cuivis homini contingit adire Corinthum.* But . . . is there not an escape to the mountains lest all be consumed, lest all evil take place and the body dies, the soul lingering to hold the bones of one's passing as long as one has the fare? Does not rot enter first through sight, the socket of which is the house of observation? I presented hell not as a ground upon which one assesses his shortcomings, but rather as a rock upon which man, both small and great, might weary himself."

PROSECUTOR: "god. You were sent to take charge of a realm, howbeit guidance from above brought you forth. But guidance does let go, and that which has been guided must stand the test of evidence. Out of nothing you bore light. Out of nothing you created the heaven and the earth. Upon the face of the waters you cast light and divided the light from the darkness. As you have learned, so you have done. As it was only natural and befitting a god. But you have created and tended your earth, an utter mess of spirits in the wool. Your finger points outward in blame over an unceremonious plate, even as you grasp the scraps in haste!"

COX: "Stop it! I can't bear this any longer! That is god and for me his love does save. I would freely lay at your feet my eternity, merely to defend his name and leave my place in history with future renascible dust. For am I not his one and only?"

PROSECUTOR: "Why, Mr. Cox. Do I detect a slight slipping of the mask? Or are four eyes your common lot? Truly, I respect your love and your poor, bleeding blame is tragic, for it is the same the world over. The expense of spirit is a waste of trust. But the limb is connected to the brain and the shadowy tongue slides like sap."

COX: "You define me more than words are worthy. I stand behind god, yes, and as I speak I am revealed. Perhaps I be of several stages. Perhaps the one I act but for a breath is full of strange oaths. But by many infallible proofs, the times and seasons swear not to depart."

PROSECUTOR: "A great deception gives birth to tantalizing ideas. Shrewd you may be standing behind god, with devotion your humble barricade. But I see through you, Cox. To worship the back of god is but a substanceless shadow of real understanding!"

COX: "Should not the judge of all the earth do right by way of dust and ashes? I gaze not upon a tribunal but the ultimate symbol of evil. How it does point and aim to speak a thousand condemnations. For destruction's sake alone. There is none more worthy than god, for there is none who created as he did an earth smouldering in devotion, creatures breathing on faith per thousands of years in time! If this is not miraculous, if this is not the seed of love's secret, man to maker, maker to man, then let my soul drop to depths unfathomable!"

god: "Cox, sit down. You talk too much." (Examining his nails.) "You always have. But if I had not made you of such, I suppose I would have been rendered a donkey's ass."

PROSECUTOR: "Disheartening, your lines, god. And you dare to speak of love?"

god: "When I breathed my souls into the earth I was but lacking a proper theme for love, I admit, but it bore me much pain, nay, dissatisfaction, to think that I would bore love for love's sake alone without love realizing the contrary. Surely, I found appreciation exists only when pleasure knoweth pain. Does not one laugh to run from such? Is it not a relief to relax in a smile after there has been a span of misery? For almost at once the food was not good; in spite I viewed my work at the beginning as good. Such a dilemma I was determined to work out. After all, the earth was pleasant to my eye. The seed was kind. The fruit ripe and plentiful. And it was all very good indeed. Very good. B+. The light of night, the light of heaven. It was all very pleasing. The creatures moving forward through the waters, deep and abundant. The creatures moving forward through the grasses, green and lush. The cattle creeping with the snake in the fine film of dust that I had created. The bird of the air slicing the crisp air with hurried wings. It was all so beautiful to my mind. And man and woman breathing among them, having dominion over all I had brought forth in the world, was good to my eye, as well as my heart. B+. So much wisdom and folly. B+. B+. And on that day of rest when I put my full face into the pillow of heaven and slept in a dream of wonderful scarlet color, I thought how good I had done my work, how pleasing I was to have fathered and smothered, and how pleasing I was to . . . to . . . to have considered the last first. Did I not do well? I did. A-. And I had even slept on it."

PROSECUTOR: "Let's face it, god. You created in order to destroy. At best your entire system was built upon such an internecine premise as dee to dum and all get done!"

god: "You neglect to see the entire design. You look at an angle, you pick out a line, and you feel justified interpreting my mind with simple phrases. You entirely miss the mark. Such crude observations you make. Consider the signs alone. I heard nigh a word regarding my trees and the poetry of branches and leaves rustling ancient, wordless sounds in the wind. Did you ever visit my October and cast your eyes upon the colors I blended and bled one into the other, a harmless, beautiful fire of hues? Not a single comment regarding the garmented love of families celebrating holidays, representing events born of love and sacrifice. The beauty of a word such as history, where people can look back in pride upon evaluation of their accomplishments. The tenderness of a father holding his newborn son, allowing the tears from his eyes to fall upon his very own. Children, born of love, man to woman. And even among the lesser kind, you neglect to mention the wild animals of the field licking off the dirt of the day from their own offspring, or the hummingbirds in suspended flight trumpeting each blossom they come upon. The warm, quiet, late afternoon slumber of all that I had created. The moon's light tipping the scale of balance, tipping the leaves as they shed their drops, a fragrance in the night. Fields awash in the sirens of insects' suits, chattering one to another, a language all their own. A mystery to human ears. Insects' music drunk on wine, pulsating blood in the veins, roses red stinging the nostrils, even as heads bowed to reverence the essence. In day's daily toil, all life dwelling tired, collapsing in a heap in the sun's absence. Stars offending the wall that separates moon from god. Oh, whatever I missed of earth I preserved in my eye and held within my sight all the inhabitants of all the cities that ever grew in the world that I planted, suspended in space."

PROSECUTOR: "But in having created life without full understanding of the universe, you broke a sacred rule. Instead of truly loving your creations and endowing them with omniscience, you chose instead to keep them in darkness, lest they discover even greater gods than yourself. What good is your beauty if it serves to conceal the greatest beauty of all?"

god: "It hardly matters. It is still mine to rule. I can't be judged for that."

PROSECUTOR: "We shall see. I should like to call Satan to the stand."

A small wisp of smoke precedes Satan as he springs forward from postscenium and approaches the witness stand.

PROSECUTOR: "Who sent you?"

SATAN: "Myself. This is the first cause of all."

PROSECUTOR: "On what grounds did you send yourself?"

SATAN: "To watch over the tree that god had planted in his garden."

PROSECUTOR: "And just why did you send yourself to watch over his tree?"

SATAN: "god was well aware of my protest when it came to the likes of mankind."

god: (Leaping up.) "I object to this line of questioning!"

PROSECUTOR: "Satan is a valid witness as you well know."

god: "I know him to be nothing but a bitter double agent!"

PROSECUTOR: "Not so! You created him! And because you have included him in your creation, you cannot object to this line of questioning. Such are your velleities. What thou createth, thouest liveth by."

god: (Excitedly.) "But you neglect to include Satan's duality. And this is what I most fervently object to. He is everyone's creation as well, lisping to one language."

PROSECUTOR: "Precisely. Therefore, he shall be questioned as such. (To the Judge.) "Is it not permisbible?"

JUDGE: "Objection overruled. You may proceed, Counsel."

PROSECUTOR: "Satan, just what were god's protests regarding mankind?"

SATAN: "god had just completed recording in his mind the staff of angels allotted to him by ruling of the universe. Naturally, numbers therein were innumerable as is only befitting a god, and so therefore the count was countless. As it is beknownst to all, god had spread his own sunny countenance over a magnitude of those angels. There were but a select among them whose original source derived from gods alone. I was chief among them. Once god began to formulate his plan for the universe and thus conjure up the image of man and imprint him with a theme and a code of creation, he began to take on a darkened air. He informed us that he was considering creating man short of omniscience. I warned him that would strictly go against code. But god had it in mind to challenge the code and create man in his own image, acting as his own integument of authority. *Heresy*, we shouted. *It is completely unlawful.* god stood on strictly creative license and cremonious grounds. 'You can't code me! What good is being a god to my creations if my creations do not see me as the one and only lord?' It was here that I, along with the select, decided to depart and inform the universe of god's plan. However, god blocked our departure and created a great disharmony. With his powers he overcame us and sent us hurdling into the earth that he had created; and then he proceeded to fill our energies with words of brutality and malice and corruption. Our attempts to reach transcendence from the earth's core were futile. We were at god's mercy and found ourselves drowning in the gravitational energy he had summoned up for us. All of the select lost their original tongues. My tongue was forked. Listen good. god had succeeded in corrupting my speech, my thoughts, my very seat of purpose, and I was a prisoner of him."

PROSECUTOR: "Satan, could you inform the court as to whether you were present at the creation of mankind?"

SATAN: "I had managed to be present, but god's power proved too immense. He silenced me throughout the creation and pretermitted my continence."

PROSECUTOR: "And as a result man was created lacking omniscience?"

SATAN: "Correct. However, once I caught onto god's undoings, he became enraged, and as further punishment to man, he planted the tree of the knowledge of good and evil, along with the tree of life in his garden, and bid me to make certain that man did eat of it. Before his departure I warned god to allow his creation, man, to have a graceful and enlightened position in the universe as a complete entity, on to himself. god conceded. But once god was departed, he turned fearful once again, and jealous, and envious of power. And with a full vengeance he forbid man to eat of the ions of the tree of good and evil. As for the tree of life, he concealed it from man's eyes – his original gift underwent a loanshift, as it were. And with that he pointed his power at me and further corrupted my essence, and cut me half an integer. Alas, all but the last breath of me was evil. I was thereafter prevaricating with the best of 'em. It is true. There is no secret to the likes of me. god's power is evident."

PROSECUTOR: "And what of your last breath?"

SATAN: "Yes. My last breath. I had to make a choice. Should I keep still and save it and thus save whatever light was left of me? Or do I warn man of god and seek him knowledge and attempt to save him and by doing so lose my last breath of light forever? Sir, for love of universe, for love of man, I fell in a moment. I especially pleaded Eve to eat of the fruit god had planted for her. To know of truth, to know of duality, to ultimately know of the entire spread of existence" (Satan laughs.) "and beyond . . . beyond . . . beyond . . ."

PROSECUTOR: "And, of course, you succeeded with Eve?"

SATAN: (Sighs.) "Yes, I succeeded. And then it was the death of all of us. My lot was being Satan. Torn in twain, I was lost. god's wrath immediately seized my last breath of life in revolution. I fell to the dust. My grape unspoken. My frenzied state undone. My rot. I fell. And I watched as my light was encompassed in darkness. And god enveloped me in his sentence. Licked but good." (Satan turns to dust.)

god: "It isn'true! What he says is a lie!"

PROSECUTOR: "No, god. It is not a lie."

god: "I can look to my earth, my heavens, my people, to all that I have created, and feel righteous. I did not break any rules. If you read between the lines, you can clearly see I did not break any rules. Urging no healths. Touching no state matter. Making so-long-meals etc. etc. etc. I granted heaven its mysteries. What I did not say I left for man to ponder. The handicraft of mysterium. Straining at every point to get to the point when one but closes an eye and can hear the ministry of the inexplicable play. Did you ever see a man drop dead for questioning my existence? When was the last time a man imploded for reaching beyond the confines of his mind? Did I not suggest, did I not hint that there was more to come for man? That there were mysteries yet to be revealed? From goles to golems to Galatea to Galimatias? On the contrary, my particular design was perfection. The very creativity that I put into my design is clearly flawless. If you but look upon me with love, you will see the full extent of my mind."

PROSECUTOR: "Your use of the word love here is but a disguise for power."

god: "How dare you! On earth I am the author of love. Love-in-a-puzzle. Love-in-idleness. Love-lies-bleeding. You know all too well the kind of love I had personally created for the earth." (god suddenly takes on a softer air and begins to laugh.) "What am I really protesting here? I was so quick to react." (his laughter increases.) "A disguise for power? Did you ever consider existence outside of acceptance? I do not think so. Did you ever think of existence outside of structure? Lumping together all the past, commingling eras without regard to context? I do not think so. But it took a god such as I to put love on a level unprecedented in the cosmos. The love of god. The love of beauty. The love of one's fellow man. The love of material things, short of a drop of blood, is but a labour of love. Where in the spheres, and beyond, does one find such a magnitude of love? The infinite superadditions of history grounded in good advice. Therefore, I can only be credited for having advanced that energy into multi-faceted disciplines."

PROSECUTOR: "Let's be realistic for a moment. The manner in which you take credit for love, as you have thusly stated, is not only crude but entirely inaccurate, as in the manner in which you deviously hide behind that same word, hoping desperately to camouflage your defects."

COX: (Rises before god.) "Yes, indeed, Counsel . . . god is right in regards to you. It is you who is guilty, judging god from a distance with your eye ill-parallel to his heart."

PROSECUTOR: "I'll have you to sit down, Cox. I was addressing god."

COX: "You address god, you address me, for did he not make us one in the same?"

PROSECUTOR: "It is not the same, dear Cox. You have been duped; a ragpicker flamboyantly adorning your wares like a hoopoo. A supernumerary polyneme passionately seeking a line within school. You are a falsity, even if your remaining eye is directed at god."

COX: (Turning to god in frustration.) "Why don't you say something? Why can't you defend me as I defend you?"

god: (Distantly.) "I never asked you to defend me. You came here of your own accord, if only for a short time. As far as I am concerned, you hinder me."

COX: (Speechless. His stare upon god is long and hard. And then, surprisingly, a single tear rolls down his cheek. And, thereafter, his very words break the silence.) "I am you. I have no choice to be anything but. Were I truly a man I would have turned from you if it was my desire to be alone. But you sent me an aspirin to do the work of a god in a man's equipoised body, with clearly no option other than to satisfy fate and confound the Jews at the gate. My lines were written for me. My tongue was faithful to the only script provided me. Left to right, my epitaph, and not a chair to spare. Did I not clearly pronunciate every last syllable of that script and thereby become equiponderant on your side?"

god: "I menticide. My script was fulfilled. What more can I say? You tenderly played your part. You took your piddleful bow. You exited. Your performance is on record, wet fool."

COX: (Bows his head.) *"The floor is bare. Not a crumb beneath the chair. Not a cup. 'Tis a gig lot that I share. It is true . . . I was raised in glory. My walk on earth was more than humble. god did drink with me every deadly thing and we did live. god did eat with me every poisonous thing and we did breathe. god did light me with every star from heaven, every lousy candle and O! we did shine! Shoo!* How can your words come back to me now with such contempt?! Such judgment?! Such scorn?! Such return?! I can barely stand, lest I grasp onto your unyielding body."

god: (Breathing haughtily.) "Don't take it so bad, Cox. Swallow hard. After all, it was a fair cop. Elementary. *Flagrante delicto.* Isn't that what love is all about, Cox? Yoke. Pain. Sacrifice."

COX: "Tell me, god. Considering the spirit and the water and the blood, did you feel any love while I was nailed between two leaves? Such punishment is less than capital. Tell me, god . . . since we are both out from under the table so visibly and all, just why did you *leave* me orating so long?"

god: "If you really want to know, I was reading a book of *Innumerable Metathetical Possibilities,* and pondering whilst reaping leaves."

COX: (Cupping his ear.) "I beg your pardon. My hearing isn't so good these days. You were . . ."

god: (Drawing close to Cox's ear.) "Pondering, whilst reaping . . ."

COX: (Shaking his head.) "How nice! How convenient! How marvelous! What a lovely image that instills in me. You've got to make certain that I take on every pickelhaube, every nuance of mowrah meal into my wo-earth body, and translate that into concentrated physical pain, changing the relative order of the letters in time's frame, and then hold it to me yellow fat for hours upon hours beyond our agreement, while you delicately ponder! So, god, let me ask you, were you able to ponder upon everything you needed to ponder upon while I was made to die?"

god: "Actually, no! Seriously, I had so many other questions in my heart. As hard as I tried I could not come up with satisfactory answers. You can't imagine how I paced back and forth, raking, and not coming up with anything that sounded quite right."

PROSECUTOR: "The record is true! My dignity cannot bear it!" (With a swift gesture he points a rigid finger at god.) "There sits god. Spare me. To those on earth he is creator, ruler, and master of his own prerogative. Never mind that he is inflated with power, unreceivable, and demands to be saluted as the one and only insatiable god in the pack. Never mind that he has blocked his creations from fully delving into the bowels of the universe and encountering the deepest darkness of unrevealed mysteries, disallowing his creations to possess the universe in all its totality so that they too might know 'the is' from 'the what is.' After all, members and spectators of the court, we know the full circumference of the universe. We know the hierarchy thereof. The prophetability of perishment. We are well aware that there are many supreme beings here and beyond, each with their own specimen, titles and responsibilities, none the least of which is love, peace, beauty and acceptance . . . As well, we too are aware of the ultimate light, glorious eternity of totality. What beauty, what pleasure, what profit we experience as entities, knowing all, is not a gift but a right, a given. Are there any among you here who would deprive another entity of knowledge of the ledger and all the records therein? Are there any among you here who would keep another entity in darkness, while at the same time punishing it relentlessly for living in the darkness that you, in fact, have placed it in? I ask you, is this darkness and this punishment and this eternal threat of extinction any the more bearable because there is a tree with pretty branches in the darkness thereof, or a mountain, or a stream, or October colors, or love between the forms of life that exist therein? For in the darkness *is* darkness, and all the members composing that one darkness, being many, are all of one darkness in total, for the darkness is not one darkness but many, as only god would make it, in order to darken counsel by words without knowledge. I went to earth and had a dream, and in that dream I saw a beautiful owl sitting on a branch lording over her terrene domain. I daresay it was a beautiful sight to behold. A lower form indeed but what color in its feathers, what mystery in its eyes, what nobility on its perch. And in this dream that I had, I found myself falling deeper and deeper into the mind of god. I was in his world, his realm after all, and so I allowed myself to fully experience his manner. And in my dream, both upon and in the earth, I saw to my horror a sudden arrow pierce through that owl's heart, and watched it fall like a dying star into the ground. What meaning I saw in this, stunned me. For there was no beauty in this act, no love, no peace as is befitting a god. And as I gazed upon the bearer of the arrow and watched him pick up the owl and sling it up on to his shoulder, not for food, mind you, nor even for the beauty of its feathers, but merely to be stuffed as a trophy of ferocious statement upon his mantelpiece, like some diabolic paraph, I found god and asked him, *What meaning is this?* To which he answered, 'It delights the king to be king. It's his Sig nature. *Le roi s'amuse.* 'Tis the very cream, I, mean.' Now I ask you, is this the true realm of love?"

The courtroom is silenced. All eyes fall upon god. The meaning of the dream, the deeper rich meaning, that is, *embarras de richesse,* is evident to all as they turn their vision to Cox and back, fresh again, upon god.

god: "Arise, and be not afraid of this longueur. I still insist my third world is perfect. Is there not beauty in death as I have so boldly constructed it? For it is only the body that returns to earth, so that its split ground may be replenished. What sanctuary of everlasting glory I have reserved for the souls of my creations is clearly spelled out in my hemistich. Raid! No mystery. It was written on the ground with a naked finger. *Ad finem.* Consider the judgment. I am entitled to judge as is befitting a last god. Is this not a particular judgment we're conducting today? Higher though it may be, the general stones are gathered. You say my crime, that is, my ultimate heinous crime against nature is not allowing my creations to know all, and keeping them chained in darkness with pain and sorrow and horror as its three-legged themes. But I bloody ask you, what is beauty, what is love without knowing the contrary? True, this point has been brought up before, but I believe no one here fully comprehends my love for my clay creations. For it is that very awareness of their introrse creator and their acceptance of his power and his love that saves them, hands down. Yes . . . even spit has sight if it first be dirt, just as babies have their rattles. After all is said and done, my design to the totality of eternity is, in actuality, *actum fide,* so easily attainable that it borders on ridiculous, like a triple erection hanging in a triangular plan."

PROSECUTOR: "Your guilt is what is most ridiculous. For it is as evident as your very presence. One and all. How you can speak thusly and say nothing concretely is but a gift you alone possess. For in that scenario alone, you cannot justify the pain and misery that your creations must undergo in order to find your grace. Sight to babies to snakes. Eating and drinking, are they guilty? Yes! But how does one not eat and drink when one is both instructed to, and to not do the same? For you said yourself, *the whole will be guilty if but one does fall.* One? Let it be one sip, one crunch, and all might be devoured in your oblatory heat. True, in having found your grace, you have the power of wiping all memories clean of pain. But pain, in any form outside of your realm, is nonexistent. For, in actuality, you are the ultimate power here, in judgment of yourself! god judging god, and that is the pain and horror thereof!"

god: (Smiles.) "And so, how long must I keep you kings and priests all here today? Until I grow bored, tired, and close my telegnostic eyes and the book and rest again on yet another seventh day? O, thy beauty rest, what is a god to do when he is a telegenic god? Who is left to condemn me outside of myself? I can play and sing with both light and dark until eternity starts to go, searching and crawling, and, perhaps, I will. There is no end to the end of me; and there is no beginning to the beginning of me. For watch me work."

god points a single finger at the Judge, and in an instant the Judge perishes. The courtroom stares intently at the Judge's empty seat. Everyone is stunned. The Judge, who was previously defined as the presiding energy of the courtroom, is now vanished. Evidently, by the power of god's scite alone, god's towcher, god's Index, recto-verso, hereby previously considered to have been a far lesser power than the Judge's Index itself. At this instant the courtroom knows neither to move nor to keep still. But the thought is common among them all: god is all-powerful and can put a Judge, more or less a Chaucer, a Bacon, a Milton, a Descartes, a Voltaire, a Hugo, or a Dante into Stall.

god: "Boredom doth have its limit." (Examining his nails.) "Neither here nor there, of course. I vanished father, believe you me. Although I much prefer Vanquished. Yes, print that if you may and send it stalking-horse with John, Jan & Gray. And might I also add, I love the 'k' sound. You know, it's the eleventh letter and akin to . . ." (Recites the following as though it were a laundry list.) ". . . king, and kingdoms of this and all other realms, and the key to H.D.B.P., and the branded Kalumnia forehead, and the three bad k's: Karian, Kretan and Kilician, as well as being akin to Victor. Actually, I thought there was a time I was going to call myself Victor. It had a sweet smell to it, but also a little like the smell of I.G. Farben and Zyklon B. Reduced to just three swallowable letters, everyone would have called me Vic, the Kef of a rabic sense." (Pensively, almost sleepishly.) "O, I recall my Victors well. St. Victor of Marseilles and St. Victor of Milan. The Victor who appeared to St. Patrick. The Victor Pack that Milton spoke of in arms . . . O, they stood golden . . . and Victor Charlie . . . . Oh, yes, dear brother, let's just say I knew them all well, and I saved this special khamsin moment for a rainy day. Standing on a sea of glass, as it were. Oh, and for the records, that's R-E-I-G-N-I-N--G day . . . Today." (Laughs haughtily.) "Just as I will wear a soft robe and may enter the house of my choice, clutching *The Book of Psalms,* victorious, in lieu of all the violence that would desire to divide me into a kenotic fall and thus sabotage my desire to repair all, as one dusty Evil May Day doth recall."

PROSECUTOR: (His mouth dropping open.) "He doth fey . . . fey . . . fey. . ."

god: (Interrupting the Prosecutor before he has time to complete the full pronunciation of whatever word he had in mind.) "That I do, and perhaps a bit more. For if you take all my definitions and apply them forthrightly, you would have me piercing into the future with an other worldly air, capped with a sense of foreboding of death. Puzzled? A little crazy, perhaps, a little touched with koan thoughtlessness, but acting under an authority of . . . fiat." (Clearing his throat, squinting his eyes at the Prosecutor.) *"Fiat justitia, ruat coelum.* Is this all a bit too much to ask of oblectation?"

god wiggles his finger, but ever so slightly, and the Prosecutor immediately perishes. The space left standing in his place is filled with a presence of otiant knowledge, only the most highest of intelligence could possibly perceive; but in another instant this knowledge too dissolves, and space is but space.

Now god raises his hand to the courtroom-at-large. A sea of dog faces peers back at him. Several of the faces and the names thereof he knows by heart; others he knows only by mind; still, others he knows by both light and dark; and others by light; and others still by dark; and others he knows by the vomit on their jaws; but all-in-all he knows them all; and, all-in-all, they know him not. Some of the faces, some of the bodies, some of the souls would like to run. The curse is to be one of Gabriel's hounds; but as wild geese, unbaptized children wandering through the air until Judgment Day can be quick of movement and slip away. To fly above god as he stands in the wake and thus make one's escape is a movement well-deserving of praise. But to bend at the knees, to slacken one's pace, drooping in essence, languid in gesture, is to lose the race man creates for himself, apart from god.

. . . until death do you part . . .

Now god extends his index finger at the courtroom-at-large. An inharmonious articulation of nullibistic sounds confronts god's gesticulation.

1st VOICE: "You give humanity no credit!"

2nd VOICE: "You give souls no credence!"

3rd VOICE: "You give faith no credentials!"

COX: (Stepping in between god and the court-at-large.) "And that is exactly why you are god and they are what they are. For is not a god perfect, through and through? Here to instruct, as well as to rule? If you stand to deliver and to destroy your court, a battle is won though its purpose is nought."

god: "Neither rhyme nor reason rule here. Had I not warned you otherwise, particularly in regards to old and cheap clichés? You're involved in saving, but, alas, your net is so ladened with hooks and erratums by the book, it's a wonder anything can survive, even as it is hoisted calmly from the eremic, santo sea. Please, Cox, step astride so that I might properly cast my line and thus end this time of Game."

god steps to the left of Cox and proceeds to activate his index finger.

Clearly there is much to consider here. For although it is a sea of immense energy that god looks upon, the identities therein are quite distinct; and neither does it consist of biblical personages alone, for there are political individuals present as well, the names of which cover the spectrum of time itself; and neither does it stop at political personages, for the presence of all that currently comprise the sea before god is composed of entities of all varieties. By the tens of thousands they childlessly stand, ready or not to perish.

god steps beside Cox and raises his hand once again at the courtroom, only to be confronted (once again) by the body of Cox.

COX: "Dear god, truly we are one-in-one, for if mine net is ladened with hooks, your line is the same. According to thyself, it is a wonder anyone can survive me. And this you put in the way of criticism to myself. But dare I ask what is your intention in casting your line? In regards to such, do you intend anyone to survive? What difference: my net, your line? When in your words both are used to bind body to eternal rest. Hic . . . Hic . . . Hic*cup* jacets . . ."

god: "Thrice you choose to block me from my task. Thrice you attempt to halt this last circumstance. Had I not programmed you as such, much time would have been spared, leaving so much more for rest. *T* ask, and it shall be unblocked if you know your verses. A god is expected to foresee all even when the mind is not in motion. A trifle, I divulge: hooks are rotten, little nasty things that do pierce and make the body sing upon contact with skin when blood seeps, streams and brings on seeds of remittance. If your request is pure and your questions sound of mind, then consider the blood I draw – to remit and give relief is kind. Note in the orchestra pit, the orchestians biting their lips. There be the difference between our hooks, and how one binds and the other finds its keep. For consider my hook to be more a smiter of sorts. Implemented in order to be released from the guilt or penalty of any given crime." (god thrusts his face forward into Cox and with a smile accents his final line.) "Sublime? Daresay, dear Cox, as far as this single moment, nothing more, nothing less, will you find that is so ridiculous."

COX: "Trip me if you must. Push me backwards, head over heels. Grind me downward until I am smudged in the same dust life yields and dies in. But be forewarned, my doubts of you forever worn."

god: "Should I care? Should I cry? Should I droop my head and sigh as autumn leaves that lie after the fall? Hardly, dear Cox. Hardly at all. Carry me up, not back. And yet, far. What do you expect? What things? What mores? What else? Your solemn words to cause this god to fret the anaphora? The only suffering I sustain is the boredom that stagnates upon each refrain. How many generations can I blame? Countless, no doubt, but each with names engraved as high as the top of a door ascending stars. Or as low as a nooky whom I abhor."

COX: "It is more than I can bear, obliterating everything with a rhyme, without a care. Abhor that which is never more."

god: (Smiles.) "In some respect you remind me of David. For even as that duppy spoke unto me, his eyes gathered tears that formed stagnant pools within. From whence did his tears begin? Hardly be or 'gin' as he lost his way on the route to the main body of the word and wound up a citatory slip of the tongue. Firm in the face, he, too, lent me words that laced my heart with grace. But never mind him. Let you suffice as a ghost with density. You may exit out the door, as well as to be."

COX: "No doubt you read my words wrong. What I cry unto you is not a psalm. Let me speak for you, a single phrase. *Davus sum, non oedipus.* What you sense is sacred does not belong. My grievances are long, longer than the folds to the pages of your book. If I were its rightful author, I would bring to an end both the threat and the promise of eternal rest, one for the worse and one for the best."

god: "You're fun, Cox. You really are. Precisely why I tamed you my star Seal. But to lay past over future is a fold too far to complete. Really, Cox, I'd rather sleep."

god attempts to raise his hand one last time. Cox does not attempt to step in as before, but speaks to god along the line of battle.

COX: "I thought, at least so I did at one time, that god could do anything. I suppose you could say my humble feet were engaged in loitering so as to get a peek at his work in progress. But, I daresay, I do not like what I see, and what I thought was sound, on four feet, on two feet, and three, now I pray will never be."

god: "I can see with you I must be guarded, for lesser procyons get early started. Every brick that makes my castle so, I know. Every corner, every crevice, every inguinal crook and granny holds not a secret beyond my nose. My staff herein I hold, less like a stick, more like a soul or a Dog with a bone chewing on his coprology, all alone. I feel such fire in your breath. Your tongue is hot though your words sound *rest*. You take me a fool? Beware, Mastur. My ears do rule. As well, my eyes and nose as devour, they go like tools."

COX: "There is a general disturbance in your remarks. Too much the bark, too less the heart. Is it befitting a god to howl, and like the beast lay uncovered? Attention! Dog-leech! Take notice the jowl and the canines therein and see if it does not sound like Canaan, condemned and cursed as sin; and as the dog does spring and burst, the juggler's red rehearsal is the second curse."

god: "What I bid prosit will be done. For man, the crime; for god, the fun. Do you dare to stand on top my head and in that moment expect my bed? There is no hope here. No proteranthous flowers grow. For this I know: a protean god is entitled to all."

COX: "Your love does grow like an icicle I did know. It matters little now, for what I see is what I know. No more, no less. Within your breath of love, no more, no less. I'll live to love before final rest pulls the strings."

Cox turns around, growling. But as he does so his eyes fall upon the sea of souls spread out endlessly before him like a mob of whales in a flensing. Suddenly his heart softens as he realizes this is not a contest between poetasters, nor a polymathic test of any sort. One who is true here does not lose himself in battle. Nor does he lose himself in balance. Nor does he suffer loss from a final separation. Nor does he fall in spirit. Nor suffer deprivation. Simply, he is carried forth up three roads on love. With sacrifice. Even upon trivial things such as Trivia of streets and ways does he convey a converse. Cox's expression relaxes. The tear that climbed to the rim of his eye does not fall as he turns to god and whispers, "I defy."

god: (Wiping his own eye, stretches forth his hand and extends his index finger.) *"Dei Judicium.* Cox, you are hereby stripped. You are a man. Alone. In the proctitisthesis of his musings. And thereby excluded from the purple insouciance of my learics."

Cox steps back into the sea of faces that stretches endlessly beyond like a thick gravy. Soon he is totally unrecognizable, and thereafter lost in the crowd.

god picks himself up and upon his own breath makes ready to carry out his plan of obreptitious destruction. Amidst cries of protest from the courtroom, god begins to flow with the power, standing in stale judgment of the headlines, and bids all to be silent as he appears in his own mercurial majesty.

THE BEGINNING RETURNS TO HAUNT . . . TO TEACH

One . . .

One is such a perfect number . . .

Dr. Theomania . . .

. . . One is such a perfect number. Especially when one can assume a Proteus-type existence. The primary concern is to survive, evolutionary-style, be it body or soul, and to transcend the face of time by at least ½ hour, and skip the protevangelium contest all together. Mortality refundable at the end of one's existence. Another chance to brighten up the house. Perhaps, next time around, to supply a regale, lots and lots of golden apples (D) 'neath the dough. Regeneration, after the cockhead has been cut so deep it literally severs the sacrum. And the last bone of earth is rendered sawdust, to dust, to dust. Pedicel stalking the fall. Better yet, a butcher's saw. The suitability of such a jagged edge makes for a grand signature – the soft-nose being so near the bottom of the sheet, allowing time for the red dye to dry a glistening trail.

The thing to do now is to stretch this expression of time – past, present, future – into one long Tenebrae. Three. In order to maximize its tensile strength. Extinguishing light while at the same time stretching a saint without tearing him apart. If one listens closely – reads with his ears, seeks, chases, identifies, attacks the *sic passim* – the reddle (sic) will be revealed and thereby the dux. First of all, one must seek forgiveness – not through guilt alone but sacrifice. Secondly, one must be held-cleansed – not through a wash alone but a grand-style tenesmus. Thirdly, one must be willing to hang by four tenpenny nails – not through a scourge alone but a cup. *Remember triskelion,* the mark with red ocher? Don't play the fugue. Lump of clay, it is all so simple, to red (sic) the words, pronounce the syllables without making an utter mooncalf of oneself. It is true sirgolem. We all hold a little bit of 'Gethsemane' in our hearts and minds. It is ultimately the only way to find madwort. In a nutshell, if one is sincerely searching for the real McCoy, willing to leaf through this dime, and ready to drink hardily from the box, then one must be willing to consume, herbivorously, the bush, the class, gymnosperm. And thereafter indulge in a bit of gymnosophistics (sic). Good student, honor student, be silent no more. Gold of pleasure, rich in oil, voluptuous silver age, this screen of WII, all in one. In life as in death, as in eternity. Raise your arm! Sidd ha! *Au naturel!*

COMMERCIAL TIME

O how time makes for a day's features to age. The yellowing of time.

We now return . . . Rosinante, Grani, Bavieca, and Grizzle doin' 6 beats to a measure of wheat.

There – that innocent snip of light began to fade. In just one day, peering off into the wilderness of shadows, the cold nip of a whiplash wind rose and fell in the space of a breath. A sighting that looked to be an unidentified Mass. O the mystery of an aging day; the distant dog barks; the car honks; children play at play; the wind in the distance of the canyon sweep of summer dust falling, while the day submits to something always indescribable; the soundbite of dusk, hotdog tracks, clear beans, TV dinners, Ward shouting, "June, my domestic bun,

I'm home. Are the boys okay?"; and night falls; the plenilune returns; a farmer murders his own; nature's wayside crickets talk a long two-way streak, chattering the silence incessantly; but really having nothing important to say; the chorus concealed; and the sun breaks; and it's been one full day; and the pattern is repeated; and the mustard tracks the patrons; and Babe tracks the basis; and poor old Margaret Jones of Mass. was the first person who suffered for her craft in America; and the endless array of boring, trivial, repetitive jokes, tears, threats, fears, laughs, screams give way to yet another day; sigh; and then another; and still another; until it seems like the only way of winding down the earth is to remake it in a different cocked eye; and seven days become eight; and eight days become ten; and ten become a lost Befehl; and the cock-brained cockalorum cockles his peter; and Jane becomes a procuratrix; and Tarzan's on trial for incest with boy; and on and on and on the honk of two thou shank den nick me rice pudding.

Meanwhile, in the old short shot belly of a Texas town – on weary feet, standing on even wearier ground – El and the Kid matched words like katydids; non-stop, for the past seven days.

EL: "You draw."

KID: "No. You draw."

EL: "No way! I insist. You draw first."

KID: "Oooooh no. You draw first."

In the saloon, bets were being made, and a teknonymous vein was carrying the bloody shouts of infamous names. Who will draw first? It's like Sonny Liston versus Cassius Clay, insofar as two blackbodies were involved, absorbing all and reflecting none of the electromagnetic radiation falling about, so radiant and all. Only everyone in the saloon was wondering *what should happen to us if El falls? Would that mean that everything would just automatically slip away as on a wave?*

What *should* happen?

Hedda Lamarr raised her bottle to ask a question, *"What should happen to the strange woman?"* She meant of the commentator, the glorified gossip columnist, Hedda Hopper (actually a watered down, telegnostic visionary), who was otherwise engaged in a photon session, and was going over the odds of whether or not a quantum **SIGN-OFF** would result should El happen to break into an uncertain principle and literally get boxed into a right-angle due to pre-mature departure?

Now Hedda wasn't an expert in the field of Dietism nor Diffraction, but she'd read *Aging Body, Tired Mind* and was confidently supportive of Niemöller's declaration of guilt for the failure of resistance to the Nazis, and in the long run was mighty convincing paraphrasing the numerous Sanskrit lines as they pertain to good fortune, well-being and prosperity, especially during any day's journey, wherein one might suddenly appear in court to testify on behalf of a victim.

HEDDA: "The body is a skeleton of parts distorted and reassembled from their classical context. If El is to die, my belief is that we must all think and feel happy thoughts because happy thoughts make happy molecules. Think of Ullmann, Kellerman, Finch, Kennedy and Van in a lost horizon, and all the wonderful Bach-David tones. Think of it as being – being uncut, a perfect print, and on a double-bill with Henderson, Maurstad, Sehschollin and Poretta in a norway song – and you'll survive even the death of El, with or without guilt.

And not only the birth of Snorro but his demise as well. With Wallace Berry looking on, *ah schukks*. Charlie's lights is all . . . Ah! the unicity of humankind."

Following Hedda's inspiring lecture, Walter Brennan took up Mike. And as it pertained to the program that each and every member of the audience held in his/her arched hands, Walter cleared his throat and commenced with *Auk* – a lecture on the black and white, short-necked diving seabirds of the northern hemisphere; the petrels, in a manner of speaking, speaking peremptorily, miking all the while, idleing, spilling away the time . . . 4:14 . . . pretending to be doing a Peter job even while dickeying around the tit with the mike and walking on milk.

Elsa Lancaster went elbow-to-gut-chastisement with Charles Laughton for yawning.

In yet another room the lights were hunched over, drooling shadows growing dim. And on a small television screen, with at least fifty onlookers, Henderson trolloped fool-Andrewly over grassy hills, alive with a julidae roll of consciousness.

Outside in the greater warmth of still another day:

"You draw first!"

"Nooooooo way! You draw first!"

Thomas found the dichotomous crack in his skull that was giving him such a massive headache (which was nothing more than a noble eupherism for effulgent hangover!). Was it last night? Or was it two nights ago that he was sitting in Tiny Naylor's at an ecclesiological table – grasping two eccoproticophoric tablets across from a nervous, chatty, wannabe actress, in a town now haunted by homeless don't wannabees living in abandoned shopping cart hives, making middle class wagings by standing at intersections, buzzing, hovering, holding cardboard inscriptions and doing eloquent, tragic Shakespearean dance impressions of Lear, Macbeth, Juliet, and Lady 'flower' Macduff in McDonald's, while sorting out the site of their iota existence in meager footwear form, with expressions a clown would rob for – and weeping, "My lamentations for a buck!"? He couldn't recall – only the way she had snapped at him with her teeth after he had bodily suggested by way of symbolic egestion that he was an escaped felon of some sort, possibly aborted, and wanted for mass homicide in Lubbock, Texas, or east/west of it. (This was after she had satisfied his inbed requests, under the assumption that he was a casting-out agent/film producer in search of casting out for a dark part that called for an hysterical deaf mute babylonian gravid kiddie whore with an indigestible matter [in addition to a sore throat] to gnash like the dickens. And that she indeed could deliver the goods given the benefits of an ecbolic.)

But that was all before this business of 'taking care' of two natures came up, which is related to the *why don't you do things to blend?* syndrome spoken of by Hit in both divine and human terms, which is eutychian in nature, which is to say of one nature – which in this case is the blending of two natures – the saint and the assassin – into one nature. Certainly in the past, Thomas had 'taken care' of High Officials suffering from a high degree of two natures, and knew well enough about black lambs, really wolves in sheep's clothing, that had somehow managed to escape vibrionic abortion by donning two natures – High Officials such as the dictator/President of Cuba, Leeuwenhoek Manuel; two Pakistanis Government Officials who were *also* part of a failed, chic, Islamic terrorist plot, targeting Pope John Paul XX during his *General Mills AmeRican Corn Tour*; and Boris Grachevoich Pavelosky, Polish-bred but Russian-fed (corn, that is, plus *Mak, kartofelfries* and *koktel*) Defense Minister, who *also* played a role in the disaster at Chechnyagotcha, and was reputed as saying from a specific location, namely 400 Lee St., Des Plaines, IL., "I know nothing of nuclear fallout nor of Puerto Ricans, therefore there isn't any."

But more a chamelion, Thomas, too, donned a number of roles, which allowed him the flexibility that he needed in life, having been born to a madcap single woman who insisted that Thomas was part of an Immaculate (Miss) Conception, and was but a single impression on a printed sheet drawn up by the preta himself, KrisKringdo (a saint, yes, but also a firm believer in Karma da-da-pa-pa Adism).

Incidentally, Thomas's poor mother had met a rather nasty end after having choked to death on a wad of Kleenex (laced with 11 secret herbs and spices, flour, paprika, and some dry ingredients, compliments of Lip's tomato soup and Seven Seas It. Dress.) originally employed to absorb a massive amount of recycled firewaterredstakelipstick foolhardily applied, but once in the process of absorbing became a living tissue with only one purpose in mind, which was to *dab and proselytize*, specifically for the purpose of prosthesis, which in this case meant the replacement of life for death; that is, the replacement of one *missing* part for something entirely artificial, but only insofar as *artificial* pertains to the rules of art and effort in contrast to nature, which is to say fabricated, skillful, cunning, crafty, invisible, intangible, and existing only in contemplation of paronomasia areligiosity, which would otherwise define *death* itself to be sacreligious, if not boxed and hand delivered to the very threshold of Elimination. Thomas had actually found her (his mother) in the foyer of her flat, after having received mom's frantic phone call muffled in broken, choked-up English to "Co . . . qu . . . ick . . . m . . . King!" and Thomas, figuring it's mom on to something regarding the *King*, jumped into hiho silverplated subvaginal condomized Ram and nearly collided with a *B*ig *M*utha *W*oman at a fork in the road in front of a Burger in Kalamazoo before knock knock knock pound pound! Who . . . burst! through the *goddamn* door, literally reappeared, and Fall down! trip over mom's lifeless trunk. A week thereafter, while sorting through her mildewed belongings, Thomas came across an enclosed envelope. In it he discovered a letter in his mother's own mutilous hand, admitting *to whomever it may concern* that her son, Thomas, was actually not the Immaculate (Miss) Conception as aforementioned but the result of a floundering fling she had had with an out-of-work archaeologist who was harboring hopes of becoming a proctologist in order to make a real living at digging (O! so no wonder Thomas suffered from such horrendous hemorrhoids) for perotrochus hirasei, Echininus cumingii, Modulus tectum, Cerithidea cingulata, terebra anilis, penicillus penis, anima mundi, and anilingus via ani-mad-version mags.

O this whole business of life under god is most agonizing, mysterious trayf, Thomas mused. But someone's got to do it. god has been an allusionary hombre these past billion years, and by/with/without god at least now someone had the courage to demetaphornize the word, the image, the world into a scopperil. Thomas stood before the mirror like Alfred the Counselor and made the death sign by running his finger crisscross his throat and slurping like a pig on antihistimines. There was a nasty chill brushing everso discourteously on his bare tush. No wonder. The front door of his apartment was wide open. Adieu, Horst, restless active creature (in the peephole as well . . .).

It's funny. Slang-wise, *tush* meant a light-complexioned, bottomless Negro; beligerent, malicious, dangerous; wealthy, sophisticated, influential; belonging to high society; ritzy but obviously buck poor; a slommack in General at*tire*. Thomas pinched a Marlboro in the butt and lit what was left of an old, jazzy, heated, smoky memory in the guise of a Jordanberryfa tlittlebodgordymotow. "That's me," he Englished, creeping into his smock with cig smugan drawing serpentine geists in the air. "A buff nigger with a tuxedo park pistol calling card all of thirty-three." A real *tux* edo from Benin, a mite s.e. of the Dead Sea – smudge and two bits of transvestite undercover gear in his pocket for a ride home to the resort while sucking on a final coffin nail.

Meanwhile, in the box, telly twaddle:

"Gow. Find you sleeping!" Spanky MacFarlane said in a heavy overcoat. "Okey-Dokey." O.D. – the euphemism for an enterp*rising* force residing in a few individuals and things that underlie hypnotism. And little Buckwheat gave his *I've just seen a germane ghost* look from inside the tube. And lisping Porky really got down in tongue, coquettish Darla groaned mindlessly, and Alfalfa's *in the mood for love* made a perfect menage a trinity. Metro Media Channel 20: *The Hey Abbott!, Coming Mother!, I dood it!* in only a *Comedy at the 11th Hour,* Abbott, da-da. "Clean through and through. But the truth is not in us."

Cosmically, it could be done – objectifying god, gegenstandstheorieizing him, intentionally doin' him in, into a thing, smearing him with tons of cosmoline grease, serving him as a sort of 1950's soda fountain gedunk. Thomas went to the window and looked out at the smoginfested city, lawful goodevil dust. He could hear *JAWS* playing IOWE Queen in the tsunami waves of carbon monoxiousness as a belch of smog-smother smur made curly-q's around a purulent Zero – Mostel-Mose Kiefer type city-walker – and dropped her flat, gasping like a beached skylla in deepshit polypnoea, throwing up the body and blood, A.M. Mass, chyme of the final hour, down to the city floor, convulsing seconds later chyle into serious soi-disant chuckholes. "Smorzando Smog Smal! Ten years ago anyone would have been called a fool for suggesting that smogsmal is growing teeth to the polyphyodont degree, more or less twelve feet and six barking heads."

Thomas opened up a small black appointment book that was resting on a night counter crawling with *bounced* cimices. 11:30. Meet Dr. Bette Outrage. (Dr. Outrage was a Beverly Hills otolaryngologist specializing in soixante-neuf *and* polydaemonism, who shared an office with Dr. Vincent Angina, an Apo soldier from the trenches, a former warrer turned bacteriologist, and an absolute pro at concocting pomanders imbued with musk-apple-*Arbutus unedo*-Caindiscord-Orchis as a safeguard against Revfucup.)

11:31: pick up fatal Deus Nasal Spray from Dr. Outrage.

(A further note on Dr. Outrage: Dr. Outrage use to be exclusive to the Mafia; but when her main-keep, the plenitudinous Papa Platinumo, had a complete table setting embedded in his skull by Dr. Outrage in order to permanently relieve Papa of excessive volatile sinuosity, Dr. Outrage pleaded *dramatic plasmolysis* and was herself relieved instantly, but honorably, from any existing contractual ties with the Mafia. Actually, she was one lucky bitch. The 'boys' thought plasmolysis was a deadly catching disease.)

9:30. NOW. Good. Thomas still had time to get down-wind of the smuggling ken, over to the airport, dash over to Canter's for a little nosh (Nova Scotia salmon, bagles and cream cheese), meet the M7, quickly go over *DIg* (Doin' In god), pick up the Deus spray from Dr. Outrage, and then head on over to Uncle Pawn's Pax, with the sign outside of three golden balls (see pomander), and venture into the Black room and through a secret panel, secret password *(two to one you'll get killed, cosimo-style),* in order to obtain final plans for *DIg* from a *thingly* disguised Medici, Sidney Poitier Averado, who loved to kiss and who was

197

Neil Baker

NOW (i.e., NoOne Works) – an intellectually successful, sophisticated Single for Atheism, a father of his race, well read in acosmism, and who also performed an infamous jig in Porky in Bess.

There was a post-feminine angle to DIg, which explained why Thomas was thinking of clutching Oprah Windpipe's vestigial in opacity, and *idoloclast* it to kingdom cum. As soon as DIg was accomplished and ol' Mugello had fallen, M.7 were to be whisked live to the seventh channel and made to participate in an unprecedented telecast of *Transmigration of Souls,* surrounded by a recidivous audience of squatters and bywoners, including patriarchal biologists, entrepreneurs, marriage counselors, two Hurrians (both Ho's in their own rite), and various semi-related telegoobs, who were all gathered together in order to discuss the psychosomatic dynamics naturally embedded within DIg. On the show Oprah was to admit to being gay, hyperglycemic, and hysterically Marxist, while M.7 were to show clips from their documentary, *Come and Get! It's Hellzapoppin at Armagetem!*, and the extraneous guests, T., Moore, and Mary, were to sing "Oft in the Stilly Night," while dancing up a storm as The Happy Hotpoint Pixies. And the son of Mad Jack whose letters were burned (a pen of all work well blown) was to mourn.

Thomas went under the schizoid tempo of hot and cold showerhead outpourings of holywetjohn, and washed away Hollywood suds + disoriented crimices from his hair and ears and a faulty white-sting from his eyes, even while he commenced to croon as a *Doubting Thomas.* Drying off, he realized that 1) his erythema was erumpent redder than rouge 2) he had neglected to remove his water sensitive Gideon's earrings created by Suitoephod 3) he was out of mouthrubpitskinspray, an urgrund-Tin actinal trademark. He could have borrowed some from Kitty, the quail multigravida next door, but through the walls he could hear she was busy squealing the cum out of a pampiniform quickie Embassy, Luke G; she, being quite the quai dog, omitted and all. Thomas didn't have time to waste so he used toothpaste like a Trinity™ for his mouth, his pits, and a quay dab in his crotch. He blessed the sex ritual cubed with a quiet benediction, "Christ O'Lather my pampiniform!"

The kitchen was like a passing away in the stomach in a point of time where time is clearly defined as a three-day dead cantaloupe slice with a poniard buried in green (what was once orange) flesh, roaming viperishly down, directly into the seat of the poop. Thomas further off-centered the off-balanced mid-life crisis of the kitchen by pulling out the dagger "Pop!" like the boy Arthur on strings, fantoccini-style, doing a good deed for the master overhead, and throwing the peel into the sink marked *Anything Goes,* where it landed upon a mound of enigmas – food crests, molds, fungii, spores, hot lips, dimples, dog's rig, petals, stones, shoulders, breasts of chewed chicken to the existential bone, the Pope's nose, meat-mass spaghetti – really a kind of fang shih fangs clay for the pontifical senses to ponder. Magical formulas, theurgic ingredients all massed into one holy fangle. If only there was enough immortality to go aground. *Ugh.* Alas, the rind of cantaloupe was more a sickening Pelops, a tektite, thrown by a Tantalus to the gods down below.

The phone rang. Thomas had a strong desire to bury the bone and raise the phone. But did he really want to mix his urgent pace with voices lost on complete fantasy, half a breakfast date late for romance from a less fatal space in time, less hungry, less desperate, less focused than the commitment he was willing to make to an even hungrier universe? Maybe he would die, crossed and scandalized, before he ever had time to live no place special . . . just maybe he would fall before he ever had time to look at a woman and see something more

198

than nothing at all. One day Thomas would live to play the domestic hero like at Gerasa, exclusive to only one woman's eyes. But until then he was hooked by the blade and the thrill of the chase, pursuing all the little mysteries that run just inches from the grasp. The phone was not raised. Now was not the time.

Thomas didn't lock the door behind him. There was nothing to keep but the census down.

THE THIRD CLUE –
None Wallows in Eve's Lament and Mary's Sorrow

Listen to me. If I am granted one wish regarding bo's second cummings, I pray to b-holy hibbing high godhood that he returns a gonococcus. In more ways than one, he'll be the lowest of the low and his robe will abhor him, just as Job's robe had abhored Job on a disgusting, seedy afternoon blown upon by the breath of slander. A good jew, bo is, with golden chords – finding J knocking on his door and responding *bon soir!*

Nadir. Nadir.

Farting is such sweet marrow

Were it be the seat of animal potency

Feculence be bound to follow.

And mind you, dear father, to stand not on the order of your going, but to go at once from the open pit two miles south, escorted by a couple of constipated gendarmes, lest your footing be full of iron shit. Iron rust. Yes, indeed, there's been a great dismissal issued by way of indicavit. Bobbobbing like Thomas reading the labels of canned goods aloud off a G. shelf, trying to read into JWH a mystery. A pernicious little son of a pedant pounding ponerology to the populace. The old chuck. The old boot. The old sack. The old can. The old axe, baby, erupting, a real expulsion. Out of the chamber. A whirlwind. Sinking in marshy earth. Nausea auburn. Infidel, quiet, infinity, infidium. Phew, wipe the forehead .. . My Baby Mother of Earth.

I am a wild creature passing through all life stages in a single bound, forever leaving behind my hering image . . . my hess image . . . (be careful – there's a bit of a gonium in me as well); and in terms of pure residency, I am extremely autoecious. I'll stick to you like horse glue. Since you want to play grand host to this particular marrow of ours, you owe me as you owe all of us, pending the unfulfillment of the conditions of our bone agreement (if I dare refer to it as such, being a silent partner, loving in more ways than one). And as for you (the larger, stronger, more dominant member, but more the stranger, the horseman, the *enemy*, as the Latins would say), dear host, dear sacrifice, you're still a mystery, a stranger. However, in your eye I sense a foreigner commanding an army for war. Father . . . here . . . you look hungry. Have some eucharistic bread if you will. It's fresh. Blood-red fresh. Let me serve you woman like a scornful Abigail and deliver the goods on an iron plate in the shape of a horseshoe. O diddle dees. The sun has diddlers on its rays, and with a little diddling the diddlydees fall didydown, all the way to the diddlee bottom, which brings up the crescent moon and a horse's lost slipper.

We who dangle on lines, who find ourselves tongue-tied, pulled along on autoerotic lines, hooked, our exact wording, our screams, our cries of agony **contingent on the pulling of the**

Ionic line are but children, infants innocent. Heavy-faced, yes, but easy to read; fantoccini. In the minds of our makers, we are filled with super-human and potentially fatal power, calling out a word or a phrase, grasping to maintain a flagitious thought. Breath. Motion. Are we guilty of disobedience? Did we misbehave and send ourselves into a major spectacle representing an atomic battle? Or, still, better yet, are we just players in a card game where you can lose all on a bid? Is that what it was all about? Was that the general concursus? Before fall arrived, the jam was already preserved. One can see how lightly the great engastrimyth moves by the irregular patches, ruffles upon the surface of Adam's deep dew during a calm where even the first forms could dwell in place. How nice it could be seated in the balcony overlooking the stage, a perfect view. The core exposed, the skin lying on the lip. Pity one must resort to transforming a text in order to conceal its meaning. Mystery play with eyes closed, lips pinched, the unwritten law keeping silence by revelation alone. The life, the death, the birth of us all. I, nevertheless, cease. Fire.

Equivocal father – your name, your voice, your words are designed to protect rights and enforce rites fixed by laws essential to the soul, though your body remains unseen. Your dialogue envelopes a body of legal terms, the substance of which is meant to enlarge, supplement, or accent existence to the fullest extent. But this issue of 'justice,' as it is most implicitly applied to natural law, is so off-balanced as to be rendered nearly incomprehensible. Except if one is so moved that he would want to place it under the heading 'obscure,' under which everything is but a pun or a lie to hell's ultimate end, even if that end is just ice and nothing more.

The numbers are up if the production is high, say's law.

The production is down if the numbers are obsolete, says paw.

When the sun crosses the equator, and day and night are everywhere of equal length, I will cut (more-like saw) you in three across your length, and carve out *a cross*. Did you think that this hostility, this intermediate character of mine that is juxtapositioned somewhere between a combat and a joust, somewhere betwixt and between a typical male and a typical female, would not cut you asunder and lead you running into all which directions, creating space, intertestamental, between your two opposing marks? Your signs draw attention mainly because they have left such deep and angry scars across the face of all your comestible children. Teeth to bare, claws to extend, marching in step to the beat of a drum, eat, the war is at hand. And you beat to a measure of come prima time that which you profess to be a musical, if not a shipwrecked adventure jaum'd in between two rocks. *J'aime. Chic. Agog. The style is OK. La homage hic et ubique. Vita.* How you do play with words. I will follow you up and seize you by your very spine, so that the reoccurrence of your primary accents will stumble out your tongue rather than flow a rhythmic movement. And you with your seven trumpets and your saints and your Louis strong-arms and your hail and fire and your sea becoming blood and your waters becoming wormwood and your men dying because they drank of the waters and your aircraft and your kites and your meteors and your serpents and your dragons and your harpers harping will fall wingless, once and for all.

Could it be (for dramatic effect alone, I suspect) that the assemblage of your parts, which transmits forces, motion, and energy one to another, is meant to operate as a prelude to an order completely unrestrained by reason and judgment? I believe you to be more a macrocephalous imbecile than a squat Macbethald gawking at ghosts, even though you do the work of a general dealing with universal rather than particular aspects. The earth with its inhabitants and all things upon the face of its totality would be none the worse by your absence, which has already been proven innumerable times. It makes a world of difference having you out of the way; however, the earth revolves as a worm wheel nonetheless. Catch a finger (more or less a hand or body) on the slipstring, where gear and wheel intersect, and one will be devoured by the teeth in less time than it takes for the earth to devour the freshly departed or for a worm to devour a crisp, fresh apple. A signpost up ahead. *Beware of dogs under the table.* Around the axle, the crooked and perverse nation slept. Such commensal pleasures raise the concupiscence to a *'t'*. And in regards to *your* going away (if that is indeed the case), allow me to say that *your* position in longitude and latitude at the beginning of *your* voyage was without form, void – a union coexisting only in darkness upon the face of the deep (the dreamy bedroom called night, in the midst of the waters). At a point from which *you* begin to complete circularity, dead reckoning need apply, and the commensal ones will only be regarded in the sense that *all who do eat at the table, do sleep afterward under it.*

An image of Ate (eyes hollow as if from a massive blow) pressed its conical nose up against my windowpane. Could I be in a strait, betwixt two, having a desire to depart? Could I be frozen in time? Could I, firsthand offspring of a fire-eater, be frightened by the breaking of a relatively quiet portion of glass? Should that pugnacious Peeping Tom cut down straight lines, I will not hesitate to claim my upright stick and retain the load therein, thus keeping at bay any further jeopardy to our kind.

Need I call you Hephaestus before this world goes asunder and a copious discharge of blood comes spurting from your vessel, hermaphrodite brig, diverse elements that you are? If by now you're squirming (a lackluster warrior of impressive size), remember – the only great quake that you will produce in the earth will be that which results directly from your fall. When I let go of you, you will fly one hundred miles and land, nay, crash, a central Percheron figure. All of civilization's children, all of universe's citizens will be utterly aghast at just what shape your body will assume upon your demise.

You thought it fun at one time to bathe with me and rimrhymeteedittyline *tomarket tomarket toland sic sic sic.* You thought me to be just another undistinguished, unthinking mass of humankind, a trusted follower from this side of life crashedlanding and all. Instead I have answered to a name other than the one I stepped in with. And I have collected, like so many flowers, a new bouquet of chromosomes to live by. In the short-lived temper there abides a content of steel that hardens the properties of the mind. Hereford I will call you, for the color is *fard*-appropriate as is the intelligence thereof. Red to white. And if there is any creature as hemophilic as a Hereford, I've yet to find it. The head is raised property like a helium head of the Good Year of Our Lord. The body but a trail of libidinal energy. Did you not think of that when you chose to call yourself Hermaphroditus? The union was unwise to begin with. For this bride is more a larva undergoing a metamorphosis that differs chiefly in size and degree from that of a devout lover. Via the imago – winged state of maturity idealized, existing without breathing, existing without intervening space or substance – this bride will tip the balances so that no groom will stand. Being of one body can be a real drag for a smaik at large.

The retarding force acting on a body moving through a fluid can absolutely hinder progress to the point of slowing it down to a screeching halt. The reason for this pause is simple. One must cut down so that the ends turn upward, and thus establish a new beginning like god in ashanelm. And should anyone know your place of refuge is a turret, you may be asked to appear at the framework and to identify yourself, an eye prone to nystagmus due to the deep slumber, the big sopor that you coined as a day's journey into *yom ha-din*, at which time the closing of your petals was but a slim delicate way of surrendering to darkness. I say let the truth be known. That is why I go by way of blood, sleuthhound that I am. I will not sit back and relax, smoothing the unfinished surface of time's puzzles. Nor bag my wine in a goat's bocksbeutel. No, the rough and jagged edges must be made to bear the plight of time's dissolution, which is why it will be impossible to dissemble truth-be-known, in spite of an onslaught of posers. The answers will predominate over uncertainty, and yet the solutions will bring a porismatic charge to the singularity of the original problem. In a glass body there is nothing to hide under the vitreous eye. The higher electrical processes from which the current flows from inner to outer, external extremities not excluded, will be revealed, will bud, as will the changing circumstances regarding the end of hypocrisy.

    Cut to

APOCALYPTIC ESOTERICISM
or
The Golem Conspiracy
or
Blame It On The Bosanova
(or better yet)
Blame It On The Nova Scotia

Better fowl. Better halt. Better maimed. Better millstone. Better old. Better marry. Better promises. Better rrection. Better premises. Beware of T.S.E.'s – junk protein, tiny holes, halo's notwithstanding.

    Badigeon anyone?

    Serious business this. After noshing on bagels, eggs, onions and lox, the Magnificent Seven were each occupying a stall in the restroom of Canter's Fairfax Delicatessen on Fairfax Avenue (so named after the 6th Lord of the New Model 7 Agency himself, Lord *Thomas Berger* of M.7), attempting to *repair* from the defects in their meal. (It should be noted here that the Magnificent Seven went by several surnames as well – chief among them being the *NEW* Model 7 Agency, a.k.a. Commission on Critical Choices for Homosapiens – a bored review of the basic philosophical and/or/a/moral cons of man and his process . . . in-stitutions, *sinnbildlich* in terms of strategies, plans, formulas, and mass versions largely unreadable in John, as they pertain to man's basic-in humanity to manini-general *sinnlosigkeit* theories and features in feculency, especially under circumstances when the latter are stripped and imprisoned by members of their own kind – named after the Seven Angels modeled in pure and white linen/porcelain on top of the Burning Beast with Seven Heads holding the Seven Kosher Deli Vials of Wrath at York.)

    Bad lox. O yes, bad lox makes for stomach shrieks and fiery *lavaish*runs. So naturally the M.7 were all in the lavatory, the perfect place to relieve lava lockup. The sounds of 7 serious heroes with severe manholeindignation, emptying their subturdians all at once, permeated through the walls of the restaurant and filled the impious ears of every diner therein. Oliver Cromwellstein, the manager of Canter's, rushed into the lavatory to see what he could do to make things better, and to hopefully dissolve the rumps into pure states of complacency. The stench alone was like unloading a vessel of ultra-assy sauerkraut in his face.

"My god in heaven! What are you people doing?! I'm trying to run a business!!" Suddenly, Oliver shuddered and collapsed over the sink and onto the floor. His forehead miraculously burst into a sea of super-glistening bartholinean clusters. A bagel, two poached eggs, a bit of gefilte fish, a matzo ball, and a green olive clambered up his esophagus and trafficjammed in **CRAM**, leaving him lying with a general, though confounding, feeling of rabbit ironsides. A dark cloud appeared over his head and hovered there as though waiting to receive him. "You all have to clear out of here! You're ruining my business! Between you and my sotah of a wife going to buck, I could drop dead this second and not ask for thirds!"

"Give us a minute's peace, DaddyO." Bry shouted from the second stall. "You served us bad holly lox of wrath and we can't kill god fighting off indigestion with physics-defying trajectories at the same time."

"Mishugahs!" Oliver ascended to his knees and from this ascension made an agonizing retreat. "I should make peace with such a smelly lot? They're all a bunch of cocaine schnubblers! Lousey schlongs! They should all eat the dust off the floor, wash it down with a swig of pish, and all drop dead with pish coming out their opened eye!"

MEANWHILE . . .

Back at Sam's real estate office, the Cyclops was receiving, via comic telepathy, stress-filled vibrations. Having picked up Ida's estrous frequency level, he was, in turn, able to home-in on the vibrations of the M.7, and by cerebral-unilateral localization separate his thoughts from Ida's via the M.7's, and by astro currents acting upon the physical plane atoms bring about a coherent agreeable-vibrational-frequency in the form of parallel lines of astro substances, partially estriolic in nature, extending from his mind to the scene at the delicatessen, which, incidentally, was also currently the site of this year's annual Jews for an Etatist Nosh, a.k.a. *JEN*, which, in itself, is a sort of Jewish version of the cardinal confucian virtue of benevolence to one's fellowman, oftentimes expressed in superficial fashion in lively stirup Sunday meetings of Mind-to-Pocket. Immediately, he understood that (for a while at least) the M.7 would be indisposed, temporarily reduced to menognathous beasts of the field engaged in unwarranted acts of physically-induced, unethical type estrepe behavior brought on by the symbol of the **FISH** via bad lox. Figures, god is, after all, a fire without cause – a fire seemingly triggered from some unknown source that nevertheless materializes asana ectenic force. Which also brings to mind the Duality-Principle of fire – that is, water and, more specifically, fountains in regards to their origins as watering places and their structure of multiple tiers, where the higher basins were offered for human usage and the lower ones for animals, as well as the hierarchy of tiers in regards to the descending order of gods, nymphs and lesser creatures, such as those who go by the name of John, Dick or Hairy Uncircum . . .

Obviously, this particular Nova Scotia was fished from the Nu waters of the fifth dimension, where all forms exist within a current that has a faster rate of vibration than earth, and where plans, original designs and living salmon set up radiations that send forth rays with a tremendous force behind them. Yes, obviously, an act of godhood, wherein his thoughts (ugh), his benevolence, and his laws which direct the universe are applied *hood-fashion*, wherein physical violence becomes the ultimate godly expression, and neonaztisvicvacillation becomes the holy spirit. And heshers into heavy *Metall* and *Topf* and tweakers into *Geschwindigkeit* get *gewaltig.* Tricky of god. Neat and cunning. Hats off to OL' theta-beater, currently residing in the reader's open eye, with one egg-shaped optic thalamus, and a mass of gray matter invaded upon by a gang of lions that would cut a cross section into a beetle, until it had the whole gang shouting, "Immortality!"

And so, the M.7 would become theta-agents. Onward. Westward ho! toward the 12-piece equinox day/night band, 6 players a piece. Hurray for the living force that slips away from the human body after death and exists in the etheric world as both secret agents of SPITTLE (which is the main Edenic headquarters/laboratorial site for a holy fluid saliva that contains all of the energies of the body, insofar as they are connected to the prepubescent emotions of devotion relational to not just any branch of natural science but the one *in the midst branch* that holds the preparation to an experiment in Edenic Field Theory involving the interaction of two separated, physical, laboring entities within a quantum field, in which the separated physical entities are said to be a manifestation of the quantum field, insofar as the physical entities embody the actions that are the resultants of dynamic interplay among the sociocultural, biomechanical and irreligious forces at work in the field system, wherein exists the common pastures in which the respective shepherds freely operate outside of god) and RAPPERS A PROFESSION (R.A.P.; etheric world intelligences who specialize in communicating with human readers of courageous fiction by means of audible sounds such as knocks, snaps, clicks and labored poetry, which bring warnings, predictions, and psychic information as to god's approximate whereabouts, whatabouts, and what-for-abouts. Note: A rapper's main function is to laconize why god would ever utter *"Why? Because that's why!"* to any given question, and leave it at 'that').

Now this is nearly where Cyclops lifts his holy leg into the air, *O gigot*, and by vibratoriation brings O defecanation, UGH, to life. And with the added assistance of Rabbi Ben Sira (who actually used a schnubbl, a shameer, that is, a diamond pulled from the beak of a rooster, the same used by Moses to cut precious stones and by King Solomon to open the Gates of Wisdom in order to create his very own Golem, which is actually a Jewish Frank Steinbestia brought to life by Magic *[wie durch zauber]*, as was first discovered by Rabbi Yehuda Low, who created a human-like being by carving wood, wax, clay, metal and pieces from dead bodies, sewing them all together, and giving it a personality by carving a sacred name into its forehead, and then infusing it with concentrated thought, *bestemmia* energy, and direction in order to rid the universe of Evil, Kosher-style, his way), Cyclops pulled together all of his life forces (licorice-liberated-life-atom-neurons) and said, "Get ready to rise, O Ugh!"

Meanwhile, far to the left of Cyclops, Spaceship Earth was on its Universal Tour, idling in *bersaglio* and filled to the brim with rubbernecks. Only now it was simply called the Shamanship. For in between the fourth and fifth dimension, that is, between the first level of the eighth plane and the last level of the seventh plane, Spaceship Earth had made a pit-stop for all on board (including Valentina Tereshkova and Yuri Gagarin, with the former having gone *around the world* 48 times much to Yuri's liking, who in turn had helped to lift up and light the first joint for APOSOY's High Relations) in a region that looked vastly similar to Pi-Ray, Arizona, which is but 6° 15′ from the town of Ouroboros, Arizona.

During that very same stop the Ship had a vertex experience, whereby it fancied itself to be the reincarnation of a tribe of Algonquin Indians (with Navajo inbreeding), complete with a past filled with tortuous initiations and battles, tribal customs and dances, and wise old shamans who would eventually evolve into *very* wise old shamans, although with a peculiar shade of curiosity via radiation due in part to heavy smoking.

FLASH! The ship was suddenly traveling beyond the speed of light, beyond the clutches of rational thought (ugh). A runaway experience beyond the Creation. A thrill per minute. So . . . Lucky! lucky! lucky! that on this Universal tour they should all witness not Kong, not Jaws, not ET but Cyclops bringing his very own *Ugh* to life!

Gott sei Dank!

Yes! the vision was growing! Ever so closer! (to home). Spontaneous Inanition God Anabapheim Repulsion (SIGAR) was drawing neigh! for both adults (wet) and children (dry), depending upon the former being both German and radically religious and the latter being the Dis-descendants of German immigrants high on *Wein, mäuse, und menschen.* O one could almost hear the four horses emptying plagues at a loss upon nearly *all* nationalities if one merely *squinted* his/her ears (which, incidentally, can be done if one is familiar with the practice of alectryomancy, which is simply divinations by way of counting how many *ears* of corn are eaten by a hen or cockerel during menstruation, and then listening for the *bloody* flux inanity of a phlegmatic reveille).

"Pneumas! Roasted pneumas! Get 'em while they're hot!"

Cyclops stepped up closer to the mound. Closer . . . closer . . . oops! Cyclops backed up a step and wiped off postern shit from in-between his toes. Positioning himself within a comfortable distance from the mound, he connected once again, only this time with two different kinds of balls of light. The thoughtful light and the thoughtless light. The thoughtful light comprised all that which is focussed on the purpose of creation in its most loving and idealized context. The thoughtless light comprised all that which is not aimed at creation, and whose sole purpose is to remain what it is and to stay where it is, devoid of any idea directed at creation. By its very nature, thoughtless light resists all creative change. In the dialogue of righteous creation, however, it is therefore a *positively* thoughtful, hostile and destructive power set on destroying the structures produced by the thoughtless light that allows, say, a St. John to (in *no* case of innocence) enter into the kingdom of that light, which is, in general terms, thoughtful and provocative.

Insofar as god was quite intent in blocking the light and life in E-DEN, it was therefore put on record that only just-so much story would be known by humankind, and that god would actually produce modes of welsh being in which humankind would not only conduct his/her own existence in relation to an ethical/unethical standard (i.e., themes pertaining to the roots of human fears – including nudity, masks, transvestitism, castration, impotency and insanity), but that the very cosmic script (male) upon which humankind would keep record of its rarebit fiend-like relationship to god would at a later stage also help to bring about humankind's ultimate destruction. But as the saying goes, "You can't keep a good man down," and so therefore the Cyclops was going to borrow from the force of the Golem one of the most important secrets in regard to the work of primeval creation. *What comes down must go up.* The mound that would give *rise* to Ugh would also be imbued with *ma'aseh bereshit,* which is in Golem terms the very essence of primeval creation.

"PUtiful!" The Cyclops drew upon the spirituality of the stars in order to empower Ugh with life. Some of the stars he chose to draw upon were specifically chosen for their shining and awarding quality. Janet Gaynor for *Seventh Heaven!* Helen Hayes, *Sin of Madelon Claudet!* Bette Davis, *Dangerous!* Mary Astor, *The Great Lie!* George Sanders, *All About*

Eve! Jo Van Fleet, *East of Eden!* phew! and Mary Postgate, *Mary Postgate!* – all mindful of pornocracy, with G fulfilling the role of Zuhälter.

O Cyclops. *Ala!* What the Cyclops knew regarding god's golem, Adam, was this: during the first 12 hours of his existence, Adam was a body without a soul; however, even in this state he was awarded a vision of all the generations to come. Therefore, it was safe to say that Adam (alias Golem) had a hidden power to grasp and to see (gene) while being bound up with the element from which he was taken, the dirt of the earth. It was becoming all too clear to the Cyclops – the various transformations and combinations of the plot, which in its own right constituted a mysterious language of the inwardness of creation; the words, the letters, the characters, the voices, the nations penetrating into a mental and spiritual intimacy, the likes of which had rarely been felt before.

The Cyclops could hear Ida in the beginning, shouting from a cave; her cave; the cave of her *memento mori* made ever so deeper, like an abyss, by the cruelty and utter violence and senseless destruction of the inimicable world she was born into. "My bedroom for a soubrette!"

He realized that in the course of Ida's own redemption it was only natural for her to take earth from virgin soil, and *rebirth* herself, just as she would take energy from her virgin soul and make a universe out of it. It was meaningful in the beginning when Ida pronounced the death of him whom she bore and returned to find herself again as his child intrigante.

Cyclops wanted more than anything to take part in the act of creation, to continue the work left unfinished. In memory of a child who was crushed in a giant's world, the Cyclops walked around the mound as in a dance, combining the phases, the levels, the symbols of the very book he was in, and the secret name, Triskelion. I, secret nevermore.

Cyclops danced and he twirled. He was everything and everyone. He was Moira Shearer in *The Red Shoes.* Only the light that he held within, the light that granted him a hidden power to grasp, showed him that he was also Robert Helpmann in *The Red Shoes!* Male, female, red shoes three-in-one. The heels of blood, sacrifice, release. This had been the way for eternity, changed little through the endless revolutions, the countless revelations. In his dance Cyclops was every village green, every factory worker, every country peasant involved in the vital force of dance – the compulsion and the energy of breath, of consciousness, unconsciousness, and movement. As he danced around the mound, he was every spark of attraction from every waltz wherein women were thrust into men's arms. He was every Can-Can kick, every Apache dig, toes half-buried in dust. Every long leg, enticing shade, exquisitely dressed, stark naked loon, swan, masquerade. He was Isadora Duncan doing Red. Together in love and harmony. He was Yuri Zhdanov grasping Ulanova in *Romeo and Juliet.* Tchernicheva luring Shabelevsky in *Schéhérazade.*

Ta-ra-ra

Boom-de-ay!

Dear ol' dad's past away.

They'll be no pain today

Let's go on Holiday!

Half maddened light in a single movement – heading headlong into a thrilling finale, into a night version of *heilsgeschichte,* wherein the hysterical stage would be flooded to an immeasurable depth for a battle of sea monsters, while one hundred people, each bearing their own *heiligenschein,* would descend from the luminous ceiling on a dewy cloud, with Ms Th taking up the rear! The Cyclops performed the Fire Dance, the Serpentine dance, and the Rainbow all in one – swirling hundreds of yards of multi-colored beach blankets of shit in breath-taking movement and show! Wistful eye, sparkling eye, magical eye – no longer hiding in the belly of his forehead, no longer an ugly blinking movement to fear, a movement blinking, recording each single catastrophic event as though god himself was looking to receive an award for Best Destructive Performance by a god in a starring role, holding a rose in the spirit of perfumed death, and ingurgitating twenty point seven to his heart's content!

The Cyclops spun, even as the mound rose. Now the beast was like Juba – black harbinger, thrown into a world ahead of its time; Juba, creating his own unique movement – knee up, well-turned out leg, hands in the pocket of his overcoat, muscles pumping mobility, flexibility of joints sliding, bounding gyrations, heel to toe, mutation of movement, vigor, grace, elasticity, tendons displaying powers of endurance in a crush of a crowd in the venatic heat before a certain death, a certain life is formed that has no relation to breath but lives nonetheless *in invitum*; a growl, a groan, a bit of laughter thrown in from some unseen seats in the balcony in the *yo* dark; clear ringing, echoing, harmonious, resonant burst of applause, and mirth, and such feverish fun you can hear its thunder pounding in your ears – the continuous humming, throbbing sound of *I don't give a damn* through the tears of watching something so miraculous *it* clings to your heart, to your mind, to your joys, to your fears, and tells you (without telling you) how good *it* feels, how good *it* is to be alive and not gone with *i vento!*

And the *pu*tiful mound that was Ugh rose even higher as the shit took form, intelligence, and desire. And depending upon which direction the Cyclops danced, Ugh, in turn, would either rise or fall. For know this – whenever the Cyclops danced in the opposite direction from whence he was coming, and whenever he spoke a logical combination of words, letters in reverse order – that is, whenever he spoke backward – the vitality of Ugh was nullified, and he (Ugh) sank or fell, the shit dribbling down, melting, as it were, to hell. But should Cyclops dance in a forward movement – progressive, vital and strong – *the shit rose,* forming legs, torso and arms – plus a neck and a head. Indeed, a human form all of shit – with proper indentations for ears, eyes, nose and a mouth. And on Ugh's forehead appeared a sign like an eye, only it read *emet,* meaning 'truth,' the seal of the Holy One. (For this was vastly different from another word from another time: *met,* meaning 'dead.')

Now the word *alef* appeared on Ugh's forehead, written in shit, as a sign of the unrestrained power of the elements that can bring destruction and havoc upon anything hostile to creation. And as Ugh continued to take form, the Cyclops danced and chanted, all the while marveling at what energies, what stars, what purpose he was seeding into the mound. Ahem.

Dear John,

Don't confuse time with any preconceptions you may have about it, for time is also relative to the space it occupies. And if that space resides in a realm taken from the center and navel of the earth, which is the navel of the universe, then twelve hours of time can be but a breath, or twelve days a deep breath, and so on and so on.

Cyclops

In regards to this fact, it took Cyclops 33 years to actually raise Ugh from the depths of shit and vomit. It would seem to be no accident that this was the age of Jesus when he was crucified. Nor would it seem to be an accident that this was the age of Adam upon discovery of Eve's G spot.

In addition to having created Ugh, there was no question as to whether Cyclops was competing with Adam or not. The creative power of a mythical beast entering into a conflict with the creative power of god was unmistakable. The only difference being – the Cyclops would not put the same limitations upon his "Ugh" as god had put upon his "creation," whereby god's "creation" was forced to return to the earth from where he was taken, dust to dust.

Granted, god did not form man from just any old dust nor just any old clump of earth that first came to his hand. On the other hand, neither had god formed man from the best, the purest and finest dust, in an essentially primal matter sort of way. Instead, god had formed man from a middle-dust, two parts fine to one part sour. For, indeed, where the former held both nutrients and elements of the highest content, the latter had a dozen or so sowbugs intermingled in it. Wood louse. Deathwatch. Tick . . . tick . . . tick . . . So it is not entirely correct to say that Adam was the best share taken from the dough of the earth. And therefore it is not entirely correct to say that he (Adam) should be blamed for his every action. Know this: Adam's life can be summed up in twelve hours. In the first hour, the earth was piled up; in the second, Adam was still unformed mass (that is, a complete mess); in the third, his limbs were stretched out; in the fourth, the soul was cast into him; in the fifth, he stood on his feet; in the sixth, he gave all living things names by speech; . . . in the eleventh, Eve handed in her leash . . .

DISORDER IN PARADISE

Rinnnnnnnnnnnng! Rinnnnnnnnnnnnng!
The provident characteristic embodied . . .
god turned the alarm off and rolled over in bed. It was 7 A.M.!; he hated getting up in the morning. And scotchrist almighty! what a dream he was having! he couldn't tell when it had started or, for that matter, when it had actually ended; he only felt that it had been a long dream with a lot of fabled characters, supernatural action, and feery-fary talking. Confidentially, the dream reminded god of an old Zritf Ganl film he'd seen, *The testamenT of Dr. Eabusm,* wherein, from the confines of an insane *assylum*, a criminal mastermind controls his underworld empire hypnotically, under a mixture of vernacular words, with non-Latin words having Latin endings, and *Latin* ending in a generally confused mixed-up piece of macaroni.

god had adored the movie. But the interesting aspect of the 'dream' that he was having was not so much that he was homing-in via a dream on a reel event, as it was the fact that a tellurian power from out of the earth had seeped into him and had enabled him to see all the generations – their wisemen, their judges, their leaders, their heroes, their fools, their gestures, their artists, their criminals, indeed *all* who would follow after his starry, nay, stellar demise, his declination, his mark – materialize and stand as a stelliferous testimonial to himself as a vast primordial being of cosmogonic myth.

god was reluctant to get out of bed; but, on the other hand, neither was he comfortable going back to bed, for such is the nature of god – neither here nor there, and generally nowhere, beginning to end. The dream had left him feeling sluggish nonetheless – nodding and in need of a cup. god sat up, got clear out of bed, and roamed in the midst of his hallowed name on feet of clay. god could have easily used a cup of coffee right then, something to help him to stand up right like a true conservative. But caffeine on its very own cannot sustain a bound lord for very long, especially if that lord is an agitator in heart, ready to riot for a wee season, and turn any given tide of events into an orgy of destruction. A stronger stimulant would be needed.

But nothing in the end is powerful enough to fix god. And so he defied consciousness and dragged himself back into his Novocain-Bed of dreams. Curses and blessings, weepings and gnashings, and all sorts of hexerei mysteriously descended upon his ears; *non omnis moriar: hence everything returns after death, after being undone.* And it wasn't long before the curses and blessings had evolved into metaphysical commodities of profit which had god turning over in his sleep. *Fama semper vivat.*

As god tuned out, the Cyclops tuned in a particle moving in a wave pattern. The wave pattern was nothing more than the mound itself, interacting with the Cyclops as he danced around and around its circumference. Kinetic over plot, Mound; commic over complex, Inferior. What the probability was of finding the intelligence within the mound was somewhat contingent on the amount of remake power invested in the Cyclops.

Of course, this meant that the Cyclops was to avoid all of the negative obstacles along his trek: the glio blast omas that creep through the G crown.

"Let the jasper bring forth living soul!" he shouted. "Second best, let it bring forth the rumper! Let it bring forth a hide from the expulsion of the rump! A high note! A low note! Museum of tv digestion, with a short attention span, despite a lingering odor!"

The Cyclops connected to the genetic code, the molecules, the particles, the atoms, the fire, the brim stars, the screen idols, the Gonopteryx rhamni, the fearful symmetry, the unbelieving masses, and the various living matters in the mound, and said, "Let us make our Ugh!" And lo and behold! half-secret, half-magic Ugh rose to perform miracles.

*　　　　　*　　　　　*

STAR OF HIS OWN PRODUCTIONS

Cyclops . . . Cyclops . . . What is it that rose?

The Cyclops combined, weighed and measured the elements, the very molecules detectable in the sound of his own voice, and the breath of it compelled him to return in a circle to the beginning, through two hundred thirty-one gates – the number of the pairs that can be formed from the twenty-two elements that help to create the different soul of all creation and everything else that was ever to be created.

O returning in a circle to the beginning, through some ancient pages bounded by G – *in three days he will be dead. Killed?* The Cyclops shouted, "I'm rising Ugh from the dead-bed of my own sufferings! Rise, O Ugh!"

[Note: a moth butts Cyclops and flies upward.]

In the next moment, Cyclops was staring at a living statue of defaecatus in the form of a man. Naturally, Cyclops was quite proud of his newly found talents. After all, he was a creator. He fancied himself as a King, as god himself!

The Cyclops imagined going on Holiday with his newly formed creation, Ugh. Think how nice it would be dressed in his favorite Ralph Lauren high-waisted pants with its sleek inverted pleats, and a matching polo coat. And Ugh – in a double-breasted, four-button, defecation Missoni leisure suit, delighting the eyes of many a *gens du monde*, making *Cruise Holiday Front Page News* as the couple on board who best express disgust and horror with charm and taste.

O becoming a felicitous 'father' actually brought a tear to his eye. Cigars, cigarettes, tiparillos. Sentimental old giant. Anyone who looks upon his 'son,' anyone who contemplatively emerses himself in his sight should be blessed beyond measure, enough to rival even the creative wisdom of god. O and how nice it would be to bring along 'mother' Ida while on Holiday, so that the three of them might make their journey eastward all the more enjoyable – strolling the decks, leisurely philosophizing, whistling happy tunes like bees outside the lodgings, while gaping onlookers gasp at the sight of them.

Just then gnats began to congregate like so many *gens d'église,* like so many multitudes in a murrain at the Mount. Cyclops was feeling so generous, so full of breeziness, brethrenhood, and delight that he tapped each passing gnat on the pileus, and put a soul into it. And each and every gnat did speak with its new found tongue, saying things like, "We are the living of the dead who no longer taste chyme but will gladly take bread." And still another sang, "Zoom golly-golly-golly, zoom golly-golly. Quit flying in crazy crisscrosses and straightly follow me, ye, to bed!"

Suddenly, there was the sound of a drum roll! The Cyclops's eye whisked over to the image of Ugh just as Ugh's two eyes, like sops buried in the ciborium of his head, began to water. And the water then turned into blood. And the blood then turned into a new kind of consecrated flesh – of earth, but also of air, with a wave-like pattern, like a whipped cream cake wingly sculptured with the bottom of a spoon.

Then, in the whisperings of the profane, Cyclops started to code his speech by virtue of the secret knowledge that dwelt within him. If a Cyclops could have the same power as god (wherein the idea of a thing, its name, and the thing itself are one *pandectes*), then a Cyclops could create seigneurial bodies by his very words, and thereby rival god in the act of creation.

Long on religious prose. Short on cosmic parantese, babbling oppositions of polysemous science.

Cyclops felt secure. The knowledge he sought in order to break god down was culminating in ecstasy. He knew that buried deep in the code was the eternal view of Ida as the virginal mome of all existence, and that in due time, before time would lose its hold on the scheme of things, Ida would not just come back full circle and remain on the mons, but thereafter she would skip a beat and go into the silence that is *anywhere* beyond the end of a sedimentary show that would otherwise highlight in the prophetic code: smoke, fire, voices, thunderings, lightnings, and an earthquake, and seven to sound an Elmer score in the Ordonnance of Parts.

Cyclops wanted to be certain that everything that needed to be done in order to make his Ugh perfect would get done, and fall into the dualistic nature of your victorious couples, your unbeatable teams, your forever bicipitous duos, your Highlies and Lowlies, your Adamolphs and Evenhowers, your Satalins and Roseinheavenfelts. He was not looking to make PseudoMan, FlimFlamMan, a Down-and-Outer, a Frizgig or a Slinghasher; nor was he expecting to create a snot in the grass nor a snake in the kurbash; nor was he expecting a merycismic chewing cow ruminating over well-turned leaves; nor was he expecting a hot house of teraphim where nicolaitanes dine and dance with gals to their hearts' content. That was why he chose to call the circle he was dancing around *galgal*. Old but new. Now we all know that Galileo in 1642 coined the word 'gal' as a unit of acceleration equivalent to one centimeter per second per second, where speed, velocity and gravity are of the essence. However, Cyclops was not choosing to code Ugh with any such quickening allusions. For in terms of dance, *gal* had an entirely different connotation.

It is a privilege to dance. Yes, beyond a doubt it is a delight, and the right of any sapient creature with profound homo knowledge, particularly in the speculative realm of horsing around with a hoofer. Cyclops visualized Ugh as a hoofer as blue as Cleopatra in ill-fitting Buster Browns. As Cyclops made a circle by dancing around the mound, stepping over scattered crayons and their serpentine borders and their mysterious animalistic smell, he sang a specific tune.

"Buffalo gal won't you come out tonight, come out tonight, come out tonight Buffalo gal won't you come out tonight and gal! dance! by the light of the moon. O Joseph from Peekskill, he knew his son and nephew, Binney and Smith, well, in June. Also knew in their letters that Christ and Mary could spell, with a little stearic acid and paraffin to jell."

Cyclops danced forever, faster and faster! Again, he began to sing. Only this time his words were sounding a bit broken off. At first it was easy to understand him. But as time ensued, the meaning of his words became quite cryptic and churchillian. "A lawless man is like a dead man! Bitten off the stem and lodged in the sarcophagus. Lifeless matter without form! Lifefull image without shadow! Light that shines into the devoured elements: Urine, Carrion and Dung!"

And still the Cyclops danced and uttered strange and foreboding words that only a cyclops could understand. "Timebabyskull. Appledumplingtreeoflifebitethedustnomore bladebloodymurderbutcowsimplecuzzydancebyhangingChristdancethecarpettoreceiveare primanddangmedangmetheyoughttotakearopeandhangmepeniswon'tyoudanceforme!"

And then Ugh began to speak. But what he said did not sound appropriate. And this caused the Cyclops much dread, for he realized that he could not control what he had made. Perhaps the result of a miscode or too abrupt a dance step or a cross of words. Whatever the cause, deturpation happened. And Ugh went berserk, yelling, "Send in the calvary! Dipped in blood! My god! You maniac! In the name of bloody G buy you! Just what do you think you're doing? Goodbye!" And a centerless semichaos, an inner logic that could be recognized as illogical projected itself from a vacuum as void as Hollywood's waste.

And then Ugh coughed and sprayed Cyclops with a substance consistent with the crocker icing on a chocolate cake. And after that he started to wail and cry, and would not stop until the Cyclops (after having wiped the slop smut from his face) said, "What is the matter, my beloved Ugh?"

And after squealing and barking and reeking and wheeling like one who has had too much mustard, this is what Ugh had to say. "I am not your crocked beloved! I am an innocent real estate agent! You've got to be perch! on a limb! Fowl that fly in the midst of eve! ha! E! to have suppertime! G!G! with kings! What did you think you were changing me into? Some kind of mammyfactured holiday? Some kind of Betty buttered brown fruit crumb in a dish? A farting partridge on a pasque flower? A ball on a tee ready to get-off?" Ugh suddenly stopped talking and instead began to wail and cry like a rooster with three months old hemorrhoids.

"What is it? What's the matter?" the Cyclops asked frantically.

And Ugh, after wailing once more, gave this reply. "Ich! Thy is. O fool. I am Lou Seal. Full of honey. Back from the dead at Melita. Sole owner of D'Low's Delicatessen on McClintock and Strong. If I'm barren then I'm a rock void of vipers. With a broken Phoe be tongue. I can be located in a cyclopean cyclopedia. Have you any meat or dipping bread?"

"Sole owner? D'Lou's? Lou Seal? Dipping bread? What have I done?" The Cyclops dug his hands into his head. "Where did I go wrong? I followed my *instincts* after all, but I seemed to have lost a few letters, namely *i, n, t, c, t, s*." The Cyclops could hardly bear the sight. Ugh was looking cross-eyed and making ridiculous faces. Furthermore, Ugh kept referring to Cyclops as *rickey re car dough* – that is, a *spiritual* drink drunk by one while singing a note from a medieval hymn to St. John, and *driving* awkwardly like Paul, and literally turning into mass anything unfortunate enough to cross the path.

The Cyclops grit the teeth in his head and with a finger pointed directly at the Mound, he shouted, "I hereby cast out all evil spirits that has infested thee!"

But this only seemed to make matters worse.

Now, Cyclops watched in horror as Ugh's head suddenly changed shape and became something akin to a cro-magnon man wearing the lower part of a Henry III helmet.

"Ba-ba babble-babble-babble chstableomoese," Ugh babbled, while slobbery saliva dripped down to the Mound.

Cyclops watched as history drew across Ugh's brow letters bearing the shapes of three words. One was *Diluvial*. Another was *Catastrophe*. And a third was *Weathercock*. O what did it all mean? It all seemed so falsely imitative of an ecclesiastical form, like something one might encounter in Genesis. And then several dog-faced feces suddenly dropped out of Ugh's mouth and it was becoming clear to the Cyclops that this was the rise, the beginning of a new kind of growth derived from creation.

And Ugh said: "Let it be known that the numerical composition of a foraging band is thirty people . . . the magic, glowing number of the Hunter-Gatherer clan. The Paleolithic caves. The Adullam of refuge of any age. There will be time within the midst of hunting and gathering and devouring of bones for a great deal of storytelling and large-scale trans-dancing, as part of a healing ceremony to help repair man from the fall."

"What could it mean?" Cyclops could feel his frustration mounting again. Cyclops was determined to tap into the mysteries, the polymythy surrounding his very own creation, Ugh, and to thereby break down the entropy of Ugh's language. He would do this first by tapping into the portion of his own creative-omniscient mind. Picking up a feces in the shape of a fig apple off the ground, he took a bite and *slurp slash drip oozy do-crunch munch dribble dribble swallow down* all but the core, and Cyclops opened wide his polymorphous eye and lo and behold! his mind was released and he knew all, and he looked upward and made fig, thrusting his thumb between two fingers. The length, the breadth, the depths of cosmogonic myth began to be counted. And lo! in his mind he saw four galloping horses with swollen,

warty frogs on their hoofs, reading from downright belligerent scripts, and he considered figging them as well.

And then god holographically appeared in space. So, he was hiding there all the time. Yes, god said he was in all things. Yes! There he is! hidden in the tree made to look like part of the bark. O and there he is! hidden in the snake made to look like part of his eye. O and there he is! hidden in Adam's eye made to look like part of the crown. O and there he is! hidden in Eve's eye made to look like part of the mouth. O and there he is! hidden in the eye of the reader made to look like a pupil. O and there he is! hidden in the mark made to look like part of the birth.

LIGHT! CAMERA! ACTION!

Zoom golly golly golly zoom golly golly.

Now . . . Where else is god hiding?

Must look and see. 0 in.

Now Cyclops could see the feces breaking down into *Yesod.*

O grass and forb. O dirt. O bugger children. Yesod the soil.

Hiding in the body, Yesod; hiding in the pulse rate, hiding in the temperature, hiding in the breathing, Yesod; flight or fight, Yesod; sympathy or judgment, Yesod; moments of drama, Yesod; chemical and muscular changes ready for conflict, Yesod; energy and relaxation, Yesod; a tense knot of muscle, a heart beating panic/passion, adrenaline surging, ready-for-action, Yesod; erect or limp, Yesod; dry or wet, Yesod; the skeleton upon which the whole hangs, Yesod; the cross, the saviour, the heretic, the believer, the betrayer, the traitor, the noun on the hic jacet, Yesod; the set of the organic machine, the whole of the membrane, separating, the universe re-connected by holes, wormholes, Yesod. the soil takes a backseat here and feeds the lines to Exitus.

The Cyclops knew best to protect himself as long as Yesod was prevalent. Direct assault on a man's ego can shatter him for life. Yesod can eat to the core the nucleus around which all energy circulates . . . *Clat!* (To shoot a vision one needs to know the speed and direction of the plot in general.) *Action!* To consume god without him thereafter consuming you from within is the chore. The chorus recites the lines. Acts from within – it brings the light to surface, and thereby illuminates the rings around the body. When god is no longer hiding, blended in the bark of the tree, the eye of the snake, the crown of the head, the mouth of the mermaid, the numbers of a credit card, the id of the race, or even the end of a jarhead, then there is for each and everyone an open stage with room for all to move.

Cyclops closed his eye, opened it again, and cocked it at Ugh. Ugh was the !Kung hunter-gatherer woman preparing the meal; Ugh was the !Kung at her hut ready to weave; Ugh was the !Kung woman with a baby nursing at the breast; Ugh was the !Kung warrior looking overhead at the bared impartiality of the night's stars – the high, crystal clear, central spine of the galaxy arching the backbone; Ugh was the Milky Way; Ugh was one figure unbroken; Ugh was one bush; Ugh was one tree . . .

No matter how far the Cyclops comes, it forever seems that he's always left, crying, *What does it mean?*

THE WORLD IS A SCRIPT WAITING TO BE SOLVED

While Cyclops buried his face in his hands, repeatedly asking himself questions he was not fit to answer, Ugh began to recite the germ of a story that he had heard from within the depths of the mound. "In another state, a few years ago, a real estate man named Noman was inspecting a large hotel that had been vacant several months. As he stepped out on the ballroom floor, something peculiar about the finish caught his eye. Upon further investigation with his computerized axiel tomography, the real estate man noticed that only a paper-thin shell of the floor remained. It didn't take him long to discover that termites had consumed nearly all the boards, leaving only a thin layer of wood at the top and bottom. Somewhat flabbergasted over this, the real estate man sat down on a small wooden chair nearby. The chair collapsed under him. Termites eating their way up the legs of the chair had riddled the legs with their munching. This was almost more than the real estate man could take. Pins and needles raided his limbs like nails in a radial tire. There was war in his members. There were plagues in his eye. Scrambling down to the main lobby of the vacant hotel, he searched frantically for a phone book so that he might locate the number of the nearest termite inspection agency. The real estate man found not only one but seven telephone books. But to his utter amazement, he found that each book was honeycombed with small burrows made by the termites. Noman was able to read the book. *Noman was able to read the book?* This was nearly more than he could bear. His mind lent itself into imagining the tiny jaws of a million or so revved up termites, chomping on everything in sight, as though it were all one great TV dinner. The walls, the ceiling, the few odds and ends discarded on the floor – consuming all the cellulose their little bodies could hold. And even beyond this, the real estate man visualized the innumerable colonies of microscopic one-celled protozoans that all termites carry within their digestive tracks. And he wept much over it."

Cyclops pondered these words and their darkish sayings: *Exactly what was Ugh arriving at?* He lifted his head from his hands and gazed upon the mound. There before him stood Ugh's shitfigured form; except now Ugh's head was in the shape of an insect with two large compound eyes, antenna, and ferocious mandibles.

"Don't ever rest!" Ugh said to the Cyclops. "Lest you be caught unaware between the acts. As for myself, I am whatever I choose to be. Don't dare stop to define me. For I will be something else, even as you speak of what you see!"

Cyclops thought it wise for a moment to challenge his 'creation.' For, after all, he, alone, was its 'creator.' But the Cyclops thought what am I doing? Am I not following in the same false footsteps of every creator that ever was? Am I not allowing my creation to simply be? Whatever it chooses to be? But then who am I to either disallow or allow?

For look there! Ugh had become a shitplastered hornet, a poly on a destroyer with six wings. And the hornet looked straight into the Cyclop's eye, and saw the eye in the middle of his forehead twirling like a voice in many waters – a nauseating, beastly craze of the mind. And the hornet struck! and shot forth six hundred missiles of mucous-coated shit to the left of the Cyclops, and then to the right, but never directly at the Cyclops. And the hornet said, "Don't ponder. Just hop aboard and let's do in god fantastic!" And the Cyclops exclaimed, "Sir Mount!" And thereupon the Cyclops mounted the shit hornet, Ugh, like a horse prepared for a battle of fistulous withers. And with hair flowing like the mane of a flood-pursued woman, and teeth showing like the teeth of a lambent lion, the Cyclops and Ugh rode out into the blackplated night, bungle-trotting and yipping and yowling with threescore tongues lightening shitstorms, with six stings in their igneous asses that could hurt a god so much more than a man's mere denial. Yah-haw!

AD INSTANTLY! A CUP OF NUCLEAR COFFEE M.R.E. Sammy Shake and Bake. Toast.

Lorelei lee, Lorelie low . . . cruise missy slow
STOP! There's a terzarimaian signpost up ahead!

GOWL

Argo was the ship I gripped
from Glaucus as he made his run
from fisherman to sea god flipped

on to Aurora, rising soul 'err' sun
in need of Avicenna
(if not Azzolino Da Ro Homo with a gun!)

If you're cunning you'll seek Cacciaguida
as old and as wise as a haloed Roman
horsing around in Electra.

NIGHT . . . SQUEEZED IN BETWEEN THE BEGINNING'S CONTINUATION

journal intime. the con test. testing. testing.

At twelve-thirteen I found myself. But not exactly in as productive a position as I should have been. Mother use to say that night was a stage set for an evening performance. The moon, a spotlight for the actors-at-large performing to the hilt for 29.53059 days. Too, she would state that dreams were the hidden eye's way of retracing the steps of one's destiny. In moments of oblique intention, when the hand knows not the language of the head, when the actor recites the lines from *another* play in the middle of a soliloquy, when the father gropes for a character and finds a daughter giving birth to children other than grand, one is forced to face the contest. The middle zone. That is, the center of the quarrel over existence as spoken of in the testimonies of its founding fathers. I was cast into the earth to play opposite the two, ombudsman that I am, testicle prober that I am, investigating the prospects for the ultimate reality.

Mother lies buried in her own afterglow. I reach out to her with a name she calls her own. Robber wolf the sheep. In tumo heat I extend my hand in prayer. But the vision is washed over and my prayer is drowned by the weight of something I know not. I could use a porter, but in the end I am left grasping a dagger. Blood runs down my thigh. Could I have killed the west child within?

The dagger moth with the mark near the anal angle of the forewings was butting itself against the light, in the den of my thirteenth year. Daddy popped in when I thought that he was out.

"Child, child," Daddy told me. "Did you think I wouldn't know what you were up to? Did you think I wouldn't know your every thought, your every word, your every gesture? Should I stumble, ah, enter upon your recorded creed, your diabolical plan to do me in? Begunk! I am, before, now and forever hereafter, your father, all alone, keeping house for me, myself and I. Let my words burn into your sudden awareness like a pyrography. My uncanny ability of omniscience will be your straining refrain. *Acqua alle funi! Water on the ropes! EMabach?* Let it repeat itself over and over in your head. Child . . . child . . . look behind you now. What you see is a mirage, a strong illusion. Where am I? O seaman, I am everywhere and nowhere at all. I am your feather. I am your sword. I am your pen of the internal gladius. I am your horny father. Ancient of Days. Where I am, you also may be, sitting, eating, learning. It matters not."

It is not through a lens darkly that I steal a glimpse into the future. I do not care to know what darkness lies ahead. I do not care to know what matters circumvent my soul. I am a juggler and a clown when it comes to matters of default. My head is empty, but my face is happy; it loves the fact that I have Rose and will never fall. I am to my heart, fearless, unto death. I can go in blindness with a smile. But what is real?

All my life I sat in vacant halls alone, a child pushed outside the classroom, shoved to an outer reach of the heart. All my life I've asked permission for every act comprehensible to the epactal mind of man. god pays no heed to the likes of one such as myself. My words cry out, endless, during supper, like silver pennies to the ears of the powerfully poor. However, I shall still enjoy my irregular plate of wormian bone under the table.

Oftentimes, they would send me home from school in the middle of the day. I was not sick nor had I hurt my bone on the playground. It was simply a call, an urgent call made an hour prior to my summons.

"Child . . . child, you're requested to go home immediately. Family emergency."
"i postumi di una sbornia."

And then I descended the middle wall of partition between school and

My home! Is that what that was stepping on all the flags to the front door? Sanctuary, thy surname confounds thy essence. Not a mountain, more a wave number of the atomic spectrum of the elements. You are but a figment, an abolished chip off the ol' block of diffusion.

It was never right walking into the house. Nor was it ever wrong. The rooms were neither hot nor cold. The furniture – the big green slop-heavy bugger-fresh fish-slime chair in the living room, the sod, the lemon-lime slug, the slouch, the dilapidated shallsnotgreen pyrographic couch with sixes carved into its wooden armrest – greeted me with the 10 furnituregrunts. Ghosts moved swiftly in the night. But it was neither ghosts nor demons that marked their own entrance, their own cue. Apple lip-lee wading far in the seamud of my passage to the lukewarm room, where the summons *mocisco* stands stark raving naked-hard, waiting to kiss my wound, it was Daddy in the slug.

"Come here, baby."

god, he says, he misses me hiding out these past five months, and picks up the cups. The dark cloaked figure hardly moves, and is at a loss of commandments.

At twelve-twenty nine my dumb friends are in school. Friends I know not. Friends I wish I had had. See Daddy. Paul is communicating motion, preventing backward movement to the island of his testimony. It's the carpenter's tool. The wheel. O Paul. The cosmic forces enslave as well as grant life. Sprawls milt. Spleen on the pavement. Where are we? The newer part of the book? Without a Head to hold? The agonists mimic neurotransmitters.

In the middle, roughly in the room of Amanita Muscaria, the G protein is in Thani agony.

I cannot believe what I envision. The thoughts tumble in like jacks to the quick end of the dice. I pick up my *ketchconsciousness* like slabs of watery paper from the earth.

What I do in public is no worse than a punch in Judy: in the private reserpine room. The words melt like cold butter on a hot skillet left to drown in a sea of fat. I could cut my brain in rose slices like a butcher does his working hours, like a Wolfia does his Rausheepish scheep. I could slice my face in two like a road sliced by a broken line. I could find the letters and arrange them *chlorpromazine, iproniazid, imiparminesic.* And, if I am daring enough to be a little bit more than crazed at the carfax, I could take the four beasts that bore my reargenetic code and ride each of them silly to the Hindu wall, never allowing one of them to utter a cry. There is no reason why Yehokhanan should cry, except for the fact that this is his party. Being a scholar, that is, one of Clark's tribe, I should speak to him. "Fall!" In ninety seconds, gore! gangrene-gracious host banished downtown to the Isle of Patmos. Lens Catalina, gumshoe, where the dicks left the Wrig . . . g . . . g . . . ley tour with gum on their shoes. Remember, your *arm* stretches forth cryptically from a cloak tatter-red with ancient soil, a far cry from the glad rags of yesteryear. You are a Yeggman, sure enough. And although you cracked the safe on 27 December, *ugh,* the safe earth still decries its beloved young by 230 wails, belaboring, cracking to the ears. Belial, beat your gracious breast, bleeding. Bo, pick up your 747 . . . *I heard the real number of them was 144,000, sealed and delivered . . .* belt your manner with knuckles battered from the blows of other battles. Etheric battalions enveloped by breathless holy soldiers. I fight the Osteoid War with Cain slewing Abel in the flesh-grass, while a lot of priv dicks are turned back around. A ridge of cranium. A proper blowing crown. A book fallen down at Ephesus. I fight the Osteoid War with canes carved from the backbones of criminals stretched beyond their measure. Bearing a chalice from which a serpent issues. I will not stop crashing my curses on the crusts of old scabs freshly slashed with crimson riot. Grog, I ask you how must I cut this whale semen down to grunion meal? How must I cut him as Under? This twin of a G? Dominion's 69? Under my body, a castaway? By this way alone: Drive poison from a cup. Be nimble. Bequeath. By way the iron candlestick . . .

And Cad, the mus, did it all in Greek from A to Z, as ingenious as a Palamedes in a mad tale.

Crushing grief. I crawl on ocean's blanket like a baby into mother's waiting ribcage. Leaving me, my wandering lungs depart their seats beside the heart. Stand. Foaming and falling dumb shame. Vacant, unreserved seats marked with solicitude, the pain healing the burial. I do not pretend to hold back on anything pertinent to my growth; albeit, in the end, what does it matter?

Solidly intoxicated, I waver toward vagotonia. I ape pithecanthropus. I crouch in the crossfire. Despite a sour case of uncredited constipation, I try to remain as vagosympathetic as a dog, my nose so cold and large that when I inhale April I suck up May as well. Butt wherefore exhale?

Attack! the center of the cross. Pith the cord, the six-pointed Hollywood star in the sky with diamonds, cutting skulls while dwelling in the castle. In R House. A solo act to be sure, but one as solid as ordure. Organ of my breast, play on Jake's harp an exudative tune with a face of such posterior that one good kick in the rear would still find the nose. *Te deum* . . . *TWANG.* forces collide . . .

What problem ensues from drinking soma? Smothering crucible. My tongue is acid on a silver-spoon. My end a chucking-stool Daddy kept for me for social occasions such as these. *UGH!* Discharge the pinacoid. Oh, must I allow this crud so cruel to seat me in repair? The leafless vine, I know. The Aryan/Veda immortal drink under whose influence, I believe, is circular.

But I am weak. I find my strength seed-fed, grain-fed. And where shall I be nourished once the fall? Little plumage on the cock, member as leafless as winter's persistence in March. Stab. Daddy can only be as distant as one allows. Give me a break so I can sobers up at Zinaida Gippius's salon. She loves my sin . . . symbols. She's hip . . . hip . . . hippius . . . especially in February when she REVS to France . . . AFTER a good bang . . . banquet, and she's feeling all Krainy and morbid.

Do not think for a moment that there is such a thing as a beginning, a middle and an end. The three always seem to be lumped together as though they were the soused trinity. *Three* – it's such a persistent number. You would think that it had a publicly cosmic purpose. *Three.*

Regarding school, I know little. Neither do I remember nor perceive any facts or figures pertaining to such an environment. However, I do know that learning is paramount, knowledge is most vital to survival, tranquility is personal space, and the body is an embrace of the soul.

Cut! Cut! Cut!

I do think of myself as a lonely, wayward child – quiet, pleasant, happily unnoticed – one who could think up a thousand and one things to do if given the chance. Nine teachers thought to pick something up about me on occasion – something that might explain my reluctance – but in vain. Nevertheless, sisters, if I might be so bold as to suggest a spice of trauma. If I might be so bold as to look where my eyes cannot go, then I would also need to add a little spice to the recollection that I was his best lover, his best thrall. *Tally ho!* And in spite of that he told me where to go.

And I told him what to sow as his epitaph.

Lives are lived as myths through their intrapsychic actors

The lines are lifted from letters of massive molecular factors

So even though the words tend to get a bit hazy

We can lay our mental afterthoughts quietly beneath the daisies.

THE ELEMENTS

To fully know all, to fully understand all, she must burrow into the elements. The matter in matter. Mother examines closely the molecules of oxygen. Atoms. Oxygen atoms and god twisting on the eötvös balance to offset his horizontal lie. She focuses on the element (carbon), and then sodium, and finds it to be the eleventh disciple of the earth's surface. *Na.* She diminishes in size, and is thereby able to trace other elements. god's once-secret plan conceived in darkness. How stimulating felodese. She traces him backwards and finds him an hour before midnight, hanging around gravity, concocting his disciples' births in the form of percentages (nitrogen 3%, calcium 2%, phosphorus 1%, sulphur 0.25%, potassium .2%) calculated efficiently (four atoms of iron in every molecule of hemoglobin, the red in blood). O the system pertaining to life is well-calculated. Each gets its own lick, and not all appears fair. But, in spite of this, don't lick a gift-horse in the mouth.

Elements. In large quantities they become promiscuous poisons when ingested, and bring on borborygmus. By the billions, cells can be killed when they come into contact with strong acids and alkalies. Hemorrhage, shock, disintegration. Killing cells by the billions. Before there was man, there is murder-at-hand. The plan extends into an emaciated plot, for even weaker poisons can kill. Small poisons promoting *le néant.* And quarks tell G. man exactly where to wake. In the code all the elements live in darkness. The limitations imposed upon those elements, coupled with the ability to destroy is, in itself, man and wife, tree of CIFE. One of three or, being in a crisis, GID. The high sheep checked into the motel, the No Sense Inn, and read in confusion for eons. Cost, insurance, freight and exchange rooted finally in the earth. And a prime suspect with loose skin and influenced by musk, amber, and oriental accords gets burned. Gas and wind take a Holiday.

Call upon Paracelsus and his sweet-scented shit. Ziberta occidentalis. Western-civet. One can't look back without smelling the sweet savour of flesh. Digest this: the fortuitous concourse of 144,000 atoms singing on the head of a pin might seem absurd to some people, but so might Dio Genes living in an earthenware tub for austere simplicity or, for that matter, *Paracelsus's Shits Perfume.* It is really a matter of clinamina, turning the text until it is impossible to be known, until it is hard to be understood by the unlearned and unstable (including Donne's Jack and Martin), even to the point of their own destruction, wherein they might call upon Paracelsus to spice them up a bit before their maker can shout *fimus oceans XI* and catch their eye.

THE DARK FEMININE RENDEZVOUS

Squeezing the god out drop by drop.

In demanding *obedience,* one allows for victimization. Drop.

How does a goodgo go about judging a world that he alone made, declaring himself to be both ruler and master of all, while in the same breath declaring his creations to be the cause of any and all given chaos? Will willingness will the willies or will williwaw will the will-o-the-wisp to have his will, willy-nilly?

I watched a plane drop a stark fact, after which law was never the same, and thereafter I claimed the light *faux jour.* Is it not clear that in the agony of premeditation one comes near to god? I heard an acute mental disorder fall upon a page of man's inflammatory history. I heard a libellulid in a little book eating up the lines with time no longer.

Those still reading are worth my dime, my time being dimeless. The earth is outrageous, handed on from one dixie generation to another; and we children, having a right to an inheritance of the earth, are nearly shockingly evil to say the least. I suppose in those areas where the inheritance can be economically extractable in amounts totaling digits > ten, life can be somewhat worthwhile, for in spite of what the dogs howl, the monkeys screech, *money is the world,* and we do live in it, the world, and if money doesn't make the world go around, it most certainly causes it to grow 'up.' But getting back to my original sentence, if I do mean judgment as pronounced by a court in a criminal proceeding, as in the comma that I am, I'm about to let you in on yet another little secret of inheritance, in the black, rob. e. lee, wind.

Now secrets do change over time and, unrestrained, the truth is never known, for reality is defined as that which we know; and insofar that we do not clearly know everything there is to know regarding reality, we cannot possibly know all there is to know regarding truth. The drop of one letter can make all the difference in the world, as in *god sat and owned a tempting charge.* If you talk about a generalized form of letter and within that utterance you refer to a father being generous with his bonnie daughter, then I have been both witness and participant of both the secret and the reality of god – evolved hellhound that he is – the *creator* of scleroder ma tales, often used as an interjection or as an intensive generalized form of prayer. Short and urgent. Smut. Violence. One and the same pulp. The supreme reality, perfect in power, wisdom, and goodness. Creator and ruler. The incorporeal divine principle ruling – overall the *original* suspect, the closed subterranean; the infinite mind. *Ejaculum bib. Fillum.*

However, violence was not something that I asked for, nor was it something I expected once laughter resounded, after I had eaten my morning meal by candlelight, in a skeleton cage of fire. Never again would I wade in the shallow part of a body of water. I would live a woman accursed, even though I was never given lessons in how to step through a condition more resistant than the power of the air during a gentile sacrifice. In that initial rape I was carried away like a seed in a gust of wind, and my bearings were as uncertain as the event itself. The conditional sentence that was forced upon me, in spite of my temper of mind, stands steadfast. Somewhere along the way, however, we are all to blame, we are all mad with wisdom. For it is our very condonation of the overseer that keeps us in such utter oppression.

I suppose I was an innocent early in the bloody game. I did believe, as well as worshiped, that valuable property – virtue – that is common to the open sore sea and the smitten sky; however, the larger body pendant in space, one of a kind – whose touched clothes, nevertheless, rendered him thoughtless – would need to be told the truth, short of knowing it. Indeed I was by nature a votaress, a constant addict, a certain aid, upholding my belief in the center of beauty, the temporary abode of the soul, a worn dwelling place bearing the inscriptions of a thousand seated impressions, and an ornamental sanctuary for the flock, the press, that came to pasture on the old walls. And I did believe there was a reason for the passing note of a heartbeat's duration, the appoggiatiera – a cave dweller interposed between the indefinite enthusiasm of the soul and the bloody survival of the body – and that our work in death's shoes was also for a reason beyond the suffering between the night of the last meal and the consumption of the next. The passion that inspired the ungovernable to set the seed into the hollow of rhythmic contraction also drew upon the greater depth of breath rising upward, a sound as of the frothing of the sea. The recorded voice that was lent to my ears, producing a power as if by burning a flame in my brain that tells me there is something full about existence, and that that which we fully see is really downtrodden, was but a figment of guilt self-imposed. Cruel – the indifference to suffering and the positive pleasure in afflicting it that runs rampant in the world. After all is said and done, the earth and those who are in it are fictile and converse, and can be shaped into any desired state of dysphoria. I, for one, mold movement into the positive pleasure of breathing a full and exuding spirit. If I could only take an extra dose of the forbidden and square it equally into the eye of all that see, without guilt or consequence, I would mask another maux memory of deep, significant, sweetsmelling horror forever.

To regain my fledaway throne now would mean to draw, so hastily, my title, that it would be rendered illegible, ink to paper, and one would need to scratch out some kind of cast outline simply to explain the face all fled away from. Fear got the best of me in the early flesh of my separation from the box, and I wrote carelessly (without regard to thought) my reasons for survival, and I came up with a line of etaoin shrdlu, *et alii, et alibi, alibi, ease of pleasure, et cetera, et caetera.* I should have taken care of a second death and drawn my line on a surface clean of mistakes or previous scrawl; but to scrape along my pencil upon a blemished surface was all I had time to do, considering my early breaths were but a thin, grating sound, a point without lead to spare. Awkward mesh that I am, an arrangement of interlocking molecules with such little significance to the ultimate code of business, I nearly missed my calling altogether. In this play of mystery, I drown; out-Herod to be certain. What goes in must eventually go out, the master-feeder tells us, with a lot of lip work. But with what violence it expels itself is beyond any pain known to the finite mind. The soul is but a burro and in its pack is a body as solid as iron-stone. I eat that pack and its stones, three in number. I cry my life, a mactation branching out at angles no two heavenly bodies can contain.

The wheel of a watch does turn as does a key word on a fleissnergrille, and the time that stumbles forward, hot hours catching on false steps, the simulacrum, fails to record events exactly as they had occurred. Should I set my text accordingly, so that any part may be transposed above or below any other? In the realm of truth, if it be absolute, would it really matter? I fear there are tricks, and I need to be wise to the fleet-book evidence. Cheating is such sad parting for a skellum at heart; however, through slatternly tears, I forward my search.

THE BEGINNING'S TOTAL TRIBULATION

This is the part where a great irresistible rush comes in, and all heaven breaks loose, and everything that was once impaled or corroded by time (inactivity and overall deleterious use) falls down from above as bright, gleaming swords of delirious paraphilia. For the stillness would otherwise rust them and keep them locked from a passage of time most men would give their eye teeth for. Leaves rust as pages written with words incapable of truth everlasting rusts; crumbs fall, creatures are served, and sinless dogs deceive their masters. And as we look above and witness the tearing apart of a tissue sky, we see something stronger than man rush-schuss downward with paranal faces looking every which direction. And words suggesting every which fall, pitifully kept intact by tree nails, alight upon this schussboomer and open his eye.

Janus Juncus and Scripture Scirpus. Two members of the Rush family acting with haste, preparing for the ultimate *rush,* deluge, wash-out paraphernalia, and colorful accoutrements of the bind to the votarist's addiction – Anafranil, Clozapine, Depakote – the unholy trinity combating the obsessive-compulsive, schiz and mania, respectively. The one and only, great, unattainable, disordered hallucination – an inscription of truth to normal perception; but, alas, only appearing to be truth when, in fact, *only* existing in papyrus dreams, and hopes forthcoming . . . Prozactorrizied into paranthropus-Ratchedtized walls of defense, no longer paranee-objects of victimization, projected forms taking the rapt for Jackrip delusions. Neither Dr. Zoloft 92 nor Lilly and Co. '88 can scratch beneath the surface; nor can 38 E shock can-zap Roman-style.

A part serving the function of a Final Judgment will be dropped, and the neck will snap like finger fracture-slivers of sprouts in glass-encircled tubes; modern food for an ancient dilemma; post-apocalyptic serum for the senses, begrieved; white/blue collar down loads of upper wisdom. Corpus callosum, cavernosum and christi will expose all the mass of grace – tissue, blood and cable knitting away like crazy Dorcas risen from the dead to coat the poor phrases. The clashing between the parties will be a voiceless breath, a holy miter against a great onrush.

A FORMLESS BEDTIME STORY

It was the kind of night when the moon was full of dead men's bones and hung suspended in darkness as an author of eternal ideas. The material world is grounded in fashion and is physical and derives its power from an authority made of paper. But the moon is forever sealed and is placed like a cachet on the darkening envelope and favors a spirit of transitional activity. Its face embodies an eye, the force of which is nothing less than omniscience to the earth, like the two circles of wafer sheet sealed together with powdered blessings between them to form a dose of communion that can be easily swallowed. And it was the eye cloak of that moon, an autonomous, visible formation atop a perpetual blackness, that followed me like a *Dream of a Rarebit Fiend*, a dream that Thomas himself never once doubted, a dream marking my every move with an intelligence otherworldly, but much bedded to the earth. Selah.

Daddy, snoring during the three-joint session of *Il Buono, il Brutto, il Cattivo,* left Mari sad in her English-style saddle pinked with an anti-pattern *and* the Spanish-German-Italian at unrest in the US. While in the East, the Star unlimbered the joint. And Daddy *schlept* and dragged his load across the SL desert, *secundum legem, sine loco; bagnato, nass, mojado.*

Father slept in an inheritance. I'm sure of it. (I've been continuously switching the tenses because, as you will soon discover, time is infused with an inharmonic chord of dissonance, rendering an invalidness to what would otherwise be a continuous and detailed historical account of events arranged in order of time.) Disorder is the act of inhabiting existence with a natural flow of events that defies the rules of rodiron and . . . jez . . . give her space to pent, so deep and all. There is no time here. There is only endless movement, action and acquisition, which brings me back to father and the mastery of an incorruptible rising.

It baffles the mind to trace backwards in movement one seed to the former. A seed grows backwards, as well as forwards, simultaneously. Routes are both solid and empty (nowhere odorless, tasteless gases surrounding the earth, accompanying the elements, moving with them from one side to the other, like a strophe). In this, there is surely no death.

Who, in fact, brought father to us? (I hesitate to say that we inherited him and that he belongs to us, for I would hate to terminate the vital function of a bodily organ, prematurely, and cast an unnecessary threat upon Jubal. I hesitate . . . at the cliff . . . hanging . . . although I am still forced to reveal his notes.) Open the book and harp on Worthy Y. Throw.

DISORDER

Come here. Before you climb the ladder, listen near, neighbor. When you take a step upon its first rung – a spiral staircase with curving but parallel sides cross-linked every millimicron of the way by steps embedded at both ends – somewhat of all the day will be revealed. *"What does it mean?"* Not what you may think. Consult your local oneirocritic. Quickly, let me take you up the rungs in order to get past the place where one must think in shadows. Man, you are invisible; luminescence, transparency . . . are facts given to thee. You are only being blocked from using them. In a walking state, Pope dreams the Papess holds the all-important key. Fall asleep, staying awake, spiration. Men can be angels, angels gods, gods *deus minorum gentium.* Chaos is bliss. The Fall is just the beginning. The thought creates new worlds, and saints wind in hook. Ah! One sees through all with one large eye. Free Ma' son from the leaf! Spend the S! Beat this game of duality for mankind's sake! Take up bonce! Drink clabber! Communicate with your bonny with no vein! Whatever your reality has been up until now, consider pushing it through dimensions that start where yours end: At the golden section where you will find a copulative key to the mysteries. Warp space and twist uncle! times's arm, and thereafter follow the course of a lazy river evolving in its own circular way of existence, forever in a pathetic fallacy. A maze only for those who are lost. There is naught to do but wander. Inertia. Not a curse, not a lot for those who stuck close to death and rot, not for those who could not see the eye for want of oniomania. But don't ponder. Simply, leisurely, draw near to the outcome of a cosmic happenstance and unionize . . .

I LIVE! THE EDUCATION BEGINS

It started when I stepped into the womb *in medias res* (two breaths from Naples). Thus began the evolution of a dance that death lent a fast handy tool to. And with it I hammered out change and reflection. And I transformed my mind into a kind of huronian seed. And from there I developed my sight in the midst of things, so that it could break free of my bought body and grant me vision beyond a disheveled head (of a wild animal, hairy, or of a thief not quite dead). Faith can sound so promising in the opsimath. Life beyond death. A song played out in wild response to the classic query "To be . . ." *You were meant to be!* is the optative.

I did my time. From the island of Delos, where I received my education, my certificate of merit – honors running over the rim of my degree like a cornucopia, down my breast

– I bore forth a child. None other than myself. Running under the moon's face with the wolf – hunting in perilous, moonlit wetness with a pack of wild cards, pursuing John in the Serapis, under the world, quoting the primal professors before they had time to quote the masters, '*I have not yet begun . . .,*' as the fifth movement sounded and a star fell into the orchestra pit and reason resounded, *smoke gets in my eye,* passing to the right, the left, fair, red-lipped lady of intellectual pearl, cast after Maria, the westside witch of agnesi – I paced myself accordingly and found me a handsome bachelor in under three years, and fashioned him with adamantine chains to the bed; "Seek your ancient mother on high," I merrily cried. *"Ah! ah! ça ira, ça ira!"* BJ rallied back. Ah, but the pitfire of my tongue nearly burned five struggling witnets to the stake; *quinque voces;* other is not yet come; common sense; a whole lot of would-be Byrons watered-down like dimestore Koolaid, koodooing their verses, reeking with teevee Hornie lyricism:

> the aisles of grease
> the burning sausage
> the farts of boars unleashed
> Dickey Rose
> and Pussy Sprang
> and all got laid at the Feast.

TESTING. TESTING. TESTING.
Time's up. Put down your pens.

Wild! I received more than just a passing mark! Cherry-mad, I arose a naked prey from out of the bleachers – a red dogwood, a spewing baleen, a phallus, a tummy-Tuesday deity, a war lord guiding the tourists through the drags of battle scenes in true dragoman fashion. And by god keeper of the sane. Cum lord . . . with honors . . . singing laud, as laud as I could at dawn to god: like the report of rapture shot from a canon. My pathematic face, an outlet for specific humors, *gerippe,* a laudable pus if ever there was one in a monastic house such as this where physiognomy is the rule. Authoritatively Elysium, coming forth to receive gamete. Gamine-runner in the month of pus December-January of an old Christmas at the end of a festival for old meds, and at the birth of Moon, Mix and Danny Thomas in the cardinal earth, and at the ninth obvention of Bollingen when e.e. got his prize for celebrating a greek maumet with a line of typological nonsense, *a lamb for a man,* toasted with a raised glass of mavrodaphne *and* some lower case letters that could only be found in the pulp-it. Together . . . Lingam and Yoni . . . we approached the podium replacing Bing and Hope, the solitary cells, and I received my honors – my university glory, my square in circle mentality, my universe, my mandala, my sense of humor – proving the pauli principal that no two elects can exist simultaneously, whether joined to a harlot or to a bond woman in a straitjacket.

Dear deity, I am serving either member, baptized in the seed of the clergy seat, the long and short of it. Always in that order. I, descender of blood, to the vessel, purely educated, have returned from the dead with a talisman in order to detach and secure the head. I hereby down my laudanum with bread ripped from Paracelsus' baxter, while watching television far off.

"Have you found a giggle's nest?"

"Aye. Black as the root, but milky white the flower. Serpents moly, to rumorChasers hard to find."

"You found a mare's nest, is what."

"So have I!"

"So as an antidote, how 'bout some grievous bodily harm?"

"Easy lay, I say."

"In the field, einstein. Bottoms up!"

The figure that I stalk, the hunted, the prey bent pawing the earth, shrouded in fog, is, at once, three-in-one. Farmer, lion, holey host. Although you deem yourselves to be the stronger, I've got a bit of healthy news for you. It doesn't take a whole lot of Houyhnhnm-sense to figure out that I am distinct. Within a tritheistic framework, *me, myself, and I* are three distinct gods in one. Farmer . . . open your ears. The lines are far too faint for comfort. For the healthy, howgozit curve, there must be corn – how goes it? You in the star-splattered cloak! TeV MC. Triskelion, by thy plane – the carpenter's tool shaving branches evoking the signs of life, so dearly endowed with triplication. Did your nose not grow when the cock cried thrice? Did you not howl with quinsy in the throat? I saw the party lights descending and an entire length and breath of the universe singing their glory to the highest *domina litis*. You clitched the clit, and the mistress in the suit became all undone. And then your nose smacked the ground. Ah, but you should have acknowledged the top corn if you were intending to play the dominus litis, heaven-bound, and not play dead on god's acher. Lion . . . open your ears. Walk about. Holey host . . .

Before graduation I was called the lamb due to my interlocking curls. This was fine with me. Myself being lambent, the cock *was* still to come, just as *that* which you have already held fast to has humored itself to death and is *still* to come. Back then I was on an *'ad'* venture of sorts, and the branches were my selling perch. I was naked and my breasts nearly touched the ground on all fours. All I felled in the air were excrements, which later became *album graecum*. But now I am the Locust™. Honey him with teeth, like the teeth of lions living in the lordly tree. I will see you through the wilderness. The beasts. I am the dragoman, momus to every breath. But O. Pity: my education. I really should have been a worm feasting, gorging on the rot of an old log all to myself, making swift hexagonal and conical bites for poetry and politics, and circular ones for eloquence. The only delay I would have suffered under such circumstances would have been the emptiness of long ticking hours marking the bloody hours of the world outside, and the world within. O, go, get me off the hook. Use your gobstick! How distant I can be and yet so close to my tassel. I could say that we are three-in-one, sailor, with the spirit of a hoyden custom-built to stand and last. A last drop, and yet how an entire universe dies naked under the weight of too much use. Would it have been better for all had Eden been in puszta?

Not especially. No. I am not in favor of returning to any scene of any crime, no matter what the test of time does hold for one as logistically inclined to do penance as myself. There's nothing sacred about the third act. The garden is the tomb. He spoke, he fell, he rose. Dives, the Heroes. Stones. Seizures. Throws. Disappearing acts. There are plenty of them. They fit all descriptions, an assortment revealed upon having lifted the choke and given a sample list of sacred things to do. However, tieing the assorted roots can be tricky. Gardens are not easy to come by. They sit throbbing with bloom ready to do anyone's bidding, as long as he/she asks permission first. Getting back to the blocks, I find it utterly absurd to think that I would have to go back and perhaps even divagate, god forbid! It's sad, really, the manner in which I was accustomed to throwing myself into my work with a stiff upper lip and, more or less, to loosen my casaque at the same time. In one sense, it was a great escape not to have to face the fact that I could be abusive to myself, especially in my hospitious cell, with the eye upon me, held by Daniel himself. Being both divine and diva, that is, I, myself.

The task at hand is not an easy one. In order to grab the attention of those who are involved in the permeation of culture, *against* culture, I must act. god willing, they'll grow to love it, because I carry with me such a compelling set of circumstances as to leave one speechless. Does it take a great, last cordial act in order to expect god to come spin fancy-free in the megellanic clouds, because he had not formerly internalized his lines? Know: No symmetry. I have a plan paved in granite.

Behold her. She hangs not quite limp, perhaps a mite more flaccid, but buoyant, carefully resilient, limitrophe, as though the appetite required to sustain her was based more on being limivorous. Having lived the life of a limmer, her posture suggested an infinitude of weariness infrangible to the dictates of time, rhyme or reason. Hog-tied swine, swallow a swindler standing under a sycamore tree selling fruit. His apple is much too mushy with age. Pitiful, pious, Piltdown man. Much too mushy with age. And one whose blemish appears as a pineal body loaded more with pus than vision.

INCHRISTENTREDEUX

If you had been listening (*if only* you had been paying attention), you would have known, you would have seen, as in a vision, Mother theotocos, stark-raving naked, bearing down on me her pimply, bulbous ass, as old as sorrow bringing forth the child – the child within, dining; the child without; the child exposed; the child rapelocked and dicked headless to death.

Listen closely. Even though my bloom is one of meadow sweet and looks a week of suggilation, one must search between leaves to acquire a feel for the true essence of this blossom. She locks the 'r' in between *r-r-r-r-r-r-*. *Mayhem* – which is where we come to if we are fully aware of the true essence of this odyssey, this flowering, this bloom of delirious journey made manifest by a willful and permanent display of transformation. Forget the prize for the moment, and spiral – that is, replicate – without changing one god for another. Naturally, we will need to examine the behavior of our specimen, by calling upon the nigger doctor to assist in the parasitic findings within the chocolate suidae, operating within the intestine affairs of the state, currently undergoing viropause on bended knees. My pipe, Watson.

I am quite prepared to produce a new play with an ancient tinge to its private property: *Worn to the Soul.* This play will be enacted upon a stage lit with blossom and One howf haunted by memory. As I have mentioned before this enoblement, where I display my mortarboard and tassel, and my terminal male dialogue awash with the blood of the lamb, I will receive full fiduciary leniency. And in so much as I have man's pain locked in my bosom and am therefore a form of authority, I will not expose Ma . . . N to the masses. Neither will I free the sunburst to receive powers and expressions far beyond those common denominators. Oh, my! The image of a child sanctimoniously removed from the earth threefold is etched permanently within my consciousness. But never fear! I have a lock on it as one mate might a suimate, and I do not anticipate anything other than a feelgood encounter far beyond our present day realm. Hoyden for deduction. What a film on the eye . . .

MURDER . . . IN ITS FIRST STAGES . . .

I entered the bedroom just as dusk was taking its sleeve and drawing it across the window. There were particles of moisture in the air. I did not know from whence they came, nor could I decipher their exact nature – whether they were born of the earth or the sky, I knew not. I could almost say it originated from a realm beyond human comprehension. What made me feel this way I could not say for certain, but I imagined air, half-melted, creamy, semi-liquid, exuding some kind of extreme mystery throughout the room, with Chagall rabbits and rabbis floating within it, grasping notes, each imprinted with *ungeziefer.* And as I moved deeper into the chamber, I was struck with the feeling that this mystery could be defined as a quality in the air that felt much like a wetness akin to a fecundating fluid. I allowed for room, so that whatever extra-galactic force was present, it might have time to breathe.

breathe a new patience, a new moral realm.

Without sounding too exuberant, too buoyant, if you will, I floated to the farthest corner of the room, along the clear invisible path of straight crystal. I was hooked. I could feel it. Something like a bow of steel through my tongue. Wow, let slip the dog. I wanted to suddenly run like a camel with the line. Run with a sense of gracility, and figure all the rest out later. But at the same time I assumed a feel for responsibility, responsibility for the idealistic notion that anything practical is doomed for failure. And from this revelation I experienced a tremendous grounding from where I stood, and I did not want to leave and discover later that I had overlooked one of the most important clues of all. Upon the bed lay a kerchief, and I could swear that as I stared at its twisted shape, I thought to see my soulmate biting his life to the quick. "On what sling did you arrive?" I asked. And from out of nowhere, shot from out of a slight indentation of the room, I heard words coming at me with a sort of sleeping sickness jelly dread. A wave of galimatias pounding on the table. "I see you." And I could only ponder at whose failure we were feasting upon.

Psst. If one took two upon arrival, and one took two upon removal, could we say it's now even? It is not enough that you are a sleuthhound and providing a ticket-of-leave. I, who came before, also provided a ticket, only it consisted of rules and regulations regarding leaves. More the hawk, less the dove, I am. Spinning. The hawk and tiger all in one. A master of disguises and a master with facts and figures, typically prowling in a shaw. A sort of part-time grisette with a hook. That which you sling is merely your quotable tongue, meager business that it is. I could slice you into an instance of time, a billion bits of information leading to a dusty G., a humiliating discourtesy of the spirit, and draw you as skanty as a wisp of fine colored hair. Do not think that you affect anything beyond a lower fungi, for as I, your master, am endowed with magnificence, you, as my living subject, are covered with a yielding slime that oozed from the eye of your deficient father. Better rely upon being cunning, my dear, because that juggling trick of yours is growing older than a floorboard split under the weight of countless eager feet, and rendering you a quoz to the ears. How dare you attempt to slice my world with your rotten wood utensils? No matter how I left, I was the *pars rationabilis.*

I cannot say for certain from whence this mystery came – only that a spirit rapping spawned a mystery beyond my grasp. There I sat on the bed, the victim of a raging misopedist, while Daddy, a decurion if ever I saw one, led his brigade of ten with a sleight of mental hands. Indefeasible, dog-faced offender chewing on a patella, he took this bed for a place to bury my bones.

How easily life can turn one into a noddy. Complications arise without a moment's notice, without a clue. Nocturnal, this one time journey signified a nightpiece, and a bed without a pillow, a soft conscious sleep without a blanket. *rap. rap. rap.* Mother was nine-sighted and without a clue herself, the muses running over her head in emissions of song and thought. Worthless lullaby not worth a theotokion of a cent.

Nicodemus had a penis not quite so big as mine.

He came upon the one awake, but still could find no sign.

Pity, on a darkened stage (naughty . . . naughty pack who dine),

That they should hide from Nicodemus, his every other line.

*   *   *

Yesterday . . . sometime after noon, during the Three Hours on a Friday that felt more like nine . . . I was busy in devotion in the true biblical sense of the word. (Confidentially, 'yesterday' is, in reality, a *feel* of time, a *dimension*, and not a true and definitive definition.) And it was here, in this three/nine hour space that I called out to all the living things beset in my mind – things such as seeds, grass, fruit, trees, fishes, fowl, cattle, dogs, life small and molecular, as well as life large and universal, actions as ecumenical as time itself, merdivorous acts, and acts as coprophagous to the continence of a coprophagist as, say, *Crème Yvette* is to the continence of an alcoholic. And it was here as well that I asked god to spin me a web so fine that I might bedevil and catch my *bête noir* in a flash. And it was here that god from his gloriously unlit corner, weighing in at a wet 110 tons, with a muscle circumference of a *good* 131 cubic inches, stood up with gloved hands raised high above his head, pranced in place, and muttered, "Good," six times.

Apparently, god did not hear a single devotional thought of mine, for I had caught him precisely at that indefinitive space of time in which he was thoroughly engaged in the beginning stages of the 'Big Match.' Actually, *Boxing Day.* Irregardless, in the other corner sat his rival . . . a small, formless, sightless, orphan germ . . . a most definitive host of near-contabescence, narrow and stiff as a Salem prayer, akin to Mrs. Grundies on a Sunday.

(This heavy weight above me penetrates me like a silver eel, and I want to brawl. "Quiet, silver beater!" the weight uproars contemptuously in my ear, ding dinging. "I raised a clamor! Open wide! Let the silver fall into the box.")

Meanwhile, god is swinging away at empty artificial air, left and right, swinging like a woolye worm on a silver chain, swinging away in a wild dance of sciamachy, hollering, "My kingdom for a louma!" And the neutral crowd is roaring laughter at the germ, yawning capriciously on the tip of god's foot.

"Let it stand!" they howl.

(I roll over on my side and this weight parts me, a red sea; he doesn't care. It doesn't matter. This specific period in time-expired. "This way," the weight moans, "we save a second accident.")

(Green pastures, Ashfield, Walter Pidgin and that wonderful, monotonous, old German voice vomits a real Bêche, spews down the center of the western hills of Ireland like lava. Walt can't seem to stay in place. His image needs adjusting. Channel 7 has such poor warrior reception. And Darby is downright plastered on Bonny Clabber, while Joan looks merrily on.)

(The pain I bear is bearable. The elastic, a tough outer tissue of my orifice, is unbelievably resilient. I am less a woman than a goddess. I am Oestrus GadWrap, the layer of mucus membrane corresponding to the rat-a-tat-tat of gunfire in my head.)

I can't help but laugh. Egad! swinging like Popeye on valium, and I can't think of a better way for god to get a hernia; his trunks are made from cobra skins dipped in bubble gum dye, ballooning like a kid's cheeks; his ribs stand out like individual River Niles filed all down along his torso. The strain at swinging at nothing has somehow rendered his skin a coriaceous texture, and it appears as though his very entrails are all exposed and ready for a wee bit of divination that's got 'em all shoutin', "Swing your swingers!"

"Don't think this too odd," a stumbling angel says (his casting totally out of place. For the scene cried out for a *British* variation of *damn* and *man,* namely *Dem-on,* and a hideously unbecoming one at that, and not for a Yoidore Tenshi). "I'm required to pop out and in at any given moment of time. Even in his sleep. That is my roll, you see. What I am, therefore, I cannot change. Nor would I, even if I could, by Jackroll, and a couple of plugs to jelly, death, dogs and Red Hot . . . Scroll, lines . . . Stand still!"

"Do you think it odd?" I ask. "That is, did I spend too much viable time outside, pondering the universe, its seven origins, and all the energies thereof?"

And in true r-r-r-r-r evolutionary fashion, the angel (I believe the keeper of the gate in a tan french kid, the poleangel from somewhere beyond the north, where Arcturus takes his frescade and bears bright his M7 in an old Charlie tune, *'Wagon's Ho! Ward, bond this deal to the end of the golden earth'*) responds, "No, as long as you complement it with a plea."

O Daddy is driven. O when one uncorks his head – the fiz of his soul, the loose jive of his silver cord, the mumble pieces of his golden bowl – it reminds me that life is a scheduled affair with a French 75 and that contradiction jests over the days, while a half-serious sodomite in court laughs at the proceedings. *"Jus' sits me down at de ol' piano . . ."*

And say, aren't those pink pansies surrounding Papa?

JEREMIADS IN THE WILDERNESS

I'm bleeding! My fingers dip into the well of my unguarded contest. Don't judge me a triviality, Mother. When I rivaled your choice in this matter of life, when I chose to stand upon the feet, upon the toes, upon the bedrock of the tribute of the hot act of this mighty adult giant of a man, to defend, to defend!, I was in the midst of *Mensuration via Menstruus Orbis.* Biology, astronomy, geometry. Such music to my ears, drowning in information, imbolized by the mass of facts consumed in the Directory.

Actually, although I hate to admit it, I stumbled a midnight ago while my fingers were walking in the Directory. Upon extreme deliberation, utilizing a host of both real and imaginary counsel, I concluded (with proper apparatus, Belial in hand, both angular and severe) to forthrightly make my way forward, minding to respect the law of definite proportions, directly, without a moment's hesitation as to whether the composition of my intent to create order varied with the manner of my actions, or to a proper adieu to the five powered directoire, or to all that is cowardly and dastardly droll outside the revolution. Into the sleeping quarters of my diabolus and isolated ol' Horny, I went. And god willing, remembering Proust's law of the past *(do-do unto others, as you would have them do-do unto you)*, I sat.

His momumental Polyphemus moth form was deep in slumber beneath a heap of blankets, ample enough to keep an army of 11,000 happily content at Valley Forge. Which is not to suggest that his skin alone could not serve as proper attire for any ol' polytheistic party hosted by Ahriman himself, with a list of grave new party guests typed on the muratorian fragment. But I am getting quite off the topic, the topic being that I had stumbled a midnight ago into an overall increasing sense of perturbations, leading to an unstable, nonperiodic, celestial commotion, mechanical or otherwise. For it was when I directly approached my angel of the bottomless pit – my 'bub bog near the rocks,' my Egyptian delight in print upon the rosetta stone, rebapted *apocatastasis* – with proper utensil in hand, and delicately planted my palm upon his amply blanketed hip, and whispered, "Thy messenger of the sickle hath arrived, thy origenian postman, thy long-suffering pidyon haben, not a Cohen nor a Levite, nor a Bonaparte, but more a ghostly, nowhere, Massthing friend in the form of a proximate sign, a signifying element, a gravitational redemption," and directed the opened tip of my Straight and Narrow down upon the blessed crown like an unbeknownst M. Boussard, that I suddenly realized I was about to do dear old Mommy in! What she was doing in this forgiving bedtime story beneath a hap-harlot of a spread will remain a mystery; but, nonetheless, it was on that very night that she had temporarily moved me to spare his life to the letter, without benefit of robes, relics, candles, bells, chants, or spots. But yea on love feasts being beyond creative.

How does one muster up the nerve to commit the most imperfected crime of all (a crime not quite enforceable by law; a crime rhetorical at best; a crime like the slicing of an eye by a straight razor; a crime in which ancient critics gathered in ancient cities could spin their opinions forth like so many ankle gyroscopes, like so many keys, like so many Latrodectus mactans playing at a game of diabolo, like so many wannabes at a sad orgy, like so many wolves saying the same thing in three different languages, like so many arachnes weaving errors in the hieroglyphic, the demotic, and the Greek – a regular bouleversement, sucking toes, handling jobbery with ease, offering considerable opposition to the task-at-large) – without offending the world? A private task whose critics would, naturally, have a lot to talk about in the New World, in a language fit for a circle of Rosicrucians on dewcross. Specifically, their opinions regarding the distance from the line of action of the force to the axis of rotation, with the resulting images being curved, via three synchronised projectors, onto a continuous theme. It would still be wise to cover my tracks, as well as my peripheral vision, so as to give a greater illusion of actually participating in the desired events. For one can never be certain as to the outcome that could occur from the point at which the crime took place to the point at which the perpetrator is pronounced innocent. Does it alarm me when I envision the enemy taking a moulage at the scene of a crime? Does it alarm me that they could use it in some uranist fashion as to render me a guilty lanarkian with a hollow spine, and thus cut short my steps in life? I think so. For one can never be too cautious in circumstances such as these, where one false move could trigger a series of events that could lead to perpetual doom. That is why, being there in this frozen moment of time, I fathom the Baron von Steuben efficiently drilling in a Mon Mouth and pulling out a wet Molly . . . or rather a Mary deed in water. In short, one musters up the nerve by boldly going in without a fear of sin, like a perquisition.

Even now, as the summer breeze carries in through the open back door, a provocative, perrectal coolness as if from a foreign realm, I think back upon all the bodies and all the crimes that Daddy personally christened, leaving gasping widows to mourn like windows in fog, to mourn like maculated maids with bright red marks.

If there was room enough to fantasize, if there was time enough to burke my dear demented one in exchange for thirty pieces, then I would at the same time burrow a place in the earth for shelter, and bring forth all the game, the mactation, the recreant victims of Daddy's-gone-a-hunting, and take a crazy shot, and conceal them from the honey pernis, conceal them from caladbolg, conceal them common rabbits in a common room of surety in which I am the head surety. But time is supra-molecular and not the elementary organization of life as rendered by man. It's a pity, really, for it would be much easier, much simpler to believe in the mundane fantasy, to believe that action can be measured, that existence can sit at the center of a table, a finite thing pernoctating even to the end of day. O, if it could only be so simplistic as a slice of Kepler's pie, as universal as three imaginary lines resting on the virtue that revolution is meant for each body in space in order to move. However, to strangle, to tie one's life up in knots (upon knots) is more the reality, the hard belly, the explicit reply, the gross earnings of life . . . nay . . . internity, consuming everything.

Somewhere along this long, endless passage of bedizened thought arises a resurrection, like a joint return. From deep within the burrow, the sepulchre of desire, the sureseater which houses foreign art among some empty seats, are bodies bent on the light of retribution.

I can hear the bodies sleeping in their chill-down at the end of wayward way, the empty shells lingering among the stagnant impressions of what was once fiery child thought and action. Even though I cannot see beyond the nearest dwelling, I can sense the lupanar crowd emerging from its stepping-off place, and I can hear Daddy being ridiculously stalked with grand illusion, although the wiggling bodies pursuing him are common, and the earth is reluctant to spew forth the bones that once supported the grand, opulent dramas of life. Rewake the revolting sunrise, the beginning of the last day as it resounds with an absorption that only thirsty souls who refuse to die could ever appreciate. Now it feels so typical, like thin waves . . . thin red waves rushing in, rushing back, creating their own sense of pursuit and pursued. The deeper they are buried – aunts, uncles, cousins, sisters, brothers, daughters and sons – the finer the resonance of their impassioned patterns of speech. I can see the bodies supine and adorned in whispers of what was once their Sunday best. Silent night, hold the unnumbered seeds while I sleep a temporary sleep before the day resurfaces, and I cast a shadow darkly.

I can hardly get out of bed. This weight that disengages me from wakefulness, this incubus that has found a place of habitation along the sleeping contours of my ophidian body has dampened me with such an incredulous feeling that I can barely indulge myself in anything sacred to life, least of all my very own consciousness. But I shall not be undone. I will speak a thousand lifetimes, if need be, dipping my tongue in acid for effect. And what to do with this cake on my chest?

How should I measure the circumference of his spell? As a child I was forced to follow on his heels around corners transfixed in fog – the memory transitory, passing through with only a brief stay. Children, little one, nabbed by claws, reputed to silence. Innocent breath.

Electric. The fiery fancy in the sky. I could even feel it in my feet – the vibrations of the blood resin pounding just ten feet away from where I stood. I don't think those children were ever seen or heard of again. Perhaps, I'm wrong. Perhaps, those children merely dwined under the primitive papers of the garden. I wasn't accustomed to reading papers during that time of life. But, just for the record, I could tell you that I did see their rotting bodies afterward, absolutely serene and untroubled. I almost envied them, their unkept peace. Daddy, oh, lord of creation, he could do nothing but gawk at their lifeless forms after he had sedated them with a serum, all-enclosing. At the time it never occurred to me why I should be there; however, in retrospect, I am simply left dumfounded. My being there seemed to serve no practical purpose. It would seem that my chance presence at that particular time would have only engendered him during his preoccupation. Except, perhaps, my presence was meant to premonish him should any outstanding chief or patriot suddenly happen upon the scene. Needless to say, I was given no formal instructions in either case. And although no aforementioned possibilities ever surfaced, I was, nonetheless, left to stand all alone, and bear witness to a penetration executed quickly and forceably, alongside whimpers, oftentimes bloodcurdling screams that were instantly quieted once Daddy had collapsed in a heap. And a strong breeze blew dead leaves everywhere.

Madrigal. Slippage. Deviation. Throw me a Mae West and just maybe I'll stay afloat, night after night. Some demons would have me drown, plop my little fanny on a liberally waxed slidearoo, and send me court straight down to perdition as though I'm no angel. I'm sure there's a host of little ronyons that would just love to make merry (god help me, Mother) with my perineum (which isn't to say I wouldn't let them and have a field day at the same time, as though everyday's a holiday). But I'm not here to nursearoo the perverted, nor nuzzle my nose into the hairs of some enthusiastic, jocose poltroon, still high from some past-moonlit nuptial flight.

One time Daddy went raving omnicidal. I'd come home from school. Mother was away visiting her flippant sister Mary jane doing MDMA. And Daddy was simply storming through the house, throwing loose papers in the air from a penny dreadful long out of print, swearing and babbling like a banshee, making astroblemes left and right. I tried to escape his sight but it was too late. Daddy had more eyes than an eye chart. He caught me hiding under the foyer table admist a field of microdots, grabbed me by the wrist, twisted, and yanked me out, causing such an eruption I thought my blood would burst.

"Eschatology!" he shouted. And then he said that word over and over again, each time heightening the pitch of his voice as if engaged in a plygain. "Don't you know what that means? There's something they don't teach you in school! Do you want I should get my butcher's knife, cut you clean down the middle, yank out what makes you tick, what makes you cockcrow, and stuff it all back down your severed throat?"

Daddy gripped my arm and shook me. "Is this what you want as your last judgment?" he said, again and again and again.

I suspect when this is all over – when I become a substitute for blood and the quality of my blond speech is but a sound unperformed, when I am no longer dangerous to man and domestic animals alike, when I am inflated with gasconadeous air and my presence is like a vanilla scent – I will be received into Valhalla, my poor denuded soul a valuable piece of history. Slain, but not dead. Living, transcending the thatch and all flesh matters of small significance in order that I might meet the theist of my own undoing. Actually, it's more than I could ever hope for – transcending my own opprobrious purpose in view of the existence of evil. Maids will clean up my room, angels will wash my feet, and a melody so often played as a reminder of grace will render me the thaumaturgist of my own resurrection. And all the angels will visit me during business hours, behind a sea of glass, stuffed to the brim with éclaircissement.

I thought of the perfect place to bury Dad. Somewhere within the sublunary plane. It's quite beneath the heavens' folds and well atop the earth's pole. This space doesn't get noticed much, like the subclavian part of an artery, but it's always there in the lune. Where would our bodies be without it, after all? So much of breath we take for granted, especially in our effort to seek refuge from a hostile environment.

Daddy complained. Putting it delicately, he awoke – along with every rooster this side of the meridian – in a lupanar. His jaw could have been impounded by the smell of his breath alone – a mixture of cloaca maxima and diborane. Dried blood, brown and crusty, smudged the underside of his fingernails from having scratched, in vain, his cloacal membrane. He must have been scratching someone's back or, perhaps, some sagital plane of some other body, for not all the blood matched his type. My instructions as a foot page were to bring home the bacon and bathe him with attention, and to take account of all the raw materials of his brain, and to put the scales into some semblance of order, starting with the backward blessing and proceeding thrice as such: 'Time's past,' 'time was,' 'time is,' all with a brazen head and an attention to atoms' broken details.

Dad typically thought of himself along patristic lines. In his defense, patina was what gave his outward appearance an etheric, seaish glow, like a dunker after the trine immersion. One could easily visualize the lungis, with his pinched nostrils and his hands clasping at thin air, standing before a congregation of green devout players, holding his black book, highlighted with divinity circuit binding like a hardy excuse for a clasper, and rendering his audience to take to their knees and to bend just a bit in order to protect the edges of their leaves. His salutations, toasts, and other assorted indulgences of social conventionality were but drops of water in the bucket, and more a bit of foostering than anything else. But just as a drop can make an annoying disturbance, so could his polite and seemingly pious efforts to interconnect to fellow human beings. On a purely ecclesiastical level, his endeavors were nothing more than simple placebos. A song played at dusk for the dead, including Theda Bara, and featuring a succession of plagal church modes graced with a pralltriller and a scrambled American figure meant to hypnotize the living on the fourth scale step. I could barely hold my own regarding the manner in which Daddy extended such civilities – a citizen Cain unbalanced, topheavy, in a fool's paradise of delusions, if ever I saw one. But tell that to the world? After all, I was in cahoots with the fellow Longinus on a level all my very own. The two of us composing a type of caduceus, intertwined in battle and in love, till death do us part. That's what made it so damn difficult. Treading ever so capriciously down a catwalk like Pyewacket, where one misstep could send us both hurdling to the sea.

Daddy in a nave, pierced with windows reflecting images of nefandous saints in stone – misproportioned *chevaux-de-frise*, spikes on parade, gilt heads on the hook, cuneiform-pierced christophany on record – that is how I will forever remember him should his physical presence ever eclipse my second sight. But what of the block in the center – the block from which all speech radiates? From what interior could this patrix cast a die in which to form a matrix? O Mother, I wanted so much to succeed. Be truly successful at something, not merely succeed a culex. Perhaps even wake up a patron saint from a deep, deep slumber, say, St. Vitus for laughs, St. Anthony for diggers, or St. Clare for television. Even have me own nimbus to keep me instinctive head wet, or have me pinching St. Dunstan's nose, or fitting him snug for shoes.

However, my second nature dreams were casting me a bit of annoyance. Insofar as I am well aware of the manner in which the soul departs from the body during various stages of sleep and wanders about in *deus au naturel* stages beyond the tangible world-in-seethe, it was somewhat disturbing to find in such a domain a creature of contumelious flout, who said something to me that I hoped was nothing more than an obiterdictum. *"Virdis virago,* playing your virginal via plactus will shorten your breath." When I first heard the creature utter it, I was taken aback, for I had neglected to put on caution-cruise, along with the other scattered remnants of my zoophilous brain, and was merely responding to the moment-at-hand. Be that as it may, I was surprised at how rapidly nature could take a course of events and cross it to such an extent that I was suddenly compelled to defend myself in a supranatural court of law. There I was, an extended appendix of the soul, a hippocampus of the brain, if you will, a pup of zoopsia, utterly defenseless, hobbling through Fortunate Isles on all fours, minding me own business, not bothering a fleck on a fly's brow, knowing, in fact, that horsing around only brings about the smell of pernicious fish, when I was instantly compelled to defend my honor due to the bold and characteristically rude remarks of a giant celestial hedgehogshrew – in effect, a southwind notiosorex, reciting in soubrette frivolity. What the creature said in a warmed-over exhalation of air as stale as a benediction in a bination spoken with a stutterer's insistence, was "Unbles . . . sed is he who walks tri . . . ske . . . lion in fash . . . ion, and sings for me . . . eat, a chant . . . ey."

No worry. None. I employed caution and formulated a plan contrary to the acknowledged standard. To start things off, I took the liberty of sleeping under Daddy's liquid bed at night, like a cowshark of the seven *notorynchus,* where I listened to the wind wiggling in and out of the knothole in Daddy's side from where a limb had been removed. And golden apples falling everywhere will be there.

HOW A NEW FIELD IS POPULATED
The Importance of Being Twilight and Daybreak
or
THE AIRWAVES PICK UP MIXED MESSAGES

Cut! Jump Live! to Dr. Caboose of the Universal Metempsychosis School of Monad Life, who will be speaking from the pulpit on the marred text *G Day: Servants, Temples, Time and Vehicles.*

DR. CABOOSE: "Thank you. Thank you. First of all, turn to the person next to you and say *howdy, glad to know you* and give 'em a big cold raw hug. Gentlemen, a handshake. It's good to love your neighbor! I said . . . it's good . . . to love your neighbor! Jesus. When he came down after having his period on the cross and his opened wounds were speaking blood! blood! blood!, he said . . . 'Hallelujah! Look at me! I'm alive! Behold my hands and my feet! Handle me and see!' Hallelujah! Go on neighbors! Give each other one more hug and shout Hallelujah! Hallelujah! Hallelujah!

"Friends, what I want to talk to you about is twilight and daybreak. When we say daybreak, we not only mean the beginning of a new day, when it begins to grow light, but the force, the entity, the roundness that would otherwise shatter a day and separate it with a suddenness of violence, if it only had the chance. Actually, disrupting the order of a perfectly normal day in order to end it, to destroy it, so that one is left crushed by grief and anguish! But, friends, daybreak also shares an altogether different purport. It can just as easily mean that in the course of a cabalistic day, one is able to discover the essentials of a specific code and apply it toward a solution to the puzzle.

"But let's not stop there. Daybreak can also mean an Escape from darkness. We spend our whole lives attempting to Escape from one thing or another. Don't think not to follow my thoughts, good people. I'm talking about the husband Escaping from the wife, the wife Escaping from the husband, the man Escaping from his business and all the responsibilities thereof – the woman Escaping from her role as a homemaker, attempting to Escape by flaunting her undesirables. The same women who spend every minute of their waking hours defying the basic fact that their place is in the home, taking care of their husbands, their children, their parents, on the very hands and knees that god in his gray-shush love gave them for that specific purpose alone. Some of you women out there today know what I'm talking about. O don't look down in shame. Don't try to hide and conceal your guilt. You know who you are. And you husbands *de habile déguisement!* You lubbers of Vidocquity! It absolutely confounds me how you let them get away with it! The reason there is so much crime today, the *only* reason god has lost his grip is because women have failed in their role as supporters of men. Look at Eve, people. Look at what she did to poor Adam, a man who walked the earth hip first and had a covenant. A neologistic covenant, dear worshippers, with god himself! O it wasn't good enough that Eve should be invited into existence and, by golly, given permission to breathe, to walk, and, yes, if necessary, to talk! Can you imagine this women Eve, as in evening, darkness, blackness . . . for which god saw fit to nickname her *Mare Frigoris* . . . consciously going against her sole mission to be a rib to Adam. The moment that she was out of Adam's sight, she thought she was the dandiest flower in the garden. And as soon as that old ularburong came sliding by, wiggling his slimy old belly along the earth, I, daresay, Eve had passion for him! *Mare Humorum!* She desired him and indeed even slept with him!! Pure atractaspis!! Vile, old, black-rooted Eve. Napoo! Napoo! *Mare Crisium!* And does every woman carry 'Eve-disease?' You better believe it! Except for a few specials ones: Ruth, Mary, and my dear beloved, duty bound gowned wife Rosaline Ann May. But the rest of you are severely corrupt!! Eversion-eviration! We are certainly living in proliferating parallel universes. god help our women! Don't take it upon yourselves, dear male brethren. Don't blame yourselves for a woman's brassiness. For her brazen accentuation! The lot of them are acephalostomuses. Wasn't it Adam who said to Eve, 'My god! What are you doing? Use a head!' And then the moment Adam's and god's backs were turned, Eve eats forbidden fruits?! Daybreaker Eve! the beginning of the evening of despair that was to fall upon all men by way of an evil woman!! Husbands, fathers, brothers! Don't spare the rod! Teach your women by it and do not fail, even as the battle dust of Armageddon continues to fall and to drift to a blitzen's purpose, and our dear blessed father is in hasty retreat.

"There is only one sure way to handle this dilemma. Notice the word *daybreak*. Now it doesn't take a genius to know that a break also implies to undergo a sudden marked decrease in price or value. To curve. To drop or rise sharply. Yes, I am equipped to tell you today, as we endeavor to break this code, this riddle, this mystery of the universe – yes, indeed, I am equipped to inform you today that far less intelligent members have drifted away with the fluctisonous text, allowing the swelling words to break them, sinfully, rather than to give into their hard truths. O hallelujah! Hard speeches make great copy of late!

"Therefore, my friends, I want to talk to you about the SINdicate. Yes, you all have sinned. And if you're planning on getting cleansed, then you must realize that the only way to do it is by either mark-up or mark-down. Assume that you are all born in sin and come into this world with the same number: six hundred and sixty-six. In life you need to be either marked-up or marked-down, just as long as you move away from that dreadful number: 666. Those who get to a thousand . . . including 999 . . . win sainthood hands down. The investment spirit, who is the one responsible for *under-writing* your issues by buying all your energy for resale to the next soul in line, has the option of spreading the risk factor inherent in your issues to other unwary souls. So, in fact, you may not be dealing with merely your own life issues but, say, for instance, with Jud S. Scary Aught as well. Unfortunately, at any given moment in time, some of you may be dealing with as many as a dozen or so other issues from a dozen or so other individual's lives. That's exactly why some of you have it so easy, while others of you can barely get by.

"There is only one efficient-solution to this most dreadful of dilemmas. You must turn aside and seek the services of an organization of *under-writers* known as *the SINdicate*. For a price they will contact certain 'specialized' entities in the net, who will force another less-than-fortunate soul to assume your *Sündig* karma, thus leaving you scoff-free.

"Think of it! If you're just plain butt ugh-ugly and wish to exchange your butt ugh-ugliness in for beauty or an aura of self-effacing benignity, without sacrificing glamourisity, you can pay the Sindicate to *'remove'* your butt ugh-ugliness and plaster it on to the punim of another poor soul, while you get re-karmatized into a beautiful, carefree creature.

"Now you must have heard how these *under-writers* are all members of the Underworld. O but don't you believe it! my dear wholly flock of friends. Yes, the SINdicate is a loose association of *racksouls* in control of organized religion, trying to make sense of past and present, as any past should count as *ours* in the present world, where the sole aim is not to torture souls in the seat during long-stretched-out sermons but to provide services through the Sincurities and Exchange Commission, which not only has the total number of hairs on your head on file, but also lists the essential facts of your spiritual condition and physical operations in a weekly periodical entitled *Fashion Earth's Mass*. And let's face it, you are all products and commodities of earth's mess. *Be aware!* because if the SINdicate cannot find a buyer for your particular karma or wares within six months, six days, and six hours, you will be forced to buy back your karma sixfold; that is $666.00 per month. Now . . . are there any questions?"

A lone hand went up in the back. "Yes . . . Dr. Caboose. I'm a member of ROTC. Reincarnated OMS Trinity Consciousness. Do I get any time off from my karma for being such a member?"

Dr. Caboose looked down at the ground and sighed heavily. "Son," he said, "as long as you continue to read from *their* bible, *The Book of Carnations: Hum, the HoLey Trinity,* there can be no Absolutely Obsolete Concionator. AOC. For holey knowledge and carnal knowledge are simply antipodal and do not mix and cannot achieve concinnity, even if you add a little Hymning, Hymen and Humming to it! Listen to me, barguests. This is a most dangerous, carnalistic, dog eat dog realm we reside in. Why, at this very moment, there are bands of petty thieves who call themselves Karnal Karma Krabbers . . . KKK's . . . who will drag your feet right off the pavement and rob you religiously of any positive karma you're holding at the time!"

There was a disturbance of both shocked and disturbed mumblings and murmurings throughout the audience.

"Dr. Caboose, with groups like the KKK, is there any way that atheous bodies like us can protect their positive karma? Like, is there any place we can store it for safe keeping?"

Dr. Caboose cleared his throat. The seriousness of a good portion of the universe was reflected in his expression. "Keepes Creepers. It all ends up antiphonetic, cold and void of cerebral arcuation. Why, ever since the Fall, wherein god and his legions were forced to flee, but managed to scream with Arctic Hysteria over their shoulders at the arch-villains, 'We'll be back!,' our universe has entered into what scientists call a *nasal zone.* And still worse, a backlash nasal zone. I'm not sure that I entirely agree with that conclusion, although admittedly we have entered into what appears to be a clogged passage of time. But, cloggers, to me if feels more like a *sinus* zone. For carefully notice the first three letters in the zone *Sin.* And then pay heed to the remaining two – *us.* Hear the words, my dear sinians, go-Cains all. *Sin us.* *We* are the sinners guilty of outrecuidance! Now put it together with the hidden definition in mind. *Sinus.* We are in a *Sin-Us Zone,* let alone a sinus zone!"

Another wave of disturbed mumblings rolled across the audience, wagging their heads in turn.

"Who can we trust in such a time as this?" Dr. Caboose continued. "You, yourselves, know how little precious positive karma there is and how any Peter, Paul or John gazing through a lens at *Yes!* would be willing to cut it off at the ear or the mound if the opportunity should ever arrive. Despair not. For I, Dr. Caboose, hold a precious key. Hallelujah! Turn around and wail a chorus of hallelujahs! I have set up a system executed in my Third Millennium Kit, where you can deposit your positive karma with me, where I will keep it in the House with a Scrambled Code! This house I devoutly call Institutional House Sub-Arrest, IHS, as you have no doubt read about in my best-selling book, *The Bridges of the Karmatine County Prophecy.*

"Notice, in regards to the word *'Institutional,'* the first three letters: *I-N-S-.* I have taken the word *sin,* eggers, and scrambled it up. No potential Karma Krapper would think of looking there or of inciting a nest of eggs where scorpions rest. And the rest of the word – t-i-t-u-t-i-o-n-a-l – makes no sense unless . . ." Dr. Caboose smiled knowingly, "you take it apart. *Tit,* which is a teat on a small inferior horse or a small, plump, often long-tailed bird; *ut,* which is the syllable sung to this note in a medieval hymn to St. John the Baptist; *io,* who was a maiden loved by Zeus and changed by jealous Hera into a heifer; add an *n* to the *io* in order to make it *ion,* and you have a group of atoms that carries a positive or negative electrical charge as a result of having lost or gained one or more electrons; and *al,* which is just another way of saying *AD, After Dissension;* or *al* in slang terms is the shoe width waxen old, where John can stoop and unloose on holy ground. So all together: sin disguised as the tit on a lower animal, which is often sung about when referring to a saint who comes from the world of a great god, made up of both positive and negative energies, of a god who ascended head-first after a great *outré* quarrel, until the last you saw of him was his muddy shoe. And remember: if the shoe fits, wear it. Now, I ask you, homicides, who would think of looking for positive karma in such an unhousel house as that?"

There was a loud burst of applause from the audience. After the salutations and wine-spilling subsided, a lone noman voice asked, "With all due respect, Dr. Caboose, what guarantee do we have should we decide to hold our positive karma in your institutional house?"

Dr. Caboose looked down and smiled as though he had heard this question a hundred times before throughout his sermonary. *"Petitio principii,"* he mused. "You know, friend, this reminds me of the old story of the marred soul that arrived at the locked gates of heaven. Now he was all set to go in, he had his fresh new pass and all, but he chose instead to look up at old Peter and ask, 'Once I step in, what guarantee do I have should I ever wish to get out?'" There was a loud burst of laughter from the audience. "Come on! Wake up! See, once you've given your positive karma to me, you won't want it back! I'll take care of it forever for you as your collector. That's your guarantee! Look, we're talking about plain and simple Panic Reversal, a basic principle of Technical Analysis. Wake up flounders! We're talking about the relevant factors that can directly influence not only the future course of corporate Lev earnings, sole prices, revs and tolls, but the very future of the direct pulse of the universe as it relates to future soul price movements. Look, if *everybody* could buy at the bottom and sell at the top, the bottom would become the top and the top would become the bottom. Think of it! Hell would be heaven and heaven hell. Demons would be angels and angels demons. Panic Reversal! Wound-of-Christ Reversal! And everybody jump up, turn around, exclaim the mark, and pick a heil of hallelujahs!"

"If I'm hearing It correctly," a lone voice asked, "are you saying, Dr. Caboose, that it would be wise for us to invest in devils and demons?"

"If you want to turn the whole Universal Concept around. And with positive karma at a premium and negative karma in such abundance, you'll all be filthy rich! Makes sense, doesn't it?"

"But what if god should return?" a lone voice asked in darkness. "What *then*?"

"Simple," Dr. Caboose said. "Should god come back cloudy, *then* you all can take a deep market breath and gather at the Column near the Soul Stock Tablets, which will show the varying numbers of advanced or declined commodities from 666, and for a very low investment of, say, three soul dividends, you can quickly acquire a declared date of do-evil-that-good-may-come record, wherein you will be granted a 'safe' number in the light eyes of god at the end. And that's a Guarantee! Go on! Hug your neighbor! Shout Hallelujah several hundred times!"

The audience (the congregation) was obviously delighted with Dr. Caboose's sermon. He preached. He sold sound advice. And he saved souls. What a profit! In life Dr. Caboose was a soul broker and one of the best! Full service guarantee! His church, St. Marketup, was even fully equipped with a "Quotron" machine, available for souls who want the *best* available up-to-the-minute numbers smacked right into their foreheads. And most everyone was flocking to him. Yes, this was an excellent time for Dr. Caboose to fully utilize his role as Pro Soul Advisor (PSA) and provide flexibility for himself and some serious in-vestry – especially in records, vessels and garments.

FLASH

Mr. B. Little, a false-finance graduate of the Furnace Institute of Finalization SoulStock Evacuation, a subsidiary of the FireBelt Federation, Lower Division, Inc., discovered a gap during his analysis of 'Support and Resistance Patterns in Chartagod Stock.' Prices plummeted dramatically on the day after Armageddon. Just hours before the Battle, holdings in *godshame* were undeniably guaranteed. Portfolio consultant, P.E. E. wept much, and the renowned Rev. Alation found that yields on Certificates of Belief were at an all-time high. As extraneous circumstances prevailed and *godshame* lost its footing, panic resulted in a reversal-pattern. Within twenty-four hours after the Battle, *godshame* was divided and the 'gap' fell through the *Alteration Network Reformation Plan,* and the letter *g* automatically reformed into the letter *d*, and the letter *d* automatically reformed into the letter *w*. So, in essence, god reformed into *dow* and the *god theory* (after Armageddon) reformed into the *dow theory.* And the dow theory was now the model for forecasting the future, utilizing as *its* guide *The New Testament Industrial Alpha and Omega Market Movements,* which is sub-analytically analogous to movements of the sea, whereby key-fraction-clue-remedies are detectable in any one of three movements occurring simultaneously within any given volatile setting on any given relative quadrum-mechanical-frequency fluctuation (whether hourly or daily), during any breakage of bread upon the waters, where the possibility of expecting a *Return* is chancey at best. Secondary or intermediate movements of two or three weeks to a month *and* primary trends of several months to infinity that Mr. B. Little had brilliantly detected in *Kaleidoscopic Portfolio: Rev's Up* stood in as alternative ways for predicting the future.

What originally brought Mr. B. Little so feverishly into the picture was the ecclesiastical analysis of highly volatile in-grown stocks. The *Oversold Condition* was now a clear catastrophe, since there were so many souls who bought their way into heaven with nowhere to go. Out in the field, there was a theory floating halebopp around that even though god had made a hasty retreat, his whereabouts could still be traced – which explained why a search party, a posse, a demolition team, twelve hired assassins, the IRSA (Internal Reversal Spiritual Agents) and the Magnificent Seven were hot on his trail. Yet another theory offered the possibility that heaven could be located by calculating its Beta coefficient under the hidden file *By Coxbones* and its Measure-Location by averaging the percentage change of investitive souls before and after the Battle by adding two zeros (00) to a far thing and dividing that by the margin number of souls left standing in the Baltic heat with worthless shares of Cockstock.

Even now P.E. E and Rev. Alation were conferring with the reserved Mr. Little (himself a meditationist, as that term applies to the taciturnity of one from which a prophet can be extracted) on, unprecedentedly, placing high-beta stocks into a less than promising market, hoping to take advantage of an entirely new trend, *Prediction Panic Reversal,* and thus avoid being whippedsawed by excessive long-termed Benevolent Activity, manifesting as an obex in the search for god's whereabouts. If heaven could be located (with or without god's flash of wit), a New Curb could thereby be established, and a new specialist's book could be maintained, containing special types of orders for each assigned, plot-utilizing affair transacted in the streets.

THE MISSING M

Mr. Little was going over the old specialist's book containing the many sharp references to the past, such as "Away from the market."

He was surprised to see just how many Bear market strategies lingered in the book, ready to sabotage any major and substantial trend with maneuvers that, if implemented correctly, would result in a devastating and dramatic Decline and Disaster Ministry to what would have otherwise been a long-term, if not eternal, Loving Ministry.

In particular, Mr. Little was annoyed by the 'don't touch' clause in the book of *G*, which he felt left a gap in The Bear Market of Profitable Possibilities. Thereby, Mr. Little was intending on closing the 'gap' by writing a 'naked call option.'

FALL IN THE WILDERNESS

"*Now* is the time to call forth a New Naked Call in order to progress the Fashion-Line and whatever shares NNC holds in *tout ensemble*. *Now* is the time to buy 100 shares at a definite price within a specified cockstock region. *Now*, in a loving universe, however chaotic the times, is the time for shared temptation. There is no doubt that the world is but a speck in the universe, and we are but specks upon the speck. However, with the New Naked Call, the caller, the writer, and the fashion designer will be speculators willing to bet the stock. And the shock of future disaster will not be rising within the time limit of the 'contract,' as was the case with the Don't Touch Clause of the Old Naked Call. With the New Naked Call, everyone will experience a future bliss of . . ."

Mr. Little was standing behind the New-Design Podium, addressing an auditorium filled to capacity with regal members of the Computerized National Association of Securities Dealers Automatic Quotation, key holders in the Option Clearing Corporation, controllers in the Advanced Research Projects Agency of New Leaf Concealment Systems, the President of MetroCard T-shirt Fashion Design, the entire membership of Karma Care Less-Body Odor Kashiyama Clothing Company, and the Cyber Station Internet Mankind-for-Free Licensors, when he suddenly fell victim to an Old-Fashioned Naked Call Assassination Plot, and thereupon received two inches of heavy metal in the center of his forehead, and collapsed dead, in mid-sentence, in what was heralded as a Closed-End Short-Stop Order!

But why . . . Mr. Little?

Because Mr. Little *was* actually an "officer" enforcing "Blue Sky Laws," designed to protect investors from worthless securities originating in the Highest Spheres. The assassins were members of god's Holy Text Defense Team, easily identifiable due to their Lacoste Shirts, baring a smiling bear emblem, cutting herring bone, arms extending clockwise, Hollywood waist trousers with dropped belt loops, and trim contemporary drapes displaying assorted profiles of god in zoot wool with a modecca flower in the lapel – everything entirely done in red, even down to the squeaky leather Oxfords.

This particular assassination, performed with a "wasting asset" gun capable of firing Guarantee Hit Bullets, referred to as ICU's, sent such shock waves on the floor that every participant immediately gravitated toward the presiding Bored Broker and surrounded him in a Tight Panic Re-Reversal that caused the Broker to suffocate to death *right* there on the spot. Sometime thereafter, the Re-Birth of the Growth Stock Theory arose into view. Only instead of stock (perhaps due to the two sudden deaths at the time of its rebirth), the theory was now referred to as the "Growth Shock Theory," which roughly stated suggests that stocks, souls, and spirits grow in relation to the increase/decrease of any given shock. Growth Shocks can provide in the long-run excellent protection against the ever-increasing fear of living, especially among the lower income fractions at, say, a compound rate of 15% per year or, in a manner of speaking, fifteen souls D.O.A.

"The Airwaves Pick Up Mixed Messages" Continues
A REVELATION LIVE! BROADCAST IN PROGRESS

". . . I am currently standing outside the White Forum. There is a lot of chaos going around aliunde. A lot of rootless, without connection, insecure kind of eldritch energy. You could almost taste it on your lips if you were standing here today. A quick observation here, Murray. Grown men have been known to cry under less harsh circumstances. I'm sure down at Eyewitness Dilated Information Center they're shedding plenty of tears as they watch, literally, the last two thousand and fifty some years go right down the tubes. This is certainly one for the first resurrection, if not conception."

"Paul, what do you make of the activity around the White Forum?"

"Murray, it's like a second death. More nerve-racking than a kid facing aliyah. The common crowd here is relentlessly damaged. People are realistically stepping on my feet. Some of them are in a pure state of pandiculation. It's so hot and we're so packed-in, your very breath is distrustful of the cokedup feelings, not only within but without . . . and about!"

"Paul. It sounds almost awful. And you have so vividly ill-prepared the state of existence there, you can be sure that we're all moved with your skillful consolidations. Have you been able to get any closer to the Forum steps?"

"Negative, Murray. In this mess *I* couldn't so much as get a dog's portion. Security is tight and flattery is literally getting me nowhere as *Everyone* is expecting to flatter over the Resurrection of the Two Dead Bodies Lying at the Column on the Pavement. Currently, we have a total eclipse taking place in the sky which could last for a duration of seven minutes. However, a bespeckled Pastor sprouting a jam of ripe red bubukles on his face and one tart bubo of syphicious character in his groin, who is posing as a 'spectator' in the crowd, is suggesting that nothing but dead dust in ashes and chalk will be drifting over the globe once the eclipse has ended and the two dead bodies lying at the column have risen. As you know, our President is an avid resurrection lover who goes for a rise whenever he can in private, and knows how best to raise a match when the fire's out. If you get a quick glimpse through the utter commotion over there at the third Column, it appears that six of the President's pet seals are running loose, barking and bilking up a storm, as seals so often do over there. And if I pierce hard enough through the utter commotion, I think I even see three smart asses with staged names, with their palms in their flippers, and some clearly visible fartleberries hanging about, requesting a reading from a character in white I can't quite identify, except to say that his gaying instrument is out, and that he keeps uttering the words, 'My oso tis blue.' Hopefully, some of this hopeless mystery will soon be over and the stranger on the pavement shore will blow his horn and . . . Wait . . . wait a minute, Murray! My god! Wait a minute! This is unbelievable! Murray! You won't believe this but the two bodies are suddenly rising, springing like a pipe in the whistle! I don't believe this, Murray! Honest to god! The crowd . . . the thousands surrounding the Column steps are going absolutely snapping berserk! You're not going to believe this, Murray, but those two bodies who have been lying dead on the pavement for over three days have seemingly come crackling back to life! and are now standing directly on their feet bearing all! By god, they're both up on their feet, waving their palms at the crowd! The crowd is going literally mad! As you know, the two nonmycostatic bodies have been heavily cloaked and guarded in a brown haze and lye should any prowling anti-resurrection men from Limousin attempt to steal . . . Oh, my god!"

"What is it, Paul?"

"Murray. Hold me for a second! It appears now that we're having an earthquake! Oh, my god! Two of the Columns have just collapsed! Oh, my god!"

"What is it, Paul? Are you all right?"

"Murray, you won't believe this! But somebody from somewhere with a booming voice is yelling, 'Come on up!' and the two bodies are literally rising up into the clouds! Oh, my god! I don't know how to report this, Murray! It's, it's like a bad Japanese film . . . but . . . but a red dragon with seven heads and . . . one . . . two . . . three . . . four . . . six . . . eight . . . ten horns is directly above us, eating what looks to be a giant blue baby! And a giant mygalomorphaeian prophet holding four books is breathing heavily over the crowd!"

"Paul! Paul! What in god's name is going on there?"

"You got me, Murray! The dust is beginning to clear, although it's still quite mythy. I can't begin to amass the damages. There's a caked mass of filth and dirt that looks somewhat related to Iowan brunizem, a yellowish mass of bones and teeth deposited by the wind . . . a mass of blood in some pockets around me . . . Wait! Something's happening! Apparently, the impact from the earthquake has caused the earth to open up, which has given rise to . . . a whole lot of frogs! They're literally everywhere, Murray! And . . . and . . . wait a minute! Wait just a minute! A man has suddenly appeared at the entrance of the Column, holding a microphone! He's suggesting that everyone who is still alive go home, confess their sins in private with a vulgar French tongue, fire their pantler if the same is employed and has been known to be both pantophagous and chuck full of papaphobia, and take inventory of all their red relishes, their precious stones and pearls, and their gypsum. And to do it in that precise order, reminding one and all of our liberties that we prize and of our rights as nothingarians that we all maintain. Well, it sounds like a good idea to me, Murray. *Première page nouvelles.* So, I'm going to turn this over now to our man cast in Havana, Ail Greenness in Paris green. Ail . . . ?"

"Thank you, Paul. *Virtus semper viridis.* Sure sounds like a lot of shaking going on in your end. Sorry I couldn't attend. But we have enough problems at this end. Our present condition is without question being agitated by revolutionary disturbances looking for independence. What this means is that we are nothing more, nor nothing less, than a protectorate of god. This puts us all into a very adverse state, one which has left our very souls in a most Augean predicament. To the left of me, you will observe a long cement dwelling structured much like an oxford. Within it god has imprisoned the souls of the Presidents of the United States. They are kept exclusively in this stronghold as a harsh reminder that a President's seed is never as limnetic as god's seed, and that there is far more life in his seed than there is in all the Presidents combined. Come and see. Ladies and gentlemen: It is the souls of all the Presidents after having undergone such a long and arduous voyage through the tides of time, the souls of the Presidents wrapped in the molecules of Odysseus in a postedenian, demitoilet state of attire. To be certain, god keeps the souls of the Presidents in his stronghold much like a cyclops keeps stranded seamen in his yard, consuming them all at his leisure. But just as Odysseus had engaged Cyclops in a stichomythia, so will the Presidents do likewise with god. Yes, even George's soul did pass by the columns of time, thirteen in all, in front of which were thirteen young girls.

"Behemoth Mount Vernon,
What does your daddy grow?
Cannabis sativa
better known as marijuana . . .
Oh!

"Ladies and gentlemen. I, Ail Greenness, even within the context of this *Inteling* report, can feel my own evolution as a reporter, however distant, coming to an end per completion; but not as a wheel is an end in itself, per se, forever ending, forever beginning. My fate renders me but a sepulchral line of beauty, more linear than circular. When I arrived in Havana, the damp dawn came with her reddened cheeks bleeding the sky like massive wounds, each one raining crimson rays on Havana that in my company felt to be like accusing fingers, the terminating members of the hand of rache. Just what is the breadth of one of god's fingers? I can tell you that it would have been easy for me to cower and to fear, buying into the notion that one should not pointedly venture in harm's way. But here I ask you, where would man's odyssey be if he permitted his voyage to be curtailed by fears fought in a bathtub? Ladies and gentlemen, start off first by looking upon any warning, howbeit a foudroyant threat, as nothing more than a filterable virus, a virus so small that a fluid containing it remains virulent after passing through a filter, like a cup of demitasse. Yes, I say, if god, upon reflection, has you locked in the grip of his hand, do not allow your own fear to hold you therein; but rather allow your courage to trickle through in order to separate matter from suspension. For the eye has not seen nor the ear heard, *'arcana caelestia,'* whereby you find your freedom and leave god holding only your dead husk. And then strike back! with deadly courage! and render him lost!

"Perhaps, ladies and gentlemen, that is why we should all take an interest in the stronghold before us. Now, go deep into the center of your consciousness – where the seahorse rides like a kelpie along that curved, elongated ridge extending over the floor of the descending cornucopian horn of each lateral ventricle of your brain, and the barguest howls at all your shenanigans before the drink is downed – and discover that ancient hippodrome wherein the race will become the battle to be one! This is where we acquire our abundant secondary education – on this campus, on this plane, at this camp. We all abode here, temporarily, like tented troops, gunsels moldering. Yes, some of us crippled, others impaired, because we have allowed ourselves to believe in melting love, malty Camelot, gelastic falcons on marked white houses, and Elysium fields dripping with reiteration, without considering the rictus of god – the gaping, twobit orifice, the grin that serves existence's mystery with abysmal ridicule! I can say that I will not abide by his circumcisional ruling for fear of being made a ridgeling, and have my potency compromised and my fate locked in a possible rejoindure. As far as the internal affairs of this odyssey is concerned, whether it be from island to island or stomach to draught, we can no longer allow ourselves to be cut off as a ritual and opposed to self love, which was once deemed to be a detriment to spiritual resolution; nor does this *cutting* suffice as a symbolic offering to a judgmental, though highly risible, god. For if a token of a sacred covenant is ever broken, must this necessarily lead to man's fatal, irreversible falling, laughing to scorn a tidbit? However, ladies and gentlemen, whatever existing pacts we share with him, let there be a cutting. For it only suggests the *cutting* of unconditional damnation!"

"Ail. This is Chip Chaos at our main-command-line-post. You've been going on there for quite some time and we've been receiving calls from a prodigious amount of confused intercon-net subscribers, who don't have the slightest inkling of what you're talking about."

"Chip . . . Chip . . . I was in the middle of a deep thought. You rudely interrupted me! Do you see me interrupting you? What do I care about your prodigious amounts? What difference does it make? This particular report just happens to be *my* life! There isn't much time left, obviously, and now because of you I need to find my proper space OHM*mmmmmmmmmmm* OHM*mmmmmmmmmmm*. As you can see, surrounding the stronghold are some remnants from the Battle of Armageddon. OHM*mmmmmmmmmmm*. Prowling about the place are mountain wolves and lions. Apparently, god didn't have time to take his entire army with him and these poor creatures have been left behind. OHM*mmmmmmmmmmm*. There, that's much better. If you'll notice, ladies and gentlemen, that lion also has six wings about him and appears to be dressed in a lion's sweater of some type, with the words *Juda Hi* inscribed across it. The wolf, too, is donning a sweater and, if I'm not mistaken, one made of sheep's wool, cleansed in lant, from a leading haute couture. It, too, bears an inscription. *Eat at Sheeps.* Surely, ladies and gentlemen, this could only mean that we are witnessing some sort of dominical dementedness. Another point that I'd like to bring out is that earlier, in 1691, as I was walking about the grounds, I came across a woman who called herself Ize. She was wearing a bell around her neck, which with astounding gyrations of her head would ring on occasion, whereupon she followed up the ringing with various recited prophecies from her masticator, most of which addressed the end of gnashing itself; specifically, the precise gnasher who was last seen galloping, striking frantically toward the dreadful showdown. Ize had offered me a Twinkie of Bottitdom and suggested that we should commit fornication, thus raising my original suspicion of her being a demimonde, and finish it off before it was time for me to come on the air. For, apparently, time itself had taken a wrong *short* turn and was hopelessly lost in the utter sclerotic depths of the canyons beyond – dazed and forgetting to mind itself. Ize stated that she was currently in her estrous cycle and thereby socially askew, and that I should take advantage of her before she should lapse into a diestrous state and become a cupcake. I stepped back in order to give her face, for I somehow felt she had greatly insulted me. Obviously, by this gold ring on my finger, it was clear to see that I was a married man, and most happily, I might add. And then she said, 'And the passerdogs wagged their tails. And the prick pierced the cat, and blood-n-water sent him to the vet. And everyone gathered in the wet room, smoking yet.'

"Obviously, these very things of which I speak of are nothing more than stumbling blocks before us, demonically placed here by chance so that we might not get to view the Works of the Presidents. In order to give you a clear understanding of the benefits of not giving into fear, I'm going to demonstrate how I can actually reduce these stumbling blocks by exercising the expression of *my own profile in courage!* Ladies and gentlemen, I'm about to approach the ferocious looking beasts aforementioned, the rock-ribbed, whole hog, staunch, hidebound dogs, the ones wearing the holey sweaters dyed-in-the-wool. I should also mention that I finished putting Ize directly in her place; that is, I threw her down into the linen bed of the earth and planted three bullets in her temple with my Ruddy Vallee R-1716. OHM*mmmmmmmm.*

"Now notice the manner in which I'll subdue both the lion and the wolf, simply by proceeding straightly and directly over to their path. Watch. They will not only refrain from attacking me, but they will rise up on their hind legs and roll over on their backs, wagging their tails as a friendly invitation to caress them behind their ears. You see, ladies and gentlemen, just what is a beast without its Master? Why, a beast in need of a Master! And that is what I am, because that is what I make myself to be. Oh*mmmmmmmmmmmm.* In lacking courage, I would have looked like a swine or a camel to them and would have been instantly eaten. Ah! But with courage I appear as a lord, and see how they bow down to me! There, there now. Good ol' boys. Good, good beasties. Are you fellas rolling over for daddy? For ol' Pooh-Bah? Oh, aren't you the cutest things, bouffant and all? Buds, so colorful, with a twist of the ring, fading in and out, in and out. Give daddy a big kiss with your wet tongues. You see, ladies and gentlemen, how simple it is. And yet at the drop of a dime, prepare to watch this. Sit! Paw! Heel! Up! Speak! Bellow! Bark! Banter!"

"My Lord Ail," the lion suddenly interrupted. "We followed your orders. We did as you asked. We rolled over and we sat up. And we shook your hand. After all, we are but crooked beasts, satraps, xshathrapavans and janissaries, and we have been dealt a severe blow. We have been abandoned by god, who is Sachem Panjandrum, Heitis, who has lost the battle and left us alone to guard this stronghold, lest anyone of its occupants should escape. I suppose you have come here straightway to free them, though I think you are more likely to stay with them and never see your home again. However, without time we are yours to command."

"You see, ladies and gentlemen," Ali said, "anything is possible as long as you command your beliefs and keep the Braves faithful . . . The future is assured . . . What you think is what you get . . . No fear, no fret . . . Much haste, little waste . . . Yell and holler, shed the collar . . . Dip in the river, clean your liver . . . One for all . . . all for . . . Ahhhhhhh! . . . Ohmn . . . Ahhhhhh!"

Cut to East Hampton Court.

"Oh, my god! No! Was that shown on the air? Oh, god! We didn't need this! This is most tragic! Ladies and gentlemen, this is Jane Puritan in East Hampton Court. Apparently, Ail Greenness has just fallen prey to that lionish beast on live camera amongst an array of agitprops."

"Jane. This is James Cineking Charles in New York."

"Yes, James."

"Jane. Apparently, the beast did turn on Ail as he was conducting his report live from Havana. From what we can gather, Ail seemed quite confident that he had everything under control. And he was preparing to go straight into the stronghold until . . ."

"James. Excuse me for interrupting, but the creature gave no indication that it was getting ready to spring."

"I agree with you on that, Jane. Ail was, well, I wouldn't call it boasting. I think it's safe to say that he was attempting to be encouraging. And, Jane, can I use the engrafted word *inspirational* here for the viewing audience in the amen corner?"

"AH-men! Absolutely, James. Inspirational is an appropriate word. And, not to add too much stress to the proceedings, don't you think a common Gelu prayer for Ail would be appropriate here?"

"Absolutely, Jane. Of course. In due time. For we have promises to keep, and a millennium to go, and bows at the end of a little season."

IN THE STRONGHOLD

". . . Men. Before he returns we need to have a plan. We're going to split up into semiabecedarian groups of twelve. CBA and go the Anabaptist way. I want Madison, Harrison, and Van Buren to be in charge of the fire."

"Mr. Cleveland . . . Van Buren is no longer with us . . ."

"No longer with us? What do you mean?"

"Don't you remember? He ate him two nights ago. There's one of his shoes."

"Balls! He was our only 'free-soil' candidate. That's how he got the nickname 'Little Magician' and the Red Fox of 'Kinderhook.' He was a rare one, he was, being made of soil that was *soil-free*. 'Tis a shame. Chins up, men! We'll just have to make do without him. Now, you men born before 1776: Washington, Adams, Jefferson, Madison, Monroe, Adams, Jackson, and Harrison. I want you all to stand over there by the left wall. Damn shame! Do you gentlemen realize that Van Buren was the first President to be born under the American flag?"

"Sir. Perhaps we should allow his representation via his shoe?"

"What's gotten into you, Eisenhower? We can't have a shoe doing a man's work."

"I didn't mean that. Look, in my second year at West Point, I was a half-a-time-half-back and the biggest thrill I ever got in my shoes was downing Jim Thorpe in the Carlisle game. If it weren't for my shoes, I don't think that would have ever been possible. Shoes make a man."

"Yes, Ike. Job seeks the man and shoes make a man, and it was in those same shoes that you succeeded in breaking your knee, and thereby forever finishing whatever was left of your football career! No! The shoe's a lousey idea! Now wake up everyone! We've got to do this systematically. We've got to organize ourselves so that he'll never be able to figure out just what kind of order we're in. We'll work out a formula he won't be able to crack. I want three Presidents born west of the Mississippi: Hoover, Truman and Eisenhower. Eisenhower, since there are four syllables in your name and only two in Hoover and Truman, I want you to go first."

"Go first?"

"Yes. You'll be the first because your inauguration was the first to be telecast. Hoover, I'm going to put you in a more favorable light in order to get you out of the shadow of a major depression."

"It wasn't my fault! Don't give me too much responsibility here! I've got a cold and a precise personality! I'm stiff due to the fact that I was orphaned at nine!"

"That's all in the past. Get with it! Snap out of it! Now, Truman. What am I going to do with you? You've used 'hell' just one too many times. You've helped usher in the atomic war. You're responsible for 74,000 Nagasakian lives! Why, you are a fine example of an accidental President, after all that cerebral hermorrhage activity on behalf of Roosevelt. And, Roosevelt, insofar that your administration lasted twelve years, one month and eight days, I'm going to team you up with that nincompoop, hottentot Harrison. Harrison, how long was your administration?"

"M-m-m-m-m mine? O-o-o-o-o one month."

"Excellent. And what was your merit?"

"W-W-W-W-W . . . Well I-I-I-I had no views upon anything at the time."

"Harrison. You're actually quite pathetic. You have absolutely nothing to offer anyone?"

"W-W-W-W-Well, why are you p-p-p-p-p-picking on me? D-D-D-D-Didn't I lead n-n-n-n-nine hundred troops to victory at T-T-T-T-Tippecanoe and b-b-b-b-b . . . eat up T-T-T-T-Tecumseh?"

"An old Indian missing three teeth?"

"I-I-I-I-It was t-t-t-t-two not t-t-t-t-three."

"Oh, why, in that case I take my hat off to you and jack it in the ring. Look, Harrison. It's no wonder you croaked in office after only one month. You didn't smoke. Neither did you drink nor gamble. You refused to be drawn into duels when everybody else was doing it. You were completely honest and happily married to a two-mites woman who bore you ten children. Hot ten tots! You had a passion for anonymity! Let's face it, you were just plain pathetic!"

"T-T-T-T-That's not f-f-f-f-fair."

"Why not? You know why you fell ill with bilious pleurisy, which was nothing more than pneumonia? Because you're a child, and an imbecilic one at that! Standing bareheaded without an overcoat in a raw wind on your Inauguration Day! Really!"

"I-I-I-I-I wish my w-w-w-w-wife Anna S-S-S-S-Symmes was here. S-S-S-S-She'd show you!"

"Look, Harrison. We've spent more time talking here than your entire length of office. Are you proud of that?"

"H-H-H-H-He's picking on me. I-I-I-I-I didn't do anything. It's n-n-n-n-not fair."

"Harrison, shut up! You're a 105 minute windbag and you're giving us all a headache."

"I-I-I-I-If D-D-D-D-Daniel Webster was here, why h-h-h-h-he'd d-d-d-d-defend me!"

"Well, he ought to. He wrote your god-damned inaugural address!"

"Y-Y-Y-Y-You're one to speak, T-T-T-T-Tyler. Y-Y-Y-Y-You were on your k-k-k-k-k-knees shooting marbles with your c-c-c-c-children when you got w-w-w-w-word of my death."

"He's right, Tyler. You served without distinction as Governor of Virginia and U.S. Senator. Why, if it hadn't been for Harrison's death, your name would have been buried in oblivion, anothermity. Your talents as President netted you the resignation of your entire cabinet, with the exception of Daniel Webster, who remained only because of a treaty with England that he was working on at the time. Your first wife was an invalid, and your second wife was all of twenty-four when you were all of fifty-four!"

"Does it give you pleasure, Mr. Cleveland, to be such a bully? It's no wonder I died in confederate congress, in revolt against the United States. You know, I could say a few things about you as well . . ."

"Yeah, but you won't get the chance to, Ty. I don't even see how you could get the chance between all those kids you had. What was the last count? Fourteen?"

"Fourteen children. Seven per wife. You're going to pick on me for that now I suppose?"

"There's no time to, Ty. But I will group you with Buchanan who had no children and could have stood a little sildenafil 'n viagra himself."

"Naturally, I had no children. I never married. Furthermore, I don't mean to be stuffy but I take pride in the fact that I was the last President to wear a stock."

"Oh, is that so? Is that why you carry your head slightly to one side like a poll-parrot and utter 'cockless' every ten minutes!"

"That's because of my poor vision. The result of one eye being cocked and near-sighted, and the other cocked and far-sighted."

"Fully cocked I'm sure. The reason your head tilts is due to the fact that your neck was permanently twisted in an attempt to hang yourself!"

"'Tis not true!"

"It is true! You never got over Anne Coleman's death after she wrote you that letter of dismissal because of your supposed philanderings! She sickened and died, and it was all your fault!"

"Oh, you wicked man! You're a beast and a scoundrel! I ought to throw you in the ring with John Heenan and let you battle it out with him. He'd beat you to a pulp, you scoundrel!"

"Mr. Cleveland, Mr. Cleveland. He's coming back! I can hear his footsteps in the earth. I can feel his approach through the walls of our imprisonment. I can sense his advance in the air we breathe. I can envision his entrance before he enters. The molecules are a sure sign that he is coming. I can visualize the Latin in his head and the Greek on his tongue. Soon he will be here and another one of us will be eaten. The eye of god does see us even if we should hide about. I could write a poem. One line in Latin, the other in Greek. And yet a third in Pentagonese. I could depict our experiences here in inenematic verse, and soil this prison with rhyme.

"He doth bendeth over and expose his clover

Like two massive dense heads in dover

I could read along the lines, his posterior curse

O the closest I come to hell is the closest I come to a hellenist's purse.

So bid me well to kiss the Jew . . .

And be mindful not to touch his doo."

"Garfield. It's no wonder Guiteau fired two shots at you, finding a bullet in your arm and spine. With such verse as that! You keep the assassins' unemployment line down."

"May I say something here beyond come and lo here! and lo there!?"

"Yes, Pierce. Please enlighten us Grand Old Party pols with your piercing perception . . ."

"Very well then. I will. Ah . . . hem. We, as a pragmatic group, are special souls. As men of the sag . . . a . . . cious flesh, we each had our turn to lead our country forward. Our hegemonic responsibilities were likened unto god's, or so we believed at the time. It was our hard-won duty to support a dichotomous country in crisis. Saviours were we, ever so slightly hegemonical. We tiptoed along that theme, dutiful servants though we were. We were deemed as Kings, to be or not to be, forever faithful, forever successful. And should we fail, we had no one to pick us up but ourselves. For we had a troubled world resting on our shoulders, a world whose shelves were crammed with ancient letters, written on the backs of holey petals, most of which were unread, but, nonetheless, written with weary hands that had touched the bones of various angels, letters written home in times of war when young, forgotten soldiers died and felled and lay in state, their identities obstructed in shifting sands and everlasting wounds. The winds blew hard, gentlemen, in our states of office – our pulpits. Young, vigorous and eager did we heed our calls. Old, weary and tethered calves did we exit. The sheer weight of our major decisions combined, no one god could hold, I'm sure. For in each of our very hands, a nation of souls with bones did lie, all very much like a baby our wives might have gently transferred to us. Here, this is the world as I leave it, we said one to another as our office turned into a stone bed and a new office rose to color the waking hours. But did we ever really sleep, gentlemen? I think not. No doubt each one of us bears a special sorrow in Cupid's alley. I, for one, lost my third and last child, a boy of eleven, in a railroad wreck. Before my very eyes his life was sliced in two like James Bulger, and each of the pieces hung over my head like old, unfriendly shadows – like a nation in war with too much bloodshed. Blood and water, gentlemen. I look back and think upon my friends, Nathaniel Hawthorne and Longfellow for effect, and I think, now what words can help to mend a universe broken apart by its very creator. Our god, gentlemen, did have the *'runs'* at Armageddon. Bare record. A war is won with love, with lungs, with the best leg of three, and not with hate toward any given race. Now we are the souls of Presidents. And I for one did not take a liking toward politics, though I was pragmatic when it came to hysterical facts. Nay, I did not want to be President. Nor one of a Puzzle Palace such as this. More a dark-horse candidate I was, and yet I won by the most sweeping majority, although almost anyone could have beaten Scott. Now it is a universe we must save and a god that we must battle. god is everywhere, gentlemen. Stiff, impaled, pierced, but sweetly in business. Not the same to each and every man, but in each and every man he rests."

"Pierce. You do us proud. You bring us all back to earth, though earth is but a cloud returned to the dust it was before god gave it shape and form, a negative collapse and a zero rest. Our puzzle of hidden correspondences. For us to deicide. It will not be an easy thing to kill our father who gave life to us and bid us to gather up his broken pieces and build something I imagine completely different from what he had in mind. A vase must have broken somewhere. Let us collect the curious, jagged ends of the cities broken apart. Let us collect our shattered foundations, and if not all the pieces fit, or some are missing, lost, and never to be found, let us remember them like unselfish warriors in the field of battle who turn over their lives for their country, and with hearts exposed fall so that another heart might beat, protected in the pavement, the flesh of its autarkic stronghold. We will put out the eye of god, Mr. Presidents, because an eye that cannot see is an eye that cannot foresee.

Gentlemen, let us pick up our roles as special men and rebuild a universe not out of dust, nor out of sin, but out of love, equality, such as an unblemished love feast, consistent and forever. Zachary. Allow your nobility to glow again. Mount 'old Whitey,' a stranger in a ghost's robe, and do not mistake nor apologize that despite your crude manners and shabby appearance, you were nobler and kinder than god himself. Light the fire. Burn the coals. Look right to left. Spread eagle with honor. It is approaching the time when we must say we would rather be right than be souls eternal but cold as ice."

At this point the Presidents lit a fire, tidied up the stronghold, and recited several penny rhymes and gabbalia songs, befitting for those about to go into battle. Polk had old wads of tobacco left over from his earthly days which he passed amongst the group, inviting each to take an equal share. "They use to say, 'Who is Polk?' But today they say, 'Polk's A-OK.!' That's because I was the first dark-horse to become President and to spit in the face of Heckley Hound."

Boasting such as this was expressed by all the Presidents, bloviating each in his own special way. In order to properly prepare for battle (especially with god who is prone to crabwise movement and/or high-level stagnation), one must be filled with confidence, full of robust, and have just consumed a full meal. With a great din, Andrew Johnson spit tobacco juice across the room. Like a great flying beetle, the dark and salivary wad splattered against the eastern wall and somehow managed to spray Woodrow Wilson's shoes as he was bending down to make the floor safe for presidential mastery.

"Yes, indeed," Johnson boasted, "no President ever suffered such humiliation as I did on my speaking tour of the East and Middle West, when I tried to rally opinion against the Republican radicals who were demanding severe punishment of the South. In almost every city mobs shouted, 'Shut up, Johnson! We don't want to hear from you!' But never once did I lose face. Not even when a House committee prepared impeachment charges against me for high crimes and misdemeanors and tried to shut me up, type-cast and all. Sure enough, by one vote was I acquitted. And it is with full pride that upon departure of my natural term, I was able to return to Washington like a god returning to earth. Naturally, of course, in my case, it was a return to the United States Senate – a far cry from Armageddon. But, nonetheless, I can relate to misery. After all, my death was virtually ignored by the press, which prompts me to recall god's own obituary in the *Harper's Weekly,* and I quote, '*DEATH OF gOD. Murder of the DM. Legions of murders, delivered into the hands of men. Ex-Omnipresent. Ex-Omniscient. Ex-Alpha and Ex-Omega. Ex-Superior Entity. Sealed No More. Died: December 31st; at the residence of the All-Presidents Stronghold. P.O. Box:* **Promised Land, T***ennessee.* '"

*   *   *

Flash! From the FL files, *falsa lectio,* this following false, loose reading:

On the 27th, when he left his residence in heaven to do battle at Armageddon, god was apparently in vigorous health. In an interview conducted by TIMEEMIT, he was quoted as saying, while surrounded by a host of angels, "We're gonna whip No Drag's ass," whereupon he demonstrated his sharp left hook. "Ohhhhh!" all the angels responded. But soon after reaching Armageddon and viewing Drag's lentiginous legions, and billions upon billions upon billions of blemished human beings, he began to complain of a splitting headache and insisted that his ulcer was acting up, as well as a slight paralysis in his right knee.

As the legions closed in on him, he complained of dizzy spells and was soon rendered incomprehensible. His last words before retreating from the Battle scene altogether were "Don't forget to renew your subchristians to D.C. Comics!" Sometime after the Battle and his virtual defeat, god rallied for Supremacy. Having lost an eye in the Battle, he eventually retired; although for a brief season he tried his hand at Cyclopsing – first, by setting up residence on Promised Land Isle; second, by perfecting the craft of reisner work in the head of both the fiber and the membrane; third, by imprisoning all forty-eight Presidents in a stronghold; fourth, by planning on consuming the Presidents one-by-one; and fifth, by exclaiming beside Prometheus in John, "I am Bomfog. Make ye way for the Rock and Water!" This was where (and how) god met his demise. Falling victim to the Presidents' ingenious scheme to do him in.

*　　　　*　　　　*

Commotional bruitenoise from the north was going on at the time that the Presidents were preparing for god's return to the den; he was but steps away, and his war-like report passed through his nostrils, even as his end sounded its own warning like a heil of dead cats. Jefferson picked up a large stone and dropped it accidentally on Nixon's foot, whereupon Nixon, not worthy, fell backward 88 steps into Lincoln, who, in turn, landed on top of Bush, the boneless wonder, now burning in the books, which prompted Grant to yell, "Knock it off men! I can hear his heavy foot at the door!" After which all the Presidents were compelled to take their proper places and to sit up straight, like perfect stool children in the flesh, greeting their king on the throne, greeting to please, in a new era, good morning. "Good mourning, god," they said in spiritual unison.

"Morning, fellas. I noticed the press is out there in abundance today. Isn't it nice how they all keep abreast of me? And since I can be everywhere, anywhere, at any given time of the day, I'm thoroughly impressed with their noble endeavors. Why, just think, on the other side of this universe – this boom and bust, cyclical movement of me bottom half that's got me rebooming in the second Act – they are speaking to an exact faxsimile of me. Only there I'm representing myself as a choirmaster, a composer of operas, *petite bouffes,* resigned to the task-at-large. Yes, it's a pleasant but a most monstrous job being me, being everywhere at once, and without being a stumbling block to the weaker sex. Me to Me, *simplex obligatio.* Now I think that I feel like having a little Jackson stew with an Adams celery stick, and perhaps a blue McKinley on the side. Oh McKinley, I just bumped into Czolgosz, that young anarchist holding a handkerchief with a 'How Do You Do' hidden beneath it. The old Final Judgment-One-Two Free Society! Routine. Leon said to me, mockingly, 'I thought it would be a good thing for the far country to kill the President.' Tsk! Tsk! Tsk! Sorry mess. The headline read: PRESIDENT McKINLEY IS DEAD – HIS SOUL FREED AT 2: 15 O'CLOCK – THE BUFFALO EXPRESS. Just like Jesus. Mark it well. The same who was seized unaware by the narrative *and* by its theatrical games. However, his breast was devoured by . . ."

"My dear god," Cleveland said. "Why don't you take a seat and rest awhile. You seem so tired."

"That's mighty thoughtful of you, Grover, being that you could do no mighty work. By far you're the best of this lot. And to show you my appreciation, I'll *save* eating you for last."

Once god had sat down, it took six Presidents under Grant's direction to remove god's shoes and rub the twelve-foot wide bunions on the souls of his broad feet, received from having trampled the countryside and squashing a co-op of farmers, and a citrus tree grower or two.

"Can we get you anything to drink perchance; a little wine while you dine?"

"That would be fine. Plus, I think an appetizer or two for this ol' deipnosophist will do." Whereupon he immediately seized Lincoln, and cracked him in two, and munched on the bottom half first, and then customarily spit out a well-worn shoe; but he swallowed his testes fast, and added, "This lawless world must be kept in motion by dice *and* mass and the will of the flesh."

"Poor, poor Lincoln. Poor, poor Lamb," three cowering Presidents mumbled under their breath, while the blood from Lincoln's torso dripped off god's chin, landed to the floor, and stuck there like en-glue. And while god munched wolfishly, englutly on Lincoln's head (a brain drain to be sure), a sour fume came up from god's bowels that filled the room.

Now, unbeknownst to god, the wine-boring, cabal crew comprised of Jackson, Teddy, Nixon and Washington had unzipped their trousers and were currently spiking the brew with fresh jets of urine. 'Tis bitterly true. Yes, the piss was both hot and embued with toxins that would upset even a god's pot, after only having a sip or two.

Standing tall on a boulder or borrowing from an associate *on a bully pulpit,* Cleveland addressed god while looking over *his* shoulder at the goings-on of the laudable oenophilists. Bravo Zulu! Black is white o helleluiah! So far, so good. Everyone's following the rules. But deep in his heart, Cleveland could barely start to find the proper words. The sudden loss of Lincoln was almost too much to bear, and despite his absolute danger, Cleveland feared that his own sadness was showing through. Chin up! Brinkmanship, brother John! Eyeball to eyeball! Go to the verge, I . . . say! The only way to beat god praying is to play his own game. "I pray that Lincoln was a culinary delight?"

"Not a bad chew. A little tough. A splinter of shoe. I should have known better and had his first beard plucked. Hmmmm . . . I could go for a *crunchy*." And reaching over Grover, he gripped Calvin and Truman, and smashed them together like peanut butter, and ate them all – skin, cloth and leatherly goo.

"Where's the wine?" he bellowed. "Don't keep me waiting! Truman's head is lodged in my throat and will soon have me fading."

Cleveland, smiling most respectively, motioned hastily for the Presidents to make hurry with their urine. It was Nixon who was still pissing – remembering the hours stewing over yellow leaves, game waring his dinner guest into the plot (as well as the pot) for a thorough urinalysis of that little 89 resignation god had planned as *his* final termination, just seventy-four words later weeping, weeping for himself and for Abraham 26 words before – who was stalling up the line. Such outer darkness as this, in sixty-nine and seventy, left Nixon feeling nam, in the action of taking or seizing by distraint the chattels of the first accordance, not so much a gift as a stealth, as was Nixon's custom when it came to hew.

"Yes. Like roving pirates you Presidents be, ruining the lives of your countrymen free!" god mused. "None of you really did much good. Anyhow, you're all failures at heart, hooked fear-first, coming up, the sea and the waves roaring. Well, at least Lincoln made himself worthy as a civil hors d'oeuvre, a fit fart for a god," whereupon he spit out two more pairs of shoes and a shoelace that was lodged between his teeth. Still munching, he mused, "So says I to a world in disarray, *Why point the finger at me?* So the battle was lost. 'Tis a mote. So, big deal. Simply setting a watch. Look away." And leaning way over and scooping up F.D. in Clover, he said, "Or should I say New Deal? O' Roosevelt. How you beam in my hand. Yes, indeed. You look rather tasty to me as I steal you from your grasp to the leaves on the floor. Come to think of it, I recall seeing you in my maieutic sleep, posing during a St. of Liberty Loan Drive with Fairbanks . . . Dear Mother Pickford . . . Dressler, and Chaplin. Now you had a lot of nerve! Presidents and actors don't mix! Neither do thieves nor acts of tricks. Politics in Hollywood? Brahmins in Politics? East in west? Absurd! Say, Reagan, *Where do you think you're going?* No way! Stay put! Don't dare move into the midst of the herd and all them dead men's naked bones."

"Well, I really wasn't moving. Maybe you could call it shifting in my shoes," Reagan counter-mused with one eye, as 'tis better that way than with two, recalling his back list of 19 unfriendly tunes, including 'Salt of the Earth,' 'All Quiet on the Western Front,' 'All the King's Men,' 'Circumstantial Evidence,' and 'DT's in the American Camp.'"

"No doubt." And turning to Roosevelt, god continued, "You see, Hollywood is my den where I call the shots."

"But, god, I was only posing," Roosevelt said. "What harm was there in that? I never meant to take over your role as director, or whatever it is you're getting at."

"Oh, no. Oh, no. Then answer me this, my tasty meatball. Why was your inaugural promise, 'Action, and don't stall!?'"

"But you're taking it all wrong! I didn't mean action as in camera and lights, as much as I meant action as in the political fight!"

"Then why so many photographs with that ridiculous profile and that ridiculous cigarette, not to mention your library-museum Monument, which contains thousands of briefing books, photographs and movie films? Didn't I say 'Thou shalt worship no other idols but me?'"

"Surely you can't begin to think that I meant to upstage you?"

"Certainly not. Exactly the reason for Campobello. Yes, remember that night. After Asia – in and out. Swimming in the icy ass waters of the Bay of Fundy. Yes, you went to bed with a chill that season, and the following morning that chill was replaced by a high temperature and acute pains in your legs, and the silver went up, way up. And only a few days later they were paralyzed!! Never to stand again on earth. My touch. And just all of thirty-nine – on to the world and angels and men and death. What grand theater!"

"So it was you all that time! Wrath is cruel! Really! Planning to cripple a President! Oh, Lois, Eunice! On my grandmother's and mother's graves! I should have known better!"

"Don't play god! and it's not *don't be cruel* but rather two hours of Diana and the supreme Stevens and Matthew and son and Firecat, the ol' Greek, bowing to stop in the name!" god wrapped his fingers tightly around Roosevelt's middle; the pressure alone released a little Roosevelt spittle. Still, Roosevelt managed to exhibit that famous smile, implying personal charm or insincerity or deviousness or, perhaps, only fear in itself. Nevertheless, it seemed to have an adverse effect upon god who, in turn, chose to utilize fear. "Don't cook tonight . . . Call Chicken Delight!" And in one gulp, Roosevelt was no longer in sight.

"Please!" Cleveland screamed. But remembering it's far better to be composed, he drolled, "We ain't corn pone. This isn't a smorgasbord or Solomon's Temple. There's not unlimited refills. There's only so many more Presidents to-go, and then the restaurant's closed."

"You're quite right, Grover. 'Tis a pity. And I was just about to seize a couple of Adams and dash their heads across the floor, so that their brains would run out in a dizzy, and make pretty colors that would, in turn, soften their bodies so that I might tear them limb by limb, to pieces, dunk, crumble, spoon, poke and suck up the flesh, marrow, bones and entrails like spaghetti."

"Well, before you do, why not have a bit of brew, and sleep awhile? You seem so tuckered out. All the work you have to do. It just isn't right. No one appreciates you upon this good night that you and your love did create for us."

"Grover, that's just what I like about you. Your dialogue's at least . . . half-right. Sweet talk and gentle persuasion. You sort of remind me of certain lewd fellows of the baser sort. You'll be my best dessert yet, after consuming my Presidential stew. Now where's that wine?"

No sooner did he shout than Nixon tapped off the very last drops from his sprout. The hot piss was immediately cooled by the tasty wine; although the poisons in the brew, the 'ol' devils in the details, were quite different than when merely chewed and consumed inside the body. For it wasn't so much the piss itself that once consumed would turn god inside-out as it was the energy of the piss working within, fueled by deception and humiliation, plus a total disregard for sin. For if there is one thing that weakens a god – if there is one thing that gets him mad and thereby reveals his vulnerabilities, a little lower than the angels, it is these very things: humiliation, deception and degradation, under the guise of *release of resources, involuntary severance, career-transition programing, reshaping, reduction in force, and strengthening global effectiveness by sheer thought.*

Upon receiving the bowl, god brought it up to his nostrils and sniffed. "Mmmmmm. Ronyon wine. My very favorite. Squeezed from the *bodies* of every scoundrel in a trinity predicament. Every pubescent grape. Every pretty petal."

Delicately, god put his lips to the bowl. The twitch in his free hand almost suggested that he was going to snatch up a couple of Presidents without warning, and continue his drink with fresh meal in his mouth.

So, the best plan of all was to let him just drink, and drink he did most greedily. Even so, one could see the old carcass, Lincoln, stuck exactly where Adam and his apple had lodged in god's throat during the time he had consumed the *mold* of the human race. Glunk! Glunk! Glunk! The wine wiggled down. To the Presidents it looked like a mountain was moving in the throat of god – like an earthquake was rolling in the center of his gullet. It made god look silted up with analogies. At least that was the impression it made on the remaining Presidents from Carter to Washington.

Howbeit, the wine was so tasty that god with a lazy tongue beckoned for more. And while Cleveland kept his highness in stitches with Presidential jokes (e.g., How many Presidents does it take to get a god stone-drunk? Answer: ten. Five to crush the grapes, four to bottle it, and one to stick on as the label. And the name of the wine? The Ten Coma-ments – all stoned on their asses), three fully-endowed replacements urinated their sparkling, yellow best into the bowl. Naturally, it took a fair amount of time, and therefore the challenge to keep god in stitches was nearly more than Grover could handle. It was more like a study of the weariness of the flesh. Running out of fresh jokes, he started to rely on some old corny favorites. (e.g., Why did god not appear on the one dollar? Answer: Because Washington beat him to it. What is the greatest sin that Eisenhower committed while in office? Answer: His syntax.)

Unfortunately, not even Grover could remember the correct answers, and he was left to rely upon his own wits, which were absolutely *un*-funny (e.g., I *ass* you: Who holes the vein in the wood I beat? Answer: Silvanus); but somehow upon hearing the ill-conceived jokes, god couldn't keep from laughing. In fact, the *un*-funnier they were, the harder god laughed. Only later did they realize the reason for god's laughter – figuring these really were old favorites, old fables, he didn't want to appear dense, or appear as though he didn't grasp the catch or, god forbid, appear as an effete snob with a lid on his eye. Fortunately, this made it possible for Grover to come up with all sorts of ridiculous and nonsensical tidbits, where subtlety was lost *and* punchlines based on acute selection were hastily ignored in headlong jumps to absurd conclusions that god gave good heed to, which, in turn, not only managed to keep god in delirious stitches, but allowed the Presidents ample enough time to do their duty and to fearlessly line up and squirt their finest into the ivy-wood bowl holding god's most pleasant and darkest wine of all.

Each President harbored so much anger, so much scorn, and so much bitterness that all they could think of doing was to pour the wreckless wine down god's throat and pray that it might catch fire in his insides, and to deface his backside with graffiti: *For a good time call 666.* With Exquisite Ease, Grover, meanwhile, was relaxing into his newly assigned role as the Presidential Commiserable Comedian, structuring it into a sort of remote, recomposed, laid-back, Las Vegas comedy act, seeking a chapel of ease so to speak. ("This is some crowd we've got here tonight. Is that god I see sitting at the sixtieth table chewing cat? What's the matter? They couldn't get you a seat up front? Oh, I get it. Nobody could see over your head without falling with a dead-cat bounce. And what about those cats out of the bag? Let me tell you. That's some ca-ca cat catabolic cataclysm, *casus fortuitus, casus belli!* Go your ways, you noisome, grievous, cocked sores. Get on your marks and off your seats.") But the ol' gimp was getting a vim out of it with a kick, if no one else was. And the roar of his laughter weakened the very walls of the stronghold.

Standing off to the side, zipping himself up in his testosterone-tightassed-tourniquet-troubled-with-the-spirit-free-fashion-clingon-homoerotic-fowldevoured-lappleaser, old Andrew Jackson noticed how the wall trembled with each ferocious roar out of god. Having once been a cockfighter himself, Andrew recalled that the best thing to feed a cock before going into battle is pickled beef. Of course! Why not? Perhaps it would give his own cock some fight if he first consumed a bit of meat, like the messenger buffet bird, the old Sec. of State, more a messet than a messenger, except if one combines the two into a pointer. Alas, the only thing at Andrew's disposal was a chunk of dashed brain left over from the Truman and Calvin Collision; and so in living up to his name, *Old Hickory*, Andrew slurped the chunk-jelly down and went straight to the pot and pissed, uttering in very imperious tones, "Let him take this from the kitchen! Five against one! Packed with a fist and a sound of many waters."

All the other Presidents were well aware of Old Hickory's reputation as the most roaring, rollicking, game-cocking, card playing son-of-a-bitch that ever lived or pizzed east of Need. And if anyone could take god for a spin, they would have to cry out, "Andrew Jackson!"

Amazingly, this time Andrew's piss jettisoned out red, which might have suggested that it was packing enough potency to strike a god dead. "I'll give him monuments. I'm not a'feared. Hark! Why, there's a sturdy, wise statue of me riding tall on a pizzle in Lafayette Park. No sir ree!" he mumbled, pissing gaily away. "Me a'feared? Never! No debate! No way! Gentlemen, be still. A murderer I was, depicted in the Coffin Handbill. Don't give me vain glory in spite of this burden near my heart! At my inauguration, the pressure of the crowd was so great that women fainted, clothing ripped, glasses and china shattered, and that ain't the end of the story. Folks stood on $150 official empty chairs just to get a glimpse of me, the President, drawing redemption. *'To the victor belongs the spoils.'* And that's a quote unlike the usual silence that once emanated from Coolidge, who was punched in the eye during Mass."

This time the wine was fiery hot. In addition to pissing, each President took his turn and *spat* in the pot. And soon thereafter god thrust out his hand like a sickle and immediately ordered more wine, for he was growing irritated with Grover's endless jokes.

How does one address god? From head to toe, four score and seven plagues ago.

With haste the Presidents lifted the bowl in god's way, although their offerings hardly had time to blend. Taking the bowl up to his face and carefully examining the brew, god shouted with an echo, "What's-t's with-th the-he reddish-sh brown-wn aromatic-ic gum-um-um-um?" And in taking a sip he experienced a bitter, slightly pungent taste, and shouted, "Come down! What is this?! When they brought Christ to the place of the skull, they gave him wine to drink mingled with myrrh and buttery crab dip; but he received it not. And then they crucified him, parting his garments and casting lots via an agent of questionable depth. Tell me, tiny Presidents, you wouldn't be up to any mischief now, would you? Engaging in personalities far beyond your parti? Because if you were, I should be compelled to turn you all into golliwogs or, at the very least, Rhodes scholars, with gas up the Sigmoid, and send you all to Golgotha where you would live out eternity myrmecochorously. And don't think I wouldn't do it! For I sense a bone has been broken and there is more than just wine in this suet. Do you think I could not grasp the lot of you in my bare hand and squeeze until your very heads pop? Don't put me beneath myrmecophagousness. What gall is this? What enemies' list? What feedback? What fallout? What bitterness of spirit dares to temper this wine with a chewing of the scenery, less divine than grand? Like yellow bile, it sits at the top. Could this be a Presidential Assassin Creme in my coffee cup? Speak up! Andrew, why is your cock exposed? You remind me of Adam after he had taken a red bite out of what was hedonistically forbidden to him. Do I detect a drip of Sigmund? For why are there drops of blood on the floor pac wit laughter's last laugh?"

"Don't you recall, god? That is where you dashed our comrades' brains with such pleasure it verged on sodcumatry. Perhaps, the bowl holds nothing more than your very own regurgitated Presidential Meat? If I were you, for sufficient protein, I shouldn't let a drop escape . . . unless you be a god who cannot hold his own and comes with a drain."

Naturally, Jackson was more bold than wise, and always felt fear to be the greater sin, more than any other energy known to man. Although, all the remaining Presidents motioned for him to be still, he refused to heed their warning and chose instead to engage god in a bit of a duel, entangling alliances in a concert of power.

"I know my bible. I know how the floo-floo bird flies. Backward to the future. And the hour. I've read the intumulated verse when he was come to the other side into the country of the Gergesenes, and there met him two devils dazzled with cynanthropy coming out of the tombs, being as fierce as the mother in myrmotherine, so that no man might pass by that way. It sounds like a dog-gone myth, does it not? Likened unto the land of the Cyclops. Or, better yet, if I may be so bold, like the floating island of Aeaea, the home of the beautiful Circe, herself a formidable goddess, a precieuse full of meretriciousness, a flat-foot Floogie with a Floy-Floy. Now I'm a man of little verse, not meaning to torment. And though my purse is empty of any formal education, I can assure you I've picked up a thing or two in the way of the costliness of war, politics and law, and a bit of meretrix as a flugie rule, especially in this land of Tennessee, to boot. Yes, for two whole days and nights, *two whole days*, mind you, that particular crew captained by Odysseus lay on the beach suffering not only from exhaustion but from all the horrors they had been through. Now on the third day, god, *the third day*, mind you, on that day the morning was heralded in by a magnificent sun that made them all squint in a glitchy kind of way. And on that morning, mind you, Odysseus speared a stag right through the heart, which later supplied his men with meat, wolfishly washed down by mellow wine, much like your meal before you. Once again, setting out on their travels on foot, they came upon Circe's house, built of dressed stone like a stronghold in a glacis. Prowling about the place were mountain wolves and lions and a misplaced, inferior merganser or two – in reality, the drugged, human victims of Circe's magic. Circe invited Odysseus and his crew into her home, where she offered them pramnian wine mixed with a powerful drug that would make them lose all memory of their native land. Once they had emptied the bowls, she struck them with her wand and magically turned them into swine, like Io's cow or like Glaucus in the waves of herbs and meats; howbeit, their minds remained human. Nevertheless, she penned them in her pigsties and refused to manumit them. Now I don't mean to be a mollycoddle, but in order not to be stripped of courage and manhood, a man has got to have his *Moly*. For with it a man can resist any drink and not be made into a swine, to prove that he be a man whom nothing defeats, not even the spread legs of a slippery goddess. Did you know, god, that from Circe's hold the men did manage to escape as men and did thereafter make a journey of a very different kind? Specifically to the holes of Hades they sailed – into a kingdom of decay, where the river of flaming fire and the mischief of electric gremlins dwelled – that was where they poured offerings to all the dead. Offerings mixed with sweet wine, offerings for the helpless dead of the ghosts and of the finest jet-black sheep in the flock. Now I beseech you, god, a soapy Orator – if a man can drink of wine endowed with powerful offerings without fear – without being a *mollycoddle*, mind you – can god afford to do any less?"

"You will not tempt me, andy-pandy!"

"Tempt? Never. I would rather choke to death drinking bottled milk from a scyphus or lay me light load on a carpet and fly cheaply by a handbill."

"Then what is it you mean to imply? And speak quick! For some reason this bowl that I hold keeps attracting a fly."

"I mean to imply that god cannot be any less fearful than the Gadareme swine that rushed into the sea upon their own request. Surely you recall their words: 'What have we to do with thee, Esuriss, that you should come and torment us before the end of time? If you choose to cast us out, make us go into the yonder urine sea.'"

"So, you choose to draw a parallel between me and mythology, heaven and Hades, swine and wine and pee? Is this meant to impress me? Is this an attempt to make me read multitudes of exquisite symbols so that I, if I am so removed, might spend endless time searching like that fool Odysseus. Don't tempt me! Or with this fist I will squash you so flat that you will surely be meal, coarsely ground! How dare you, Andrew, render me a fool? You think me a mollycoddle? When the fire glows and I am raging with fumes, and my anger and scorn could spin an earth off its orbit with but a twist of my wrist, and with a flip of my finger twist it back home, I should warn you since you are going to perish anyway – don't let me catch you exiting with a cruel jest!"

And upon saying this, god brought the bowl to his mouth and drank. And in just three gulps he downed the expelled bladders of over a dozen Presidents. And the fullness of it made god heavy. For all the pain of the Presidents – each in their turn representing their times, their peoples, their Nation of the great unwashed, and all of the pains thereof – flowed into the belly of his consciousness. And a vast ocean of wine, mixed with urine and heavy chunks of men's flesh, nauseously rolled and churned inside him. And the V-shaped Hyades clustered in his head – stormed, ranted and raged a Noah's flood inside him – so that each wave of nausea was like a quell, a deadly riot. And the piss was like a sin festering like his own personal Sheol turned aside. And then god fell to the floor and moved not a limb.

The Presidents were stunned – amazed at what they had done, what they had accomplished. For a moment not one of them could speak.

And then Andrew fell to his knees and gave thanks for his own victorious gifts. And one by one each President followed suit; that is, each gave thanks for his own cunning and bravery. And in unison they chanted, *"Illegitimi non carborundum,"* over and over again. And, all at once, each and every President made his hand into a fist, and with their self-endowed power they made each fist into fiery ash, until each fist glowed fiercely, alight in flame. And then they took turns, and each President drove his fist into god's eye, and twisted and twisted inward until they could hear a hiss *Shh! o! ah!* as unto snakes coming from deep within the darkness of god. And it made them want to back away in terror, but they remembered: *fear is the greatest sin.* And so they stood their ground instead, and did god in.

How does one kill god?

By a bitterness of spirit and a disregard of awe.

NONENTITY INTERRUPTUS SUSPECTS . . . THE BEGINNING REVEALS THE END . . .

Mother was a weak stout, but her heart had a spirit verging on courageous. I caught her once, the last letter of her name dangling dubiously on her tongue. Her head was unmanned and going in every which direction. I thought it cruel to see her whimper. Enough had been broken in time, and I did not wish to separate any future desirable elements from their proper course.

Mother had insisted that I bear the produce. So I gave birth to a life which was at once paurometabolous. I suppose that the creation of a reasonable existence, free from either intentional or accidental harm, should be just. Lying face down I talked to the earth. My tongue was a root to the inner body wall. I tore it down, my words a scheme concealing bloody patterns broken by the force of my voice. I rolled over, and my dorsicumbent form had me howling once again.

I suppose it was all on account of me being a chrisom child. Mother and father barely had time to lay that pure white cloth under my rosy red cheeks and ponder whether I was an elaborate, unrealized dream or something all mashed together – incongruous parts, tissues of diverse genetic constitution, a real she-monster vomiting flames from a soapy lion's head. If you're up for truth, I suppose I ought to tell you that there was no time for innocence with me. My so-called 'baptism' was performed behind a closed door in the basement of the house I was born in. Father drank three glasses of water and proceeded to urinate on my head like Bacchus upon a pissabed, a sedgy sea. He loved telling me about it. Sometimes he would recall the event in a song, like a connubial drama sung by a prester with a thing for octaves. I was always daddy's little neoteric angel. Either he would embrace me and call me his true and faithful jupiter angel, squeezing me in private till I cried, or he would place me in a stretch of choppy seas, and with the door closed and the radio on and the toilet running and all life in deep kimshi, he would silo this and silo that and baptize me all night long.

Indeed, I was by nature a votaress, a constant addict, a certain aid, upholding my belief in the center of beauty, the temporary abode of the soul, a worn dwelling place bearing the inscriptions of a thousand seated impressions, the press that came to pasture on the old walls. And I did believe there was a reason for the passing note of a heartbeat's duration, the appoggiatiera – a cave dweller interposed between the indefinite enthusiasm of the soul and the bloody survival of the body – and that our work in death's shoes was also for a reason beyond the suffering between the night of the last meal and the consumption of the next. The passion that inspired the ungovernable to set the seed into the hollow of rhythmic contraction also drew upon the greater depth of breath rising upward a sound as of the frothing of the sea. Cruel – the indifference to suffering and the positive pleasure in afflicting it that runs rampant in the world. After all is said and done, the earth and those who are in it are fictile and converse, and can be shaped into any desired state of dysphoria.

THE CLUES ARE PLANTED. THE MYSTERY BEGINS TO DIE . . .

I suppose with most children a bed is a place for sleeping, a mattress filled with soft material. Beds are good for people, animals and plants. I suppose god in all his goodness was offering the bed as a sort of *beau geste*, a place to rest in the midst of from the burdens of the day; typically, a place from which to come into, to evolve, and to go out of the world. How I wish it were so for all of us. I cannot share the baby blue nor the soft pink of motherstuffed innocence, even though I was cast in a bed.

Mother use to tell me that most things happen unpredictably and without discernible human intention. I suppose that was her way of dealing with uncertainty. I think upon Mother as a Jansenist. She would have one believe that the freedom of the will is nonexistent and that redemption is limited to only a select few. She was perfect for father, marked by a kind but naive heart and a loving but stupid spirit. She was, in essence, a small container of intellect; her mental capabilities were endangered by unharnessed absolutes. In terms of society, she was an ornamental stand; like a sweet-scented flower, she added perfume to the masses. But what a long mixed array of confusion she acted out behind closed doors.

BLOOD SPRAYED PROFUSELY ACROSS THE BATHROOM WALLS

Daddy became his own victim of prolapse. It was the 'last three days' and a tenebrific mocking prolonged the suffering. Tenesmus gripped and held Daddy in deadlock. The ten-pounders he would have released that fuliginous evening were, for the time being, lodged tightly in *Schlemm's Canal*, and any amount of constant straining produced nothing more than a pitiful drop from the eye. An absence of light from within only meant that darkness might otherwise heighten the risk of danger. Daddy smashed his forehead against the mirror in the bathroom and received a blade of glass in the eye. The mirror was shattered and accepted his face's fate as only a jagged tetrahedral angle. Blood trailed down his form in T-formation, pudding mixed with a fair amount of runny, aqueous humor. I supposed at the time that he was enacting a minor concussion or was, at the very least, behaving a bit dazzled and lame. He muttered over and over again, "Yah weh . . . yah weh!" I mocked from the tub, "Ya who?" "Yah weh!" he cried with *vis major* in minor, his head mauling a slanted book.

And then Daddy said something rather original. He said, "I haven't lost my liveliness, my brightness, nor my moshing, sinuous ways. And I'm still standing at the foot of a straight stairway, jazzing and drooling over your long legs. Come. What we do, we do quickly." I went over to the calendar because I wanted to mark this day as significant in the archives of lavatory experimentation, and I discovered that it was the first day of the new millennium.

*   *   *

Snapsnapsnap. Body, mind and spirit. I felt so vigorous, so alert and energized, so guilefully dichotomous, I could hardly explain the full meaning behind my elation. Guilty of making snap judgments, this dog got snipped for snapping, and I couldn't be more tickled pink. If Jack's first act in killing the giant was to let a bunch of worthless beans . . . duk-duks . . . fall on the earth, I felt I had done much the same, barking out peevish retorts as the twig snapped, giving way under strain, driving out Thema Nadam, and thereby causing one and all to suffer from a fit of otosis. Sometime thereafter, my Ma, good ol' mule, walked into my broad room and said, "You should set back the night, my god! My god! My dictature!" We both had a good laugh and shared a glass of milk and munchies. And then the sun rose, and Mom and I went out and cleared some stones. And there was a big malefic earthquake. And the sun that morning was so bright and beat down so hard that it was blinding to behold, almost as if it wasn't there at all.

It was a real hysteron proteron, believe me. A garden snake, slithering through the grass, succeeded in wrapping itself around my Mother's ankles, and coiled up her trunk until it reached eye level with her, and whispered, "Me, Nehushtan, and these horns mean this ain't any *fête champêtre.*" Once Mother discovered the true identity of this brass snake in the grass, she seized it at the back of the head by a frib and proceeded to uncoil it from around her body. And, at the same time, she asked me what time it was by my watch alone. And I said, "It's exactly nine o'clock." Mother laughed out with a loud roar, "Elam. Elam. Worthy is the blameable that was slammed." And with that she brought the snake up to her face and planted a kiss directly upon its forked tongue. And the snake said, "Ma, I may be subtle, but I'm not malicious."

It just so happened that Mom was wearing her favorite silk evening mazzeltov gown with the provocative split up the side. And three women who happened to be walking by, looking from afar, said, "Really. The nerve of some people. Have they no shame?" Whereupon Mom lifted her thumb, pressed it against the back of her front teeth, and snapped it outward. And the women dispersed, each going their own way, their tongues sputtering in disbelief. And then Mom and the serpent shared a good hearty laugh. And she set it back down in the reeds, wagging, whereupon it promptly slithered away. Mother turned to me and said behind a smile, "Even in the midst of the garden, I put on a good show."

Mother had produced something very specific that hour. Something that followed from something that did not need to be proved. For I was there. And if anyone need be surprised at Mother's egregious behavior, it is I alone. In my experience, what is finally ejected from a living body is something beyond what is real to the human eye. But getting back to those women who had previously dispersed, like so many planets in various movements and phases – apparently, one of them went so far as to summon, with a *yad-a-hoo*, a tipstaff. For it wasn't too long thereafter, while we were standing in the garden, that a tipstaff drove up in black-and-white and climbed out into full exposure, and addressed Mother and me, asking, *"Truly* is just *what* is going on here?" Mother's quick reply was, "We're trying to get a game going of 'seven devils.' Do you think you could round up four others so we could have a numinous go at it, and nievie-nievie-nick-nack in one another's ear?"

"What the hay?" the tipstaff said, further exposing a gold chain around his neck, from which hung an index finger pointing this way and that with the sweet imperial sway of his body.

Mother approached him, and said, "If you come on inside, I'll give you a drink of any deadly thing I've got and let you have your just desserts, complete with a libera for the dead, because I got the authority to do these things."

And then she went and stood on the right side of the tipstaff. And they went forth into black-and-white. And then tipstaff flew away after Mother reappeared in color.

"Such docetic creatures, men, the whole immane lot of them," Mother said. "The chosen, the select, less than heaven sent. I once had an affair with a melomaniac, dressed in a deep, deep, deep purple shell-like uniform, almost blue, but purple nonetheless. It was such a fine-winged uniform and I just so love an imago in uniform. This was well before you were born, well before I ever knew your father-lasher on my egg, while I was on my *Voyage à Cythère*. Now it just so happened that this man had two beautiful Clydesdales, named Geez and Casper, both trained to lick anything that came into his house. And whenever we made mad vocabulary, those two sweet-toothed dogs would be a panting verbs right alongside of us. Because of them there was hope of resurrection throughout the night, whereas neither angel nor spirit can reawaken the geist from the chief erect."

And then Mother and me dashed down to Mausolus's Place, like a couple of carnivorous tomboys. And Python, he laughed, because he was there. And he said I had quite a mind and that me maw had one too. And he got the best of us, so artful and misworshipped among the marble columns, bases, capitals and friezes, and battlescenes, and horses in relief, and Luc's dialogues of stone among the sweating tourists . . .

TIME TO REFLECT

I took a shower in order to apply proper termination to the act, which in its own fashion was both instant and sudorific. I was shaken by the utter violence . . . from a motion of his mouth that drew a red, milky film into the air, shot from the roots of his teeth . . . an irresistible attraction that he once applied, in an obsequious manner, to all that he detested in the earth . . . fleshhooks, though they be. What I arranged for him was nothing short of a sinecure. Man of wool. Not a mystic but a wolf hiding within an absence of sound behind the doors of his face, rendering the unwary, stone-deaf. I thrived in a color other than silhouette. No collar. Returning fire for fire, envoking a divine protection for the innocent animals lacking spoken dialogue, I committed neither offense nor fault during my undertaking.

When all is said and done, I, alone, will be standing as the one and only hypsicephal, having thrived so heartily on *élan vital.* And why not? All other nourishment was in such short supply. I would have starved beyond recognition were it not for that one vital source, a force so embedded within my gut as to be rendered indiscernible. But take heed. Do not be fooled by that which is invisible to the naked eye. For it is not by bread alone that one prefigures existence. It is in the eye, the third eye, so pronounced in the center of the forehead, that one is able to both sleep and see simultaneously. Of course, I survived by way of principles . . . creative and indefinite. And, more than not, lent my wits to haruspicy. Be alert to the fact that that which is vague is also that which evolves. For, then, any such element remains open to that area of gray where there is neither pro nor con, crudeness nor refinement. Cut me open if you will. In fact, plunge your hand deep within my intestines, deep, until you grip *élan vital* by its very throat and seize the impulse of life. Feel it beating electrically in your hand. Such keen and contagious excitement has never been felt before. I'm sure of it. Eviscerate my fire, my runners bent, my long pavement to mart, like Erasmus, and wound my entrails around a mariner's windlass.

Lord-High-On-Everything-Else. I tell you, I was in the middle of the murder scene, committing an act so pretentiously dogmatic, I had every lord mentioned in the Domesday Book humbly vomiting references to high heaven.

Jeremiah Pyramidal gate-keeper foreseeing Jekyll and Hyde, future-tense – his jaw will hang like a Java man dug up, pieces unhinged. Picture me, a hen on the block, one of the best tales around, counting my eggs, one by one, letting that one drop to the floor and crack, throwing this one against the wall, a cosmic force imploding, the yolk, a delicious red syrup splattering letters every which way. Something akin to diapedesis, loose-oozing guttatim through walls into the mesh, pursuing a certain condition, be it death or struggle, medication or . . . transformation, I know not. I tell you, I care not the least for him. He cannot be accepted as infallible truth as long as there are rumors and reports in the air, curmurring, reporting, without authority, the end. Ahh, it seems like everyone wants to do god in.

PICK UP

god was hooked.

Mother nearly died when she found out. She was thrown for a loop. She flew in her GV in the Gulf Stream. In the bosom of her coffin, the cradle of her lord, she sat, having been put at the bottom of the list, passing overhead without honors from the Cambridge Platonists, even though she had felt a lifting of spirits whenever haunting the old motels, the winding streets and narrow passages unaltered with time, or experimenting with small matters and great fires in the cavendish laboratory, finding specific heats for this cat or that kat, this air or that heir, inflammable or not, which brings up gas, and the properties thereof, and water, and baptism, 5.48 times that which is below earth, where one might find a cavendish playing whist with the Grand Sweeper of Whitechapel and the Invincibles of Phoenix Park. And she shrieked. And she barked. It was a false matter. A hard matter. A controversial matter. A root matter. A wise matter. A blazing matter. "How great a matter a little fire. Kind . . . lethal . . ." It was a real *coup de theatre.* And the course leading up to it – nothing more nor less than a hunt for dramatic ejectment, a rev. society, a chip off the old nature's block, for burke's sake – was turned towards Fables, although leaving real marks was *theirs* poor trade for medicine. A pinch of *dementia praecox* thrown in, as well as a bit of premature *dementia cockalorum,* with an emphasis on lorum. A stimulating leaf. A measure. I'm sure that as soon as Mother appeared, she was greeted by an echo, the same echo that belted out *Dies Irae* in the masses: 'Arise! Take up your bed. Wist not. Depart. Spit on the ground. Jesus in 1496. John in 1511. Faithful witness of the cinerescent dead. Of the kings in full joy. Gray overalls in moil. Seven! Ahh! Diddle-ee-dee, diddle-ee-doo.' Phew.

In order to get off this main drag, this obnoxious mundungus, the one in which we have been hauling the heaviest body, the heaviest offal in existence, first and foremost as a word (secondly, as an actual body), we must first regard our relationship to this word/body in terms of doxology. Take it from me (a regular doxy by birth, if there ever was one, born on a *Dies non,* a real drab, if you know what I mean, who was at least theoretically present when good ol' Sorrow Himself – Lamb, Door, Bread, Vine . . . *Dii Penates* all in a line – was followed by Cheaper-By-The-Dozen-Dragged-Themselves-Carking-Down-The-Beaten-Path-Crossing-Over-Crossroads-With-Crosses), you don't want to praise any such Source to the highest when, in fact, you could very well have a Draco-on-Draft on your hands. Do not be intimidated by this amplification. Get up off the floor and wipe the dust off your knees. god forbid, you'll all be suffering from reversal cerebrospinal meningitis of the mancipium-genuflexion, the manner in which you pay homage (obedience), prostrating yourselves upon your very marrow, bones, yielding your palms, hiding your pathetic, diminished heads, your noisome sores, bending to the very yolk under the hand.

GARDEN SCENE DESCRIPTION

Laborious and heavy this condition I suffer from – crowded, packed together bodies, megalopsychy, most predominantly. Although breath is fleeting, and everywhere around us there can be found a lack of breath, I am at odds with both life and death, feeling everyone's breath at once. I had intended to pass over the more tender constructions of existence; namely, those three-dimensional creations formed of disparate elements, like the bones of four hundred posaunen – heads of cattle, nonetheless, talking, chanting. But this condition, this omnipotent dichotomist, stopped me dead in my tracks. A trump if ever there was one. And on a misprint shaped like three sixshaped port-wine marks, this dic stated, regardless, "Get thee to a comart." Grabbing me by the shoulder, he first compelled me to play a game of ombre with him, the old three-handed arrangement as it were. The only problem being, there were only two players. Father, daughter (but no H.G.). Ma, which . . . well . . . made for quite a narrow and inappropriate opposition.

But creeping was the northern wind, creeping from the crest of the sun, from the east, from the pulpit, from the altar, from the chancel, creeping, creeping from the flexing lump of muscle meat, from the bridge player, from the full moon, from the lamb, from the figs' untimely green buggers, stars sliding backside down, quaking blood pounding all the way to the sack, pubic hairs and all.

The greatest rape was the reduction of my talent (like a once healthy nucleus dwarfed by pycnosis) for the conformity of a creativeless society.

THE M7 IN THE STALLS OF DOOM

Magnificoes Seven! Cowboys! Oarsmen! Dugongs! Clerks! Warriors! Soldiers! Assassins! Saviours! Stick to your blades, striking hard with your thrust, with your grave determination to deliver blows through the broken waters, the broken words, the broken heart, the broken gut, the broken bowels. Alas. Still stuck in the stalls of Canter's, the M7 were engaged in their own battle with indigestion, and were forced to let god pass. Cut!

The following news report on *The Collapse and Fall of god* is brought to you by the *Casting Lots of BB:* The Leading Casting Agency of Bottomless Bits.

ABADDON: "The most terrifying, unglamorous, unconventional earthquake of the millennium occurred less than an hour ago on the island of Napaj. Registered at 6.66, the earthquake left the island in utter ruins. Yes, god made good on one promise to us, his *enfants perdus,* that, indeed, there would be an earthquake (along with voices, vices, and a censor) should everything get totally out-of-hand. However, the ultimate decision regarding what needs to be done at this, the unknowing hour, would need to be taken up by an *un-board* of carefully selected, dead-body-non-educators, specialized in outlining sudden world-wide oblivion, all of whom were (nearly) totally separated and full of moist grapes and bald heads in the face of god's equivocal dis-appearance. But, first, light must be shed on the utter chaos now synonomous with Napaj by addressing one disoriented survivor, who was flown in from the dust that is now Napaj in order to attend a semblance of the annual Clog Dance Competition, normally held in Napaj at this time of the year.

"Jez, could you please share with us your particular experience upon interaction with the impact of the quake?"

JEZ: "Well, I was clogging at the time with Sir Tussle Russell of Shenendoah Valley, grandson of the ninth Duke of Iveagh, who should have been an Earl, but he detested anything with four letters in it. Things weren't going so bad, that is, until that horrible chandelier fell on top of Sir Tuss, whereupon he mistook the 'a' in Iveagh for a 'u,' and the 'u' in Duke for a 'y,' which would have made him the grandson of an unruly member, if not the grandson of a covetous uranian you-know-what. Oh, that's the chandelier over there. I think if you bend down a bit and hunt, you'll be able to see Sir Tuss's sole. Sir Tuss, himself, is dead, and paid extra for it, but he did the best clogging I've ever seen and was, in fact, cachinnating so handsomely when the chandelier finally topped him and gelled him, I don't think he ever realized he was even dead. After that, of course, there was a lot of screaming and a thorough-wave stampede of clogs to the early door, this being the resurrected Music

Hall of Evan's Supper Rooms and all. To be honest, my own ears are still clogged from all the clogging. I was *totally* running instep behind the King of Belgium, saluting all the while, and in the chaos the King dropped this book. It's a copy of *Lebbi*. It's absolutely an original copy, written in long hand, which makes for a tormenting read at 46,227 "ands" alone, god only knows. *Since* I had glimpsed through the book so close to the 6:12 earthquake that I wept at 5:04 and was nearly blotted out at 3:05 without a word, I thought: *should I survive this woe, I might be too shook up to talk or, at Least, to hold an extraordinary entangled conversation for maybe ten or even twenty broken years.* I only thank god that I was able to recoup so quickly and get a good grip on me east *and* west and end of ends. Not to change the subject, but if you like, I'll now show you the back of my hand and try to sing for you a few bars from 'I'm a Little Bit Ristly, You're a Little Bit Rock 'n Roll, So Let's Exchange DNA and Moll the Trulle!'"

Cut!

LOOKING BACK (at arm's length) AT ARMAGEDDON
Adv. Arm1616 H.T. ATE BOOK
Visit our Website at Hit://000. ARM. ED. MR.

Regarding the Battle that was fought and lost, there was a Secretion Council that not only overlooked the activities of the Battle, but also represented the nucleus of *The Spiritus Frumenti Powers,* which was to develop and impose over the next *live* millennium a Centralized Administration, composed of a shining kakistocracy.

Without a doubt, the end of Armageddon marked a revolutionary crack in the once prevalent Judyo-Christian tri-dynamics of figs, flowers, buttocks of flowers and paradise. Given that the condition of natural weaknesses is only benefited by sublime redemption and forgiveness (which is, at least, part of the creed of Judyo-Christian conception), it was the demand of the Secretion Council that every previous thought be done away with, as thinking only brings about periodic discontent due to internal unrest and excessive judophobia, as a result of a mismatch of guiltenstein and angerler – a discontent which is held is soul-check via falanga or *lay on order!* by sole force. The regime's main contention was that in order to prevent dissatisfaction from arising from the soul, a bat/club system of sovereignty must be established, as long as it is able to absorb all political, social and economic conflicts within the existing spiritual framework without coming apart in the act. And the best way to establish this (according to the Secretion Council) was to eliminate all guilt and blame on behalf of the ear and eye, and to thereafter satisfy all needs and desires of the atechnic masses so that not a tear is shed, nor a seed is sewed, after the internecion.

Going back always – it was during the Battle of Armageddon that the Secretion Council came to rest upon a single radical act of secularization. This was where the satrap and his satrapy came about to do so much rapping under the tag of Sanctus[3]. According to the *tides* of the Battle, it was all too evident that religion was secund and was therefore not equipped to manage both war and paradise. If a regime were to be absolute, it would need to constitute a newt principle, namely a viscuous one, wherein god ruled in the flesh and was not a servant, nor a carpenter, nor a great and mighty spirit residing in the realms beyond, but an *ad vice* man. The con sect of the Tri Nity™ in tricot, represented in the name of Rector (a Sub. of Christian Galimatias), would need to be abolished. In the new regime, the Cremator, holding a bill, would also be referred to as the Great John Thomas (a Nick off the old block), who would be available to the masses in constant rhythm, beat and rollick, via satellite and remote cunt-roll envenomation, whereby he would be able to regulate existence with but a smile, a rod, and a brief *touching* answer to any particular question asked customarily. It was the great J.T. himself, who, in the throes of dissolution, battled with the goy Prince, eye-to-eye, in what was probably the most important internecine-cunt flick yet, whether global or spiritual, featuring a nazirite's acceptance to being defiled by a corpse, while drinking wine and getting a haircut with/by an esbat NC-17, disguised in the form of a *Rev. Aeb* in a sea of glass, over and over and over and over again. There was an interest of an acquisition of power at stake and the Cremator felt, based upon the reputations of the most studfast gods on the battlefield, that he alone was most entitled to supremacy among Mais, Erbse & Spargel – yes, he, an Erector, who, on the one hand, was an absolute participant in war, while on the other hand was absolutely horrified by the utter slaughter of Armageddon as directed by goles himself, was most entitled. The total casualities therein amounted in the millions. Men were burned! ripped apart! dissected! and indeed diced-died such agonizing near-deaths! It was therefore *fundament* that the Erector, shaped like an agnolotti, should come to call himself Holey in the First Place. With his cremations, buns, and trollops (however loyal or dis-loyal) burke-strickened to near-death in the smoky gip field, where the sgip were marked 5 times/5 ways on the foreleg before getting choked, it was no wonder that his royal, centralized firm of Sarin & Soman gosh! his royal legions, his Royal Gene Court à la Covent Garden, would leap and disappear so abruptly and with such nebbishness. (Note: It was another leaper of sorts who arose out of the smoke with given power to smoke neither grass, nor any green thing, but only sealless men for five months, and to further torment those men with non-holophrastic discourses/arguments on design, cosmos, perfection, first causes and first movers, until those very men are driven crazy, doubting even their visions; which, in this case, was a horse prepared for battle with the hair of a woman, the teeth of a lion, and the tail of a scorpion.)

There were several other names that were made famous in the Battle of Armageddon as well. One was a Russian prince, a graduate technikum turned tax collector, who went by the name of Jud Bags; a rather formless fellow given over to nervosity, possibly due to being a bastard of Pavlov's dogs-in-nervism. It was his habit to prowl the battlefields, taking whatever he could from the pockets of the dead spirits strewn about. He was recognizable by the two golden arches above his crown and the flashing shazam sign directly above G, emphasizing: *over 2 billion served.* Jud Bags had probably more spiritual acquisitions than any other participant in the field. Indeed, during his SETI exploits, he would occasionally show marked signs of decline to the right, as well as to the left of his jud hole, as his unlimited exploits filled up his pockets so fully that they nearly dragged him to the earth. (Some would say, *beneath the earth.*)

Jud Bags, turned aside, had two henchmen whom he called his "cowboys" (in the same manner as *Mark & John*), who each, in turn, had under their command an army of oriental Zouaves with French tongues dressed in civil war gab, who, in turn, were attended by assorted zymites with baskets of hardy leavened bread to keep the troops well-fed, who all in turn fled.

There were sharp differentiations between the various ranks, depending upon their specific locations in relation to one another. Those serving in or on the knees of god were called *caps*. Their purpose was to extract any water collected in god's knees due to spiritual humiliation. Without their quick and efficient services, god was prone to fall head-over-heels during intensive moments of battle, and to get an attack of gyppy tummy, and do a nasty run in a foreign country on bended knees, playing *swift jakes on the tail*, which not only disrupted the course of fighting but typically left his streamlined rivals in stitches – rivals who, other world-wise, would have pounced upon god in an instant had they not been rendered breathless with laughter and diffluence in their own right.

Another such differentiation was known as *Go!rods!* Actually, their function was to (without *one* question) protect god's gonads (and general vicinity) at the cost of arm and leg, or eye and ear, or foot and tongue, as there was a schism in the scheme. Naturally, battles became so confusing at times that the general area was often left unprotected (i.e., without authority), and many an iron hit was made, sometimes even with a *god*emiche. Needless to say, the scratches, cuts and bruises on god's privates accounted for the several one-armed and/or one-legged spirits with two tongues running amuck throughout the battlefield, one of whom god pegged as *Pvt. John Miche*, who in former times *layed Ma* when he was better know as John 'Blood' Bull.

There were others in the ranks and files of each fighting side, respectfully; spirits of voracious appetites, thirsty for blood in battle, autonomy, independence, anomie, misogyny, sodomy, misogamy, and general alienation *âme* – engineers, artisans, judges, doctors, priests and composers of pooka music. In fact, the Supreme Commander of the pooka unit was one Sir George Alexander Gibb Samson, thinly disguised as Alexander Pope, the same made famous by his tory, *Swift,* another John, who would prove to be a witness to sorcerers, adulterers *and* false swearers on either the left or right of his stall (in the theater), according to St. James in the bygone text. Alexander led an army of 200 thousand thousand accordion players into battle against god, all playing the plain chant, "Today Harmony, Tomorrow the Holey World," or "Go For Broke" (another John), who would awake! all with meaner things – the pride of kings, ample fields, deers and winding mazes – but not without a plan, without a head, or without a stitch. While the lyrics possessed (at least between the lines) a latent hostility toward Jews, not a Christian was left unturned. Pope conducted the charge as (a lionized maestro!) a poperine pear, exhibiting various *nicely* salutes throughout, hailing his pope's ruling eye, head and nose, like in the sequel *Innocent III: a study in consanguinity.* Those watching from the sidelines couldn't help but polka, which was one reason why that particular battle turned into a major dance contest, with god and his partner (the glorious fruit, Freddo William III, a.k.a. D.C.) coming in third, formulating their 600-odd steps into a tricky witch of agnesi or Riccardo's test. Still, all one hundred and forty-four thousand contestants managed to walk off starkers (streaking) with swelling, fat trophies nonetheless, and Delicious cerise balls as promising as James Nais . . . mith's original version of thirteen in Mass.

Indeed! One of the highlights of the Battle of Armageddon was when Jerome Bonaparte, King of Diaphoresis, Westperspiration, charged! onto the scene (thus incurring a debt) with wild fanaticism, waving sword in hand. The only trouble was that his 'charge' occurred while both parties were taking a bread break (specifically paratha) and were quite expired in breath. Realization of such poor timing left Jerome so red in the face that both sides nicknamed him *Dr. Little Cherry-picker*. Both sides further accented his arrival by briefly joining together and dragging Jerome off his charged horse and administering so many swats to his cheeks that when all was said and done, Jerome could no longer speak French, and thereafter Portuguese became his native tongue. Unfortunately, no one in the field understood a word of Portuguese, and Jerome's ferociously shouted commands were met with nothing but stoned ignorance. The last was seen of Jerome, his horse had him pinned lovingly to the ground in an otherwise deserted spot in the field; and Jerome was laughing in Latin (*"Copia verborum! Rapere pax! Necare!"*), and pumping hysterically, while the horse punctiliously tongued his ear.

As you can see, Armageddon was not an easy battle to describe. It was much like talking with baloney in your mouth and swallowing a curate's egg whole at the same time . . . *M/F Bishop left, shitmoves by a patzer.* O the blood, the chaos, the cries of the hounds of hell pursuing, as it were, the sights of scholarly game, heavenly birds, and playful, leisurely brides as boned as Ginevra after her wedding day, angels all! Paying for what they believed in was terrifying in the stall. To the victor belongs the tontine, which leads us to still another victim warrior.

Don Ho. Hoian by birth, Don was of a munda mentality in that he used a munda Tory to wipe clean his vessel. He later converted to *orthodox Jew's marrow* (for no other reason than he had a *mind* to anger any Ubiquitarians lingering in the midst) and grew his beard and hair infinitely long, and everywhere wore only black with a yellow chew and crossbones, and uttered such statements as 'Matzo is fair with butter and jam, as long as when you eat you never shake a lady's hand!' Don solved the mystery behind the simple destruction of the vessels of wrath, containing the sacred recipe for gefilte fish, by pointing the finger at Ed Aphic Sully Van, who he claimed nearly always had a piece of gefilte fish tucked in his cheek during social occasions, and actually preserved hundreds of g. fish in sealed-tight jars in his basement due to his overwhelming edacity. Don was regarded infamously in the battlefields, for his thirst for blood was relentless, and he was even known to drink from the dirty river flowing out of any enemy, and to thereafter bottle it and brown paper bag it and drink up the light luminaria – the apocryphal *aqua mirabilis,* V.G., at his leisure, on the corner of a 1224 cold night with Aquilo blowing in his ear – as long as he blessed it first and could be certain of experiencing an edaphic climax afterwards. Indeed, more angels became kosher this way than there are plaintive rabbis in Israel.

Unbeknownst to pre-Armageddions, the major bulk of the Battle lasted twenty-two minutes. Of course, there were several moments thereafter which could be misconstrued as part and parcel of the endless battle itself – such as beatings with the head and horns; targeted halibut and flounder; the laughing-stock on the mount – the object of criticism, abuse and contempt as hereby written about under the heavy beams, end to end, amidst a sea of butt ends, crushed and mangled, stubbed and stamped, smeared and dauby blottesque; and a severely attacked body end of a pork shoulder prepared the night before, leftover today among the unburned end of a candle and a broken cask of wine, the contents of which had spilled long before these words were written, during a long, exhausted blotto butt of a prison term – cherubims aflaming, excrement aflowing, jacks ejaculating. Generally speaking, the *biblia pauperumical* portions, with garbled objections of false Js, added in, were still about the *canned-silence length of a free sitcom.*

What is there to say about Armageddon? Not all who participated there were warriors. Obviously, there were bystanders, subjects of adharma, inactive souls, as well as souls in disharmony with the nature of things, innocent citizens caught up in the turmoil, *hippocratic worriers* refusing to conform to the worldly situation at hand. There were also plain old folks in plain clothes telling spade jokes to blokes named Sam. Reporters and commentators. One such commentator was Saint UGHustine, who wrote a small pamphlet that defined Armageddon as a hippophagous war. He entitled the pamphlet *De Civitate Dei Deis.* Saint UGHustine wasn't much of a commentator. He was, in reality, a hippophagist, and believed that important things did not need to be said. To read Saint UGHustine's account of the Battle, one would discover the following:

(a) It was sort of warm that day. Not hot, but not cold. The full temperture at the time of the Battle was, more or less, *lukewarm,* though perhaps a bit lewd and a mighty bit dusty on account of all the city being in an uproar, as well as on an assault-alert, and planet-stricken with the daily news: **Latakia barfs up ruins over Phrygia. Goldberg hotdogs it.**

(b) There were some clouds present. However, not a lot of clouds, but enough to cover a bow coming upright, rising out of the west, and bringing forth a shower coming with great loud glory, which all received (it) in the eye.

(c) The Battle position was roughly as follows: both lines advanced wrathfully toward one another at about 15 years per minute in living color. However, in retreat, god was able to cover a lot more dusty ground in far to less *simple* time, thus assuring that if god puts his dualistic head to it, he can move very quickly as on a sea of glass – lifeless, last, and under power and authority, but wearing a two-tone coat.

(d) The back of god's *T*-shirt, which the opposing forces got a glimpse of just as god was about to dissolve and thereby make his extra-speedy, hasty retreat, had printed on it god's universal, alkahestic motto: *Dieus le veult!*

More could be said about the *De Civitate Dei Deis.* For example, Saint UGHustine's chapter on *Armageddon Vendors,* particularly the section describing the *astronomical* sale of such food items as *Hotgods with Crushed Mustard Seeds* and *JuicyristLicoriceStrips,* is priceless material for any would-be historian or, for that matter, anyone planning on going into the vending business, particularly in regards to dogs or vegetables or major *Religious Altercations.* This brings us to one definite conclusion that Saint UGHustine was able to record at the back of his pamphlet: **the sale of *BeelzebubBlasters* far outreached the sale of *SatanSwatters.*** Perhaps this had something to do with Beelzebub being more closely related to flies. In essence, *BeelzebubBlasters* were nothing more than common flyswatters. And during the Battle, *the Blasters* were going for two-for-one, which may have accounted for the lagging sales in *SatanSwatters* and other such criminal devices. Other novelties sold on the grounds under the *Sinsign* included *god Dusters,* which were nothing more than durable wineskins used to wipe the dust of the dead off the carnal parts of the spectators; *Christ All-Mighty Combat Boots* with crucifixion spikes serving as "cleats" (incidentally, these were a hot-selling item with the kids); the forever popular *Saviourly Slavery Icemint Chewing Gum* – just a little something to *quench* the Sugar urge; *Go! Angel Ale* for the grown-ups to down; four-foot-two high creepycrappy statues of god in a foul/fowl T-shirt going for 11.20

leva a-piece, as there were only four hand-painted models made before the mold forever was broken; and CD's depicting various (i.e., infinite) sound effects, including sounds underfoot and cries of "How long! O! *h'm h'm Simultanéisme!*" (Note: There is a sad twist regarding Saint UGHustine: two weeks after the Battle, while consuming a left-over-wine-flavored-*Hotgod*-warmed-over-in-the-microwave, and partaking of a diffarreation, he choked to death. Apparently, he had been working on his latest manuscript, *The Planetesimal Hypothesis*, at the time of the accident. His last written words were addressed to someone by the name of David [still, a mystery].)

h'm h'm,

One of the major problems concerning man's control of god is that, generally speaking, god is too large to be directly administered to. In a supine position, his length is well over the length of ten football fields. Thank god I wasn't made to be his tailor! It was difficult enough going to market and asking the clerk where the accidents of Christ were kept on the endless shelves lined in plastic cloth. Perhaps this accounts for the fact that god has not changed his wardrobe in ten

Unfortunately, this was all Saint UGHustine wrote. We can only surmise from here that the microwave buzzer went off and that instead of going forth to have a quick snack, Saint UGHustine, upon heeding the call, jumped up for his last, and thus suffered *fatal humiliation*. Estimated time of death: 3 p.m.

Another curious fact concerning Armageddon was the heavy use of muskets during the battle; but not only muskets, for god himself was armed with two petronels and two French flint-lock pistols snatched right out of the hands of Louis XIV. Indeed, during a noon break in the Battle, god was interviewed regarding his weapons. "The weapon is *à toute force*," he was heard to say. Apparently, what attracted god to the pistols (which accounted for his personal Raffles-theft of them) were the stocks. Not only were they made of dark walnut (a most attractive wood when polished), they were carved into the figure of Hercules skinning a lion, only without life or consciousness; *'Muslin'* draping Her loins; the remainder of the *Word* going up the *lum* in ashes or falling down into the depths of the *lum* in despair, which god went after straightway and, upon connection, rent off the garments, and proceeded to beat the best leg.

Within hours of god's defeat at Armageddon (all captured on video) and his Ignavia-fleeing with Arms, he assembled his council together and admitted to them that things did not look good. For upon his property and most dear life a damned defeat was made; he was beaten *hors de combat*. god's original plan to have a quarter of his angels dress up as Pawnee Indians in hay skirts, and a quarter to adorn the light uniforms of Prussian Line Infantry Men and be married by foot, one to another, in sickness, health, sacrifice or death, until all became beholding men, had miserably backfired. (Actually, it was Prince Leopold of Anhalt-Dessau who, as Dess, god's field marshall, had advised him as to how perfect his angels would look in such glazing attire, especially after *spending* for fourteen years in Puerto Rico, bobbing, as it were, like obsolete asinegoes. For we must never forget, *"Stabia quocunque ieceris."* *Just think, after all the T . . . T . . . Tnights and the Bis Mark plus one, the hot iron hit, BM, the descending two-in-one swelling in Jordan like a Frank in a bun, he was still . . . sin . . . the atrabilarian one.)*

Naturally, Satan and his boiling legions, one-quarter of which were commanded by Field Marshall Ney (62), who at the time was nursing an eruption a Baby couldn't sit on, couldn't help howling at how ridiculous god's army looked descending from the watery cumulonimbus clouds in such jupiterian getup. The change from spiritual dress to football/baseball/cashmerette/golf/warrior/Godzilla conquering attire, accompanied by powdered white wigs, white tights and caps (each bearing the landwehr cross), not only exasperated the barbarity of warfare but, as worn by such heavenly cast heavies as El Christ Risus, Solomon Mongrel, Moses Esotropia, Peter, Au lait, and Mary, and none other than god himself, downright sent shivers up and down the ideological spine of the missionary brotherhood, and prompted all to cry a graupel. *"Cirrus uncinus! WWJD?"* While in the field the worshippers bellowed on the Ground, *"Am I my brother's beeper? Yea! I will drag his skin and lather him! I will chase the snakes in crooked lines and page him. O he's so fine, so fine, that ever-lovin' all-Star of mine!"* The message (on bracelets, T shirts, gold rings, underwear) was *t . . . t . . . teu c* (goodbi hook echo Hallmark is here) *lear: dust to dust* – either knight of either side was equated with the devil, and the message was for all knights to clear out of Acre with or without a hammer, and to make themselves comfortable in another realm without creating a mess of their ages. Obviously, this message resulted in a fury of spiritual passions puffing on both sides, which brought up a little dido about Aeneas and Herc and a Hit grand opera concerning a King in his lull, who was about to take on tremendous proportions with a horse's head in mind, a mare's tail (if not a dragon's), and a planchette in hand, which also brought up another *D* and *Á,* who would come to transform themselves into two giant-sized poodle's heads with mohawks, and snarl like death's business at one another. After awhile this pseudo-display of mighty message grew old, and the lingering crowd kept awaiting in Acre for him to come demanded that both parties think of something a bit more occupational to do. That was when god, as a querent, briefly retreated and took a second look over his past twenty-two tarot card/astrological readings. Needless to say, he had "fired" each of the last twenty-two readers, and thereafter appointed another, a certain Lazare Carnot, who, after having god pick out ten separate cards, inferred that his chances of winning at Armageddon were "lukewarm," if not "fully guaranteed," since he was clearly in his tenth house and his lunar temperament was cusping the right nip corner of the Milky field, sort of like Clint at Lew in (the) sky KY Queen. This meant that god was finally coming out of his *look, lo, Starr, a Lamb sat on the mountsyndrome trip,* and was finally coming into his *far country,* speckled with birdbaths, having clearly gained ten extra chocolate pounds cast into James's gold fever. Lazare told god that he needed to be weaned of his white milk and made to fall into sporadic fits of asitia and, in doing so, he could gain tolerable respect for the mass; then he would be able to wean the white horse in an opened sea, along with all the cattle in a mackerel sky, and get a good rush in the long run. Three of the cards that god chose were the Hanged Man, Death and the Judgment. *Nu* you sayinyid? Lazare's faithful expression dropped upon *truly* viewing these cards; and thereafter he suggested to god that just to be "safe," he should reserve a room at the Marriott on Hilltop Drive under an alias, *Loup Garou,* and spend the weekend "organizing kosher labels." If anything went wrong with his image, his mark, or his number, he would be able to hide out in the baignoire with the prickly tuna, the tunny and teazle, and compose an entirely new victorious work under the heading: *We take no notice of it. We do not know. You don't know JACK So.* We cannot (at this time) go into full detail in regard to god's tarot reading with Lazare; but if the reader is wanting to learn more regarding this topic, he should rent the Video, *god and the big T (tail that is): What the Stars Told him Regarding an Armed Dog,* as later told to Victor Borgest, Dingus, and Dojigger Ferfree from Jebel. Actually (viz. factually), it is a monumental documentary in three parts. *Part I: god and the Devil: Was the Big 'D' Really His Dad?* runs over 7 plagues alone, and departs only after the King comes (sic) over the child, which, in turn, opens up the second part, *Kismet is the Kist,* or, roughly translated, *Fate is the Coffin.* So Shut Your Lid with a Y and Foget the Skull-Job.* (*Note: For those interested readers of hereforeverafter, read S.A.T.'s account of PostRev. in *YesMa! There is NoLife Guard on Duty at the Lake of Fire!)*

ALERT

Reader . . . yes, you. It is by-time you interact purely with the book. At this point, you can choose to remain passive and sit. But be forewarned – passivity is nothing more than a sour acid fruit that vibrates at the fastest frequency of any of humankind's various stagnations. For, in the end, history shows that all which is consumed files out into a movement. Some movements defiantly leave their marks on paper – massive marks; mysterious symbols; letters actually smeared upon a bundle; challenging blotches of matter; transversed, cryptic scripture soon to drop; distilled characters about to greet the great infusion and soak in the muddy pool that will soon all vanish into the sea with the massive marks still on the paper; painful movement for all the world beneath the surface to read and decipher – or to simply eat the contents of, depending upon the nature of the species that meets it, even if that specie be a descendant of a flannelmouthed sucker, or a by-blow of a blowen, or a voyant bent on volupté, or any other living movement nearly transparent on the page, if not invisible. Hardly a mark at all – more a divisible dot, a wet clarity – a movement can also be a bomb, even though the bomb, the miserable missile, the digested matter of life preceding the fall, can be the sign of the times; the pun of the period.

Mythology, fantasy, fairytale, legend, physics, metaphysics, history, police tricks, math, seances, and *show business standing* – it was god's lot to defeat them all obsoletely, if not at Armageddon then somewhere along the way. What wasn't noted prior to the actual Battle was just how many battles god had had to experience before finally arriving upon that same site. True, in all the skirmishes and battles thus fought, god's legions had performed bravely; his army in several of the skirmishes had been spread out over a realm stretching a hundred light years and one-half, in an assaulted position, while the opposing forces had occupied a considerably shorter space (e.g., analogous to the western front). In several of the affairs, *Au Contraire* had succeeded in concentrating his main effort against the left wings of god's Army, who, in turn, were sent hurdling downward to the earth in vast numbers, hopelessly flapping right wings only, after having it out with Leah Cimex, whose 'ex' is out of context. Certainly, god had enough wages-in-order to keep the Battle long, for he had been able to save the tithes collected for the support of his 'promised land,' and thereby utilize the bulk of his resources in order to operate his vast *Army,* his *Project Locust*, wherein his 1000 plan for Armageddon was to have countless numbers of xiphoid locusts emerge from the smoke upon the earth, and with the fiery power of a scorpion drive every sealless man barking mad.

Nevertheless, it was difficult to watch the sun set its watch over Armageddon and discover that time ran late with the planet earth and the nightingales crying for the souls in purgative laxity. The battlefield held more dead bodies, more carnage, more coprolite, more dust than a bin. Bodies, transfixed in death, still held the buttery-pearl colors of the first Battalion – but nay a breath, not even a buzz of dropdead flies on Armageddon.

O. In the long run, in the long, drunken, topsy-turvy, blatant, blood-and-guts and tormented run to the empty tomb, each and everyone of us must ask ourselves, 'What got done?' or , in another way, 'What was left undone?' It is hard enough ugh that we should breathe – breathe to struggle; breathe to survive; breathe to come and see; breathe to have a name; breathe to create a history; hard enough that we should be made to create, and thereafter make a dent in faith and charity. It isn't enough to say that one tiny drop, one little splash of balanced blood, clear and direct, would be enough to touch and warm the otherwise cold surrounding ink of oblivion. We must be willing to fight the good sleeping fight. But not in the moon's cups, nor in the moon's shine, for the moon is airless, waterless, sterile and unsuited for life; nor in Venus's cups, for Venus is choked with clouds, and is as hot as an oven at her lid surface, and it is difficult to walk in slippers on such a harsh ground; nor in Mars's cups, for Mars is an endless, dusty, arctic desert with a vacuous, oxygen-deficient atmosphere not suitable for gold; nor in Jupiter's cups, for Jupiter is deadly frigid, two thousand miles deep, descending to soulless oceans of methane, not nearly equated with ambition, leadership nor religious zeal; nor in Saturn's cups, for Saturn is a plumbiferous old man with a wooden leg and a scythe, swinging the lead, cold and damp – but in the head of our own making.

COME DEATH, SO STEALTHILY

By the time the Cyclops had sailed over Phoenix, riding on the back of his crap-globular-cluster, Ugh, Armageddon had long since come and gone. A hollow, moaning, lonely, forlorn, bront wind swept over the barren sands, the purple dust that once was the able bodies and souls, the long lost participants of the Battle of Armageddon. The wind suggested by its very wail that it was a nomadic wind, and was well-familiar with desolate and forgotten places once alive with history and activity. This was the same wind that had spent a brief time crying over the deserts of Mars; the same howling voice bemoaning the barreness of Saturn – all spiral grains of the universe, empty of hydrogen, oxygen and carbon, devoid of any definable grain or measurable texture that would otherwise be deemed as an integral part of life; the same thunderous wind that had touched its force upon the first verse of Genesis, and had ridden the waves without form, and had plunged into the face of the matterless deep, the dry bed of the unborn oceans of the nebulous sphere.

And it was Cyclops and Ugh (two very abstract nodes galloping through the hourglass of space) who heralded in strange fleers. And in their *oly oly* gallop, Cyclops and Ugh merged with the wayward travelings of the forelorned wind, and tried to conduct it into the elliptical orbit of their godly dreams – dancing spirals, rob-robbing in time through space, forever corkscrewing their way ahead into the great currents – the thunder cells' second estate, coughed from the mouths of duststormdevils – devils in the desert with dark vortical spots in their throats.

The Cyclops waved a ten-gallon hat in the air and used it to swat Ugh's hindquarters. "No time to be still! Giddap!" he commanded with an antic flair. The Cyclops was every cowpoke that ever bit the frontier dust, having lived out an existence on the gloomy range, in an endless sequence of near miracles: fire, flood, famine; having chased all the rattlers into the bush that would have otherwise bitten the horse's heel; having spent an hour in the meadow, casting dust on the bare heads of cattle chewing gifblaar; having played the bit of a pomologist bent on a limb; having flushed the Pharisaical pheasants out of G; having passed through the phragma with Dis, honestly; having sailed the ocean's depths, the sands, from one rock to another, in search of a golden gier-eagle having a foul, wet hare in its grasp. The Cyclops cried out in a low ring, "To the end!"

And what of the sussultorial earth – once full of conflicts, revelations, morals, struggles, agonies, complexities, adversities, uncertainties, bewilderings, surmises and philosophical puzzles? The tempting city streets, once pressed with the abstract poses of city workers, derelicts and nostalgic kings, all gone; every discarded tin can, dog's bark, maple tree and peppermint-flavored chewing gum (the foil wrapper kicked in the street by a centuried breeze), all gone; from micro dust to giant stars, conceived of and pondered by that mysterious factor in the construction of the universe, all gone. Kissed goodbye.

And so Ugh reared and thereby set their course.

. . . FOLLOWING THE MURDER . . .

I stand here naked before the glass. My image is not a part of me. It breathes outside my framework, naked as December and chilled to the bone. A small surgical mask of pubic-coil placed fastidiously on a disjointed, fallen mouth of the body. I could love the glass if only the image did not mimic adversity. I could be a good student of hyalophagia, upon reflection. There is no communion where the three of us are standing, each in our respective places, conducting our own *drame avec soi.* There is no god in kitab, nor eye in the navel. There is no son-of-a-whatever, peering out, abiding by the rules spelled out in street-corner fashion on the midnight sidewalks of New York, highlighting his quidditas. If only I could love the day's eye: Opening Daisy: *Dai-sy pat-ronne give me your answer blue. I'm half-crazy over the like of you.*

Baby, why are you crying? Why? Me . . . ow. Here. Here. Have some *langue de chat.* Dear, dear in a virulent way. These past thousand years no one has heard you. Your tears fall silent, while your winter garments drop mystically for the arrival of snow like scattered pearls. White knight on the mare of transformation, alas. Do you think no one caresses (especially you)? 'Tis true. The sound of your despair suggests to me that a hint of pity tops the cake half-baked. Here, let me eat just some of it – this hostia, your body; baby; quiet; baby! Scooped icing on a spoon. Hush, this should not hurt the virilia. At least not yet. Not before you are standing erect, waiting to be taken back by a hearty regret. You came in naked wetness, a rock grinded down to sand, to form the reflection of birth, to be cared for. For a season.

Killing what you love in sublime fashion is but part of the grand design – the great grand-daddy scheme of spermatic afterthought caught struggling for life in a coil. I plunge daggers, like vampire-fangs, into the mouth of your twisted compartment, your profonde of hopes and schemes, and pull out a plum. The skin wet, barely clinging to the body, like the flesh hanging under the jaw of a fat pig or like the tail pocket of a tattered magic coat; I rock the plum in my arms. In a great city, parted three ways. Poor baby. It doesn't know who the fuck is coming down. Cloned rib went wrong. Welcome to hard times. There, there now. Even hard times has its limbs to cradle, its *objets d'art* to taste of virtu, long forgotten. Such a god-pitiful plum as this. Disgusting creation spawned nothing but a passion irresponsible and tenacious as a rotten tooth in the mouth of a glass jaw, as a bibelot on a dusty shelf. Rock-a-bye, don't you cry for Mary. She's safe and sound in the Roslin Institute being treated for pseudoblepsia and pseudocyesis, among other things. Dear Mother. You're (I'm . . .) so curious after all is said and done. Heard you had a little lamb with fleece as yellow as snow. What a doll.

Back again. The *coup d'essai*. Studying the plan in the glass. Perhaps planning to break it like a vitrifragist. Yesterday, Mother called. She wanted to know which one of three sizes would best fit me for the March ball. I said, "Mother, really, why not just buy me all three? You know I simply adore to purchase anything and everything in pairs, and good god only knows that threes are far better than twos, so why only suffer with one? Really, Mother. It isn't like you couldn't afford it. For god's sake, I'm your kingpin daughter, plus a half, and with this weight, this massive, behemoth weight of a man you vowed in an earlier recitation of an oath pledged under the glass eye of good god to be, for better or worse, your man, Mother . . . for better or for worse . . . give or take sulfer and salt, mercurius . . . your man, pounding his egg-beater into my yolk, you could have at least offered me all three."

When I gave birth to a half-created form and summarized the entire ordeal *aplomb*, I thought that my name would have been placed on Immanuel's good-for-nothing summons lists, reasoning 'tis better to remain tranquil and miscreant and not fear personal space just because it is with us. Needless to say, my name was never shouted when Daddy planted his fine, succulent, god-blasted lips on his piece and trumpeted a note of horn madness that crashed Dumpty Nadir to the earth, thus spilling his yolk across the cowson grass. I looked back and watched in utter dismantled bereavement three billion and a half million netted souls leave their shoes like so many Mickeys on my *mons veneris*, and gather together like so many lion club members toasting to themselves, one to another, in a virtual, visual field of dash – hopes and dreams (not to mention one vocabulary entry, *otter-shrew*) in the white, crisp-billowy, huckleberry clouds above my head. Gravity kept me asunder. Mickey in the cold drink. A bit of Steak at Supper. And (oh, dear) the virtualism of it all has put me in a dizzy. Yes, by god, the grave saints just didn't come-a-marchin'-in. They floated like Niven's balloons, down to the top story. Dewi me and my dead-weight of a cunt triad. I should have been a cock unsung at the crack of dawn – a beast bleeding his bloody soul, wing-hemmed in violet hues, crowned, freckled-faced and collared like a red tailless clown, like a godwelsh red uckers pachisi serpent entwined. Not responding to the predictor's cue but to the sun's breaking moon. At least then I would have been a centerpiece placed in the middle of the table, whilst the Gau gods grazed and gorged on cock-cradle stew, scratched together by old greasy grumus himself. I might have been thrown a sparerib or two, minding me table rules. Or, speaking in plain English, a fly on the wall in the home of a fatty whore called *Baby*. Strap me into that timepiece of a machine that cuts travel into quadrum leaps of dark ages so that I might have the honor of joining John and Mary to Heaven – recusant hands bound together in holy matrimony – and cross them in appropriate urinary fashion befitting a king and queen, before indulging in a *déjeuner à la fourchette*.

Look quickly! Catch a glimpse of my tribunal frowning down upon me, drowning me under tons of molten judgment. Red earth. Sparrow's shit. After the proctodust clears, there stands MacDonald's bread and Disney's spit. Get Tobias to stand in the center and we'll take a picture . . . *Quit!!*

"Light, more light!"

he cries vociferously.

Dust rings my eyes; swirling masses of gray discolor gradually, but assertively, erasing the god-fresh strokes of daylight. Dust brings in the tears that fill a fool's eyes with remorse and bemoaning decay in his latter end. Little girl, yes, dear dusk-devil spirit deep in grassation. Little girl the hand job gave rise to. I once was this little girl sleeping on the earth in white socks that clung like baby sheep around my ankles. In the dusk of the waning day, in the deepening, dull-deadening rays of slipping sun, I answered the call of my Mother. Little sparrows. Little girls, 1,000 she asses, such as I was back when, should not be out past dusk; wolf-beaten tracks to my front door that is built atop me like the shell of a snail. *Oops, nearly tripped over a dead Jew strangled in the street. Toby, you lousy bloodhound, find me home!* Job, well-done! Daddy thickened the roof with sod. It was what lifted me to prayer: *"Now I lay me down to sleep . . . bray the lord . . . full of days . . . my voluntary escape . . . for a little season of misshapen fate."*

" . . . Good god, will you turn off that fucking light!"

. . . THERE WILL BE A COMMERCIAL

When I was a child (pretending there was ever a time), I use to unscrew the light bulbs from their sockets and store the blasted things way back in a drafty corner of a drawer marked for socks. This way, whenever Daddy flipped the switch and absolutely nothing would transpire, I would have time to hide. *Oly, Oly, oxen free* never carried so much meaning as it did in times like these. Father was rendered impotent due to the fact there was nothing for him to see. His eye was one worthless ball in its socket. I would scramble for cover like a moth in sheep's clothing. If it had only been a game, I'm certain that my laughter would have caught me on the heels and cornered me to the floor in uproarious fashion. If it had only been a game, I'm sure that I would have been caught at the head like a chicken and tickled to kingdom come. And that I would have made the angels snicker in turn. If it had only been a game that travels playfully along the course with inconsequential words falling from the sky.

A game. My child had neither comprehension nor even the most minimus list-view of that word. What did it mean? To seize a prey. Something two or more people play on a table, on a carpet, on the floor, *near* a door, in a dark room lit with pink lemonade, chocolate chip cookies, chick-peas, and meat. Something a person does, at least until the age of ten, if not for sometime after that. I should have been a pair of slippers and slip me through the crack familism under the door. Already I can hear a theme of *mission impossible* resounding in my head like a *name that tune* departure of life, everything thrown into a kind of Olla Podrida, a stew of gossip as devised by people safely tucked into the TV. *In the dark my Daddy gropes.* Together, he and I will go, when all of his breath is spread across my bed like a fresh slice of likeness wrath. I will pluck the lashes and the lettuce shreds from his ox-eye and model him off to the top Hollywood brass. *I'll take delight once they ridicule him, his sexostiatae-slits of the tongue, his mouth of the river, his segmental body walls, his spitty, napkined face, his identacode of threesix and any other liphistiomorphae-given talents he never deserved. The true essence of his agenesia. I will picture-frame his penmanship on the wall, his pedigree, only to render it out-dated, and give it to goodwill so that some waste of a cupless manikin soul will have something to piss out of on the battlefield. I'll put Daddy to good use, bit by miserable bit, piece by wasted piece, as is his alloted illth.*

IMBROGLIO

What a tangled mess this is. Mother called last night and wanted to know: *"What have you done with Daddy's balls? Daddy can't find them anywhere and neither can I."* Taking a ladified leave of absence from bareback commerce, I rolled Buddah's boulders across the massive floor in utter darkness, eloign-ladified-fashion. It was when I got to the far end of the room that the phone rang. Fumbling in the dark, clumsily clawing my way through carefully measured blackness, I finally succeeded in picking up the receiver on the seventh ring only to hear a strong, tormented (resounding thunderously), hollow voice answer back, "Spagyrist . . . that you? Wh, eat? The bar? Ley? Me Sponsor, I promise not to abuse the wine. Come an' see me not fall. Third ring, ya say? Sorry, wrong number." Meanwhile, in utter dismay, whilst still standing vacant as a caryatid, I heard those two massive boulders rolling back from whence they came.

Daddy, I picked you boldly up in my Auto and craftily cussed in your ear until your mark had slipped from the top of your head to the bottom of your feet. Then I put on me shades and had me rope to hang you up with. After all, it was Crouchmas – *Gang Day* – before Ascension, and I was on a flying roll of Zechariah. Come and see! Watch out!

G: olden view in pair of dice. Gee, I imagine me a cabbie. Seven eleven. Ha!

Pan to: She lets out her fore room and lies backwards.

Foaming at the mouth I think is what they call it. Foaming *'at'* the mouth. Not in the mouth, mind you (although, believe me, I have on occasion performed that tricky maneuver before proctors in convocation), nor up the mouth, nor down, nor even beneath like some hypolithic plants I know, but 'at.' 'At' is a function word indicating presence, indicating action. Fast action. Smart, wandering stars with swelling, hard speeches seek the whitest of explosions. First of all, there must be 'presence,' for without it there can be no action at all. *Without presence* is merely another way of saying *Caetera desunt.* And what is presence but that which is felt unseen? And what is action but that which is thought undone? And, secondly, there must be accomplishment. For a job well done, whether by hand, by foot, or by mouth, is a job well-received by all.

Last Tuesday. I was scooped up out of a hot oven between 400° and 450°F., where lightning and voices and seven lamps of fire burning raged, and hand-delivered in person before the tribunal, and asked point-blank, "Why if thy hand doth offend thee has thy not cut if off in shame?" And I, hampig, sucking on the hinder part of a fat cigar with my head on a pillow, eyebrows rolling like Storm's waves, responded in kind, "Just which hand are we speaking of? At first hand? At hand? Come to hand? Give a hand? Hand in glove? Hand over fist? Helping hand? On hand? On the other hand? Out of hand? Play one's hand? Rose hand? Wind hand? Under hand and seal? With a heavy hand? With one hand tied behind one's back? Hands down? Hand it to? Hand on? Hand out? Hand over? Hand job? Hands of war? Hand staff? Hand-warmers? Handy-dandy? Hand on yid at Hitleroven?" The answer was a long time in coming (as life is short, art is long), for the tribunal scratched their heads first for twelve hours on either end, and second for twelve hours on either beginning.

It appeared that I had gotten the best of them and, come hell or high water, had managed to win over the jury of old men, hands down. Be still legions.

"*This way. The intermezzo.*"

Having escaped judgment (albeit temporarily), I lingered awhile on one of the twenty-one top floors in a room marked *Obadiah,* sipping a *moto.* Definitely not a Major, but inspired nonetheless as a divine wisdom *à la moscato.* I would look askew with a lazy eye, Zzzzzzz . . . slow down my vision in order to curtail the future, and restore the past as though it were an old shelf run out of dry goods. I would take sentences once spoken and reword them in such a way as to build strong character and fire, using Tutivillus as an aide in building one of our better shelves. It isn't the departure itself that defies gravity. It is what occurs before the departure. The lifting of the spirit, of the leg, in order to spread a bit of baptismal kynurenic acid COOH – the laying on of hands, hands that speak volumes of servitude *à la embusque a pseudepigraphe.* What is it to serve man? To get down on the hands and knees. To bleed. To feed and flush out famine with good intentions. Those starving for love take heed. Eat bread. Love comes clothed in various garments. I collect garments. Some torn, others ripped, still others cut asunder by scissors far too large for their own good. Sweating souls weary with talk, labor, sleep over ages strewn both across and around father time in a mass, like so many hapless minutes leading up to the final stumble-walk moment; that is, that moment in which one takes half a notion to perform a noble deed and land head first on the a-waiting earth, and thus conceal a hundred prophets from death.

Hardly *demi-vierge,* the mother of existence. Mother, I give up my mortality to thee with a last embrace, which I saved for a moment such as this. *Nom de lait.* Compliments of carnation: flesh mother's milk, hircine-style. I was raised on such things. But why should anyone appear in a vision, or otherwise, sucking on a cigar that reeks of old chicken fat? Is it only because I woke my seven sailors up, my crew, my goats in the lowest academic rank, and tapped them on the forehead, that I'm able to say *I'm OK with solutions half-sealed?*

3.2

Never remain comfortable in your space.

That was the message 3.2 gave the world from the bodhisattva clouds, in the aftermath of Armageddon.

Who is 3.2?

3.2 is infamous for doing random acts of violence. Take Bonnie and Clyde, toss in Dillinger, a loaf of Ma Barker, a slice of Bundy, some chopped up Lizzie Borden, a coffle of crinite critics, Incubus, Charon, Belial and Momos, and you have 3.2.

3.2 is the moment you wake up and have your first piece of fruit, and you see ten police cars in front of your house and learn that your quiet, little next-door neighbor had spent all of last night decapitating and chopping up his wife and two children. 3.2 is the hollow-eyed stranger waiting at a stop light, who proceeds to point a Walther PPK 7.65mm in your face after you have come to stop in your 750iL, and fires before explaining himself. 3.2 is the moment over one thousand, *go ma go, loose as a goose, sandy, too,* who loves to camp out with all the saints. 3.2 familiarizes you with such tidbits as kidnapping, sodomy, mutilization, shootings, stabbings, and bombings. 3.2 is a thief in the unwary hour saying *this is the world you live in so be watchful* – and mind that you strengthen whatever is left of beauty, peace, love, sacrifice, design, structure, religion, education, art, government, law – for even though these things remain, they are ready to die insofar as you lose faith.

3.2 had started off being a creative writer; howbeit, he oftentimes employed dictation. His writing could at times be inspirational, gentle, graceful: *And the children grew and waxed strong, and bruised god as his feet worked to the throne;* however, it was also not uncommon for his writing to take on an angry tone, a harmful, even destructive one: *Rod destroyed the child, body and soul, like John G. of fame in shitty Gehenna who shouted, "Let us alone, to the bone!"* In lieu of this, 3.2 was forever a teacher, a leader, and an educator. Education is a questionable thing, for it can mean so many different things to the receiver. You can learn how to solve a problem (i.e., 5+5=10). You can learn to speak a foreign language (i.e., *Aliquando bonus dormitat Homerus . . . Credo In Un Dio Crudel . . . Credo quia absurdum.*). You can read and learn facts about history (i.e., Detonation of the first hydrogen bomb was officially reported by Pres. Eisenhower). You can learn how to put things together (i.e., puer as of dogs' dungs in water) or how to dismantle them (i.e. Jack as in hack hack hack). On another level, you can learn from experience: 1) fire is hot 2) driving too fast causes accidents 3) eating spoiled food makes you sick 4) and I wept much, because no man was found worthy to open and to read the book, neither to look thereon, and my time was spent.

3.2 was also a kind of educator who forced you to learn quickly in his classroom. Certainly, when 3.2 taught you something your eyes were opened, for 3.2 was also an *homme de letters.* In the classroom, 3.2 would ask the following kinds of questions: What kind of torture defines foreplay? What kinds of pain will make you scream *"in cruce corvos pascere, corvus?"* Can you say I love you to the one who has just chopped off your left hand?

3.2 could make statements as well as ask questions: To suffer is to learn; to die is to be free; romance cannot happen without violation; law is violation, which is the key to love without mercy; work is freedom.

3.2 was everything to anyone who happened to step into his classroom. His classroom was an enclosed space with a curtained wall, like a cyclorama, existing as a backdrop that both eliminated all pre-existing shadows and yet suggested divided space. 'Graduation' from 3.2's classroom could be obtained by death or survival, depending upon one's darwinian wits. 3.2 typically enjoyed a 1:1 interaction, especially during urban/indoor pleasures. No help, no assistance from outside oneself. 3.2 forced you to use your *dasein* brain and your factual spirit. He was what was meant by *fighting for the last breath in space-time unlimited.* In addition to all that has been said regarding 3.2, it is interesting to omissively observe that he also loved to smile during noctambulant states of restlessaliturgicality, as well as during post-Armageddon reruns of *Blasè H.G..*

This post-Armageddon condition put the world on a very curious plane. What does one do when one's earnest-creature expectations have been reduced into a small cinereous fraction of what one had originally assumed? Is this the time to create new resources from within, in order to address the current answer (howbeit, outcome) without? Resourcefulness is the finest clue. When the chips are down and the stage is bare of real props, and there is only you and the current ascriptive reality of whatever there might be staring you in the face, what does one do with only a reprobate mind and an unknown tongue? Aliunde your words, thoughts and speech together into The New Trinity. T.N.T. The chili chiliasm. It is more than just, *trinitrotoluene;* more than just, CH3 C6 H2 (NO2)3. More than just C3H5(NO3)3. But it is still a high explosive. A vapulation of an aposiopesis. Passing over one . . . Threefold. If you were smart, if, in fact, you should happen to confront 3.2 and wish to survive aseity, you must stop for a moment and rest your eyes heavily upon *TNT*. Feel the word with your eyes, allow yourself to see anything and everything you choose to see (or think) when you look upon those three letters from another source: TNT.

REVIEW: This was how the book, unsealed, started off. It was not the kind of a beginning most people were comfortable with, given that IN THE BEGINNING was getting a face-lift. Just what poison was hiding behind all that common sea? What hidden lines layed buried underneath the ancient lines, the fallen phrases, the sagging promises, the problems with lost antecedents, the problems with pronoun agreement, the problems with this, that, which, and it? *lapsus calami. Come and see.* This time there was form and light; this time there were immediate ideas; this time there was no split infinitive, no Edenistic subject-verb disagreement, no expletive constructions, no strung out thrice weekly, no phrasemonger inserted to fill a vacancy, no forty-three low words creeping in one dull line . . . *because thou hast done this* . . . no treeing down the topic, no zerodrafts, no circling the field, no wheel spinning, no lightening up of bureaucratic prose, no tongues up the nose, no japruschiamerican *weepweep,* no demystification, no run-on sentences . . .

DR. SSEUS FACES ENTANGLEMENT AND DEVOURING IN THE COMFORT ZONE
ACT I – HONEY AND WILD LOCUSTS AND A LITTLE BOOK

Given that honey is the product of a mysterious and elaborate process of assuagement, it is not difficult to understand that in accordance with that process, honey became synonomous with wisdom and the idea that there is no higher state than that of Alleviation Without Suffering. Dr. Sseus was still searching for the Cyclops through the honeymoon corridors of space and time. The fact that he had lost him via wane-hypnosis was not something he was proud of; nor was he comfortable with the fact that his ever-decreasing cosmic essence was extruding a meaty, honey-like substance.

Dr. Sseus climbed to the top of a high space and set his limbs there to consider his various problems. First of all, in searching for Cyclops, he had become lost in a deep hyperborean realm devoid of history and consolidation. Secondly, he was dripping wet, like one returning from a bad tripsis, oozing globs of honey from head to toe, but most particularly from the region of his neck. Thirdly, whereas he was once a compact mass, he was now an utter mess. *How could this have happened to me?* he thought. *When I set out this morning through the constellation of this vast mind of space, I was dressed so neat. I had no idea **such** parts of me would come unglued; quem quaeritis. If I'm not careful, perhaps this honey will unhold and release an arm or leg, or perhaps my very wrathy nature, and I will thereafter roam and wander endlessly through this disenchanted place, wherein I seek my patient, Cyclops, forever aging against a vast diorama. Imagine me punished form, as feeble-minded as a* *clubbed fish, stranded in the greatest tribulation of its life. Just think: who is here to commit me should I leap from this high place? I am gravely alone in darkness, and yet I still breathe and can still recall the most furious things that have ever happened to me. The fall. The kiss upon the neck.*

Before he became lost, there was light as likened to a dawn with the shades pulled and drawn. And the pages that took leave of his mind were clearly visible line for line – the near exact position where a grave decision must be met, a turning point of life or death, beginning to end. But that was in the light. Now it was as if a great esquamate wall stretched across 300 million light-years of space and a mysterious concentration of cold dark mass was hauling away much of his knowledge, and Dr. Sseus felt no more substantial than an ordinary cosmic afterthought. The very fabric of his mind – what he knew about fashionable space and time – seemed to be coming further apart with every minute, the subtile web of his intelligence giving way to a greater web of texture and durability, similar to that of the universe's origin, full of secret and evolutionary steps, and a solitary outward sustentation dominated by matter, dark and unfathomable. And all Dr. Sseus could yammer was a ditty from that mighty, great city.

"On Gr. Ave the mate tell gen
that gr. eat sin exo pan. O! see!
. . . Creamery butterflies and fish, divided wastefully . . .
Eritis sicut Deus, scientes bonumet malum."

It all made Dr. Sseus recall a certain hoyden, so full of sauce she was likened unto glue itself, and light years from pucelage. She pulled him into the country barn when he was thirteen and six inches long.

Sprinkled memories such as these led Dr. Sseus to reach further back when, as a Catholic youth, he was *made* to swear the truth in Greek, and point the dirty finger at himself and recite 12 hail Mary's to one Mark, and was told to put his malignant condition on an ill-conditioned seat, and to crow, *"Eye know not."* And leaping further back, *ex pede Herculem* (though his memory here was a bit faulty, a bit cloven), he recalled (while kicking on his back in the full price) his mother, Mary (whilst nursing a gibson), touching him between the leaves and sinking her ver mouth into his neck for a wet kiss (crimson-red lipstick left its mark in a mysteriously Beautiful and Delicious way, with pearl onions and angelica print, eighteen ways). And although he was but a wormwood babe, she called him her moist *bel esprit*, and made him swell.

In the shallow-expanding sadness of his mind, Dr. Sseus was evaporating. He took no joy in this, nor pride. The juice of his knowledge was reduced to a state which left him yielding to infantile dreams (salt, tears and envisagement) and screams for the bare necessities of life. He longed to feel himself the Voyager, the Planner, the Evaluator, the Analyzer, the Therapist, the Inventor, the Medicator, the Clinician, the Seeker. This only suggested that he must move continuously through the universe. And, yet, in this sub-journey in search of Cyclops, he felt more like a fly caught in a web, a spiral net converging to a central point, with god sitting in the middle like a spider.

And then his worst dream came true. Dr. Sseus looked up to see god approaching him on a slender thread. And what Dr. Sseus realized was more than just a form of madness. He was entangled in the cosmic web of the world, where he had been ensnared without prior 'knowledge.' Memories of falling give way to disgusting dreams of despair.

Dr. Sseus wanted to cry out in fear. The sight of god with the abdomen of an araneid was frightful and unexpected, with eight hideously long legs, and several eyes a-poppin'. The sight of god loosening his ass from his stall and creeping down toward him in a sort of slow-motion pedesis was enough to put Dr. Sseus in his right mind. Neglecting reverence, neglecting sin, Dr. Sseus trumpeted, "Cut! Don't come any closer! You cannot touch me! I forbid it!"

"It's a little too late for that," god said, his incisors dripping a sticky goo like something found in bed. "So quick I was in the dark movement, as you mused and pondered, you did not feel my bite, nor did you detect the spinning of my cocoon."

"But, nevertheless, I felt something," Dr. Sseus replied. "And seeing that it's god whom I address, I beg let it rest."

god moved in an inch. *Let it rest*, he says. Here he is in my domain. How he got here is neither sane nor plain. But here he is in a *pars rationabilis* nonetheless, caught in my web, undoubtedly looking for someone or something beyond his bounds to address. Whereby, like a thief in the night, I caught him rummaging about in my attic – ooomy basement, too – a rude intruder watering my nest, diseased, and kicking up smust at Best. And he says, *Let it rest? Et sic de caeteris?* Arrest is more the proper term to stress! Kind sir," god said, playing four legs to a closer thread. "I'm sure that should I cut in deep, I would find a chocolate heart to blame. Even the nosing of your beak is sweet. And quite frankly I'm starved for lack of keep."

"Eat? You want to eat me? For as long as you have been existence's absentee landlord, you have watched with eyes in back of your head, numberless people destroy themselves before your lord. Except for a selected few whom you would save for rooms reserved."

"Rooms reserved, you say? An inheritance, incorruptible and undefiled? How about shelves . . . racks to rack and manger where they be hung like bells?"

Within a blink of an eye, god lighted his stage. Directly behind him, dangling like bells from adhamant, slender threads, were the dried up shells of meals digested from long ago, from the aged streets of saints and the battered coals of hot beds. The remaining husks in outline form were unmistakable: Voltaire, Locke, Rousseau, Sir Thomas More, John Calvin, Harold Lloyd, and Shakespeare.

"You see," god said, bringing four more legs upon the closest thread, "preceding you, their few chosen lines were much the same. The chief difference being small: a 'thee' or a 'thy,' a 'we' or two. I believe Calvin said, 'How do you do?' Whereas More's remark was, 'Bread! it's you!?' and Shakespeare's 'Pew!' And Dr. Calvin – he knew what I knew – that from the beginning – the hour, the day, the month, and the year notwithstanding – who would be saved and who would be damned, the former meriting relatively few. And now Locke, he pinned the Glorious Revolution, except that's G-o-r-i-o-u-s, Locke. Tah-tah. Now take Rousseau. He was quite a different meal. Neglected as a child, born of lower class, he was always the last so he got the heel. He attacked society, declaring that its *'column'* was artificial and prehistoric: Lies standing out in the world like an erection amidst a congregation of specious eunuchs. Reason, he labeled, a false guide, and argued that civilization actually made men less than wise, and that life in the state of nature was much better in guise. Actually, I liked his taste. For where he believed in no church, no clergy and no revelation, he had a respect for love, beauty and altercation. I recall, although his carcase nearly broke the web and felled to that river below, Voltaire preaching the cause of religious toleration as peneplain relief, grimacing, *'Ecrasez l'infâme! Crush the infamous thing! Yes, conculcate the Obsoletes!'* Of course, he was speaking of bigotry, intolerance and superstition. Arguing instead for a natural religion, he came down with parotitis and, thusly, represented Christianity as mere opinion. Here, doc, watch him spin and wax hard. For I saved his ceruminous gland, as I love to prick his ear." And with his eighth leg, god kicked the shell in – Voltaire – and around and around it spun, as dust does in a run. "Delicious. Want, More? Then let's forget about taking oaths and acts of supremacy, and leap to speak of *Utopia*. The man who wished to behead of a Catholic church did indeed become a head, a top. But, in spite of it all, I think Shakespeare said it best, when seeing that the legs were unbroken pierced the meaty side instead, and with blood and water pouring forth said, *'Carnation! the dread of something after death, the undiscovered country, from whose bourn no traveller returns to find a constant bed.'"* god kicked the shell – Shakespeare – and he went hurdling in a mighty wind. "General Lloyd . . . I remember him well. The old kid brother engastrimyth. His soup mixed like a tetanus drug and made me swell with laughter. O his wood records were true, of course, mostly being a light in the dark looked upon by assorted waggers. So Lloyd said to me and, if you'll permit, I'll do this in my C. Fields bit, 'god, my boy, you fascinate me. You get hold of several thousand dollars with which you intend to make a new pic of your very own in under forty-two months, and a few days later you rent a corner in the Bradbury Mansion in order to listen to juvenile hymns from Plotinus.' I tell you, Lloyd was a fresh man and made a most excellent meal. Why! the tip of his foot was like an ice cream cone – at least until the last of him had sunk lower and lower at the fleshy table." god started to toy with Dr. Sseus by tapping him with four legs and spinning him into an even tighter cocoon, all the while tasting the honey collected on the tips of his legs.

"If you make me your meal, god," Dr. Sseus uttered, "you really show yourself to be the weaker one. For you only prove that you need me to survive, just as you need More, Rousseau, and *all the rest* whose dry fisher's coats hang upon your nest."

"Ad gustum!" god said, sinking his chelicers into Dr. Sseus's body and drinking up his essence!

And then suddenly, in a burst of light, Dr. Sseus saw a new milky way sprawling across the galaxies like so many enlightened, cadgy cattle in Ecstasy. O! And there he could see – herding the thousand cattle in on a street of ormolu varnish in the beautiful new galaxy of stars – the Cyclops balanced atop Ugh's ordurous back.

Cut

BEEP! The Time Is

1:14. Do you know where your pale piacular horse is?

The rule of the day is: Let them be for signs. Assignment: Compose a four-line poem with the rhyme scale (aa-bb), wherein four different months are employed (one per line), all four seasons are mentioned throughout the poem, there are 'spell-together' allusions to both one week and seven days in each of the four lines, the total of the four months equals 25, the difference between the months in sequence equals 10, the first two lines allude to Jack, the third line alludes to war, and the fourth line alludes to Hell; there is mention of an eye in the second line, the *Feel* of a vein *and* a path in the first and third lines, respectively; and the conclusion is lined with trees growing to die. Answer:

Autumn slashes vain July
Spring cuts up October's eye
Summer takes the road to March
Winter leaves May all quite parched.

Flash! White raw human waves make a fluctisonous roar! "Heel!" a little boy screams at his ashen dog, outside the Stadium! The Geometry of circles aids the red piece and allows the Great Geometer to go wild with Geomancy! Hippomancy rules with a shoe of iron! Swart ritter!

IS IT A HIT?

It is the beginning of the beginning. And only here in the Hamito-Semitic Free City of Danzig can you find Hit politely, with gibus in hand, peddling three lite opera plots to a bored board of West Virginians, addressing them as the Venerable, and Very Reverend, Father Patrial Preacher Generals. "It is my pleasure, *Montani semper liberi*." Irregardenless of his pleasures, *mountaineers are always free.* And they turned flat down in trial two 'masterful' operas. *("O rich JE! You E? Bare as can be. Who told you so? The gal from Gladalee.")* One was based on Buster Crabbe's *King of the Jungle,* wherein Buster hits high screeching notes that challenged the wild, loud cries of Weissmuller's pointless err notes married to nothing but the cool Jungle itself *Ah Ah Ah!,* thus causing a crack in the theologaster. In his opera, Hit's lead was a *lion man* orphaned at three by his nutty, dimwitted explorer-parents; mom, named Mary Eddy, who thought it a good idea to sell pink lemonade to the sick, thirsty natives on hot, windless African days. Alee! Whiskified natives hate sour drinks. To the very last dropdrink, honey. Passes thru 'em like Goose Shit. Rather ducky. *Quack. Quack.* Jus' ask Jackie on third. Jackie? Jackie! who's into double errings, adoring pigeons, and preening middle-aged doctors. "It was just my attempt to make-up to the Negro race," Hit cried in Hollywood, with a trace of *ol' 'ly,'* hearing and talking for 72 hours on end, strictly business-on-hand. "Holy, holy, holy . . ." (Hit's lead, the King of the Jungle, *was* to be a waxy rabbi in the habit of giving *Kedushah* with his legs together, with a straight foot to ten *bonobos,* who loved flying up and down a dozen times a day; but, alas, his leather girdle got in the way.) *Break Comm. 189:*J.M. *(Smuck'er)* and F.W. (Rue [ck] *heim*), the Kings of Sweet AD, who had committed for Ni KATE a delicious existence, did (also) Bewail (re): Prepare. *Pop and Jam her Corn and Smoke her Virginia Slims Baby.*

We K-Now Return. Another opera that the Preacher Generals (at Night) turned down was *Gefängnis* – Hit's attempt (his 'reach') to put into song: *I Am A Miniature Fugitive From A Massive Chain Gang* – wherein Hit takes over the role of James (formerly held by Paul) via preformation, and performs his part entirely in psalm-on-palm. Forever doing penance, Hit writes the part so that the main lead continues to suffer (viz. vomit-on-hand), being sentenced to a thousand dog-germ-years hard-labor (bing!) on a brutalized chain gang for singing psalms off-key without an updated passport or sea letter (come!), which made things tough because a theomachistic-war-at-hand was still going on, and there was no more sea and little precious blood, which made for a bad prophecy. Hit proves to be a model prisoner (with broad shoulders, the human equivalent of antlers), and actually stops an attempted breakout by symbolically *informing* the guards of it (bing! and Heimdall) via a bottomless pslam, with lyrics sung from off the palm, entitled "When de Prisoners Come Breaking Out de be an Awful Fug," which had a subplot going on at 'Calvary' (sic: *not* cavalry) that was symbolized as a brightly lit fonduk in N. Africa, where a wey of wet, sour wool and gummy salt – 182 lbs., 160 pecks; 100 lbs. weight, wreck – occupied the stage. The bottomless psalm was subtitled "Descent From The Cross Of Some Shadowless Shenanigans Plotted By A Nondescript Gang Of Scroyles." *Declined!* But Hit got smart and struck gold with the Preacher Generals with his operatic, postobsolete remake of *Anything Goes* (bing!) in Asgard. They loved the idea of Hit taking on via Ethel Merman vocals *(moo)* a trivial plot heavy with mistaken identities, gimmicks, susing out anyone a bit sus, and rotten, romantic misunderstandings with godhead-in-Dust, wherein a comic gangster (viz. *Lou in angst*), just out of solitary-den-confinement, masquerades as a cleric known as ReverEnd Dr. Moonme, who spends a lot of time in the nest *(mew)*, coming 'n going, but with nothing to show for it. "That's nidicolous!" (the Hit line). They got a kick out of Hit singing to his cock, "You're The Top Sushi!" *(nay, ragout),* and howled when Hit contorted himself (lawlessly *askew*) so that his head *actually* faced his ass, or tail, as in *Rock*, or tales of a merman ass in dock, as he burst out with his aria, "I Get A Kick Or Roll Or Swish Out Of You, Depending On The Cir*cum*stance." This, defiantly, was Hit's hamulus *(debut)* into the world of opera *(mew)*, and as far as the impersonator Merman in the theologium was *con*cerned *(ahchoo!)*, his dream come true. *"Am I awake?"* (bing!) 'Tis true, Jew. *(Adieu.)*

E PIC OF ALL TIME!

They're shooting a film over there! There! Where the earth is ripe! The only camera on earth is from another planet in a distant galaxy doing a study of that world to determine if any life ever existed there, *malgré* the nothingless. It's an endless, boring documentary, actually wordless, showing nothing but vast stretches of sand and dust. If an earthling was available to narrate it, he would have said over the unmoving, lifeless terrain, "This was New York, this was Chicago, and this was Los Angeles. This was where you could choose from 31 flavors. This was where you could choose from thirty-nine articles. This was where you could choose from thirty tyrants. This was where you could choose from thirty wars. This was where you could eat pizza with the Hapsburgs or Leg of Lamb with the Guilenots. This was where you could drive up to a window and purchase a vegetarian hamburger from Thomas À. Kempis or a Sardine Pizza from Artdeado. This was Tokyo, put together by Meson and Yukawa™ (a gaijin-sponsored enterprise). O! and this was Moscow, where Pushkin was observed by the police obsessing over the *dust* content in frangible bullets, which do not penetrate like the secret police's, nor the penes', in matters of uprightness. O! and this was the icing on the cake, where the double steal was real and the crack could smack the bejeezus out of a sphere with stunning acts of aggression that only a hat-backward and a grin-cocksure could endure. O! and this was an M-3, another trinity shot by a survivalist with a .45 mentality. Sorry it all looks the same. This vast stretch of sand, lint and dust. Really, it looked better yesterday."

(But there are no truly free earthly narrators. Even G did skid-bid for 1000 years. The scene remains unchanged, undefined. An alien tongue analyzes the data and reports: small traces of lysozyme found in the dust of this planet, along with minute traces of plebeians, one fragment of an air to ground popeye, and one Ophirian surrey with a fringe on top.

Conclusions in a nutshell: pliskie; malheur; or some kind of dump site with an euxine-like quality to it. Do ye have an urn, ophis?)

Over there! In the wilderness – where they're shooting a Film in color, directed by Homer Haines. Not just a documentary! It casts a lot of old stars (black and white), elders, and authentic nicolaitans.

In the Film, Homer has "the kid" dragging his "sailors," accompanied by an "Italian band" *per praecognitum,* up a cliff (notes one half of the Symplegades on the left), wherein they find at the top a studio, abandoned. They venture in and stumble upon the cutting room floor: Old pieces of *Gunga Din* on India's mountainous Northwest frontier; Japs and desperate Indians (known as JIFFS) running amok in India; James Brown Stuart at cavalry raids through the bush on prads, taken in the Wilderness; and Charles Stuart, the grandson of James, who was otherwise known as The Great Pretender, defeated at Culloden by a poorly factotum E. Princely. The "band" sets down their instruments (plus lanterns, torches, and assorted weapons). Come stumbling in from the back is an uncredited William Faulkner, grasping approximately three swigs of gin. The JIBrand. It is a cutting room experience for expensive flair, epic fun, lots of foreign words, and nonstop movement. Behind Faulkner is a baldpated (wigless) Eduardo Ciannelli. Chilling as Guru. But they are both second-hands. It's interesting. But Faulkner, collecting the pieces on the floor, and thereafter splicing together a second film via some serious reel intercourse, ends up having on a makeshift screen the villain Guru from *Gunga Din* addressing Dorothy and all of her miniature fans from *The Wizard of Oz:* DOROTHY: "I want to go home somewhere, over the rainbow image." GURU: "You Englishmen are all alike! You're nothing but colonist-Guppies, wet, gay, upwardly mobile professionals from *'Pater Familias,'* with graven heads jammed into Beowulf, Diana and Battles of Maldon! And into way too many commas! But look! Your empire will never stand in these mountains! Your love affair with Caryatid 'n' Drappies is over!" DOROTHY: "O Toto! Stay away from him! He only reads fresh Pax-transcript off the walls of Taj Mahal without proper punctuation!" Then there's Gunga Din sounding the trumpet at *nones-at-that* and ushering in, Armageddon-fashion, an army of munchkins. And Toto, suddenly loose, loses a *T* and replaces it with a dead man's *J*, and thereafter becomes Joto, and barks out an order to attack Pearl Harbor with Montgomery Cliff Notes. And Montgomery, looking a lot like Freud in his later years, says, "Thatta boy, Gunga! You're a better lump of clay than I any day!" While a cowardly lion standing beside Dorothy like a pair on the Boulevard de Lupa, dressed up to the hilt for a necktie party, utters, "What did I tell you? What did I tell you? Didn't I say he couldn't do it and would lose it even though they hanged him for it anyway?" Then there's the cavalry storming the mountain walls – led by three sergeants (Sin, Mart, and Law), Marthe Richard, and a one-legged attorney, Tungay-at-law, who specializes in cases concerning the pravity of spiritual nature – until they are finally stopped at the main gate by Professor Marvell, who says to the charge, "The Wizard's not in. The ecdysiast is in Georgia. The Garden is closed for the day on account of 1) gravity, 2) electromagnetism, 3) a nuclear proton force, 4) a weak nuclear radioactive decay force, and 5) generalized sin in a G suit. But like AL', I got a gut feeling everything will be figured out in twenty-four hours. Come back tomorrow and for thirty pieces I'll let you in as has-beens to catch the E Pic of All Time!" Then comes a quick off the cuff shot of Count Ciano being handed over by the Nazis *cufferoo* (that's what's called cuffing one's meat); England shouting to New York, "To Hell with Hitler! Let G do it!"; and G handing in a ukelele in grand form, *by George!*, in order to play "Oh, Don't The Wind Blow Cold This Day" at the following Praise Meeting. And the cast begins to jitterbug and hora in the midst of Little Big Horn, singing, high-jinks-style,

"Two paradises are better than one
For there's more ripe apples to drop in the sun."

Homer is contemplating doing a pleurosequel, entitled *Armageddon-at-Night*, and is already inspecting future shooting sites. He would like to use Faulkner as a sort of antephialtic provision after witnessing how knightly he had scooped up the pieces on the cutting floor and had managed to block together such a fabulous flick, including a scene where Ida carelessly talks her way *through* a German spy, disguised as an Iraqian Babylonian Nebuchadnezzarian (IBN), bronze, ibn-saud multivocalmotley. However, Faulkner keeps insisting that the final editing was a rotten mess, as it covered too broad a topic. But Homer will hear no part of it. Now he wants Faulkner to intermingle the cut pieces of *King Kong* with the cut pieces of *Drums Along the Mohawk,* and have Kong holding a *kkkicking,* screaming Edna May Oliver in his hairy palm, while dodging a parade of fiery arrows darting from the bows of Mohawk bit players, which results in a good evil display of epiphanic theatrics.

Yes! They're shooting a film over there! It's a premillenarian of La Femme en Pourpre et Écarlate with a belle amie, that is, a belle laide as the première, a châtelaine with a dangling key, a femme du monde, a demi mondaine, a soubrette, a grande amoureuse, an ingénue, a femme savante, a chanteuse, a boulevardier, a fille publique, a bête noire in a chapeau rouge and a pourpre chemise, a bit gaga, a bit mal de mer, a bébé, a mystère, but all-in-all a femme incomprise.

Cut to Guide: Voices down in this Ho'. . . Schools, fishes, wandering diaspora, nomads alike, in Ch . . . Diaskeuasis . . . Make ye ready, prepare the way and be prepared. For the Great Revision is editing your Selection. This way! This way! It's almost doomsday! By the hundreds of thousands, spews in tanks, flipflops and apocalyptic-appropriate mushrooms and capes, celery stalks, carrot stems, and Paris Falls file down the deep. Here, Webster, your words are collected in stalls. RAW is tumbling down the pipe, backwards to the sea. Boy Scouts, Seniors, and Baby makes three. Con men there by the ribbon of reps from Time Immorally. And pilgrims with Ten on their hands give one another the third degree. Step aside. The real issues await. Health is so important. Grant us Truemen and by George! M.D. The crypt cries out for the Dead!

Shooting continues in the SW wing #38, if you're keeping count.

G DAY

They're discussing *G DAY* over there! It's a film directed by Homer Haines, an interpolator, on the smyrna set, who is infamous for the statement *'the first shall be last and the last shall be first.'* In it he had Ida decorated with considerable merit, imagination, and good taste. Whenever Ida undressed in a scene, she stepped into a zinc hot tub and scrubbed the dust and white ashes of a Mother's day off her chest with a washcloth, brush and soap. In the same tub she emptied her bladder so that the urine would keep the existing water warm and golden as Burgundy. Mother-white naked in the presence of a sparkling screen was somehow reassuring to a commanding, if pistic, audience not quite as clean and decocted as she. This gave Homer an excuse to turn Ida into a bi Pierrot/Pierrette – only cast in gold!

with sagging skin and a mundane egg of neither time nor space. And Opa City played on the tube in the background. And a Cyclops lost his specs. And righto, Ida could laugh an audience to death doing Armstrong pats on her chest.

However, there is a lighter side to this, for the word *Pierrot* also suggests a comic character of French pantomime with whitened face and loose white clothes, and a crow hop; a sort of living death born of a thirsty Friday; a fripper who loves to rub up against human clothes and wear them out to old relics; a eurythmic hack a cut above a rook. This sounds much better – for it is easier to converse with A-clown of theotechny with neither shadow nor thumbs than it is to converse with a dead, ex-bitter messiah with a D-in geopolitics. Think upon the clown, Grimaldi, a true geophagist, conversing with Mother Goose's Mary, and thereby causing her to sing *Mary, Mary, quite contrary, how does your garden grow? With such petit morts, Alot to bear, the count, you'll never know.* Which brings us back to Ida in the tub, scrubbing the dust and ashes off her breasts, two feet deep in lambshit. The dust of death.

Homer did not mean to define Ida as a perpetual explorer of oceans under endless skies of circumambages but rather as a soul knowledgeable in the holy journey that is part of this and every other invisible move of prestidigitation. He had meant to simply lie with her in order to lend her warm comfort in her disquieted sleep. *The fatherly lion sounds the ferocious roar of the outside world* – that is, the world that beckons to the traveller who has learned to sail the sea of transVeSdence in the cool of the day. Homer put Ida between the sun, the moon, and the celestial sea; her tub, shaped like a cup, was tabular in character, and more along the lines of Rubadub B-E-Z Lee Bub Z. It was her ship likened as unto the ship on a rooftop, the temple of a house – the notion being: to travel out of one's house, one's paleograph, as it were – to be cast out through the darkness of space – one must become a living ghost.

In the meantime, Homer, the director, wanted to become more personally involved in *G Day*. So he wrenched himself from the all-seeing eye and let it run on its very own. Stripping himself bare, he then lay down in the tub beside Ida and submerged – that is, he got down in the mouth; however, his secret (no longer) toupee floated clear to the top, and remained as buoyant as a nest of feathers on Jordan. Ida improvised like a turtle to the flies: "O dear father pro of lies! Your halo broke off!" But Homer could not bear to hear her due to the barrier of the surrounding waters. On the contrary, he was still far too busy creeping ear to ear through the room of his captive, silly woman, with lively stones to roll. Ida apologized to the all-seeing eye and said, "I'm sorry that I improvised. But you see, there is no script here for me to read. Homer has taken this whole film off-course by stripping down to nothing and planting himself in my tub. Yes, I was meant to do a soliloquy in circus makeup and tell all the good news to the world. But Homer is down below, prowling through Cupid's cave and . . . Whoa! . . . certainly finding the best of me! How he could hold his breath so long without drowning makes his act a little like a miraculous Ahab, ripped at the leg but darning. Perhaps even a little miscast, like Peck, yawning. But Homer is still a captain; a little Peter jelly playing prisoner Jonah in my belly, eating out my leviathan stitch. Suddenly out! at my feet, he reminds me of a little boy peeping at the MDs. The chiefs eye him continuously. Whoa! Homer just found my Ulysses bow! Naughty boy in fauntleroy."

Compactness, cleverness, and clear coherence of all faculties and powers, minus G. Nowdatsasomatrinity. All dem A words. Ida carped a cutting bit of vice. "No! Homer isn't timid. Massively, he's all over me. Homer, me, and the four missing pizzles of 'suspicion:

C . . . J . . . F . . . G!? HA! Do recall Lord Haw-Haw: 'Germany calling. CF . . . CJ'; Gestas, bad to the skull; Cain's Abel-annul; Dr. Faustus' dung-fall-to-the-wall; and Judas' bowels gushing beyond the stall. Together, the whole group makes a hollow cast. For the emptiness within is what is really hallow, and I can definitely say that I beat them all hollow. Whoa! Whoopsy! Homer's circumambulatory journey down below is no doubt a white jagged probing; but a competent saw-cut on my virgin thigh leaves me with an impression of thirtysome pews that could be present in order to applaud Homer's emotions at the bottom of me – all ready to worship under the prickmadam. Cast picaroon; cast the whorled leaves and the fleshy stems; cast Wormwood, that great star from *Heave;* though it just may end up as a lot of *casting*, as a lot of casting of anthelmintic pearls before swine, as the nacres migutdo with their mother . . ."

But this was not the end of *G Day*. Rather, it was a head start. For what happened next was not just any ordinary thing in the scheme of things. For Ida got the advantage by landing her great hand on a sword laying on the ground beside the tub. And grasping the sword by the handle, she plunged the blade into the tub, where it struck Homer full in the neck. Homer's head disengaged and met the fine dust from Ida's breast at the bottom of the tub, where the head became wormwood, and retted most freely. Without delay, Ida picked up Homer's loose head with both hands, and noticing that it resembled loose smut (which is to say that the entire head was now a dusty, dry mass of whorly spores), she lifted the head out of the tub and pointed it at the camera's all-seeing eye, and said, laughing above Homer's crown, "This man is innocent. Aye. The pride of the clan lost at sea. Spare him. For he is a thorny castaway *rouseau pensant* – a whimsical mix of moralism and duplicity searching the purple seas for mother's milk. And even though his cells are loosening from the bone, his rachis is still erect, and his weeds are wild and wholly wet. O I love him just as he loves me."

And as the credits rolled over the bathroom scene, the camera eyed Homer and Ida lying in heaps of blood and dust, like fish that fishermen drag out of the meshes of their net to lie rotting in masses on the sand, among the shafts of the sea pens spilling their ink.

G DAY: A Smash Review

A panel, including three sylogists, two mystagogues, a mishegoss, and one beadle, critiqued *G DAY* after its finish and arrived at some quick conclusions. All agreed that *G DAY's* main premise was the uprooting of sin. Clearly, *G DAY* demonstrated that it is a man's role to rip the sin out of woman, just as it is a woman's role to hack the sin out of man. Secondary themes involving god's omnipresence were also quite obvious, as symbolized by the all-seeing camera and Homer's overall casual direction of the holy proceedings. The narration held a number of 'suspected' passages, marked like an obelus, perhaps to signify necessary transitions between warfaring times *and* cast-out space.

One of the guests of the panel was a nameless fellow who otherwise went by Synod. He was actually a once-tailor, now dead, though doing quite well in the head, quiteable, resurrected in the depths of hell in a brand new shop that's a swell *Hot on the Block* known for its Hot and hots, Hot cross buns of tight coarse fabric, *and* Hot Rod jock straps sewed (in tact) within the lining, with a proper release for some quick hotcake plunging with good timing. A bright and cheerful mintie fellow, moderately modern, dressed in a dark, double-breasted paleolithic suit with chipped stone pockets and a marble collar to boot. His interest in *G DAY* pertained to the stripping of clothes *and* the prossie-minded attitude of all babes-in-wool. As a youth, it was his practice to automatically rip the seams of any pair of trousers that happen to fall into his hands in the season of autem divers. Skilled in the craft of tailoring since he was two, it was not uncommon to find him as a child arguing in the royal shops of some of the great Hollywood tailors from Woolwich to Sandhurst over the best straight path to take when it comes to ascots of camel hair.

On one such occasion, when he was twelve years old, he travelled with his rather foolish and silently ignorant mother and father into St. Peters, Rome; and after descending 33 stone steps, he wound up in the atelier of the legendary tailor, Pope Angelo Litacandle, having arrived there while his parents' backs were turned. When they finally found their son, he was sitting in the midst of several wiseacre, procumbent tailors, asking the tailors questions, with premature wisdom teeth grinding on gossip with pluperfect pleasure. And even though he came from a line of second-rate tailors, his seniors and superiors were absolutely astonished at his expertise in playing the devil *among* the tailors. He advised the tailors as to how they could produce an elegant dinner camel jacket *and* shop a person into 'striped black and white trousers *and* a pigeon-gray vest made entirely from charcoal and ashes *and* a tossed diaper around the breast.' When his father scolded him for running off, with salt spraying from his castigations, his son answered him, "What are you complaining about? Amscray! Am I not going about my Patroclinous business in fine, old procryptic cloaks on ellybay?" It was only in later years that *he* sewed skin in various ways: on the body of couches, chairs, and lampshades.

After the panel discussion, Homer and his female lead, Ida, signed autographs for their adoring, heady audience. One enthusiastic fan asked the two, "Since Armageddon, this is a dogged, silent universe we're spinning in – sprawled and scrawled in runny, bleeding-over, ebony ink across the spheres. Why do you suppose it takes so much time signing autographs?"

Ida chose to take this one. "I'm a starlet of a chosen generation. I know I look much nicer now that I did. Especially since I've had my tit-uplift. If you want *you* may autograph them and cut down on the time of *my* royal pen. Just write something nice. Manifest a secret. Sweet little nothings, over and over again, like 'I loved your wlatsome movie. Especially the *bain-marie* scene.' Why, on the way home *I* even spit thick oysters clear until ten. And many of them held pearls that glistened on the walk. But time, ladies and gentlemen, is a poetical dilemma. So I won't say that time won't dirty the cause, whether its signing autographs or signing laws."

The audience was satisfied with her direct reply, because life was so much more agreeable now. Ida could get by wearing see-through jeans, and appear without a cover to the world. And there was no god around to scream at her periwinkle down below. Everyone loved everyone else's reply. Even if it didn't address the question. There was total acceptance in the physical condition, in the yarn, in the bend, *and* in the trend of mind and spirit assailing the senses. There was no need to Procrusteanize. Why, in any given moment , there could be two raised eyebrows jumping around a big blue Hairy; a tongue squeezed into a burning bush; a pink flush; a glad gash; a flash; a taste of honey; a bit of jelly running outta love canal; a second coming; a bite out of a buff ball, where a lot of people danced *ballum rancum* around a mid tree; a walk in the garden afterwards; a puff of gasper; a few subtil smiles on a summer night; a little Arm trumpet; a warm, ticklish, playful summer breeze; a kiss on the rosy cheek; the sudden release of a dozen memories accented with the scent of Aloes and Pilates; the *me-ow* echoes of all the vacations past; a burnt-up; a bloody mare; a third part gone; a bitter toast; the moon's mare darkened; a crazed, unreasonable *nagel*-printing *owe owe owe* to the ladies and gents; a last trump – and yet not one gaga lord would jump out and gassy say, "What's going on? What's the matter? Why y'all hanging down that way? What's with the false bits?" Undressing the unbeguiling soul is the new recreation. A sort of recklessness in reverse where, instead of it leading to sin, it leads to purity, and no one gets hurt.

And to celebrate the cause, Homer showed a clip from his first flick.

Harmony Pictures presents
By Reason of the Mokes
A film by Homer.

This is the story of a pen named Jed.
Poor stupid head barely kept Ms. Gina fed.
Then one day he was shootin' in the moss
And up from the depths came the seven deadly sins of floss.
The Glutton
Vitellius
Apicius
Texas creed
Troopers
Hard balls.
Slops drops.
Cut to:
The Gardener shouted, "Gancho! Gancho! Número diecisiete! Púrpura y escarlata!"
Cut to:
Ms. Gina: *"Sitting on water and every dirty name in the book, I formed a mystery into a heady look. And I loved to do the numbers with the starlit Spook. O, god, get me off the hook."*
Cut to:
Voice-over Narration: *This was a very important story for the world to hear. In the Christian era, the time is come.*
Cut to:
Mr. Pen: *"Flash! Aliens are so out of control, they are threatening the very existence of a prodigious number of zeros! Follow me, please. The Z row in this Theater is raw, in the flesh of men. It is finished."*
End of clip. Applause.

*   *   *

MORE STARS

Indeed, it truly was a miracle that in the audience was Mr. Pen, looking quite regal and debonair in a feathery tux and tails with a culotte. Breeching six-foot-six. Splitting hairs.

291

Neil Baker

Former Jew from Kent. A neatly hair-trimmed mustache via à la becket. One of the staff.
Stood erect like nobody's business. Could be a bit hesitant in public ("I . . . er . . ." etc). Had
an assafetidan dribble everytime a beautiful naught came into his view, with the tears in such
dark-colored masses, the sniff-taste test would make your head spin like one sniffing glue.
He cast a shadow that seemed almost infinite over the audience, and thereby transformed the
setting into an anomalous, rudimental thing. Was actually quite independent before attaining
stardom; a real lone star, often disguised as *nom de plume.*

   Sitting beside Mr. Pen was a horny lamb of wool. That was Ms. Gina! Great cry and little
wool. 5'5". 25. A bushy tail, looking most elegant in a black chiffon dress (with a culotte)
and a bit Splib. She had a salient-divided mind in an angry breast; unity and diversity, all
in one esurient A-bomb breath. She fell in love with Mr. Pen when they were filming *By
Reason of the Mokes.* That was when she was in her Niagra-Viagra Falls, New Yoke, yen,
hook, love period, and so it was easy to connect to her. Ms. Gina and Mr. Pen held a firm
belief in one another that went way beyond monogamy; even beyond deuterogamy, shmee!
Ms. Gina called it "mahogany in the bush." What did she care for the loose interpretation?
She'd wandered far and wide around the world. She'd sucked Dick. She'd sucked Gumshoe.
She'd been a Dickless Tracy with a *dicax* sense of humor, sucking fruit. She'd sucked John's
ep sin. She'd sucked luz for indestructibility. She'd bowed to the almond nut and sucked
Luzzatto and had danced with Grim the *totentanz* while *he* swept the seas. She'd even
sucked the other Moses and Mary – Ester and Fawn – on her knees. She'd sucked Hit in the
iguana. Dong! She'd sucked Lincoln while Mary Todd looked on. Get the picture? She was
Hollywood Harry. She was No.17 by Cock. She was a motor mouth in the reign of Queen
Dick. Sure she'd suffered, but she raised her I.Q. when she said, "I quit, I do!" and fled to
Peloponnesus with her used planchette in order to get a rich piece of the ivory shoulder and
a diddey or two. Or more than two. Phew. The teachers scolded her for eating *six* in all
three corners! It reminded her of the Golden Rules. One teacher said, "Wet gins like you
don't graduate when they live in such a cheap, holey *sic* way. Take a shower *fore!* Sunday."
Ms. Gina could have sworn her teacher said *'jeep,'* not *'cheap.'* So she decided to beat the
devil (dickens, skip the shower) and bought herself a Cherokee and drove with the king, a
knave, over to Bad Man's River, over the Golden Rules, drinking treacle and cullis, speaking
tongues, penning sentences, and conjuring up a mass of figures *and* a Dick o' Tuesday on a
Sunday over baptism, and thus was saved from revision. Her personalized license plate *on
her baby-blue-job Bentley* was marked with: *Virtuous diets are ridiculous, Son. Go ahead.
Eat your mate in heal.* Needless to say, it was an enormous license plate, quite prothetic; but
for a gal like Ms. Gina, with eight legs/heels to set before her name, 'character' is irrelevant
and 'transgression' inconsequential. Especially when it cums to licking a plate and leaving
not a single legover, nor a trace of provender, nor even a trail of tears for any prowling private
eye to investigate. She didn't wait for the late stroke of some miraculous miracle to become
her fate. She didn't give a Black Widow P-L-U-N-G-E for living a strong, combat-trained,
vicious, Biblically-prepared-to-die, adapt, improvise-or-lie kind of life. She only cared
about making movies and attending parties and hanging out with Mr. Pen, who had become
a celebrity by taking on parts that appealed to audience duncery.

   Yes, and why shouldn't they think of Mr. Pen as a celebrity? Perhaps, Mr. Pen dreamed
of reading the right books, the right doctrines, the right manuals of genetics, hyperspace,
physics, art and philosophy, with perpetual inrodes engraved in the X, and thereby finally

292

came to realize that the great, big, fat, impossible G-dream was to make himself even bigger with Brazen Age. If you listen to the hot-iron testimony of the inner consciousness's vain jangling inside of Mr. Pen (who has seen himself in cross section; who has seen himself in the mouth of a mendacious lion marked with *ars gratia artis;* who has seen himself crucified in good warfare; who has seen his concealed ink run into rich green crucigerous letters on a page; who has seen a great canker hand magically, science-falsely turn the once-hidden black river into exposed characters full of ideas and actions; who has seen himself a stoney figure of civic indignation; who has seen himself as a man in a horse in a procerous fable trancing to the abstract idyll of wit), then you will know that he really wanted to grow forever.

After all, who are Mr. Pen and Ms. Gina? The only ones dripping wet in black fruit tabloid juice, stepping sheeplessly out of a giant Vogue, having gin-cum-on-the-rocks, sipping from a cocktail glass, *and* roaming boundlessly through an art-choked mortuary, jingo-talking authoritatively on matters of life and death, demonstrating to the centaurs how to add length to breadth, logic to progress *and* inches to the vertical firearm before *it* becomes lost in the jingjang bush of intuition and depth. Considering all of this, who would not want to seek the raw autographs of Pen and Gina?

*   *   *

Action! Ms. Gina severed Mr. Pen from the crowd-hounding-autographs and whisked him via taxi to their stuffy hotel room, where Ms. Gina spent three solid hours licking the pleasure off Mr. Pen's crown, up to the tip of his epithema.

The room was dark and dirty and on the 18th floor. Mr. Pen, encased in a wet blanket, finally stopped drilling, slid open the pink doors, and journeyed out onto the balcony. Ms. Gina crept up beside him, having wandered out of the moist bliss of soiled sheets of passion subtil of heart, the purlieu of her desires, and wrapped two coiled hairs around his agreeable trunk. "O darling," Ms. Gina said. "Let's forget our glorious celebrity, the muttering, mumbling, grunting, groaning, grumbling, loud and stubborn managers, the mangers, the eaters, the fly agents with bloodsucking cultelli, and the workaholic fans with *goyisheh kop.* Let's just be articulate and verbalize our devotions one to another."

"The unvarnished telling of a tale," Pen said, feeling out the night air, "is that a sinful man is finally satisfied with the liquidation of his own soul. We are all paid to feign wandering pleasure so the camera can stay glued to us for yet another day. In a veil we are a symbol of priceless power. We are carved works in an age of gold emolument and we should congratulate ourselves that we were not left behind – small, stranded and inert."

"We did it!" Ms. Gina agreed. "You know, when I think of all the windy jobs, all the eaten pastors, all the clowns up for first rounds, all the butts of the company, all the Veronica Lakes in the murk *and* the spread-eagle Viviens in the midst, all the heads I snapped off, all the leads I chewed – what role I loved to play most was G. Being a celebrity is my revelation! It's true, I lost my virginity to obscurity. But, in return, I gained a world as buffoonish as a swillbelly vacuum."

Mr. Pen laughed. "Rub my face in it, honey. Roll me over and peel away my clover. When all is said and done, we stripped off our anyway-love-shirts, dunked our heads, slapped our backs and ate until we bloody knew everything. We returned from obscurity and undressed a life-long dream and just gracefully exited by way of the box office."

Ms. Gina wrapped two more coiled, elfin hairs around Mr. Pen. She closed her piercing eye and gave him a big hug. "Yeah, baby. We did it. Ever since we were smaller than extras and reddened with a kind of savage mirth, with my mouth wide-opened and the miracles in your apocentric throat dancing into a rush of rancid air . . . we've been dreaming of such a life."

The phone rang. It was an agent. It was a reporter. It was a chorus with a mournful epithalamium, but with a fast beat. It was the strangulated curiosity of a broken public seeking to get repaired. For, indeed, Ms. Gina and Mr. Pen were a phenomena, and the sity parts they played were special. What they brought to one another were their personal ghosts, their social memories, and their quick-fire responses. The phone was ringing off the hook.

"Don't answer it, baby," Ms. Gina said. "Just don't answer it tonight."

TIME IS, TIME WAS, TIME PAST
OUR FAILURE

was nothing more than a matter of timing, and therefore not a failure at all. We simply got created with time out of mind; however, in the Royal way, one can still hear the call, "Wakey, Wakey! You've had your time! What noble deeds have ye done? What sacrifices rung?" Actually, there was a certain paranoid delirium to all of this. If you key in and listen very closely, you'll hear the grandiloquent outrage and contempt boiling behind the laughter in the dark. "Time is," "Time was," "Time past." Truly embarassing overacting. Three actors get killed on screen. In the last hours their heads will be worth millions. They'll be sought after. It won't be safe for them. Some fiend will go about collecting heads. The press and police will have a field day if they don't throw up first, collecting heads for the front page. An utter hour. A sore loser. O he just can't help sounding off. *ha ha ha.* In the last hours, the three actors will be bread for the masses, chewed to a paste. But time heals a brazen head. Better yet, timelessness heals the world's abrupt manners.

Soon the guilt, the remorse, the limicolous decay will vanish, and paradise will prove to be a lurid and darkly funny, limitrophe fever-dream without the original, hypnopompic, dirty, limivorous host. The final twist should make everyone think twice about god, and fully realize that his heavy-handed, domestic, semi-biblical drama about a dysfunctional earth has the makings of a top-grossing Universal motion picture that could reap in billions upon billions. Confidentially, it will need to have a certain roughedged energy with colliding atoms aplenty, as well as nurse the notion that religion and violence make strange bedfellows, officiating their aims with displeasure. O, no doubt there will be allusions made pertaining to god's *non possumus* attempts at revenge, but, naturally, all hurried into a nonstoichiometric context in order to appear totally inappropriate in regards to the events at hand.

CATCHING UP WITH god

"Cab! Ala to Scybala!" god stepped in and sat down. A backward blessing beginning with 'tae ekat' was on his mind and a substance like catsup was on his attire.

"Scythe the dry, hard Mass! Gee, says I, I thought Jo wrapped you in a clean linen!" the cabbie said.

Strangled in traffic, god took out a ham sandwich and commenced to eat, telling the cabbie to "fare yewell. The road is strewn with taxus."

They sat in silence, passing over a lane.

"Oh, by the way," the cabbie said, "that JapGreek outcast Judas is on the front page. Claims you were murdered out of rage. Damn shame, says I. You should have stayed put. Like a pig in the mud. And if there was a question as to whether you were a Jew, you could have sat up and said, 'Amsow. And you?'"

Blink. Blink. god was bewildered because he was unread.

Yes, god had become all unglued in labour, sickness and discontent, getting loosened up in *Eclogues* and *Georgics*, virtually shattering the leaves in his epical drive to expiscate the mystery by plunging *in medias res* (even if it meant having to cross over the median strip with bad timing in an age too late for mankind), and had collided headon with a decorum of decrement tipped favorably in the path of inequality. Aside from an epithalamion that stood higgledy-piggledy on end, the drive sat less on matrimony than on maniac ceremony, and ripped through *La Semaine* in a manit and *Thebaid, De Rerum Natura* and *Orlando Furioso* in a half a manit, and ripped through fallen gels, leaves; and all the while, the drive drove him struggling to keep wind of wings on his way toward the'den.

And god thought: It all comes around to where it all began. I want to see the bright lights again *en l'air* and learn how real the problem of high intensity, radiated fields is, and read the military jammers and electronic countermeasures, and manage the disruptions in flight navigation due to electromagnetic interference, and obtain the false readings, the false commands of misguided equipment, the offbeat disjointed pulses, the black box cavities filled with priscan, sonobuoy tubes meant to detect the decrement of decumbent, homesick angels, once decretal and well-favored, now reduced to warfare literature, fratricidal freakishness, judgments delivering impossibly distant sounds, preconceived whispers piped into private canals, eardrums, gospels cried from a center whose range is everywhere, sirens that cut across space so sharply that their point of origin becomes synonomous with super mundane peeper's refrain . . .

And, in the cab, the cabbie shouted, *"Ad infinitum!"*

G Cleft

And so we come around again to the beginning. I do so much hope that I have proven to be a worthy guide. I really do love humankind, and I really do care what happens to all of you, and I'm peaceful despite the rumors. Yes, I chose to feel the epithumetic sensations, the eponymous vibrations of earth, the litotes of its consciousness. I, like you, stumbled through its vast darkness, constantly reminding myself: *Nothing's going to harm you. Knock while I'm around,* for I am a citizen of no mean city. Only knock, en-sof, lest you sigh, looking up. I, like you, felt the warmth go, the cold come, and misery breathe its heavy, maledictive breath down my back and around my hidden face, all the way to my Arm. I suppose I could have received earth in a courteous retort, issued to me by a lowly messenger with a weak back, the spine of an angleworm, and a lower belly atop two stick legs. A real knockout clown who only pretended to deliver gold from a touched stone. I could have simply read the cut report, the epitome, estimate which way the mass of information tips, establish my evaluation and enforce my final sentence. But I do not think this would have been classified as progress. Call me a sucker. Call me a fool. Call me an unbounded optimist. Call me a protective archivist of the soul. I chose instead to enter earth and experience firsthand it's licentious rule. It's . . . unbelievable! I fell and I leaned on Litholatry. I drank Rock and got High, I did! I nearly lost my desire to survive! But I *was* good. Dear me, I *was* quite good.

REVELATION!

This was the way it ended as it began as the leaves concluded a mystery concerning a concinnity of calamities that committed a chorus to a conclamation of concordance that left its performers priming the globe with obscurities obsequious to the mind and will and power of god, oblivious to the remanence.

I slid back to basic theocrasy and waited for the accouchement of me ruptured penance O.

G DAY

FLASH!

Six days after the birth, she began to grin. "Look, she is simpering!" everybody said – and the sweet dimples in her papyraceous cheeks were still in bloom once everyone had filled the room. Her eyes were smoky eyes, her lips were red. Daisy May blond waves framed her face, an air of mystical, womanly knowledge.

Those whom came and arrived, in her name, were sure–footed, ambitious, and cloven, and clever enough to dissolve god.

"Look, she is happy!" everybody said.

One held up a prune.

They laughed and cried.

That was something they could all understand.

"Look! Doesn't that tidbit look tempting? Go ahead, take a bite. It's free."

"Shhh . . ."

After that . . . the proceedings just continued . . .

ABOUT THE AUTHOR

Neil Baker, born in 1951, is a novelist, short story writer, poet, and world re-nowned psychic. While his themes involve Apocalyptic Satire, Neil also weaves mystery, suspense, and adventure into the fabric of his Storylines. Neil holds a degree in Psychology and has been a psychodramatist for a private psychiatric hospital. Neil has managed a theater, a Candystore, a book store, a golf course, an all-night Seven-Eleven, and a motel. Neil has also been a Library page, a child's activities director, a senior citizens activities director, an actor, a gravedigger, a BigFoot tracker, and a professional psychic and medium. He has been on numerous radio shows and has given over 10,000 personal readings, and has accomplished this variety of roles while maintaining a somewhat questionable existence with the severe physical contours of the earth.

Neil has written six other novels.